Worth Their Colours

Martin McDowell

WORTH THEIR COLOURS
Copyright © Martin McDowell 2010

First Published in the UK by
Paul Mould Publishing
p.mould@yahoo.com

In association with
Empire Publishing Service www.ppeps.com
P.O. Box 1344, Studio City, CA 91614-0344

A CIP Catalogue record for this book is available from the British Library or from the US Library of Congress.

Simultaneously published in
Australia, Canada, Germany, UK, USA

Printed in Great Britain
First Printing 2010

US 13 ISBN 978-1-58690-097-7
UK 13 ISBN 978-1-904959-89-2

"It is impossible, by any description, to do justice to the conduct of the men."

General Sir William Beresford, in his Despatch to General Lord Wellington on the Battle of Albuera, 16 May 1811

Contents

Chapter One

From all Walks and Stations

English rain! Closer to mist than honest rainfall, bleak and dank, it folded grey and cold across the tired green of the late Autumn Wiltshire Downs. Like starlings in their daydone swarm, more flying than falling on a bullying wind, thick closing curtains were hung across the hills and slopes of the wide and rolling landscape, but, once hung, they were then quickly drawn out into thin veils that poised, shifted, sagged, and then lifted, to reveal small details, soon lost again as stars in a ragged sky. The wind blew holes in the layers of murk. A battered copse showed itself, desperately hanging onto its shivering leaves, then a winding chalkstone wall with sheep huddled in its lee, then a low hedgerow almost leafless, pierced by a lopsided gate. Real winter had come early to 1805. Neither sky nor scenery gave any cheer, nor was any gained from the trudging, hunched figures inching along a distant chalk track.

Coloured more grey than white, it would eventually feel its way through the mist and rain, to run over the slopes and high pasture, then on down into a harbouring valley which gave at least minimal shelter from the gusting wind. Their stubborn progress slowly revealed a pattern in the shape: six figures, in two lines of three, maintained themselves either side of a central single file of 12 or so. The six slowly became identified as soldiers, a stovepipe shako covering a head hunched into a greatcoat collar, below that a knapsack, alongside this, the conspicuous butt of a reversed musket, muzzle down against the rain. These six walked with the easy marching gait of men used to many miles rather than few, thumbs tucked into straps and fastenings, but their charges, whose status soon became apparent, walked with feet only, although carrying no burden. Their hands were fixed before them as would be for bound prisoners.

Corporal Jedediah Deakin, first in the right-hand column, looked back at his command. His eyes dwelt not a second on his five comrades, but several of his prisoners were showing all the signs of unfit men being asked to do what they did little of. The cold and the march, three days old, were taking them

1

through tiredness, to exhaustion and beyond. He had enough campaign experience to have seen men simply fall out of rank and give all up by the roadside. His orders were to deliver twelve men from Devizes Assize to Taunton Barracks and some were in no good state. All had been given good boots and a greatcoat to help them through their journey, but this was a bad march for men unused to fifteen miles a day, a daily soaking, and poor food.

A small stone structure grew out of the rain and mist, a shepherd's hut just off the track with the door firm shut, but smoke spilling from somewhere in the roof. Deakin gave three blows on the door, which soon opened so that he could feel a moment of warmth on his face, but it was soon gone, away in the wind. Around the door appeared first a cudgel, then the fingers of a large and filthy hand complete with black and torn fingernails. This was followed by the brown and wrinkled face of a man of indeterminable age, framed by hat, smock and whiskers, a cold, clay pipe jutting challengingly at Deakin. Both stared, waiting for the other to speak, but Deakin was a Corporal after all and he used the initiative that was his.

"How far to some shelter, mate? Farm or something?"

"On down, two mile or more, Downgate Farm, they got a barn. No reason why she shouldn't let 'ee use it. Can 'ee pay?"

"If it'll serve. Two mile you say?"

"Right. Stay on the track and it'll come."

With that the conversation ended, the cudgel withdrew and the door closed. Deakin turned to his fellow escorts.

"Two miles, and that's the end for today. There'll be a barn for rent."

Private Tom Miles had slept more of the nights of his 25 years out of a bed than in. He had heard all and was not content.

"You spend that coin, Jed, and there's less left for us. What's wrong with a blanket behind a wall like last night?"

"You take a look at them prisoners, Tom, some is like to arrive more dead than alive, more like died, 'specially the Parson. I've been given twelve prisoners to get to barracks, and my stripes be worth more to me than coin in your pocket. Tonight we take's shelter."

One hour more all but ended the feeble light, but it brought them to the first farm off the high downland, made up of squat,

2

blue stone buildings, closed up to confront weather worse than even this day had brought. Its grey thatch was now showing over the fold of the downland, giving the first sign of comfort in a day best ended, this added to by curling smoke from a thick chimney. Deakin led his men into the yard, ignoring the sentry dogs that approached to set up an indignant barking, but they yet retained a healthy distance, intimidated by the group of large, dark figures. Deakin detached himself from the halted column and approached the door, but it opened before he could knock. A harsh, but female voice spoke from a large, bound, upright, bundle that now filled the doorway, framed in firelight from within and holding high a candle lantern.

"Soldiers? You'll be seeking shelter, but don't think 'ee's welcome. I seen too many like 'ee through here to bid thee welcome."

"Peace, Mother, 'tis too bad a night to take so ill with anyone. 'Sides we've coin to pay. Fivepence each, for the night, and all found. Sounds fair?"

"Six would be better. There's no farm on now for some miles."

"Then 'tis behind the walls for us, Mother, like last night. Five, or we move on."

The bundle heaved and gave vent to a deep sigh.

"How many?"

"Eighteen."

A pause, the maths was not beyond her.

"There's a barn behind the house. It's dry, with a fireplace for lambing and wood at the back. Good enough for 6d, I'm thinking, with a bowl of stew each, and bread?"

"You could sweet talk a Quartermaster, Mother. It'll serve nicely, and we do thank you."

"Enough from you and away round. Take this lantern, I'm fair chilled from this talk with thee. I'm back in. The food'll come soon as 'tis warmed."

However, she stayed long enough to make a knowledgeable examination of the men filing past, but learned little in the gloom, except that some were prisoners, hands bound, with a rope from the hands of each man to the neck of the man in front. A good soul, not inexperienced in either tragedy or the ways of Assize Courts, the misery of their slumped and lurching figures chilled her the equal of the keening wind.

The barn loomed dark and solid, the blue lias stonework glistening wet even in the poor light of the lantern, but the door was sound and well made and swung inside with the lifting of the bar. Inside was no warmth and the smell of generations of sheep, but the wind and rain no longer beat and blew on the shoulders of the hunched figures that entered through the low, but welcome door. The lantern showed the fireplace and the kindling. Deakin gave his orders.

"Harry, get the fire going. Pat, secure the door, then release the prisoners. Tom, make sure there's no other way out of here, then you're on first sentry. Loaded, bayonet fixed, hammer down. You two," gesturing to the last two of his command, "get some wood from round the back."

Private Harry Stiles made a fire appear in the fireplace with a rapidity that cheered them all, through the simple expedient of pouring the powder from a cartridge onto the kindling and then pouring another into the priming pan of his musket. He then released the hammer with its flint onto the steel of the "frizzen"; the striking plate. The burning powder was then tipped onto the fire and the "firepower" of the two charges quickly ignited the kindling, to which some dry logs were added. The light from the burning fire made the lantern redundant and Deakin blew out its candle. The rest of the wood arrived, not too damp, and all gathered or shuffled to feel the first of its warmth. Haybales were dragged over and most began the business of repairing the damage done from the day's march, now past.

The soldiers, from habit formed from many marches and campaigns, began to shed themselves of their knapsacks, to open, but not remove, greatcoats and clean their weapons of any dirt or damp. It was a scene they had created for themselves countless times before and there was comfort in its familiarity. They had reached their evening billet, which meant the day was ended, this day's duty was finished.

One that did not attend to any improvement of his affairs was the ex-Reverend Percival Sedgwicke. He slumped onto the floor, as close to the fire as he could get, subsumed in abject misery. He was numbingly tired in both body and mind, and hungry, as only one can be who is accustomed to filling his belly as least twice a day. He'd had nothing for days but army biscuit and

4

water. His legs ached and his feet pained. The lyle stockings, as worn by one of his ex-calling, had soon worn away in the new boots and large blisters soon followed. Now he waited for one of the coarse soldiers to release his bonds, being the last on the tether.

The stew arrived, brought by a young lad, who disappeared at the instant of setting down a black iron cauldron, a sack of bread, and a variety of crude, earthen, dishes. Not enough for eighteen together, there would have to be two sittings. Lance-Corporal Patrick Mulcahey, one of many Irishmen in the British Army, at last reached Sedgwicke. A gentle Irishman, slow to condemn, he turned him over to release his wrists. Raised a Catholic, he addressed the cleric using the title that he had used all his life to men of a religious calling.

"Come on now, Father, we can't have this, this won't do at all. Sit up now, up against this bale, and I'll get you some stew."

He turned to the soldier carrying the food around the gathering.

"John, give me some for the Father quick. He's fair done in. Needs something hot inside him soon, now."

A bowl was prepared, a large lump of coarse clap bread torn off the huge loaf, and brought to the Parson. Mulcahey tried to be cheerful.

"There now, Father. Get that inside of youse, it'll make all the difference, now."

Sedgwicke sat up, saw the food, then fell perplexed as to how he would eat it, there was no spoon. It smelt wholesome; an impression that could not be spoilt by appearance, for it was too dark. Mulcahey again administered unto his needs.

"Here Father, borrow this spoon. I've got two. We often have more than one, it's handy. Easy to come by when you're soldiering. Dead men have no needs, if you take my meaning."

Oh Lord, dead men! The words hit Sedgwicke like a hammerblow, piercing a mind already numb with exhaustion and still reeling with the growing shock of his present circumstances. Tired as it was, his mind worked on it. He was now in the same Army. Previously death had come into his life as an issue of salvation. His close conjunction with death in this form was something new and not far from terrifying.

The stew revived him, its heat before its nourishment, but what was revived anew was his misery. Always jealous of his status, the misery was compounded by the realisation that, only days ago, all in the barn, including the soldiers, would have been at his bidding. Now he was their's to command, forced to enter the Army by a Judge who demolished his comfortable life in less than the time it took to eat a good dinner. He was now branded a felon, one of the "King's hard bargains". The thought rose vividly, that just days ago, he was riding around his scattered Parish in his favourite state, one of moderate intoxication, being greeted by his equals and respectfully acknowledged by all the lesser members of his flock that he encountered.

He had been the Parish Vicar for over ten years, his first posting, for he was still a relatively young man, early-thirties, if neither strong nor sound of wind. He had graduated from the Ecumenical College at a lowly level, but the unfashionable and difficult Parish of Chorlton Sage on the high Wessex Plains had become vacant. None wanted it and so when he put himself forward, the Bishop welcomed the solving of the problem and the position became Sedgwicke's. It was a Parish hard to minister, scattered hamlets sunk in deep and sheltering valleys, many of them some distance from the small church. He fulfilled the job well enough at first, but, with an adequate income and few expenses, a little luxury came into his life, especially a taste for good wine. This grew from a requirement to a necessity, which eventually governed and shaped his life, a life unrestrained by any female influence. Zealous not so much for his Faith, more the social power and standing it afforded, both his cold and over bearing character and the bleak isolation of the high downlands of Wiltshire quickly repelled any prospective wife. Two, in fact, had attempted to generate a more then affable acquaintance, their parents having looked upon him as a possible suitor of sufficient income and social position, but his scarecrow figure and argumentative hautiness, killed any affection before it could influence either's affairs.

Almost equalling his requirement for good wine, with no woman in his life, his attention fixed on the young women of his Parish. Too much and too often for Mothers, Fathers, and even husbands, on whom he called, hands would stroke and fondle. Casually, yet intimately, such as would produce angry looks from outraged, angry, but helpless parents and relations. They soon learned to send the young women away when he arrived

6

in the village, or stand between them until she could make an excuse and affect an escape. They knew how useless it was to complain, nor to try to bar him from their threshold, for the Vicar had connections, something very absent in their lives. Rising out of the common herd to complain to the local Constable about a Cleric could cost them both their tenancy and their employment. This rendered him safe from his conduct being the possible cause of any fall from grace, if that ever occurred to him, for he could see neither harm nor crime within it.

Even his laggard performance as the Spiritual Leader of his scattered flock gave no cause for concern; hangdog and hungover at Matins, slurred and swaying come Evensong. Problems arose, however, as his income did not quite run to accommodate his expanding toping habits and it became more difficult to place bottles on the table for both luncheon and dinner and also make one available to fortify his evenings.

An annual event within the Diocese was dinner at Grangemore Manor, the country seat of the Duke and Duchess of that title. Sedgwicke attended every one, with high expectation that grew with the years. The food was sumptuous, more so the wine but, on the last occasion, more so again the silver cutlery. This year the place next to him, for some reason, was vacant, and over the course of the evening the full placing found its way into his copious cassock pockets. Within the next week he had taken half to the pawnbroker at Warminster. However, this worthy proprietor, being of the Jewish persuasion, knew nothing of English Heraldry; a portcullis, with coiled chains either side, surmounted by a lion rampant. He did not notice that this design, on each item of the cutlery, also matched the carefully painted inn sign hanging just down the road, swinging above the door of the Grangemore Arms.

Chance would have it that the Head Butler of Grangemoor was ambling by on his day off, glanced in the window and saw a half set of his beloved cutlery on display in a place so dreadful as a Pawnbroker's window! The Town Constable was fetched and soon it was ascertained that the Vicar of Chorlton Sage had made the sale. A search was made of the Vicarage; in the absence of the incumbent, for he was off on his rounds. The remainder of the set was duly found and Sedgwicke arrested on his return, the shock mercifully reduced by the amount of alcohol running through the passages of his befuddled brain. Not even his status as a High Church Vicar could stave off the wrath of a High Duchess and within days he was charged, tried, and sentenced, "Service in the Army until discharged by the King", then ignominiously de-frocked in his cell by the Bishop. Mortified by these final thoughts on his shameful story, exhaustion at last overcame him and he fell into a troubled sleep.

The company settled to rest. The soldiers had completed their cleaning and inspection and Tom Miles began the first sentry duty, leaning against the wall by the door. His musket grounded, with bayonet fixed and the hammer holding closed the frizzen, behind which lay the charge of priming powder. Jed Deakin took a last turn around his command; most were asleep, save one who was still making preparations. It was the prisoner he was most concerned over, the one he felt the most liable to make an attempt at escape. He was the one he had named in his mind "The Gypsy", although there was nothing to confirm that origin. This one was tall, 5' 10", muscled and well proportioned. The exertions and privations of the past days had inflicted no more on him than it had on the soldiers, perhaps less so. What he was doing impressed the veteran Corporal. He was lining his wet greatcoat with dry hay from the back of the barn, making a thick lining between himself and the sodden material. Impressed with this old soldier's dodge and recognising someone of the same ilk as himself, Deakin felt no hesitation in beginning a conversation. He settled himself on the nearest straw bale

"You'd be Davey."

The prisoner looked up and studied his interlocutor. His expression remained unchanged.

"Correct."

"Why'd they bring you before the Beak?"

"Poaching."

"Poaching! You could've been hung!"

"Depends what and who from. A pair of coneys off a farmer's land don't count the same as pheasants off the Duke's."

"How'd they catch you?"

"Gin trap."

"An' it didn't break your leg?"

"No, I had on leather gaiters with slats down inside. It hurt, but that were all."

8

"You've been out more than once, that's plain. And you couldn't get it open?"

"No, and the Bailiff and his mates got to me on the following morning."

"It must've been a new one. You been hauled up before?"

Davey felt his temper rising at the questioning, but he knew enough not to start a quarrel when not needed and besides, this was the Corporal in charge. He had the power to make life hard and, besides again, it was hard to take too much offence at Deakin. His temper subsided. It was obvious that their backgrounds were alike, he could easily have come from the next village to his own, Far Devening, with both standing talking, whilst leaning on some field gate. He found himself becoming less terse.

"Three times, but I went out many more times than that. Out for simple stuff, coneys and hares, took just for the pot. Had to, widowed Mother and three youngers. 'Twere that or starve, if you understand?"

"Oh, I understands, well enough! Oh my, yes."

Deakin nodded in accompaniment, he understood perfectly. As a child he had fed often enough on poached meat; crow, badger, and others of an even less savoury variety.

"What did they give you those times?"

"A whipping and a fine. That's what I expected this time. Things is now different, that's plain."

"Aye, you're right. More and more the Courts is sentencing time in th'Army. Not hard to work out why, with Boney just across the Channel. Now, a word of advice to 'ee. Deserting won't be far from your mind. If you got a family behind you, like you say, don't try. The first place the Provosts go to is your home, and they be none too gentle. They'll smash the place up, just out of spite. Even if they catch you or they don't. The Army isn't so bad. It don't let you starve, and you do get paid. You shot before?"

"Yes, carrion shoot. It put food on the table."

"Were you any use?"

"Better than most, I'd say."

"Right then. If you're a good shot, like you say, try to get into the Light Company. Promotion's quicker and there's a better chance of plunder. If you want, the Regimental Purser will send home your pay, and any other money besides. Most Purs-

9

ers are straight, it's too soft a billet to risk with a little crookery. Think of someone you can trust, and he'll send it on."

With no more conversation from either, Deakin rose and moved to his own place in the barn, leaving Davey wrapped in his greatcoat. The fire began to die, but the barn was a place of succour, the warmest place they'd been all day, and dry, despite the rising wind howling between the gaps in the tiles in the roof above. All fell to sleep, save the sentry and one other. He lay on the edge of the group of sleeping bodies. Seth Tiley, thief, robber, thug and footpad, lay with eyes wide open, watching the sentry, considering choices, thinking and scheming.

* * *

In a setting of deepest contrast to those in the barn, Mrs March-Markham stood in a state of profound delight, hands clasped over her ample bosom. Almost as round as she was tall, her height was doubled by a pink turban and a swaying peacock's tail feather, set about by others, smaller but equally lavish. Trussed about in numerous sashes, she resembled a collection of lustrous orbs of various sizes, all gathered roundabout by finest satin. Her round and heated face bore a permanent smile of gleaming contentment. Arranged before her, she viewed, as would a miser his gold, the cause of her glorious state of exuberance. A society ball exhibited itself in all its grandeur in the main hall of her own home; Newcombe Hall, recently purchased and sumptuously refurbished by profits from her husband's plantations in the West Indies. A social success had plainly been achieved; a "place", surely, had been established amongst the local high placed gentry, both for herself and for her merchant husband.

New to the area, the March-Markhams had anxiously issued invitations to all of local society, all had accepted and, to her utmost satisfaction, all had attended. Newcombe was one of the more substantial properties in the area, set in extensive grounds and all came, if only out of curiosity, to see what the cavalcade of builder's wagons over the past months had accomplished. Also, adding brilliant scarlet, the entire officer corps of the fashionable King's Own Royal Fusiliers, the "King's Royals" were present, having been billeted in the surrounding area. The dancing was glorious, the music well played and in mode, the conversation loud and mirthful, and the food plentiful and exotic. Moving as on casters beneath the shimmering gown, opening and closing a huge fan as the occasion warranted, she drifted amongst her guests, bestowing her obvious pleasure to all, who in turn greeted her as their generous and accomplished hostess.

Nothing existed in either her view or knowledge that could in any way mar the joy that welled within her bejewelled chest and throat, of enough acreage to show off the lavish display gifted to her by her thoroughly moneyed husband. However, beyond the scope of what she knew or saw, events were progressing in an upstairs room that would soon develop into the confrontation that would mark the occasion beyond the memory generated by the opulence and grandeur created by the host and hostess. The young gentlemen of the County, plus a few of the younger Officers, were lolling and lounging in the smoking room, which was living up to its name with a fug of cigar smoke building nicely. Some drank of the fine wine and spirits available that evening, but all were watching two players, one a well-dressed young gentleman, the other a young Officer. Each sat at the opposite ends of a small colourful board that neatly covered its supporting table. The young Lord Frederick Templemere, recent inheritor of the Hampshire estates and fortune of the late Lord Josiah Templemere, was losing heavily at his favourite and major gamble, backgammon. Having never met his equal, Templemere justifiably counted himself as one of the best players in the country and, in truth, he was invariably proved correct. Usually he found himself happily fleecing minor players on such social occasions as these, to provide the small change that a gentleman such as himself really did not need. Such coinage, though, proved useful at the racetrack; his other, if more minor, gambling activity, where a bet added interest to each race. Templemere was strong featured, dark eyes under dark brows, healthily complexioned and generally considered by his close circle to be good company. He was always ready with the "bon mot" that usually arrived in the form of some cutting remark aimed at someone out of favour.

However, Templemere was reaching an undisguisable level of agitation. They were on their third game and both that had gone before had been lost. In fact, at the conclusion of the second game he had suffered the deep humiliation of being "backgammoned", for at the close of the game he had failed to "bear off" any of his checkers, because there remained two in his opponent's home board. Worse, being Lord Frederick Templemere and playing to the crowd, at the onset he had goaded his opponent into five pounds per pip. Worse still, he had doubled and re-doubled during that game in the hope of making his opponent concede the game, but he had doubled also, making the final reckoning eight times the original stake. Templemere had lost over three hundred pounds so far and this third game was going the same way. All his tactics, blocking and priming, had been demolished and circumvented and so, coming to the end, "counting pips" told him that he was, again, about to lose heavily. His opponent had to move but one checker to his home board and, subject to "bearing off", a long way away for Templemere, this game also would be his.

Opposite, on the far side of the board, sat Captain Henry Carr, languid and relaxed, displaying just the level of effortless sangfroid that Templemere most often demonstrated himself when gambling in this way and all the more irritating for that. Carr's open face, just too full to be described as aquiline and too pale to be described as healthy, sat above the full collar of a fully buttoned Officer's jacket. A jacket not perfectly tailored, nor perfectly new, but clean and certainly becoming an Officer. Clear blue eyes calmly regarded Templemere and a confident smile moved one corner of his mouth to one side of his face as he threw a five and a three which moved his last checker the eight points needed to both oer'leap Templemere's block, and also clear all his checkers from Templemere's home board. Templemere still had five to bring home and one on the bar, which he had to attend to first. He threw and obtained a three and a six. This brought the checker off the bar and enabled the movement of one of the other five checkers, but not to his home board. Losing was now almost certain. The doubling cube sat unused. Now that his throw had arrived, Captain Carr picked it up and turned it to show the two. Templemere had now to accept a doubling of the stakes or concede the game. His temper finally broke.

"You, Sir, are a damned cheat!"

The words exploded into the silence. All present sat up, alert and now paying rapt attention. This was developing into much more than a match made for interest in gambling. Carr looked

12

more quizzical than astonished, still retaining an unruffled countenance.

"A cheat? Come now, Sir, how can it be possible to cheat at backgammon? The board is in full view, the dice also. How can any manipulation be possible?"

"Nevertheless, I say you cheated."

Although they were equal in years, Carr spoke as an indulgent adult addressing an errant child.

"My Lord, pray calm yourself. If you saw cheating, describe what you saw. I'm sure it can be explained."

Templemere drew himself up in the chair and delivered his accusation via a stabbing finger.

"You primed the dice. Too often you threw exactly the number you needed. I say that's clear evidence of cheating."

There was not a sound in the room, nor movement, not even to draw on a fine cigar, nor sip the fine wine. All knew the absurdity of what had been said and all knew the stage that it had now reached. Carr spoke in tones that became progressively more clipped and formal.

"My Lord, the rules say that the dice must be delivered from the cup, onto the board, and lie flat. That was ever the case, never once other than. Please accept that."

However, his loss and humiliation had taken Templemere beyond reason to near hysteria. Reason had gone absent. He screamed,

"I don't. I've never seen dice favour a man as they have you. It's the work of a cheat. There's no other explanation."

Carr's face became blank, showing no emotion.

"You have accused me of cheating, within hearing of this honourable company. I require you to withdraw the remark."

Some of the company now spoke up. None wanted what now seemed likely.

"Come on, Fred. He beat you fair, fair that I saw. All good players try to prime the dice inside the cup. It's all within the rules."

"Fred, he's not asking for an apology. Just let it go. The man's a good player. That's that!"

Templemere felt further humiliation pressing in from all sides, but worse, no support.

"Pay the man, Fred. You'd expect the same if he were the loser. Pay up for fair play, and let's get back to the ladies."

But Templemere was not used to such a defeat, especially not before an audience of cronies. His jaw clenched so hard that muscles and veins protruded from both the cheeks and temples of his now liverish face. None agreed with him, none had offered support; none would say that they had seen what he had just accused this repulsive Officer of. There would be a reckoning. He took out his pocket book and opened it, never taking his eyes off Carr. Through clenched teeth,

"Will someone provide me with pen and ink?"

An inkwell and a quill were duly found and the note duly written. Templemere offered the note across to Carr, who took it and read the sum. £315, the exact amount for the first two games, nothing for the third.

"And the withdrawal?"

There remained a thunderous, drawn out silence, suddenly broken.

"Now hold there, Carr."

Carr recognised the Lancashire tones of Nathaniel Peak, Major of the King's Royals. He looked around to the source of the words and saw Peak coming to the table. Had he been summoned, or had he been there some while? Carr had no way of knowing. The Major spoke,

"Take your winnings, Captain, and end the matter. The sum has been paid; take that as acceptance of fair play. Now take yourself back to the dancing. That's an order."

Carr rose to his feet, the note still in his hand. To throw it back meant a challenge, to accept it constituted exactly that, acceptance. Without taking his eyes, now icy blue, from Templemere he unbuttoned his jacket, placed the note inside, and then rebuttoned fully, taking care with every one. He then turned on his heel and left.

An uneasy silence settled on the room, then, with uneasy glances towards each other and Templemere, who remained sitting, the group began to break up and leave. Friends of the defeated Lord came to offer consolation, a hand on the shoulder, a pat on the back. All were shrugged off, all felt it better to leave, and did so.

The company of gentlemen and Officers descended the main staircase, some noticed by the other guests below, but most of these guests were deep into the distractions of the evening. Mrs March-Markham continued to circulate, cementing the good

14

work of the evening and basking in the complimentary comments: "glittering occasion", "such a pleasurable evening". Major Peak watched and then followed Carr all the way down the staircase and at the bottom caught up with him.

"These are your orders. If you have the need, get a bottle, get something to eat, portable, then get your cloak and take yourself back to your billet. Use my carriage. I want you out of here in ten minutes. Clear?"

"Sir."

Carr took himself to the buffet table, much reduced but still displaying plentiful fare. He was very hungry. He emptied a breadbasket, refilled it with food that would travel, chose a bottle and then turned, to find himself nose to nose with Lord Templemere. It was Templemere who stepped back, but only to give himself room to throw a glass of brandy full into Carr's face, then shout loudly and from a range so close that spittle was added to the brandy.

"I still say that you are a damned cheat. You cheat from the cup, and that's how you beat me."

Carr carefully returned the basket of food to the table behind, withdrew a large kerchief from his cuff and wiped away the brandy that stung both his eyes and nostrils. This took enough time for the room to go very silent, the dancers to stop, and the music to die away, the last notes discordant within the ragged ending. This was not all that "died away". On seeing the two antagonists in full view in the middle of the room, one evidently having assaulted the other, who seemed about to strike back, Mrs March-Markham collapsed; the disaster of what was unfolding took her legs from under her. She could not be held up and was allowed to sink to the floor, but remained unattended; all eyes were on Carr and Templemere. Carr was icy calm. He made a point of carefully returning the kerchief, then made his reply.

"My Lord, this has now become a serious affair that must be settled in the proper manner. Do you have Seconds?"

"So you make a challenge?"

"No my Lord, for I pick up yours. Do you have Seconds?"

"Yes. As for weapons, I choose pistols."

Mrs March-Markham had regained enough equilibrium to enable herself to roll to a sitting position, but at the mention of pistols and Seconds, she thoroughly fainted off, resuming her impression of a badly made satin bed and bolster.

15

"I'm afraid, my Lord, that is not within your right. As you have accused me of cheating, and in addition, struck me a blow by throwing brandy at me, according to the Code Duello, you have issued the challenge. You are the challenger; I am the challenged. That gives me choice of weapons. I choose sabres. Any fellow Officer here will act as Second for me. Appoint yours, and make arrangements."

Both stood the ground they held. Templemere had recovered some composure. He had been out at dawn himself many times before and knew the rules, but Carr's cool correction of him had renewed his high level of agitation. For a short but tense period, he said nothing, but it was not he who broke the silence.

"I'm afraid he has the right of it, young fellah!"

Both looked in the direction of the voice. A thin but elegant man, his elegance stemming from his gorgeous blue and gold Hussar's uniform, was close to the front of those who stood as audience. His face bore the scars of combat, whether from battle or from duelling, it was impossible to tell.

"An insult, or as in this case, a glass of brandy thrown between you, counts as a blow. He is the challenged. If you want a change from swords to pistols, you must give your word of honour that you are no swordsman. He is then honour bound to accept."

"I am aware of this, but I had the right to hope that such as the Captain here, evidently not a Gentleman, would not. I now do so. Captain Carr. On my word of honour I am no swordsman. The weapons should be pistols".

Carr allowed a moment of silence to stand between them, the contempt on his face clear and palpable.

"My Lord, in my dealings with you I have found honour to be conspicuous in its absence. The weapons are sabres. Of course you may now withdraw if you wish. Please inform me through my Seconds."

A nod to two fellow Officers stood close by, established their role as such, then he strode across the empty floor, past the attempted elevation of Mrs March-Markham, arduously being undertaken by several maids and footmen. He continued to the main door, but was intercepted by Major Peak.

"Carr, you can't do this. You know what it means, the end of your Commission. Orders are clear and strict on duelling, as

16

you well know. If you survive you'll still be up before a Court Martial and cashiered. Your Army career ended."

"Thank you Major, this I know. If needs be, I resign my Commission. I'm going to meet him. I can do no other thing."

With that, he took his cloak and shako from the footman and boarded the waiting carriage. On reaching his billet, before preparing for sleep, he wrote a letter resigning his place as an Officer in the King's Royals, carefully dated. He addressed the letter to his Lieutenant Colonel. He awoke to no word from his Seconds. He was now a civilian.

* * *

The dawn of the next day came dry but restless. The wind continued to harry all that stood upright in its path, but the rain had gone, blown inland. Bright patches of sunshine raced over the autumn green countryside, painting their changing shapes on the downs, fields, and valleys alike. The first of the morning raced over the imposing edifice that was the front of Farslake House. A climbing elaboration of Tudor redbrick, crowned by Tudor chimneys, Farslake had changed hands many times during the Wars of the Roses, but, with the peace of Henry Tudor, it stood in the hands of the Coatsley family. They had rebuilt it in the style and it had remained in such ownership ever since. Surrounded by paths of immaculate, white, sea dredged gravel, it was a red and cream confection in the middle of its own well managed woodland and pasture.

One of the paths crunched to the good boots of a lone figure, who trudged past the side of the East wing, the strap of a stout leather satchel holding down a good half coat, it being of the same ivy green colour as a good tricorn hat that completed the apparel of Joseph Pike, ex-fenceman of the Farslake Estate. He was a young man of classic good looks and could have been the model for any of the statues that he passed on his exit towards the main gate. Tall, well muscled, and well proportioned, even under the depressed circumstances of this ragged morning, he walked with an easy athletic elegance. To crown all, a queue of brilliant blond hair hung just behind his collar, protruding beneath the rear of the hat. He looked up at the top windows of the side of the East Wing, an imposing creation by itself. Did a curtain move? He stopped, but it was impossible to tell. He resumed his long walk to the Main Gate.

17

The youngest son of four boys, Father a carpenter, at seventeen he had no choice but to follow the next brother above and leave home. He had gone to the Farslake Estate looking for work and found himself before the Estate Manager, Jacob Tilsley When asked what skills he had, he had replied, "Carpentry". The Manager needed a fenceman and so Joe was required to demonstrate his skills by making a side-gate. When given a pile of good timber and a set of tools better than his Father could ever dream of, Joe had made a gate of sound construction and proper proportion. He was duly hired and given lodgings above the workshops. For almost three years all went well. All were impressed with young Joe; he proved himself a good worker; when given any job it was carried out in good time and carried out well.

None of the female staff could resist a soft spot for Joe, certainly none on the catering side, yet he formed neither attachment nor liaison with any of the girls on the staff. Though several there set their cap in his direction, he had no experience of girls and no capability to recognise the signs. Also, his humble background and limited experience rendered him shy and awkward in so lofty a place, but he was polite and respectful and always with a ready smile. Needless to say he was "mothered" by the Cook.

His job was the fences and gates all over the estate. The Manager would set the work and, being Joe, soon he was trusted to arrange and carry out the work, ordering the timber and loading his work cart. Jacob Tilsley soon noticed that there was little waste and the tools and the cart with it's horse, were cared for. One summer's day he was ordered to replace a section that fenced off The Ride, a wide earthen pathway used by the Coatsley family for exercising both themselves and their horses, its long sweeping curves designed for a good gallop, and all within the confines of the estate.

This generation of the Coatsleys was not a large one: two sons and one daughter, Jasmine. When she entered her late teens, riding became a daily, even twice daily, occupation, at least once along The Ride. Now, at the age of eighteen, she was allowed to go alone, with neither her groom nor her brothers. Inevitably, like all the females on the estate, she also had noticed Joe, and now, as she took her fine gelding on a rising trot out for a morning ride, there he was, working on the fencing.

18

She slowed her horse to a walk. She had all the confidence and poise of her breeding, thoroughly instilled by her own Governess, but nevertheless, she was yet a teenage girl and not sure to look or look away. Joe stood up and turned to pay his respects. His fellow estate workers had quickly drilled it into him that you ignored one of the family at your cost. All expected you to acknowledge their arrival. He lifted his hat, and turned full to face her, as he had been taught, but being Joe he added a smile.

"Morning, Miss."

From any other worker on the estate, to any other member of the family, such over familiarity as a smile would have brought a withering look, or even a verbal rebuke. However, what was returned was nothing of the kind. He waited for an acknowledgement, in case one came. It did, a nod, but Joe noticed the discomposure that entered her face. She looked down, she looked up, she looked away, she looked back, then recovered herself and set her horse back to a trot. Joe returned the nod, although it wasn't required and followed her with his eyes as she rode past, then returned to his work.

She could naturally see no reason why the afternoon ride should not take the same route. Joe had finished about four sections and was taking a break; bread, cheese and an apple. He himself sat leaning back against a lower rail. Again, he rose to his feet, but he had just taken a mouthful of bread and cheese, both still in his hands, and so he began chewing for all his was worth to enable himself to speak the required acknowledgement. He was still chewing mightily when Jasmine reached the distance from him at which the words and gesture should arrive. At last he managed the last swallow, exaggerated and comical. The humour was not lost on him and showed in his face.

"Sorry, Miss. Good afternoon. Miss."

She reigned in her horse. She looked down, he looked up. She wanting to say something, but knowing not what; he waiting for the customary nod or lifting of the riding crop, or even some instructions. Joe broke the moment.

"Is your horse alright, Miss?"

She seized the subject gratefully.

"I'm not sure. Could you check his left rear hoof? He doesn't feel quite right."

Joe knew little of horses, but he had enough common sense and experience to know what a shoe on a hoof should look like.

"Yes, Miss. Certainly, Miss."

He approached the horse and again knew enough to calm the horse by running his hand along the well-groomed brown flank, then down the leg to the hoof. He lifted it and made an inspection. All sound, no stone, nothing loose. He returned to Miss Jasmine.

"All's well, Miss. As far as I can tell. There's nothing wrong with the hoof. Perhaps a stiff tendon or somesuch, but there's nothing obvious."

"Perhaps you're right. Could you give him some water?"

"Yes, Miss. I have some here."

He moved to the workcart. His own small workhorse stood nearby, hobbled and contentedly grazing. A bucket and pile of hay were nearby. He picked up the bucket and returned with it.

"Could you get fresh?" she asked. "I don't like him drinking from the same bucket as the workhorses. He's bred. You can't be too careful."

Joe halted and looked for the stream. It was 100 yards away.

"Yes, Miss, I can. Just give me a moment, and I'll fetch some."

She watched him all the way to the stream and she watched him all the way back, at least until he returned close enough for her to grow concerned that he would become aware that she was gazing at him. The water was set down and the horse drank. She broke the silence.

"Why are you working here; is there a problem? Are stock escaping, or something?"

"No Miss. Mr Tilsley thinks the fence could soon go, and has set me to replace what I think is close to rotten."

"He trusts you to decide such a thing for yourself?"

"Why, yes Miss. My job is the fencing, I make the careful check of the wood and gates and such, and decide what needs doing. He's made no complaint to me so far."

He smiled and so did she. The coquettishness of an eighteen year old surfaced.

"What's your name, fencer?"

This being spoken with a wide grin banished all hint of any attempt at superiority.

"Joe. Joe Pike. Miss."

"Are you a good fencer, Joe? What needs to be done when you "fence"?"

20

"Well, as I say Miss, no complaints so far. I just mend the fences with good timber."

"And what do you do to warrant yourself to be called a "good fencer?"

Joe, surprised at so detailed an enquiry, obediently began some explanation, naively going into details about fence joints, rail splitters, woodgrain, augers, tar, and so on. She watched and listened with amusement to his description, all well illustrated with gestures and waving hands, but she looked more than she listened. She was fascinated. She knew few boys and fewer still of what she felt the right age, that being just her senior, and here she was talking to one, and one very much out of the ordinary. Joe had stopped.

"Well that's about it. There's not that much to it, really."

"I feel I could be a fencer. I think I'd be very good, as well."

"Yes, Miss. I'm sure the stock would be fully safe and sound with you looking after all the gates and rails. And they'd feel it, too, that's for certain."

She laughed.

"Well, Joe Pike. I'll leave you to your wood and tar. I've enjoyed our conversation."

"My pleasure, Miss."

She fixed her eyes on his, and then kicked her horse into a trot. Joe stood, stunned and dazed. He'd talked to a girl and she'd listened. The small details of his lowly life and work had entertained the daughter of the estate! He watched her back as she grew smaller down The Ride, but the significance of her turning her head was lost on Joe, for when she did look back, her face was lit by a smile that matched the smile in her eyes.

In her innocence, with growing frequency, in the days and weeks that followed, before her ride she would ask Jacob Tilsley where Joe was working. He didn't like what he knew was happening, even less when sometimes she would walk there and the pair would talk as equals. The family talked from above, which didn't just mean from horseback. Tilsley was not an obsequious man such as would grovel in his place, but he feared for Joe. He could do nothing to prevent it. If the daughter of the estate asked him something he had no choice but to answer and answer fully. Often he would follow and was relieved to see that they never touched and were always in full view, but it was plain that they were special to each other. The language of their hands and faces could give no other impression. She did not remain with Joe long, but their meetings were a daily occurrence.

One evening Tilsley called on Joe in his room above his workshop. He knocked on the door and Joe opened it, his right holding the door, his left a book. Tilsley stepped inside.

"Joe, I didn't know you could read."

"Yes, some. We were taught a little at Sunday School, and Miss Jasmine is helping me to improve more. This is her book, she lent it to me."

Tilsley's spirits sank. This was worse than he had expected. What had grown between these two could cause nothing but trouble, but both he and Joe were powerless. If a Coatsley decided to take a course of action, any course of action, how were any such as themselves to alter the run of the outcome?

"Joe, now listen to me. You must be careful. If she wants to sit with you to read, or visit you whilst you work, I know you can't turn her away, nor anything, but don't 'ee touch her. Don't even look at her for more than a second. Keep it worker and Mistress; apart and respectful. She'll get bored, they always do, and then she'll leave 'ee alone, but by Jesus our Saviour don't touch her and keep a distance between yourself and her. No matter what she says or does. You do have that with you. Same as a Master can't touch a maidservant, she can't touch you."

Joe looked astonished and not a little concerned. This was beyond his thinking; beyond his understanding of himself with Miss Jasmine.

"I understand you, Mr Tilsley, but I never thought otherwise about how it should be, and stay. I know my place with the likes of her, and that's how it'll stay. I'm grateful for her helping me with my reading, but, like you say, how do the likes of us turn away the likes of them? Besides, she acts like a good friend."

"You're right lad, I know, but I also know that you're meeting too often. I'll do what I can to keep her away. It's best, I hope you know that."

"Yes, Mr Tilsley, I do, and I do thank you for your concern."

"Right, Joe. Good night."

"Good night, Mr Tilsley."

But the next morning, the Earl strode into the Estate Office.

"Tilsley, what's this I hear about Jasmine spending time, a lot of time, with this fencer boy? I'm told they even sit together reading books. What do you know?"

"It's true, Sir. She spends time with the lad, and she is teaching him to read, but there's nothing to fear. He's a good boy. He knows his place. He's just grateful that she's helping him with his learning."

"Learning be damned! I want him gone, off the estate, do you hear? Gone, so's I don't see him again, and neither does she."

Tilsley replied in a tone that carried his sorrow the equal of the carefully chosen words he spoke.

"But what would you have me tell him Sir? He's as good a worker as we've got here, skilled and diligent. He can do any job on the estate, with never a complaint. On what grounds Sir, what do I tell him?"

"That's of no concern to me. I don't care what you say, as long as you say "you're dismissed!" Just get him on his way. I leave that to you, I care not."

Tilsley had no choice but to resign himself to the inevitable.

"Yes Sir. I'll see to it. He'll be gone by morning."

The Earl left the office and Tilsley followed him out, but Tilsley turned into the stable and began saddling his good steady mare. His jaw was clenched and his brows knitted together in a deep frown. Sadness, and no small amount of injustice too, lay upon him as profound as he could remember. He was the Estate Manager and though it felt like a ton weight, it fell to him to dismiss Joe. He leant his forehead onto the smooth leather of the saddle and paused in thought. Then he mounted.

He set the mare to the track that led to the field where Joe was working and soon reached the section along it where Joe should be found. There he was and, as if by solemn edict, Miss Jasmine was there, holding the end of a rail whilst Joe set the other end into its post.

"Morning Miss Jasmine."

"Mr Tilsley."

"Excuse me, Miss, but I need a word with Joe here."

"By all means."

"Joe, when you've finished here, come by the office, will you?"

"Right, Mr Tilsley. I shouldn't be too long."

"Fine Joe, I won't be far away."

Tilsley couldn't smile, nor give any kind of cheery word. The dismissal of a good worker for such a reason was new to him personally, but he had heard of it and could find no comfort that such things were not unknown to workers on any estate. He acknowledged Miss Jasmine with a forefinger to his forehead, remounted his mare and let her walk back at her own speed. He didn't, however, return to his office. He went instead to the saddler and obtained a good leather satchel. Then he went to the kitchen. He shared the news with all there and not a few white pinafores went up to cover sorrowing faces, but he had only to show the satchel for the cook to fill it with as much travelling food as was easily available. Next, to the Counting House, where he paid for Joe's boots, coat, and hat from his own money, collected Joe's wages, then back to his office to await Joe. There he waited in silence, with no company but the sorrowful tick of the old clock. When Joe arrived, it didn't take long. Tilsley handed over the satchel and the wages and wished him well, adding that he need not leave till dawn; he would have till then to gather up his things. Joe took himself off to his room and gathered his few possessions, making good use of his new satchel. He slept until dawn, which woke him as it customarily did. Then he set off, not fully understanding the events that had befallen him, but nevertheless wiser in the ways of Nobles and Commoners.

* * *

Henry George Aloysius Carr; the second son of the Carrs of South Hatherleigh, these being landed, but secondary gentry in the Parish of that name. At the age of 17, after a good education at a lesser Public School, he had been packed off to the Army by the simple expedient of buying him a Commission in the 6th Regiment of Foot. By the fortunes of war he too quickly found himself as the Junior Officer in the single company of that good Regiment that saw action in the second Irish Rebellion of Summer 1798. The landing of over 1,000 French Regulars had re-kindled the rebellion and so 2,000 French and Irish Rebels under the French General Humbert met 6,000 British, mostly Irish Militia, under General Lake outside Castlebar in County Mayo, Western Ireland. When the Militia in the British centre gave way before a determined French column, the whole line collapsed and the 6,000 retreated so fast that the aftermath became known as the "Castlebar Races", save the lone company of the 6th fighting its way off the stricken field. With his Captain dead, Carr became the Officer in Command, with not enough military knowledge to fill an eggcup! However, his Sergeants of long service quickly made suggestions amidst the mayhem that regularly met with the reply of either,

"Yes, make it so", or "Yes, carry on."

Usually his agreement was little more than a confirmation of an order already being carried out. It began with a rallying square in which they fought their way off the battlefield and then two steady lines each firing alternate volleys at a rate of three rounds a minute. When a battle-maddened Irish Patriot reached their line, it was Carr that advanced out to turn the bayonet aside with his sabre and the Senior Sergeant who ended the threat with a shot from so close a range that it set the Irishman's coat on fire! The six rounds a minute gave them respite, so then followed an orderly retreat with the first line filing back through the second to reload. Their numbers grew as veterans from within the Militia, mostly old NCO's, joined the company, recognising the steady conduct of the 6th as the safest route out of what could easily become a massacre. Thus, this company of the 6th completed their retreat with twice their original number and with Carr as the lone Officer.

They marched on unmolested and approached Tuam where the "Races" had finally run their course and the defeated Militia were mostly gathered. One of his good Sergeants again made a suggestion.

"Will you march the lads in, Sir?"

Young Carr looked puzzled, but agreed.

"Yes. Make it so."

The 200 or so formed fours on the road.

"Say a few words to the lads, Sir? They fought well, Sir. Got us out of a bad business."

"Er, yes, if you think I should."

"Yes Sir. The lads always appreciates an Officer taking the trouble."

In this way, Carr, the shaver Officer, found himself mumbling tangled sentences of congratulations at 200 odd hardened veterans, all dirty, some bloody. However, they all stood stock still with shouldered arms and even gave three cheers for Lieutenant Carr. The order came for "Right turn, quick march" and with Carr at the head and the Sergeants and Corporals ranged down the flanks they marched into the camp.

Carr fell back alongside the Senior Sergeant.

"I don't see how I deserved that, Sergeant. Their cheering, I mean."

"Begging you pardon, Sir, but yes you did. You stood with the lads in the front rank, always the front rank, and set a good example. That's all that was needed, Sir."

The lesson was not lost on Carr. Battle drill and steady conduct had won their way out of a perilous situation, a full defeat, but more so, the simple facts of keeping his head and sharing their dangers, had won him the respect of the men.

Lake was soon massively reinforced and renewed his challenge on Humbert who was moving around the country, trying to link up with other Irish Rebels. However, defeat soon came for him when his mixed force was caught at Ballinamuck between both General Lake and the new Viceroy, Lord Cornwallis. The French were later repatriated, having laid down their arms, but the Irish Rebels taken prisoner were massacred on the spot by the Militia. Carr and his company, back in reserve, took little part in a battle that lasted but minutes, but they were part of the force that were given the task of taking the rebel stronghold of Killala. First amongst those ordered to the assault, the intimidating column of veterans was easily the first into the town and the first to the plunder. They found themselves facing the town bank and the door was quickly stove in and soon they came across a hoard of gold coin, in thirty neat leather bags, each marked with the black silhouette of The Emperor. The money was part of the finance for the French invasion. Carr took his first military decision.

"Those Militia bastards are not getting their hands on this. Get the Sergeants. I want these in their knapsacks. Any man that remains in this town loses his share."

Carr and his Sergeants pulled their men away from the town to begin the share out. There was no argument from the men, to them the coin was easily preferable than the alternative of rapine and drink that could often finish on a rope's end, either knotted as a noose, or combed out into a lash.

Carr had held both himself and his men out of the scenes of rape, revenge and slaughter that finished the Irish Rebellion of 1798 and he returned to England substantially richer. Within the ranks of the 6th his military skills improved and, after three more years, with good references, he obtained his advancement by buying a Captain's Commission in the King's Own Royal Fusiliers.

However, now, as a civilian, he rode a closed carriage with his two Seconds, through a cold, but dry and still October dawn. The atmosphere was sombre, no conversation; this was a first for all three. The appointed place was a lonely meadow close to a sluggish stream, picking its careful way through a bed thick with reeds. As the carriage swung around to face the open space, it was clear that they were first. Nevertheless, despite the cold, Carr stripped down to his shirt, took himself off to a corner of the field with one of his Seconds and ran through a few fencing exercises. Minutes passed, the opposition was late, but eventually a huge, black, open carriage appeared, with the crest of the Templemeres gaudy on the side. The current Lord descended, followed by two Seconds, both with a "routine", even amused, set to their faces, one carrying a long case, the other, a short. Templemere walked to the river edge, whilst the two Seconds approached the single Second that remained by the opposite coach. As they approached, both watched Carr exercising. One spoke to the other.

"He'd better watch out that he don't get tired."

Both chuckled and then reached the object of their walk.

"Good morning. I am Lord Charles Hopgood, and this is Lord Anthony Mahon. Whom have we the honour of addressing?'

"Lieutenant John Kerriack. King's Royals. And the Officer over there is Captain Harry Rogers."

"Just so. Now, we are instructed by our Principal to say that he states, on his honour, that he is no adept with a blade. Not much of a swordsman, if you take my meaning. He calls upon your man, if he counts himself a Gentleman, bound by honourable conduct, to accept this and conclude this affair with pistols. We have a brace here. Would you kindly put that to him?".

Kerriack nodded and turned away to walk the distance to where Carr stood. Having now ceased their practice, Rodgers was wiping the handles of the blades, prior to a dusting with French chalk.

"I've just been talking to his Seconds. Their man again asks that the weapons be pistols, as he is no swordsman. On his word of honour."

"He can go to Hell. Twice he called me a cheat and a liar, and then emptied brandy over me. Tell them that I do not feel that his Lordship would be obliging were the positions reversed. The weapons remain sabres. Tell them that. Exactly."

Rodgers returned to the two figures, who had strolled, in his absence, closer to Carr. He relayed the answer and waited for their reply. None came, other than a curt nod of the head from Hopgood. Both then returned to their side of the meadow. When within earshot of Templemere, Hopgood spoke.

"He says no.

His face became quizzical.

"What was it you used on that insolent bastard Hinshelwood, the last time you were out?"

"Sabres."

Smiles all round. Mahon opened the long box and Templemere extracted a sabre. All then walked to the centre ground. As they advanced so did Carr, but alone. Just beyond five paces the protagonists stopped and regarded each other, Templemere flexing the fine blade, Carr with the point on the toe of his right shoe, his fingers flexing forward, his palm upon the pommel. Neither spoke, but Templemere's expression gave a clear message of deep loathing and contempt. Carr remained impassive. Lord Hopgood moved to the space between them.

"Gentlemen. How is this duel to be? Until first blood, or until one can no longer continue, or to the death? No quarter."

Templemere spoke first.

"Until it is finished, be it death or otherwise. No quarter."

Carr spoke.

"Make it so."

Hopgood spoke again.

"This is a duel with edged weapons. The clear rules are that you both use only that weapon to lay a blow upon your opponent. No other type of blow is to be struck. Agreed?"

A pause, but no response.

"It is time to compare weapons. Please lay your blades alongside each other."

The blades slid along each other, both points seeking the guard of the other. Carr's was found to be longer, Templemere's was short of Carr's guard by an inch. Templemere took the brief moment to inflict a jibe.

"Where did you get your weapon, Carr? Kings Lynn Farmer's Emporium?"

Hopgood's formal pomposity vanished into a smirk. The sabres were indeed, in marked contrast. Templemere's was a finely crafted weapon. A shining, lightly engraved blade extending from a hilt with a single crosspiece and a slender silvered handguard. Carr's, on the other hand, was a far more workaday weapon. A plain, steel blade, extending out of a wide dull metal bell guard that protected the knuckles of the hand. Carr replied with force.

"This sabre has seen me in and out of battle, Templemere! What about yours?"

Templemere ignored the repost and Hopgood continued, still amused.

"Lord Templemere, do you wish to take issue with the length of blade?"

"Get on with it."

"Very well. Gentlemen, you should now open your shirts, to show no protection".

Templemere pulled his open. Carr's already was.

"Take point, and approach."

Each adopted the "high point" and approached each other. Hopgood took both points in either hand.

"En garde. Allez!"

Pale dawn sunlight ran up and along the opposing blades as they touched, then parted, to menace the other or counter a threat. The duellists circled, then counter circled, each content to touch points, one side, then the other and feel for the mistake that could create an opening. There was no sound; as though the drama and frail mortality within the moment had halted the still awakening dawn. No sound, save the small tinkling ring of one blade tip upon another and the sound of their feet upon the still upright grass. Kerriack and Rogers stood stiff and tense, whilst their Lordships leaned upon their gilt topped canes, as though regarding something rather more commonplace.

It was Templemere who attacked first. Circling the point around his wrist, he whirled a cut at Carr's left shoulder. Carr moved his blade across to his left and took the sweep on the underside, so that the arcing edge slid down to meet the guard. With Templemere's weapon now down low, Carr swept his own weapon at Templemere's right sword arm, but he lifted his sword hilt high and made the parry on the crosspiece, then dodged back. Both now resumed circling, but again Templemere took the initiative, attacking with both guile and ferocity. This time the exchange was furious, the flashing blades almost impossible to follow. Carr met the attack, not quite desperately, but it was clear that Templemere was no "dunce with a blade" and had the edge between the two. Carr tried an attack of his own, but Templemere turned Carr's blade low and turned it into a platform for his own offence and pressed in again, fencing quickly, then thrusting for the chest, but Carr took the point over and they came together, hilt locked against hilt.

"Sweating yet, Carr? You should be."

This time Carr's superior strength told. Thrusting forward, he forced Templemere's hilt back against his chest and pushing forward again, sent him back off balance and followed up with a cut of his own. However, Templemere made the parry cleanly, continued backward and regained his stance. With his body he feinted left, then went right, his sword arm moving all the while to execute a flick at Carr's left shoulder. As the blow came, Carr passed his sabre across to his left to meet it, but the connection never came. Templemere had pulled back the sweeping blade so that the tip just missed Carr's upright blade, then, with perfect timing, he thrust it forward. Carr reacted by ducking and dropping to his left, but the blade dug into the top of his right shoulder and slid on, creating a deep cut halfway between neck and shoulder point. Blood flowed. Hopgood stepped in.

"First blood to Lord Templemere. Carr. Do you concede and apologise?"

"No concession, nor apology. I fight on."

Each again came to the high point, Hopgood took both points in his hands and signalled the resume'.

"En garde. Allez!"

Templemere immediately attacked Carr's right side, forcing him to use the cut muscle to lift the blade to make a defence. The parry was slow, but it was completed. Templemere disengaged, but immediately his sabre whirled in, finding the awkward angles, thrusting and cutting, forcing Carr's blade across and back in a defence that was becoming increasingly fragile. Templemere's strong fencing, using wrist alone, was sending the arcing point flashing wickedly across Carr's open chest and right side, the side now red from the open wound. Templemere for once attacked crudely, a simple attack from on high, the gleaming blade ringing onto Carr's high horizontal parry that slid off to Carr's left. However, Templemere had perfect control of his blade and flicked quickly upward for the very tip to connect with Carr's forehead, perfectly dissecting his left eyebrow. A cut opened, deep to the bone.

Templemere remained just beyond reach, not quite threatening, but not quite neutral either. He wanted his opponent to feel the blood that was immediately running down into his eye. Lord Mahon had sidled around to stand beside Lieutenant Kerriack.

"Did we say that Templemere was no swordsman? Well, relative to his skill with a pistol, that is. I'd say he's done just under half of his men with a sabre, the rest with a bullet. I'd say that things are getting a mite sticky for your man. I hope you've plenty of clean rag, to plug the holes I mean, or even enough to make a shroud! Ha."

Carr felt again the pain in his shoulder and now pain high on his forehead. The blood from his shoulder was soaking his shirt and that from his forehead was blinding his eye. That itself was a stinging pain and he could now also feel the ache and stiffness growing in his shoulder. Templemere held off, his face lit by a mocking derisory grin. Carr felt a bitter, fighting hatred welling up inside him, his eyes narrowed to malevolent slits and the jaw muscles at the side of his face stood out as his teeth clenched together. He took one pace forward and circled to his right. Templemere followed the move, sabre "en garde", clearly biding his time, waiting for the attack, then to judge the damage done to Carr by both injuries. The contest was plainly moving his way; either wound to Carr should be enough to help him finish it.

Carr came to the high point and tapped Templemere's blade, once left, once right, then, pushing off his left leg, thrust straight forward directly at Templemere's chest. Templemere took the thrust cleanly away to his right and withdrew his sword arm to make a thrust of his own that would have impaled Carr had there been time to get the point across, but Carr was coming in too fast. His forearm was up, his relaxed wrist dropping the sabre low, point down, protecting his left side by engaging Templemere's blade, preventing it moving across to thrust for

Carr's body. Carr's forearm connected with Templemere's throat, their chests touching. He pushed Templemere back, just enough to give himself room, then, with a vicious backhand, crashed the pommel of his sword into the side of Templemere's face, breaking his right cheekbone. That done, he drew back his arm and smashed the bellguard into the exposed jaw, just left of centre.

Templemere's eyes rolled upward and his knees sagged and buckled. However, as he sank to the ground, by some reflex his right hand came up, the sword dangling by the hand guard around the limp fingers. Carr took the proffered sword by its guard with his left hand and remained standing above the now prostrate Templemere, his own blade upright, his new acquisition pointing down. Hopgood sprang forward, incensed.

"A foul blow, Carr, not fair. I say you are forfeit. A damned ugly, illegal blow."

Carr remained staring at the unconscious Lordship at his feet. Dramatically he speared Templemere's sabre into the earth beside him and the hilt oscillated above the delicate blade, its shadow describing arcs upon the flattened turf. Eventually he turned to confront the enraged Hopgood.

"You and him to The Devil and be damned. I came for a fight, not some kind of dance. I fought with my sabre, so don't complain. He said no quarter. I could skewer him now and there could be no argument. It's done."

Carr walked forward, roughly shouldering Hopgood out of the way. Kerriack handed Carr a wad of bandage, which he pushed inside his bloodied shirt, over the still bleeding cut, then Kerriack bound a strip around the bleeding forehead. As Carr began walking back to the coach, Kerriack and Rogers fell in beside him, but slightly behind. Neither spoke a word to Carr, but both exchanged glances. Rogers handed Carr his coat, but did not look at him. Once in the coach, all sat in silence, Carr staring fixedly out of the window, his expression grim and angry. Kerriack wrapped both sabres in the grey linen in which they had travelled. After a while, Rogers broke the silence.

"Duelling has a strict etiquette, Henry. I know the rules talk of only using your weapon, but it means the point or edge, nothing else. Templemere's a rotten piece, I know, but he did stick to the rules, at least as gentlemen understand them. You struck a foul blow. I'm afraid your name is sullied. Because of this you won't be welcome in the Mess."

Carr made no reply and no one spoke further. Clearly, they knew nothing of his resignation, but what did that matter? The coach pulled up at Carr's lodgings, he gathered his sabres and stepped out, but paused after the step down and turned to look back into the coach.

"I thank you both for your support. If we meet again I hope that it will be in friendship."

Both the remaining occupants nodded in acknowledgment, but made no reply. Carr closed the door and the coach drew away. He watched its diminishing form, focusing on the rear window, black with its drawn down blind. He entered his lodgings, found some clean cotton and stitched up both cuts himself. He then began to pack.

* * *

Seth Tiley had found what he needed. For a march of two days he had been thoroughly examining the ground over which he was being led. Limited though his powers of intellect were, cunning came as second nature. He had grown desperate, which made that cunning wholly focused and intense, himself knowing that the barracks, the same to him as a prison, could not be too far into the future. When at last he spotted what he sought, he pretended to stumble, sprawling full length upon the road, his tether rope jerking down the man in front, the ex-Reverend Percival Sedgwicke, pulling him also to the ground, the rope cruelly straining around his neck and throat. The nearest guard, Tom Miles, swift into temper, quickly ran over.

"You great clumsy ox, Tiley. They taught you to thieve, but not to walk."

All was accompanied by kicks and blows from the musket butt, but Tiley had what he wanted. His rough hands had closed over a small shard of metal that had gleamed at him on the road, unnoticeable now within the palms of hands already bound together. That night, another spent in the shelter of a field wall, he had patiently used a flat stone to grind an edge to one of the sides. The morning check of their renewed bindings now past, he was ready. Feigning a long call of nature, he had manoeuvred himself to the end of the line, one man in front, none behind. The day's march began and, taking every opportunity, the blade held in his teeth, he had cut at his bonds. If a sentry

33

seemed too near, he transferred the blade into his cheek. Only once did a sentry notice Tiley's hands going often to his mouth.

"What be up with thee, Tiley? Summat wrong with thy face?

"My nose is wet. I got an ague. Leave I be."

The reply was no more than a guffaw, but Tiley was making progress. The edge was keen and now naught but a few strands remained of his bindings. The question now was when and Tiley had clear in his mind the kind of country he needed. An hour more brought them to the hills of South Somerset and, as the road topped a gentle gradient, Tiley saw what he needed. The road ahead followed the contour of the side of a well-defined valley; the down side to the right separated from the road by a low stonewall. Beyond that, the slanting field fell down to a wood that was narrow, but seemingly dense. The valley bottom deepened back in the direction they had come, then curved away into the distance. This was perfect, but he needed the last sentry between him and the wall to be just in front, not behind. He began to jerk on the rope. The prisoner in front lurched back, pulling back the man before him. Soon the whole line had extended back and Tiley was just behind his guard's left shoulder, just out of his sight.

He jerked his arms apart and the last strands gave. He was free, but his cunning told him still to hold the rope and give no appearance of no longer being bound. His next move was to edge right, until just behind the guard. With a prodigious strength made greater by the desperation strong inside him, he brought his huge hands, locked together, down onto the exposed neck of the soldier, who collapsed to the road senseless. Big, but still agile, Tiley was over the wall and running with huge strides down the descending hill, rapidly closing the distance between himself and the wood.

The soldier had gone down with a clatter; musket, boots, and accoutrements hitting the road with a noise that turned all heads, all to see Seth Tiley disappearing beyond the wall. Tom Miles ran to the wall, cocked his musket and fired, but Tiley never even heard the ball sing three feet over his head into the trees. He was well over 100 yards down the slope, bounding on further, well over the accurate range of a Brown Bess. Deakin issued his orders.

"Tom, follow him. Harry and Peters, go round right, stay high, out of that wood. Keep him moving left. Pat, you're in charge."

With that, he took himself over the wall and set off left to skirt around the higher end of the valley that lay ahead to the right. Whilst covering the remaining prisoners with a cocked musket, Mulcahey went to the downed soldier, lying ominously still. He feared him to be dead. Irish temper rising he raised his musket to his shoulder.

"Lie down, the damn lot if you! Lie down."

All obeyed.

Tiley was in the wood. In the centre, at its lowest point, was a stream, fast flowing in a narrow bed. Just beyond that was a track, the drove that came up into the field, hidden from above by the trees. He leapt the stream, got to the firm ground beyond and onto the track. Beyond the track the valley side was much steeper and covered in thick undergrowth, he had no choice but to turn right and use the track, wherever it led. He ran on down, the stream to his right, his route curving to the left, as it followed the valley bottom. One gate, then another, slowed him up, but he could hear nothing of any pursuit. However, the track, once firm and level, now turned into rutted channels of thick mud, that sucked at his boots and slowed his running to little more than a staggering lope, his feet treacherously sliding away into the ruts at all the wrong angles. The track had reached its lowest point, continuing its leftward curve but from now on it went upward. However, Tiley saw what he was hoping for; another way off that led sharply to the right. With all the speed he could muster, he headed for the near corner and turned in.

Tom Miles was Light Company. His red jacket had shoulder "wings" and his shako had the hunting horn badge with a green plume on the circular peak. Wiry, strong, and with lungs that could cope with any kind of running, he reached the stream quicker than Tiley had managed, but still some time behind. However, skirmishing experience told him that a streambed gave firmer running than any muddy track. He leapt into the shallow stream and began his run, always keeping an eye on the track in case it separated from his chosen course. His running was unimpeded by neither mud nor gates, but there was yet no sight of Tiley. Nevertheless, expecting some kind of a fight with his quarry, with practice borne of years of service, he drew his bayonet from its scabbard and fixed it to his musket on the run, his pace barely slackening.

Tiley turned into the new opening and stopped dead. It was a track out of the wood, but it led through a cattle pen that was, as was its purpose, full of cattle. Worse, the penned animals had churned both the streambed and their pen into a deep quagmire. He stopped to ponder his next move. It was made for him, because one red figure, then another, was running down from the valley side beyond. He could not get through and make enough time to affect an escape. However, not unused to making an escape from authority, criminal guile told him that a return to the main track would leave the two pursuers to fight their way through the nervous herd and the knee-deep mud. A shout of recognition from one of the red figures spurred him into action and so he turned and re-joined the main track.

This ancient way now ran up and through a deep gully. The bed, worn by centuries of wheels, feet and hooves through the soft red sandstone, was firm but deep, within steep sides that were almost vertical and at the top grew thick undergrowth. Tiley had no choice but to continue on up, apprehension growing. He liked a choice that would give pursuers the dilemma of "which way did he go?" and himself the chance to make a smart move, but now there was no choice but to keep climbing.

Miles heard the shout from up ahead by one of his comrades, which told him that Tiley was indeed up ahead and perhaps not too far. He saw the red figures coming in from the right and so he left the stream to join the track, calculating that Tiley would be found on it, not in the stream. However, when he reached the turn to the cattle pen, he felt disappointment. Tiley was nowhere to be seen and his two comrades were making little to no progress through a pen thick with panicking cattle and thicker mud. He saw the gully leading up and resumed his running pursuit, hoping that Tiley would also have taken what seemed to be the only way.

Tiley was a huge man, immensely strong, but his bulk and strength made for neither speed nor endurance over distance. His breath was laboured through aching lungs and his hammering pulse was surging in his ears. His well muscled legs, useful in a fight, but not in a running escape, seemed to grow in weight as though slowly being cased in lead. He was slowing badly, but the gradient was lessening and the nearness of the horizon told him that the flat of the top could not be too far.

36

Almost all houses in all villages in that deeply rural part of the South West kept dogs. All bred and kept for speed and aggression, dogs that could bring down rabbits, hare, or even deer when working together with the dogs of neighbours, were a valuable addition to any family and worth their place at the fireside. Most were cast-offs from the local deer pack, but still strong, agile, and aggressive. At the top of the drove there dwelt a small hamlet, some cottages, some little more than hovels, but each could show the family hound lolling or sitting just by the door. To the villagers this was a home; to the dogs, the road was pack territory.

The panting, large, and threatening figure of Seth Tiley set off a cacophony of indignant barking and defiance that brought the rest of the local pack from back yards and dark rooms. He found himself surrounded by ten to twelve sets of bared teeth and angry eyes that poured aggression at him from large heads above powerful necks and shoulders. The pack had formed and were mounting an offence enough even to make a man of violence such as Seth Tiley halt and hesitate rather than attempt to fight his way through such a surging, leaping, wave of black and brown, all with the clear ambition to sink their teeth into whichever part of him was in reach. Two fastened to his loose trousers, each taking their own leg. He could make no further progress. Kicks and swinging ham-sized fists did nothing to make a way through. He was trapped against a cottage wall.

Miles heard the uproar ahead over the brow and knew that he had made the right choice. Soon the buildings grew in size above the horizon of the track surface and soon he saw Tiley's beleaguered figure surrounded by the barking and berserk dogs, fending them off with kicks and no small amount of noise of his own. Miles came in behind the dogs, bayonet extended, but he could get no nearer to Tiley than the width of the street. His arrival gave some relief to Tiley, for this new additional stranger gave the dogs a new target for their aggression and some, distracted, turned their attention to Miles, who had to hold them off using the bayonet at the end of his musket. Tiley kicked off one of the fastened dogs, clubbed the other senseless and used the reduction in their numbers to inch his way along the wall to the cottage door. This immediately yielded to the pressure of so heavy a shoulder and Tiley was inside, soon he had closed the door against two baying dogs that were both intent on following him in.

Miles ran around to the back of the cottage, scrambled over the logs and barrels and then around the privy. Then he saw the back door and stopped. Tiley had emerged, but he was not alone and screams were heard amongst the noise of the still barking dogs. Held in the crook of his left arm was the petrified figure of a small girl, a terrified face above a filthy shift, thin arms dangling from wide sleeves and dirty legs dangling down beneath the tattered hem. Mother emerged immediately after, grey apron gripped in tight fists, all raised to a face fixed in an agony of fear and terror; above the fists were eyes wide with panic and horror. Miles stopped, musket and bayonet pointed to Tiley, but he made no further move. In Tiley's right hand was the sharp metal shim, held against the jugular vein exposed by the small tilting head.

"Keep away, don't you move, you bloodyback bastard! One step more and I'll slit her open, wide open. Well enough to see her life all over these cobbles. You stay back."

All the while he backed away himself, threading his way through the barrels, pens, and rubbish that cluttered the back of the rank. The dogs, confused at the front, were no longer there to impede his progress. Miles shifted his gaze, to Tiley, then to the Mother, and then to the child, she rigid with terror, but Miles held his place. He had little choice, for Mother's thin hands were pushing at his chest and shoulder, her shivering voice, between gasping sobs, imploring him to go no further. Miles knew that Tiley would kill her if he showed any move that would threaten capture. Mother was still frozen to the spot between them, her head furiously working to both look at her child and then turn to ensure that Miles was making no threatening move. By now Tiley had edged along the back wall and had reached the last alley between the last two buildings. Laughing with triumph and still holding the girl, like a doll within the crook of his huge left arm, he dodged into the alley and regained the street. Throwing the girl over his shoulder, he ran across the front of the last building and gave a last look back before turning the corner that finished the houses. He then ran smack into the expertly wielded musket butt of Jed Deakin, the brass soleplate connecting conjointly with the point of his chin and his misshaped nose. He staggered back and slumped to his knees, his eyes seeing nothing but flashing lights and his mouth tasting the blood from his nose that mingled with that of

38

his split lip. The released girl ran off in a flurry of bare feet and whirling arms.

"What you didn't know, Tiley, you shitten whoreson, is that I was raised in just these very parts, and I knows every track, gate, hole and hovel. Lash the bastard's arms tight behind him, Tom, and let's get back to Pat and the rest."

* * *

Henry Carr was no stranger to London, but where he was, what he saw, and what awaited, caused an uncomfortable knot of anxiety in the pit of his stomach. He was crunching his way across the gravel of Horse Guards Parade, towards the imposing Renaissance façade that was Horse Guards itself. Within his mind he was hoping that the interview that he had arranged would indeed take place and would prove fruitful. He was there to attend an 11.00 o' clock appointment with the Secretary to the Commander in Chief. The yellow Portland stone shone pale in the weak late October sunshine as he drew closer, passing elegant ladies sitting in gleaming open landaus, engaging in languid and frivolous conversation with tall, equally elegant, Household Officers. This was the meeting place for many, prior to the ride up The Mall and onto Hyde Park and the vital drive along Rotten Row. This poor sunshine could be providing the last day of the 1805 Season. Carr's gravel-crunching brought him close enough to reveal some of the details that existed within the shadow of the arch set in the centre, particularly a sentry guarding the main doorway, set deep within the interior. He passed through into the chill shadow.

Immediately Carr had reached the capital he had taken himself around to this, the solemn centre of the British Army's affairs, submitted his papers, and booked himself a time during which, perhaps, to resurrect his career. He had worked on his uniform long into the night. Buttons, leatherwork, and boots now gleamed, and he presented enough of an impressive sight to bring an immaculate "present arms" from the Coldstreamer on guard. With his sabre scabbard grasped in his left hand and his braided shako under his right arm he used that free hand to turn the huge brass ring to open the door and approached the desk.

"Good morning. Henry Carr to see the Secretary. I believe that I have an appointment for eleven o' clock.

The soberly dressed man, coat and cravat as dark as his eyes, looked up. He counted all within his gaze, from the detailed plasterwork on the ceiling, down to the polished tiles, as his own command and empire and had seen many such an officer, from Ensigns to Generals, cross that floor with a look in their eyes that more often carried dread and anxiety rather than hope. The desk was his citadel; it was almost of sufficient size. With his eyes still upon Carr, he sent a bony hand on the end of a bony wrist to stretch further from the spotless white linen that emerged from his left cuff. Unhurriedly the hand reached the black leather of the plain book that held a place in the top left quadrant of the desk. Using the red silk marker the diary was opened and the page studied, enough to form a reply.

"You are correct, Mr Carr. Please take a seat and I will inform the Secretary that you are here."

Carr nodded and backed away in retreat from the black bastion that rose on his side of the desk. He then turned to select his place, a huge, polished, winged armchair, resplendent with burnished brass studs paraded across the front of the seat, and immaculate amongst a rank of exact copies. With no mistake, caused by neither sword nor shako, he sank down and back into its soft comfort, but he was in too high a state of tension to either notice or enjoy it. Unknown to Carr, the Outer Secretary to The Secretary had been watching, hoping, for some kind of calamitous fusion, between Carr's feet and his sword perhaps, but none came and, mildly disappointed, he disappeared off through a wide, tall, gleaming black door, to the left of the Hallway. Carr was left to himself in the total silence, relief coming only from the loud beat of the giant grandfather clock, off to his right. He studied his surroundings, noting the tall, dark, oaken panels that stood sentry around the walls, adding their height and dour colour to the military ambience inevitable in so august a place as this. A minute passed, no more than two, and to the thunderous accompaniment of the clock chiming eleven, the door re-opened and the Outer Secretary returned. He stood in the doorway and, with no words, merely gestures, waved Carr towards the imposing portal and ushered him through. He was announced.

"Captain Carr, Sir Henry."

Secretary to the Commander in Chief, General Sir Henry Livermore, raised not his face, just his eyes to observe Carr march forward, halt, and come to attention. At this point he raised his head and sat back, elbows on the arms of his huge dark leather chair, fingertips of both hands poised in opposition. He studied Carr for what seemed to Carr to be an eternity, but was only a count of five for Sir Henry. Carr maintained a steady gaze over Sir Henry's left shoulder, a choice that made unavoidable his realising that most of Sir Henry's left ear was missing and there was a noticeable concave furrow along the side of his head, leading directly to the missing section of earlobe. Sir Henry took stock of what was before him, noticing the cut and age of the tunic and the half healed wound bisecting an eyebrow, but all was soldier enough for him to find no fault with this aspect of this tall ex-Captain.

"Rum business this, Carr!" This spoken in a voice that sounded like rocks being washed around on a beach, spoken whilst still retaining his balanced position in the armchair and also adopting an expression that could only be described as disapproving.

"Sir?"

"Your papers here say that you resigned from the King's Royals two weeks ago. Now you present yourself here, presumably with the ambition to rejoin His Majesty's Forces."

"Yes, Sir. I need to know if I can regain a Commission and then approach an Army Agent. I have some money and I am hoping to be able to purchase a posting somewhere. I expect a reduction in rank to Lieutenant."

"Not in the King's Royals, eh?"

"No, Sir. It has been made plain to me that I am not welcome there."

Livermore let the silence hang whilst studying Carr some more.

"So, here you are, not welcome in your old Regiment, and wishing for a Commission, two weeks after resigning one. Explain."

"I resigned to enable me to settle a matter of honour, Sir. A duel."

"And you're not dead!"

"No, Sir."

The faintest of smiles passed across the face of them both. Carr relaxed, a little. Sir Henry continued.

"Who with? What about? You'd better sit down."

"Thank you Sir."

Carr came around to the front of one of the two chairs before the desk and sat, but he did not feel confident enough to place his shako on the edge of the desk before him. He retained it on his right knee, his left hand holding his sabre erect. Sir Henry now leant forward, elbows placed on the desk, evidently curious. Carr could have replied "a personal matter of honour" but saw little point. He felt his best course to be open and frank.

"Lord Frederick Templemere, Sir. He accused me of cheating at backgammon. He also threw a glass of brandy over me. Sir."

"Templemere! I've heard. I've heard he'll be dining on soup and nothing else for the next month. Broken jaw, or somesuch. Ha! Funny wound to come out of a duel with, though. What happened?"

Sir Henry sat back again, evidently cheered up, plainly now in good humour. Carr remained on guard. An inferior reporting to his superior. He continued to look over his superior's shoulder, but had enough sense to no longer use the left, which could seem as staring. Now he chose the right.

"I punched him with the bellguard of my sabre, Sir."

"Punched him with the bellguard. Be damned! Hee hee! In a duel! All against the rules that, Carr. Tut tut. I'm not surprised in the least that you are no longer welcome in polite society".

"No, Sir. But as I said at the time, I came for a fight, not for a dance."

Sir Henry gave vent to a snigger, his large wounded head jerking back in unison with his right fist thumping the chair arm. He sat forward, conspiratorially.

"Well Carr, here's how it is. Boney's still just the other side of The Channel with 250,000 men, all veterans. What Nelson did at Trafalgar, God rest him for it, means we still hold the waters between, but he's still there. England needs every man, even those who can't fight a duel in the right way, which means that you may be in luck. This is the best that I can do. The 9th have been shipwrecked on their way back from Ireland. On the French coast. They've lost a lot of men, but some survivors, about 200, I believe, managed to get to Dorset in the ships boats. What's left of the 9th want them back, but the powers think otherwise. Along with Militia and other odds and sods, they have been collected into a Detachment Battalion at Taunton, not too far from here. It could get up to 700 men, perhaps more, the Militia are strong down there. They need Commissioned Officers of experience, and you can keep your rank of Captain. Also it won't cost you a penny, purchase into a collection of Detachments is unheard of. It's what's available, and I don't see how you'll do better. Militia Officers are being called in, and using their money to buy their postings, in the more, er, well known Regiments. But you'll be back in the Army, and still a Captain."

"I'll take it, Sir. And thank you."

"Don't thank me too soon, boy. Detachmant Battalions are usually the most God-awful rabble, but we need every man, in some sort of order. Mark my words, sooner or later, somewhere, you'll be muzzle to muzzle with Napoleon's forces. Have you ever seen a French column?"

"Yes, Sir. A small one at Castlebar. It went right through our line."

"So have I, only at Marengo. That battle was near as damnit won, when a whole collection of French columns, Division strength, mind, went through the Austrians like they weren't there! Boney's men can fight. When you come up against them, it won't be easy. With Boney leading them, they haven't lost a battle!"

"No, Sir. But I am ready to do my duty."

Livermore looked at him hard, examining his face. The mouth was steady, the eyes fixed and unblinking.

"Right, I'll tell Wilson out there to create your papers and a letter of introduction to Colonel William Lacey. He's in command. They are called the…"

There came the opening of drawers and the rustling of papers. At last the right one was found.

"…5th Detachments, the collective noun for odds and sods and sweepings, Colonel Lacey commanding, good man that he is. Come around at this time tomorrow and collect your orders. Good luck, Carr."

With that, Sir Henry rose out of his chair and proffered his right hand. Carr, recognising the traditional soldier's farewell, both the words and the gesture conveying respect, rose from

his chair, shook the hand gratefully, came to the attention, saluted, did a smart about turn, and marched out. Only then did
he permit himself a smile.

* * *

Now, in thus varied a manner, the body of men that would
come to be known as Lacey's Battalion, the 5th Detachments,
converged to their point of muster. Some came as bound prisoners, some as soldiers obeying their orders, some as officers
obeying the King's Commission. And some came as volunteers,
as a cheerful column marching their way West to Taunton. This
included Joe Pike. He had found his way to Chard, and there a
Recruiting Sergeant had found him, a perfect recruit, strong
and lithe, taking a drink outside the local Coaching Inn. "Take
a drink with me", was the cheerful beginning, "I've stories to tell
'ee," but at the bottom of the dull pewter tankard was the shiny
shilling. Joe was recruited, but he felt neither anger nor sadness. The Army seemed as good a course for his life to take as
any; hunger, no work and nights spent in ditches and barns
had taken their toll on his spirit. He wrote a letter to his family
and lodged it with the Post House, then went back to the Inn.
The Army was paying for his first square meal for days.

Chapter Two

Arrival

Taunton Barracks had been built in the required style; that required by an age during which social rebellion from their own population was as much a fear for any Government as any foreign invasion. With this in mind, it had been designed as much to repel any form of civil unrest, as to keep in the common soldiery. It sat squat on it's hill, its profile only broken by a high centre arch, such as could contain the necessary forbidding gates. The new "prisoner" recruits, these recruited by a Judge rather than the blandishments of any Recruiting Sergeant, saw the pale, brick orange, loopholed walls from a considerable distance as they crossed the last flat plain of the River Tone. The walls were highlighted enough by the weak early November afternoon sunlight, dissipated by the unseasonably high cloud.

Feelings were mixed throughout the equally mixed members of the column. For Percival Sedgwicke it meant the welcome end of the most physically gruelling requirement of his life, but also it meant the beginning of his time as an anonymous soldier. Once a social notary, now he was merely a cipher on a Regimental Muster Roll. Almost impossible for him to contemplate, he could now be ordered and bludgeoned into subservience to become no more and no less than an effective "ranker", able to load and fire a musket, and to survive or fall in any future bloody conflict. For John Davey, it meant a very new life, separated from the freedoms of a country village, he was now to be locked into the restrictive regime of a soldier's life. For Tiley it meant prison, but he could see nothing of the squat building that could call that state to mind. He was marching forward not knowing what lay before. He had a canvas bag over his head!

As chance would have it another column was also approaching the tall, narrow, yet imposing gate arch, topped by a firing gallery that glowered down onto the road below. This column did comprise the gatherings of a Recruiting Sergeant and it contained Joe Pike. On present progress the prisoner column would arrive just in front, a fact not lost on a tall, aristocratic Officer who was Officer of the Guard for that day. Captain Lord Charles

Carravoy decided to alter matters. Left hand sunk into the hand guard of his elegant sword, he strode forward to confront the head of the prisoner column.

Deakin had seen the imposing Officer leave the shadow of the gate and march forward. He had wondered which column he would challenge, but the answer was soon provided, if not by the direction of his march, then certainly by the direction of his gaze.

"Corporal, halt your men"

"Column. Halt".

The dishevelled and tired men shambled to a halt. Carravoy continued forward, this bedraggled collection needed investigating, also they needed a thorough berating for their appalling appearance.

"What the Hell is this, Corporal? Report."

"Corporal Deakin, Sir. Six escort and twelve prisoners. Now arrived from Devizes Assize. Sir."

"This is a damn shambles, Corporal. Report."

"It was a tough march, Sir. Most of the prisoners b'aint used to this kind of trek. Also, we had trouble, Sir."

"Why does that man have a bag over his head, and why is that soldier being supported?"

Carrovoy gestured to the almost slumped soldier being supported by one escort and one prisoner.

"That's what I meant by trouble, Sir. The one blindfolded tried to escape and assaulted that guard in the attempt."

"Right. Him to the Guardhouse, wounded to the Surgeon, the rest onto The Square. Enter after this other column, and when I see you on the Parade Ground, I want you smartened up!"

"Sir."

Carravoy departed to place himself at the head of the other column that was up and passing the junction of the two tracks to the Barrack Gate. Deakin's experienced eye knew exactly what this column was made up of. He knew the Sergeant, knew of his role and recognised the gaudy cockade and the smirking grin being delivered in his direction. This Sergeant, experienced in his task, had managed to drive some semblance of military bearing into his charges, all now marching in step, left foot matching the beat given out by the accompanying Drummer Boy, resplendent in gold jacket with scarlet collar and cuffs.

Deakin leaned resignedly on his musket; wrists draped over the muzzle, leaning slightly forward and his weight supported by the long Brown Bess with its butt on the soil just before his shabby boots. He turned to the nearest figure to him, first in the prisoner line, who happened to be John Davey, still bound at the wrists and a halter from his neck to the wrists of the man behind. It was not lost on Deakin that Davey had worn the march well.

"There you see it, Davey. Them's Volunteers, and Officers like him will always see them as better than you. Unless."

"Unless what?"

"Unless lots of times you does things that makes you look very special."

"How special?"

"Every time it has to be something, the doing of which, makes it very likely that you'll get your head blowed off!"

Davey sniggered and Deakin permitted himself a grin. By now the Volunteers had passed. Time to move. Deakin lifted himself from his musket, then raised the same to his left shoulder.

"Escort. Shoulder arms. Forward."

The column resumed its progress, but there was little in its appearance that could be described as military. Besides the incongruous giant with a bag over his head, wrists bound before him and being towed along at the back of the line, few backs were straight and most legs bent with the weariness of the past week's march. Weariness refused to allow those legs to straighten even over the last few yards, the result being that their feet moved in no unison at all, giving the column more the appearance of a disjointed insect that anything associated with the British Army. In thus manner Deakin's command progressed up the main track just yards behind the column of Volunteers. Deakin's remained a dishevelled and shambolic spectacle, one column of swaying, bound men flanked by guards and made worst by the final ignominy of walking wounded supported by others. In stark contrast the volunteers strode ahead, even with swinging arms, now in rhythm to the drumbeat of the cocky Drummer boy at the rear. He thought the occasion secure enough to turn around and treat Deakin to a highly insolent grin. The taunt was intensified by the eyes in a dirty face that flashed from Deakin to his charges, but Deakin knew enough of Drummer boys, and the stony look and the lifting of his head told yon Drummermite that he had best face his front if he knew what was good for him. The young face fell and the head quickly turned.

The Volunteers reached the high arch and they passed into dark shadow, but the sound of their marching feet and the sharp drumbeat echoed back from the curving stonework above them. They passed on into the weak light and further onto the Parade Ground. The clean rhythm of their feet and arms and their upright backs and shoulders, set the heads nodding and the eyebrows lifting of those who happened to be there watching the events of that post noon. However, any feelings of high optimism for the Battalion were soon dissolved by what emerged next from the darkness of the gate arch. It was obvious, and the well-used phrase entered the many experienced heads amongst those who looked on; "King's hard bargains". Before the anxiety of 1805 the argument had raged about patriotic volunteers soon to be stood, in equality, with criminals who had opted for the Army rather than the lash, deportation, or worse. Here was the argument eloquently arranged before their very eyes. The "hard bargains" shuffled and lurched in, nothing soldierly in any of them, and one plainly so poor a recruit that he had to be denied the sight of even where he was. Heads that had been set nodding with pleasure, changed immediately to being shaken with censure and disapproval, emphasised by eyeballs rolling skyward and mouths set in grim lines.

The Officer of the Day, Ensign Barnaby Rushby, emerged running from the Colonel's Office to discover what was about, scabbard held safely away from his feet, right arm pumping furiously. Close to the object of his concern, the run reduced to a rapid birdlike walk. Unsurprisingly, he had targeted the Volunteers first, now drawn up, stood at ease in four good lines of 10. Salutes were exchanged.

"You'd better hold your men here, Sergeant. I'll fetch the Colonel."

"Sir."

He moved on, to Deakin's party, halted glaringly in the middle of the Parade Ground. This gave the prisoner party a chance to appraise their surroundings, whilst conversations, of which they were the subject, continued around them. The sight before them would have dampened even the cheeriest of spirits in bright

Spring sunshine, but on such an afternoon, the inevitable emotions of such as they, were of gloom and despondency. The whole aspect of the barracks was inward and functional; plain narrow windows and doors stared at them from the plain fortress stonework, some windows guarded by threatening bars, plainly the prison within the prison.

"Better to draw yours up before The Guardroom, Corporal. Is that man wounded?"

He indicated the Private, barely holding himself up, between his two supports.

"Yes Sir. He was attacked and wounded by that prisoner, I mean recruit, there, Sir. Captain Carravoy said he was to the taken to the Guardroom."

Deakin indicated Tiley, facing the wrong way, with a bag over his head.

"Well then, er, wounded to the sickbay, and carry out your orders."

"Sir."

Deakin saluted the disappearing back, now jogging off to find the Colonel. He turned to Mulcahey.

"Pat, you and Stiles get Tiley to the Guardroom. Take him off now. Tom, get the rest over to the Guardroom windows and see if you can't get them to stand up straight. I'm going to the office to get these papers signed."

Only Pat Mulcahey made a reply, "Right you are, Corporal," whilst Stiles released Tiley's tether from the neck of the man in front.

Tom Miles' answer was to turn and shout at the party,

"Now listen. You about face, that is turn around, and follow Peters over to those windows with bars."

None waited for a command, all just did it, haphazardly, increasing the tangle now caused by their tethers. What had once been a tidy neck back to the wrists of the one behind, was now wrists back to the neck of the man behind and so each had to hold their tethered hands out to the side to allow the rope to extend back. Private John Peters motioned for the leading prisoner to follow him, which he did, bringing on the others. Miles had moved to the wounded escort and was supporting him alone.

"Come on, mate. Let's get you to the Surgeon. He'll fix you up, plus a drop of strong stuff too, I shouldn't wonder."

The reply was a weak grin in the sickly pale face.

Ensign Rushby rushed into The Messroom, sword scabbard clattering against the doorframe, and was relieved to find the Colonel there, seated at the long table, going through some papers with Quartermaster Sergeant Harold Sleightman. Rushby was a tall, slim, callow youth who always seemed to be living up to his name; always giving the appearance of being in an anxious hurry. However, he came to the attention well enough, saluted correctly and reported.

"Two parties of recruits have just marched in, Sir. I say, "marched", Sir, but that may not be quite right. One is a party of volunteers with the Recruiting Sergeant; the other is a bunch of tethered felons, marched in by Corporal Deakin. Do you have any orders, Sir?"

Lieutenant Colonel William Lacey had responded to the noisy entrance and was studying Ensign Rushby calmly.

"Mr Rushby."

"Sir?"

"You are the Officer of the Day. What would your solution be to the arrival of two new parties of recruits?"

"Well, Sir. I'd get them issued with drill whites, first. Then see them off to their billets. Get them clean, and then some food. Sir."

"An excellent solution, Mr Rushby. Then you don't need me."

"Yes, Sir. But I thought that you might want to say something to these men, having just joined the Regiment, Battalion, I mean. Especially the Volunteers. Sir."

Colonel Lacey adopted his thinking pose. His left index finger came to the space between his upper lip and his finely chiselled nose.

"Hmmm. You may have a point. Two parties just arrived, you say?'

"Yes, Sir. Two parties, 40 Volunteers, and 12 "Hard Bargains", Sir."

"Desist with the "Hard Bargains", Mr Rushby. You may well find those same men stood at your shoulder in a murderous firefight, or going up into some even more murderous breach! Then we'll find out who the "hard bargains" are."

"Yes, Sir."

"Right. I'll address the Volunteers. You find Captain Heaviside, and ask him to do the same for the, er, "Assize Volunteers". Perhaps a bit of his religious fervour won't come amiss in their case."

"Yes, Sir."

Rushby gave a perfect salute, turned on his heel and marched out, this time managing to control the wayward scabbard. Colonel Lacey turned to his Quartermaster Sergeant.

"I'm not happy, Sarn't Sleightman, but we'll leave it there for now. We've not been here one month, and already what's in your stores doesn't tally with what's in your ledgers. If you say that your Clerks can't read, write, and cipher, then get some who can. There must be someone in this Barracks who can do a competent job as a Stores Clerk. I hope I am clear. Dismiss."

Sleightman rose to his feet, gathered his ledgers and papers, tucked them all under his left arm and with his right delivered a blistering salute, which Lacey briefly acknowledged.

Lacey was a Colonel called back from retirement. 47 years of age, he still had the figure and bearing of a much younger man, but his face carried the weariness of a man who had contended all his professional life with disillusionment and defeat. As a young Ensign, younger than Rushby, in 1775 he had carried his Regiment's Colour up the bloody slope of Bunker Hill and, as the Colonel of his own Regiment in 1781, he had led them out after the defeat at Yorktown, marching to the tune of "The World Turned Upside Down". Until the Treaty of Paris in 1783 he was stationed in Canada on the de facto border, expecting a repeat of the new United States Continental Army's attempt during the war years to invade Canada. He had then spent 21 further years on Garrison Duty around the North American Continent, dealing with threats and rebellions and enduring the fierce heat and freezing wastes of the high Canadian Plains.

Both the defeats and the victories that he had lived through had distilled one salient item of wisdom within him; that it is the role of the Senior Officers in any Regiment to ensure that every man knows his duty and has the capabilities to carry them out. Then, everyone has a good chance of finishing any kind of battlefield encounter in one piece or, at least, still alive. He did his best to apply this maxim wherever he was in a position to, but worn out, he had retired in 1804. However, he was now back in uniform, called back by his old friend General Sir Henry Livermore, who needed experienced Staff Officers who could pull together the mix of volunteers, gaol sweepings, Militia, and survivors from shattered Regiments that were being gathered together to meet the invasion threat of Napoleon.

Lacey walked to the Mess Cloakroom, retrieved his shako and buckled on his sword. He then walked out into the growing gloom of the November afternoon. The cloud had thickened and threatened rain. He saw what was obviously the parade of Volunteers and walked smartly over. The Recruiting Sergeant spotted him early.

"Parade. Atten shun!"

In a not unsoldierly manner, the 40 Volunteers brought their feet together, lifted their heads and straightened their backs.

"Stand the men easy, Sergeant."

"Parade. Stand at ease."

As they had been taught, their left foot moved eighteen inches away from their right.

"You've done a good job, Sergeant. Well done."

"Thank you, Sir. And, if I may say so, Sir, this here's a good lot."

"You may, and thank you once again."

Lacey turned to stand straight and upright before the Volunteers.

"Now, men. It falls to me to thank you for answering your Country's call in her hour of need. You haven't come to a Regiment as such. We are a Battalion of Detachments composed of men from Regiments that are now too small to remain independent, and so they have been gathered here to await orders. Plus recruits like yourselves and Militia. Thus we are called the 5th Detachments. We may be sent to fight as a Provisional Battalion or disbanded and sent to make up the muster of other Regiments, but that is in the future. You are amongst trained men and some are real veterans. Learn from them and you will become good soldiers, worthy of your red jacket.

He paused. The Volunteers remained stock still.

"Bonaparte is stuck over The Channel, but he is still there, and who knows what he may yet try. England needs men ready to stand up and defend these shores, and, we hope, carry the fight to him on his own soil. We stand for freedom, he for tyranny. We fight for our King and Country, he for conquest and personal glory. He hasn't fought the British Army yet, at least not in open battle. He's got that nasty surprise coming, and if we're there, on that day, he'll find out that the British Redcoat is a very special soldier and doesn't give best too easily, if ever!"

The Recruiting Sergeant's smile had broadened with every word.

"Three cheers for The King and The Colonel. Huzzah! Huzzah! Huzzah!"

"Thank you, Sergeant, and thank you men. Now, Sergeant, get these men off to the Quartermaster, get them their drill whites and get them to their billets. And get them fed".

"Yes, Sir. Very good, Sir."

Lacey turned and headed off to his office. It was a short walk but it crossed the path of Captain Jacob Heaviside, him hurrying to address the much smaller group of prisoners. Heaviside also lived up to his name. He was of medium height, but he looked smaller, his muscular legs and shoulders making him look squat and powerful. Salutes and greetings were exchanged.

Heaviside hurried on, and then he noticed Sergeant Major Gibney watching from the side of the Parade Ground.

"Gibney. With me."

"Sir."

Gibney fell in step with the Captain, but remained a respectful yard behind. They reached the sorry rank of prisoners, now rid of their tethers, at least, but shapeless in their grey greatcoats and some ridiculous with bare legs emerging from army boots. Deakin had rejoined his men. Gibney took command.

"Parade. Atten shun."

The soldier escort came to the smart upright. The prisoners mostly just looked bemused. Heaviside drew himself up, three yards before his audience. It began to rain.

"The wicked man travaileth with pain all his days: Book of Job, chapter 15, verse 20. You are all wicked, ungodly men. Were you not, you would not be here. You would not be here, because it is not in your character to volunteer. Although your country be in peril, you would not have stepped forward to answer the need of your King and his people, but it is now so. Be sure your sin will find you out: Numbers, chapter 32, verse 23. The Courts have now sent you to answer your country's call, and you now find yourselves amongst us."

For Percival Sedgwicke, for the first time in days, hope welled up inside him. He raised his face and eyes to study this obvious Man of God. He could not stop himself. He cried out,

"Christ hath redeemed us from the curse of the law. Galatians, chapter 3, verse 13."

Gibney strode forward.

"Listen. Filth! Tha' speaks only when an Officer asks thee to. Clear?"

This was delivered six inches from Sedgwicke's face, close enough so that he could smell the beer and onions the Sergeant Major had consumed for his dinner. Sedgwicke's face just registered shock and fear, but Gibney returned to his place, just behind and to the right of the Officer. Heaviside continued.

"You are all now Soldiers of the King, and subject to his discipline. The light of the wicked shall be put out, and the spark of his fire shall not shine: Job, chapter 18, verse 5. Any transgressions against the orders and instructions of your superiors and betters will result in the lash. Make no mistake; you will "kiss the drummer's daughter!" But: With his stripes we are healed: Isaiah, chapter 53, verse 5. You now have the chance to redeem yourselves. You will wear the King's uniform and fight his enemies. You will recover your honour and you will turn to Christ. Church parade will strengthen your salvation, each Sunday......"

Again, Sedwicke could not contain himself, and besides, he felt himself wholly misunderstood.

"Behold the Lamb of God, which taketh away the sin of the world. John, chapter 1, verse 29."

Heavitree stopped and waited for Gibney to, once again, stride forward. He was a big man. Sergeant Majors often had to enforce discipline with their fists and Gibney was no exception. Over his time he had learnt to judge the weight of a punch against the weight of a man, and most often, as in this case, his judgment was perfect. His huge fist slammed into the left corner of Sedgwicke's mouth, just enough to knock him down, but not enough to knock him out. Sedgwicke was sent spinning out of the front rank and into the man behind. He remained on all fours shocked at the blood that was dripping from his stinging mouth.

"Get him back on his feet."

The two nearest reacted speedily to the order, fearing the same treatment for themselves. Sedgwicke was hauled back upright and shoved back into line. Heavitree continued, making no reference to what had just happened. It was an issue between rankers.

"Each Sunday you will attend Church Parade and you must convince me that you are singing and praying with every fibre of your miserable beings and then, believe me, you will be cleansed. Turn Thou us into Thee, O Lord, and we shall be turned: Lamentations, chapter 5, verse 21. Now, Deakin, isn't it?"

Deakin had been stood to perfect attention all through. Facing his front.

"Sir."

"Get these men off to the Quartermaster, get them some drill whites, into their barracks, and get them fed. Eat that thou mayest have strength, when thou goest on thy way: One Samuel, chapter 28, verse 22. Gibney, dismiss the parade."

Gibney took Heavitree's place as he strolled off.

"Now listen, cowdung! I am going to give thee an order. I will say parade dismiss. Thee turns to tha' right, stands still, and when I say so, Deakin will lead thee off. So thee turns towards him. Here we go. Parade diss miss."

Most knew where Deakin was and most knew right from left, but two found themselves nose to nose with the next along, and, all four became confused, with each not sure who was correct, they or he? They had to be turned around to face the right way.

"By the right, forward march."

All but one this time lifted the correct foot, but the step was soon lost. Led by Deakin with two other Privates, the two lines traversed the Parade Ground.

* * *

"Officer of the Guard! Rider approaching. Sir."

Captain Lord Carravoy lurched resignedly off the inside wall of the entrance arch. He would have to go outside into the steady rain, but at least he had his greatcoat, recently tailored, just brought to him by his servant and it with it's double layer of fine broadcloth to protect his upper back and shoulders. He walked a short way down the track, accompanied by the Corporal of the Guard, the one who had just called him. A lone rider was being carried up the right hand track by an evidently tired horse. The rider wore an issue greatcoat and a black bicorne hat, "fore and aft". The dark grey of the wet greatcoat, the black hat, and the dark wet of the dark horse were details only just becoming clear in the rain and the gathering gloom. Behind the rider swung two portmanteaus, one large, one small, and a large sabre. After three damp minutes the horse gratefully halted before Carravoy and his Corporal. The rider spoke first.

"Have I found the 5th Detachments, Colonel William Lacey commanding, at Taunton Barracks?'

"You have. And you are?"

"Captain Henry Carr. Late of the King's Royals. I have orders to report here"

"Do you have papers?"

"Yes I do, but is there any chance of us getting in somewhere, out of this rain?"

Carr dismounted, and without waiting for an invitation, led his horse towards the shelter of the arch. Carravoy broke the silence.

"Would you be the Carr that had a little to-do with Fred Templemere a while back?"

Carr turned his head towards his interlocutor, a move accentuated by the front point of the bi-corn hat. It was a while before he spoke.

"Bad news travels fast! Yes, I am he. You speak as though you are acquainted with my Lord Templemere."

"That is so, and I haven't introduced myself. I am Captain Lord Charles Carravoy, friend of the family. The Templemere family, that is. So you'd be "puncher" Carr?"

Carr ignored the question. They had now made the shelter of the arch and so he reached inside his greatcoat and produced his papers.

"My papers, that being my Commission and my orders to report to Colonel Lacey. Could you tell off someone to take me to the Colonel's Office, please?"

Carravoy scanned the papers quickly and returned them. He turned to the nearest Private.

"Take this Officer to the Colonel's Office." Then, turning to Carr,

"Welcome to the 5ᵗʰ Detachments, Carr. I hope to see you later, in The Mess. I'm sure we have much to talk about."

Carr replied without looking. He was studying his horse.

"Yes, I'm sure. I look forward to it."

Carravoy replied,

"Not much of a horse, that. Carr."

Carr looked up, and with his indulgent, half mouth smile, replied,

"Just so, but he got me here, and, in my experience, Captains fight on foot."

With that he led his horse after the disappearing Private and followed him across one side of the Parade Ground, until they reached an imposing door surrounded by the only ornate stonework in the whole barracks. Carr removed his belongings and told the Private to take the horse to the stables. With the horse gone, Carr did his best to shake out some of the rain from his soaked greatcoat, the wet having now reached his red jacket, darkening the cloth across his shoulders. He entered the door and, leaving his belongings in the hallway, he went through another and approached the Sergeant Clerk behind the desk.

"Evening Sir. How can I help?"

"Captain Carr reporting for duty. Here are my papers."

"Yes, Sir. The Colonel's in his Office. I'll take these in, and if you'll just wait a moment, I'm sure that the Colonel will see you directly."

"Thank you, Sergeant."

With that the Sergeant rose and went through the door behind and to the left, leaving it ajar. Therefore, Carr heard the Sergeant tell of his arrival and the brief reply of "Send him in. And we need candles." The Sergeant re-emerged and held open the door.

"Colonel Lacey will see you now, Sir."

Carr entered the Office and found Lacey standing behind a smallish, plain mahogany desk, ready to receive him and shake hands. The room was utterly sparse and cheerless, made more so by an empty colour stand, the two "O"s on their long stalks waiting to take charge of the shafts of the two Colours of a Regiment, but both gaping with dismay at the absence of their honourable occupiers. The two tall windows on the inside wall, showing only a slate grey sky, added to the gloom.

"Welcome, Carr. Welcome to the 5ᵗʰ Detachments. Pleased to see you. Not too unpleasant a journey, I hope."

"It was tolerable until the rain started, Sir."

"Yes, quite. The infantryman's curse, eh. To soak and freeze. Well, I see that Livermore sent you. How did you find him."

"Well enough, Sir. In fact in good health, I'd say. I must say I liked him. He impressed me as a "soldier's soldier. Bluff and to the point."

"He is that, and a good friend of mine. An old comrade, you see. We saw some action together, against The Colonists. Have you seen any, action that is, there's no mention here?"

"Yes Sir, but not on the same scale as yourself. In the Irish Rebellion of '98, with the 6th Foot."

"Hmm, yes. A bad business, rebellions, as was that one. It always gets nasty, bad things are done which shouldn't be part of soldiering. You'd agree?"

"Yes Sir. I saw things at the end of that affair that I hope not to see again."

"Amen to that."

The candles arrived to be placed at either end of the desk and Lacey continued.

"So, down to business. We haven't told off Officers to their companies yet, I need to form an opinion of what I have. The main game, as we speak, is to train, both the men and their Officers. You know what we are, a collection of all sorts, even for a Battalion of Detachments"

"Yes, Sir."

"The best I have are the men from the 9th; they were Norfolks. They've only just dried out, but they're all good soldiers and they know their business. You know about that sorry business, do you?

"Yes Sir. General Livermore told me."

"I wouldn't have a hope of making the battalion fit for the field without them. The rest are Militia and recruits, both good and bad."

He changed the subject to Carr himself.

"I understand that you spent some time with the King's Royals. A high ranking Regiment, but clearly you aren't with them now."

"No Sir. It's a long story, but it was with them that I learnt how to serve as an effective Officer. Them, and the 6th, my first Regiment, taught me all I know about soldiering. I'll do my best, Sir."

The words seemed to chime with Lacey. His head rose and he gave a ghost of a smile, for the first time.

"I'm sure you will. That's good, I'm pleased. I need Officers who at least know the Drill Book, and battle experience is a bonus. Too many of my Officers are Militia. They're keen and they know the book, but when it comes to facing a determined foe like the French, veterans too; who knows?"

"No Sir. When it comes to that, we can all only hope to do our duty."

"Well said, Carr. Well said. Right, you can stay in barracks for now, until we find you a billet. The Sergeant will explain what that means. Once again, welcome."

They shook hands again, and Lacey called the Sergeant. Outside, Carr set off around the Parade Ground, following two soldiers who carried his bags. He carried his sword.

* * *

By now the recruits were entering their barrack rooms, carrying their collection of "whites", just issued. Most had never possessed so many clothes before, but one, Percival Sedgwicke, mouth no longer throbbing, merely swollen, remarked to himself the coarseness of the cloth, very similar to Naval canvas, even the shirt and drawers. Upon entering the barrack room, he was struck, mortified, by three things, the smell, the noise, and the lack of privacy. Each barrack room was designed to hold a fifth of a company, 20 men maximum and in some cases also their families. Sergeants and a small proportion of the men were allowed to marry, but in this case that seemed to have been exceeded. This one room, an area no bigger than a small church and not so high, contained the living space of about 50 souls, of all ages, sexes, and sizes. There were few windows and these high up on the walls, with, unsurprisingly, only one open; it was November, after all. Consequently the place stank worse than a stable; of bodies, tobacco smoke, damp, urine, soap, and candle wax. In the centre were four plain, wooden, trestle tables, sitting at which were all kinds of occupants, gambling, talking, mending, making and playing.

The hubbub of adult conversation was punctuated by the cries of children and the arguments of anyone. Privacy barely existed. All around the sides were large cubicles that really did resemble the bays of a stable. Some had a rope hanging between the dividing posts and some of these had a blanket draped over the rope to provide some level of seclusion, but plainly, few bothered. Sedgwicke found himself staring in shock at the naked back of a large, middle-aged matron who was washing both herself and her children within their family area.

John Davey followed Sedgwicke in. To him all was familiar; simply on a larger scale. Large families, such as that from which he had sprung, lived in just this fashion. You lived cheek by jowl with your parents, brothers, sisters, and sometimes uncles and aunts and you just made the best of it. The Room Sergeant seized the shoulder of both him and Sedgwicke and shoved them in the direction of a vacant cubicle.

"You two, in there. Clean it up, and I'll be back to inspect."

Both entered their new home. It was about five yards by four, formed from rough wooden boards that in places had been worn smooth by use. The floor was on two levels, the inside half was a platform three boards high that was covered by two straw mattresses. Davey immediately began to make good use of the many pegs and single shelf. Sedgwicke looked forlornly around, unsure of what to do next, and when not doing that, he cast anxious, even suspicious glances at his new acquaintance. Davey saw his confusion and took him in hand. His pathetic appearance drained away any level of impatience that he could have harboured against his hopeless "stablemate." He had no experience of his character, they had exchanged no words on the march and so he genuinely felt sorry for him.

"Come on now, Parson, this is how it is, and you've got to make the best of it. Hang your clothes on those pegs there, and use that shelf for what won't hang up, like your plate and mug and such. There, that's fine. Now, let's get the mattresses out, and try to clean the place up. There'll be some food soon, I think they must have some kind of evening meal."

Davey dragged out the mattresses and looked around for some kind of broom. He saw one and fetched it, a large "witches" broomstick, made of twigs and a rough pole and gave it to Sedgwicke. He looked at it and then ineffectually started to use it, but progress was made. Davey, meanwhile brushed off the dirt, straw and waste from both mattresses, then he found a cloth and dusted all round, sides, shelves and corners, removing the cobwebs. With the place clean, he looked to himself. He found an unused bowl, went to the row of buckets on one of the tables and half filled the bowl. Returning, he stripped himself naked and began to wash, using the bar of mutton fat soap they had been issued with, modestly choosing to face inwards. He then shaved. Sedgwicke was mortified with embarrassment. On the march, by a stream, they had made space between each other, but this! This was outside of any of the civilised standards that had governed his life so far. Davey finished, dried himself and put on his drill whites. By contrast Sedgwicke now looked filthy and unkempt. Davey's attention returned to his messmate.

"For the love of God, Parson, you've got to clean yourself up. The Sergeant will be back soon and you'll be in for more trouble, and I'd have thought that you'd had enough of that for one day. There's still water in those buckets. Get yourself clean and get into uniform."

Sedgwicke obeyed, again only after a fashion. He obtained a measure of water for himself, took the bowl off to the furthest corner, took off most of his clothes, washed and shaved and then, gingerly, and with great distaste, donned the coarse shirt, thick woollen hose and breeches. Just in time, for the Sergeant then returned and looked around.

"Hmm, that'll do. And see it's kept that way!"

He then turned to shout across the room, voice rising even above the general hubbub.

"Dan. Over here!"

A ranker detached himself from the press of bodies all around and came at the Sergeant's call.

"You two. What're you called?"

They introduced themselves.

"Parson."

"John Davey."

"Parson? What sort of name is that?"

"Its what I was, and it's what people call me."

"Right, sounds fair. Now. This is Dan Smith. He'll show you what's what and how to keep out of the Officer's line of sight. Do like he says, and you'll be alright. Don't and you watch out. Watch out from me, an' all!"

With that, he left. Dan began his instruction.

"That's Sarn't Hill, Obediah Hill. He's not too bad, his bark's worse than his bite. Now, you've got yourselves clean, but there's two things. Your boots and your hair. You've been given gaiters. They're clean, but your boots are dirty. It'll show. Candle grease and soot will do for that. Second, rankers is required to wear their hair in a tight pigtail. In some Regiments, it has to be greased down with wax and soap, and powdered with flour. None's been told to do this yet, so we be waitin' to see what the Officers want. Us bein' Detachments, they might not insist on that. "Ere's hopes. It feels 'orrible and takes ages to do, and I've known men get summat wrong with their scalp and their hair falls out. So, clean your boots and just pull each other's hair back, and tie it with the bit of black ribbon you've been given. Right, I'll leave you to it, then."

With that he returned to the bustling bosom of his own family.

"Right, Parson." Davey said cheerily. He was trying hard not to let the Parson's dour and miserable countenance affect his own good spirits. He was in a warm, dry place, amidst what seemed to be decent folk. All he needed now was food.

"I'm for doing my boots, then some sleep. Perhaps some food will arrive meantime. We'll leave the hair business until later, perhaps morning. Does that suit?"

Sedgwicke nodded once in glum agreement. For one, this place was terrible, for two, the idea of another man grooming his hair and he doing likewise, was utterly repugnant. In addition by a man from such a lower social order, that being a gypsy in this case, he felt sure. Davey then left and travelled around the room. He returned with a large spoon of candlewax, covered in soot, took himself and his boots over to one of the tables and set about his task. Sedgwicke slumped down to sit on one of the mattresses.

Meanwhile, in another barrack room, the twin of Davey's and Sedgwicke's, Joe Pike was settling in with Tom Miles. Tom had, until now, occupied a cubicle all alone, but now Joe had been billeted with him. Tom set about cleaning, organising and giving Joe his instructions, mostly about how he should not, in any way, disturb Tom.

"Now, you uses the pegs furthest from me. That way, when our kit gets wet, yours won't drip on mine. Your eating kit goes at your end of the shelf, furthest from mine, so that it don't get muddled up. Even on campaign you still always uses your own plate, spoon, and such. And your boots and gaiters, always down your end. Boots smell bad enough, so keep yours away from me. I'll smell my own. Oh, yes, and…"

His instructing tailed off in mid sentence, he noticed movement. He looked to see that very many of the younger females therein were moving to their part of the room.

"Who's your friend, Tom?"

"B'aint no friend of mine. Just a messmate so far. His name's Joe. But there he is. He can speak, ask him!"

Joe spoke. "My name's Joe Pike, and I'm pleased to meet you."

The pleasant and formal greeting was met with a flash of her eyes and a sway of her hips.

"I'm very pleased to meet you, Joe."

Their interlocutor was a dark eyed, dark haired woman, who looked mid-twenties and in other circumstances of place and clothing could have been taken for a beauty. As it was, her hair was scruffy, but it could be described as "arranged"; thick and lustrous, it tumbled to her shoulders. Also her clothing was worn, patched and mended. Her bare feet added to the impression of poverty just sufferable, as did the poorly clothed toddler at her right hip, cradled crudely in the large shawl that draped from her left shoulder down and across, with her arms subconsciously steadying and rocking the sleeping child. A warm smile was sent in Joe's direction.

"Be you a Volunteer, Joe?"

Miles answered.

"Yes, he is, damn fool."

Another female now joined the conversation, she the exact opposite of the first. She was middle aged and, frankly, burly. Powerful arms and shoulders bulged at a blouse too tight, from which points it then stretched across her ample bosom. Her hair was tied back, and out of the way. However, her face was comely and kindly, but now her voice was heavy with sarcasm, its tone and cadence marked her as a "Past Mistress" in such exchanges. If the Room Sergeant was the King of the room, Nelly Nichols was its Queen.

"'An of course, you didn't volunteer, Tom Miles. Oh no, gaol sweepings is how you ended up with the King's shilling!"

"I b'aint no gaol sweepings. I did volunteer, but that don't mean I don't regret it."

Joe joined in.

"Actually, I suppose I can say that I didn't volunteer. I had a drink with the Recruiting Sergeant that he bought me, and when I had finished, I found a shilling at the bottom. I could say I was tricked."

Now it was Tom's turn for sarcasm.

"Hadn't you heard of that one! Oldest recruiting trick in the British Army. Damn fool!"

"Well, I'll tell the truth. I wasn't angry, nor even upset. I was cold, wet, hungry and tired. I'd spent weeks on the road and got little work, of any kind. The Army got me out of that, at least."

The younger woman quickly came to Joe's support.

"There you are, Tom, he was tricked and that makes him less of a fool volunteer than you! Now Joe. If you needs any cleaning and mending done, you just come over my way. Molly Dixon's my name."

This accompanied by a beaming smile and another swing of her hips, but the older bridled fiercely at the idea and she some-how became wider and taller.

"He don't need no help from a doxy like you! You come and..."

"Who are you calling a doxy? You fat baggage!"

"You. Three husbands and not widowed once! Just moved on by common consent. There's a gypsy, new, I've heard, in the next room as would suit you, if another move is needed. Joe here needs proper help, and you've got that one to care for. My three is now growed, and can help out."

Molly was fashioning a reply, but a glaring look, clenched fists and lowering gesture that narrowed the gap between them, made her think better of it. Her face was her fortune, even if it as yet remained in the future, and she knew it. She turned her back and took herself and her child away.

"Now then, Joe. I'm the one you come to. Nelly Nicholls is my name. I'm a Mother, too, and if you've got one, don't forget to write to her."

"Yes, Mrs Nicholls. I do have a Mother and I do thank you for your kind offer of help."

"Lord love him, Mrs Nicholls he says. Mrs! I'm in the next bay. Just come over when the need comes."

She too, with Grenadier strides, took herself back to her family.

Meanwhile, Tom Miles was in a state of near apoplexy. He had been in the Army more years than he could count and never had one woman offered to help him with his domestics. Now here was a raw recruit, not been in barracks one day, having two women fighting over who should be doing his washing, cleaning, mending and suchlike! He fixed Joe with a look that could have carried lightning bolts, eyes narrowed, mouth working above a clenched jaw and fingers opening and closing. Joe just returned the look, innocent and blank. Tom let out a healing curse.

"Lord love us and save us!"

He returned to arranging his kit and bedding, although most things were thrown rather than placed.

All was suddenly interrupted. The Sergeant had entered their room, with a burdened Kitchen Orderly.

"Foods up! Left over stew and potatoes for the recruits and their escorts. Bread, cheese, onions and smallbeer for the rest."

The Orderly approached the nearest table and set his two baskets of the latter on its surface. The Sergeant added the small cauldron of stew. Joe reacted first and reached for his pewter plate.

"Come on, Tom. There's hot stew. Potatoes too, I 'spect. We need to be quick."

Tom gathered his own plate and spoon and pushed the boy forward, but in a way neither rough nor vengeful.

"Its stew alright, boy. But don't expect it to be anything like your Mother makes."

* * *

As this meal was starting, so was another but in a different place. It was just before 7 o' clock and all the Officers, save those on duty, had gathered in the Officer's Quarters, a collection of rooms accessed by only one door from the parade ground. Now they were moving out of a small social room to table, which they could see, long and plain, but well polished. The Dining Room itself was one of the largest rooms in the building, but as cheerless as any other. Each Officer, as they passed, placed an empty glass of what had been very agreeable sherry on the small table just behind the door. Colonel Lacey took the head of the table, on his right a sturdy Officer of medium height found his seat. This Officer carried the epaulettes of a Major on his uniform, him being the Senior Major, then, on down the table, a mixture of Captains, Lieutenants and Ensigns. To the Colonel's left came the Junior Majors and then the same mixture, 30 in all around the table, gathered for the Evening Dinner. The tableware was plain and sturdy, such as would be used on campaign, the only decoration some evergreens in a vase. As the soup was served to each Officer, Colonel Lacey rang for the table's attention by tapping his knife against a large wine glass. The silence was instant, all realised the direction it came from.

"Gentlemen. Good Evening. We welcome here this evening a new member to The Mess. Captain Carr, please stand, if you would".

Carr eased back his chair, then stood, looking both up and down the table.

"This is Captain Henry Carr. He has been sent down to us from Horse Guards. Captain Carr is an experienced Officer, who has seen action against the French. I look upon him as a valuable addition to the Battalion. I'm sure that I can rely on you all to make him welcome and greet him as a Brother Officer. Captain Carr, I formally welcome you to this Battalion."

"Thank you, Colonel Lacey, thank you for your kind words of welcome." He paused and remained standing.

"I am pleased to be a member of a battalion that will soon be in action. I intend to do my best, and to do my duty, as I'm sure does every Officer here. Forgive me Gentlemen, for stating the obvious, but we are soldiers and we are at war. At some time, sooner or perhaps later, we will meet the French. Stout hearts and strong arms will do the job; and not forgetting the Roast Beef of Old England."

Smiles and chuckles were seen and heard from around the table. All now looked at Carr. He had their attention.

"I've met the French, as have others here. I've seen then in action, I know what happens. They come on at you, in column, all noise and capering, shouts and drums, but one thing to me is clear. Things don't work out for them when they're stood up to. They don't like a good steady line to their front, standing up, and off to the flanks. There are no better soldiers in the world than us at defending the ground we're stood on. If that's how it is, we'll beat them; nothing more certain, each man standing his ground, and our men getting off their three rounds a minute. So; a toast, if I may Colonel. To stout hearts and three rounds a minute!"

A cheer and then the toast was echoed around the table and all drank. Then the applause, hands drumming on the table.

"Well said, Carr."

"Hear him, hear him!"

Whilst both rapped the table in applause, Lacey and his Senior Major exchanged querulous looks. The Major spoke first.

"What have we here? A fool or a firebrand?"

"I suspect a little of both."

Each nodded agreement to the other. Meanwhile all were showing their approval in some way, except Carravoy. He was sat almost opposite Carr. He showed no reaction, save a knowing smile accompanied by a quizzical frown. Lacey rose to his feet again and resumed his address.

"Thank you, Captain Carr. In truth, I didn't expect a speech, but those are good words, and wise ones too. Now, the soup's getting cold. Gentlemen, time to eat."

It was a good meal. Plain, but hot and wholesome. After the soup came boiled mutton, followed by figgy duff, Carr's favourite, all washed down with a good claret. Carr sat between two other Captains. One was Militia, just joined. The other, as Livermore had said, had been washed up with the 9th, but he also was no veteran. He had embarked on the 9th's fateful voyage, but, not long before that, he had joined from the Militia. As the last plates were cleared away, the Colonel established silence again in the same fashion as before.

"Ensign Rushby. The Loyal Toast, if you please."

Rushby was the most Junior Officer present. It fell to him to make the Loyal Toast. He rose to his feet, as did all the others.

"Gentlemen. The King."

"The King!"

That done, many Officers took their leave and the port and nuts circulated. Carr and Carravoy remained and the port did its work on top of the claret. From a Lieutenant sat opposite Carr, one Nathaniel Drake, came,

"Captain Carr. A glass with you Sir."

This meant that each should fill his glass and then empty it, in accompaniment with the other. Carr showed his half empty glass to the Orderly. It was filled and then quickly emptied in unison, one with the other. With the Loyal Toast done, the conversation could move to "shop"; soldierly concerns. Lacey leaned forward.

"Carr, I don't know if you've met my Senior Major?"

"No Sir."

"Then may I put that right? Captain Henry Carr, please meet Major Padraigh O'Hare."

"I'm pleased to meet you, Captain Carr. May I welcome you to the Battalion?'

This delivered in the smoothest, most lilting Irish brogue that Carr had ever heard.

"I'm pleased to meet you, Major O'Hare. Thank you for your kind welcome."

Lacey rejoined.

"Padraigh was with Abercrombie at Alexandria, in the year one. He has something to say about lines versus columns."

"That's right, Colonel. I was a Captain in the 28th Gloucesters, and it was a damned hard episode. We had to fight front and rear for a while, you know, but if I understand Henry correctly, he is saying that lines beat columns because of superior fire-power delivered from a steady line. A French column is often between 50 to 100 files wide. That means only those in front can fire. Only up to 100 replying to something like 800. He's right, a steady line will win every time, but only if it stays steady. The French soften you up with cannon fire and sharpshooters before the column arrives, and it works. Certainly it has against the Austrians and Prussians, and they know a thing or two about fighting."

Lacey joined in,

"And I saw the answer against the Colonists. Sharpshooters out front. Theirs brought down our gunners and Officers so badly that our lines lost cohesion and we lost our advantage in cannon. Light Infantry out in front, protecting our main line until they close, to within 100, perhaps even 50 yards I'd say, now that's a good thing. I hear that Moore has been developing Light Infantry tactics over in Shorncliffe. That gives me, at least, some cause for optimism."

Carravoy had been listening to the conversation but made no contribution. Until now.

"A heady speech that, Captain Carr."

Carr made no reply, instead he regarded Carravoy with his usual blank but indulgent stare.

"Where was it that you faced the French? Exactly?"

"During the Irish Rebellion in '98. I was at Castlebar,

Ballinamuck, and the taking of Killala."

"But we lost at Castlebar. Notwithstanding what Major O'Hare has said, in your view how does that square with your idea of lines against columns?'

"The French column went straight at the Militia. They had the advantage of being in line, but they didn't stand. It's all very well talking about superior firepower, but if you're a ranker in the path of that column, you know that if they reach you, you're dead. It's intimidating and that's what the French column relies on. You fire, one, two, volleys, but the French come on, the following ranks stepping over the dead. They look unstoppable. The men in their path very soon take on a severe fright, and if they don't see that column stopped, and soon; they run and you've lost. The French come on with their shouts and drums, and they look unbeatable, and they feel unbeatable, especially if you've just endured sharpshooters and grapeshot, as the Major says. The men in the way of that column have to feel that it's being stopped. If not, they run! On the Militia, it worked perfectly. These French tactics prey on the mind you see, as well as the body."

"True," added Lacey. "But I feel that we can also prey on their minds. A steady, long red line, all trained and moving as one, now that's intimidating. Never mind their shouts and screams and drums and what. A long, silent, red line. Disciplined and standing firm and steady. That's something that will prey on their minds, and I think I'm right."

He paused and placed his hands on the table.

"But, ah! I'll leave you Gentlemen to another glass of port. Early rise in the morning. Trouble with the stores. I bid you goodnight."

All rose and returned the Colonel's goodnight. The port circulated and all sat in silence for a minute or so. Carravoy broke the silence, his sarcastic tone carrying thinly veiled menace.

"Captain Carr. I wonder if you could help me to settle something. I was in a discussion, maybe even an argument, about duelling. I maintained the position that in a duel involving sabres, only the point or the edge may be used to lay a blow on your opponent. Do you have a view?"

Carr made no immediate reply, but to sit back, fold his arms, and regard Carravoy with a relaxed stare from under his eyebrows, his head tilting forward. Carravoy returned the look with an amused smile. All others were silent. Padraigh O'Hare felt the tension and leaned forward on both elbows. He was worried. After a moment, Carr replied.

"In my reading of the Code Duello, which controls these things, nothing is said at all about how you fight your opponent. Convention, not the Code, is that you use only the weapon, but were you to throw a stone, you would offend no written part of the Code."

"But would you not agree that duels occur between Gentlemen, and Gentlemen should use a weapon as it was intended. One fires a pistol at an opponent, one doesn't use it as a club, or hurl it at his head. The same applies, don't you think, to a sword. It has an edge and a point and that is what you use."

"My Lord. I have been in a duel with sabres, as I think you know. Perhaps you haven't. I was being beaten, I admit it. I still carry the wounds."

He pointed to the lurid diagonal line dividing his left eyebrow.

"It was clear to me that soon I would be dead. Facing death, and I put it that strongly, I chose to make a fight of it the best way I knew; it was that or be slowly cut up and killed. I fought as though in battle, and I came out alive. As the winner? Well, that's debatable."

"Debatable. I'll say! Faced with evident superiority, a Gentleman would have lowered his sword and given best."

"Given best? Given in, you mean. Also, that would have made me guilty of what I had been accused of: cheating. Does not a gentleman's code tell him that honour comes before life? It certainly should for an Officer. If you can still fight, you fight! If Templemere thought it was all taking place as though in a ballroom or on a ballet stage, not a battle field, then he was mistaken. For me, I was in a fight for my life, so I fought. I make no apology. All I can say is that you so-called Gentlemen, expecting your opponent to obligingly carry on the duel according to your rules until he's skewered, should be much more careful about who you pick a fight with. Some may actually, and justifiably in my opinion, turn it into a real fight."

"And I still say that a Gentleman would ...."

O'Hare intervened. His Irish accent giving bite to his commanding words.

"Carravoy, Carr. That's enough. You've both made your

70

points, and frankly, Carravoy, I'm disappointed that you should raise such a thing as an Officer's past encounters at the Mess table. Especially his first time at this table of comrades. Leave, now, both of you. Off to your billets, and let this argument between you occur no more. Do you hear?"

"Yes, Major," came in unison. Both left the table, collected their shakoes and left into the night. One turned left, the other right.

* * *

The barracks was settling for the night. Corporal Pat Mulcahey was tucking up his four children, two boys and two girls, onto a mattress divided by a long rolled up blanket. They were getting older and boys and girls in the exact same bed just wasn't proper to one such as him and his good wife Bridie, both firmly of the Catholic persuasion. Bridie had a younger sister, Mary O'Keefe, Bridie the eldest of six, Mary the youngest. Mary slept in what can best be described as a "lean to", only it was a blanket that did the leaning, being suspended from a shelf above and slanting down, giving Mary a secluded sleeping space. She was settling herself in the one place in the day that she could call her own, when Jed Deakin arrived in their living space, as he usually did at the end of the day, to talk to Pat. Mary saw his boots pass the end of her "bothy" and she looked out and up from around the blanket,

"Hello, Jed."

"Hello, Mary."

The head was withdrawn.

Bridie Mulcahey, warned by Mary's greeting, gave the same, and Pat looked up from lavishing affections upon his children.

"Hello, Bridie. Everything alright? Pat, we'll be needed in the morning, best get up early. There'll be drill for the recruits, and Tiley's trial, too, I shouldn't wonder. We'll be needed for that. Some of our new 'uns will need shifting, and if they don't shift, it'll be us as gets it. Could be a busy day, then. I'll see you in the morning, Pat."

"For sure, Corporal."

Deakin turned to leave, but an elfin face had appeared above the blanket of the children's mattress and held up her arms in Deakin's direction.

"Uncle Jed."

This prompted kisses and hugs for all four of the Mulcahey children, administered from "Uncle" Jed, and, with all the tenderness he could find, his rough hands smoothed hair and hoisted up the blanket to just the right height below their lined up faces. A last smile at Bridie and Jed was gone.

The night began, but for Percival Sedgwicke it was the worst of his life. His mattress seemed to be filled with everything that bites and the night was filled with the sounds of snoring, grunting, farting, fornicating and shouts from those dreaming of far into their past. Such words as he could discern clearly were born from the depths of nightmares and the sentiment that they carried was of battle and terror, and it did little to ease the gnawing fear and apprehension that was large within him. For much of the night he consoled himself in prayer, his despair giving potency to his ability to compose the correct litany, asking his God to forgive his past transgressions and praying for deliverance from this place of sin and wickedness. At some stage he fell into an exhausted sleep, but it seemed that after no time at all, he was being kicked awake.

Chapter Three

A Soldier's Life

Breakfast came and went. The meal was bread and either small beer or tea, brewed from second-hand leaves used once and now donated by the Officer's Mess. Plus whatever was left in the copper stew pans, the contents of which were re-heated and thinned with water. The occasion took place at the barrack room tables, amid the din of wives, children and shouted orders. All was to be done within 30 minutes, including dressing and preparations for the forthcoming parade. Coincidentally with eating, grooming took place, particularly to achieve the regulation hairstyle. Davey took care of Sedgwicke's whilst he was eating, for which Sedgwicke was thankful. It took his mind off the distasteful process and, his hair still being Parson length in the clerical style, it was long enough to tie back quickly and easily. He was even more thankful when a woman from another barrack room, whom he described to himself as "of the same ilk" as Davey, offered to take care of Davey's hair. Neither Davey nor Sedgwicke objected.

All were to parade outside with full equipment, in the ten companies that comprised a battalion; with the exception of the "new men". They were to form up outside the Guardroom, in four ranks, facing across a short side of the Parade Ground. At 7.30 each man was in his proper place in his company, waiting for orders and waiting for the slow breaking of a November dawn that would replace the deep November night. The moon still shone between the scudding clouds, whilst all, including the recruits, stood still and observant. The silence of the parade ground was uncanny, made more so by the solid ranks of hundreds of red-coated soldiers eerily making neither sound nor movement. If there was a moment when the recruit's life as a soldier began, then this was that time. Orders were barked out and the ten companies marched out of the gate and away, marching to regulation step with shouldered arms. Off to what the recruits could only guess at.

With the last echo of the marching feet fading from the four walls, the recruits found themselves confronted with Sergeant

Major Gibney. Gibney was immaculate. His height would have made him imposing even were he not, but everything about his uniform was in perfect order, right down to the silver topped Drill Cane tucked under his left arm and the shining hilt of his Sergeant's short sword. It was now, despite yesterday's noteworthy events, that they noticed that Gibney had a peculiar accent.

"First. Inspection. I desires to take a good look at thee."

With that he began a slow march up and between the ranks of four. With little kit issued, he did not expect too much to be wrong, nor, in fairness, could he complain too much about kit that was only issued hours ago. As long as they were clean and buttons were in the right holes, this time he would be satisfied. All right, so far. And so far. He stopped.

"Name."

"Percival Sedgwicke."

"Percy. My boy! Thee has a first name that I does not want to hear, but thee has a rank that I does want to hear, and so has I. I wants to hear both, mine and thine."

"Private Sedgwicke. Sergeant Major."

"Better. That's correct. Yes; but there's nowt correct about the cow-herd boots that thee has decided to wear this morning on my parade. Tha' boots are so filthy, I can smell 'em from here!"

Sedgwicke had done nothing to improve the appearance of the boots that he had been issued with at Devizes and they now showed as more mud than leather. What Davey had done, he hadn't, and the clean gaiters accentuated the boots' filthy state. All else was quite satisfactory; he had, after all, once dressed for society.

"Can thee smell tha' boots, Sedgwicke?"

"No, Sergeant Major."

"Then us'll put that right, because I can. Why should I suffer what thee doesn't? Corporal, get me a length of twine."

A length of twine was found and Sedgwicke removed his boots. There were no lace holes. The boot was really a heavy shoe that the foot was thrust into like a slipper, but nevertheless the pair were tied together around the arch between the sole and heel and Sedgwicke suffered the indignity of both now being draped around his neck by Sergeant Major Gibney. The inspection continued. Some buttons were wrongly fastened and some slouched in their uniform more than stood, but Gibney was content with the start.

"That'll do for first off. But now, harken. Not from here on. Boots must be blackened and buttons polished. Jackets and

74

breaches must be clean and hair tied back. And especially clean, when thee gets 'em, shakoes, muskets and bayonets. Especially tha' muskets and bayonets. Right, inspections done. Now, take good notice. After what thee looks like, the next thing that we has to teach thee, is to come to attention. That way thee'll keep out of trouble with th'Officers, and wi' me! Attention should give thee no problem. Up straight, feet together, arms straight down. Right. Attention!"

All managed after a fashion, some were straightened by the Corporals that had arrived front and sides to help Gibney with his educating.

"Not too bad. That'll do for a start. Now, the second thing that we has to teach thee is to march. Tha's no good to any General, or whatever, if thee can't get th'selves to where tha's needed. This battalion marches at something like 90 paces each minute. For those of thee that knows, that's three every two seconds. Now; each of thee, hold up tha' left hand."

Most got it right. Those that did not were quickly cuffed and corrected by the Corporals.

"Now. Put forward the foot that's below the hand thee has up in th'air."

All managed this.

"Good. Lower tha' hands, straight down by th'side. Now, I'm goin' to tell thee to right turn. Remember that foot thee pushed forward? Yes? Well, on the command, "right turn", thee swings it around tha' right foot, to tha' right, letting tha' right foot spin where 'tis. Then, thee stamps in ont' ground, next to tha' right. So; let's try. Ready? Right turn!"

Many calamities. Some kicked the man in front with their rotating left foot, some toppled forward into the man in front and some overbalanced altogether. However, Gibney's Corporals restored order and Gibney continued.

"I'll put that down to over enthusiasm, which is better than none at all. Now, time to march. Thee starts with that left foot again, and this little Drummer Boy here," indicating a lone child supporting a drum almost the size of himself, "will give thee a beat, and each time he beats that drum, that left foot hits the ground. Now, hold up tha' left hand."

All did.

"Now, lift up tha' left foot."

All did.

75

"That's the foot that begins thee off. Thee steps first with that one. Time to march. Ready? Company, quick march."

Thus all set off, not just to the furthest end of the Parade Ground, but into the life of a soldier in the Army of King George III. Once up and once back, Sedgwicke was allowed to double over to the well, clean his boots and resume his place. All morning, until the midday meal, they were marched up and down. They were halted at one of the two end walls that were their only destinations and told to about turn. Not yet according to military regulations, simply by stopping and spinning, coming to attention and then they were marched back. All saw only the man in front as he strained to keep time, therefore few saw the huge figure in ill fitting whites, being walked between four burly, yet still diminished by comparison, soldier escorts. The drumbeat and Gibney's barked orders dinned in their ears and then once again, as it echoed back from the high barrack walls. The sound impinged into the Officer's Mess through the open window, the messroom now arranged to serve as a Military Courtroom.

"Close the window, Sergeant."

"Yes Sir."

The Clerk Sergeant moved at Lacey's command. The window was closed and the Clerk Sergeant had resumed his seat when Tiley was marched in and placed physically before the Colonel's table, the bare boards resounding to the stamping feet. The room was simple. Lacey at his desk, with O'Hare at his right side. The Clerk at a right angle to them both. 10 feet from the Colonel's desk and facing him were placed three rows of chairs, utilised from the Mess Room. Those at the front were occupied by a variety of Battalion Officers, those at the back by NCO's and Private soldiers who were witnesses.

The Clerk Sergeant came and stood before the imposing figure of Tiley. Holding his head at an uncomfortable angle, he began the proceedings by addressing him.

"State your name and rank."

"I be Seth Tiley."

"Your rank"

A pause and a blank look; no answer. The Clerk Sergeant spoke to him in a hushed tone.

"Your rank is Private. Say Private."

"Private."

Colonel Lacey took up the proceedings.

"Private Tiley. This is a Field Court Martial being held to hear your case. The Clerk Sergeant will now read out the charges that exist against you. Proceed, please, Sergeant."

"Private Tiley, you are charged with attempted desertion and assault. That on the 27th October 1805 you attempted to desert a party of recruits and in the process, you assaulted Private William Maltby. How do you plead?"

"It were I, right enough. I never wanted to be in the Army in the first place."

"Please answer guilty, or not guilty."

"Guilty."

Colonel Lacey resumed.

"Private Tiley, you have pleaded guilty. You now have a choice. You can accept my sentence, or you can choose to accept sentence from a Military Tribunal by three higher Officers than myself. This will take some time to arrange, during which time you will be held in the Guardroom cells. Which do you choose?"

"I'll take the sentence that you gives me."

"Very well. But before I pass any sentence I need to hear the facts of your case. There are four witnesses, as I understand it, and the first is Private William Maltby. Call him, please, Sergeant."

Maltby marched from the back, came to attention and saluted, but was then allowed to sit, he still not being fully recovered. His position was close to Major O'Hare. Lacey began.

"You are Private William Maltby?"

"I am, Sir."

"Please describe the events of 27th October that involve Private Seth Tiley."

"Well, Sir. I was the escort at the back on the right. Tiley was the last in the line. He was alongside me, then he wasn't. He dropped back. The last thing I can remember was the rope to his hands going slack, then a blow on the back of my neck. Then I woke up and I was sitting against a wall with Pat, I mean Corporal Mulcahey, looking after me."

"You did not see Tiley come at you?"

"No, Sir. But there was no one else after him in the line."

"Thank you Maltby.

Maltby was dismissed, and then Mulcahey, Deakin and Miles were called. All told their stories, Miles laying particular emphasis on the terror and distress caused by Tiley's threat to the life of the child. All three were stood down as witnesses, but remained in the room. Lacey turned to Tiley, who had been stood before him throughout the whole proceedings.

"Private Tiley. You have pleaded guilty to attempted desertion and assault. You are a bad lot, Tiley. You came here as a prisoner, and whilst the other members of your party are being trained in their duties as we speak, to turn them into soldiers, it has not been possible for you to shed the description of prisoner. I will now pass sentence upon you, but before I do that, I want to make it clear that if this were a civilian court you would hang. You would hang because added to the civil charge of assault would be kidnapping and possibly even attempted murder. Any day, this battalion could be marching off to fight the French. I'm not going to take the chance of you being left behind because a just punishment for crimes such as yours, has rendered you unfit for service. Do you have anything to say before I pass sentence?"

Tiley shuffled his feet and lifted his bound hands.

"I want nothing to do with the Army."

"You will be given two dozen lashes, punishment to be carried out at 4 o' clock tomorrow, before the paraded Battalion. Escort, march him away. This Court Martial is at an end"

Tiley was turned around by his escort and bodily shunted towards the door. The Clerk Sergeant had already prepared the orders, which were placed before Lacey to sign. As he did so Lacey angled himself towards Major O'Hare,

"We need to watch that one very carefully. I'll wager he's a devil in a fight, but he'll run first chance he gets. Make sure his Corporals and Sergeant are well aware, will you?"

"Yes Sir."

Colonel Lacy rose from his place, which was the signal for all others to rise. The Clerk Sergeant called for attention and all obeyed. Lacey left and O'Hare dismissed the assembly. Deacon's good friend of long standing, Corporal Tobias Halfway was waiting outside the Colonel's Office. One soon joined the other.

"Anything on, Jed?"

"Not till kit issue before tea."

"Time for a quick one in town, then."

"If you're buying!"

Both made the gate, subconsciously in perfect step, marching in quick time. The nearest Inn was just down the hill towards the town proper, The Turks Head, a drinking tavern well frequented over the years by the occupants of the barracks. As they walked, they talked, and talk came easily between them.

"What do you think of Tiley's sentence, Jed? I think he got off light."

"I'll say! Assault and desertion! I've seen 100 lashes given out for just one of those two. And that Tiley is a huge man. That cuff he gave Maltby could have killed many others, and now he'd be waiting to dance on a rope's end. Instead, just a two dozen tickle from the lash. I'd call that light!"

"Ah, he's lucky, and that's the truth. You're right, we've had Colonels and Majors would have given him the hundred, march or no march. And given him another 50 if he didn't parade next day. Two dozen! I'm thinkin' this one's soft."

"You might be right, but I don't know. He's seen some service, and come out the other side; he strikes me as different, somehow. He's certainly not a parade ground stickler who'd flog you for a tarnished button; and I think the Army's changing. We're seeing a new kind of Officer, they approach it all sort of different. He could be one. The old style hasn't worked, has it? It used to but it doesn't any more. Apart from Egypt, and that was down to the lads pulling that one out of the fire, it's been defeat after defeat. The old ways didn't work in The Colonies, did they? The lash doesn't seem to come out of the bag as much as it used to, and I'm for that. It changes nothing, flogging a man's back off. Just makes the men more fearful and hating of their Officers. I don't see how that can be good."

Silence fell between them, but Halfway soon ended that.

"I reckon a damn rum billet, though, this one, Jed. Detachments in the middle of no-where, at the back-of-beyond."

Deakin chuckled.

"I'll not argue, but it's better than the bottom of the sea, or a French prison, where a lot of the lads are."

"That's true, but I can't see us getting back to the 9th. This looks too set, more so by the day."

They entered the Inn; inside both took off their shakoes, tucked the chinstrap up inside and placed them on the bar. The Inn was a drinking place, little more, but it was homely enough, with its oak tables and chairs and a good fire beneath a Hamstone fireplace. Deakin tapped the Regimental Plate on the shako's front, showing the Britannia of the 9th East Norfolk.

"That'll have to change. To common GR, I suppose, and some number."

"A shame that'll be. Not many Regiments has got special headgear, outside of The Guards, that is."

They ordered their drinks, two quarts of ale, and resumed talking.

"I reckon we've been lucky, Jed. With what we've been through, we should be dead. Or missing something! In '99, we came out of that North Holland mess in one piece, and that shambles of a battle, what was it called? Castrica? Sounds Spanish."

Deakin lowered his tankard, even though in mid swallow.

"Castricum."

"Castricum, aye. And I'll say this, I can't see this lot that we've got now fighting their way out of a mess like that, like the old 9th. Can you, Jed?"

"Not as they are now, that's for certain sure."

"On top of that, we had the shipwreck coming back from Ireland. I never thought we was going to get off that ship, Jed, I never did. I was sure we was goners, but we was lucky, that boat was there and we got into it and got back here. But this b'aint lucky. Here is the very bottom, Detachments!"

"It don't look top drawer, I'll grant you, but I'll settle for it. To me things don't look too bad. We've still got some good Officers from the 9th. Drake for one, and I've got a lot of time for Lacey and O'Hare, like I said, they've seen service. O'Hare was at Alexandria, did you know that? Heaviside's the worst bloody Biblepuncher I've ever come across. No wonder the Good Lord held him up off that ship, but he's a good Officer. I'd trust him in a fight. I s'pose if you look on religion the way he does you're not too worried about an early trip to the Pearly Gates, but for a Holy Joe, he knows his stuff. His Company was rearguard at Castricum and he got 'em away, with French cavalry ranging about."

"I've heard French cavalry is the best there is, Jed."

"Ah, I've heard that too, and I don't want to be around when it's put to the test. Anyway; Carr and Carravoy, a rum pair both. I don't know, we'll see. Carravoy; bit of a fop, likes giving orders. Carr, too early to tell, but seems a cold fish. I heard he was part of that Irish Jig back in '98. Anyway, don't forget; we've good Corporals and Sergeants, like I and thee, and Gibney, that Yorkshire bugger. He didn't sink."

"Pulling this lot together is going to take some doing Jed, all the same, I saw them "hard bargains" you brought in, and the Army don't look good in the eyes of civilians outside. The Navy's the people's darling right now."

Both nodded and silence fell between them and both drank. Deakin broke the silence.

"But this I do know. I'm not wantin' that much to get back to campaigning. We're in the middle of nowhere, but it's a soft billet, and like I said, that I'll settle for. Training what's back there in the barracks suits me just fine as of now. What after? Who knows, but sometime we'll be sent to fight the French; later, I hope, not sooner, but I'd put my money on us staying as a Battalion of Detachments. If we're trained and ready, they won't split us up. Makes no sense. 'Sides, I'm not sorry to be spending some time home. I've been away a long time."

"I didn't know you was from these parts, Jed? How'd you end up in the East Norfolks?"

"I joined up in '89, with the 13th Somersets. I was driving sheep off the Mendips to Bridgwater, and there was a Recruiting Sergeant there. It just seemed a better life, is all. We was sent to the West Indies in '90, a whole Battalion, and the first action I saw was against rebel slaves. In '95 we was sent home, just 60 strong. Disease practically wiped us out, swamp fever they called it. Me and others spent some months in the hospital. The Doctor reckoned my early life on the marshes saved my life, gave me some "resistance", was his words. After, when I got better, the 13th was away, and so we was scattered around, including me. I ended up with the 9th."

"Disease! Ah. 'Tis a common thing, right enough, Jed. Disease kills more than any enemy. I reckons you got to be unlucky to be killed in a battle, but lucky to come out of a campaign without some ailment that could kill you just the same."

"From you, that's wisdom! Come on, drink up, we've just got time for another."

* * *

"Greatcoat, one. Shako, one. Foraging cap, one. Stock, one. Haversack, one. Canteen, one. Knapsack, one. Pouch, one. Musket, with sling, one. Bayonet and scabbard, one. All were either piled onto proffered arms, or jammed on heads, or slung around shoulders and necks, and all delivered with an authoritarian bellow by Quartermaster Sergeant Sleightman. Each recruit then manoeuvred themselves out through the narrow door of the Quartermaster's Stores, hoping that nothing would be dropped before the disapproving gaze of Sergeant Major Gibney. Once through the door, they joined the growing parade of the "kitted out", whilst the line of those waiting for their issue slowly diminished. Eventually all had received what was required. Gibney placed himself before them.

"Thee now has full kit, apart from tha' red jacket and grey trousers; they come later. Right now, tha's raw recruits, and not yet worthy. There will be full inspection of all kit, morning parade, tomorrow. We expects it to be clean and shining. Parade, diss miss!"

The recruits faced right and then shuffled off to barracks, peering to find their way over and around the pile of new possessions held in their arms. Joe Pike returned to his cubicle, where Tom Miles was waiting for him.

"Hang up what you can. Then come back here with your jacket, musket and bayonet."

Joe did as he was bid and laid all on the table with a clatter.

"Right, here's the rule. If it's metal, you polish it with brick dust. That's yer musket, bayonet and buttons, crossbelt badge and shako badge."

He examined the badge and plume.

"13th! Somersets, I think, with a beige plume. They're a local Regiment. It must be some stuff from local stores. Anyhow, here's some of what you need."

He placed a small canvas bag before Joe containing a red powder.

"If it's white, you rubs it with damp pipe clay. We calls that "blancoeing". Here's a dish. But start with what's metal, and you may as well learn now what some old sweats calls those two," indicating the musket and bayonet.

"Some calls yer musket, yer "bundook". I've not heard it much, but I'm hearing it more. That comes from service in India. Some of the natives out there calls guns that, or similar.

Most Regiments, though, calls it a "Brown Bess", don't ask me where that comes from. Yer bayonet is yer "brummagem", that's because it was made in Birmingham. Right, if that's clear, get to polishing."

Joe obeyed, his actions being duplicated all over the barracks; all recruits now knew what awaited transgressors of a kit inspection. Only the others of his kind didn't have the female audience that Joe soon gathered, nor the two elder daughters of Nelly Nichols, who, unbidden, had sat and begun on the second task of whitening his cross belts.

Similarly, John Davey and Percival Sedgwicke sat at the same table together, burnishing and cleaning their new equipment and clothing, Dan Smith having given both the benefit of his experience. There had not been one companionable conversation between them since they were placed together, but each was growing used to the other, not as friends, but at least as a familiar face. Sedgwicke felt able to begin a conversation, but not so much as to use the over-familiar, as he felt, Christian name of his fellow soldier.

"Are you a church-goer, Davey?"

"Yes, Parson. I am, or was, and I believe in Jesus Christ as my Lord and Saviour, but regarding church goin', the likes of me didn't have too much choice.

"How do you mean?"

"Well. The likes of you went to worship and to meet others of the same standing. We had to go to keep ourselves in work and shelter. If the Squire didn't see you in a pew behind him, with your family, and then you paying your respects after, outside, you was one step down the road to losing both your job and your cottage.

Sedgwicke looked quizzical and gave a slight shake to his head.

"Ah, you can shake your head, Parson, but I've seen it, and often. When times got hard, and some had to go, church goin' or no church goin' was something that could help them decide. Especially when, as often happened, the Squire asked the Parson for his opinion."

"Does that mean that you went to church not for worship, but to keep your job and your standing with your betters?'

"Betters! I'll let that go, but it means both, Parson, and I'll level with you straight. The job was more important than the worship."

"You mean you place your standing with your employer above your love of God?'

"I mean I place food on the table, a roof over our heads and something burning in the grate above my love of God. But don't get me wrong, Parson. I went and was glad to. Sunday is the Lord's Day, but I know what would happen if I didn't, and that's something that was never in your life, but a big part in mine. The lives of the likes of me aren't our own. You works in with what those above wants of you. If you don't, then you suffers."

"But you didn't work in, did you? You were condemned as a poacher and sent to the Army."

"Pots and kettles, Parson. Pots and kettles!"

Sedgwicke felt his ire rising at so effective a reposte from someone who, not so long ago, would not have dared even to have met his gaze.

"But that's right Parson. I did some poaching, but again, there's hard times that comes around. If wages is cut and rents go up, then you can't buy meat nor even bread sometimes, and so it has to come from somewhere else. Hunger isn't funny, Parson. Neither's cold nor no roof over your head."

"Stealing's a sin!"

Davey chuckled.

"You're right there, Parson, but I knows a bigger sin, and that's throwing a good family out of their home because you've both cut their wages and increased their rent. And then getting all high and mighty, saying they should have worked harder, or saved during better times. For the likes of us, there b'aint no better times. Just time to get through with the family kept together."

"There will always be social order, Davey. That's natural and God's way."

"Then I'd like your God to come down and get a basinful of it for himself, then, being Almighty, He might decide to make a few changes."

Silence fell between them. Despite the blasphemy, Sedgwicke made no reply, he could feel Davey's temper rising and now appreciated his situation well enough to realise not to make an enemy of someone who, at least, had shown him some measure of kindness and acceptance. Sedgwicke was grateful when Davey moved away. His "hairdresser" had returned and they sat at a table quietly talking for some time.

Acceptance was also close to being fractured at the Nag's Head, another Inn in Taunton, but larger than that of the Turk. The Inn itself being larger, rather than the "Head", which helped distinguish it from that of the Turk. It was the billet of Captain Henry Carr; Lieutenant The Honourable Nathaniel Drake; and Lieutenant Royston D'Villiers, and was one of the more comfortable Inns within the town, a Coaching House on the pike road. All three had just enjoyed a quiet dinner, their first together, made more pleasant by agreeable small talk and all were now in Carr and Drake's room. It was a cosy room, warm and well furnished, but a little cramped for two.

D'Villiers had his own room, being of independent means. Over dinner he had been freer with the wine and port, a more than carefree attitude and ability towards spending had helped there, and both were beginning to work on his discretion, rarely at a high level at the best of times. He was sprawled before a good fire, feet half way up the fire place, one heel resting on a bas relief of a child carrying a sheaf of corn, using the head as a convenient projection. A bottle of port that was by his side was regularly suffering major attrition.

"I mean, how can one tell one's friends that one is an Officer in a "Detachment Battalion? It just sounds too ridiculous; it turns one into a laughing stock. Also, it's so damned underhand for Horse Guards to suddenly say to Officers in the Somerset Militia, "Get yourself and your men to Taunton Barracks by the 1st October." It's presumptuous and underhand. Even fraudulent! It's understood that an Officer in the Militia will move up into at least a regiment with a number and name, and even one with some small standing should not be too much to hope for! It should at least be the one we're in reserve for; the 13th. Also, there's The Mess. Its so "trade", and provincial, and, well, suspect. I thought that Irish Officers only served in Irish Regiments"

Nat Drake was polishing a pair of pistols.

"This "suspect". Does that include present company, D'Villiers?"

"No! Oh God no! You're both good company, good fellows, and all that. I do think so, really. I just mean that, well, I do think that social rank should count for something within the Army of King George."

Carr looked over the top of his newspaper.

"Good company! That sounds suspiciously like damning by faint praise, D'Villiers."

"Well I don't mean it to. I'm disappointed, that's the "up and down" of it. I mean a "Detachment Battalion" and all that goes with it! In Taunton, of all places!"

Carr and Drake looked at each other, a "what's wrong with him" look on their faces. Drake made the first reply.

"And what's so bad about Taunton? I find it most agreeable, apart from the weather. There's nothing wrong with this billet, and the food's most plentiful, and palatable, even a 'cut above. Excellent pork and fowl, and the cheese, most good."

"My dear Drake, what's food and lodging got to do with it? There's no society. None. At least none that I would care to be invited to."

The port bottle suffered further dimunition.

"You mean, D'Villiers, that it's intolerable to find yourself in barracks in a town where the women only wear last year's fashions, a "ticket to the show" means going to some kind of agricultural display, and you could wake up one morning to find that a goat's chewed a hole in your breeches!"

Conspiracy grew between them. Carr took up the theme.

"Yes, exactly. How can a chap be expected to put up with a society where a sheep shank is what you use to tie your cravat, a "rising trot" means running your carthorse up a hill, and the only question your tailor wants an answer to is, in which pocket does Sir carry his pork pie?"

By now, Drake had dropped his head below the table, only supporting himself by holding onto the pistol that remained upright, it still wrapped in its polishing rag, his shoulders quaking with silent mirth. Carr had crunched his paper between his two hands and was holding all before a face going through paroxysms rather than utter a sound. D'Villiers, by contrast, was oblivious to their barbed ribaldry and was off on another subject.

"Do you think he'll give me the Light Company? Or even the Grenadiers? It could be either. It must be one of the two. Or what about the Colour Company? Oh, yes, we haven't got any have we? Hmmm. Well, him and my Father knew each other, you know, the Regional General too, but I've forgotten his name. They attended all the County occasions together, dances, point to points. I think they were in the same Hunt, even. That must count for something."

By now, Drake had sagged almost completely out of his chair, chest on his knees. Carr was hoping to get out of the door in order to release his pent up hilarity, but Drake recovered first and managed to fire off yet another barb.

"What County was that, then, D'Villiers? Blastedheathshire?"

Both Drake and Carr resumed shaking.

"Good Heavens, Drake, no; not in the least. I've never heard of such a place! Why, the family part of Somerset. Bath! Surely you've heard."

Both had recovered further. It was Drake that answered.

"Oh, yes. D'Villiers. We've heard, and we're both sure that you will be assigned to a Company the best measures up to both your social status and talents. Whatever your undoubted attributes are, I'm sure Lacey will make good use of them. I mean, who else can tie a cravat like you, or has a horse with such breeding? As you keep telling us."

Hearing this last, and observing their mirthful faces, the realisation that he was the butt of their wit began to dawn on the social warrior D'Villiers. He began to take umbrage.

"I say, you two. I don't think you're taking this seriously at all. This is career launching stuff, you know. And at least I haven't been thrown out of one Regiment and ended up with a bunch of sweepings. Nor been washed up on a beach! I'm at the start, and I intend to get it right. Right from the start."

He paused and fixed both with an alcoholic, hurt, and disapproving look.

"I think it's time I left, and took myself off to my own room."

This he did. With as much dignity as the early bottle of claret and most of the bottle of port would allow, he rose, accompanied himself with what was left of the port, navigated himself to the door, found the handle, carefully twisted it, pulled open the door and left. Carr and Drake exchanged mirthful smiles, accompanied by head shaking, and resumed their reading and polishing respectively.

"Has he really got a thoroughbred horse?"

"Oh, yes. There's some racehorse in him, I do believe."

Carr screwed his mouth and nodded his head.

* * *

Second day and once again the recruits had to be kicked awake. Breakfast arrived, the same dull combination of bread, small beer, and tea, although the bread was fresh and plentiful. Davey and Sedgwicke sat in silence, whilst Dan Smith gave a cursory inspection of their kit. Tom Miles did the same for Joe Pike, but he could find no fault at all. Joe had taken good care of the metalwork, and as for that needing pipe clay, not all the veterans in the barracks were male! The Room Sergeant shouted for quiet.

"Orders has come through about hair. Hair is to be tied back, but not soaped and powdered."

Cheers rang out all round.

"But; stocks is to be worn on any parade, and during drill."

This last greeted by heavy groans.

"What's the stock, Tom?"

Tom rose from the table and fetched Joe's stock from his part of the cubicle. Joe had wondered what it was and how he wore it. It looked like a badly made shoe, thick black leather and two long rows of lace holes. Miles placed himself behind Joe and opened the stiff collar of the tunic further. The stiff front of the stock went under Joe's chin and the rest, with the laces and lace holes, came around the back of his neck. The instant it was placed around his neck, Joe felt it to be stiff and uncomfortable and the stiff edges dug into his skin, both under his chin above and the sides of his neck below. That was before Miles began to lace it up. The effect worsened with the joining of each lace hole. When Miles was finished Joe could only move his head from side to side with difficulty and he could not look down at all. He felt uncertain if he could chew food, nor swallow, even.

"What's this for, Tom?"

"This is to keep your head up, so that you looks right on parade. The Officers likes to see all our heads at the same slant, and this is what does it. Its called your stock and we all hate it. The only good thing about it, is that you won't have to wear it all the time, not with this lot, at least, just on parade. And the stiffness does go, especially if you hammers the edges to make them soft, but not too much, mind, or it'll show and that could mean the lash for damaging the King's property. Better still, if you can get a bit of linen, like a kerchief or summat to pad out where it digs into your neck, then its not too bad."

The two elder Nicholls girls, who had been sat at the end of the table, immediately disappeared and re-appeared almost as quickly with a light blue kerchief that they passed along the table with nervous smiles and lowered eyes.

"Why, thank you girls, that's a real kindness. I'll wear it always."

Tom Miles ground his teeth, clenched his fists, smote the table and looked in the other direction, whilst rising to obtain his own, well worn and sweat stained cloth object of the same; also the stock itself, from a far peg in their cubicle. An order rang out.

"Parade, in five minutes. Full kit."

All responded, haversack first, then the white crossbelts with bayonet and ammunition pouch, then the knapsack, then the canteen, with its bright leather strap. Last, each hefted his musket onto his shoulder. Thus began the second day, Morning Parade with all in their same places. After a brief inspection, as before, the Battalion marched out and the recruits were left with Gibney and the same crew of Corporals.

"What a fine body of men! What a fine, fine, body of men, but thee b'aint "stood on parade in the regulation manner.""

All were in correct uniform and uniform correctly arranged, but their muskets were held in whichever way the owner felt comfortable.

"Thee remembers that left foot?"

None could have nodded, even if they felt a reply was required. Their stocks held their heads straight ahead and high.

"Well, think about tha' other one, tha' right. Tha' musket goes alongside tha' right leg. Do it now."

He paused whilst several muskets shifted over.

"Trigger guard forward, butt close alongside tha' right foot."

He paused again, whilst some muskets swivelled.

"Right hand reaching down the barrel, fingers reaching around the barrel and hold it where it's comfortable. Do it now."

All obeyed and some muskets toppled over. Some hadn't realised that their thumb went around in the opposite direction, but order was soon restored.

"We calls that, "Order Arms.""

He marched to the furthest recruit to his right.

"What does we call it?"

"Order arms, Sergeant Major."

"Now then, yesterday we learnt to march, today we learns to march with a musket. A soldier's not much good without his gun, now is he? But thee cannot march with tha' gun dragging along the ground. Right. Keep tha' left hand where it is, down by tha' side, but lift tha' fingers to make a kind of cup."

All did eventually, after some thought. It was their only free hand.

"Lift up tha' musket so that the brass plate of the butt drops into tha' left hand. But don't yet drop tha' right. Hold tha' musket steady with it"

All did.

"Without dropping tha' musket, slope it back onto tha' left shoulder, and return tha' right hand to tha' right side."

All did.

"What fine soldiers, what fine, fine, soldiers. We calls that "shoulder arms.""

They spent the next hour going from "shoulder" to "order", finishing with a performance to the beat of a drum. To many, the 10lbs and more, coupled with the awkwardness of its five-foot length, turned the musket into a ton weight, and it was a great relief to all when Gibney ordered shoulder arms for the last time and set them off marching. Dinner, the main meal of the day, came as an even bigger relief and enabled the removal of the hated stock, at least for a while. The afternoon saw the introduction of "present arms" which taxed, even more, muscles that were not used to such weight shifting. At 3.30 they were paraded in their usual morning position, before the Guardhouse windows and told to "Stand with ordered arms." A short while passed and the rest of the battalion marched in and formed up with practised ease, forming on them as the first company on three sides of a square. In no time, all was silent, each company with Officers before and N.C.O.'s behind. A chill wind ruffled the hair queues of some and the shako plumes of most.

They had not stood thus for longer than two or three minutes, when three drummers marched out of the Guardhouse, each carrying a long Sergeant's halberd, a long, almost medieval spear, each with shining steel point and a short cross piece just below, that bisected the shank that held the point onto the shaft. A single drummer boy and another drummer, he with Sergeant's stripes and carrying a beige linen bag, followed the three. On reaching the centre of the square the three halberds

90

were lashed together using the crosspieces and thus they formed a tall tripod. The five drummers then lined up to form the fourth side of the square.

With this complete, as though all took place with practised regularity, Seth Tiley was brought up to the tripod, not led, but walking unaided, flanked by two Sergeants, with another behind. His hands were bound before him at the wrist and he was stripped to the waist. Quickly a tether was fixed to his bindings and one of his Sergeant escorts threw the tether over the top of the tripod such that it ran between the spearheads. Both Sergeants then hauled Tiley's arms up the tripod to pull him against the wooden shafts, but such was his height that Tiley easily supported himself upon his own legs.

Gibney detached himself from the parade.

"Parade, shoulder arms."

The whole parade, in almost perfect unison, obeyed. With this done, Colonel Lacey and his Majors rode in on horseback, Lacey walking his horse around to face Tiley.

"Private Tiley. You have been sentenced to two dozen lashes, for assault on a fellow soldier and attempted desertion. Drummer Sergeant, carry out the sentence."

The Drummer Sergeant opened the bag and took out the lash, the regulation Cat 'o Nine Tails; one long strand that split into three, and then each of these into three "tails", each tail having three knots. He approached Tiley and combed out the strands. One of the Sergeants gave Tiley a length of wood to bite on and then lashed it behind his head. The Drummer Sergeant placed himself four yards behind Tiley and threw the tails of the lash out behind him. The Drummerboy began a roll.

The first stroke gave an eerie whistle as it travelled to meet Tiley's back and connect with a sickening slap, like a wet sheet being swung against a wall. Tiley lurched into the halberd shafts, his mouth wide open, such as would have caused the wooden length to fall out, were it not tied. All the wind had been knocked out of his body. His knees buckled, then he recovered himself, stood, and sucked in breath. The second lash made the same connection, but Tiley had tensed himself and his bulging back muscles took the blow. Each lash was delivered carefully by the Drummer Sergeant and soon blood began to flow, slowly at first, then more quickly and the lash, equally quickly, spread it further over his back. Tiley bit hard on the wood tied into his mouth, but each lash brought a deeper gasp of pain. After one dozen, the Drummer Sergeant combed out the tails of the lash. The Medical Officer looked at Tiley and nodded his head, the punishment could continue, but when seventeen was reached, the carefully choreographed performance took an unrehearsed turn. Tiley bellowed with rage, seized two of the pike shafts and lifted up the whole structure, turning around to use the pikes to ward off the next lash. The Drummer Sergeant stopped and Lacey spurred his horse forward to confront the defiant Tiley. His face contorted with anger.

"Private Tiley. You will take your punishment or you'll hang for mutiny. Do you hear me! Mutiny. In the Army that's a capital offence. You'll hang!"

Tiley stood defiant before Lacey, shoulders heaving as his lungs fought for breath. For what seemed an age to those who watched, he held up the pikes, maintaining his defiance, his glaring eyes locked in fierce hatred against the Colonel. A long stare passed between them, then slowly the wooden shafts were lowered and Tiley turned his back towards his tormentor, the Drummer Sergeant. He jammed one of the shafts into the ground and leaned on it for support, the other two hanging loose at odd angles. Lacey motioned to the Drummers and the two ran forward to re-arrange the tripod. With that done they remained, holding them in place, each looking up at Tiley, but neither spoke a word. Spittle issued frothily from Tiley's mouth.

"Drummer Sergeant. One dozen more."

"Is that from now, Sir, or on top?"

"On top. Now do your duty."

Thus Tiley received three dozen lashes and their delivery seemed to go on forever. Lash after lash on a back already shredded and bloody intensified the horror of what was taking place before them. Many in the Recruit Company, seeing such medieval brutality for the first time, felt their senses leaving them and began to sway. Joe Pike, next to Davey, lurched into his shoulder. Davey pushed back, returning him to upright. He whispered,

"Up straight, lad. Close your eyes. You don't have to look, just count. That's 31."

Joe Pike took a firmer grip on his musket and recovered. He closed his eyes, as did many others.

"36. Punishment complete, Sir."

"Cut him down. Off to the Surgeon."

Tiley was hanging from the tripod, attempting to raise himself upon legs that seemed either disobedient or absent. A bucket of salt water was thrown over his riven back, turning the back of what had begun as white drill trousers into different shades of red and pink. He was cut down, then supported by his arms around the shoulders of two drummers, and then dragged off, face down towards the sickbay. However, just as they were passing through the gap between two companies, he gasped out,

"Stop, stop! Leave I be."

His attendants released his arms, but he sagged down onto all fours, and remained there for a short while. Then, his massive strength asserted itself and he raised himself up. He stood, swayed, and then stood again with his hands on his hips. He took several deep breaths. Then, from there, he walked to where the drummers were indicating and disappeared into a narrow door at the far end of the barrack square, a trail of water and red spots on the hard packed sand marking the route of his passage.

* * *

The polished shank of the steel bayonet lazily described slow circles across the background of the swept cobbles of the billet. Joe Pike held the sharp point between his finger tips and absent mindedly allowed the bayonet to rotate, one way, then another, whilst he stared dully through the tube of the shank to the floor, focusing from one, then back to the other. He had removed none of his kit, merely unlaced the stock, and now he sat hunched over on the nearest stool, haversack still in place along with all other bags and pouches. A morose figure, head supported on his left hand, elbow resting on his left knee, his right hand rotating the bayonet.

The men had been dismissed by companies and none had dawdled whilst returning to their barrack room. Whilst nothing was different from dismissal from previous parades, the events of only minutes ago had cast a pall over the mood of the battalion, more so on the new recruits and none more among them than Joe Pike. Likewise, John Davey and Sedgwicke had arrived in their cubicle in similar mood, and both divested themselves of their kit, but from then on, their reactions had been very different. John Davey placed both hands on a high peg and leaned forward, head between his forearms, thinking revolutionary thoughts. Percival Sedgwicke had quickly sunk into a corner of his part of the cubicle and was now mumbling a barely audible prayer. Davey could hear emphasised words such as "forgiveness" and "salvation" but how, when, and for whom were beyond his hearing.

Within their cubicle Tom Miles turned angrily on Joe.

"Snap out of it, boy, and quick. There's worse than that waiting in your future, and that's no mistake. You think you're the only one that doesn't like a flogging? Get up and see to your kit. Food'll be here soon and you're still togged up. Now move! Do as is needed."

Joe rose to his bidding and began the ordered removal of his equipment, each onto its peg or into its place.

"But it was all done so careful, Tom. Like it was measured out, in a play or something. Cold blooded and careful."

Tom ceased his own arrangements and turned angrily towards him, thumbs locked into the top of his belt.

"Listen boy, you have to understand what you are to them. You're not a man, you're a musket. They want to make sure that you will stand and fire that musket no matter what your state of mind. You could be in a fight where the enemy is so close that the paper from their cartridges is setting your clothes on fire. You're so close you can see if they've shaved, if they've any teeth missing, and you can hear them curse you. What will stop you from running? Not much without the terror that they make inside you. The lash or the rope. They think they have to make you fear that, more than you fear getting killed, and you just saw some of it."

"But what about fighting for your country, and your King? What about not showing yourself a coward? Doesn't that make you stand and fight?

The outburst had relieved Miles of much of his anger. He spoke more calmly.

"You may be right, lad. It may be in there somewhere, but that's not for now. Right now, get yourself ready to eat. After, you change your shirt and linen. Tonight's Saturday night, washing night. Tomorrow's Sunday, one of the better days."

* * *

94

The order came for Church Parade. No weapons, nor packs, nor pouches. The parade assembled with each company in their allotted place, the recruits forming an eleventh company as part of the three sides of a square. All the family members gathered behind them, against the walls, to also partake of the Sunday devotions. The weather was dry and mild for November and most had thoughts that were less than Holy, more concerned with what followed this Sunday ritual, but it was nevertheless a welcome diversion from the endless drill and preparation. Gibney marched up to Colonel Lacey and reeled off an immaculate salute that was returned with equal quality.

"10.30, Sir. Parade assembled. I am informed that the Vicar is at the gate, arrived on his donkey. Shall I let him in, Sir?'

"Yes. Make it so."

"Sir."

Further salutes were exchanged and Gibney walked to the gate, nevertheless showing more military bearing than most could manage on a march down Whitehall. He took himself through the space of the missing side of the square, passing what occupied this vacant side, seven drums piled in a pyramid to form an altar, three on four. Gibney disappeared into the darkness of the gate arch. Five silent seconds passed, terminated by a cacophony of baying and shouting. What emerged from the arch was not a Vicar, preceding Sergeant Major Gibney, but the lone donkey, saddle down on one side, baying and kicking then galloping into the centre of the Parade Ground. Feeling itself hemmed in, it galloped back to the gate, found that occupied by humans, so it turned again and ran along a wall, using the space between the paraded soldiers and their assembled relations. It reached a corner, felt safe, and so stopped. At peace, it turned its head to look at the long collection of humanity, raised its tail and defecated. However, it did now feel sufficiently tranquil to allow a nervous Orderly to gather its trailing halter.

Smiles and smirks broke out in the ranks and sideways looks were exchanged. The Sergeants felt, more than saw, the disturbance and more than one mumbled dire threats about teeth disappearing down throats. Hoots of laughter issued from amongst the civilians, quickly terminated by fierce looks from nearby NCO's threatening a taste of the cane for anyone who couldn't "hold their rattle."

By this time, Gibney had returned.

"Ah'm sorry, Sir, but the Vicar has fallen off, and can't get up. We've tried to make him stand, Sir, but he just falls over again. He doesn't look ill, nor seem injured, but he does smell of drink, Sir. And his clothes are all out of good order. He hasn't shaved. He smells of drink, Sir. Sorry Sir."

"Nothing to do with you, Sergeant Major. Not your fault. You are excused the Parade. Order a carriage, and get the Vicar home."

"Sir." And Gibney hurried away

Lacey half turned towards Ensign Rushby, who was stood just behind his left shoulder.

"Rushby."

"Sir."

"Take yourself over to Captain Heaviside. Do try to maintain an Officerlike appearance. Present him with my compliments, and ask him to take over. A psalm, a prayer and a hymn should cover it. I'll produce a Sermon"

"Sir."

Rushby saluted, described a reasonable about turn and took himself off in the direction of Captain Heaviside. He did his best on the question of "Officerlike", but few could attribute that high adjective to the marionette march that took him to the said Captain who was at attention in front of his Company.

"Colonel Lacey presents his compliments, Sir, and asks if you could take over. The Vicar is indisposed, Sir. The Colonel added that a psalm, and a hymn, plus a prayer should serve the purpose, Sir. The Colonel will do the Sermon"

Heaviside made no reply, instead he turned to face the Colonel, came to the attention and saluted. Lacey replied in kind. Heaviside marched smartly over to the drums and stood before them, not behind. He stood at ease and remained silent, not so much to gather his thoughts, more to gather his audience unto him.

"Book of Psalms; 40. I waited patiently for the Lord; he inclined to me and heard my cry. He drew me up from the desolate pit, out of the miry bog, and set my feet upon a rock, making my steps secure. He put a new song in my mouth, a song of praise to our God."

Heaviside continued on, sonorously enunciating six of the seven verses of one of the longer Psalms, and the thoughts of many drifted away with each line. Order had been restored; all was as normal on a normal Sunday parade. This was neither orders, nor instructions, that could result in punishment if not followed. This was orders and instructions for the good of their mortal soul, such as had been dispensed in their direction for all their lives, since they could stand in Church and sing and chant. The thoughts of many drifted away, off to fix on what they may, thoughts of family, future, friends and enemies, hatred, home and hunger, but the good majority listened. Heaviside's sepulchral voice slowly and gravely intoned the weighty words of David in the 40th Psalm. Fear of God dwelt amongst the ranks of soldiers as much as the populace outside, probably more so. Any soldier, either deeply religious, such as Heaviside, or more loosely persuaded, knew that he was more likely to keep an early appointment with his Maker than most that were not of his calling.

When the time came, all joined in the Lord's Prayer. Softly spoken by a thousand voices and more, the comforting words rose in surging waves of cadence beyond the confines of the four square parade ground, even through the windows of the Sick Bay where many, even in their beds, joined in. It was a communal act, into which each felt joined, an element of a common humanity, united by their collective recitation of the familiar words of their childhood, coupled together by a shared canon of certain belief. Equally did all join in the hymn, Love Divine, All Loves Excelling. Soldiers and their kin were no different from any other congregation and enjoyed belting out a good tune, and the rendition may not have been up to choir standard, but it could not be faulted for lack of volume nor enthusiasm.

With the advent of the last lines of the last verse, Colonel Lacy strode forward to turn and stand just before and to the left of Heaviside. As the last notes faded away over the grim walls, Lacey allowed the silence to gather and settle. All looked and waited to listen. The Colonel had something to say.

"What is the worst sin that can be committed by a soldier? Theft and rapine are most often associated with soldiers and we all know the punishment for these crimes. "Thou shalt not kill" sits more loosely upon ourselves, for it is our trade, to kill our country's enemies, those that would march through our streets, depose our King, and overthrow our way of life. These are sins and crimes within our law, both army and civil law, but what is the greatest moral sin that a soldier can commit? I say desertion. The soldier that deserts his comrades commits both a crime and a sin, a moral sin, to leave his comrades in the lurch, alone to face the lot of a soldier, whatever that may be. Whether it be to run from a firing line at a time of mortal danger or to run from his post in time of peace, both are moral sins, the worst a soldier can commit. To run from the ranks in time of battle means one less musket, one less foe that the enemy faces, and this gives him succour against us. No less, in my view, to run in time of little danger, whilst home and safe in barracks such as this. They desert our side as we prepare to face our country's enemies, and with their sinful absence we know that we are one fewer. They run from a future that we are prepared to face. We prepare to meet what the future brings, binding ourselves together as comrades. The deserter sins against God and his country, and he sins against us, soldiers who will one day endure the danger and shock of battle, standing together shoulder to shoulder."

A silence and stillness filled the square with the ending of his last words. Lacey made no move, nor any other sound, allowing the message to sink in. Finally, he addressed the Officers opposite him across the parade. Gibney was absent.

"Major O'Hare. Please dismiss the parade."

"Sir."

The orders rang out and the companies disassembled. Lacey turned to Heaviside.

"Wesleyan hymn that, Heaviside, unless I'm mistaken."

"Yes Sir. It's my opinion that a good tune carries the Holy Message that much better, no matter the composer."

"Just so. You'll get no argument from me."

"Sir."

* * *

The return to barracks found all in better heart. The connection between Lacey's sermon and the flogging of Tiley had not been lost, but there was more coming in the next hour or so to raise the spirits further; Sunday dinner. Not long after they had removed their tunics and stocks, it arrived, hot from the kitchens, roast pork, peas, and potatoes. The drink was the common small beer. The meat was the lowest cut from the animal, rolled belly and flank, but it was well cooked and looked tasty.

The room Sergeant cut the meat into slices and two "matrons' dealt out the vegetables, sternly dealing with any complaints of short measure. Soon all were at table, and the communal mood was one of good cheer. With the meal completed, pipes were filled and the small beer finished off, whilst the women dealt with the serving dishes and wives with their husband's plates; single men took care of their own. Conversation ran up and down the tables and cards and dice were produced. The barracks was enjoying its leisure time.

Davey and Sedgwicke did not remain at the tables, but returned to their cubicles, each taking a stool into their space to add to their comfort. Davey attended to some loose stitching on one of his boots, whilst Sedgwicke read from his Bible.

"Must have done you heart good to see all that going on, on the Parade Ground just now, eh Parson, a thousand souls or more?"

"Yes. I'll not argue with the event itself, but I would have much preferred the service were it conducted by an Ordained Man of God."

"I don't doubt that, Parson, but, if I read it right, all we got from the due Man of God was his donkey. Why that was, I can only guess, we aren't made privy to the doings of our betters, now are we? But I thought that there was strength in what we got. Devotions brought forth from amongst our own, as it were. Sort of wove us together, like. You know, so far, this army doesn't strike me as being so bad, but perhaps I'm saying that because I'm warm and dry, and with a full belly."

He opened his clasp knife and sliced off the cotton to complete the stitching. Sedgwicke lifted himself from his Bible and regarded Davey.

"Brought forth from amongst our own" That does have strength in it, yes. You know, Davey, I do think that you may have the potential to serve as a Lay Preacher."

Davey chuckled and shook his head.

"Not me, Parson. No kind of God Botherer am I. I'm content to sing your hymns and chant your prayers, but I know where the pew is that I sit on."

There was equal conviviality in the barracks of Joe Pike and Tom Miles. Dice and cards, the common leisure of all soldiers, were also indulged in, and Joe joined in the dice. He soon began to lose what little money he had, but Tom pulled him away from further punishment by taking his purse and stowing it safely in the pocket of Joe's tunic, hanging on its peg.

"But Tom, how do I get my money back."

"You've got as much chance of getting your money back as I have of riding a horse to the moon. Them men is long players, they can judge the roll of the dice better than any alive. Keep your money, lad, 'tis too hard come by to risk it on rolling whale-bones. Turn yourself to something useful, like carving or something. You used to be a carpenter of sorts, didn't you?"

He held up a fine piece of beech wood that he was turning into a whistle. It was already a hollow tube and he was attending to the finger holes.

"Alright Tom, if you'll teach me."

"Teach you nothing. All you need is a sharp knife and a nice piece of close grain wood. The rest comes with experience."

He reached into a canvas sack.

"Here's a piece of oak, see what you can fashion from that."

And he threw it over to land on Joe's straw mattress. Joe picked it up and regarded it carefully, thinking creatively. Whilst he mused on the possibilities, the conviviality within the barrack room was growing. Someone had produced a fiddle, and the children, and no few of the grown ups, were dancing country reels, whilst many kept time by thumping on the table. Good cheer increased considerably when the door opened and in came a Corporal Orderly carrying two pails of dark, pungent liquid. Rum.

"Spirits up! Compliments of the Colonel."

All fiddling and dancing ceased as the men ran to get their mugs in which to receive their half pint entitlement. Soon there was an unruly gathering around the Orderly and his containers, who was rapidly dipping the half pint measure into the rum and tipping it into the eagerly proffered mugs. Tom Miles soon reached the edge of the crowd where he could see what was going on. He soon took umbrage.

"You get the top of your thumb out of that measure, you chiselling sod! Damn your tricks to save rum for your sodding self! Give us full measure."

Joe Pike, at his side with his own mug, looked quizzical and the Orderly returned a hurt and pleading look.

"Listen, Tom. It b'ain't my fault. The Colonel gave the order for a rum ration and whilst there should be enough, there ain't.

'Tis either eke it out, like this, or water it down, as some has done. Most like their rum neat, and can tell when 'tis watered. So, I don't fancy my face being smashed in, so I'm doing it this way. Here, here's a drip more. No more moaning."

Tom received the extra tiny measure, but not in good grace, and treated the Orderly to one of his especially black looks of contempt and annoyance.

"And for the boy, here," was his parting shot before turning away, and he left as Joe received a tiny extra. Nevertheless, it was good Navy rum, such as Miles had not tasted since leaving Ireland and survived the shipwreck. Returning to a table, Joe sat beside Tom, took a large swallow and began coughing and choking. Between gulps from his heaving chest he gasped out the question.

"What in the Lord's Name is this, Tom?"

"Navy rum, boy, and it don't come often, this side of a battle, anyways. Get it down you, it'll do you the world of good."

Joe obeyed and the chokes subsided. However, it was not long before a glazed look came over his eyes and he slumped forward over the table. Tom grinned and took up Joe's mug, but it was not tipped into his own. Instead he went to Joe's canteen and into it he carefully decanted the remainder.

Concurrently, another Orderly arrived in the barrack room of Davey and Sedgwicke. Davey reacted before Sedgwicke, who was deep into his Bible. He saw the commotion caused by the arrival, rather than hear the Orderly's shout; the room was full of so much noise. All the men running to the man with the buckets carried its own message.

"Come on, Parson, I think they're standing us a drink. Get your mug."

And with that, he took his own off its peg and joined the throng. Sedgwicke looked up. A drink! The dependence on alcohol, created during his previous life had not left him. It surfaced within him and quickly asserted itself. He seized his mug and hurried after Davey. The wait in the throng seemed interminable, especially as, being someone of more minor stature than major, he was twice shouldered to the rear, but eventually the dark, strong smelling, and mysterious liquid was dispensed into his mug.

Having indulged himself in the past on fine wine, his first sip told him that this was liquor, ferocious and strong, but the

101

warming feeling now growing in his stomach was far from unpleasant. His half pint was soon consumed and the effects of such a measure, of such a libation, soon grew also. For the first time in weeks, he actually felt cheerful, such that he took himself over, to the astonishment of John Davey, to the rowdy group that were singing to the accompaniment of two penny whistles. He didn't know the words, but they made room for him and he clapped his hands in time, the social level of the company, at least for a time, forgotten.

Chapter Four

A Soldier's Trade

"Well, this is peculiar. Most odd. What's he got in mind, do you think? Was the "Old Man" a Headmaster, or something, before he joined the Army?"

Lieutenant D'Villiers shrill and nasal tones drifted down the Mess Table to the other Officers, a dozen of them, each having a small pile of plain foolscap, with pen and ink before them. Lieutenant The Honourable Nathaniel Drake leaned forward and gave his opinion.

"I think he wants to test you on your Latin grammar, D'Villiers. Get you to decline the odd Latin noun, perhaps. Dominus, domine, dominum, domini, domino, dominorum."

Carravoy joined the banter, but his tone was acid and more like to kill it.

"I think you'll find, Lieutenant Drake, that the declension of a common masculine noun ends in "o", not "orum"."

Drake raised his eyebrows in surprise and screwed his face in feigned shock that his attempt at humour should fall on such stony ground, but at that moment, Colonel Lacey and Major O'Hare entered the room. There was instant silence and all stood. Lacey and O'Hare strode to the head of the table.

"Gentlemen, please be seated."

Ensign Rushby had not caught on and had sat himself at a place that had no writing materials and, nonplussed and confused, he looked down the table at the Colonel. He had failed to notice the vacant place with the paper, pen, and ink.

"Ensign Rushby, please to bring yourself down to this place here," this said whilst indicating the vacant space, which Lacey assumed Rushby would have had the common sense to choose in the first place. Rushby bustled and clattered down to the correct place and the Colonel began.

"Soon, Gentlemen, I will be allocating you to your Companies. I'm going to set you a military problem that I want you to answer using the paper before you. Your answers will aid both Major O'Hare and myself in that decision which we will soon have to take. Answer in words or diagrams, or both, as you choose."

He paused.

"The problem is this; you are in command of the battalion, which could happen to you Captains, especially those senior. Lieutenants; that is unlikely, but the next hour, I feel sure, will teach you something of a soldier's trade and do you no harm. The problem's as follows. As Commander, you have been ordered to advance at the enemy's extreme left flank. The end of his line is anchored on a large copse, whilst yours will be "in the air" as you advance. You are in open country, and there are enemy cavalry clear and present, but not in contact with you. What do you do?"

Many took their gaze away from the Colonel to look at each other and exchanged puzzled, even worried, glances. Carr and Carravoy, as so often in the Mess, found themselves opposite each other. Carr, demonstrating his usual languid style, picked up the pen but leaned as far back in the chair as it would allow. He began twirling the pen in his fingers whilst giving the problem his consideration, his mouth adopting the insolent half smile that many who felt he should better know his place found so annoying. Carravoy, in contrast, leaned forward, elbows on the table, fingers interlocked, with his upper lip touching the index finger of his right hand. He spent some moments studying Carr, who soon began drawing. Carr felt, more than saw, Carravoy studying him and looked up, and met the look with his own challenging, expressionless stare, countering Carravoy's own examining look.

Carravoy took his questioning gaze onto Drake, sat next to Carr. Drake also noticed himself being studied, and when it was clear that Carravoy was taking more time to study him than to attempt the question, Drake being ever ready for any opportunity for humour, he knotted his eyebrows quizzically, adopted an amused expression and placed his left arm over the top of his paper. The gesture conveyed the jest - heinous cheating! Carravoy was trying to look at his paper! Drake raised his head further and grinned, adding to this attempt at amusement between them, but Carravoy's face remained expressionless and showed no sign of seeing anything funny. Drake's smile faded and he returned to his answer. Carr noted Carravoy's chilly rebuff of his friend and stared coldly at Carravoy for a long moment, before addressing himself to his own answer.

"Is there any artillery support, Sir?"

"A good question, Mr Rushby. Yes there is, from the left."

"Thank you, Sir."

"Any from our own cavalry? Sir," from a voice at the top end of the table.

"No. None."

For ten minutes silence reigned around the mess table, save for the scratch of pen on parchment. Lacey broke the silence.

"Enough. That is about the time you would have in battle. Gentlemen, name your work and pass it up to Major O'Hare. Now take yourselves off and re-assemble in 30 minutes. Dismiss."

Chairs scraped back and all left for an anteroom where an Orderly had prepared coffee. Many formed small knots, which anxiously discussed the merits of various answers, but Carr and Drake took their coffee and themselves out of the building for some fresh air and a rare smoke. Drake turned to Carr.

"What did you make of that?'

"New in my experience."

Drake nodded, but further conversation was unnecessary. There was enough to divert them already on the parade ground. Sergeant Major Gibney was teaching his recruits how to load a musket, using Deakin as his visual aid. Deakin was holding his musket before him, both hands either side of the flintlock, making clear what the recruits were to focus on. Gibney began by pointing at the flintlock, giving instructions that Deakin obeyed as required.

"Now listen and listen good. This is the flintlock part that makes tha' musket fire. Point to these parts, please, Corporal. Pan. Frizzen. Hammer, with a flint, at half cock. The Corporal's frizzen is down to cover the pan, it has a spring to hold it closed, which it has to be after thee's primed it with gunpowder. Frizzen down puts the striking plate up. The Corporal here, will now fully cock the hammer and pull the trigger. Ah wants thee to watch carefully."

Deakin pulled back the hammer and pulled the trigger. The hammer hit the striking plate and the frizzen slammed forward.

"Didst tha' see that? The spark it made. That sets off the powder in the pan, which sets off the main charge inside the barrel. How does it do that? All of thee, look inside the pan."

All raised their muskets, pushed the frizzen forward and studied. Gibney chose a recruit in the centre, the least likely looking, and pointed.

"Thee. What can th'see?"

"A small hole, Sergeant Major."

"A small hole, that's right. Smart lad. That small hole is called the touch hole and the fire in the pan goes through it to the main charge. Now, after a number of firings the pan gets fouled and the hole clogged."

He pointed to another recruit, this time, John Davey.

"What did we get thee to tie to tha' knapsack strap, thee?"

"A small spike and a small brush, Sergeant Major."

"That's right. It's called a brush and pricker, and what does thee think it's for? Thee," pointing to another.

"Cleaning the pan with the brush and cleaning out the touch hole with the pricker, Sergeant Major."

"Didst tha' hear that. He called them by their right names. What gradely recruits ah has here now, right before me now."

He took from his pocket a paper cylinder, about four inches long and held it aloft.

"Tha' sees this. This is a cartridge. It contains just enough powder to prime and charge tha' musket, and at one end is a musket ball, at the end that's not folded. Right, Deakin, load tha' musket and fire, salute angle. Now."

Deakin swung the musket to his hip, pulled the hammer back to half cock which fully exposed the pan. He took a paper cartridge from the box just behind his right hip and bit open the folded end. Some gunpowder grains adhered to the side of his mouth. He ignored them. A small measure was tipped into the pan and the frizzen closed. He then grounded his musket before him and tipped the rest of the gunpowder into the barrel, whilst still holding the ball through the paper. Once empty, the paper containing the ball was then stuffed into the top of the barrel. He extracted the ramrod beneath the barrel, rammed all down tight and then returned the ramrod. He lifted the weapon up, fully cocked the hammer, set the butt against his shoulder, raised the barrel high and pulled the trigger. There had been not a wasted movement throughout. The priming in the pan flashed into white smoke and the musket went off with a sharp bark. Deakin returned to order arms. The whole had taken just under 20 seconds. As the smoke cleared and the report echoed away, Gibney resumed his lecture.

"That is what we wants from thee. A good soldier can manage three reloads a minute. The best can get close to four, but over four is rare. Has thee ever heard of a man getting over four, Corporal?"

"No, Sar' Major."

"Just so. Now, tha' turn. Step by step. Take out a cartridge from tha' box. Feel the ball in the end not folded."

He paused whilst all obeyed.

"Tha' cartridge is full of dried sand. We doesn't want thee blowing someone's head off, now do we? At least not yet awhile. And sand doesn't pack down like gunpowder, so 'tis easy to tip out, but only if thee doesn't stuff in the paper. Let the ball fall out, and let the paper drop. So, half cock the hammer and open the frizzen."

The worthy Gilbey now took his charges move-by-move, step-by-step, through the procedure to load and fire their heavy muskets. Deakin moved up and down the line, giving help and advice where he could. When the time came to ground the butt to enter the main charge down the muzzle, much sand was added to the parade ground; several had forgotten to close the frizzen. Eventually all had a "loaded" musket.

"Now then, my men. When tha's loaded and ready, tha' has to give th'Officer some sign. Tha' points thee musket straight up into th'air. We calls it "make ready". Show this to our fine lads, please, Corporal," and Deakin obeyed.

"Now, all of you, make ready."

All obeyed. 52 muskets pointed skyward.

"Present, which means aim tha' musket."

All came to the "present", and Gibney strode forward and walked along the line. Eventually he found what he knew he would. He seized the end of a ramrod protruding from a muzzle and worked it in and out of the barrel, like a plunger.

"Percy, my boy."

It was Sedgwicke.

"Hast thee been given some special kind of ammunition?"

Sedgwicke's face took on an agonized expression. Yet again a focus of critical attention.

"No, Sergeant Major."

"So, what's this still doing down tha' barrel? Can thee imagine, Percy, what a mess thee'll be in, if thee fires this away?"

"Yes, Sergeant Major. I won't be able to reload."

"Just so, Percy. Don't do it again."

He watched as Sedgwicke returned his ramrod to the guides below the barrel, then he left the line and resumed his teaching post.

"Now look along the barrel. Nothing in the way, is there? Muskets have no sights. Thee just points it at what thee wants to hit. It's that simple. Now, let's try for speed."

Time and again the sand and the ball were tipped out onto the ground and the priming pan emptied. Discarded cartridge papers, balls and sand soon littered the ground at their feet. Some were achieving beyond two reloads a minute, as observed by Drake and Carr, when they heard an Orderly calling the Officers back into the Dining Room. They entered silently behind the others who were also making no conversation and took their places. Tension was high. When the last had taken their place, the silence was total, each with an anxious expression that conveyed their anxiety over the Colonel's judgment on their answers.

"We are both pleased. All of you, but one, has produced a solution that at least has some merit, but some, as you can imagine, are better than others. However, it is clear that I am in the good company of professional and knowledgeable Officers. Ensign Rushby."

"S,sir."

Rushby sat up like a startled rabbit. Was he "the one"?

"How do infantry defend against an attack by cavalry?"

"That'll be a defensive square, Sir."

"Just so Mr Rushby. Now, Captain Carravoy."

"Sir."

"You have protected your exposed flank with a closed column of three companies, Light, First and Second. What are the merits of that?"

Carrovoy stood to address his superior. He looked anxious but also annoyed, the normal confidence and poise of the aristocracy were not bearing him up. His voice was testy, as though addressing an ignorant estate worker. He greatly resented being asked to justify himself.

"Well, Sir. Three companies closed up would form a block of men similar to a square, to give the protection needed, and, when we reached the copse, the column could launch forward with enough men to capture it and secure our own flank. Sir."

"A good solution, Captain, I like what you say. A good compromise between defence and attack. What are the disadvantages?"

Again, the impatience was audible in his voice, almost sarcastic.

"It would shorten our line for the main attack."

A pause. Then he added, "Sir."

"Correct, well done."

Carravoy resumed his seat, but praise from his Colonel seemed to have done little to reduce his irritation.

"Captain Carr."

"Sir."

"You advocate three companies forming three sides of a square. The open side away from the cavalry, the Light Company in the lead at the end of your main line, the Grenadiers facing out to the threat, and Number One company marching forward in the rear. What are the merits of that?"

"Well Sir. At some stage the cavalry will attack you. If you can see them, they can see you, and a line of infantry advancing in open country would be an irresistible target for them. When you close with the enemy line, the Lights could take the copse, but you must have some protection against a cavalry attack against your flank and rear, Sir, whilst you are in a firefight with the enemy's main line."

"Just so. And the disadvantages?'

"As Captain Carravoy said, Sir. You are weakening your main line."

Lacey nodded.

"Ensign Rushby."

Again displaying deep consternation, Rushby looked up.

"S,sir."

"Well done, Mr Rushby. Your solution has merits. One company facing the cavalry as you advance, but I agree with Captain Carr, another would be needed in the rear."

Rushby beamed with relief.

"Yes Sir. Thank you Sir."

"All of you have described a solution based on those just described. In my opinion it is the correct course of action. Well done, but with one exception. Lieutenant D'Villiers."

"Sir."

"What is a cavalryman's favourite target?'

"I wouldn't know, Sir. I'm an infantryman."

Stifled sniggers and amused grins broke out around the table, their relief at their own solutions not being selected for criticism gave an easy avenue for humour.

"Then I will tell you. It is broken infantry, scattered, all formation gone."

"Sir."

"And you heard Ensign Rushby's meritorious answer to the question on how infantry defends against cavalry?"

"Yes Sir."

"Then what, pray, can be the merits of sending your Light Company out in skirmish order to provide a screen against a cavalry charge?"

D'Villers' mouth opened and closed, and his fingers stretched forward and back upon the polished table. His eyes bulged in a reddening face as he stared helplessly at the opposite wall.

"I, I, well Sir, I thought that the Lights would be able to retreat quickly, Sir, if attacked."

"So, you expect your Lights to outrun a horse, and when they have retreated, what then?"

"Yes Sir. I suppose there could be some confusion, Sir, but I would expect them to rally."

The amused expressions resumed.

"Confusion, Lieutenant D'Villiers, would be the least of it. Massacre would be more likely. If you had a Light Company that knew what they were about, they would refuse your order. You would have a mutiny on your hands and I would have some sympathy. I, personally, would rather be shot than sabred. If you have a tactics manual, I suggest you read it."

The last sentence was spoken with some venom. After some moments, Lacey took his austere and withering gaze away from D'Villiers, who remained red faced and dismayed, and could not bring himself to do more than study the table surface.

"Gentlemen. Myself and Major O'Hare thank you for your efforts, and the serious approach you have taken to this exercise. I ask your forgiveness in that you are being examined in front of your brother Officers. This is something I know you are not used to, but I ask you to accept that soon you could find yourself being examined in a far more unforgiving place, and by a sterner examiner than myself. Upon our decisions rest the

110

lives of our men, and the outcome of the day. Thank you, once again. This has been extremely useful and, after your hard work, I feel some refreshments are called for."

He waved forward an Orderly, poised in the doorway, who quickly came forward with several bottles of port, and he was followed by another Orderly with a quantity of glasses.

'Gentlemen, please enjoy your wine, and please remain seated. Thank you, and good morning."

Nevertheless, many stood at the parting of their Colonel and Senior Major and returned his good morning. Drake seized a bottle, wrenched open the cork and pushed a glass at D'Villiers, which he then quickly filled.

"There you are, Royston. Get yourself around that, and put it behind you. Be of good cheer. You aren't the first to get a roasting off your Colonel and you won't be the last. We've all been there, am I right?" he said, regarding the rest of the assembly. Several replies came down, "yes, of course", "well chewed up", and "part of the game", but D'Villiers was both incensed and inconsolable.

"Well, I think its all damned wrong and unfair on top. To spring that on us without some kind of warning. Who does he think he is? I'm going to write to my Father to see what he can do. That was public humiliation. Uncalled for."

Carr also tried to mollify the aggrieved warrior D'Villiers.

"Calm yourself, D'Villiers. This is our trade, and we have to know it. Like he said, life and death depend on it. He treated you harshly here so that you get it right when it counts. Now have a drink and then another. You are amongst friends and we know how you feel. We all have sympathy, no one thinks any less of you. He's the Colonel; you're a Junior Officer. It's a Law of Nature. Junior Officers get verbally scragged by their Colonels, and I can see his point. Many here now, know what they didn't before and may well be grateful for."

Carravoy sat forward, his face black with anger, and no glass of port before him.

"I don't see it that way, Carr. You set yourself apart. I tell you it's beyond justification for him to treat one his Officers in such a way. Damn him! I know plenty who would now call him out on a matter of honour. That was in front of peers and inferiors. I know the D'Villiers family; on a par with my own, his Father's a Knight. I object to my thoughts and opinions on his

111

damned puzzle being openly discussed. I'm taking my leave. Damned "call back" that he is, him and his Irish lackey. D'Villiers, are you with me?"

He rose and left at speed. D'Villiers had his second glass of port poised for despatch, but he gulped it quickly, rose from his chair, and with all the bruised dignity that he could muster, followed Carravoy out through the door.

* * *

The King's Sedge Moor, the name for this part of the Somerset Wetlands, stretched away over flat, grey miles to merge with a thickening mist that shrouded the surrounding range of low hills. In the hidden distance, these emerged just enough from the chequer work of square water meadows and ditches to mark an end to that table flat area known by that name. Bleaker than most in any December, this featureless expanse of identical farms and fields had given its name to the last battle fought on English soil and witnessed retribution of the most savage kind. The Recruit Company, their grey drill coats in marked contrast to the bright red of those worn by their several instructors, marched smartly along the raised bank that carried the burden of a gravel track out into the dank emptiness that contained, for them, a destination unknown. A necessary good dinner of hot stew fortified them securely against the damp chill that pervaded all on that drab winter afternoon.

Grey bark willows, pollarded into alien shapes and standing sentinel at the margins of the track, they loomed up beside them, then fell behind with their onward march, monotonously beaten out by the lone Drummerboy at their rear. Seth Tiley, marched alone at the rear, under special escort. Tall reeds dripped moisture gathered from the mist and hid their progress as they marched on through a landscape that seemed unfamiliar and hostile, although it was but a few short weeks previously that they had marched through it as recruits, either as prisoner or as volunteer.

"Company. Halt."

The reeds beside the track on their right had ended to reveal a wide, rough grass expanse that had been levelled and drained up to the wilder areas at its margins. Fifty yards from the track, and parallel to it, was a long rank of vertical poles sunk into the ground in pairs. The left hand pole had a number. Deakin was the NCO commanding and, as such, he began to arrange his company as he required.

"Both right hand files, stand fast. Both left hand files, by the left, march."

As commanded, the two left hand files marched on beyond their comrades until the order came to halt when the last pair were past and clear. A "right face" and a "two paces forward" produced his command in two ranks facing the poles, each pair of poles by now being linked by a white sheet. With this complete, his fellow escorts ran back to take their places at either end of the line. Preventing possible desertion was on their minds. A deep rhyne was behind, but they were there to stop escape either way along the track. Deakin strode up and down the line, 52 men, 26 in each line, his own musket loaded, but slung over his shoulder.

"This is a firing range. You now have cartridges that contain real gunpowder. On the command, you load your muskets, but this time you leave the ball inside the cartridge and stuff all down the barrel, ball inside the paper, like you saw me do this morning. Load your muskets."

With some precision, practised all morning, the recruits began to load, but their real cartridges contained an unpleasant surprise. The sand had been gritty in their mouths when they bit into the cartridge, the real thing was both gritty and bitter and some tried to spit or wipe the grains away, to Deakin's annoyance.

"Never mind all that. Get your pieces loaded, and then grounded at order arms."

Within a minute all were stood with the butt of their musket besides their right boot.

"Now. You in the rear rank. You can't see anything. Front rank's heads are in the way. I wants you to move, to your left, just enough so that you can look between the heads of those in front. We calls that "locking on", and that's the command. Rear rank; lock on."

All in the rear rank moved and their heads appeared as though a child had pulled a string to which all were tethered.

"You will fire by files, one in front with one behind. Now, the "brown bess' has a kick. Get the butt hard into your shoulder. Private Stiles will tell you your target."

He waited for Stiles to instruct the first two, one in front, one behind.

"Make ready. Present. Fire."

The reports from both muskets, almost simultaneous, were subdued in the wide stretching space, the opposite to within the confines of the barrack square and the sound quickly rolled away to be absorbed into the lonely emptiness. The smoke slowly drifted away on the breathless wind. Number two target had jerked.

"Stiles. Who fired at number two?'

"Davey here, Corporal."

"Right. Keep a record of who hits. From you now Stiles, give 'em their targets and order to fire. Peters, the same, but start from the middle. Keep 'em firing. I want ten shots each."

Thus it began. The firing by files rolled up the line, about half the targets twitching with the passage of the half-inch ball. The smoke and crash both rolled away to be lost on the moor, leaving each man hurrying to reload before his turn came again. Deakin walked up the rear of the line, giving advice, making judgments. His attention was pulled away. He heard the fall of a hoof on the gravel, then the jingle of a bit. A horse meant an Officer. He came to instant attention, just as Captain Heaviside reached the lines of men, all furiously working to put a hole in their targets.

"Afternoon, Sir. Musket drill, Sir. All present and correct."

"Just so, Corporal. How are they doing?"

"Not too bad, Sir. Reloading is about two a minute, and at the 50 yard target just over half is hits."

"Well done. "Their arrows shall be as of a mighty expert man; none shall return in vain. Jeremiah, chapter 50, verse 9."

"Yes Sir. Just so, Sir."

"Carry on Corporal."

"Yes Sir. Thank you, Sir."

Heaviside allowed his horse to amble past, his left hand holding the reins, the right his coal-black Bible, cover worn and pages well thumbed. He was there for his daily sojourn in the wilderness, to read his Bible and compose his daily prayer. He rode on, through the cheerless landscape until the sound of the musket drill became no more than a dull thump and the image of the firing line lost in the mist. He dismounted, took a blanket from his saddlebag, along with a cross on a stand and then a small miniature of a pleasant looking, but unsmiling woman. Still folded, he placed the blanket on the ground and the stand and the picture beyond. He knelt on the blanket before both cross and picture, grasped the Bible in both hands before him and bowed his head.

"Oh, Lord, thou knowest that I am away from the bosom of my family, preparing now to march against my country's enemies. Soon, but I know not when, I will be leaving these shores to fight overseas. Whilst I am away from her side, may I commend my beloved Mary into thy safe keeping. Give her comfort and hold her in thy mighty hand away from all harm. Also, please take under they merciful gaze, my two dear children, Joseph and Matilda. Keep both safe and well. For Jesus Christ, Our Lord's Sake. Amen."

His prayer done, he opened his Bible and read out loud, to the thickening mist and the glistening trees, their thin willow branches pointing up from their pollarded heads to the Heaven he addressed. He also gave accompaniment to the silent, scurrying creatures, tracking their way home. Reading finished, he rose and stood a while in silent contemplation, then he packed away his items of prayer, remounted his horse and turned her back to retrace his route. The sound of the musketry grew louder and soon the figures at their practice appeared in detail through the mist. As chance would have it, Deakin was again the first he encountered and again he came to instant attention.

"Sir. Welcome back, Sir. We was just finishing. I was going to finish with volley fire by ranks, but with you here I was wondering if you would like to take over, Sir. They've been listening to me since we got out here. A change will do them good. I'm hoping that they can get off three shots in a minute, with two reloads. Sir."

"Why, yes, Corporal. I'll do that with pleasure, and after I'll lead the men in."

"Yes, Sir. Thank you, Sir."

Heaviside dismounted and handed the reins, without looking, to a nearby Private.

Deakin turned to his charges and raised his voice to Parade Ground level.

"We are going to finish with volley by ranks. That means one rank fires, while the other reloads. You will get the order; front rank fire or rear rank fire, and you has to reload in time to meet the order. When you are reloaded, adopt the "make ready". I wants three shots in a minute, from each rank. That means two reloads. Captain Heaviside will give the orders. Attention."

The company came to the attention as Deakin saluted and stood aside for Heaviside to step forward.

"Now men, this is, as Corporal Deakin has said, volley fire by ranks. Against any enemy this is the most effective way to organize our fire. It means that an enemy isn't hit wastefully by two balls when one will do, and they come under fire twice as often. Now, reload."

Deakin stepped forward and whispered.

"They're already loaded. Sir."

"Just so. Now, front rank. Make ready. Present. Fire."

26 muskets went off with a deafening crash, and the 26 in the front rank immediately lowered their muskets to begin reloading. Most of the white targets had jerked back. Heaviside allowed the smoke to clear.

"Rear rank. Make ready. Present. Fire."

Again the angry bark of 26 muskets shattered the evening silence. Heaviside knew he had to wait for about 25 seconds for the front rank to return to the "make ready". This came and the round of volleys continued.

For ex-Parson Percival Sedgwicke this was far worse than anything previous, and in this opinion he was not alone. The musket, after two hours of firing practice, seemed made of solid lead. His throat and mouth burned with a raging thirst which each bite of a cartridge made worse. Either side of him, three feet forward, were the muzzles of two muskets that exploded into dense white smoke that stung his eyes, assaulted his nostrils and deafened his ears. Within a foot, either side, were the flintlocks of the two accursed muskets, the pans of which flashed more smoke around his buzzing head and, finally, burning embers from the pan on his left had stung his face more times than he could count. Within this, he was expected to load and fire his musket and he knew he was falling behind. In the front rank, he had just made the second volley, bringing up his musket and firing just as the others had fired and were dropping their muskets to begin the reload, but he was going to miss the third. Heaviside saw the time arriving and called for "present", but Sedgwicke's ramrod was still down the barrel. He pulled it out and thrust it behind one of his straps, then pulled the hammer to full cock, came to the "present" and fired, again just after his comrades, but enough to be counted as one of the volley. The three shots from the front rank complete, along with the rest, he ordered arms and waited for the flash and explosion from the two muskets beside him. It was not long in coming and again his face was enveloped in the stinging, foul smelling smoke, but it was finished.

Heaviside walked along the front rank and stopped in the centre.

"Well done, men. Three shots and two reloads in a minute, well done, and as far as I saw, not one missed his volley. Ye shall chase your enemies, and they shall fall before you by the sword. Leviticus, chapter 26, verse 7."

Deakin was a pace behind.

"Yes, Sir. I'm sure the lads appreciated that, Sir. Shall I form them up, Sir?"

"Yes, Corporal, do. Soldier, my horse!"

As Heaviside took himself off to mount his horse, Deakin studied Sedgwicke.

"Sneaky trick that, Parson, b'ain't it, stickin' your ramrod down behind a strap. But," and he leaned forward to whisper conspiratorially, "that's exactly what the lads does, when things gets a bit hot. Smart move, Parson, you must have some brains!"

Sedgwicke looked shocked but this couldn't disguise that he felt pleased. Deakin turned to Lance Corporal Mulcahey.

"Pat, take over. I has some totting up to do."

Orders were given and the Recruit Company formed up in fours behind Captain Heaviside. They were marched off, again to the flat beat of the bleary Drummerboy, who had been shaken awake, asleep through all the firing. Deakin did his additions. Davey and Pike were equal with each other and superior to the others by four shots. At the other end of the scale, Percival Sedgwicke had not achieved one single hit.

* * *

The throng of young Officers around the Orders Board more resembled the scrum around the Notice Board of a Public School when Prefects were announced; the notice upon it being studied just as avidly. Those on the back were on tiptoe, whilst most craned their necks and bobbed their heads to get a view.

117

Lieutenant D'Villiers shouldered his way back and out, the scowl on his pallid face immediately conveying his disappointment.

"Lieutenant in Number Three Company, under Captain Heaviside. Not much more distinction than being a damned ranker! An altarboy for Holy Joe Heaviside!"

However, his complaints were ignored as others looked to see their allocation within the battalion. Carr reached the board with Drake and both exchanged broad smiles and shook hands. Carr was Captain of the Light Company and Drake was one of his Lieutenants. Carr looked again. At the top of the list was the name Captain Lord Carravoy. The Captain of the Senior Company, the Grenadiers, which made him effectively the Senior Captain in the Battalion, but this merely reinforced what was already shown on the board, his seniority stemmed from his Commission date. Neverthearless, both Carr and Drake were delighted and took themselves off to their billet in town for a good dinner and a fine bottle.

Soon, just one Officer was left studying the list; Ensign Rushby. He knew enough of his role in a Numbered Battalion with its two colours, the King's and the Regimental, to know that he shouldn't be in any Company at all, but the bearer of one of these two standards in the centre of the firing line. However, here he was listed for the Light Company, to act as a Lieutenant. He was turning away when an Irish voice stopped him.

"A moment, Ensign Rushby."

Rushby turned to see Major O'Hare approaching him along the corridor. Rushby sprung to attention with his best salute.

"Don't take it hard that you are assigned to a Company. You understand that we are Detachments and we need to make the best use of all our Officers. The Colonel and myself feel you have a lot of potential, so we're making you an Acting Lieutenant. You're young and untried as yet, but under good Officers like Captain Carr and Lieutenant Drake we're sure you'll learn and turn into a fine Officer.

"Yes Sir. Thank you, Sir."

"Now, a word in confidence. I feel certain we will stay as a battalion and be sent into action and who knows, eventually perhaps we'll get a number and be granted Colours. Then, an Ensign, indeed, is what you'll be!"

"Yes, Sir. Thank you, Sir."

"Ah, right, that's fine. Now, cut along."

Rushby saluted, which was returned, and then he scuttled off to his quarters.

Lacey and O'Hare had debated long over which Officers to which Companies. O'Hare had argued that experience in the field should take absolute priority and had argued for the veteran Heaviside to be given the Grenadiers. However, Lacey knew that he had to be politic. Carravoy had been a Gazetted Captain for longer than anyone; even though solely in the Militia, he had to be given some measure of seniority. Besides, the Grenadiers were a strong Company, with a strong leavening from the 9th, they would take care of him as much as he would them. D'Villiers was a different case. Although an aristocrat and from a family known to Lacey, he judged him a poor Officer who should be placed where he could do little harm. In a line Company under the experienced Heaviside, seemed the best compromise. Both had agreed; Carr and Drake were perfect for the Lights.

Rushby had exited the door by the Colonel's Office and took himself across the Parade Ground, just close enough to interrupt Sergeant Major Gilbey, who had to halt his address of the Recruit Company to perform the required salute. This done, he continued.

"Thee's been training, now, just on two month, and we feels that we knows enough about thee to put thee into the company that can make the best use of tha' talents, such as they are. This marks the end of tha' first round of training and now thee can receive tha' red jacket and grey trousers, for we finds thee worthy of the title "Redcoat in th'King's Army. If ah calls tha' name, thee can fall out, then take th'sen over to t'stores and get a jacket and the shako that thee should have. Grenadiers and Light Company have shoulder wings on their jackets. If we thinks thee worthy for a Grenadier, thee gets a shako with a white plume and a grenade badge. Roberts, Tiley, and Hughes. Fall out and get tha'selves over t'stores. Tha's Grenadiers."

He paused whilst the commotion from leaving the ranks subsided.

"If we thinks thee worthy of the Light Company, with tha' red jacket, with wings an' all, thee gets a shako with a green plume and a hunting horn badge. Wilkins, Pike, Garwood, and Davey. Fall out. Tha's Light Company."

The four took themselves out of the ranks and walked towards the entrance to the stores, in time to see the last "Grenadier" enter the door. They began talking, Garwood first.

"What's "Light Company" all about? What's the difference?"

A pause, none could really answer, but Davey gave what he knew.

"We're supposed to be fit, brainy, and good shots."

All laughed. Davey continued.

"And from what I've been told, we're often the first in, so we gets first go at the plunder."

Joe Pike took it up.

"First in where?"

"Well, anywhere. Town, village, house, hilltop. Anywhere." Garwood replied.

"I've heard it means dodging about between the armies. Sharpshooting like. Can't say as that appeals."

Wilkins finished the exchange.

"First go at plunder sounds best to me."

They had reached the stores and entered, to be greeted by Sleightman.

"Light Company?'

All nodded. He shouted back into the depths of the stores.

"Four green plumes."

The shakoes appeared in the grimy hands of a Storeman, held by the chinstraps, who then gauged them for jacket size and these also appeared. The same did not seem to apply to the grey trousers, either "long or short". Long seemed to be the size in fashion. Walking back to their barrack rooms they heard Gilbey finishing reading the lists of names with Company numbers. He then sent the parade, by ranks, over to form line at the stores door.

Joe Pike, with all haste, soon returned to his barrack room and sat at their table with the Light Company shako placed before him. His first act was to smooth up the green plume, and then shine the hunting horn badge with his sleeve. Then try it on.

"Light Company, Tom. Just like you."

"That's fine, boy. Have you made a Will?"

Nelly Nicholls had noticed the bright face of Joe Pike enter the room, she saw the green plume and was now stood close.

"You shut your gob, Tom Miles, you miserable bugger! The

lad's pleased and I be pleased for him. B'ain't no point, as I see it, you spreading your misery no further than 'tis needed."

She turned to Joe and placed a huge, red, motherly hand upon his shoulder.

"I'm pleased for 'ee, Joe. I wish thee well. My first husband was in the Lights, and we did well out of it, till he got his head blowed off somewhere in Holland. But you take no notice of this miserable tripehound!"

She delivered one last withering scowl in the direction of Tom Miles, and took herself back to her family. However, half her family, the two girls, were sat at the table gazing in adoration of the elevated Joe. Tom turned to him, but there was no anger in his voice

"All right, boy, let's see to your jacket. You've now got a new set of buttons to polish."

Joe obeyed and went to fetch the brickdust.

At the same time, Percival Sedgwicke was returning to his place in his barrack room. Davey saw the misery in his face.

"What ails thee, Parson? What company?"

"Three."

Davey was busy polishing his new buttons, but the Parson was as depressed as ever he saw him. He had no ambitions for Lights nor Grenadiers, but his being given to a Line Company had come as a new and singular reminder, in some ways worse than those before, that he was now no more than what upper society would term as "a common soldier". He genuinely was, now, just a figure in a rank, "uniform" in his uniform. His days of status, deference, and comfortable living were now as remote as the Court of an Archbishop. When once he could have counted on his name being embossed onto the record of the incumbents of a Parish Church, to remain there for evermore, now he was the practically anonymous Private Sedgwicke, Number Three Company. At his death, his name would be merely scratched through. He slumped in his corner, seized his Bible and held it closed to his forehead. He remained thus for some time. Davey let him be.

* * *

The year was approaching it's close, and this meant the festival that all could look forward to. The children could be heard chant-

121

ing as they danced around, meeting their partner's hands with their own;

"Christmas is coming, the goose is getting fat.
Please put a penny in the old man's hat.
If you haven't got a penny, a farthing will do.
If you haven't got that, well God bless you."

The women and children were improvising decorations, holly and ivy and such scraps of coloured bunting as could be found. Three groups of children were re-painting wooden decorations, that had been produced from some family possessions, and would form a Nativity. Some new figures that would add to the Nativity needed to be painted; a shepherd, a donkey, and a wise man. Two produced by Tom Miles, one by Joe Pike. Tom had placed his two before the inevitable organiser of the festivities, Nelly Nicholls, who had greeted the gift with her usual hostile tone when dealing with Tom Miles, but perhaps the tone of the greeting was not quite so belligerent.

"Well, thankee for that, Tom Miles. Week of wet Mondays you may be, but you has the knack when it comes to carving."

Tom had glowered back, but nevertheless, it was plain that the acid between them was significantly diluted, at least for the festive season. Joe Pike's effort, the wise man, and of a significantly lesser quality than Tom's, had been greeted with effusive praise and thanks, for which Tom blamed Nelly rather than Joe. The truce held and day by day, the cheer in the barracks grew as all looked forward to the two days of Christmas.

With less communal cheer, but with more opulence, preparations moved forward within the Officer's Mess, only here the work was undertaken not by the occupants, but by Mess Room Orderlies. Their labour had been halted for the Officer's Luncheon and, whilst this was being eaten, the conversation was of leisure activities that would occupy them over Christmas leave. Orders were that Officers were to lodge close by the barracks, but there would be at least four days of idleness that could be taken advantage of. Carravoy and D'Villiers were discussing the same across the table, Carravoy making the suggestions.

"I have an invitation to a local Hunt, D'Villiers, the Blackdown. How do you feel about that? Is your horse up to it?"

"My horse is most certainly up to it, and I do accept. Is it a social hunt, anyone of note?"

"Why, local gentry, no more I feel sure, but it could be amusing. A ride to hounds would do us both the world of good."

"Agreed. I'll send for my hunting togs."

Carr and Drake were also discussing plans for Christmas, but with less volume and less publicly.

"Any plans for Christmas, Nat? Are your family near?"

"Yes, they are, at least enough to send over some Christmas cheer, but I have no plans, other than Carols with the local choir."

"Carols in a choir! Really? I had no notion that you were in any way musical."

"Why yes, and there's a certain party there who insists on my attendance."

"And she's young and pretty, of course."

"I think so, but what of your musical talents?"

"Well, I've been known to manage a few notes in the lower registers. Not exactly Basso Profundo, but I can get down there, or thereabouts."

"In that case, you are exactly the man we need, women bass singers, surprisingly, being somewhat rare. Do come. Can you read music?"

"Yes, enough to get by."

"Rehearsal this Wednesday evening, tomorrow, and I can recommend the post vocal refreshments."

"Wednesday evenings, eh, with a pretty maid involved. That explains your regular disappearance from our lowly lodging on that particular time of the week, but yes, I'll come along. Pleased to."

Drake turned his attention to Ensign Rushby, at his place at the end of the table, drinking his coffee, but not taking part in any conversation. Instead he was turning the leaves of a large manuscript, such as artists use.

"Is that a sketchbook, Barnaby? May I take a look?"

"Yes. Well, no. It's just a few doodles, really. You know, when the mood takes I like to spoil a good piece of paper.

Both Carr and Drake laughed. Drake took it up.

"Come now, Barnaby, we are all in the same Company now, the much vaunted Lights. We can have no secrets between each other. Slide it over, I pray."

The book was closed and nervously pushed within reach of Drake. Drake placed his hand on the cover and drew it towards him, then placed the book between himself and Carr. Carr was in the best position to open the heavy cover and he did so. The result caused both to take a sharp intake of breath and Carr continued to turn the leaves, turn and turn for some time. The contents were astonishing, mere pencil drawings they were, and there was a huge variety of subject matter, but each strongly conveyed the mood of the moment; the tranquillity of a riverside, the cheerlessness of cattle out on the moor, the misery of a women returning from the same, bent almost double with a burden of firewood. But most striking was the life and verve in the portraits of members of the battalion, some Officers, some NCO's and some rankers, some in a military setting, others plainly at their ease, but all came off the page with their lifelike quality.

Carr looked at Drake and both shared a look of astonishment.

"My word, Barnaby, but these are damned good. Have you had lessons or something? These are absolutely excellent. You'd agree, Drake?"

"I most certainly would. Can you do oils, Barnaby? If you can, there's a career waiting for you, after the army. How often do you get out, mostly local, yes?"

"Yes, mostly local. I hope to get out into some of the local villages this Christmas. I'm looking forward to it."

"I'm sure you are, if the result is such as this. Wish I had such a talent. Wonderful work, Barnaby. Allow us to see the results of your work post Christmas."

"Yes Sir. I will."

* * *

Wednesday evening came, cold, with soaking rain slanting off the moor, carried to them on a wayward and gusting wind. Carr and Drake, both in long greatcoats with collars turned up to overlap their glistening black shakoes, strode in step up the long garden path to confront the imposing front door; panels and studding both of medieval proportions. Carr felt, rather than saw, the heavy stonework stretching upwards and above, into the rainy dark, as Drake lifted the heavy knocker and allowed it to fall, the resultant sound appropriately resembled that of a medieval battering ram.

"The residence of Lady Constance Fynings. A nice old dear, who likes choral music, but, more importantly, keeps a very good table."

The door was opened by a maid of indeterminate age, who quickly and gratefully closed the door upon the two Officers crossing the threshold. Drake addressed her as she took their damp greatcoats.

"Are we in the usual place?"

"Yes, Sir. The front drawing room."

"This way, Henry," and Drake strode forward to enter a well lit corridor off to the right. The light from many candles reflected off the polished dark oak panels on the wall, from the glass of many display cabinets and the equally polished light oak flooring. Once in the corridor, choral singing reached their ears.

"Seems we're a bit late, Henry," and he turned the gleaming brass handle of an ornate, panelled door to reveal a brightly lit room containing above 30 people of a variety of ages and gender, but, Carr noted with relief, none in military uniform. On their entrance, the singing stopped.

"Evening, Constance. Sorry we're late, but I've brought reinforcements for the bass section. May I introduce Captain Henry Carr? Henry, this is Lady Constance Fynings."

Carr stepped forward and saluted, rather than bowed.

"Your servant, Ma'am."

This was delivered in the direction of a late middle-aged, but evidently noble and definitely well dressed woman who stood before the assembly. Her hands were held together at the waist of a well tailored grey satin dress, and she evidently occupied the role of the Musical Director. Her countenance did not convey approval.

"I'm very pleased to meet you, Captain Carr, and yes, Nathaniel, you are late, but I forgive you on this occasion, especially as you have brought us another member. Please add yourself to the right of the choir, Captain Carr, that's your left, their right."

Carr smiled and replied, "Yes Ma'am," as he took his place. He had noticed the smiles and grins that greeted Drake's entrance, but, unmistakably, the face of one particularly pretty member of the soprano end of the choir had lit up appreciably, not least of the light coming from a long and unblinking gaze in

Drake's direction. As Drake took his place, his last act was to meet her affectionate gaze delivered to him as she leaned forward out of the line.

"Captain Carr, we are singing "Come Thou Long Expected Jesus." It's Weslyan. Does that give you any cause for concern?"

"No indeed, Ma'am. None at all."

"Do you know it?"

"I'm afraid I do not, Ma'am, but if you find it acceptable, then I will just listen. At least for a while. I'll join in when I feel able."

"Very well, here is the music. I'm sure I have no need to point out the bass line."

She reached behind her to an elegant beech wood table and picked up a sheet, and held it in Carr's direction. He, remembering his manners, left his place to accept it. She called the choir to order and nodded her head in the direction of a girl of about middle teenage years who was at the piano. The bars of the introduction sounded out and off they went. Carr, indeed did not know the tune, but he did have an ear for music and a good sense of rhythm and so, by listening to his fellow bassists and reading the music, he was able to join in after not too long a period and his mistakes became less frequent and, more importantly, less profound. They sang two other carols and, quickly as it seemed to Carr, the session ended. Lady Fynings thanked them all for their attendance and remarked favourably on the quality of their singing that evening. Carr formed the opinion to himself that the praise was not mere flummery, the choir genuinely made a fine sound. Finally, she announced what he and Drake were most keen to hear, that food and refreshments were in the next room.

The members filed out, some singly, some in pairs, but Carr noted that Drake and his attractive acquaintance had gone to each other as though magnetized and were the last in the line, her arm as far through his as convention would allow, both clearly very special to each other.

"Captain Carr. May I introduce Miss Cecily Fynings? Niece of Lady Constance."

Cecily Fynings met Carr's gaze confidently, before respectfully lowering her eyes of striking blue as she made a light, girlish curtsey. Carr placed his right hand over his midriff and bowed.

"It is an honour to make you acquaintance, Miss Fynings. I trust I find you well?"

"Quite well, Sir, thank you. It is a pleasure to meet you."

Smiles all round; the atmosphere was genuinely warm and pleasant. Drake looked from one to the other.

"Food!"

Cecily Fynings playfully pushed his shoulder.

"I swear that's the only reason why he comes. He can't sing, he can't read a note!" but her hands were on his forearm, gazing up.

"I am much maligned! That is a malicious rumour, put about by those who wish to discredit me. I eat because of the effort I put into dragging this choir up a level of acceptable quality."

They led off to the next room, their playful banter flowing back to Carr as he followed them to the table, which was, indeed, full and resplendent with a well cooked and well presented variety of dishes. Drake and Cecily soon took themselves off to a corner and were lost in each other and the items on the plate, which they both intimately shared.

Carr helped himself; he was hungry, but finding himself alone he looked around the room and saw that it was a library of sorts and began looking at the titles on the shelves. He felt at peace, the food was indeed excellent, the company and setting civilian, thereby calm and comfortable, and he had enjoyed the singing. He was wondering if it would be ill mannered to extract a book and read some of its contents; he decided yes and his choice was half out when a voice that he now recognised as that of Lady Constance, spoke from behind him.

"Captain Carr."

He turned immediately, the book he had half extracted tumbling to the floor. Lady Constance ignored it.

"I have someone here who would like to meet you, Captain. May I introduce Miss Jane Perry?"

Carr's greeting of "Your Servant, Miss Perry, and a perfunctory bow were harshly terminated as he bent to retrieve the book. As he regained his height, she was just finishing her curtsey.

"Do you count yourself as much of a reader, Captain Carr? Do you have a preference, prose or poetry? Or do you just throw the books around? "

He was struck with how carefully each syllable and each letter was spoken, all by a young woman almost as tall as himself, slim build, pleasant face and complexion, fair hair, but deep brown eyes that literally shone as they calmly regarded him, waiting for an answer. Carr was thrown, and stepped back, to collide with a chair. His questioner gave a slight smile.

"No, Ma'am. Not a great reader. I was, but lately? No."

He paused, thinking of more to say.

"I play a little backgammon, and have been known to sing from time to time, but these days my talents stop there."

"What talent does it take to read a book?"

Carr realised he had chosen the wrong word.

"No talent at all, I agree, but we are soldiering hard in these worrying times, and access to books is none too easy, nor the time to read them."

Lady Constance, who had been standing as a silent observer of the frosty exchange, interrupted.

"I'll leave you two to your conversation, if that's the right word," and she turned away. Carr bowed, Jane Perry curtsied.

"You may have heard of my Father, General Perry. He's the General for this area."

"I'm afraid I have not, Miss Perry. I'm only recently into this area. Prior to here I was more to the East of the country. Almost all here is new to me."

"Almost all?"

"The army. That, of course, is familiar."

She paused and studied his face. She saw eyes that were not cold, but contained little emotion, and a mouth that tried to smile, but couldn't quite make the last effort. She noticed the scar of the half healed wound dividing his left eyebrow. She spoke again, her diction as precise as before.

"When you do read, what is your choice?"

"Was, Miss Perry. History mostly, rarely novels. I enjoy, or rather did, reading about Elizabeth I, and the Civil War."

"Violent topics, Captain Carr."

"True, up to a point, but both are not short on drama; nor on plot. I enjoy them as much as any novel."

He smiled slightly. She did not and she reached out to twist the book in his hand to enable her to read the title on the spine.

"The Plantagenets. History, as you say, but your topic is widening."

He remained silent and she changed the subject.

"And where did you take up singing?"

Carr was grateful for the change and strangely, he felt happy to be so thoroughly questioned.

"My Father insisted that I learn an instrument. The piano was his choice. My Tutor failed to teach me to play the piano, at least to any standard, but I did end up able to read music. In my last Regiment there were many Welsh, of all ranks, and I was sort of roped in."

He hoped that that would cause a smile, at least a mild thaw; but none came. Instead, the conversation took a considerable turn for the worse.

"Your name has been mentioned within my family circle. At dinner, quite recently and not with pleasure. It seems Father has just received notification of your posting."

Carr sighed, the old subject. Her precise diction, clinical questions, and, tediously, the old subject. Just another kind of stone-faced Carravoy. Gentility suddenly deserted him and irritation surfaced. It showed in both his voice and choice of words.

"I think I can guess what it was in connection with; and at dinner! So lofty a setting. After which course? The soup? Or perhaps the roast would be more appropriate. Carving knives and things!"

She ignored his sarcasm and his obvious annoyance.

"I thought I would come and see the infamous Captain Carr for myself."

"Infamous! Yes, of course, and your conclusion?"

"I'm keeping that to myself."

She swung her hips, girlishly, from side to side, as though winding herself up.

"I don't approve of duelling. I think it ridiculous. Such things can be settled by argument. And evidence! It's like some kind of feudal trial by combat. The winner has the right! How is that proven just because one is a better shot, or better with a sword? It's absurd."

This calmed him, but he still felt impatient at having to justify himself.

"Well my experience leads me to agree with you, but amongst society gentlemen it's different. It's part of the time in which we live. Good name and honour do matter, greatly, if you want to keep your standing and position. The pressure is huge."

It was now her turn for irritation.

"Nonsense. You stand up and argue. Where's your evidence,

you say? If none, you've won the argument, and to the Devil with whoever and their swords and pistols! Those with the argument, they're in the right."

The vehemence of her reply took Carr aback.

"Well, it's forbidden in the Army," he replied weakly.

"That didn't stop you. Did it? You resigned your Commission, didn't you?"

"Yes, Miss Perry, I did, but you see an Officer who's called out and doesn't respond, loses the respect of his fellows and he'll find himself cut out, even within his own Regiment. What's more it could effect how he carries out his duties. You'll get no support, no co-operation."

"Then you're just a bunch of silly boys! That's no argument at all. It's time to grow up."

Carr sighed, and rubbed his cheek with his left hand, before raising his eyes to look at her again, measured belligerence in his tone.

"Miss Perry. Did you come for an argument, or did you come to meet me?"

"Both."

"Well, in reply, us "silly boys" will soon be off to war, to fight the French. I do think we should be given some credit for that. That said, you may be right, in fact I'm sure you are, but facing danger is our trade, Officers, I mean. If you back away, there is a question over your courage, you'll be shunned and, what's worse, not trusted.

"I still say its absurd."

"I've agreed with you, but it happens. I'll be truthful; I wanted to fight Templemere, after what he did. Calling me a cheat and a liar and emptying brandy all over me. I'd have been happy to fight him there and then. There is such a thing as self regard, at least in my book. Nations declare war over insults and minor incidents; a duel isn't so very different. In many ways it does come down to self-respect, and there is much talk nowadays of national honour. One extreme gives rise to another. Reading history taught me that. In my defence, by the rules I could have killed him, but I didn't."

"But from what I hear, you broke the rules."

As she spoke, at last she smiled, and Carr's irritation, at a low ebb anyway, disappeared as smoke before a gale.

"Yes I did, but, as I say, one extreme provokes another."

There was a pause and each regarded the other. Carr managed a half smile, he had detected a slight thaw between them, but then she continued the argument, with undiminished intensity.

"I'm still not convinced. Settling disputes in such a manner proves neither right nor wrong and I've heard of some who are happy to start arguments, knowing that their duelling skill is very likely to get them through as the winner and, on top of that, a reputation as a duellist increases their standing in society. Does that apply to you?"

"No Miss Perry, it was my first and I've decided my last and you've raised another issue. I'd go so far as to say that causing a duel knowing that you are highly skilled at it, certainly applies to our Lord Fred Templemere. However, as I say, it is forbidden in the Army and I for one think that to be a step in the right direction. I hope that the lead given by the Army will transfer itself across into what calls itself society and changes attitudes. Duelling has gained me nothing, I can say that without fear of contradiction."

"Except notoriety."

"Except notoriety."

He looked at her and it came as no surprise that he didn't want to take his eyes away from what he saw, but he sighed again. He could see she was not content, even offended. Her last words were delivered as a judgment. He wondered if he could engage her on another subject, but his time had expired. A chubby, bespectacled Gentleman was calling out.

"Jane, the carriage has come round. We're leaving."

She looked around Carr to her informer.

"Thank you, Edmund, I'll just get my coat."

Carr stepped aside to allow her passage, it had been a disastrous introduction, but she remained and held out her hand for Carr to take, which he did, but when he relaxed his grip, she did not hers. Her words and tone were both in stark contrast to what had gone before, which both surprised and confused him,.

"Good bye, Captain Carr. I would like it very much if we could talk again."

"I too. Goodbye, Miss Perry."

She looked into his face once more, and then was gone. Drake and Cecily came to his side.

"Do you know who that is? She's Jane Perry, daughter of our General, General Perry.

"Yes, I know who she is, and she doesn't like duelling and she doesn't like me. Which the most, I can't tell."

They did meet again, but not to talk once more at length. With Christmas so close, their choir went carol singing around the town and at various churches and concerts. There were no more post practice socials and always there was the General's carriage to whisk her away, her Father not trusting the more remote parts of town, nor the villages. Most concerts were held in the homes of local notaries, including that of General Perry himself, but he exchanged not a word with Drake nor Carr, acknowledging their salutes with no more than a punctilious nod. Their final concert was in a local church and, their performance complete, the choir returned to their pews. Carr managed to manoeuvre himself into the pew behind her. When the time came to leave, he spoke to her as she passed.

"Miss Perry."

She stopped and walked out of the aisle to join him in his space. The brown eyes shone just as before even in the weak candlelight, but this time he felt sure she was glad to see him.

"I just wanted to wish you a merry Christmas, and a happy New Year. And I hope that things are well with you, and you are keeping ...er... healthy."

The last word jarred clumsily in his throat, but she really was smiling, what at, he wasn't sure.

"Yes, Captain Carr, I am keeping healthy, and I wish a merry Christmas and a happy New Year to you also. How are things at your barracks?"

"Oh, good enough, you know. Everyone's making preparations for Christmas, it's really quite pleasant. Just about everyone's good company at this time of year."

She made no reply, only to look at him and continue smiling, but it ended. The same Edmund was calling for her.

"I must go. If you see me again, do approach. You will, won't you?"

"Why yes, yes. You may count on it."

Then she was gone, but she did turn and wave at the transfixed Henry Carr. Drake and Cecily halted their own exit at where he stood.

132

"Carr. You know what they say about the likes of us court-ing the General's daughter. A one way ticket to the front rank."

"I really don't know what you're talking about, Drake. Miss Perry and I were merely exchanging Seasons Greetings," but both Drake and Cecily, especially Drake, saw a cheerfulness in his face that had not been seen before, over the cold months of their acquaintance so far."

* * *

Christmas Eve eve. There were few Officers in the barracks, most were using their leave, but in the barrack rooms the over population remained the same. All was good cheer, the decora-tions were complete, holly and ivy, each cutting carefully se-lected for its berries, hung from every beam and windowsill and coloured bunting stretched across as diagonals. Someone had managed to produce some Naval Signal flags; what they said no one knew but their bright colours certainly added to the overall effect. Each family had a collection of presents stored in whatever could be found, box or sack or netting, each wrapped in cloth which did much to hide the contents, although the children took much time in studying each present, trying to identify the object through the encircling folds. Those adults who could write had written names in ink or charcoal on the wrapping, and most children could recognise their own name, which gave added urgency to the identification of those marked as theirs.

The Christian importance of the time was not absent from any of the barrack rooms. Most had a Nativity and if not that, then some picture or symbol of the Sacred Birth, and it was upon these that the most careful attention had descended, mostly evergreens around it, but within the Nativity the detail was as good as could be produced, even the straw of the man-ger carefully sliced down and cut to scale. In their barrack Nativity, Joe Pike's wise man was well to the fore, whilst Tom's excellent donkey and shepherd were makeweights at the back, but even Tom Miles could see no cause for umbrage. This time of laughter and good neighbourliness had permeated even into him.

For some weeks Davey and Sedgwicke's barrack room, along with all others, had been preparing for the communal Christmas meal. The pork, peas and potatoes came as rations, but not, because they were in barracks, the highly popular figgy duff. All had been saving money for the vital ingredients; flour, sugar, suet and raisins, and these necessaries had to be obtained from outside in the town. They were to be boiled with great care and attention, tied as puddings in white sheets, on the barrack room cooking fire in its wide grate with its heavy metal range, under the supervision of the senior "wives".

On the morning of that day, ration duty fell to Davey and Sedgwicke. After their obtaining the pork, peas, potatoes and flour from the kitchen stores, the savings were handed over to them both and safely pocketed. Wearing both knapsacks and haversacks to carry back their purchases, they obtained permission from the Officer of the Day to leave the barracks and shop for what was needed for the much anticipated pudding treat. Davey, at least, knew the weighty responsibility he carried, such luxuries were rare and precious.

Sedgwicke, however, had never shopped for food in his life and told Davey such. Davey gave him the simpler task of obtaining suet.

"Suet, Parson. It's white fat. Any butchers will do, and you want 8lbs weight."

He only trusted himself for the other two, sugar, and raisins in particular, needed to be searched out. Besides they were more expensive and he trusted himself more with the heavier purse. They reached the Market Cross and Davey told Sedgwicke to meet back at that spot. He pointed out a butcher, watched Sedgwicke shuffle nervously away, but in the right direction, then went off on his own errand. There was no market stall selling such fruit and so he had to search further. A good costermonger's shop was eventually found and in went Davey to obtain 10lbs of raisins. Such a quantity merited some bargaining and Davey did so and obtained a good price. The sugar proved easier, so time came to return to the Market, and there was Sedgwicke, with bulging haversack and presumably equally filled knapsack.

"Well done, Parson. Let's get these back, now. Figgy duff takes a long time mixin' and makin'."

They re-entered the barracks and carried their purchases to their table. Davey emptied out his parcels, making much of displaying the plump raisons, whilst Sedgwicke struggled with what looked like a soft and slimy parcel from each of his carriers. Davey opened the greased wrapping of one and ran his finger up the side of the soft white pile inside.

"Parson! What have you bought? You asked the butcher for suet, yes?"

Sedgwicke took umbrage, born of a growing anxiety.

"No. I asked for white fat and the butcher pointed to this, and so I said yes. He said he was a pork butcher and lard was all he had. He said that lard was used in lardy cakes. That's a sweet dish, is it not? The difference between various kinds of fat lies outside my experience. Fat for a lardy cake or fat for a pudding. I bought what he had and spoke of."

Davey placed his hands on the table and hung his head forward. Meanwhile the cooks were gathering. The Head Cook spoke up.

"Where's the makings, then? We needs to start. What in the Lord's name is that?" pointing a condemning finger at the two offending piles before Sedgwicke. This accompanied by comments such as "Damn fool", "He must have lard in his head!" Davey raised his eyes and looked across to see a horrified and shrinking Sedgwicke, terror growing by the second as the cooks and mothers surrounded the table and them, both. Something describable as compassion rose within him; he couldn't leave Sedgwicke to carry the blame and so he addressed the cook who had spoken.

"Beg pardon, Ma'am, but it seems we've bought you lard instead of suet. That won't serve, will it?"

Several heads shaking told him all he needed to know, followed by comments that were all variations on the theme of, "What kind of addled numbskull doesn't know the difference between suet and lard?" but after came the threat, this time from a male voice, Dan Smith.

"Put it right, or it's a "cobbing."

Davey had little idea what a "cobbing" was, but it was clearly a punishment and to be avoided. On top of that, and much worse, no figgy duff for the room; for which he would never be forgiven.

"We will, we'll put it right. I promise. Give us an hour or so."

Most walked off, but a few remained to listen. Davey turned to Sedgwicke.

"Parson, we've got to put this right. I'll put in all the money I have, you do the same."

Sedgwicke looked horrified, but horror of a different colour caused by the fear of being "cobbed". He made no move. Seeing this, Davey went to his own belongings and took out his purse.

"Parson. Get your money. Get your money! There's mine. We've got to put this right."

Reluctantly, Sedgwicke copied Davey's actions. Both emptied their purses out onto the table. All copper.

"Right. One shilling and a penny. We're going to need four shillings at least. We'll take back the lard and sell it back. What did you pay?"

"Four shillings."

"We won't get full coin, but he'll give us half. That leaves us short by about eleven pence. Wrap up the lard and put one in each of our haversacks. We have to find the difference."

They left the barrack room and out onto the parade square. The only people with any money were Officers and so Davey, followed by Sedgwicke, crossed the square to the Officers Mess. Desperate situations required desperate measures. Davey entered the main door but saw no one. Anxiously, he knocked on other doors. Depending on the Officer he found he was taking a huge risk to be in such a place without any orders giving him permission. Finally one opened. It was Major O'Hare.

"Begging your pardon, Sir. I hope you'll forgive the intrusion, but I was hoping that you may be able to help us out of a problem that could spoil Christmas for our room. Our cooks is making a figgy duff, Sir, that needs suet and, because of a mix up," Davey turned to look squarely at Sedgwicke, "Because of a mix up, we got lard instead of suet. We need another eleven pence, Sir, to buy the suet needed. I was hoping to borrow it from an Officer, Sir, as our only hope. Could you see your way clear, Sir?"

O'Hare's face broadened into a wide Irish grin.

"Lard instead of suet. For a figgy duff? Now, what kind of gombeen eejit thinks you can make figgy duff with lard instead of suet?'

Davey made no move, but O'Hare also looked squarely at Sedgwicke, who lowered his eyes and shrunk, both in height and girth. O'Hare noticed Davey's shoulder wings.

"Light Company, are you?"

"Yes Sir."

"Well, I'll tell you; this is just the kind of initiative that we hope from such as yourself. I think I can find the necessary."

He put his hands into his waistcoat pocket and extracted a silver shilling.

"There's your finance. A penny more than you need. Pay me back when you can, and tomorrow I expect to come around and receive a portion. Which room?'

"Number three, Sir, and thank you. You've just saved us from a cobbing, Sir, whatever that is."

"Oh, it's nasty. You don't want to know."

"Right, Sir. I'll try to avoid it, and thank you once again."

Davey looked at Sedgwicke, expecting an echo of his thanks, but none came. He motioned with both head and hands towards O'Hare. At last Sedgwicke got the message and added his mumbled thanks. O'Hare stood in the doorway, enjoying the grand humour, as both crossed the parade ground and disappeared through the gate arch.

An energetic half hour saw them return, with suet of high quality and sufficient quantity. The butcher had taken the lard back, but, as Davey said, only for half the price. The ingredients delivered, both lay back on their straw mattresses, penniless and in debt, but free from the unknown but plainly dire punishment as threatened. Davey, relief now thoroughly run through him, turned over and addressed a passing roommate.

"Hey, Walter. What's a cobbing?"

"* * *, serious. You don't want to know."

"Oh. Right."

* * *

Christmas Eve had broken. Whilst Christmas Day was for family, this day was the celebration day for villages, but for soldiers and their families their barracks was their village and all took their chance to join in whatever went on, in whichever room. Breakfast was the usual bread and tea, but all knew of the communal feast that would be served at dinner, each room having been given the rations for its occupants, and they were left to prepare it, as best they may. Rolled joints of pork, not the poorest cuts this time, turned before the fire, and a long line of mothers and daughters prepared the vegetables, tossing their

137

carefully pared item into the appropriate pot. Meanwhile the children and the men, with a few of the females who had finished their tasks for the meal, set about entertaining themselves. The be-ribboned hoops of Game of Graces raced between the opposing sides, and elsewhere quoits, hopscotch, and games of chase, sent shrieks of laughter and excitement along the halls and corridors.

Tom and Joe's room had fewer small children and so the older children and adults set about their Celebration Day with dances and jigs, performed to the accompaniment of fiddles, fifes and penny whistles. Their room had a Drummerboy and so they had added percussion. Tom Miles revealed hidden talent with a Jew's Harp and joined in with the growing band that was whipping up a frenzy on the centre space that was now a dance floor. The full repertoire of jigs and reels was gone through, and with that done, then tricks of all kinds with all objects; ropes, chairs, broomsticks and juggling with bags of beans.

Joe Pike took the floor and proved an adept tumbler, with cartwheels, handstands, and somersaults in profusion across the length of the room, end-to-end, and corner-to-corner. As if this didn't endear him further enough to the female members of the room, when the dancing was done, solo's were called for and he was amongst the first, singing in a fine clear voice, "They bid me forget thee". During this rendition no vegetable was peeled nor pots stirred, the only stirring occurring within the emotions of many of Joe's admirers as they struggled to maintain a steady breathing but found that lumps in their throats were making that difficult. Many followed to perform their party piece of song or recitation but soon it was to table.

All plates were hidden under pork, potatoes, and greens, with bread and small beer to accompany, followed by the magnificent size and glistening countenance of the figgy duff. O'Hare arrived in Room Three and wondered if the two crates of beer he had brought would be fair exchange for a plate of the wondrous pudding. Shouts of agreement and welcome were his answer and he sat in the midst of about 50 revellers, all common soldiery and their families. Once established, he gave free rein to his Irish temperament within good company and with good cheer, amongst people he well understood. After the meal the revels continued, although with stomachs so full, not so energetically. Nevertheless dancing and singing were the main entertainments and Major O'Hare got up and sang two songs before he took his leave, one a comedy ditty, "Courting in the Kitchen", the other one a ballad of deeply poignant sentiment and sorrow that only the Irish can both compose and sing, the "Isle of Inisfree".

The evening wore on in similar tone, but eventually became more subdued. Time was approaching for preparations for Midnight Mass. The families prepared and dressed themselves in their best clothes and husband soldiers donned their full dress uniforms. At 11.45 all filed out along corridors and out through the many doors onto the parade ground. There was no formality of parade by companies, instead, by the light of candle lanterns all assembled, soldiers with families, mingled with NCO's and Officers. Each stood amongst faces that were familiar, the power of shared worship creating a time for friends and comrades, not the military formality of salutes, orders, and dress by ranks. The Vicar stood waiting and, mindful of his last appearance, stone cold sober. When all were assembled, and quiet had descended to match the silence of the black and starless sky, the service began. The Vicar led his congregation faultlessly through the hymns and prayers and, had he known, he would have said a prayer for the cause of the absence of one family from Room Three.

A child had fallen ill. She had joined in the gaiety that began the day and ate heartily from the Christmas meal, but, come late afternoon, she had returned to her family and lay down in her bothy, plainly unwell, faced flushed, then grey, forehead damp with perspiration. Through the night the fever grew. The Surgeon was away for the Festival and so there was little anyone could do but fall back on the folk-lore that had, or had not, got the sick children of families such as theirs through the diseases and ailments that so often added to the graveyards, but occupied little space. Her poor dress and shift were removed and she was wrapped in wet blankets, or dry, as the fever waxed and waned. As neighbouring families drifted back in, their enquiries were met with shaking heads and anxious faces. All through the night such was done as could help. Christmas Day came and presents and gifts were exchanged, but the mood was subdued.

On the opposite side of the room, on Christmas Morning, Davey took himself over to Sedgwicke and handed him a small bundle wrapped in green cloth.

"Here you are Parson. Happy Christmas."

Sedgwicke looked up astonished, first at Davey's gift, and then his friendly face. He took the gift and unwrapped it. It was a clasp knife, not new, but serviceable.

"I noticed that you haven't got one. You'll need one, it'll come in handy, and often."

Sedgwicke returned no thanks; his mind was fixed on the fact that he had nothing to give in return. Over the weeks leading up to Christmas the thought had never crossed his mind to obtain a gift for this gypsy that he shared with. He could think of nothing to say but an apology.

"I'm sorry Davey, but I have nothing to give you." His sorrow was genuine.

"Never you mind, Parson. If you see something that I could count as handy and it's within your means, well, that'll be nice."

Sedgwicke sat on his stool and looked at the gift, his mind in turmoil. This was an act of kindness, as also was Davey's support with his shopping failure. Together both were wholly undermining his low opinion of the capabilities of the lower social orders to understand and be motivated by what he described as "higher feelings". The knife opened and closed as did his thoughts on his hitherto well established judgment on the likes of John Davey and those that he called "as myself". Not unintelligent, Sedgwicke appreciated that there were questions that needed answering and his previous life was not providing the answers. Davey left the cubicle. His "lady" acquaintance had come into the room and both exchanged gifts before sitting together for their usual quiet conversation. She had brought a piece of mistletoe which was put to good and frequent use.

With the evening, it was plain that the child was losing her fight. Delirium and shallow breathing were telling their story. At midnight, she died, her little heart unable to sustain the effort needed to keep her body alive through the assault that many thought must be scarlet fever. Not one family in the barrack room, and plenty from elsewhere, failed to come and pay their respects to the anguished Father and distraught Mother. Marjorie Smith, wife of Dan, came over to Davey and Sedgwicke's cubicle. She addressed herself to Sedgwicke.

"Won't you go over and say a few words, Parson? For the pity of the Lord's Sake."

Sedgwicke was readying himself for sleep. He looked up at Marjorie Smith, and then to Davey, he was surprised and unsure. Davey nodded to him.

"Take your Bible, Parson. Put on your red jacket. Full fig and up to the mark."

Sedgwicke reached inside his canvas bag and found his Bible. He took his jacket off its peg, put it on, buttoned it fully and brushed it down. He motioned to the woman to lead on and he would follow. He reached the bothy and found both Mother and Father kneeling beside the lifeless figure, the rag doll that was to have been her Christmas present lodged under her right forearm.

"Would you like me to pray with you?"

The Father replied, "Yes, Parson. That would be nice."

Sedgwicke kneeled beside the child. As he knelt, so did her parents and almost all around besides. Sedgwicke was moved. The sincerity and gravity of this simple act of faith were not lost on him.

"Dear Lord, thou hast chosen this child to come to thee and be amongst thy Heavenly Host. As was said by our Dear Lord Jesus, suffer the little children to come unto me. Give succour, please Dear Lord, to her Mother and Father, brothers and sisters. Comfort them in their sorrow and in their hour of need."

Then, surprising himself, he departed from the stock phrases that he had used so often before.

"She was but an innocent child, Dear Lord, born and raised into a life of toil and disappointment, but she was well loved, Heavenly Father, and held dear, not just by her family but by all her friends and neighbours around her. Her riches she already had, not silver coin, but the love of her family and all who knew her, and counted her as one of their own. As thou loved thy only Son, take her unto thee, and let her dwell in thy Holy House. For Jesus Christ's Sake. Amen."

Amen echoed from all present. When they were all upright, the Father shook Sedgwicke's hand.

"Thank you, Parson. Those were fine words and a comfort. We're burying her tomorrow, first thing. Would you do the ceremony? She was a soldier's daughter and we bury our own. We'd like you to, as one of us."

"One of us." The poignancy of the moment and the Father's genuine request had both made a profound impression on Sedgwicke.

"I will. Yes, of course."

Come the morning the sorrowful figure was laid out on one of the tables, dressed in her best dress, with the rag doll still in the crook of her arm. Then she was wound in the best white sheet the room could provide, and her face was kissed by each of her family, her Mother last, before the final folds closed over and around. Then her Father picked her up and carried her out. They were followed by all others in the room. Few had any clothes that could be described as appropriate for mourning, but all had managed something dark or at least dark armbands. The men wore their dress uniforms that needed little cleaning nor burnishing having been prepared so recently for the Midnight Mass but were nevertheless checked for perfection. As they walked the corridor and traversed the parade ground to the gate they walked between two silent rows formed by all the occupants of the barracks, all also in their best clothes or immaculate uniforms.

The small cemetery lay behind the barracks and so the mournful procession continued its way through the weak December light to the small grave, dug not an hour before in the growing dawn to be prepared and ready. As the small body was passed down to her Father, Sedgwicke read the familiar ceremony. When all was done, the Father shook his hand again and the Mother thanked him for giving what was a "good and right ceremony". Whilst the grave was being filled in, he stood with the family and for the first time in his life, he felt he had a clear understanding of what it meant to be a "Christian Man of God".

Chapter Five

Change upon Change

It was the fourth Day of Christmas. The festivities had come and gone, but not yet the New Year. It was the evening of the last day of Christmas Leave and all Officers had returned and were assembling in the Mess for evening dinner. Carr and Drake were already established together at the table, sat at their usual place, the halfway point along one side. The Mess was quiet, despite being over half full, a "post holiday" atmosphere pervaded and conversation between the two was relaxed, but slow. Drake, as ever, sat up alert, whilst Carr lounged back in usual languid manner, subconsciously toying with a piece of cutlery. Everything changed with the entrance of Carravoy and D'Villiers, the latter with his left arm in a sling, splints on his forearm clearly making angles through the white cloth. Carravoy was clearly in very ebullient mood.

"You may congratulate me, Gentlemen, I am £250 richer, won yesterday at a Steeplechase. Not a bet, I wish you to know, but as the victor in that same race. On D'Villier's horse; he fell off him the previous day, hence the broken wing. This evening the claret is on me," and he turned to the Mess Room Orderly,

"Rogers, this evening, the better stuff."

Inevitably, as if by magnetism, his gaze fell on Carr, who raised his hand in salute, forefinger upright.

"Give you joy, Carravoy, on your splendid victory, and thanks from us all on your generously sharing the proceeds in the form of …er…improved claret. Do we take it that bad luck robbed Royston of the victory, or do you feel that your horsemanship brought some special quality to the performance?"

"Modesty forbids, as I'm sure you understand, but I will say that he is a very spirited animal that does require a level of skill above and beyond. He unseated D'Villiers here at a plain fence. Simply flew over it, and, damn me, if he didn't turn in the air and off came Royston."

"Oh, I say Carravoy, that's putting it a bit steep. Could've happened to anyone and it's not a break, just a sprain. I stayed on him well enough during the hunts; just a bit of bad luck, that's all."

143

Carr sensed D'Villier's embarrassment and raised his now filled glass in his direction.

"Well, whatever. Royston! My congratulations on your owning so splendid a horse, and I'm sure that your previous horsemanship ensured that he was well broke in for the substitute jockey!"

Carravoy's face changed. He sensed an insult, intended or not.

"And what, pray, did you two get up to over the holiday?"

Drake looked at Carr and spoke.

"Shall we tell him? Has he the level of sophistication to permit appreciation, do you think?"

Carravoy bridled further at the notion that he was being toyed with. Carr smiled slightly and answered.

"Yes, I believe so. Yes, of course. We...." he said, turning to Carravoy, "...had a very pleasant and uplifting Christmas, singing in the Choral Ensemble of Lady Constance Fynings. Carols, good food, and good company."

Carravoy sensed an opening.

"Carols? Singing in a choir? You two? Hardly an activity for two Princes of Mars; whom being vigorous and enterprising Officers of the King."

Drake and Carr looked at each other and Carr soon mirrored Drake's look of astonishment, which carried over into Drake's voice.

"He doesn't believe us!"

"Oh I believe you, well enough. Now I think of it, it fits perfectly. Off tune pianos and descants and whatnot. I trust that neither of you let the side down and gave vent to any "bum notes"?

Carr took up the verbal jousting. So far, it had remained just on the right side of Mess Room banter. Grins and sniggers could be seen and heard elsewhere around the table.

"Bum notes! Dear me, the very idea. No indeed, it was a choir of the very highest accomplishment, well schooled and tutored by Lady Constance herself, a lady of estimable quality in the musical line of things. Would you not say, Drake?"

"I would, and I would go further by saying that our performances were appreciated by the highest echelons of local society, including that of our Regional General, no less."

Carr nodded and inclined his head towards Carravoy, his expression making the silent question, "So what do you think of that?"

Carravoy was indeed struck by the fact of the pair circulating in the same society as the Regional General, but he quickly recovered.

"Well, as long as you didn't let the side down with anything too discordant or off the beat. If that is the case, then I pronounce myself untroubled. Gentlemen, I propose a toast, to our two choirboys. May their notes come in the right place, fivers preferred, and their keys be never off, always safely in the lock," and he drank to his own toast.

Carr replied.

"And here's to our noble horsemen. May they have a long rein in the saddle," groans at the awful pun, "but their stirrups short, and their gallops fast and fruitful, at least in proportion to their prize money," and he and Drake drank to this toast. Laughter sounded from around the room, accompanied by good-natured rapping on the table. The banter stopped. Colonel Lacey and Major O'Hare had entered the room, timing their entrance until all were assembled and all Officers rose. Lacey and O'Hare reached their places and Lacey addressed the table.

"Gentlemen, good evening. I wish to welcome you back, and I trust that you all had an enjoyable leave over the festive season. Please be seated."

Carravoy bit back the temptation to add a comment about "festive singing in the sweet choir". To make such a quip as an addition to the Colonel's greeting would be gravely ill mannered. Throughout the meal, he and Carr exchanged glances, but Carr, more than Carravoy, was grateful that he had "fought a draw". However, Carravoy's repeated humming of several well known carols as the various courses came and went was not lost on him. Meanwhile, Drake had forgotten the whole thing and was busy extolling the virtues of tarpaulin over waxed cloth as cover in a rainstorm.

* * *

Their entrance was fierce and loud, both violent and shrill, such that all in the room turned to see a Corporal in the Grenadiers, dragging Molly Dixon, plus child, into the barrack room, he shout-

ing at her, she shouting back, and the child the loudest, screaming wails of distress. However, it was the shouts of the Corporal
that drew the watchers attention, here was domestic drama,
which always presented worthwhile entertainment.

"Where is the bastard, where is he? You point him out. I
knows you 'bin comin' 'ere, so now you show me."

Molly wrenched herself free and adjusted the child in its
shawl on her hip. She looked over to the cubicle that she had
visited so often and saw Davey. No words were exchanged and
she made no indication that he was the one, but that changed
when Davey looked steadily at her and nodded, twice.

"It's him, there, John Davey."

The room fell totally silent and Sedgwicke, in the midst of
tidying, instinctively took a step back to feel the boards that
defined their space in the room. He expected violence, a premo-
nition that seemed accurate, for the Grenadier Corporal, with
Grenadier strides, was heading straight for Davey; stools, buckets, and people being ploughed aside to create a direct path to
his quarry. No more words were said, the anger on his face and
the fierce hatred in his eyes told all of what was about to happen.

Davey stood his ground, but his feet had shifted, poised to
give him purchase for any required move. The Corporal came up
to Davey and reached out with his left hand to seize Davey's
shirt, whilst drawing back a huge right fist, but Davey shifted
left, then right, ducking under the outstretched hand. The Corporal released the punch anyway, but Davey swung his body
back and ducked again. A haymaking left met only thin air as
Davey again bobbed and weaved his head away from danger.

Meanwhile, many men were closing in on the Corporal. Two
seized his arms and one held him from behind, arms looping
around his shoulder and waist, but the Corporal continued to
struggle, driving himself forward to reach Davey.

"Let I go, the bastard's takin' my Molly. Let I go!" but none
obeyed. Instead the Room Sergeant, Obediah Hill, had reached
the scene and placed himself between Davey and the Corporal.

"Now hold hard, Corporal. You touch me and it's your stripes
and the lash. Hold hard and stay."

The Corporal, chest heaving and still wild eyed, did cease his
struggling. Hill motioned to those holding him and the Corporal
was released.

"Now, what's all this about?"

The Corporal took two deep breaths and then spoke, through clenched teeth. He pointed at Davey.

"He's takin' my Molly, took her away, stole her from me."

He paused and breathed again.

"I'm here to do something about it. I b'aint letting this go."

Hill stood for a moment regarding the Corporal, then looked past him at Molly. His authority in the room was absolute, all were waiting for him to pronounce on what should happen next.

"If he stole her, like you say, he must've come into your room, to start things off, like. Is that what he did? Have you seen him in your barrack room?"

"No, but he got to her somehow," and his anger reasserted itself, "Gypsy bastard!" and he moved forward to be halted both by his escort regaining their grip on his arms and the raised hand of Hill. With all still, Hill gave his verdict.

"Now you listen. We've all seen her in here, she comes straight in and goes straight over, to him," jerking a thumb in Davey's direction. "She's not forced, she comes as she pleases and goes the same. In other words, she comes by choice. Now, listen some more, and I knows I be makin' sense. You b'aint the first man as has failed to hold onto Molly Dixon. We all knows her story."

Molly leaned forward, nearly as angry as the Corporal.

"Now just a minute, I've......"

"You keep your gob shut! This b'aint the first time you're wandering ways has caused ructions in this barracks. So keep shut!"

Molly shrunk back and Hill turned to the Corporal.

"She's gone! Her wandering nature has took her elsewhere. You had your time, but now she's gone. Be this child thine?"

The Corporal shook his head and Hill nodded.

"There, 'twer there for 'ee to see from the onset. She's now gone, gone from 'ee. Mother!" shouting to his own wife, "Fetch a piece of rope."

All was quiet, save the subsiding, but still audible, breathing of the Corporal. Hill looked from the Corporal, to Molly and then to Davey, standing behind and to one side. He regarded Davey for the longest. The rope arrived. Molly knew what the rope meant.

"I b'aint one to be swapped about by a piece of rope!"

For the first time Hill raised his voice.

"We all knows what you be, and the list of men you called husband. Now, shut your rattle, and we'll get this settled."

He presented one end to Molly, who reluctantly took it, the other he gave to the Corporal.

"You've lost her. 'Tis up to another to take her, so's you be no longer responsible, not for her nor for the child. You has to offer that rope to him, Davey here, and if he takes it, she's away from you."

The Corporal looked pained and distraught, but the violence was gone. He looked in anguish at Molly, but could see only the curtain of her chestnut hair hiding her left cheek. She had eyes only for John Davey. Hill turned to Davey.

"If you wants her, take the rope. That makes her your wife, your woman and in your keeping. The child too."

All eyes were focused on Davey, studying either his face or looking for movement from his right hand. Davey looked carefully at Molly, her eyes wide open and the anxiety in her face plain and painful. She nodded, hope and apprehension still in her eyes and face, but Davey decided. He reached out and took the rope; it wasn't offered but it came easily from the Corporal's fingers. Davey smiled; Molly was overjoyed, but her look was cut short by Hill.

"Now try to make this one last more'n the others. I think you've got a good man there, better than you know."

The crowd thinned, the matter settled, the diversion was ended. Davey moved forward.

"Now then, Sergeant, you are speaking to my wife, and didn't you say she was now in my keeping?"

Hill turned to Davey and nodded. He started to turn away, but paused, to regard Davey carefully.

"I'd say, from what I've just seen, you've seen the inside of a ring."

"You're not wrong, Sergeant. Fairgrounds and such brought a bit of prize money that never did no harm."

Hill nodded again.

"I'd keep that to yourself, if I was you. In my time, that, as common knowledge, does more harm than good."

Hill was the last to move off, but he did, his part in the settlement complete. Davey looked at Molly.

148

"You'd best off and get your things."

Her face exploded into a radiant grin; she nodded, turned and hurried away. Davey and the Grenadier Corporal remained facing each other, each studying the other's face. Davey spoke.

"I swear to you, I did nothing to start this. One day she came, and it went on from there. I promise I'll take care of her, and I'll take care of the child."

The Corporal nodded, released a huge breath and then turned for the door. His time of leaving sketched a forlorn figure and inevitable sympathy attached to him, but his sadness was too deep for him to notice the compassionate looks that followed his passage. However, he didn't reach the door, a table of fellow Grenadiers called him over and shared some beer with him and he sat with them, while they explained why it was "really all for the best".

Molly returned, child on one hip, possessions on the other. She moved straight into the cubicle and began arranging, joy unconfined and obvious to see. Sedgwicke was at a loss. Was it this simple? What would happen to him? He moved closer to Davey.

"How now, Parson? I'd like you to meet my wife. Perhaps one day you can do the full jig for us in a church."

Sedgwicke grinned but still looked confused, adding to the impression by both nodding and shaking his head.

"Molly, this is the Parson. He's an educated man, so stick to talking about things that you know something about."

Molly extended her hand and bestowed upon Sedgwicke her warmest smile; he took her hand then released it, but said nothing, still too confused. He turned to Davey.

"What happens to me? Do I move out? If so, where?"

"I don't see why, Parson. We've gotten used to each other, haven't we? All we needs is another mattress, next to mine for Molly, then we goes on as before, although it would be nice if you could start educating Tilly here," placing his hand on the child's head, the same chestnut brown as her Mother's. "She turned five a while back, bit young perhaps, but bright as a button. It's time, I'd say, that she started learning her letters and scripture. She may not get a better chance."

Sedgwicke nodded, although inside he wasn't sure. Would such a child, sprung from such a spring have any capacity for learning? However, he held his peace. An extra mattress was

149

found, and a small one for Tilly. Domesticity soon settled in, Molly began cleaning and tidying and Tilly ran off to find new playmates from within the room. Their first mealtime together proved to be more than pleasant, Sedgwicke sat with the new "family", saying little, but Molly and Tilly chatted away, with Davey acting as the calm but genial Father figure, joining in as and when. Lights out came and all settled down. Sedgwicke slept in his usual place, but this time with a blanket pulled tight around his ears to block out what he didn't want to hear. Not only did he have a rustling child not two yards from his own bed, but also he knew and expected the sounds that would come from Davey and Molly sharing their first night together. So intimate, and yet so public. Deeply tender and caring, but, he knew, so much not for him.

* * *

The next day was New Year's Eve, but it would not be wasted. The whole battalion was assembled to march off for battalion exercise. No soldier was to remain in the barracks, this was battle drill and each man in the battalion had a part to play. All companies were paraded in marching order in four ranks, each with their Captain and two or three of each of Lieutenants and Sergeants. Sergeant Major Gibney marched up the long ranks of those assembled, the verb "to walk" could never be applied to him, he would be insulted and puzzled, him examining and judging all that he saw. Finally, he marched up to Colonel Lacey, saluted and pronounced the parade ready to march off. With that, Lacey with his Battalion Staff and two Junior Majors, turned their mounts for the gate and walked their horses forward, leaving Major O'Hare in charge of the parade. O'Hare placed his horse before the centre, at the junction of number four and number five company. He issued his orders, all satisfactorily obeyed, that achieved the whole battalion at attention, with sloped arms, facing the gate. He gave the final order,
    "Battalion, quick march."
    892 left feet lifted and fell as one and the 5th Detachments, for the first time, marched out of their barracks as a whole unit, drummers between each company hitting a marching beat. Their progress took them out onto the flat plain to the South East of the town, slightly higher than the moor and better

drained, with no deep, water filled rhynes to interfere with their battalion manoeuvres. It was a clear, mild day, unseasonable for the final day of 1805, enough clouds that could perhaps gang up and cause rain, but also enough bright light from the low sun to pick out the dull winter greens and browns of this winter barren moorland. However, the sun chose to alight, not on the common scrub and grassland but the bright scarlet coats and badges of the impressive marching column of King's Redcoats, their Colonel leading them on. When the track gave out onto a wide-open area of rough grassland, the column halted. Lacey turned to O'Hare,

"We'll start by advancing in column of companies. About half a mile up and back should do it. I want to see how they perform in 'open', 'closed' and "half distance" between companies."

"Sir."

O'Hare rode down the column.

"Open column of companies. Advance in five minutes."

The leading company, the Grenadiers, wheeled 90 degrees from their line of march, and the rear two ranks marched to the end of the front two ranks, doubling the length of their front. Each company followed their example into a two deep line. Then all advanced with "open column" intervals, enough space between each company to enable each to easily wheel 90 degrees either way to quickly form up as a continuous firing line on either side. Then the order came for closed companies and the space disappeared and the whole battalion became one solid block of men. This was practiced up and down the half mile and, as the order came for "closed" or "open" or "half", Captains, Lieutenants, and Sergeants screamed instructions, "close up" or "fall back", their voices adding words to the signals beaten out by the drummers. After an hour, Lacey was satisfied. As the battalion marched past as a column of open companies, he turned to O'Hare sitting his horse beside him.

"It's a start. Now, firing line; left flank."

O'Hare spurred his horse away, relaying the order to each Captain. The column halted and each company swung around to the left, the last two men on the left of each company holding their ground to act as a pivot. It was performed with satisfactory speed apart from number three company, Captain Heaviside's. Lacey had not failed to notice. He turned to the Lieutenant on his Staff.

"Present my compliments to Captain Heaviside. Tell him I want his outside half company moving quicker than that."

"Yes Sir", and off went the messenger spraying up a cloud of turf from his horse's hooves.

"Colonel Lacey's compliments, Sir, but he asks that you speed up your outside half company. Yours was the last in line, Sir."

Heaviside looked up at the mounted messenger and immediately angered. Without replying, he strode off to find the errant Lieutenant in charge. It was D'Villiers and Heaviside didn't bother to hold his peace until he reached a distance for quiet conversation. He gave his opinion at shouting distance.

"D'Villiers. Your men are moving like a collection of worn out washerwomen! Next time, be the first, not the last."

Many men in the company sniggered and D'Villiers saw shoulders shaking with laughter. A "Holy Joe" he may be, but Heaviside was liked and respected by his men. D'Villiers was incandescent at such a public humiliation.

"Face your front, the damn lot of you," although there wasn't one man not already doing so, "And silence in the ranks, or there'll be bloody backs before this day is out."

He took himself up and down the line pushing and shoving with the pommel of his sword at any back more than an inch out of alignment.

Whilst the exercises in column had been taking place, a line of posts had been erected with three strands of whitewashed rope stretching along the whole length, forming a length of about 230 yards, the frontage of a battalion in a two deep line. It was 100 yards distant, and just overlapping the length of the battalion at either end. This was to serve as their target. Again, Lacey turned to O'Hare.

"Volley by ranks, 10 rounds per man. You take the left wing, Major Simmonds, the right."

"Sir," and he was away again, shouting orders and finally instructing Major Simmonds. Soon the orders rang out, "lock on", "load", "make ready" and "present". Each Major gave the order to their own half of the battalion and the appalling noise began, front rank, then rear rank; load, present, fire. Burning paper cartridges, blasted from the muzzles of furiously worked muskets, fluttered down from the dense white smoke before them. The daily practice had enabled almost all new recruits to achieve three reloads in a minute, but Sedgwicke was still well short, two was his best. After five, he fell badly behind and his musket gave its lonely bark, whilst all around in his rank were busy biting cartridges. D'Villiers had noticed and he was still in a foul mood.

"Sedgwicke, you damned lazy shirker, meet the orders or I'll see you flogged and in the Guardhouse. See if I don't, you idle waster!"

The threat didn't help Sedgwicke's composure in the slightest, in fact he dropped his opened cartridge, but the soldier in the rank behind gave help, whilst subconsciously carrying out his own reload, that soldier being Corporal Toby Halfway.

"Don't worry, Parson. Just bring up your musket loaded or not. No one will notice in all the smoke if you don't fire, 'specially not that bloody tripe-hound. If 'tis loaded, all well and good; if not, well, no matter."

Sedgwicke half turned and gave his thanks. He managed eight shots, but by taking the advice, he made false "presents", and came no more to the attention of Lieutenant D'Villiers. Then the "cease fire" came; ten rounds and nine reloads completed.

Lacey turned again to his Lieutenant.

"How long?"

"Just over three minutes, Sir."

"How much over?"

"Six seconds, Sir."

"Hmmm, we're getting there. O'Hare, let the men take a drink. And clean muskets."

Canteens were eagerly found behind their left hip and the men washed the gunpowder from their mouths before swallowing. Then, as best they could, they cleaned their muskets of the fouling that remained after ten rounds. They could see, after the smoke had cleared, that most of the white ropes were cut and all the posts severely splintered, but it was not over.

"Do it again, O'Hare," and it was, and again after that, achieving three minutes 3 seconds, each time.

After the third time, the posts were uprooted and driven in to form a rectangle with a front facing their centre of only two companies width. The remaining posts stretched back at right angles. Most recognised this figure to be the outline of the columns they had been practising earlier, an impression made stronger by the addition of more white ropes. All complete, Lacey turned again to O'Hare.

"This is what we will most likely face. Our line against their column. Now, each wing independent, you start the left, Simmonds the right. I want half company volleys, ten rounds per man. The front ranks of outside companies fire first, following on into the centre, then the rear ranks, starting from the outside again. Fire when reloaded, and encourage the outside companies to wheel in upon the target's flanks."

Again the orders rang out and many Officers took the short time to explain what was needed. Sedgwicke stood confused.

"What's happening now?"

Again Halfway spoke up.

"Don't worry Parson, just listen to Heaviside. He'll say when to fire, front rank, then rear rank. Do as he says, concentrate on what he says, he'll be just over to the right. When he says "front rank present", do just that, loaded or not."

Over to their right and way over to their left, the half companies responded to the order to fire, and the volleys ran down the front rank towards the centre, then the company half volleys began along the rear. For the recruits and anyone new this was a hell of noise and smoke that surpassed anything before. The crash of muskets was continuous, the volleys, each of about 40 muskets blended one into the other to form one continuous wall of sound that made their ears ring and their heads spin. Captains didn't wait for their turn to fire to reach them, they looked for their men to be stood at the "make ready", either front rank or rear rank, then screamed their orders above the din, "present", "fire" at the tops of their voices. No Captain wanted to cause a break in the rippling volleys. In the midst of this ordered mayhem, all in the ranks endeavoured to reload in time. Eventually the rear rank of the centre companies, Four and Five, delivered their last volley and "cease fire", "order arms" rang out all along the line. Again Lacey asked the crucial question,

"How long?"

"Ten rounds in three minutes and 27 seconds, Sir."

"Hmm. Get a message to Heaviside about D'Villier's Company. He fires too soon, they'll be putting bullets into men already falling over, tell him to pause. Now; do it again, O'Hare," and it was and, as before, once more after that. The final time was three minutes 19 seconds.

"That'll do."

Lacey rode out before his men, placing himself halfway along their line and half way between their target. His tone was in marked contrast to the formal way that he addressed his Officers. His first act was to point at the cut ropes and shattered posts.

"Well done, lads. If that were a French column, they'd be halfway to the Dorset border by now! That's how we do it, boys, ten rounds each man. When the time comes, get off your ten rounds and you'll cut 'em to bits, just like you cut these ropes here. Alright lads, time to take a drink, and when we get back to barracks we'll all have something stronger. At least you've no full cartridge box to weigh you down!"

Suddenly, all was good cheer as the men again opened their canteens, but many raised them to the Colonel before using the longed for water. Lacey rode back to O'Hare.

"Good enough, O'Hare. Enough for first off, but I want better. Tell the Officers so, but tell the men well done. For first time, that's pleasing. Perhaps we have the makings here? D'you think?"

"Perhaps Sir, but one's things for sure. Any animal that was once alive in that column is for sure dead by now!"

Both laughed as they turned their horses to the track back to barracks, leaving the men to be formed up in fours ready for the road home. The march back began and Lacey exchanged a knowing and satisfied look with O'Hare as singing came up to them in time to marching feet. "She Never Blamed Him, Never" more than once, but not as often as "Yankee Doodle".

* * *

The return to barracks had never been more welcome. Column exercise in full kit, followed by sixty rounds rapid fire had taken its toll. First a wash, then a thorough clean of all kit, the very fouled muskets taking the longest, but all was done in time for the evening meal. This eaten, then, with perfect timing the rum buckets arrived. This time there was enough and all received their full half pint, even Tom Miles being satisfied having carefully noted that the Orderly's thumb was well out of the measure. All drank some, but all left some for later. This was New Year's Eve and in every barrack room the atmosphere was cheery and neighbourly, whilst waiting for the significant hour. Around

155

all the tables sat the occupants of each room, talking, jesting, and telling tall stories.

In the Officer's Mess, this was an important Dinner. Drinking too much on this occasion was excusable, almost obligatory, in fact drinking too much was almost impossible to avoid, the usual three courses, being extended to five, each needing to be washed down with their own glasses of claret. Come ten o' clock, Lacey and the other Majors toasted all present, wishing them a happy and prosperous New Year, hoping they would all see the end of it, and left the Junior Officers to their revels. These began at something around 10.30. First, all furniture was cleared away to the anteroom and the Mess table disassembled, leaving a very satisfactory space for a long succession of roughneck games that required a significant level of inebriation in order to ignore the danger of taking part. First came piggy back fighting with rolled up towels, then "hobby horse" where two teams had to compete to be the first to be all sat on the backs of other team members who were braced against the wall. Both teams collapsing was the usual result.

More drinking was required, so came "Snap Dragon", where a basin full of brandy and raisins was set on fire and each had to fish around in the bowl to obtain raisins, which, when eaten, still on fire, constituted your turn. This being done with the lights out, so Drake, in a state of acute inebriation, couldn't understand why his hand was surrounded by a blue fire and regarded it stupidly until Carr, himself the worse for wear and concentrating furiously on accuracy, blew out the flames, much to Drake's joy and surprise.

It came to five to midnight and in came Old Father Time, on a pair of sack trucks filched from stores. On close examination Old Father Time proved to be the eldest Captain, William Reynolds, draped from top to bottom in some old grey dust sheets, still dusty, which added to the effect. On his feet, obtained from where was a mystery, he had a pair of Arab sandals, over his shoulder was a giant scythe and on his head, for nothing else could be found, was a black bicorn hat, worn "athwartships". He was wheeled helter skelter several times around the room, at all times being pelted with anything that wouldn't do too much damage; food, screwed up paper, and the odd half glass of wine. He didn't seem to care too much about this assault upon his person, for he was swigging copiously from his own bottle.

156

At two minutes to midnight he was despatched through the door to make way for the appearance of the New Year, on a second pair of sack trucks. This was not hard to recognise as Ensign Rushby, the youngest Officer. He was in the guise of a new born babe thereby naked as the day he was born, save a white sheet bundled around his loins, supported in the folds of which was a giant wooden safety pin. On his head was a frilly blue bonnet and in one hand he had a giant rattle, but in his mouth was a huge wooden dummy painted pink. In the other hand he also had his own bottle, but it was plain that he was so much the worse for wear that it was doubtful if he had any idea what was going on, a conclusion supported by the fact that he was lashed to the sack trucks with some of the white target rope. He, too, was whisked several times around the room. At seconds to midnight the mess clock began to chime and those who heard the venerable instrument called for silence. "This is it". At the last stroke "Happy New Year' rang out around the room and everyone toasted whoever was nearest. In this sudden reduction in the level of wild and raucous revelry, the sounds of "Auld Lang Syne" could be heard from outside on the Parade Ground. The soldiers and their families had issued out of their rooms and were joining each other out on the barrack square.

Carr turned to Drake, he didn't have to turn very far because each was supporting the other. Speech came with difficulty.

"I think we should join the men. 'Specially our Company. Wish them a Happy New Year."

"How will we tell who they are?"

"Well, they won't be very big, and they'll have those shoulder wings."

"Ah, yes. That's why you're the Captain."

Carr returned a drunken nod and both lurched out of the room, giving a good impression of competitors in a three-legged race. All in the Mess thought likewise and out they went, leaving Rushby on his trucks, slumped as far down as his bindings would allow. On reaching outside, it was clear that Carr's clever wheeze was not clever at all; very few were wearing their jackets. Not to be beaten, they ambled around the square, greeting all whom they recognised, which included Davey, with Molly on his arm, Joe Pike and Tom Miles. All politely and respectfully returned their Officers' loud and hearty best wishes that were accompanied by claps on the shoulder. Except Tom Miles, who, thoroughly disconcerted to see his two superior Officers in such a state, including one from his old Regiment, thought that the best thing to do to avoid embarrassment was to spring to attention. Drake gave him an extra, "Good man, Miles", and Miles replied, "Thank you very much, Sir," keeping his eyes averted by staring between both, as an experienced ranker should. On and around the pair went, wishing "Happy New Year" to anyone who looked familiar, until they encountered Sergeant Major Gibney. By this time Drake had very much lost the plot and greeted him with," Congratulations, Sergeant Major."

"Congratulations, Sir? Don't thee mean Happy New Year, Sir?"

"It is certainly one of the two, Sar' Major, and I wish it to you most sincerely."

"I think thee two would be best off to tha' beds now, Sirs, if thee don't mind my saying so."

Carr replied, accompanied by vigorous nodding.

"You are right," he turned to Drake, "He is right. Time to be off to our comfortable billet. Good night, Sar' Major, and we both wish you well."

"Thank you, Sir, and good night to thee both."

Gibney had drunk his half pint of rum, but a constitution such as his had not even quivered. He wasn't shocked and he didn't condemn. His feelings towards both could best be described as Fatherly. He had enough of that sentiment in him to appreciate that they were two young men, both good Officers in his estimation, enjoying what could be their last New Year's celebration. He watched them guide each other away in the wrong direction and waited for a correction in their course that never came. Instead, they found themselves at the door of the Sick Bay, found it inviting and took themselves in. They told the Orderly that they wanted a bed, he pointed anxiously at a room for Officers with two beds, both made a choice and collapsed upon it. Their last words to each other before oblivion claimed them were,"Happy New Year, Nat."

"Happy New Year, Henry."

"I wish you well with Cecily, she's a lovely girl."

"Thank you, I think so too."

"You don't deserve her, you're a drunken bugger."

158

Lacey, mindful of the exertions of the previous day and the celebrations of the evening, wisely decided to give the battalion a rest, although Reveille was sounded and many were up and about at their usual time. Unsurprisingly, the Officers in barracks woke late. Carr and Drake woke together and Drake looked around, immediately confused.

"Are we wounded? Has there been a battle, or some similar kind of strife?"

"Wounded, no, dead, yes," replied Carr, dragging his throbbing head off the pillow, but failing to open his eyes.

A question arose in Drake's mind.

"Do you think anyone took care of Rushby? The last I saw, or should I say remember, was him sat on those sack trucks in the middle of the room. We should go see."

"We should. Yes, we should. Have I got my boots on?"

"You've got everything on, minus headgear."

"Is it raining?"

"Can't tell."

"Come on."

Carr opened his eyes, felt a stab of pain, but resisted the idea of closing them again. They left the Sick Bay and took themselves into the Mess. All was as normal; table, chairs and furniture. A few Officers were sat in their places, drinking coffee and eating bread rolls. The two joined them and were grateful to receive their share of the coffee and bread. Drake looked both up and down the table.

"Does anyone know what happened to Rushby? He was in no position to move, as I remember. Things did get a bit out of hand."

Shaking heads were the reply, but at that moment Rushby walked in.

"Are you alright, Rushby?" asked Carr, "I'm afraid you got a bit abandoned last night. Where did you wake up?"

"On Major O'Hare's sofa, as it happens. My uniform was there with me, and it seemed the right thing to bring myself here."

"No damage, or anything?"

"Well, now you mention it, I've got some frightful chafing under my arms, sort of like rope burns. Odd."

All smiled and settled into grateful silence, but each had racked up their opinion of Major O'Hare another notch. The silence pervaded until the Sergeant Clerk came into the hallway and tacked a notice onto the board, the hammering of the tacks reverberating around the inside of skulls that were aching quite enough.

"What's that?" asked someone, and Rushby replied, "I'll go see." He did, and on his return,

"There will be a full dress parade, late afternoon. The men will be given leave until midnight, but Officers to remain on duty. There's a list there of those who are to remain in the barracks, and those who are to patrol the town."

Someone down the table was the first to react.

"Leave for the men? That's rare, even for a few hours out. What's the "old man" about, do you think?'

By now Carravoy and D'Villiers had made their appearance and were settling into their places as the question was posed. Carravoy was not slow to give his opinion, which was not in any way softened by the hangover he was nursing.

"Namby pamby, I call it, and we've got to act nursemaid all evening whilst the rankers go out on a spree. The man's a fool! A dolt! I'll bet a dozen claret that more than a score desert. Twenty. Who'll take?

Carr looked across,

"Please don't mention claret or anything as such this morning, Carravoy, but I'll take you up."

"And I'll have some of that," added Drake.

"Done."

* * *

The word quickly circulated around the barracks. Leave till midnight for those that wanted it, after inspection on a full parade. It was unspoken, but fully understood, that those who failed the inspection would be confined to barracks. All kit and uniform was carefully checked and polished and at 3.00pm the whole battalion paraded in immaculate scarlet, white, and black. Order arms, shoulder arms, and present were completed with immaculate precision and the inspection began; Lacey, O'Hare, Simmonds, and Gibney forming the inspection party. Very few went into Gibney's notebook and at the end of the inspection, Lacey turned to Gibney.

"Good turnout, Gibney. Dismiss the parade."

Gibney peeled off his usual immaculate salute.

"Yes Sir. Thank you, Sir."

The parade was dismissed and all took themselves back to their rooms to shed the unwanted parts of their parade uniform. Then slowly, but then in greater numbers, the men issued from the doors of the barrackrooms, onto the parade ground and turned towards the gate, then queued at the table where the Clerk Sergeant entered their names, by Company, into a register of those taking leave. However, many remained in barracks; almost all family men who saw no cause to spend their limited family funds on a night's drinking. John Davey was one; for one reason he had no money, having spent all correcting the 'figgy duff' fiasco, and for another the domestic warmth of Molly and Tilly suited him far better. Inevitably, stronger friendship bonds had been made with other similar families and he was well content to sit at table with Molly, with her arm through his, keeping an eye on the children and yarning with new friends. All those remaining had made their choice for similar reasons. All save one; Seth Tiley sat alone at a table and nursed his anger. An attempted deserter already, to him leave was denied.

Percival Sedgewicke, on the other hand, had received replenishing funds from home and family, specifically his sister and he had the choice; he could go out into town and he decided he would. Firstly, to experience independence after such a long time and secondly, he could get drink, as much as he liked. So out he went, into the arch, gave his name, through the gate and onto the barracks road, then he found himself followed by much of the escort party that had brought him there as a prisoner, weeks ago; Deakin, Mulcahey, Miles, Stiles and Peters, with Joe Pike added to the jovial crew. Toby Halfway was remaining with his family.

"How now, Parson," called out Tom Miles, "Off for a drink? You'd best get yourself off to the far side of town, this here's the rough end, and if I knows it right, that'll show before the night's done."

Mulcahey caught up with Sedgwicke, stopped him, and added his own advice.

"He's right there, Father. Get to the main turnpike, turn left, take the long straight road to the church and there's a couple of Inns there that'll serve you; and you'll keep out of trouble. That Miles is right, there'll be some shenanigans, most like, and he's most like to start it, if I knows him with drink inside him. Remember now, Father, get up to the Church and use the Inns there. Take good care now, and we'll see you later."

Sedgwicke nodded and took the advice. Mulcahey watched him go and then caught up with the others.

"Where to first, me bhoys? The Bush is just up here."

Miles, more animated than usual even for him and certainly more in high spirits than the others, replied.

"I'm for a couple and then a doxey. I don't mind payin' for a couple of hours. After that, I'll drink out the time."

Deakin couldn't resist the comment,

"I'm damn sure your brains be more inside your breeches than up in your head. You sort yourself, I'm for a good drink."

"'T'aint too often that we'm allowed near women and I means to get near as I can, whilst I can."

Stiles spoke up, "There's women in barracks."

Deakin replied, "Ah, and 'ee don't touch if 'ee knows what's good for thee. That John Davey were lucky. I've heard of killin' over such as that."

He turned back to Tom Miles.

"An' who'll watch over the boy?" said Deakin, thumbing towards Joe Pike.

"He's a soldier now, he can watch for himself. How often do we get leave into a town? 'Tain't something I can remember. Can you?"

"You're not wrong, but 'tain't somethin' that I be goin' to question."

They entered The Bush, the first Inn encountered. Joe was confined to pints, whilst the rest drank quarts. Jed Deakin bought the first round and began the first subject.

"Well, we'n all in third Company, bar these two "elite" troops, one with the humour of a fox in a chicken run, and the other that's goin' to start shavin' any day now!"

He jerked his thumb in the direction of Tom Miles and Joe Pike. He continued.

"But there's no complainin' from me. I don't relish the idea of having to break in a new set of messmates, and old Holy Joe will do for me."

Tom Miles, to the surprise of no one, took umbrage.

162

"Is it my fault I'm handy on me pins and can hit most things inside 100 yards? How much choice do we get?"

Deakin pushed a full quart in front of him.

"Cease yer bellyaching and get yerself around that. Here's to the Lights!", and he waved his own tankard in Miles's direction. Miles scowled and drank. After two, he kept to his plan and took himself out to comb the seediest parts of the seedier end of town, to find the requirements of his desires. The rest settled to an evening's drinking. Deakin carefully monitored Joe Pike's consumption, but before long, a bleary look came over him and out of him came incongruous sentences concerned with the quality of the carpentry of the table and a girl called Miss Jasmine. He was humoured and indulged for both, and it wasn't long before the conversation around the table turned to their own battalion circumstances. Stiles threw out the question to no one on the table in particular.

"How do we reckon to that caper last night? Officers roamin' round, drunk as Lords."

Peters took it up.

"Ah, if Lords they be, but I saw none like that, but I saw they two sparks Carr and Drake. Couldn't hardy barely stand, they was, proppin' each other up. Officer class? I'd question. That's a good 'un for they two."

Deakin lowered his tankard.

"Well, I fails to see why we should hold that against 'em. Drake's old Norfolks, and that'll do for me. Carr I like, more by the day. I don't see why they shouldn't come out on New Year's and wish their men Happy New Year. I calls that building a good spirit and I knows that helps, when there's balls and bullets in the air."

Peters replied, developing his theme.

"Well, 'tain't something I feels at ease with. I like's us here, and them there. They gives the orders and we does the job. It's clean and simple, with no awkward feelings."

"Well, hold there a bit. Just what is it that ails thee, seeing 'em drunk, or them wishing you a Happy New Year?"

"Both, I d'reckon. Them there, and us here. We takes care of our own, and from each other we gets all the wishin' that I d'need."

Mulcahey had listened and delivered his verdict.

"Well, I'm inclined to give a man the benefit of the doubt that wishes me well for the season. Captain Heavside did the same for all of us, but, of course, he was sober. As for the question of getting drunk, well, we're well to talk, sat here drinkin' quarts. I pass no judgment, and on top of that, Peters, it's your shout!"

All laughed and pushed their tankards in his direction. Peters gave a mock scowl and took himself up to the bar. Mulcahey continued.

"If there's an Officer I am impressed with, it's our present dear Colonel. We've all been in action and knows that what matters is having a lot of what he's tryin' to put into us. That range practice yesterday was close to standard. A few more weeks and we'll be as close to that of any regiment I've served in, and that includes the 88th; and what a gang of fightin' berserkers they be!"

Stiles leaned towards him, a friendly arm around his shoulders and speaking in a mock Irish accent.

"And, of course, O'Hare is as foine an Oirish gentleman as ever walked this God's Kingdom!'

Mulcahey smiled indulgently.

"Just so. You have the very right of it."

Deakin returned to the exchange.

"Ah, you Irish, 'tis always the best from your Emerald Isle, even though you lives on nothin' but potatoes and sheep's bollocks, and sleeps on one side of the bed leavin' your cow to eat the other!"

All laughed, none louder than Mulcahey, and Peters returned with the refilled tankards. For about half an hour the conversation continued in similar light-hearted vein, until Miles returned, to the surprise of all, the more so because he was accompanied by a young lady of the required occupation.

"This is Suzette. I've brought her here, because she said she wanted a drink in the better end of town."

Better end of town? All stood, Pike was hauled up by Deakin, and Mulcahey fetched her a chair, but their table was full with them all, so Suzette and Miles settled on the next table up.

"I wants a gin," was the request made to Miles and he took himself off to the bar. The quintet looked along their table to regard Suzette. Peters broke the short silence.

"Suzette, now that's not a name I'd call local."

"No, 'tis French. My Mother be French, she done raised I Chard way, and I've ended up over 'yer."

Each clenched their jaws to prevent themselves laughing. If there was ever an absence of French influence in anyone's speech and upbringing, then this was it. Deakin was first to recover.

"Well, we're all pleased to meet you, Suzette, and we hope Tom takes good care of you."

Suzette was sat with her back to the window, looking into the room. Miles returned with his own drink and a double gin for Suzette. Sitting opposite, he drank his quickly, anxious for her to do likewise, so that the important business could begin elsewhere. Miles said little, other than to maintain a leery sparkle in his eye, but he soon noticed that she was looking at him less and less, and beyond him more and more. On top of that, also with growing frequency, smiling coquettishly in that direction. Miles turned to see four apparently farming men, sat at their own table. The two nearest him were eyeing Suzette lewdly and lining up shiny shillings at the end of their table, facing Suzette. The score had got to six and, as he watched, a seventh was added. He turned to Suzette to find her picking up her bag and preparing to leave.

"Where be you goin'?"

"I think I've just had a better offer, than thy half crown. A girl has to do the best for herself, and over thur' be better."

Miles placed one hand on the table, the better to lever himself round. He looked back at Suzette, who was just easing herself out from behind the table. Miles rose and reached the four men in less than a second. He scooped up the shillings, opened the coat of the nearest and threw them inside.

"You keep your eyes off my doxey and go find your own! Take your money and bugger off! I got her. And paid for!"

The four men were all, indeed, local farmers and had the weight and muscle that went with their occupation. The one with the shillings down his coat stood up, put a meaty hand on Miles' face and pushed hard. Miles lurched back to collide with his table.

"It's you that's buggering off, bloodyback! We think the young lady would now like to spend her time with us."

This was said just as Suzette crossed with Miles, he going one way, she the other. Miles response was to pick up a chair and hurl it in the direction of the four doxey stealers, then follow the chair into the fray, both his mood and limbs primed for combat. All four were still recovering from the chair when Miles reached the speaker, seized his coat and headbutted him perfectly onto the point of his nose. Blood spurted copiously. Suzette screamed and ran out the door, crying "Murder." Miles was kicking and punching for all he was worth, but against the other three it was a losing battle, he was lighter than any of them and sinking under a rain of blows. He was almost on the floor when the other five reached him in his peril. Not unfamiliar with brawling and street fighting, the four, minus Joe Pike who stood in confusion, quickly despatched Miles's three assailants. That done, again as their experience taught them, they did not press home their victory by inflicting more damage, but hastened to make a speedy getaway. The barely conscious Miles was hoisted between Stiles and Peters, his arms around their shoulders. In this formation, Deakin in the lead, with Mulcahey and Joe Pike bringing up the rear, they made a quick exit through the door. Experience again told them to get off the road and so they turned the first corner, to collide, almost, with two patrolling Officers.

"Halt. The lot of you. We've just seen a woman, running across this road, yelling murder. What do you know?"

Deakin recognised neither Officer, but he took the lead in making a response.

"Murder, Sir? We knows nuthin' about no murder, Sir. We've just come down the road and turned in here, Sir, hopin' this is a way back to the barracks."

The Officer looked at Deakin in the light of his candle lantern and then shone it on Miles.

"What's the matter with him."

"Bad beer, Sir. We'm all feeling a bit queezy, Sir. Bad choice of pub, Sir. Right, lads?"

Vigorous nodding and words of agreement came from all around. Peters gave a gulp and lurched towards the gutter as though about to vomit. The Officer didn't hesitate.

"Very well. On your way. Get him back quick."

"Sir. Yes Sir. Thank you, Sir. Quick as possible."

Coincident with this, Percival Sedgwicke was also rolling and stumbling, though in his case, through a churchyard, the one that had formed his navigation point. He had indeed found an Inn close by and had entered. The Landlord looked at him suspiciously, but Sedgwicke's cultured accent satisfied him partly but what mostly eased any suspicion was the new crown that Sedgwicke placed on the bar and asked for the best bottle of red wine in the house. Not unfamiliar with "gentlemen rankers", although Sedgwicke looked anything like the kind of "gay dog" who spent money freely, a glass and a bottle were handed over. There followed a second and half a third. This was not fully imbided because at that point of consumption Sedgwicke started singing hymns and quoting psalms and so he had to go. With one drayman's hand he lifted Sedgwicke, took him to the door and propelled him out.

Thus Sedgwicke found himself in the churchyard, wondering, through an alcoholic haze, which was the best way to go. The churchyard was dimly lit by the light from nearby windows, these in houses that pushed up to the low church wall. Tombstones dark and brooding, silhouetted like broken teeth, crowded up from all sides. He couldn't see any kind of gateway, lychgate or otherwise, but what he did notice was the now familiar uniform of a fellow soldier, dull pink in the poor light, he being sat on a raised grave close to the church wall. Sedgwicke approached, his choice of words and diction remaining cultured.

"Excuse me, I wonder, I seem to be somewhat lost. By any chance can you point me back towards the barracks?"

The soldier looked up and Sedgwicke could see that he wasn't annoyed, nor likely to rob him, just very puzzled at being disturbed.

"No need, plenty of time yet. Sit down, have a drink."

He thrust a bottle up towards Sedgwicke. He recognised that it was not a wine bottle; an impression confirmed when he sampled the contents and found them to be the now well favoured rum. He needed no further bidding to take a seat beside this generous drinking companion, who began the conversation.

"Who might you be?"

"Percival Sedgwicke. They call me Parson."

"Parson, oh yes, I've heard. Educated man; who came in with that bunch of "hard bargains" a while back; but, no offence, hard bargains I mean, that's past. I don't mean nuthin' by it. That don't mean nuthin' no more. We'm all just soldiers. Am I right?"

Sedgwicke was pleased at this generous appraisal. Despite his drunken fog, he maintained a polite dialogue.

"May I know your name?"

"Quartermaster Sergeant Harold Sleightman. At your service."

Something lurched into Sedgwicke's sodden mind that did something to clear it. The stores; a storeman, those anonymous people that came and went, always in the background, but it was Sleightman who moved the conversation on.

"An educated man, and, I take it, you like a drink. Quite right, partial to one myself from time to time. An educated man," he repeated," Read, write and cipher, can you?"

"Well, yes. Of course."

"Then I'm thinkin' that us two meetin' here, like this, is pure providence. Pure providence. How are you findin' life as a company ranker? What's your company number?

"Three."

"Ah, Holy Joe Heavside, and that piece of wet rag, D'Villiers. So, how're you finding it?"

Sedgwicke didn't reply instantly, but turned to look at Sleightman. Even in the poor light, Sedgwicke could see that Sleightman was regarding him with a most ingratiating look, eyes wide above an oily smile, both of which showed that he expected an answer deeply negative.

"It's foul, appalling, like being in Hell."

Sleightman laughed and drew deep from the bottle, before handing it to Sedgwicke.

"And didn't I find it just the same! Drill, cleaning, gunpowder down yer gob, snotty Officers, and a stinkin', noisy, lice ridden barrack room the only place you've got to rest up in. Am I right?"

"Yes."

"Now, an educated man as you are, I think you'd make a storeman. I needs storemen. In fact, I've been told I 'as to get storemen. How would you like to be added to my list? And I see you likes a drink. You could be just the kind of storeman recruit that I needs. What do you say?"

"I say yes. What kind of fool would say anything else?"

"That is just the right sentiment that I was hoping for. Percival Sedgwicke, you say? Well, Percy, I think we should finish this bottle, then get ourselves back. You can trust me to know the way."

Many others had already begun finding their way, the Town Hall clock had struck half eleven and the barrack road was now feeling a steady stream of soldiery returning in the opposite direction to that of a few hours before. Many were wholly the worse for their feats of drinking in the nearby inns and were making progress only because they were supported either side by comrades, their feet incongruously moving out of step and at half the rate of their overworked "brothers of the bar".

Lieutenant Royston D'Villiers was in a black mood. The foundation of his ire was the underlying memory from the battalion exercise, all too vivid, of humiliation, both in front of fellow Officers and worst of all, in front of the men. This mood was deepened by a headache that yet remained from the previous evening and deepened yet further at having to be Officer of the Guard whilst the common rankers returned from what had obviously been a very merry evening of drinking, wenching, yarning, and fighting. The atmosphere was maintained almost universally as those first back had themselves signed in and then took themselves off to their barrack rooms, still in good cheer and high spirits, unlike D'Villiers.

Sergeant Obediah Hill, the family man, the ex-Norfolk, the NCO of vast experience, was the Sergeant of the Guard and knew exactly what the pitfalls and dangers of this situation were. An Officer that few of the men had any time for and them, many of them, worse for drink. It was a powder keg of potential for charges of insubordination and a series of floggings. As the first of the men came back, he did his best to reduce the risk.

"If it's all the same to you, Sir, I can take care of this. I'll deal with the men, Sir, see them through the gate and on their way. No real need for you to get involved. Sir. Just remain in the arch, and that'll serve, Sir, as you being here and present as the Officer of the Guard."

"What are you suggesting, Sergeant? That I should remain out of the way, in the shadows, unseen?'

"Well, if I can speak truly, Sir, the lads have been drinking and some don't recognise when an Officer is near."

He realised almost instantly that he had used the wrong word.

"Recognise, Sergeant? Recognise? They'll recognise this coat I wear whether they be drunk or dying. I'll truck no disrespect of my rank at any time, whatever."

"Beggin' your pardon, Sir. I meant no disrespect, it's just that, well, that way we won't get any avoidable trouble, Sir. We can just get the men through and off, and then off ourselves, Sir, when our relief arrives. No harm done."

D'Villiers pent up anger exploded on hearing a counter argument from a plain NCO.

"Damn you, Sergeant. I'll take no argument from you! Any more and it'll cost you your stripes. D'ye hear me?"

The last was delivered so loud, that it echoed around the arch. Hill sprang to attention; it was the only response he could give.

"Yes Sir. Very good, Sir."

D'Villiers was now awash with released anger. Hill didn't need to see his face, even if he could in the poor light, for D'Villiers projecting jaw and clenched fists at the end of arms bent in front of him told him that his cause was lost, but D'Villiers, even through his anger, knew he had to think of some way to demonstrate his will. Two soldiers arriving with unbuttoned jackets gave him his answer. Inspection! Before any soldier was re-admitted into the barracks he had to be presentable enough to be called one; all would be properly dressed; all must pass inspection, by him.

"Get those two against the wall, Sergeant, and get their uniform up to the mark. They left here in proper state, they'll come back in proper state."

"Yes Sir. Right lads, against the wall, and get your jackets properly buttoned."

The two looked bleary and confused, but drink did not have so great a hold on them that they failed to obey. They took themselves to the wall of the arch, buttoned all buttons and stood to attention before D'Villiers.

"Dismiss."

The two turned to continue their journey.

"Halt."

The two halted, the first first, the last last, so that the two collided.

"Don't you know to salute an Officer?

Both spoke on unison.

"Yes Sir. Sorry Sir," then they saluted. D'Villiers repeated, "Dismiss."

They executed an instinctive right turn and went to the Sergeant Clerk to be signed in. D'Villiers turned to Hill.

"All men to come before me for my inspection upon entering the gate, Sergeant. See to it."

"Yes Sir."

Hill was both in despair and in a quandary. He knew what this would mean. An Officer in plain sight with men returning drunk from leave was bad enough, his inspecting them could only lead to one outcome; men ending up on a charge. Also, hundreds returning and only entering after inspection would cause long delays when what was needed was to get the men quickly in and off to their rooms. He sent out his Corporal and four men as an advanced guard to warn the men and get them in some sort of shape before approaching the gate. For over 15 minutes it worked, but the late arrivals were the most worse for drink and the inevitable happened. One very tipsy soldier buttoned up his jacket using the wrong buttonholes. D'Villiers at last had someone on whom he could further vent his anger.

"You, soldier, are a damn disgrace. A disgrace, do you understand? Get your jacket buttoned up and correct."

The soldier, confused and unknowing about his buttoning error, replied, or rather the alcohol did for him.

"I don't see why I'm a disgrace. Don't know what you're talking about. I thinks I'm just fine."

Not for the first time that night D'Villiers erupted.

"Sergeant, take this man's name. He's on a charge; insulting an Officer."

Hill, as he was bid, wrote down the name. Before midnight the name was not alone, eight more were added for various levels of insubordination; despite Hill adding himself to the warning party and applying a pre-inspection as best he could. The Sergeant Clerk wrote out the charges there and then and D'Villiers signed them, then he took himself away, whilst the Sergeant Clerk took himself in the opposite direction, to place the written charges on Lacey's desk, ready for the morning.

* * *

"How many?"

"Six."

"Damn me, but you lie."

"Careful, Carravoy, those are strong words. The answer is six, two injured and being cared for somewhere, two arrested by the Town Constables and in their cells, and two unaccounted for. So, strictly, the answer is two. I believe, therefore, that the claret is on you."

Carravoy stood silent, more amazed than annoyed; he was genuinely surprised. He had been told, certainly by the more elderly and superior Officers of his acquaintance, that the men would desert given the merest opportunity, yet here was an almost complete rebuttal. Over half the men had gone out, yet only two remained at large. His expression changed to one of resignation. He had lost the bet

"Very well, Carr. You win. To where shall I send your winnings?"

"Oh, to the Mess. I donate it to the Mess. Drake will do the same. I'd send some to the men, if I could, it was they after all that won the bet, but I'll hold that back for some other time, some other way."

At that moment the Sergeant Clerk emerged, Carr and Carravoy both being stood outside the Colonel's Office.

"Excuse me, Sirs, but does either of you know of the whereabouts of Lieutenant D'Villiers? The Colonel wishes to see him."

"He billets in the same Inn as myself and Lieutenant Drake. Not an hour ago, he was sat in the breakfast room, off duty. If you send a runner to the Nag's Head, you should find him, either on his way here, or still there."

"Yes Sir. Thank you, Sir."

Carr nodded in his direction, then turned to Carravoy. Carr's tone was coldly professional, with neither warmth nor concern.

"I hear there was a lot of bother with the men coming back in last night. D'Villiers was Officer of the Guard. If you see him before the Old Man does, my advice is for him to get his story clear and straight."

He then left, out onto the Parade Ground, leaving Carravoy alone in the hallway of the Colonel's Offices. He knew that Carr was right and therefore he lingered, hoping that D'Villiers would arrive soon, but his own duties as Officer of the Day called him away. D'Villiers duly appeared and presented himself to the Sergeant Clerk.

"I have been made aware that the Colonel wishes to see me."

"Yes Sir. I will tell him that you are here."

172

The Sergeant Clerk rose and noted that D'Villiers' uniform was not all it should be, done in a rush, and experience told him that a proper uniform would be to his advantage over the next few minutes. The collar, at least, was poorly adjusted. The Sergeant Clerk put his hand to his own perfect collar and cleared his throat, hoping that D'Villiers would somehow take the hint and put things right, but D'Villiers drew his brows together in puzzlement and the hint was lost. At that moment, through the open door, he heard the words, delivered hard, as though carved on steel,

"Send him in."

The Clerk Sergeant went to the open door and remained by it as D'Villiers entered, as though holding it open, whilst in actuality he was waiting to close it, tight and shut. This done he returned to his desk. The silence of his own office was soon torn apart as the tirade began and grew in volume, clear and plain, even through the solid oak door. Even through the dense, dark wood some words came plain and prominent.

"Common sense", "Sergeant Hill", "experience", "causing trouble", "ridiculous", "bad feeling", "showing yourself a fool", "unnecessary inspection", "none needed", "idiotic", "absurd", "no flogging" and it went on, several phrases being repeated for effect. Eventually D'Villiers emerged, shaken and agitated, but lividly angry. He had held his tongue, but, now out of Lacey's presence, he was almost beside himself. He went looking for Carravoy and had no trouble finding him, he being stood outside, overseeing events on the Parade Ground.

"He's failed to back me. A night in cells is all he's given them. Says he's got to back me up for the sake of appearance, but he didn't even want to do that, and he'll order no flogging. Damn the man, insubordination and disrespect of an Officer is what it was, plain as you like. A night in cells! I expect he'll take along their supper himself, and tuck them in. Damn him, Charles, damn him. Well, I've had enough. I'm getting in touch with my people and asking them to purchase me another Commission, somewhere, anywhere. The Commissariat, I don't care. I'll not spend another day under his command longer than I have to. I'm buying myself out.

* * *

173

General Reynier was very proud of his horse, a pure bred Andalusian, 16 hands high, spirited, strong, and obedient. So taken was he with his mount that he had felt no qualms at spending almost 400 francs on the finest saddle, reins, and head harness that he could find. Now, himself and his horse, were atop a hill overlooking the Great Road from Rome, South to Naples, a road that was now filled with 30,000 French veterans. On the orders of Napoleon, this Army, part of the Armies of the French Republic that had just crushed the Austrians at Ulm during the last month of 1805, were ordered to see that Napoleon's writ was run throughout the whole length of Italy, which included Naples and Sicily. General Massena was given the task and Reynier sat watching the army's advance as part of Massena's Staff.

January was indeed proving to be a fine month for Jean Louis Reynier; benign Italian weather and here before him, the splendid French invasion force and within himself every hope of an independent command. The future held the chance for him to prove himself further in the eyes of Napoleon, against the British and Russian forces in Naples. They were there to shore up the Kingdom of the Two Sicilies, and surely, now, its King, Ferdinand of Naples, and both enemy forces were anxious at the news that such a French force was marching South, descending on them with their full attention.

Chapter Six

Orders, Large and Small

The year was marching on, January gone, advancing through February and looking on to March, but as yet the bleak stretches of moor beyond the barracks remained as sombre within their Winter guise as ever. Spring lay far away and unwoken, and so cheerless days progressed on in various shades of grey. For the 5th Detachments life reflected the same cold progression of identical days that rose and set across the giant Somerset sky; drill, marching, and firing range, or marching, firing range, then drill, or some other mixture. All were learning to respond to the different rhythms of the drummers or the different notes and cadence of the bugle calls, that conveyed across the battalion the orders for the required formation. Only their Colonel remained grateful for the extra days that they were being granted before orders came for deployment to a conflict as yet unknown. His battalion could perform to a standard that met the requirements in the Drill Book, but the big question hung over their readiness for a set piece battle. Only practice and rehearsal could chip away at that doubt and so he maintained the pressure. Days were spent on the moors doing what he was least satisfied with, always watchful, always with a critical eye.

Almost as the year began Lacey had called Carr into his office for a brief conversation that did not even justify Carr taking a seat. Lacey handed him two books, both military manuals, these being; "Regulations of the Rifle Corps" and "The Exercise Book of the Rifle Service". Carr's orders were simple, read the manuals and train his Light Company in what was recommended. Also, to discover who were the best marksmen. It may come to something, it may not.

Understanding the first order, but mystified by the second, Carr was marching his Company, 90 strong, out for yet further training in the basic principles as recommended in the manuals Lacey had given him. He had ridden out the previous day and discovered a small wood, stood alone atop a low hill, perfect to practice advancing in open order and clearing a wood of any enemy. Light Infantry, as recommended, needed to operate in groups of three, and for this he had taken the advice of Ethan

Ellis, the Sergeant he trusted most. Ellis was young for a Sergeant, but tough and wiry, this reflected in the hard look in his eyes, and supported again by the fixed set of his mouth. He rarely smiled, nor showed any humour, but it was undeniable that what he was ordered to do, he carried out and the men obeyed him instantly.

Their march brought them around a bend in the lane that revealed the wood, but also the farm that held ownership of its surrounding fields. The buildings did not speak of any level of opulence, but they were well built and functional, a solid farm for solid people. Carr sent Drake to see if he could find the farmer; it seemed the right thing, to ask if they could exercise on his land, rather than just march on and march up. Drake returned bringing the farmer with him. Drake introduced Edwin Farriner and Carr introduced himself.

"Good morning, Mr Farriner. My name is Henry Carr, and I was hoping that we might use your field and wood there, to practice our manoeuvres. I do hope that's possible. I don't anticipate any damage."

"You can use that wood there as much as you like, Sir. I can't get none of my people to go in there, nor even near. "T'ave been like that since time beyond memory, so I've been told. People say 'tis haunted. Bad spirits. No one goes in there and if any stock is lost in there, 'tis I that's got to go in and fetch 'em out. That's why I don't let stock graze this field, so you carry on. There's nothin' planted, so use all as you see fit."

Drake turned away to grin at the description, but with this he saw the expressions of the men; that being those who had overheard what was said and many of these wore a look of deep concern. Nevertheless, this he ignored as he heard Carr's reply.

"My thanks, Mr Farriner, it sounds just the place for us. No one in there means we can blaze away to our hearts' content. Thank you and good day to you."

They marched on into the field and Carr gave the order to deploy in files of three, which saw his men in three ranks facing the wood, with thirty files from left to right. At their request Tom Miles and Joe Pike had asked to be kept in a "three" and Ellis had added John Davey. An "old soldier", a good shot, and a young athlete seemed a good combination. Thus, Tom Miles was in the first rank, Joe Pike ten yards behind in the second, with John Davey last in the third. Each file had a seven yard

176

gap either side between its neighbours, the requirements of "skirmish order". Once formed up, Carr, now on foot, gave the order to advance and forward they went at a rapid trot. Using an empty barrack room, Carr had explained to all what he wanted and was pleased to see the spaces between the ranks and files being maintained. The soldier's instinct was to group together, shoulder to shoulder.

Drake gave the order.

"Enemy Light Infantry has come out of the wood and are opposing you. Advance firing by files."

At this order Tom Miles fired at the trees, then stopped to reload, to be overtaken by Joe Pike who advanced further to open fire. John Davey came up and past for his turn, and thus it went on. Tom Miles couldn't contain his impatience at what he was being asked to do and as he came up past John Davey to fire for a third time, he gave his surly opinion.

"Call this fightin' drill. 'Tis more like a bloody barn dance than any kind of moves I've ever been part of."

Davey grinned, but not so the nearest Lieutenant.

"Enough of that Miles. You follow orders and keep the advance going."

Miles replied, but only to himself and under his breath, as he reloaded.

"Alright, alright. I can hear you, and you won't find I falling behind."

Soon the edge of the wood was achieved and Carr reminded his men of what was now needed.

"Well done. Firing in files as before, but this time from cover. Number one fires from cover, two advances forward to his cover, fires, and so on. Now, deploy."

The groups of three spread out along the edge of the wood. Drake gave the order, number one opened fire and in went number two to find cover and open fire, followed by number three. For a wood never maintained, nor visited even for firewood, the undergrowth was surprisingly light and the advance continued easily through the wood to the green field beyond. Carr took them well beyond the edge of the wood, down into the field and turned his men around. They then practised retreat, filing back up the field and back through the wood, number one firing, then falling back behind number three to reload, leaving number two with a clear field of fire. This done once, they practised retreat again from the opposite direction. All was going well, they had retreated to the middle of the wood when a howling and wailing was heard out on the left, cries of dire distress, such to signify that someone's very soul was in jeopardy. Carr looked at Drake.

"What the Hell is that?"

"Only one way to find out," and Drake took himself off in the likely direction. What he found was Ellis, kneeling over a crevice in the ground, about a yard wide and yelling down into it.

"What's happened Ellis? What's down there?"

"Murray, Sir. He fell down in and now he's yelling blue murder about ghosts and spirits, Sir. I can hear him clattering about, but I can't get him to shut up, Sir."

Drake decided to try. He looked in, but an overhang covered in matted ferns prevented him seeing any further.

"Murray. Keep quiet, do you hear me, keep quiet. You're still alive, not dead, so keep quiet."

"Oh Sir, Sir, I've fallen into Hell, Sir, I'm down yer with a load of bones, Sir, and I think they be human. Oh God, there's a skull, they are Sir, they be human. And there's a load of metal stuff an' all Sir."

"Alright Murray, keep calm, you're not in Hell because I'm not, not yet anyway. We'll get you out. I'll come down to you as soon as I can. Are you hurt?"

"No Sir, I be just damn scared, Sir."

He turned to the nearest Private and told him to double back to the farm to fetch a rope. Carr arrived.

"Murray has fallen down this crevice. He's not hurt, but there's something down there with him that's frightening the life out of him. I've sent for a rope."

By now, all had gathered at the scene, some looking most uncomfortable at what had befallen and what was being talked about. The rope arrived and Drake secured a loop under his arms. With the rope bent around a tree he was lowered down. There was little light, but enough to see Murray hunched at one end of the crevice, cowering as far as possible away from what was clearly the remains of a skeleton, complete, as far as Drake could see, but scattered. There were other dull, flat objects that looked very much like pieces of armour.

"All right, Murray, get this rope around you and we'll get you out."

"Oh Sir, thank you, Sir," and Murray obeyed and was quickly, and gratefully, hauled to the top, to be quickly surrounded by his mates to tell of blackened bones and spirits of the dead.

Carr shouted down.

"What's there?"

"I think it's one of King Arthur's Knights. There's a whole skeleton, just about, and lots of bits of armour, and the biggest sword I've ever seen."

This time Carr ordered an errand.

"Back to the farm. Get a sack, two, big as you can."

Then he resumed shouting at Drake.

"Some sort of Knight? Can't be."

"No, it's not. There's not enough armour. Some kind of soldier, though."

The sacks arrived and they began the job of hauling all up to the top, bones first, all laid out as best they knew, then the armour. Drake and Carr stood regarding the bones, then the collection of armour. Drake spoke first,

"What do you think?"

"My best guess is a Trooper in the New Model Army."

"New what Army?"

"Model. Cromwell's army. Surely you've heard of him? Had King Charles' head cut off. The helmet's the giveaway, a lobster tail down the back, and a single piece coming down from the peak to protect the face. There's your ghosts, Nat. There was a lot of fighting in these parts during the Civil War and my guess is that this wood saw some and he was killed or wounded and tumbled down there, not to be found by his mates. As it was the scene of killing and bloodshed, and burial, the locals shunned it and have ever since, since 1644 or thereabouts. The overhang kept the metal from rusting too much and there it is."

"What should we do?'

"Well, I think we should bury him. They were strict Puritans, were the New Model, and it's very likely that no local church will accept him into their churchyard, them being Anglican and all that and him being fanatically Puritan. Besides, I suspect that the other casualties were buried here, so I say bury him where they are."

Drake's silence spoke of no argument and so two more were despatched on the same journey, this time for shovels. Awaiting their return all crowded up, fear of ghosts now gone, to

179

examine what such a soldier wore and carried. Most attention was focused on the remains of a huge horse pistol, the wood rotten, but the barrel and flintlock clearly identifiable. The shovels arrived and many helped to dig the grave, not easy to dig in the shaley soil, but the men were eager to help with such a task and all took turns. Drake's curiosity was aroused.

"Religious Army, were they?"

"Yes, all strict Puritan. A weird bunch, absolutely Religious, every man. They sang psalms before a battle, thanking God for delivering the enemy into their hands, but don't be deceived. No one could best them, ever, not Royalists, Scots, Irish, nor even the Spanish. They had the nickname "Ironsides", and they were just about the closest this country's ever come to having an invincible army."

"Is that a fact? Well, we could do with them right now."

"I wouldn't argue, and Lady Constance could teach us the psalms!"

By now the grave had been dug and the men, without orders, had begun arranging the bones at the bottom. Ellis looked up to Carr.

"Say a few words, Sir?"

Carr was surprised and looked it, but quickly recovered.

"Yes, yes, of course."

He cleared his throat.

"Heavenly Father, we send to you this soldier. We think him to be a Puritan soldier of a long time before now, but he was part of an Army that carried your Word with them. They fought in your Name. They feared your wrath and obeyed your commandments, as much as was possible during war. They always believed that they were doing Thy Will. Please take him to you, and look kindly upon him. Amen."

All repeated the final word and the grave was filled. This left the armour.

"What should we do with this?"

Carr thought for a moment.

"Well, it must be of some interest for some antiquarian. As far as I can tell, it's just about complete. We should bag it up and take it back to town. I'm sure the Council can find it a home. I can't think of anything better."

"I can. Our esteemed Regional General Perry. He's a fanatic about this sort of stuff. Put it in a box, and send it to him, with our compliments. Maybe next time we see him we'll get a glad look instead of being ignored, like last time. At least we know that he'll take care of it, instead of dumping it down some cellar."

"Right. Yes. That's the move. You three, get all that into the sacks. As much as will fit; the rest we'll have to carry loose. And by the way, all of you, what I saw was well done, clean and professional. Good Light Infantry. Well done."

* * *

Davey returned to his barrack room to find Sedgwicke packing his belongings in such bags as he possessed.

"What's happening Parson? Found a better billet?'

"In a way, yes, but don't think I mean that in any bad way. I'm grateful that I had you to share with, John, but I've been made a storeman and they sleep, well, in the stores. Seems my education has made a difference, finally."

He looked at Davey, hoping for a look that spoke a kindly goodbye and he was not disappointed.

"Well, we'll still see you about the place then, Parson."

Davey paused.

"For the best, really, don't you think? You'll make a good storeman."

"Yes, better than a ranker in a firing line."

Davey smiled and nodded agreement. Molly had come over, having noticed that Sedgwicke was packing. She looked at Davey enquiringly.

"Parson's off for a storeman. He's just packed and ready to go. I'll give him a hand to take his things over."

Molly went over to Sedgwicke and kissed the side of his face and he grinned with surprise, not expecting anything as such.

"We'll, goodbye, Percy. Thank you for starting Tilly with her letters. I'm grateful."

"Oh, not in the slightest. She's really quite bright. I'll try to come back as often as I can. To maintain progress, as it were."

Davey picked up the heaviest bag.

"Come on then, Parson, let's get you to your new lodgings."

As they left, greatly to Sedgwicke's surprise, almost all wished him well and raised a hand in goodbye. The Father of the child who had died took the trouble to come over and shake his hand.

181

Sedgwicke was moved, but also confused and could but mumble clumsy appreciation.

They reached the stores and Davey placed the bag on the counter. He could go no further, only storemen were allowed in the inner sanctum.

"Well, goodbye Parson, although we'll still see each other, won't we?"

He looked around and nodded his head, then looked again at Sedgwicke.

"Yes. I'm sure it's for the best."

He smiled, clapped his hand on Sdedgwicke's shoulder, and left.

Sedgwicke needed two journeys to carry all his effects back to the dark, dusty, but silent reaches of the stores, beyond the shelves and fixtures that carried the full needs of a battalion at war. He would sleep and eat by his desk; pens and ledgers already neatly arranged and labelled. Sedgwicke's head and shoulders slumped down with a huge sigh of relief, then rose, as he straightened up. He felt renewed, as if returned to his more natural, even rightful, element. Here, at last, was a world more familiar, more in keeping with the character of a Priest, de-frocked or otherwise. He unpacked and sat at the ledger desk. Some dockets needed entering so he opened the required ledger, inked a pen and began.

He was not long into his task when Sleightman arrived, oily grin matching his oily, slicked down hair.

"Ah, Percy! Settled in and started, I see. Good, good. I likes a man as is diligent about his work, and mark my words, Percy, you mark my words, 'tis diligence as does it. When the Colonel of Commissariat comes to call, the first place he goes to is; the books! Yes. Good and careful ledgers. So you go on as you mean to stay, Percy."

He stopped and thought, that didn't seem quite right, but by now Sedgwicke could smell the rum on his breath, even though it was only early afternoon. What came next confirmed it. Sleightman approached closer, mouth almost touching Sedgwicke's ear.

"Now, Percy. This is how things be. You see, being a storeman has its advantages. The odd perk can come your way, in all kinds of forms. Here's your first," and he placed a full bottle of rum on the desk before Sedgwicke.

"Now then, you get that into your canteen. It don't make no sense to have a full bottle of rum out in plain sight, now do it? What the eye don't see, the heart don't grieve over. That's my motto, and 't'ave seen me well so far. If you needs a second canteen, just get one. The numbers haven't matched for months. So, ha ha, welcome to the stores Percy," and he left.

Left alone, Sedgwicke sat staring at the bottle. The temptation was huge, so much so that perspiration broke out on his forehead. He stood down from his desk, went to his possessions and found his Bible. With it clasped tight between both hands and tighter still against his chest he prayed for strength and help. It came, and he took the bottle and decanted it into his canteen, which he hid, then he wondered what to do with the bottle. Finding no answer, he hid that too, then resumed his work.

Days passed, then weeks, and Sedgwicke learned his duties, counting, storing, booking and recording. On campaign, so Sleightman told him, their place was in the rear, with the supply train. The only danger came when the battalion needed to be re-supplied, then someone had to load a string of mules, or a cart, and go up to the fighting, but, "You're always in the rear," Sleightman emphasised, "Always in the rear." Sedgwicke kept his word to continue teaching Tilly and he returned each evening. So good an act as this justified in his mind using the rum that came copiously to him from Sleightman, and most evenings saw him slump down on his mattress, fully clothed, sleep irresistible after a day at the ledgers and an evening with the equally irresistible bottle, drawn from its hiding place. If Sleightman found that the previous bottle was not empty when he brought another, then he reproached Sedgwicke for not taking advantage of the generosity that he, the munificent Sleightman, was bestowing upon him.

Sleightman began spending more time with him, being social and personable, but mostly ingratiating with extra food and small comforts like decent shaving soap. On his return from Tilly late evening, they began drinking together and, with both drunk, in small doses Sleightman drew out the story of Sedgwicke's fall from grace.

"A couple of bloody knives and forks! If 'twern't for this national emergency, they could've shipped you off to Australia. A couple of bloody knives and forks. It b'aint just, Percy, you owes them nuthin'. Truth of the matter is, they owes you!"

Sedgwicke, well in his cups, nodded in firm agreement.

"I likes you, Percy! You're a man after my own. Tomorrow, we'll talk some more. There's something I think you can help me with."

Sure enough, the following day Sleightman found Sedgwicke at his ledgers.

"Right Percy. Break off and come into the office."

Sedgwicke did as obeyed and entered the small cubby-hole that served as stores office and Sleightman's billet. Once inside, and he had started talking, the ingratiating and wheedling tone Sleightman used disappeared entirely, to be replaced by a hard, businesslike demeanour that came as a shock to Sedgwicke.

"Right, Percy. I knows you likes your bottle. Right?"

Sedgwicke nodded, now fearful.

"And you doesn't have to pay. Right?"

Again, Sedgwicke nodded. The oily grin returned

"Now, I likes you Percy, and I wants to see you right, but time's come for you to do something for me. Do this, and things stays as they are, if you takes my meaning."

He paused and Sedgwicke waited, expecting something terrible.

"As a storeman you is able to leave barracks and get into town to see merchants, and shopkeepers, and such."

Sedgwicke nodded.

"Right. From time to time, I needs a letter delivered to the Innkeeper at the Five Feathers, that's the Inn that you came out of when we first met; and bring a letter back. That's all I wants you to do, Percy. Deliver that letter and all stays as before. Let me down, and there'll be changes, and I don't just mean the end of the bottles, if you takes my meaning."

Sedgwicke saw nothing that could be made an issue of. To deliver and collect a letter as part of his duties in town could present no problem, as far as he could see.

"Yes. Of course. I'll do that gladly."

"Right Percy. Knew you'd be sensible. Start now."

He produced an envelope from a drawer in his desk, sealed with bright red wax, but no name.

"See that this goes into the hand, and I mean into the hand, of Wilberforce Johnson. He's the Landlord. If he's not there, wait. Go."

Sedgwicke went.

* * *

Other envelopes were in transit around the barracks, one of vital interest for all, one of specific interest for just one. The former rested on the desk of Colonel Lacey. It was addressed to himself, with "confidential" written on the quality paper, sealed with red wax, and that imprinted with the seal of the Horse Guards. He picked up his plain, workaday paper knife and used it to extract the contents. The heavy vellum paper opened reluctantly, then he scanned down over the usual opening blandishments to read what he knew it would contain.

Colonel William Lacey: Officer Commanding 5th Detachments.

You are to prepare your command for embarkation at Weymouth on the 20th April 1806. In future correspondence your battalion will be referred to as the 5th Provisional Battalion. Further orders will be conveyed via General Perry.

It stopped there; no indication of destination, just the simple order. One more month, less with embarkation preparations, to get them up to standard. Too many were still green, too many were still too slow.

On the other side of the wall, in the Mess anteroom another envelope was being opened, of equal quality, but this time by Lieutenant D'Villiers. The contents of his letter were equally disturbing but whilst Lacey's produced anxiety, D'Villiers' produced disappointment. His parents had failed to find him a Commission. It was proving difficult. Money was not the problem, it was the fact that he was recently in the Militia, he had no experience, and Commanding Officers were being careful about who they took into their Regiments. Fighting was in the offing, not society balls. On top of that, there were few vacancies, most Regiments were reaching full muster and, on top of that, an exchange was impossible, no-one wanted to exchange into a Detachment Battalion. Anxious times these may be, but young Officers saw the chance of advancement on the field of battle and were more than content to remain in Regiments where they were likely to see it.

Both left their discarded covers where they lay and then passed each other in the corridor, each bearing their own letter. Such was the anxiety that the letters had raised in the mind of each that no salutes were exchanged. Lacey was looking for O'Hare, D'Villiers for Carravoy. Lacey found O'Hare first, sat in his own Office.

"It's come, Padraigh. Orders. We are to embark on the 20th April, it doesn't say where, but it's plainly overseas. They are calling us the 5th Provisionals. We are remaining together."

O'Hare consulted a calendar.

"Four weeks, four days."

"Yes. Start making preparations. We need transport and we need supplies, all the usual, flints, dry food, boots, spare equipment..."

O'Hare interrupted. He could both see and hear the anxiety this had raised within his Colonel.

"Yes Sir. I'll see to it. I've done it before."

Lacey stopped, and grew calm.

"Yes. Yes, of course. I'll leave it with you."

He paused.

"We haven't had enough time, Padraigh. Do you think that they're anything close to ready?"

"They're not bad, they won't disgrace us. Only the real thing will tell, of course, but we still have some time. We'll keep working."

Whilst Lacey's state of agitation decreased, that of D'Villiers did the opposite as he searched for Carravoy. Eventually he found him.

"Damnable news, Carravoy. No luck with a transfer. My people have contacted God knows who and got nowhere. Damn this half baked Battalion, damn my luck, and above all damn him!" and he jabbed his finger in the direction of Lacey's Office.

Carravoy grinned and tried to look re-assuring.

"Don't take it so bad, D'Villiers. There's still time, we're still stuck here with no orders for anywhere, so don't give up all hope. It can still happen."

D'Villiers dropped his arms, one hand still holding the letter and he fumed, his face screwed with anger and unfamiliar frustration . Still holding the letter, he stalked off.

The next day saw D'Villiers state of agitation increase. The notice for embarkation appeared on the Mess noticeboard, with the date underlined, also their new title; 5th Provisional Battalion. Next to that was a notice that drill and practice were to be stepped up and, at the foot of that, the notification that the battalion were off on four days manoeuvres in three days time. All Officers to prepare themselves for life in the field. His misery was complete; days under canvas, marching, drilling, lousy food, little wine, dirty clothes and linen. He slouched off to consult Carravoy on what to pack in two paltry portmanteaus, which he knew, as a mere Lieutenant, were his sole allowance for the baggage train.

* * *

On the dawn of the due day the Battalion paraded, all men with full packs and equipment, greatcoats rolled and strapped on the top of their packs. It began to rain, and then, for the number of occasions that no-one knew, for all had lost count, the battalion once more shouldered arms and marched out through the barrack gate. The baggage train had assembled outside and, as the last company quit the gate, they joined on, under the command of Quartermaster Sergeant Sleightman, his command of carts and mules almost doubling the length of the marching column. Sedgwicke was grateful, he rode beside the driver, well back in the wagon under the sheltering canvas. This time, however, he could quickly see that the destination was not out onto the practice moors, this time was on into the town, through it and up into the hills to the West.

Carr was entitled to ride a horse, being a Captain, but he elected not to. He preferred to march in front of the company where he could at least talk to Drake and, wearing his greatcoat, there was less of him exposed to the rain, rather than up on a horse. However, it was Drake as usual who did most of the talking, mostly about his dearest sweetheart Cecily, how she could ride a horse, embroider wonderfully and sweetly play the piano. Behind them there was no singing and little talk. Soon full packs were digging into shoulders, besides the other straps of knapsacks full of biscuit, water bottles full to the brim and cartridge boxes full with their maximum sixty.

The observer with an eye for detail would have noticed that some of the Light Company carried a musket shorter by nine inches than the majority, also that they carried a bayonet more resembling a short sword. Any with a keener eye for smaller detail would have noticed that the Sergeants of the Light Com-

187

pany also carried a weapn of the same, not the standard spearlike "Badge of Office"; the halberd, as with Sergeants of the other battalion companies. Two weeks previously Lacey had summoned Carr and Drake to the Armoury and showed them the contents of three long boxes. His words to them were brief and to the point.

"Three dozen new Baker Rifles, Carr. Bought at my own expense. You remember I told you to identify your best shots. Well, here's their weapon. With their rifled barrel, this musket is accurate at 200 yards. They go to your best marksmen."

Carr had consulted Drake and Ellis, but both agreed with him. He decided to give one to each file, not to the best shot, but to the one prepared to learn the use of the new weapon. The Baker was slower and more intricate to load, it could use the standard paper cartridges, but, for full accuracy, the ball needed to be wrapped in a piece of leather to ensure it gripped the rifling inside the barrel. When Ellis presented the Baker to their file, Tom Miles refused point blank, saying he could hit most things with what he already had, and Joe Pike felt he had only just mastered one weapon and he didn't fancy having to learn a second. John Davey, on the other hand, very much liked the look of the new weapon. It was well made with a walnut stock, a flintlock whose oiled click sounded of precision manufacture, but, most appealingly, it had a front and back sight. He took it on, and when practising on the range on straw dummies he was impressed with the level of accuracy. He was more than content with his choice and so now he carried one out into the wilds to the West, the high moorland, ignoring the quips that came from his marching comrades about "that new short-arse bundook".

Their march took them up and up, leaving behind the first signs of the Spring that was breaking out on the lowlands. Cultivation fell behind them, neat fields became moorland, divided, if at all, by stonewalls and wind blown hedges. The rain ceased, but after the rain came the wind, not cold, but sweeping up the slopes, in off the Bristol Channel. It blew the clouds off to the East, and the Westering sun, now revealed, edged across to the grave of the day within a reddening sky. At the opposite end of the widening heavens, a half moon grew out of the thickening dark.

The time had come to make camp. Veterans scuttled about, doing the necessary and shouting bad tempered instructions to those new to the game, those who should be doing what was "bloody obvious", the verdict and opinion of those already with the knowledge. Officers' servants pitched their tents and arranged the camp tables and chairs to create at least a modicum of comfort and civilisation, whilst the said Officers looked to the arrangements of the camp and the preparations of the men. However, all were wet and most welcome of all, was the starting of good campfires made from wood gathered from the many hedges and copses that occupied this high terrain of West Somerset. Rations were issued and the camp kettles set upon the fires and soon came the equally welcome aroma of cooking.

Tom Miles thought that he knew it all, but was both surprised and pleased with the shelter that John Davey quickly fashioned from poles and branches gathered nearby. A sloping shelter for the three of them, which would, as John Davey put it,

"Keep off any more rain and, even if no more came, the morning dew could give you a soaking, just the same."

Miles made some comment about "thieving poachers tricks", but he recognised a good addition to the small number of comforts that their open camp afforded. Many tried to dry their jackets, but taking them off just brought a chill and so they were put back on and left to dry in place. Not so for the Officers. They at least, had one change of clothing and so all took advantage of this, leaving their servants to dry the day's wet casualties as best they may. This gave rise to several washing lines being strung up, hoping for the continuance of the drying wind.

One of the more onerous additions to a soldier's life caused by field manoeuvres was sentry duty. It broke up precious sleep and took men away from the comfort of their billets. The first sentry duty fell to the Grenadier Company and Carravoy went about placing his men, 20 paces apart, establishing a rota with his Sergeants for the men and a rota with his Lieutenants for inspection of the sentry lines. Gradually the camp settled to stillness and a degree of quiet. The one benefit of field manoeuvres was the absence of drill and the strict cleaning of uniforms and so, their hunger satisfied, the men lay or sat in their mess groups, waiting for full dark and time for sleep. Miles, Pike, and Davey lay or sat under their improvised shelter. Miles, knowing himself the veteran thought he would have to teach the other two from scratch, but it was plain that both knew as much, perhaps even more, about living out in the open. However, what he did know was what a soldier needed to add to these country skills and he made sure that each placed their clean and dry equipment in a set way, so that it could be easily found if "some enemy comes sneakin". Miles fell to musing about their lot.

"Just think, Davey, you could be in Australia by now if Boney weren't kickin' up over the water. Instead, you'm up 'ere trying to keep warm and dry, and cuddlin' that fancy bundook."

"From what I hear about Australia, there's no problem with warm and dry, and if there's any cuddlin' down there it's with some sheep or somesuch. I think I got the best of it, 'specially with my Molly and me now paired up".

A short silence settled, but Davey resumed.

"There's the rumour that we're off, sometime next month. It's got to be abroad, hasn't it?"

Miles replied authoritatively.

"Can't be nothin' else. On a ship and off somewhere. Could be years."

"What happens to families?"

"Some families comes with us. We draws lots, about ten per company, so the odds aren't good. Also, those as follows must be of some use. They 'as to be able to cook, fetch, and carry, and care for the wounded. So even if a family's drawn out, not all can come."

"So, even if my Molly's drawn out, we'd have to leave at least Tilly behind?"

"I'd say so. Sorry John, the answer's yes. You'd do well to be thinkin' of what she could do. I has to say this, John, but this an' all could come. With her reputation of a string of husbands, she could be turned out of barracks into the Poor House, after we'n gone, without your knowin'. You b'aint church married. You'd best be thinkin' of where she could go. You can have some pay sent to her, there is that. I don't recommend barrack life with us away. 'Tis like prison, they'n forgotten, poor food and nuthin' to do all day. And they could be turfed out if a new battalion arrives. If you 'as family, try to get her and Tilly over to them; and send 'em money. If they stays in barracks, the Army docks yer pay anyway. That's the best way."

190

In the half-light from the dying fire, Tom could see Davey nodding.

"That's good advice, Tom. I do have family, over Devizes way. They'll care for her, take her and Tilly in. And I'll send my pay. I'll see what can be done."

Tom turned to Joe.

"You Joe, what do you think you'd be doin'? If you weren't 'ere?"

He got no reply. Joe was wrapped in his greatcoat, head on his pack, sound asleep, the sleep borne of both innocence and inexperience. The last to settle to sleep were the Officers, these being able to maintain their society in the dark, as they had tables, chairs, and, most importantly, a candle! Carr and Drake, closeted in their tent, were both sat at the table, Carr reading, Drake writing.

"What's the book?"

"A book of poems, "Poems on Various Subjects" by one Samuel Taylor Coleridge."

"Any good?"

"Well, it's not exactly a good read, and I don't think this chap is the happiest fellow in the world at present. He rumbles on about lots of stuff. Most of the titles begin with the word "effusion". I wish he'd have left most of them in the bottle! "

"And yet you persist in reading it. May I enquire as to its source? No, don't tell me, I'm sure I can guess. One Jane Perry, fondest daughter of our beloved General."

Carr grinned, thoroughly found out.

"Yes, it came the other day. I'm reading it out of politeness, actually. I mean it's very likely that I will be questioned on it, next time we meet."

"Yes, nothing more certain, and I'd better make a note of your opinion, to be sure that it is conveyed accurately to her."

He made a show of writing on a spare piece of paper.

"Rumbles on... lots of stuff... not the happiest fellow... left in the bottle. Got it."

"And you are doing what? Exactly."

"Writing to Cecily."

"When was the last time you saw her?"

"Yesterday."

"And you're writing to her today? Has anything noteworthy happened between then and now, that justifies so urgent a letter?"

"Well, not exactly, but, well, you know, absence makes the heart grow fonder, and all that."

Both grinned and returned to their occupations, Carr out of duty, or so he would say, but Drake out of something much more uplifting.

The camp was asleep, except the sentries and their patrolling Officers. As the night turned through its small hours the half moon strengthened above the trees, giving an eerie half-light. Carravoy took his turn inspecting the sentries, satisfied when each time he heard the correct challenge and the correct reply to his own response. The routine was becoming monotonous when suddenly a shot rang out, behind and to the left.

"What the Devil? Who fired?

"Me Sir. Wilkins."

Carravoy had passed him, three sentries ago. He ran back.

"What on earth for? What did you see?"

"A shape, Sir. It ran across my front, right to left, but it was holdin' aloft what looked like clothes, Sir. Could be some locals tryin' to rob the camp."

"You definitely saw something?"

"Yes Sir, as I just described."

"Right, well done. You kept alert. There's nothing we can do now, just wait till morning, and then see what can be seen. Reload and keep alert."

"Yessir."

Carravoy passed the rounds onto one of his Lieutenants and morning came. What was discovered was a dismantled clothesline, with the contents strewn on the damp earth. Carravoy walked forward to investigate, then stopped. The prints in the damp earth were confusing. He gave an order.

"One of Carr's hard bargains, Davey I think, used to be a poacher. Get him over, see what he can make of this."

Davey was summoned and approached the scene. He gave it but one glance.

"Deer, Sir, of some sort. Came through here, hit the clothes line and took off that way, past the sentry."

Carravoy turned to the servant.

"What's missing?"

"Some breeches, Sir."

"Whose?"

"Mr D'Villiers', Sir."

D'Villiers had been standing by as a casual observer, but now he took an especially keen interest. His recent bad temper, still bubbling, quickly came again to the surface.

"Dammit, Simpson. I'll have you flogged for this. This leaves me with just one pair. Flogged, and returned to the ranks!"

Simpson looked at Carravoy, his face showing all the anxiety he felt. Carravoy looked at D'Villiers, but said nothing, only shifting his gaze when Davey spoke up.

"I think I can help, Sir."

"How?"

"Deer are slow grazers, Sir. Once they find what they want, they generally stay a while. He could still be near, Sir. I say he, I suspect the deer came through and his antlers got tangled with the washing. I can probably trail it, at least to find out, Sir."

"Right, get to it. Take whoever you need, but we move in an hour."

"Sir."

Davey summoned Miles and Joe Pike and they followed what was an easy trail, but nevertheless he frequently checked the wind, to be ready to move downwind when the quarry was found. Over a slight rise and they saw it, a young buck, the breeches caught in its immature set of antlers. It frequently shook its head to rid itself of the annoying addition, but the clothing was stuck fast.

"We move left, downwind."

His two companions followed, but the available cover only took them to within 250 yards of the deer, perhaps a little less. Davey loaded carefully, wrapping the ball in the piece of thin leather. Miles was puzzled.

"That's over 200 yards. You're wasting your time. We've got to get closer."

"Can't be done, Tom. Deer has good eyesight, besides a good sense of smell. Any movement or scent and they'll be gone, and they're quick."

He settled into the undergrowth, wriggled forward as much as he dared and set his sights for the distance. He then took careful aim and took a deep breath. Miles and Joe Pike looked from him to the deer. When Davey fired; what had been comedy, a set of breeches bobbing with the rhythm of the grazing head, quickly turned to pathos. The deer shook, staggered three paces on drunken legs and then collapsed. The rest of the herd took off at speed the instant on hearing the report. Miles looked at Davey, astonishment replacing his most common look of impatience.

"Well, I'll be. Well, I'll be!"

All three went down to recover the deer. The ball had entered just behind the left shoulder, but there was no exit wound. Miles was still amazed.

"Took him clean. Clean as you like."

He took Davey's weapon from him and hefted it in his hand.

"Seems like this fancy bundook really is just as much as it's cracked up to be."

Davey eviscerated the animal and Joe disengaged the breeches; the merest of examinations would have shown that they were of the finest. Joe and Miles carried the carcass back to camp and Davey carried the breeches. Once in camp, Davey saw D'Villiers and approached him.

"Sir. We had some success, Sir."

Davey handed him his missing clothing."

"Any blood?"

"No Sir. Your clothes were on his antlers, out of the way."

With no more words, D'Villiers walked away and threw the breeches at Simpson.

"See that these are clean."

Miles stood, regarding the disappearing back, and spoke just louder than under his breath, just enough for his two messmates to hear.

"Did you see that? No thank you, no well done, no bloody nothin'. If it hadn't been for you and that Baker, John, he'd be goin' bare arsed before we was done up here. Not even one bloody miserable coin!"

He pointed to the deer carcass.

"Best take that to the Officer's cooks. But if they'n as generous as 'ee, we won't see no share of it."

* * *

They broke camp and marched out, but they were at the summit of the range of hills and Lacey took full advantage of the gently rolling uplands to march and counter march, form line, form square, and form column. They attacked in line, with the

194

Light Company out before as a skirmish line, they retreated in line with the Lights and Grenadiers forming a rearguard. They deployed from line to square, they attacked in column, deploying into a firing line just before the objective, all measured by the pitiless movement of the second hand of Lacey's silver half-hunter. Thus the two middle days were occupied and, after each day, the men were as exhausted as their empty cartridge boxes, dragging themselves around their new camping ground, each time forming and pitching on ground that needed to be cleared and tamed before tents and billets could be formed. However, Miles was proved wrong. At the end of the second day, a Servant came to them in their billet and tipped a joint of venison into their cooking pot. Miles asked of the servant,

"Who from?"

"You particular who you gets extras from, or are you goin' to quibble over the joint you got? Well, here's the facts of it, it ain't the best and it's from Captain Carr. He says to tell you that you "improved the standing of the Light Company in the battalion". His words."

They toasted Captain Carr with the evening's rum ration.

On the last day they were joined by General Perry and he assumed command from Colonel Lacey, but for the men there was no discernible change, formations came and went and volleys began according to the signal from the drummers. The men cared little about the source of orders, only to quickly obey to avoid the ire of Officers or Sergeants.

The day wore on and the battalion was advancing in column, half distance between companies, along a shallow hogsback that carried a small wood, down over, off to their right front. Close to the wood, Perry ordered a two deep firing line facing the right, and Lacey, now merely an observer, was pleased with the speed with which it was formed. Suddenly from around the wood, came a Regiment of cavalry, lancers, in column, two squadrons wide and advancing at a fast canter, bright yellow guidons contrasting with their dark blue uniforms. Their objective was clear, the 5th Provisionals, and within a minute they would be at the foot of the slope, 300 yards before the 5th's firing line. Lacey waited for a response from Perry, an order, but none came, instead he turned in his saddle and addressed Lacey.

"A little surprise I've arranged for you Lacey. Those are enemy cavalry, so give your orders."

Lacey spurred his horse forward, but time had been lost. He reached the middle of the line and bellowed to the drummers.

"Beat Form Square."

The drummers responded immediately, but their signal was competing with the pounding hooves and other sounds of 900 charging cavalry, not to mention the hypnotic effect of such a sight. However, the line began to break up as Officers recognised the new order. Three companies in the centre quickly condensed from a two to a four deep front line and the two outside companies at each end swung back to form one behind the other, achieving their four deep line at the sides. The front two ranks fixed bayonets and knelt. However, the remaining three companies had furthest to go. They had to retreat back and form the fourth side and by now the cavalry were up to the fronting companies and sweeping past the bayonets of the corners and sides of the square to turn and descend upon the confusion of the unformed fourth wall. The men were running to position, fixing bayonets as they ran, but they were too late. The heavy horses, spurred on by eager riders, crashed in where the back line should have joined at the corner. Men were pushed aside, knocked over and trampled, and then self-preservation took over; in the face of the hopeless cause many ran to the shelter of the ranks already formed.

The cavalry reached what would have been the centre of the formed square, a trumpeter sounded and all came to a halt, some in, some out, of the square. Their Colonel emerged from the melee and approached Lacey; his good-natured smile conveying all that was needed to say about who lost and who won.

"Good afternoon, Colonel. Jamieson of the Border Yeomanry. I'm afraid we've broken your square. Your colour," looking around, "if you had one; would be ours."

He saluted General Perry.

"General Perry, Sir. Permission to withdraw."

"Granted. Pass "well done" to your men."

From a scene of frantic activity, all was peace and stillness within the square, save restless horses shaking and nodding their heads. The cavalry, wearing pleasant, indulgent smiles, looked down on the infantry; the infantry stared back with implacable hatred as winded and injured men were attended to by the drummers. Conversation between the two, such as it was, was significantly less than amiable, mostly a variation of what Miles called out,

"Don't let yourself be found in town over the next few days, mate."

Carr, on the other hand, his Light Company in position close by, ambled up to the Captain of a Squadron, fondled the muzzle and forehead of his horse, and introduced himself.

"Captain Henry Carr. Light Company. 5th Provisionals."

The cavalryman replied.

"Captain Jonathan Tavender. Border Yeomanry."

"Well done, smart work, you have your men in good order. However, I wonder how many of your men would have got round the back had we been allowed to open fire?"

"Casualties from one volley? Less than 50. It wouldn't have stopped us."

"At 50 yards, I doubt it. Be pleased it wasn't put to the test."

Carr raised his voice so that as many as possible would hear.

"The musketry of this battalion is the best I've seen. Provisionals or not."

Many in the ranks behind raised their muskets to accompany their shouts of agreement, but Tavender merely smiled and jerked his horse's head away from Carr's reach.

"Let's hope so, but the fact remains, we broke your square. If you don't move smarter than that, musketry or no, you'll be dead men."

With that he turned his horse and walked it back into the ranks of his men. Just to make the extra point of who held what ground, the Yeomanry formed up within the square, then rode out in immaculate order. Deakin watching events, turned to Halfway.

"Didn't you say French cavalry was the best there is?"

"I did, but perhaps ours have learned a thing or two."

"All the same, Carr's right. By the time they got round the back, there would've been a lot of empty saddles, and riders with no horse!"

Lacey and Jamieson exchanged salutes, but no words, and Jamieson rode to the head of his men as they trotted off. Lacey was annoyed, he knew that precious seconds that had been unnecessarily lost, but it was clearly useless to complain. Perry turned to Lacey, clearly satisfied with events, something had been proven which seem to give him pleasure.

"You failed the test, Lacey. Your men were too slow. Against French cuirassiers, you'd have been broken and slaughtered. They will have to improve; your square was taken before it could be formed. We'll talk again before you embark. I bid you Good Day. Oh, by the way, D'Villier's Father sends his best regards."

With that he and his Staff rode away, following the Yeomanry. Lacey turned to O'Hare, his voice and expression showed how deflated he was.

"Form Fours, we're marching home."

O'Hare allowed himself the chance to ride along the ranks before giving the orders, his voice matching his cheery expression.

"Never mind, boys. It wasn't your fault, late orders. You nearly got there."

Many shouted back, brandishing their muskets.

"Never mind late orders, Major. We'd have turned round and blasted their smug faces right off their damned horses, to Kingdom bloody Come and all!"

"Indeed you would, boys. Indeed you would, but we're off back now. You've done well, as good as I've seen."

He reached the central drummers. "Beat Form Fours."

* * *

It was full dark when the head of the column reached the barrack gate. Most expected the orders of "Halt" and "Dismiss", but instead, as each company entered, a full parade was formed before the silent and still figure of Colonel Lacey. Tired and dirty as they all were, each could feel that something important was soon to be said and all waited with grounded arms, no talking, all waiting. The Light Company came in last and formed up, so that now all stood facing their Colonel, all colour banished in the gloom of the square, only the glint of the candle lanterns lighting on the badges and buttons to give eerie shape to the assembled ranks. However, none cared about what they could see, all were concerned about what that were soon to hear. The parade came to order, with Gibney bellowing "Order Arms."

"Men. I want you to know that your conduct and skill as soldiers over the past four days, has been as good as I've seen. Anywhere! I would have no hesitation in leading you against any enemy force, and be proud to do so. It was a pity that we couldn't see off that Regiment of cavalry, but no harm done, and perhaps it makes the point; speed is everything. You must respond to your orders as though your life depends upon it, for indeed it does, and indeed it will. Our orders have come. We will be treated as a battalion in our own right. We are now the 5th Provisional Battalion, as good as any, which is as much a compliment to you as it is to me. We embark for overseas on 20th April, which means we leave here, ready to fight, on the 15th. I can't say where, as yet I don't know. All I can say is that it is overseas, and wherever it is, against whoever it is, I know that we will give a good account of ourselves. Major O'Hare, dismiss the parade."

The orders rang out, and the ranks dissolved. What had been silent anticipation now turned to a buzz of conversation as speculation ran from one soldier to another, but the noise on the square died away as they entered the doors that led to their barrack rooms. Sleightman, Sedgwicke and the other storemen had been stood waiting in the entrance arch, waiting but also listening. Sleightman turned to his men.

"So, off abroad. Back to campaignin', and not long. That's goin' to keep us busy, boys, campaignin'll need twice what we've had to deal with here, but that's not for now. Get the wagons in and get them unloaded. We need's to be off this Parade Ground by first light, with all tucked away."

The wagons were drawn in through the gate, up to the stores entrance as the unloading began. From fussing and bustling about at the beginning, Sleightman soon disappeared, to where no one knew, it wasn't to his private quarters. It was long into the night before the last supply wagon left empty through the arch and they could all take themselves off to their beds, only to be thrust awake by the Reveille that came, for them, far too soon. After breakfast, Sleightman was still nowhere to seen, but the stores business moved on to meet the requirements of the day. In their absence much had arrived in their sacks, barrels and boxes, and all had to be opened, booked and stored. Sedgwicke found himself in charge of a large brown parcel. When it moved it made a wooden rattle, and the address was Sergeant Sleightmen, The Stores, Taunton Barracks. There was nothing unusual in that, everything had that address, but it was unusual in that it was just one item. Usually they dealt in dozens and scores, but this was one unique parcel.

"Is Sergeant Sleightman back yet?" he enquired of a passing storeman, but the reply was in the negative. He looked again at the parcel. Should he leave it for Sleightman, or open it? He decided on the latter. He was a storeman, his job was to deal with what arrived. He opened the parcel and out came five barrel taps, brand new and made from soft pine, but very long. Sedgwicke had little experience of such mundane items but they did strike him as longer, much longer, than those he had seen before, hammered into barrels at village fairs and such. However, they were not common stores items; they had neither bin nor box in the stores and so Sedgwicke could not book them in. All he could do was place them outside of Sleightman's office; not inside, for he kept it locked. This he did and returned to the other work that came crowding in. His head was bent over his Ledger when he heard Sleightman's voice, yelling in a state of high agitation. He was coursing up and down the aisles of the store, waving the wrapping paper of the box of taps.

"Who opened this? I wants to know, now. Who opened this?"

Sedgwicke recognised the wrapping and instantly spoke up.

"It was me. I opened it this morning, about two hours ago."

"I wants you in my Office, now!"

Sedgwicke eased himself off his stool and followed Sleightman into his exclusive burrow and waited whilst Sleightman sat in the only chair. On his desk were the barrel taps.

"Who said you could open these?" His grating voice and glaring bloodshot eyes told Sedgwicke that something serious was amiss with this, his Sergeant.

"No one, Sergeant. I opened it, as I would any package, so that I could see what it was, find the docket and deal with it. It wasn't a stores item and…"

Sleightman exploded.

"It damn well had my name on it, Sedgwicke. My name. You should have left it for me. Me!"

Sedgwicke stopped his explanation and fell silent. Both let the silence dwell, but it was Sleightman who finally broke it.

"You never saw this, Percy. You got me? Never saw it. You breathe a word and it'll go very hard on you, very hard. Have you got my meaning?"

"I understand you perfectly, Sergeant, but after all, why should I want to start a conversation with anyone about a few barrel taps?"

Sleightman's face lightened.

"No indeed, Percy. You has the right of it there. Why should you want to talk with anyone about barrel taps? Now, if you keeps it that way, I'll forget, and you mark my words, so should you."

"Yes, Sergeant. It will be just as you say. I can promise."

"Good Percy. Man after my own heart, you is and will stay as such. Here's my gesture of goodwill."

With that he fetched up another bottle of rum and pushed it in Sedgwicke's direction.

"That's yours, and I wants that delivered. Same as before. Now, be off."

He had pushed across the desk another plain envelope. Sedgwicke took it and left the office. His route back to his desk took him past the rum barrels, all with a tap and their fronts slanting forward, the back slightly higher, each held that way by their individual cradles. He also passed a group of his fellow storemen, all deep in discussion, but there was only one topic. How many would accompany the Battalion on campaign? There would be a draw for them as individuals and in their draw, what were the odds of staying or going? Sedgwicke grew anxious, about everything.

That night, in all the barrack rooms, that also was the sole topic of concern, but there was little conversation. Who went would be decided in the regulation manner and Sergeant Obediah Hill was organising proceedings.

"You all knows how this goes. Any family as wants to go into the draw, get your name written on a piece of paper and ready; the bags'll be around soon, but you also knows that no babes nor toddlers is able to come. All must be able bodied and able to pull their weight."

His eyes lighted on Pat Mulcahey.

"Be your name goin' in, Pat?"

"Yes. All mine is able bodied, able to fetch and carry and be of use around the camp. If I'm lucky, mine will come. What's the number?"

"Eight families each company is what I've been told."

Mulcahey nodded and returned to his family.

John Davey and Molly sat in gloom.

"She's too young Molly. Even if you were drawn, they'd draw again until they've got families all that can pull their weight. Besides, from what I've been told there's danger, for you both, and disease. Too many men has to bury their families in the faraway places they serve in. I don't want that to happen to you. Campaignin' can be real hard, too hard for the likes of a mite like Tilly. I'm too fearful for her."

Molly seized his hands and chewed her lower lip. Tears were starting in her eyes.

"You could be gone years, John, what'll happen to us?"

Davey misinterpreted the meaning of "us".

"Me 'n' you, we'll always be together Molly. Far or near."

Now the tears did come, but Davey continued to answer her real question.

"I've got family, not too far, at Devizes. Place called Far Devening. They'll take you in and care for you, better there than you'd be here. I'll get Parson to write a letter. You take it to our local Vicar, Reverend Blackmore, and he'll take you to my Mother and Sisters, and read out the letter. They'll take you in. One sister is married with children, they'll be playmates for Tilly. It's for the best, and I can send you money. You'll get all my pay. The Purser says he can do that. What use will I have for money in some foreign place?"

Molly sighed and dried her eyes. To Davey, she looked re-signed and he felt content. Tilly came up onto the bench and embraced her Mother. Davey was re-assured. It was sad, but it was settled. At that point the ten draw bags arrived, one for each company and according to their company, the men placed their names into the bags, which were then taken away.

Morning came and breakfast, but no result of the draw, but elsewhere one name had been decided. Sleightman called in Sedgwicke and told him that he was going on campaign. Sedgwicke's stomach turned over in horror.

"But I thought there was a draw, for the sake of fairness."

"Well, yes and no, Percy. It's not quite like that, not for us storesmen. I has to name someone that can be trusted, some-one that will keep the Colonel happy. That'll be you Percy."

"But I'm not even a Lance Corporal Storeman. Mitchell and Stevens are Corporals. Why am I selected over them? They've been in the stores for years, whilst myself, barely months. Also, they've been on campaign. If someone should have their name taken out of the draw, it should at least be one of them."

"They're old, Percy. You're young and spry. You can cope; the Colonel will ask if they can cope. I'll tell him no."

"That's not true, both are strong and fit. You've seen them around the stores, and I reiterate, both have been on campaign before. I'd surmise that they are just what Lacey would want."

"Now never mind your fancy words, Percy. "Tis my decision and 'tis done. Now out. I've work to do."

Sedgwicke left, much disturbed. He was desperate not to go, but would have accepted as God's Will being one of those to go, if drawn, but this arbitrary decision of Sleightman raised the potent question; why did Sleightman pick on him in particular to go? There was no justification. He went and told his fellow storemen and their comments disturbed him even more.

"Better look out your bayonet and musket then, Parson, because back in the ranks is where you'll be."

Sedgwicke was horrified.

"But I've been told that storemen stay in the rear, only coming forward to bring up supplies. Not needed to fight."

"Everyone is needed to fight, Parson, everyone. They can call you forward if things gets tight, they can give the supply job to local hired help, freeing you up, and also, God forbid, Light Cavalry can come calling. They specialises in raiding the enemy backlines."

He held up his left hand with three fingers missing.

"How d'you think I got this? Caught my hand in a drawer?"

All laughed, plainly at Sedgwicke's expense. He withdrew to his single and friendless billet, deep in gloom. There, he slowly became resolved. Service abroad and battle terrified him more than Sleightman or anything. Sleightman had taken him out of the draw, the removal of Sleightman, perhaps, would put him back in it. Whatever needed to be done to get himself into the draw would be done. The outcome was then in the hands of God and prayer would save him.

Lunchtime came and with it the lucky names. Mulcahey was chosen, also Private Henry Nicholls, wife of Nelly. The topic was also discussed over lunch in the Officer's Mess, but not of a draw, this didn't apply to Officers, simply the decision, should the family come or not? Carr addressed Padraigh O'Hare.

"May I ask, Sir, if you are taking your family?"

"You may ask, Captain Carr, and the answer is no. Both my wife and I think it best that my family remains here, at least within the Isles. They will return to Ireland, to our family home. There I know that they are safe and well cared for, leaving me to concentrate on my duties, which will be many, you can be sure."

"Yes, Sir. I'm sure you're right. A good decision, certainly for the best."

"You may be right, I hope you are, but there's many a young Officer, with a young bride, who thinks me wrong."

"Perhaps, Sir, but different circumstances. It's children that make all the difference, surely?"

"You are right, and I have five. They make the difference."

At that point, D'Villiers, late to lunch, came bursting in, waving a piece of paper.

"Something cheerful at last, I've just taken this from the board. We are all invited to a Ball at the General's. 14th April, the day before we march. I must send for my best togs. Boots and breeches."

* * *

Sedgwicke left the bottle unopened and lay awake, his mind alternating between fear and puzzlement. Fear of the firing line in a battle and puzzlement at why he was being taken out of the draw to remain in barracks or to go on campaign. He dwelt mostly on the latter, starting with the obvious fact that Sleightman had singled him out for the campaign because he wanted him gone. Was it because he was a threat? No, surely. Sedgwicke knew that he could not be a physical threat to anyone. Because of what he knew? What did he know? Sleightman could obtain copious amounts of rum, far above the legal ration. He had some dealings with a local Landlord, letters to and fro, and then there was the barrel taps. Oddly long and definitely not standard. He rose, lit his candle and took it through the stores to the barrels. He studied the row, 12 in all, the candle shining dully on the steel hoops, all barrels tilted forward to place the tap at the lowest point. Suddenly, it came to him, simple and obvious, but only if you knew what Sedgwicke did, that Sleightman used a tap of extra length. Sleightman was stealing rum. Sleightman was a criminal. It could be proved and criminals were taken away to gaol.

He returned to his bed, thought out his plan, then slept. The day after next came his chance, another letter to be taken to the Five Feathers. The envelope was standard paper, sealed but with no writing on it. He went to the Colonel's Clerk and obtained the duplicate of the paper. He wrote nothing on it, neither inside nor on the cover, he simply folded it and sealed it with red wax. Being careful to keep Sleightman's letter separate from his, he took himself off to the Five Feathers, surprising himself that he felt so calm. His plan received a boost when he found Wilberforce Johnson busy at his own ledgers, making it likely that Sedgwicke's letter would only be opened some time after his departure, which would give him time to get back inside the barracks. This was confirmed when Johnson merely indicated where to put the letter and then simply waved the reply in Sedgwicke's direction. He took it and hurried away.

He both ran and walked at the best pace he could manage to reach the safety of the sentry at the arch, then over to the Colonel's Office and up to the Sergeant Clerk.

"I need to see the Colonel."

"He's busy."

"It's urgent, very urgent."

"I can take you to Major O'Hare."

"That will be sufficient."

They both went outside the building and walked to the next door. Sedgwicke's heart skipped a beat when he saw Johnson, just inside the arch, straining against the muskets of two sentries and shouting at an Officer. Inside, Major O'Hare was at his desk. The Sergeant Clerk made their presence known.

"Excuse me, Sir. This man needs to see either you or the Colonel, Sir. He says it's urgent."

"Right, Sergeant. I'll deal with it. You may go about your duties."

Sedgwicke waited until the door had closed. O'Hare sat patiently waiting.

"Sir, I have evidence that Sergeant Sleightman is stealing rum and selling it to an Inn in town. The Five Feathers, Sir. Here is part of my evidence," and he placed the two letters on O'Hare's desk, pointing to each.

"That one is from Sleightman to the Landlord, one Wilberforce Johnson. That one is Johnson's reply. Both are unopened and are as written by them. Sleightman gives me the task of delivering and taking delivery of these letters. I believe that inside there will be proof that Sleightman is selling Johnson Army rum."

O'Hare looked at Sedgwicke, then at the letters. He took his paper knife and opened first the one from Johnson. It contained a Five Pound Note, drawn on the Somerset Agricultural Bank. When the other was opened, there were only two pieces of information. A date, 4ᵗʰ April, and five characters XX4BY.

O'Hare looked up.

"Sedgwicke, isn't it?

Sedgwicke nodded.

"They call you Parson."

Sedgwicke nodded again.

"This proves nothing. Money is changing hands, as it does with local suppliers, and this, what looks like code, proves nothing."

"On the contrary, Sir, I know how it is done. Any payment should show what it is paying for. The £5 letter does not. The code on the other identifies the barrels that Johnson must obtain from the drayman when he collects the empty barrels and then delivers new. Sleightman always loads two or three barrels himself, all with some chalk mark such as that. He calls the barrels "ullage", that is rum left over in the barrels with sediment and therefore undrinkable. The date is the date of the delivery, tomorrow; the drayman is coming tomorrow. Also, Sir, evidence is in the stores. Sleightman obtains the rum for his own selling by using long taps. A long tap in the front face, sloping up with the slant of the barrel, will be exposed sooner above the rum inside as the level falls. This leaves much more in the barrel than a shorter tap. It's a question of simple trigonometry, Sir, if I may show you," and he drew a diagram on a spare piece of paper.

"You can prove this?"

"Yes Sir, but I think we need to go now. I saw Johnson at the gate. He may have got to Sleightman who may, as we speak, be destroying evidence."

O'Hare rose from behind his desk and hurried to the door, putting on his coat as he went. On their way to the stores he gathered up as many soldiers as he encountered and once inside the stores, what he saw chimed with what Sedgwicke had said. Sleightman and Johnson were busy extracting the offending taps and replacing them with standard. They had two barrels to go. Sleightman had a mallet in his hand and was in the act of withdrawing one of his special taps. Johnson was stood close by, holding one of standard length. But Sleightman wasn't going to submit that easily.

"Good morning, Sir. We'm just changing some taps here, that are not standard. Me and a local Landlord, Sir, Wilberforce Johnson of the Five Feathers, I relies on his expertise, Sir."

O'Hare looked at Sedgwicke.

"Sedgwicke?"

"There are three barrels in his office there, Sir. All should have that code XX4BY."

O'Hare looked at Sleightman, who was plainly becoming worried, then O'Hare turned and entered the office. Behind the desk there were indeed, three rum barrels with the code chalked on their tops. He tested their weight. He couldn't easily lift them, they were all full. He returned to Sleightman.

"Explain those three barrels in your office, Sleightman. All full, all with a chalk code. Why should Mr Johnson here need to know that code?"

Sleightman grew more nervous and began to shake. Johnson stepped back into the shadows.

"Ullage, Sir, left overs. Undrinkable, Sir."

"Three full barrels, Sleightman. That's a ration for nearly half the battalion! And why should you take five pounds from Johnson here? He sells nothing that you need to buy; you get your beer and spirits from Army Supplies.

He paused to let the facts sink in.

"It's clear to me that you are selling something to him, and the answer is the men's rum!"

"No Sir, you got it all wrong, Sir. Johnson here buys the ullage and then......"

O'Hare was no longer listening. He turned to his accompanying soldiers.

"These two are under arrest. Take them to the Guardroom. They are to be locked up."

O'Hare's escort needed no further bidding. Here was a culprit caught "bang to rights" in the act of selling their rum, one of their few comforts. Both were seized and hauled roughly away from the scene of their crime. As he passed Sedgwicke, Sleightman hissed his threat,

"I'll see the colour of your insides, Sedgwicke, you bastard, you see if I don't."

This prompted even rougher handling from the escort and, once out of sight of O'Hare, there came back the sounds of blows being landed and cries of pain. O'Hare turned to Sedgwicke.

"Well done, Sedgwicke. Stealing from your messmates is one of the worst crimes within the army. Look in the accounts to see if there is any record of any money being booked in for sales to the Five Feathers. There won't be, but check."

"Yes Sir."

Sedgwicke went into the Office, found the accounts book and checked. As O'Hare predicted, no sales were recorded and no money was booked in. Sleightman was finished. Sedgwicke took the ledger to O'Hare's office and wrote a note that described his findings, then he returned to his store duties.

Sleightman and Johnson were arrested and escorted off to gaol. Sedgwicke's star was in the ascendant around the barracks, he had stopped the thieving of the men's rum and he received many pats on the back and many accolades of "Well done, Parson." Two days later a Prosecuting Attorney came and took statements. Four days later a Militia Quartermaster Sergeant, a Sergeant Pearson, arrived to take over the stores. He arranged a draw. Two thirds of the storemen would go and they drew for those who would stay. Sedgwicke's name was not drawn. He was going anyway.

* * *

Taking any excuse, Reynier rode his horse along the cliffs over the Straits of Messina. It was a beautiful clear day; early April at the extreme tip of the toe of Italy was the best time of year to gain the benefit of time spent in Calabria, and the view was made more interesting by two frigates of the Royal Navy, coursing up and down the Straits, less that half a mile off, guarding against any French invasion across this narrow stretch of water to Sicily. Had they been able to read his mind their Captains would have returned to the harbour of Messina where the rest of the British forces were. Reynier had troubles of his own on the mainland.

Grateful that he had not been given the duty of besieging Gaeta to the North of Naples, he had been even more grateful to have been given his independent command. He had crushed the Neapolitan Army at the Battle of Campo Tenese and had soon reached the Straits. He had prepared for an invasion, as Napoleon ordered, but the Royal Navy held sway on the waters before him and now irregular warfare was exploding behind him. The Calabrians, finding out what it meant to be occupied by a French Army that lived off the local population and didn't care what methods they used to find stores of food, were in rebellion, tying down a large proportion of his army.

He watched as one frigate detached itself from the other, spread more sail and gained speed in his direction, heeling over to the added leverage from the wind in the taut sails. 400 metres from him, the course changed to parallel to the cliff and with sharp efficiency, the foresail was backed to the wind, bringing the vessel to a halt and holding her stationary. Reynier watched, fascinated, but this soon changed when he saw a large puff of white smoke emerge from her side, then heard the report, then heard the "whoosh" as a cannonball ploughed into the cliff, perfectly in line with him, but 5 metres below. His horse bucked and reared as a thousand or more seabirds, thoroughly disturbed, rose and wheeled from the cliff face all round. Reynier raised his hat to the frigate and then turned his horse away from the coast. The sea had suddenly lost his interest, invasion was impossible and his thoughts turned inland. What was now paramount was the question of how to subdue a partisan war?

Chapter Seven

Of Texts and Privateers

What the Ball lacked in opulence it made up for in scale. Being the Regional General, Matthew Perry had more than sufficient weight of authority and influence to secure the Town Assembly Rooms. A recent addition to the town, built in Renaissance style with distinctive Roman influence of columns and triangles, the bath stone frontage rose powerfully from the flat expanse of the town square. Inside was an entrance hall that could alone rival many ballrooms, but its own ballroom stretched for what seemed endless yards to a raised platform that boasted its own acreage. For this roomy space General Perry had arranged the massed bands of two local Regiments, conducted by a local Colonel of Music, who happened to be a good friend, and the area was indeed now occupied by their serried ranks, all in immaculate musical uniform, bearing shiny instruments, behind a palisade of bright silver music stands.

Outside the carriages were drawing up, shiny black in the remaining bright sunshine of the April evening, each carefully taking turns to allow their occupants to alight with the minimum requirement of walking. Few carriages were adorned with any form of heraldry, but those attending were, nevertheless, the great, and the good, and the wealthy of the County of Somerset and in some cases, beyond that. What an observer would have noticed, however, was the high proportion of guests that represented the military, of all arms; Infantry, Cavalry, Artillery and even the Navy, and most without female accompaniment.

Many of the Officers of the 5th Provisionals rode there on horseback, but an equal number elected to walk, which included Captain Carr and Lieutenant Drake, their billet in the town being just a few minutes away. The walk had been a pleasant stroll, but the conversation was, as usual, wholly one sided, with Ned Drake extolling the virtues of his dearest Cecily Fynings. He extracted from Carr a promise to dance with her once or twice, so that no one could accuse him of monopolising her. They reached the fine portico of the entrance and, before making an entry, they checked their uniforms and brushed any adhering dust off their carefully polished boots.

At this point arrived Carravoy and D'Villiers, wishing to make a show, both on their fine mounts, which were burnished to rival the black carriages that had preceded them. With a flourish both dismounted and handed the reins to the ostlers, then mounted the steps, to observe Carr and Drake making the final rounds of their uniforms. D'Villiers was as good as his word, he had sent for his "best togs" and he certainly looked the part in white doeskin breeches, high black boots with a golden tassel at the peak and his immaculately tailored Lieutenant's jacket. Carravoy, of equal means, matched him stitch for stitch and it was himself who made the quip, as they passed Carr and Drake, about "high society Officers being most fit for high society occasions". Carr thought about a reply but let it go, even more so when the next carriage brought Colonel Jamieson and Captain Tavender to the steps, both dazzling in their mid blue Light Cavalry dress uniform, with the fur-trimmed pelisse jacket hanging, as required, across one shoulder by the regulation golden cord. Carr and Drake immediately came to attention and saluted at the sight of a Colonel's uniform, but in return came neither reply nor acknowledgment. Instead the two stalked past, on and into the interior. Carr looked at Drake; he was annoyed at such a snub, which ran wholly counter to any military etiquette he had been brought up with, and he followed the pair with angry eyes as they vanished through the imposing doorway.

"Oh, like that, is it? Right."

Drake picked up his tone of annoyance.

"Never mind, what's it matter? Cavalry always have had a strange idea of superiority. Why should those two be any different? I expect they were worried that if they saluted then that weird jacket thing they wear might fall off! Or slip to the wrong angle. Come on, let's get inside, there might be something to eat."

Carr was soothed and regarded his companion amicably.

"You and your stomach."

Both entered and felt the warmth already building from a thousand candles and hundreds of humans. They both took their place in the queue that was waiting to be greeted by their host, the General, who was stood with his wife and Jane, his daughter. Carr and Jane Perry noticed each other at the same moment and Carr felt his spirits lift at the light that came into her face as she saw him and returned his gaze. At the appropriate moment she stepped forward.

"Father, may I introduce Captain Henry Carr and Lieutenant Nathaniel Drake. You may remember them from the Christmas just passed. They sang in Lady Constance's choir."

General Perry did not offer his hand.

"Yes, I remember Captain Henry Carr, but not for that reason. Still in the Army, are you, Carr? Not resigned again?"

Carr felt his teeth clamp together, but he relaxed his jaw enough to answer.

"No, Sir. I'm still here, Sir, and ready to do my duty."

"Hmmm, yes, as are many others. However, I suppose I need to thank you for that set of Cromwellian armour you sent."

Carr felt no need to remove the cold edge to his voice.

"Yes, Sir. I hope that you are pleased with it. I thought it belonged to one of Cromwell's Ironsides, and I hope it was complete."

"This time you are right on both counts. Now, I wish you both a pleasant evening."

General Perry turned abruptly to his next guest as Drake spoke his thanks, but Carr took a step on, to deliver a bow to Mrs. Perry and Jane together that was returned with delicate curtsies. Once inside Drake quickly spied out Cecily and no soldier ever marched a straighter line to take himself to his objective, taking Carr in tow. Cecily was with her parents and the introductions were made. Drake soon went off with Cecily to investigate the whereabouts of anything to eat, leaving Carr with her parents. Her mother turned to Carr.

"I understand that you sang in my sister's choir, Captain Carr."

"How kind of you, ma'am, to call it singing! But, yes, I did, Christmas just gone. It was very enjoyable, and a welcome escape from Army routine. I would go so far as to say, but with only comments afterwards to judge by, that we made a reasonably agreeable sound. I credit Lady Constance with that, she is a very fine Choir Mistress."

Mr Fynings took over.

"And you're off to fight the French soon, eh, Captain?"

"Yes Sir. We march out tomorrow, to embark at Weymouth. More than that I cannot say, for I do not know."

"Eager to capture a couple of Eagles, eh?"

212

Carr couldn't bring himself to humour so ignorant a question, but politeness required at lest some measure of indulgence.

"One can only hope, Sir, but my understanding is that they are held deep within any French column that carries one. They don't always, and a French column is a tough nut to get into. I'll be happy to see them turn around and carry it away."

"Now, now. No modesty, let's have some ambition. They're only a bunch of Frenchmen. Frogs and crapauds! No match for the likes of you."

"I can only say that I hope to justify your confidence, Mr Fynings. One thing I can say for certain is that Napoleon's men don't give best too easily, but we are determined not to let anybody down."

"Napoleon! Despicable damned little jumped up Corporal. He made himself an Emperor when he started life with no more than one pair of breeches. If I…"

Mrs Fynings interrupted.

"No politics, you promised! Captain Carr doesn't want an argument, he wants a pleasant evening. Tomorrow he marches away."

Carr had had enough.

"Yes, ma'am. Politics and soldiering really don't mix. One is too subtle to mix with the other that is too certain. But I've seen someone I was hoping to meet. If you'll excuse me? It's been a pleasure meeting you."

He bowed and left. There was no one that he had seen, but he wanted a drink and wondered if Drake had found something to eat. He looked for Jane Perry, but she was nowhere within sight, perhaps still greeting guests with her parents. That was true, for Jane Perry and her Mother were standing stead for her Father. He had gone to a side room with Colonel Lacey who had been "summoned" to attend the Ball. The conversation was not social, in fact, all such niceties were dispensed with, frozen by the frigid atmosphere between them. It began with General Perry handing Colonel Lacey a packet of papers.

"Those are your marching orders, Lacey. At Weymouth, you are to meet Captain Fallway of HMS Ipheion, he is your escort, and Captain Smallcombe of the Bidewell, he is your Senior Captain. Your other two transports are the Llewellyn and the Tansy. The last two are smaller than the Bidewell, but not by much.

You will receive further orders once you are on board, but they are not to be opened until you are well out to sea. Is that clear?"

"Yes, Sir. Perfectly."

"Buonaparte has spies everywhere, and secrecy must be protected at all times."

He looked coldly, almost angrily at Lacey.

"So, Lacey, they're keeping you together. As a Provisional Battalion."

"Yes, Sir. We remain as a unit. I'm quite content. I feel that we have built up sufficient cohesion and, as for musketry,......

"I don't agree!"

"Sir?"

"First, I didn't forget that damn shambles when you tried to form square. I wrote to Horse Guards immediately after, recommending your being broken up and sent to reinforce Line Regiments that are under strength. It seems Horse Guards think otherwise. Desperate times require desperate measures, it would seem. Perhaps your final orders will show that they have adopted my recommendation. Secondly and above all, I don't like your appointments. Carr should not be Captain of a Senior Company, he's far too unpredictable, and D'Villiers should be in a Senior Company, with the rank of Brevet Captain, under a Gazetted Captain, such as Carravoy, whom I would earmark for Brevet Major when the possibility arises. Both are from good families with the right background. D'Villiers especially has been abominably treated. I know you leave tomorrow, but I want you to be aware of my opinion before you embark. I think you've done a poor job and my prediction is disaster."

"Sir. This is neither the time nor the place to debate this in detail. I don't know what your experience is, but mine has been to serve through the only major war that this country has lost. Defeat teaches lessons, and I have tried to put into practice what I have learnt. I am prepared to stand by my decisions, Sir, come what may. I have made my judgement and I will carry the consequences. Now, if there is nothing further, Sir, I still have arrangements to make for tomorrow's march. My regards to your wife. I bid you good-night."

Lacey moved to the table to collect his shako, cloak and gloves, leaving Perry to talk to his back.

"I still say you're not up to it, Lacey, and time will prove me right. My advice is; take no risks. They'll fail you!"

By the time Perry had finished his last condemnation, Lacey had his cloak on and had his shako containing his gloves tucked under his arm. Standing by the door, he turned to face Perry, his face bearing the anger that he felt. He saluted and left.

* * *

Carr found Drake and Cecily at the buffet table and selected some of the items displayed. None were what might be called delicacies; all were rather what might be called "solid, from a good Officer's Mess". Carr stood, mostly silent, whilst Drake and Cecily indulged themselves in frivolous, but to them deeply important, conversation. Carr looked around. At least two thirds of the male guests were in uniform, many of them familiar to him from the 5th. Carravoy and D'Villiers stood by the fireplace, both drinking, D'Villiers with a disdainful expression, aping the dandy, left arm on hip, elbow jutting out, glass in right hand held before his face at just the correct jaunty angle, right boot up on the fender.

Carr grinned inwardly at the display, but the mood was soon lost. For him the evening was not going well, and he felt it. When the orchestra started up, Drake and Cecily disappeared, leaving him to his own devices. He wandered between the rooms, meeting one or two people that he knew, fellow Officers, and engaged in conversation with them that inevitably was concerned with their embarkation and where they might be going. He thought about dancing, but with the preponderance of male soldiery, very few females that may even want to dance remained without a partner. More wandering of rooms ensued until he stopped before a picture that looked like a depiction of a battle scene from the Monmouth Rebellion. He approached to study it more closely and was examining the detail, when the voice he recognised from all others spoke from behind.

"Not just books, Captain Carr, but a student of art, also."

He turned and there she was, and she brought a second smile to his face, just as the sight of her had brought the first.

"Ah, yes, well, perhaps not the style and composition and whatnot, more the subject. Soldiers have, after all, more than a passing interest for me."

A pause and one studied the other. She spoke first, her voice carrying genuine concern.

"How are you, Henry?"

"I'm well. Vigorous soldiering, you see. Good for any constitution."

The both laughed, then the pause again. Carr's turn to break the silence.

"I was hoping very much to see you again. I hope that you are well. It's been a long time, well, since Christmas!"

"I was hoping just as much to see you. Did you get the book I sent?"

"I read it."

"What did you think of it?"

Carr looked around, hoping not to see Drake.

"Erm, well, he writes all round a lot of things. Clearly a man who thinks a lot, and he likes the word "Effusion".

She laughed, "You hated it!"

"Well, no. Well, a bit. I did get to the end, however. I did give it a full go and I did read "Lines on a Friend" twice."

He paused, whilst she smiled.

"Truth is, I prefer history to novels or poetry. That's how it is, I'm sorry, I wish I could speak better of it."

"Never mind, at least we got you to read it. Anyway, Father was pleased with the armour you sent. He spent ages polishing it and fitting it around a dummy. It's now in his study. Pride of place! And he's having the cloth and leather bits made, whatever they are."

"I'm pleased to hear that, because it frightened the life out of the soldier who found it. He fell on top of it, complete with its original occupant inside."

Her face showed genuine concern.

"What did you do? With the original occupant, I mean?"

"We buried him on the spot, or at least my men did. I'm sure it was the right thing. He's amongst his comrades. Most soldiers would want it that way."

Her face grew fearful.

"So many end that way, away from home. Is that what you would want?

His own expression changed to mirror her concern.

"Yes. Absolutely. The men at your shoulder in battle are special to you. That's how it is."

He paused and tried to smile.

216

"Enough of all that, this is more morbid than your famous "Effusions"! This is a Ball, and perhaps we should dance. Shall we go into the ballroom and see if there is any room. Hey, that rhymes! Coleridge would have been proud."

She laughed, "No it doesn't rhyme. They're the same word!"

She took his arm and they followed the sound of the music. In the ballroom the military orchestra were volleying out a Muzurka. They joined in and Jane proved to be an expert dancer, whilst Carr made a reasonable fist of keeping his place. He, however, made a thorough hash of the Quadrille that followed, but counted it a draw when he completed a Polonaise with some style. He heard with gratitude the call for the main buffet and they took their places to wait, during which Carr held forth about Army food, especially on campaign. Each was obtaining a necessary plate, when General Perry came to them both, clearly not content with developments. Carr he ignored.

"Jane, there is someone that I wish you to meet. Never mind the food, you can get some later." This reinforced by his hand through her upper arm to lead her away. The General turned to Carr, his tone dismissive, barely giving Carr a glance.

"You will excuse us, Captain Carr, but I need Jane elsewhere."

Carr fully felt the contempt in both the voice and face of the General and felt no need for excessive courtesy, nor to reassure him about the future.

"Of course, General. It has been a pleasure to meet you again, Miss Perry. I hope we can meet again before we march away."

"I hope so too, Captain Carr. If you'll excuse me, I think I'm needed elsewhere?"

Carr bowed to both, but not before he had caught the anxiety in her eyes. However, the General was impatient.

"Perhaps, but I doubt it. Now, we go, Jane, if you please." She was led away.

Carr studied the food before him on the table, trying to make a choice, even whether to choose anything. His deliberations were interrupted by a voice from the far side of the table, again one he recognised, but with a very different reaction.

"You seem out of favour with the General, Captain Carr. Not fit company for his daughter, was it?"

Carr raised his eyes to see Captain Tavender, still resplendent in his dress uniform, an amused and insulting look still on his face, which matched his tone. Carr changed his gaze to the uniform itself. It was the most amazing collection of brocade and embroidery, cords and arrows going in all directions, doubled by the pelisse jacket.

"Well, Captain Tavender, at least in my uniform I look like an escort, however much in passing, rather than someone who needs to be carefully chaperoned and escorted onto the dance floor!"

He returned his plate and walked away, giving Tavender no further regard. He kept moving, in black mood, wondering whether to return to their billet, but he remembered that this was his last night in England and he should make the best of it. Luckily he found Drake and Cecily, both at the peak of cheerfulness and his spirits rose.

"Ah, Henry. There you are. Cecily wants to dance with you. Something about higher military rank causing a move up the social strati. She's decided I'm too lowly."

"You're talking nonsense again, Nathaniel, be quiet! Yes, Captain Carr, I must insist that you honour me with a dance."

"The honour is all mine, Miss Fynings, but I can only hope that it is not a Quadrille. I've just made a most fearful jumble of one of those."

Drake had been listening.

"So you have been dancing, not prowling about like some "out of sorts" bear. With whom?"

"You can guess, I feel sure," and he and Cecily joined the lines for a Polonaise, to Carr's great relief. However, that was short lived. Tavender was in the line and clearly smarting at Carr's earlier jibe. As they passed, and it was quite often, Tavender lost no opportunity to deliver a goading "hurry up, Carr", "close the line", "must be quick". For the sake of Cecily, who was thoroughly enjoying the moves involved, as was her nature, Carr said nothing, but he was grateful when the music ended and he escorted her back to Drake. However, Tavender was not done. He followed Carr and, whilst stood behind him, leaned over to say into his ear,

"You know, Carr, it is my understanding that in some parts of the Americas they have such a thing as a square dance. Perhaps you should take yourself over there, you might learn a thing or two."

Luckily, Cecily had moved off to talk to friends, only Drake heard. As Tavender walked away, Carr made to follow him, but Drake seized his arm.

"I'm going to hit him."

"No you are not. The last thing you need is another duel. Look, over there. There's Jane Perry, with Carravoy. He's talking to her, no doubt being as insufferable as ever, talking about some staggering achievement of his, but she is looking at you. Get yourself over there, "Sir", and get her out of it."

Carr saw Jane and immediately his mood changed. Then he grinned at Drake's reverse use of rank, something so rarely mentioned between them.

"Go on, Henry. Forward march. The cause is hers."

Carr looked at him and received no further words, just a nod of Drake's head. He looked again and Jane Perry was still studying him. Squaring his shoulders, he crossed the floor. He decided that it would be best to be as civil as possible. He began with greetings.

"Miss Perry. Charles. Excuse me, Charles, but I wonder if you would allow me a quiet word with Miss Perry? There is something I would ask her to do for me, whilst we are abroad."

Carravoy turned and showed his irritation, partly at who was asking, but mostly at the idea that Jane Perry could be taken from his company, he felt he was doing rather well and building a good impression. However, habit and breeding did not allow his irritation to show within the effortless superiority of his voice.

"I'd like to, Carr, but you see, the thing is, her Father the General, has required me to keep you, away, from her, for the rest of the evening. Nothing I can do. General's orders, so goodbye!"

Jane Perry had heard all and it was her turn for irritation.

"I'll make any necessary excuses to my Father, Captain Carravoy, I will ensure that you are blameless. I know what Captain Carr wishes to speak to me about, and I also wish it to be finalised."

With that she took Carr's arm and began walking, almost pulling Carr, who quickly followed. Carravoy was not done.

"This could go hard on you, Carr."

But it was Jane Perry who turned to answer.

"The choice is mine, Lord Carravoy, not his!"

She was taking the lead, and she drew him to an alcove behind the colonnade that ran down one side. She turned to him and lowered her face, but raised her eyes to his and placed her hand upon his forearm.

"We haven't much time. Father will send out a search party, I'm sure. What was it you wanted?"

"Only to seek your permission to write to you, whilst I'm away."

He placed his hand on hers. The dam burst.

"When you're away, it's good to have someone to think of and better still, to know that they're thinking of you. For me, that's you. It matters to any soldier, especially this one, to have someone special to them back home, perhaps waiting, and someone that he can say things to, even from a long way away, and even if it reaches them long after the time. When I'm out there, wherever it is, when I'm writing, I can picture you, and ………."

She halted his rush of words by squeezing his forearm.

"Hush, you're wasting time. Yes, of course you can write, and I will write to you, but you mustn't send it to my home. Father will almost certainly intercept. Is there anything that we can do instead?"

Carr's face screwed up in thought. He formed an answer.

"In the barracks there will be a Deputy Purser left behind to look after the financial affairs. I can write to you, care of him. He will receive a great deal of mail, any extra letter won't make much difference. Wait a month, then letters may start to arrive."

"Yes, but don't address them to Jane Perry, rather Jane Emily, that's one of my middle names."

He smiled and she giggled at the conspiracy, but it was short lived. The General had found them, informed by an Aide de Camp who had spied their whereabouts.

"Jane! Come, we're leaving. Come, this instant, if you please!"

Jane looked at Carr and saw a warm smile and eyes that she saw smile for the first time. She withdraw her arm and said 'Goodbye' which Carr returned, then away to her Father's side, then to be swallowed up in his retinue. Carr followed her fair hair through the varied light of the ballroom and then she was gone. He took himself off to find Drake and Cecily, his spirits at their highest for some time.

Back in the several rooms of the barracks, the mood was more sombre. All had a four-day march to prepare for and old soldiers prepared and the new ones copied and listened. Boots were checked and hose mended, pack straps tried and adjusted to spread the load that would be their burden throughout the long marching days. There was little humour, just fond looks and fond touches between wives and husbands, children and fathers. Of course, not all families were staying behind and so they, too, made their preparations, particularly the families Nicholls and Mulcahey; they were all adjusting their straps and buckles like the veterans they were. If there was any cheer, it was amongst these old hands, all born up with the excitement of a new life in the offing, a major change, and if not one for the better, well, no matter.

Not so Molly Dixon and John Davey. With Tilly on his knee he was using the last few minutes before lights out to explain his plans. Having packed and arranged all his kit ready for the immediate parade in the morning, he had placed before Molly a leather purse and an envelope, but it was Molly who was doing the talking.

"But I wants to come down to Weymouth with 'ee, John."

"That's no good, Molly, 'twon't serve. It's a four day walk. Think of the time and money it'll take to get you back, even to here. When I go, you go on."

As anxious as she, his instructions became rambling and fretful.

"There's the money, Molly, all I have and some borrowed. Far Devening is the place, and the man you need is Reverend Blackmore. That's the letter; I got Parson to write it for me and I've signed it. It says that you are my wife and it asks him to take you to my Mother's cottage and explain what has happened to me. If you get yourself to Devizes and go to the Matthews Corn Chandler's in Devizes, they've always got wagons going out that way and they'll give you a ride to the exact place. I've been to the Purser and he's goin' to send on my pay to the Reverend where you can collect it. Parson says he'll help me write to you, and I'll send it to the Reverend and he'll help you read it. There's two things more that will convince my Mother to take you in. One's this."

He removed a leather wristband from his left wrist. It had a chased design on the outer surface.

"She'll know it comes from me because it was my Father's. The other's this," and he pushed across a thin silver ring. "I made it from a shilling, I bored out a hole, then filed it down. You wear this, and it'll at least look as though we're some kind of married."

Molly took the ring and tried it on the third finger. It was loose, and she turned it around her finger, but it stayed.

"Don't worry about that, Mother will fatten you up!"

Molly reached across the table, got her forearm around his neck and kissed him, then everyone kissed everyone else, Davey, Tilly and Molly. Lights out came and all made ready for bed. When the candles were robbed of their flame, many a husband and wife lay together in intimacy for the last time, but many also lay awake, both wife and children in the crook of each arm.

* * *

Reveille came too soon and also the end of their last meal. Too soon also, came the order to parade outside and all took themselves across the parade ground to their familiar positions. There all stood to wait, arms grounded, hands either grasping the muzzle of their musket or making last adjustments to their kit and pack straps. Another grey day, some blue sky and another "Channel wind". A band had arrived and were tuning up, their discordant notes adding to the general hubbub of conversation, shouted orders, and horses hooves and harness. Sergeant Major Gibney, now, since marching orders, appointed Senior Sergeant Major, called the parade to attention. The familiar orders rang out and led by the band, as yet silent, they marched out of the gate for the last time, Grenadiers behind the band, then the Light Company, then the Companies by numbers. Outside was the Supply Train and the families that were to go, the familes of the rankers on foot, those of officers in carriages, mostly closed or hooded for comfort. Those staying lined the route down into the town and as the soldiers marched through, there were many shouts of "Goodbye and good luck", terminated by the name of the soldier that it was wished upon, this accompanied by the tearful and vigorous waving of hats and handkerchiefs.

222

All too soon the road was empty, all that could be seen were the backs of the camp followers as they brought up the rear behind the supply train. As the column passed the first buildings of the town the band struck up the tune of "Kemp's Jig" in marching time, as much to clear the route as to add to the drama of the occasion. At the sound of the martial music the good citizens of Taunton, such as were near, brought themselves to the edge of the road, to watch and cheer the fine sight. Carr marched on foot, at the head of his Company, Drake just behind to his right, Rushby to his left. He could see Colonel Lacey up ahead, on horseback with his Majors, the first of the battalion behind the band, but nothing else could he see but the backs of the last rank of the Grenadiers and the passing faces off to the sides. Soon the gaps between the buildings grew larger, the town was falling behind and the cheering now came from individual voices, but one individual voice stood out, from the left, one he recognised from all others.

"Henry."

He turned and there she was, her face both smiling and tearful framed in a blue bonnet trimmed with white small lace, her coat decorated across with mauve coloured bands, her hands in matching gloves. It was one of those hands that was waving him across to the side of the road for she was keeping pace with the parade. Irregular as it was, still carrying his erect sword, he took a swerving course across to her. She spoke.

"No one knows I'm down here. Here, take this, it will bring you luck."

He looked down and in her hand was a silver medallion complete with chain. There was no time for an examination, he took it and thrust it into his pocket. The chain still dangled out, but she corrected that.

"Thank you. It's... I'll... keep it close... and wear it, always."

"It'll bring you luck. Don't forget to write, and don't forget to come back!"

Then, scandalously, she kissed his cheek, waved, and was gone. He felt a wet tear remaining on the side of his face.

All this had not gone unnoticed in the front rank of his company and the comments came forward.

"One there to come back for, eh, Sir?"

Drake took charge,

"Silence in the ranks, there," but all were wearing broad grins.

223

* * *

The band had long past fallen out from the column, but they had added their shouts of good luck and good fortune as the column marched on by. After that, the day passed to the accompaniment of 1,000 pairs of feet, or more. Old hands were glad at the return of winter weather for the first day's march, not too cold, but above all not too warm. For a public parade their stocks were required and it was not long before sweat trickled down inside collars and the hated stiff leather began to chafe all it touched. All were mostly sombre and grave, there was little conversation, minds were elsewhere, if not with families left behind, then with their possible destination, the subject of what talk there was.

Deakin and Halfway were marching together in Number 3 Company, both thinking over in their different ways the meaning of Captain Heaviside's brief Christian homily to his men, prior to their outward march. "Upon this rock I will build my church; and the gates of hell shall not prevail against it. Matthew: 6. Verse 18."

"What do you think he was goin' on about, Ned?'

"Blessed if I know. It meant something to him, if not to me. If he takes comfort, then he can spout all he likes, long as it don't cause him to volunteer us for any double dangerous doings when the bullets starts to fly. When's the first stop, do 'ee reckon?"

"Two hours more."

"How much water you got?"

"Full canteen."

"Right, then we've spare for a bit of a wet."

With that he pulled a red kerchief from his pocket, wetted it, and shared it with his friend to cool and clean their faces.

Campaign habits were soon resurrected. They loosened their stocks and reset the straps that criss-crossed their chests and shoulders. Soon after they changed their muskets to a different shoulder.

However, one amongst them felt more reason for cheer than all others. For the first time since entering the barracks, all those months ago, Seth Tiley was looking upon the outside world. He had expected by now to be bound behind a wagon, but no. Perhaps he had been forgotten, perhaps no one thought of it,

224

but here he was now, in his Grenadier uniform, his packs and equipment spread over his huge frame, marching free with all the others. He knew that they were ship bound and, once aboard, he was an army prisoner forever; which was just how he saw it. Years to him constituted a lifetime and these final days marching presented him with his only chance. The cunning that had seen him through his malevolent life so far, now told him that night would present his best and really only, chance. The battalion had a deadline to meet, then to board ship. If he escaped now, none could be spared to search for him. He marched on, keeping step and keeping counsel with himself and making plans; once he was away, what was his best course? One thing was prominent in his mind, the further South he was taken, the lower his chances. He would be trapped against the sea when the Provosts began their search and he knew his height and bulk pointed him out from most others.

The first halt brought the most welcome order, "Remove stocks". Once removed, some, the new recruits especially, thought of throwing them away, what use would they be abroad, but the likes of Tom Miles, Ned Deakin, and Toby Halfway counselled otherwise, "If they calls for a parade for some foreign bigwig, and you don't have, it'll be a flogging" and so they were stored down into their packs. Using the break, whilst sat with Drake at the side of the road, Carr studied the medallion. He had glanced at it on the march, but now was the chance for a careful examination. The front showed St. George slaying his dragon but the engraving on the reverse was the subject of long study, "To Henry, from Jane."

"What's that?"

"A medallion, from Jane Perry."

"Well, that's that, then. Exchanging medallions and suchlike means that you are practically engaged. On which subject, I have some news."

"Which is?"

"Cecily and I are engaged. Unofficially, that is. We've told no one. You're the first and I've only told you now, being as we are now on our outward march. Couldn't tell you earlier, you being such a blabbermouth."

Carr grinned. "My dear fellow, my heartiest congratulations. Do you anticipate any opposition, parentwise, that is?"

"I'd say not, we get on fine, but we won't spring the news until I get a Captaincy. It isn't the pay, coming from a family calling itself "Honourable" does have its pecuniary advantages, but a higher rank will all add to my chances. Don't you think?"

"Yes, my dear chap. Absolutely."

"May I see?"

Carr handed the medallion across. Drake looked at the front, but thought better of examining the back.

"St George. Patron Saint of soldiers. You'd better put it on now. Losing it and not being able to produce it on our return, spells catastrophe. No explanation possible."

Carr obeyed. He loosened his collar, put the chain over his head and let the medallion slip down the front of his neck. It's bulk felt cold against his chest, but it soon warmed.

* * *

The day's march ended and camp was made in fields beside the road. Some Officers took themselves off to any local town or village that had an Inn which could provide a more comfortable billet, Carravoy and D'Villiers included, but this did not apply to either Carr, Drake, nor Rushby. One thing the manuals said and Carr agreed, was, "Stay with your men, share their hardships", and so he was touring the campfires of the Light Company, having sent Drake and Rushby off on their own tour, asking after the men's welfare, giving help and guidance where he could, sharing a cup of tea when offered, and answering their questions, all except the important one; "Where are we going, Sir?"

Seth Tiley welcomed the fall of the sun and the dismissal off the road. He had quickly made his own fire and camp arrangements on the very edge of the area occupied by the Grenadiers. He had no messmates. Those who had approached him, impressed with his defiance at the flogging, were quickly spurned and all quickly learned that he was best left alone. Those that he shared his rations with had learned to give him his share and then leave him. This suited him well, as he chewed his ration of boiled beef and ate all he could, unlike those around him who knew to eke out their rations. He planned to leave all behind and food was best inside his stomach, not weighty around his shoulders. Stealing and sheep killing would provide for his

226

future needs. A mist fell with the dark and he knew his chance had come. As dark grew thicker, hastened by the mist, "Lights Out", came and he unrolled his greatcoat and smeared its back and arms with mud. He threw on grass and sweepings to stick over that, then he lay still and waited, covered by the greatcoat; camouflaged side in, clean side out.

His position was deliberately close to the sentry line, sufficient to let him know when an Officer had made his rounds. Past midnight he heard a challenge, the reply came and he took this as his time. Sentries would know that they now had time to themselves and heads would go down into collars, minds more concerned about the cold; why be watchful, they were still in England? He doused the last glow of his fire, shed his red jacket and lay on the ground, covering his head, shoulders, and back with his mudcaked greatcoat, then he slowly crawled forward, aiming to bisect the point between two sentries. The mist helped, he made no noise, moving inch by inch, and anyone looking across would think him a shape on the rough ground. Finally, he was confident that the mist and dark were hiding him and he moved more quickly. Further on still he stood up, donned the greatcoat and was gone, running and stumbling in a direction that he thought was back North, away from the sea and, above all, away from this hated life as a soldier. The luck that had given him the mist held further. He came across an isolated cottage, smashed his way in, pummelled the occupants until either senseless or paralysed with terror and stole what food there was and any useful clothing. Seth Tiley, thief, thug and footpad, was back on the road.

His absence was only discovered with the dawn, his kit left behind, bar the greatcoat, providing clear testimony to the fact that an escape was intended and that it had been successful. Carravoy was the Captain of Grenadiers and Colonel Lacey called him to his tent for an explanation, but none could he give. He had not been in camp. Why had Tiley not been watched or even tethered? No answer; no one had thought of it. Lacey did not hide his displeasure at so valuable a man, a Grenadier, being so easily lost. Carravoy was left in no doubt that he was responsible and such a dereliction must not occur again. Carravoy left the tent, smarting and angry.

* * *

227

If there was a green that spoke of England, it was the Dorset green of the Spring of 1806. The elder bushes were long out, wasting no growing time, but the pure new green of the bursting chestnut, beech, and elm trees along the way did not pass unnoticed by any in that column that made it's way, march by march, down to the sea at Weymouth. Nor the quintessential Dorset villages, colours bright in the clear sunshine, mothers and daughters stood in doorways, white aprons showing bright from the shade, children laughing and cheering, keeping step and old men, some old soldiers, who could remember Woolfe and the Plains of Abraham, or even the perilous march forward at Minden. Labourers waved from the barns and pastures beyond the road and feelings were mixed within many in the ranks, as they thought of those in the fields with a life of little danger, but each day one of drudging labour that did little more than keep body and soul united. Themselves, now with the adventurous and varied life of a soldier, but marching to who knew what perils.

Dorchester was the last major town they passed through and those citizens that were about their early morning business and were near enough, came to the roadside to cheer. On then, out onto the straight Roman road that led down to the sea, the low ramparts on the high hill of Maiden Castle provided passing interest for many, but for more the sight of the sea through the valley beyond held their attention fixed. Just before the port of Weymouth, the column swung off the road and onto the downs to make their final camp. Lacey had suffered one desertion, there was not going to be another. Guards were to be paired and regularly changed, Officers were expected to remain in camp and be assiduous with their rounds. The camp quickly spread across the rolling green upland and all settled to their business, be it repairing the damage of four days marching, or writing last letters home. The latter occupied both Drake and Carr, but whilst words came easily to Drake, not so to Carr, letter writing being consistently outside of his experience. He sat with the medallion in front of him, hoping for more inspiration than the simple "miss you and will be thinking of you".

"Do you think I should say that her medallion is big enough to stop a bullet? Keep me safe that way?"

"Absolutely and completely not! Of all that is dunce and dunderhead. Dangers are not to be mentioned, ever. Tell her about the last time you saw her, what you thought and felt, lots of it. Let it go at that. Close early, tell her that duty calls. Stop a bullet! I don't know where the poet lies in you, Henry, but it's deep, deep, down."

He paused, movement at the camp entrance caught his eye.

"Developments! The Navy has arrived, on horseback. I think things could be moving, perhaps quickly."

Two Naval Officers had arrived, one with the epaulettes of a Royal Navy Captain, the other in more plain garb, but also Navy colours. Carr and Drake followed their route through the camp; plainly they were being conducted to the tent of Colonel Lacey. They entered and the tent flap closed. Drake drew the conclusion.

"Orders soon, I'll not be surprised."

He was not wrong. Within an hour Lacey called Captains and Majors to his tent. Carr arrived at the tent anxious for what Lacey had to tell them.

"Gentlemen, we sail on the night tide, if this wind holds. We embark at night. Napoleon has spies everywhere and our escort, Captain Fallway, does not want anyone to see which way we go, once in the Channel and past Portland. The French have fast, well armed Privateers that range up and down their coast and we have only HMS Ipheion as protection, a two masted brig, all that can be spared. We will be in three ships, the largest, the Bidewell, will hold the Grenadiers, the Light, and Companies One, Two and Three. The Llewellyn, will hold Companies Four, Five, and Six. The last the Tansy, will hold Seven and Eight Companies, our stores, that are being loaded as we speak, and the camp followers. See that your men are fed and paraded at sunset. Thank you, Gentlemen, that will be all."

Carr returned and spread the word, to Drake, Rushby, and his Sergeants. They were to eat at four, parade at six. Ellis spoke the question all wanted to ask.

"Do you know where, Sir?"

"No Sergeant. I suspect that the Colonel does, but he's not telling anyone. The French have spies here, we can be certain, and would give anything to know our destination. Even just to know if we are going up or down Channel. So, we have our orders. We will be marching soon after six."

Soon Ration Call was heard and soon after that the sights and smells of cooking, campaign food, boiled salt beef, dried peas and biscuit. As the men ate and the afternoon waned into evening, the Officers took the chance to bid farewell to their families, those that had decided to accompany them down to embarkation and were dismayed at the speed with which they would be leaving, not even one more day, nor even half a day. Padraigh O'Hare was one such and left the camp to see his family safe into an Inn, before returning back to the camp. On his return, clearly heavy spirited and saddened, the Officer on duty at the camp gate happened to be Captain Carr.

"I trust you left them all well, Sir, and they are not too down-hearted."

"Thank you, Captain Carr. Yes, I left them well, although somewhat down, but only to be expected. But having said that, I've been away before, they all know how it happens, and it's not for ever."

"Yes, Sir. Will they take ship to Ireland or cross country?"

"Cross country, to be sure. My wife is not a good sailor, and our home is up North. A short voyage from Liverpool is the best she can manage. I want them at sea as brief a time as possible. As the Colonel said; French Privateers!"

"Yes Sir, sailing across, that far up the Irish Sea will make them as safe as can be hoped."

"Yes, Captain. I'm sure you're right. Now, let's all see to our business."

* * *

The parade formed in the dying light, the offshore wind, so desired by departing Captains, played with the shako plumes above their heads and the new grass at their feet. The Light Company was second to the Grenadiers and Carr paced up and down before his men, impatient for why he knew not, and his anxiety was matched by all around him. He came up to Rushby and found him, with a small knife, packing soil into a small box, much like a snuffbox.

"What are you about, Barnaby?"

"I, well, just wanted to take a little bit of the home country with me, Sir. You know Sir, something to look at whilst we're away. A bit of nonsense, really."

"No, Barnaby, not nonsense at all. But I'm anxious that you take that sketchbook of yours. I hope you are taking one with plenty of spare capacity. You're sure to see much that you'd like to record. We'll all want to see the results, when we get back."

"Yes Sir. I will be taking my sketchbook, but returning to this, Sir," indicating the soil in the dying light, "if the worst does happen, you'll see that this goes in with me, Sir, won't you?"

"Enough of all that, Barnaby. You'll be looking at that box when you're a retired General, but, yes, of course, be assured, I'll make sure."

Orders were resounding around the camp and the Grenadiers had faced left. Soon they marched out and Carr repeated the orders to his own command. In no time at all, the whole battalion was marching downhill along the main turnpike into Weymouth. Such civilians as were out, mostly homeward labourers, stood and watched, but in silence and also in homage, perhaps? They knew the time they lived in and it took little imagination to realise that many of the men they watched marching past, of the same clay as themselves, would remain where they were destined for, and not see England again. They followed them with their eyes as the column of common soldiers marched to the quayside towards the three sets of masts silhouetted against the last dying light.

As they progressed along the quayside, Carr studied the names embossed beneath the wide cabin windows of each ship as their sterns loomed up beneath the thick latticework of rigging, spars and masts. Tansy, Llewellyn, Bidewell, their ship was the last. The Grenadiers were already aboard and filing down the several hatches to their berths below. Carr held his men back until told to come aboard and he led the way, following the seaman and taking his men along dimly lit companionways, which seemed to have every conceivable obstacle built into them to hamper their progress without totally halting it; low beams, buttresses, steep ladders, and tight turns. Eventually, in what seemed the deepest bowels of the ship, their place was indicated and Carr watched the men take a hammock from a pile and claim their places. He was there to check the quality of their quarters, also to halt any squabbles and arguments, but he was very satisfied that none arose. The Bidewell had been built as a troop transport and he left them arranging their equipment on the many hooks and pegs, the experienced telling the inexperienced to "keep your kit off the deck".

The embarkation was rapid; what had earlier been a thronged and busy quay now held just the few of the Officer's families who had followed in their coaches to wave their last goodbyes. Carr, Drake, and Rushby, content that their men were safely lodged below, leaned on the side of the ship watching the last events they would see in England for some time. Mostly it was last conversations, shouted up and down, Major O'Hare and his family being the main contributors. Mrs O'Hare, whom the three saw for the first time, was clearly a handsome woman, well dressed and above average height, but they could see little of her face behind the white handkerchief held permanently to her weeping eyes. The other events told of imminent departure, mooring lines were being loosened along the quayside of all three ships and the activities on each forecastle confirmed that towing lines were being attached to the longboats of each vessel, so that each could be eased out of the harbour to pick up the fortuitous North wind.

The moorings were loosened and fell away into the inky black water to be retrieved in an instant by the skilled efforts of the sailors. The gap between the tumblehome of the Bidewell and the quayside grew and the features on the quay began to fall back astern, all that kept pace were the final few members of the families on the quayside, anxious to prolong the send-off as much as possible. Eventually the end of the quay came and this gap also grew so that faces could no longer be discerned in the dark, just the last shaking of white, tear damp handkerchiefs. The ships passed across and beyond the lights on the high peak of Portland Bill and then sail could safely be set for the open sea to take them South, down to The Channel proper. The longboats were recovered and all felt the ship heel to the pressure of the wind on the spread canvas and after came the motion of the sea. The Ipheion was waiting in the bay and she became more discernable, as her canvas, pale but just visible in the dark, appeared out in the bay above her riding lights. The dark bulk of Portland Bill passed to starboard and all Officers took whatever vantage points offered themselves to look at the disappearing lights of Weymouth town. No one spoke.

A French agent, high on the downs of their recent camp, sat a fast horse, secure in the dark, and watched the lights of the four vessels converge together as the distance increased. He waited for them to make their turn, either up or down Channel, but then he cursed. At a signal gun all lights went out together and out in the Channel, beyond the Bill, was nought but all concealing darkness.

* * *

"Shoot me!"

"I will not. I have only one pistol and I am saving that for myself. Besides, Cecily would never speak to me again."

"Oh, this is death, how much more? This up and down and side to side, and the noise. The permanent creak and groan and rattle. When we get back, I'm transferring to the Militia and manning a well built fort. Can this get any worse, Carr, do you think? I don't see how, I've never felt so bad."

Carr looked over at his companion, whose green complexion did nothing to reduce his own feeling of wretchedness. Drake had just returned from one of several visits to the leeward side of the ship and he was contemplating another of his own, but there were always at least 50 competing for places. He sat up from his cot, seized the door handle in both hands and thus anchored tried to convince himself that he felt better.

"How's Rushby?"

"Absolutely fine. The scut's up on deck, sketching if you please. Says he quite enjoys the "pitch and send" as the sailors call it. Oh God, excuse me, old fellow, but I feel I must return to the deck."

Drake took his exit, in a hurry. Carr groaned and again resumed his position, leaning his forehead against the door edge and staring at the deck between his wrists as the ship performed another reel and curtsy.

Above them a meeting was in progress in the main cabin, Lacey, O'Hare, Captain Fallway and Captain Smallcombe, Commanding Officer of the Bidewell. The latter two looked at the two soldiers, trying to detect any mal-de-mer, but saw none. Fallway asked after their wellbeing.

"Are you both coping? This is a wicked sea."

Lacey answered.

"Yes, we are both well. We have both endured long sea voyages, and we know the correct manouevres."

The ship made another swerve and the decanter of Chablis, put there for refreshment, took on a life of its own as if by some ghostly hand and slid alarmingly across the polished table. With his left hand Lacey halted its progress and placed it in the fiddle of the serving table behind. His right was occupied with a bundle of oiled cloth, tied about with red ribbon, not yet undone because of the red wax seal that bound the knot together. Lacey quickly broke it and found the most important piece of paper, their orders and their destination. They confirmed their Naval orders to sail down Channel. He read the necessary himself then turned the paper around so that all could see. Their destination was Sicily; after a call at Gibraltar for supplies, their orders were to join the force at Messina under the command of Major General John Stuart. Lacey looked at those about him.

"Gentlemen, I'm sure I do not need to tell you that this information must remain with us four only, even after our call at Gibraltar."

* * *

Immediately after leaving harbour, the small convoy had quickly picked up the fast ebb tide off Portland Bill and, under easy canvas, they had made good progress down Channel until dawn, keeping both France and England down over the horizon. However, with the dawn, the wind backed to almost due West and blew strong against them, setting up a regular sea, equal waves, separated by equal distance. The ships had no choice but to tack diagonally across, starting a corkscrew motion of up to the crest and down, simultaneous with rolling side to side as they slanted down into a trough, or up and out of one. There was no change for three days and almost all the soldiers aboard were suffering in this, the worst sea of all for the unseaworthy.

Joe Pike could barely move, sprawled mostly on the deck, shoulders and back propped up against the ship's side. His eyes were closed with exhaustion and his head lolled forward over a jacket stained with vomit from days before. Tom Miles and Ned Deakin were bending over him.

"Something's got to be done, Ned. This boy's not drunk nor eaten nothin' since dawn on the first day. He could go from thirst, at this rate."

234

"You're not wrong. This sea's makin' the worst passage I've known. Half the battalion's fit for nuthin'. We needs to ease the feeling of a movin' ship. Get him in his hammock, that'll at least take away some of all this rollin' and pitchin'. Here, Pat, Davey, give us a hand."

Joe's hammock was slung between hooks and all four lifted his almost lifeless figure up and into it's welcoming shape. Deakin gave his orders.

"Now, Davey, you seems able to cope, and you too, Tom. Let it swing side to side, but try to hold it steady end to end. Now..."

He leaned over Joe and pulled up his own canteen, drawing water to wet the ailing Joe's lips.

"...Joe. Can you hear me?"

The water seemed to have revived him somewhat. He opened his eyes and gave a groan.

"Joe. Take a drink of water. You must drink. Then, keep your eyes open and fixed on a point above you. You'll feel more steady. As soon as you feels able, take a drink of water, often. That's vital."

For the rest of that day, the four administered unto the desperately seasick Joe, but Deakin's solution began to bear fruit. After a few hours, Joe did feel better and began to drink more regularly. The next night in his hammock held onto his progress and the next day their course turned South and the wind dropped and veered back to North West. The motion of the ships eased in the irregular sea and while not steady and still, to all aboard, after days of rolling and rising, by comparison the ships felt firm and stable. The ships held a permanent heel to larboard as the steady North Westerly came over the starboard quarter and soon all aboard began to feel new strength in their sea legs, as the convoy progressed on and into easy sailing in the Bay of Biscay under a late April sky.

* * *

The two white shapes, far out on the Western horizon, had caught up, drawn level and were now moving ahead. Since dawn, together they had been the subjects of every telescope on every vessel and now, as they took a course that brought them closer, their worst fears were confirmed.

"Two heavy French Privateers, probably twins and built for the job. Topsail schooners, probably six 18's each side."

This was the conclusion of Captain Smallcombe, emphatically closing the sections of his ancient spyglass.

"What are they trying to do?" asked Colonel Lacey.

"This wind is almost right against us. They are heading us to get the weather gauge, then they can turn and come down on the wind and choose whatever suits them best. Depends on what the Ipheion does, but they probably plan for one of them to keep her busy whilst the other takes one of us. I expect that to be this ship, we make the biggest prize."

"Why are they overtaking us so easily?"

"They're schooners, fore and aft rig. They can sail closer to the wind than we, and so on the same heading, into the wind, they're faster than we. Very handy vessels, perfect for commerce raiding."

He pointed to the spars above, strained around their masts as much as possible, but only gaining leverage from the wind for little more than two knots.

"That's the best we can get, without tacking, and we can't do that, with them to the West and the Spanish coast to the East. They could have us against that. With this wind, we're almost becalmed. They've got us bottled!"

Three days sailing across the Bay of Biscay had seen the wind change to a hampering South Westerly. Both the Llewellyn and the Tansy were poor sailors into the wind and through the night they had dropped behind, almost a mile back. They showed as little more than white shapes over the Bidewell's stern counter. Half a mile off to the West the Ipheion had cleared for action and her 9 guns showed through their gunports, White Ensigns at her stern and mastheads. She had hauled her wind and was closing with the Bidewell. Smallcombe continued his analysis.

"If the Ipheion sails out to meet them, they'll take her, one each side. They can dance around her and hit from where she can't hit back. A British warship is a good prize by herself, and then we'll be at their mercy anyway. They won't pair up on her close to us, because we can come to her support, just about. So, they know the Ipheion will guard one side, and one of 'em will keep her occupied, tacking and turning, just keeping away from her broadsides. The other will come t'other side, board and capture one of us, put on a prize crew, then sail on. The Ipheion will have saved two of us, the French will have got the other."

The Ipheion had come within hailing distance. Fallway was up in her rigging with a speaking trumpet. He confirmed what Smallcombe had said.

"I'll hold this side. They'll split and come on, one at me and one at you. Do your best. Good luck."

With that, the Ipheion tacked away with immaculate seamanship and made some distance to hold off the attack when it came, but the two shapes, pure white but malignant to all, continued to gain heading. It was not yet Noon, they had plenty of time.

Lacey turned to Smallcombe.

"May we use your cabin, Captain, for a council? Will you join us?"

"Yes to both, Colonel."

Lacey turned to O'Hare.

"Call all Officers, Majors and Captains, to the Captain's cabin. Five minutes."

All arrived sooner and Lacey lost no time in addressing the assembly.

"Soon we will have a heavily armed French Privateer sailing down on us. They want to capture us and take us into a French port. We are the biggest prize, and the nearest. The Ipheion will deal with one; we have to deal with the other. Any ideas?"

There was stunned silence, but it was Carravoy that broke it.

"Sir, we have over 400 trained soldiers aboard, surely we can do something?"

Smallcombe spoke up.

"We must hope that they think us to be supply transports. They have to board us to capture us as a prize. If they think that we are stuffed full of soldiers they won't try, but they'll stand off and pound us to matchwood with their guns, then go on to do the same to the Llewellyn and the Tanzy. They'll get a fine payment for sinking a whole battalion of British soldiers."

Silence again, then Carr spoke.

"Sir. If we can convince them that we are supply ships, merchantmen, then they will come alongside. That will give us a chance to board her ourselves. Captain Smallcombe, what would they expect to see as they sailed down onto a prize such as ourselves, if we were a merchantman?"

Smallcombe paused, then answered.

"She would expect to see the crew give her up and sail for the two astern. They appreciate that the crew would not want to be taken prisoner, that the crew would know that they had no chance and so the crew takes themselves off. It's the common result. If we slacken the sheets and let the sails hang limp, they'll think that we're giving her to them, in return for being allowed to escape."

"There, Sir. It's a start. If the French see no soldiers and a crew taking off in the longboat, giving her to the French, then they will come alongside, and that'll be our chance, Sir."

Lacey took it up.

"Right, we've got them alongside, what then?"

Carravoy grinned. "We're all waiting behind the bulwark and we stand up and give 'em a volley."

Smallcombe spoke up.

"Beggin your pardon, Sir, but 'twon't serve. These Privateers is stuffed full of men. You won't down a quarter of 'em. They'll sheer off and man their guns, just like I said."

Lacey spoke again.

"So we must hold them fast to us to give us a chance to board them. Any ideas, Smallcombe."

"They will throw over grappling irons to pull the two ships together. All right, you blows away their boarding party. We then have to use their grapnels on their own ship, and our own that we have, to hold the ships together. It won't be easy, after seeing you they'll be doing their damndest to sheer off, cutting the grappling ropes and setting sail, which, with this wind, will move them away."

Lacey gave his orders.

"Right. Carravoy, your Grenadiers are on the grappling hooks, our own, and also to use any thrown over by the French that can be pulled aboard and then used on them. Carr, your riflemen and any other useful marksmen are to prevent any Frenchman from cutting a grappling rope. No. 3 will give the first volley. One and Two will hold the ship and wait below. O'Hare, you're in command of our deck. Good, I think we have a chance."

Carr gave voice to his idea.

"The longboat, Sir. It doesn't have to be seamen in it. The seamen will be needed here. If the longboat had our soldiers, dressed like sailors, when the fighting starts they could come back and take the French from the other side."

But Smallcombe interjected.

"Again, beggin' your pardon Sir, but it'll be a long pull back to here against the wind. You can sail off, the French will expect it, but a row back will take some time. It'll all be over. You'll be more use aboard."

"Then we'll pay out a towing rope to pull us back, then row round to her bow. Will that work."

"Yes Sir. Yes, I think it will. I'll get some cable spliced together. It'll have to be a long one!"

Lacey turned to Carr.

"Right; Carr. You're in the longboat. Choose your men."

Drake's face broke into a smile.

"Sir, what if the French thought that there were French prisoners aboard. Then they'd be even less likely to fire and even more likely to come alongside. Some Officers, including myself, speak a bit of French, or at least pronounce it. If we were up the front, I mean bow, as they came in, shouting out in French, that could add to the effect, Sir."

"Good idea, Mr Drake. You see to it."

He looked up and looked around.

"Gentlemen, I think we have a plan that gives us a more than even chance. It'll need careful timing, but well executed, it'll work."

However, Carravoy wasn't smiling.

"There's just one danger, Sir. We can keep redcoats hidden on our deck but what about the Llewellyn and the Tansy. If they spy redcoats aboard them, they'll put two and two together and take no chances. They'll use their guns on us."

Lacey's face fell.

"You're right. How can we get a message to them? They are way back. What about your signal flags, Smallcombe?"

"Almost certainly the French will have a captured British signal book aboard. They'll read whatever we send."

The meeting fell silent, as all fell to thinking. It was Captain Heaviside who spoke.

"You can send Gen. 37. 3. Matt. 9, 30. Ecc. 3.6."

From Lacey. "What will that say?"

"He made him a coat of many colours. See that no man knows it. A time to keep, a time to cast away."

Lacey turned to Smallcombe.

"Will the French have a Bible?"

"Some do, some don't. It depends on the Captain. Whatever, it'll take them a while to work it out, even if they do."

Carravoy looked worried.

"Won't the French smell a rat, us sending cryptic messages, Sir?"

"Perhaps, but it can't be helped, it's a chance we'll have to take. Besides, it is Sunday. Perhaps we're exchanging texts for Sunday service?"

All laughed, the tension broken, at least for a while.

"Good luck to you all."

* * *

Carr went below and gathered his company.

"We are going to be boarded by a French Privateer. They think we are a Merchantman, and we must keep it so. You must not show yourselves above the ship's side, your redcoat will tell them that the ship is full of soldiers, and they'll keep off and sink us with their guns. When the ships come together, our job, as good shots, is to stop any Frenchman from cutting the rope from a grappling iron. Take care with each shot, but I need 20 men to come with me in the longboat to attack them from the other side. Volunteers? You'll be first for any plunder!"

He grinned and, and soon he had more than he needed, so he chose the 20 he thought best suited to close quarter fighting, which included Tom Miles.

"What will they be armed with, Sir?"

"Cutlasses, but that's fine. Just think of them as cavalry. Longboatmen, leave your jackets here. You'll get some shirts to make you look like sailors."

After removing his own jacket and donning a large blue neckerchief, he led his men up to the deck, to find the Grenadiers and Number 3 Company already squatting against the ship's side. The longboat was being swung out and he wondered at the haste, but a walk to the forecastle and a look South West told him why. The Privateers had gained all the sea-room they needed and were making their move, even from a mile away he could see their creaming bow wave, forced aside by the bulk of their sleek hulls, which looked small by comparison to the tower of white canvas that forced them on towards their intended targets. Another look out to starboard saw the Ipheion, stationed off their starboard bow, ready to meet any attack down that side. At that moment the Privateers split and Carr watched fascinated as the gap grew between them. He was called back to his task by Major O'Hare.

"Captain Carr. Into the longboat, if you please."

The Bidewell was stationary, the sails now hanging limp. Carr slid down a rope into the crowded vessel, noted the bayoneted muskets lying in the bottom and watched two of the three sailors hoist the sail and spread it to the wind. He looked back. One of the Privateers was visible from their side. They could see him, so time for the off. The rope began to pay out through a rowlock from its perfect coil in the bow. Carr was set on his part of the plan.

The roar of gunfire drew all eyes that were able, over to the starboard side. The Ipheion, with perfect timing, had tacked around to parallel her Privateer and present her larboard broadside and each gun, carefully aimed, was holding the Frenchman out from the Bidewell. However, the Frenchman, with equal skill was holding his ship just out of range, as shown by the fall of shot, thus forcing the Ipheion to hold her position to protect that flank of the convoy.

Davey and Joe Pike crouched down on the deck, as low as they could despite the discomfort of many like them crowded up under the ships side. Davey could read clearly the fear and anxiety of Joe's face.

"John, d'you think we can do it? John, I never shot at no one, never mind killed anyone."

Davey smiled and squeezed his upper arm.

"Neither have I, boy, but I knows one thing. This is soldiering and if we don't win, it's a French prison or the bottom of the ocean for us both. You'll soon change when you see's what they'n tryin' to do to you.

He smiled again.

"We'll be all right, Joe. Both of us, once it gets goin'. Just do what you've been told. Think of 'em same as those straw dummies you blew apart on the range! Now check your priming and your flint."

Joe grinned and nodded, and did as he was bid, then looked up. O'Hare was passing amongst them, crouching just as they were.

"Now remember, you gang of scoundrels. No. 3 fires first, then the Grenadiers, then you Lights, and you Lights especially, choose your targets, like you've been told, not just anyone. When you've fired get back out of the way, make room for the next. Good luck to you all, boys; they're in for a nasty surprise trying to pick a fight with the 5th," and he slapped as many on the back and shoulders as were in range.

Royston D'Villiers had much more of a view than he wanted. The Privateer was growing in size, rushing on in puissant confidence, so quickly that details rapidly emerged within the terrifying picture that was building before him. Her guns, run out and ready on the side that would come to face him, muzzles speaking their own threat, the huge tricolour billowing off to the left, and, worst, the men milling about and busy on her crowded forecastle, many clearly armed.

He was stood with Drake, Rushby and five others, all able to speak French and all scruffily dressed as though prisoners. He studied the Privateer and his fear grew worse, such that he gripped the arm of the man before him.

"Steady up, D'Villiers. Must make the right impression, you'd agree."

Nearer and nearer, was she going to stand off, or was she going to board? Her course said the latter, but it could change. Did she know? A puff of white smoke issued from her bowchaser on the forecastle, followed by the report, then a splash of shot 30 yards before them. What did that mean? Nearer and nearer. Here was the enemy, in all his strength, ability and power. Now he could see their faces. He doubted that he could speak anything, but then came relief so strong his legs gave way, he had to seize the nearby rigging. She was running in her guns, he could hear the squeal of the gun trucks and the portlids were closing with a thump. No doubt, she was coming alongside. He heard Drake yell, to be taken up by the others.

"Ne tirez pas. Ne tirez pas. Nous sommes prisonniers Francaise. Ne tirez pas. Vive la France. Vive la France."

The others were waving and cheering, and, unbelievably, the French were laughing and grinning back. D'Villiers started shouting for all he was worth.

242

"Merci. Merci. Vous etre notre secourireurs. Merci. Merci. Vive la Revolution."

With superb seamanship the Privateer slackened her own sails and glided to a halt just off the Bidewell's hull, both mainmasts opposite, but the Privateer shorter, measuring somewhat over half the Bidewell's length. The distance between them was not quite enough to leap over, but almost. Joe Pike and Davey looked up to see the towering sails with Frenchmen on the uppermost spars. The realisation struck him hard: Frenchmen! If he could see them, they could see him, and they were shouting something, but he could hear nothing above the gunfire between the Ipheion and the other Privateer and the yelling from the forecastle. Joe's attention switched to the grappling hooks that arced over the sides and jerked back against the rail above. The barbs bit into the woodwork as the Privateer crew took the strain. Seconds passed, surely the gap was closing. Then he heard,

"Allez, mes enfants, en avant, en avant!".

Carr turned in the stern of the longboat and decided his moment had come. The Privateer was stationary beside the Bidewell, her rail and rigging black with men waiting to swing over and board. Not quite yet going over, but he decided to take the chance. Time to return.

"Strike the sail! Onto that rope, all of you, and pull for all you're worth."

The longboat spun with the new strain on the towline at her bows and Carr and his men began the long haul back, rapidly closing the gap, but not fast enough for Carr. He studied the gap between the two ships. It was narrow enough, the boarders were away, swinging on ropes from the French yardarms.

O'Hare stood up. "No 3 Company. Up. Present. Fire!"

His timing was as good as could be hoped. The Privateers, their ship left behind and in the act of swinging across, were suddenly confronted by the muzzles of 85 muskets, at point blank range. Practically the whole boarding party were blown away to fall between the two hulls. The few that, by a miracle, made the deck of the Bidewell were quickly bayoneted.

"Grenadiers. Up. Present. Fire!"

The volley from the Grenadiers added to the confusion on the French deck, then they dropped their muskets to use their own grapnels, some hauling in the rope of those thrown by the French, to use them as their own.

"Lights. Up. Independent fire."

Smoke was everywhere, despite the breeze it was moving too slowly to see any target. It was caught in the eddies around the slack sails, but what could be heard was the sound of chopping from the French deck and many grapnel lines were going slack.

"Sod this smoke," and John Davey climbed the rigging to get above the clinging white fog. Once above, he could see down clearly onto the French deck and with his first shot he downed a sailor about to wield an axe against a grapnel line. Others joined him and at last the smoke cleared. Many Privateers were shot as they frantically used their axes, but there were many of them and they were winning the contest. Many Grenadiers had no line to pull and although they joined onto those lines that were left, the gap was too far for the redcoats to simply jump and it was not closing.

Carr's longboat was rapidly closing with the stern counter of the Bidewell, now only yards from her rudder. He could hear the laboured breathing of his men as they hauled in the last yards of rope, but they needed to get to the bows of the Privateer. There was no time for oars; he had to gamble that they would have enough momentum to run up to the woodwork beneath her bowsprit. To pull anymore on the rope would just take them to the Bidewell.

"Stop pulling. Take your weapons."

The longboat glided around as it's tiller altered course. The distance closed but they were slowing, finally stopping short, under the Privateer's bowsprit. Carr stood and grasped the rope that ran from the bow to the "dolphin striker", a stout rod of metal spearing down from the bowsprit and using all his strength he pulled, then he was joined by others and they reached the complex of woodwork that would take them up to the French forecastle. A face appeared above them, it shouted then was gone, but soon it re-appeared, joined by others and pistols came over the side, but Carr was ready. Ten in the boat were at the "present" and they fired first. The faces disappeared in the white smoke, but one pistol had been fired and the ball took the man next to Carr in the chest. He fell over the side and was gone, leaving his dropped musket upon the gunwhale. Carr seized the musket with it's bayonet in place, tucked his own unfired pistol into his waistband, then latched onto a convenient piece of woodwork and hauled himself up.

"Come on!"

244

The gap between the ships was not closing. It only needed the last lines to be cut and the Privateer would be free. The Lights were protecting the last few lines but knives were appearing from below the Frenchman's rail, sawing away from where they were safe. The French Captain had reset the huge driver sail at the stern and, with the good breeze still holding, its massive leverage was taking the Frenchman's stern away. Lacey, from up on the Bidewell's Quarterdeck, looked in despair at what seemed to be the defeat of all their efforts, but, as quick as despair rose within him, hope came to take its place. Every headsail on the Bidewell was running up the stays that ran from the foremast to the bowsprit. The ship's Bosun had gathered as many of his crew as he could see and the Bidewell was spreading her own acreage of canvas, which soon caught the wind and pushed the Bidewell's bows over towards the Privateer's stern. More than this, the spread canvas robbed the wind from the Privateer's driver and the gap began to close, more rapidly, until the two hulls crashed together. O'Hare drew his sword and jumped up onto the rail, steadying himself with the mainmast rigging.

"Come on, me boys. 'Tis but a little jump!" and he was over the side and gone, followed by all that were near him. Carravoy saw the figure disappear and waved his own sword as he climbed up.

"Grenadiers, with me!"

He was soon copied by Heaviside.

"No. 3!"

The redcoats followed them over, like a wave topping a sea wall. Davey looked at Joe.

"Come on, boy. It's time to follow the band!"

Carr was fighting for his life. The Privateer's forecastle rail was crowded with men, all stabbing with cutlasses and boarding pikes and Carr was just below the rail. All he could do was fend off the blows with the bayonet and musket, he could make no attack of his own. All that was keeping him alive was the accurate shooting from the longboat. A deep cut on his hairline was bleeding into his eyes, the cut made by a cutlass that was in the hand of a Frenchman who had been intending to use it to cleave Carr's skull in two. Instead it only dropped onto him from the lifeless fingers of the Frenchman when Miles had shot him from below. Carr had looked up helplessly at his assailant when suddenly the Frenchman's mouth, upper lip, and nose merged into a huge hole with the passage of Miles' musket ball.

Others from the longboat were assaulting the forecastle rail further along, but making as little progress as he. He allowed himself to drop lower as he heard Miles below him, "To your left, Sir," and looked above as Miles ball took another Privateer just under the chin; blood and brains spraying skywards out of the top of his skull as he jerked back out of sight. He ascended again, bayonet before him, and was surprised at no opposition. He drew back the musket ready to make a stab forward, when what appeared above him was a perfectly tailored red coat and an elegant sword.

"Carr! What the Devil are you doing down there? And don't you try to stick that thing in me. Ah, I see you've gained another hole in your head."

"Carravoy! I think I preferred the French. Well, aren't you going to help me up? Pipe me aboard, or something?"

Carr threw the musket over the rail then followed it onto the deck. Miles came over just behind.

"What was that about plunder, Sir?"

The forecastle was cleared of Frenchmen and was now occupied with Carravoy's Grenadiers. The main deck below was also full of red coats, many with bayonets levelled at French chests, holding them prisoner, but shouts and the bark of muskets below decks told that the fighting was not yet over.

Joe and Davey had been ordered down the starboard companionway beneath the quarterdeck. Supported by five others, bayonets forward, they found themselves in a corridor with two cabin doors to each side, ending with another ladder that descended down into the ship. The first three cabins were empty. Davey burst open the fourth to find himself staring into a pistol. He ducked instinctively and the time it took for the hammer to fall and the main charge to fire was just enough to save his life, but the ball ploughed a furrow along the side of his skull. Davey spoke no words, but simply smashed his rifle butt into the man's face, caving in his cheek and eye socket. Leaving him moaning, they went on, but a shriek told them that someone had used their bayonet. The lead had fallen to Joe, and below the stairs was almost total dark and his eyes were unused to the gloom. He could see little and heard only the sounds of continued combat.

Robbed of both senses, Joe edged forward, bayonet before him, the barrel of the musket of the man behind over his right shoulder. Eyes were becoming accustomed to the dark and they saw that they were down in the hold, sacks and barrels neatly stored.

"Madelleine!"

An Officer had jumped out from a hiding place, sword in one hand, pistol in the other and he was not alone. More than could be easily counted in the dark narrows of the hold had responded to the cry of their ship's name. The pistol came up, but not quick enough before Joe's guardian behind fired and the ball took the Frenchman in the chest. Joe fired into the gloom as did others and now the hold was full of smoke. Joe's group spread across the hold in a defensive line, bayonets before them, expecting a desperate charge onto them along the gangway, but up ahead came renewed firing. All that came out of the murk was one Frenchman, his cutlass raised ready to stab forward, blade beside his right ear. When the thrust came, Joe slid the blade over with his musket and the Frenchman's momentum took him onto the bayonet of the soldier to Joe's left. The soldier stamped down to free his bayonet, then they left him choking and moved on further. The sound of fighting ahead had ceased. Davey called out.

"Up ahead. Who's there?"

"3rd Company. Who are you?"

"Bloody all sorts. Just keep your fingers off your triggers!"

The ship was theirs. All that remained of the Privateer crew were being herded below deck or being searched prior to imprisonment below, but the combat was still rumbling on between the Ipheion and her Privateer. Smallcombe looked over at what was happening between them. When her sister ship's colours came down the second Privateer had two choices, to run off North with the wind behind her, or the other choice was to evade the Ipheion, which she could, and run past, delivering a final broadside. The Bidewell and her prize had swung too far in the wind to be raked, but a broadside into either ship as she passed could do great harm and the prize was the most likely on the quickest route away. She was spreading sail, she knew she was alone and needed now to escape, how and which way remained to be seen. Smallwood ran to the rail of his quarterdeck to hail O'Hare.

"Major. Get your guns manned and run out. The other Privateer, she may run past. Load chain shot, if you can find it. If you hit her sails she'll take fright and go."

O'Hare ran to the exposed side, gathering men and giving orders. Deakin and Halfway found themselves in charge of the first 18 pound cannon, lashed and tethered against its gunport. Deakin issued his orders to the men he had.

"Get those lashings off and get the thing further in. You four, we needs gunpowder and something called "chain-shot". Shouldn't be hard to recognise. It must be down below somewhere."

The lashings were removed and the gun hauled in to give access to the muzzle. The gunpowder arrived in two white bags and also the chain-shot, obvious as two cannon balls linked by a chain. Deakin looked at Halfway.

"How do you load the bloody thing?"

"Same as a musket, Ned, only with a damn sight more. Break open a musket cartridge and use it all to prime that touchhole there. How many charges, do you think?"

"Stuff in both. First one broke open, second as is, then the shot."

This was done, then the gunport hauled up and the gun ran out. The slow match was lit by sparking gunpowder in the firing pan of Halfway's musket. They looked along the barrel to examine the empty sea. O'Hare climbed the rigging enough to see the Ipheion and her opponent, but he just saw the former. A look North saw the Privateer running for France under a cloud of canvas. The fight was over. O'Hare climbed down onto the nearest gun and sheathed his sword.

"Now, there's well done! Well done to you all, thieving gang of fighting villains that ye are. Now, didn't I say that we'd make them wish that they'd all stayed at home?"

The cheers and shouts of agreement accompanied him all the way to the French quarterdeck, then he returned to the Bidewell, carrying the several folds of the French ensign. He went over to Lacey.

"Our first trophy. Sir. Not many Regiments can say they've captured a French warship! In a sea action!"

Lacey took hold of one end, but they still had to share the burden.

"Take that to the Captain's cabin. I know just what we'll do with this once we reach Gibraltar."

O'Hare offered his hand and Lacey took it. No words, just a grip of fearsome intensity. Both then looked over to their prize, their moment broken by the sound of cheering. The Ipheion was sailing past, her sailors all in the rigging, cheering for all they were worth. Fallway was up on his own quarterdeck rail, waving his hat. Lacey's own men were making an enormous din, cheering and shouting in reply. Officers and men, waving muskets and swords, joining with all others who had helped to fight it out, celebrating the relief, and the joy, of still being alive and on the side victorious.

* * *

The same day also saw a French defeat, but of a more minor nature. Because of it, Captain Roul Linois lay in the dust of the road, smiting the dry and stony surface in anger and frustration. Around him lay the bodies of several of his company from the 1st Legere, and another behind screamed in agony from an almost severed arm. He rose to his feet, ignoring the now filthy state of his fine Voltigeur uniform to scream obscenities at the figures now disappearing into the scrub and gorse that covered the far side of the valley in which he stood.

The ambush had been perfect. Stones, rocks and boulders had been dislodged down upon his patrol followed by a musket volley, then a charge down the hillside to inflict as many bayonet and sabre wounds as possible on his confused men as the partisans passed through, before continuing down and away, to cross the stream below and escape up the hillside beyond. The partisans had left three of their number behind, two dead and one soon to be as the French soldiers, besides themselves with anger, stove in his skull with their musket butts. Linois had been sent out to find partisans, but they had found him. He cursed them and he cursed himself. Had he sent them ahead, three scouts would have discovered the ambush, but this was a new kind of warfare and there were lessons yet to be learned, but this, at least, was no longer one.

Chapter Eight

Laurels and Celebrations

The gentle swell rose and fell under the five ships as they turned across the wind onto their first Northing course in weeks. Now, at last, before and around them was Mediterranean blue, so different from the washed out blue of the wild Atlantic. Nearest to the shore were the three transports, in line astern and each crowded with canvas above their blunt and bulky hulls to make the most of the, now favourable, South West wind. Further out, like sheepdogs to three strays, and much more pleasing to the nautical eye, was the Ipheion, tailed by their prize, the Medelline, both now spreading canvas and pulling ahead of their three charges. The Medelline proclaimed her status as a French prize, flying the White Ensign above the French Tricolour from the end of her driver yard at the stern. The Ipheion would lead on, the better to display the prize, and the two warships swooped over right to left, across the intended course of the three transports.

The Rock of Gibraltar was growing before them, rising out of the heat haze that shimmered on the near horizon that blended with the clean blue of the tranquil sea. As the distance decreased, the white buildings of the town of Gibraltar became clear as details around the Rock's base and also around the shoreline, like white shells thickly decorating the margins of a child's finished sandcastle, piled up and abandoned for other pursuits on a high summer's day. Last to come into view for the watchers on the two lines of vessels were the innumerable masts of the Naval base and the glowering guardian that was The Fortress.

Deakin and Halfway leaned on the rail of the Bidewell, whilst close to them, Miles, Pike and Davey used the nearby rigging as support. Rushby was closeby, sketching furiously whilst sharing their vantage point. Gibraltar was new to them all, but such sights were most unique to Joe Pike and John Davey, both of whom stood transfixed at the sight of their first foreign shore. As the details of the view appeared before them, it was Tom Miles who broke the silence.

"What're the chances of us gettin' ashore then, there?"

Deakin fashioned an answer.

"None, almost nuthin'. We'll stock up, quick as can be done, then on, to wherever. They won't like us runnin' about in a cooped up placed like this. All around is Spain and the Spanish, they'm our enemies," and to give emphasis he waved his hand at the panorama that formed both the sides and the centre stage of the theatre before them. He pointed to their left.

"Over there is Algeciras, a Spanish base, which is why we'm comin' in at such a wide angle. There b'ain't much room, this place bein' just about under siege, with the Spanish army crowding up, close as they dare. A battalion our size would fill the place up, on top of all the sailors and citizens."

Miles changed the subject. He pointed to the Madelline, now tailing the Ipheion, both ahead and to their left, each adding their casual beauty to the olive green hills and burnt brown mountains, which formed the backdrop behind each picturesque vessel.

"Captured enemy vessels means prize money, and I'd say that Frencher over there should fetch us a nice sum of coin. I wouldn't say no to being able to spend it in yon harbour town. If they looks after the matelots, then they'll look after the likes of us."

Again it was Deakin that made an answer.

"There's you thinkin' from the inside of your trousers again, and as for prize money, you can put that outside your head! I've been talkin' to one of our sailors and for one thing, it takes months before the sum is agreed, and for another, every Tom, Dick, and Harry that was anywhere in sight of the Madelline when we took her, gets a share. Topsails up, as he said, whatever that means. That includes all the lads on the Tanzy and the Llewellyn, besides the crew of the Ipheion. So, I reckons you might just get enough to buy me that drink what you owes me!

All laughed, whilst Tom Miles scowled. Joe Pike gave his opinion. It had not been missed by those around him, that since the fight on the Madelline, Joe had grown in both confidence and stature, and was now more willing to speak his mind amongst his fellow soldiers.

"Well, that don't impress me. That Recruiting Sergeant made me all kinds of promises about booty and seeing new places, and here is one, and you say we're to stay cooped up on this ship some more. A stretch of my legs around that place would not come amiss at all, certainly not in my case."

It was Tom Miles who fashioned the reply that all felt.

"If you think that the Army's goin' to be just like what that Recruitin' Sergeant told thee, before he put that shillin' in your drink, then your thinkin' has turned out to be much more suspect than I've thought up till now. If you think he told thee right, then, boy, you needs yer head read!"

With that Joe Pike was the subject of an outburst of much roughneck behaviour and was pushed and pummelled by all that could reach him, which was all four of his fellow companions, but all accompanied by much laughter. However, events around the harbour regained their attention. They were slowing, sails were being furled above them, and the Ipheion and the Medelline sailed on towards the Naval Base, taking in their sails as if by magic, and both were then warped up against the harbour wall. The three transports dropped anchor in the bay, within long hailing distance of their escort and prize. It wasn't long before an Admiral's Barge, so recognised by the Port Admiral's flag at her stern, left the steps of the Naval Harbour and pulled strongly for the Bidewell. Ensign Rushby was the first to recognise that the Bidewell was its intended destination and he turned to the nearest soldier.

"Get yourself to the Colonel's cabin and inform him, that what looks like an important Naval Officer, is about to visit the ship."

Lacey and O'Hare arrived quickly, both buckling on their swords, and all watched the progress of the barge. In no time the barge was alongside and the Admiral was climbing the ladder to board the ship through the entry port that had been removed from her side. First into view was his bi-corne hat, worn Admiral style "athwartships", to show the cockade of his rank, then his beaming countenance as he pulled his slightly tubby, middle aged figure up the last few steps. Once on deck, he looked around for those that appeared as authority and saw the three Officers at attention and at the salute. He chose the correct one and headed straight for Lacey, hand outstretched and with a smile that, if anything, had broadened.

"My dear Colonel Lacey, permit me to introduce myself, Rear Admiral Staveley, in command of this port. May I congratulate you and give you joy on your victory. A splendid, a most splendid, heroic effort, and a marvellous success. I can't tell you how good it feels to have one of those damn pirates tied up against my quayside. Those two have been plaguing this coast for months and have cost us dear, but you, my dear sir, you have broken the pair and no more can they play their damn tricks up and down my piece of ocean. Marvellous. Marvellous."

All this whilst he pumped Lacey's hand up and down with both hands of his own.

"Thank you, Admiral, but may I introduce Major O'Hare and Ensign Rushby? Both played a significant role in the action."

Staveley transferred his hand pumping to O'Hare and Rushby."

"Major. Rushby. Capital. Capital. Yes. Yes. Now listen. You are all invited, with any other Officers you choose, to dinner in our Officers' Mess. This evening. I'll brook no argument and, I feel sure, you'll not be sorry to stretch your legs off this old tub. What? Not wrong am I? Hmm? Now, I want to hear now, all the details, before I leave, about how you took her. Every detail, you understand, for my own satisfaction."

Lacey stood aside and motioned the Admiral to the door under the quarterdeck.

"Our pleasure, Admiral. The Army likes to boast about its Naval victories, and all accompanied by a glass of madeira, if you partake?"

"Partake? Does the tide go in and out? Lead me on."

The small party entered the great cabin, which contained Captain Smallcombe, who was quickly introduced, but Staveley had eyes only for the French tricolour draped over a table to the side. He made a beeline straight for it and seized a portion in both fists. To the onlookers it seemed as though he were about to rend it apart, but he simply lifted it up, emitted a sound that could not be identified, then cast it back down onto the table, with what could be identified as a grunt of satisfaction. Lacey asked the question that all were thinking, as he handed Staveley his bumper of madeira.

"The battalion's first battle trophy, Admiral. I do so hope that we are entitled to keep it?"

"Indeed you are, my dear Lacey. Oh, my word yes. Wouldn't have it any other way. Now, first things first. How many will you be bringing to dinner?"

Lacey looked in puzzlement at O'Hare.

"About, eight, nine, would you say, Major?"

"Oh surely. Yes, about that Colonel. For certain. We can find about that number from amongst us who were involved in some way."

Staveley walked away from the discarded flag and beamed anew.

"Nine it is. I'll send some boats for you at seven. Now," and in the time honoured Naval manner he cleared a space on the desktop and began assembling a collection of inkwells and paperweights, "Show me how it all happened."

* * *

Two longboats arrived at the due time, six oars in each manned by sailors in immaculate navy ducks and each steered by a young Midshipman, even more immaculately turned out than his crew, which had to be assumed, for it was impossible to detect. Five embarked in one, four in the other. Rushby sat with Carr and Drake, the first and the last wearing their headdress; Carr not, he was sporting a bandaged head, thereby he was "excused shako". Rushby was clearly enthralled with the spectacle. The Great Rock, pink in the Westering sun, the ships and small boats sitting above their own reflections, the small details of the harbour, and the buildings and houses, tumbling in random up the steepening hillside.

"I wish I'd brought my sketchbook. This is wonderful. I couldn't arrange the subject better, even if I had the power."

Drake answered. Carr had gone into quiet mode.

"Well I'm afraid you haven't, and you couldn't have brought it anyway. Not good manners, you understand. You must commit it to memory, and Carr and myself will each remember three things that you must add in. Won't we, Henry?"

Carr smiled and realised that he had a part to play.

"Yes, yes. Of course. Three things. I'm doing mine now. Which way are we looking?"

Rushby and Drake replied in unison, with Drake pointing for added emphasis.

"That way!"

"Right."

They were met on the harbourside by a Captain and two Lieutenants of the Royal Marines and led off to a low whitewashed building, which, nevertheless, managed to look important and imposing. Once through the door and into the mess room they were greeted by a roar of cheering, loud huzzas, and clapping by all present, and nine of the assembly came forward with bumper glasses of good sherry for their guests. The glasses were raised high, to nothing in particular, just more cheering and huzzas. All quickly took their places and the progression of courses began. From the onset it was a rowdy affair, good cheer in large measure ran up and down the table. It was plain that the capture of one of the Privateers was a double welcome triumph and this set the tone for the evening. As each course came and went, all in the 5th remarked on the quality of the food; the fish and the lamb and above all, the wine. Lacey, Guest of Honour on Staveley's right leaned over to his host and remarked the same.

"Ah, Lacey. This is Spain and the old Dons are never too inclined to take this warfare thing too seriously. The Spanish fishermen regularly come over from opposite to sell their catch, and each day along the causeway between us, sort of neutral territory if you understand, there's a regular market. And, if a cart comes a bit far and unloads on our side, no one cares too much. Especially if the old Generalissimo, my opposite number, gets a share of the lucre and a box of cigars with my compliments, then all goes on in just the way that we would want it. They're no strong allies of the French, you know. Especially after Trafalgar. They've worked out what they're up against. Trade matters to them, and they haven't a fleet left. Can't get to their own colonies, even."

Lacey nodded.

"Then Amen to peaceful coexistence."

The good wine was extensively imbibed by all and the noise level rose to that of a small skirmish. A Midshipman was hoisted up to propose the Loyal Toast and with that Staveley decided that a speech of some kind was required. The factual substance of his discourse was that "the French had been given another drubbing" and that the success of the 5th was "on a par with the boldest example of cutting out that he had ever heard of." However, most of the speech was a vehicle for yet further toasts to the "Good Officers of the 5th" and the "boarders who took her". Lacey made a reply complimenting his host on his excellent table, pronouncing to all that "we've shown that against the likes of us the French are very beatable", and, lastly, making his own toast to the "excellent Captain Fallway, now present, of the Ipheion, and his good crew of stout British tars", which drew the loudest support and placed the glassware, and table itself, in some peril from the furious drubbing of all hands upon its thick tablecloth.

With that the port arrived and the assembly sunk into an even deeper state of inebriation, with even Carravoy and D'Villiers eventually shedding the caricature of aristocratic posturing and finding themselves thoroughly caught up in the intoxicated merriment. Toasts arrived thick and fast. They toasted the 5th Provisionals, "good as the Marines". They toasted Major O'Hare, as the first man aboard, and then they toasted his sword, as the piece of good English steel that struck the first blow. They toasted the Grenadiers, the 3rd, then the Lights, all "damn fine shots". Then they toasted Carr, Carr's bandage, and the hole in his head, the last proposed by Drake, who couldn't find the chair that he had just risen from and, in a state of abject confusion, instead sagged to the floor.

Lacey and O'Hare, knowing from the onset what was coming, managed to stay relatively sober, as also did Heaviside, as was his nature, but their fellow Officers of the 5th, all young men, were determined to match the Navy glass for glass. Come the end of the wine soaked affair, all staggered off; Infantry, Navy, and Marines, providing communal support in two's and three's, all enthusiastically proclaiming each other as, "Damn fine fellows". The bonhomie continued, even to the quayside, and cries of mutual admiration, both for each other and the service they belonged to, carried across the water as the longboats pulled away. For Carr, Drake, Rushby, and others, the last double toasts did their work on the journey back and the notion of them climbing a rope ladder up the ship's side was out of the question. Instead, a rope was lowered from the davits on the end of the main yard and each was hoisted, as an incapable bundle, to land on the deck. Deakin, on watch with Halfway, stood on the forecastle and watched proceedings.

"Does any of this look familiar to you, at all, Toby?"

* * *

Colonel Lacey sat at the desk of the Captain's Cabin, penning a letter with the help of Major O'Hare. On the end of the desk, neatly folded and sunk in brown paper was the French tricolour, the letter was to be placed on top before the parcel was finally sealed over.

"I've asked General Perry to take charge of this ensign until our return, and I've commended the courage of both yourself and Captain Carr. What other names should I mention?"

"That's very kind of you, Colonel. Sure, I was only doing what I was supposed to do, but I do think that you could mention the initiative shown by Drake and Heaviside, those were good ideas of theirs. For Heaviside again, and Carravoy, say that both led their men as good Officers should. That will about cover it, I'd say."

Lacey made the additions, signed it, sanded it and placed it on top of the tricolour. Then the parcel was bound and addressed. At that point, Ensign Rushby knocked and entered, plainly the worse for wear from the previous evening, head down, eyes to the decking, neither of which could he have elevated, even had he wished to. He was bearing a letter.

"Letter just arrived, Sir. I think it's from the Admiral. It came in his boat, Sir, and they are standing by for a reply. Also, I thought you'd like to know, Sir, there's a ship leaving for home this afternoon."

"Thank you, Mr Rushby. Please take this parcel and see that it gets safely into the Admiral's boat. I will make a reply directly."

"Yes Sir."

Rushby gathered the parcel and gratefully exited the cabin. The sunlight reflected from the sea beyond the windows was causing him acute pain in the centre of his forehead.

Lacey opened the letter and quickly scanned the short message.

"It's from Staveley. The Ipheion has a wounded mast, whatever that means, and it must be repaired before sailing on. Staveley estimates something short of a week, they have to take the mast out altogether and step in another, as he puts it. He says that he has an empty Marine barracks that we can all use, the families too, off the Tansy. It will be a bit crowded, but it'll serve if we want it. What do you think?"

"I think we should accept his offer, Sir. Stuck a week on board these ships, looking at the shore, will not do much for anyone's good feelings. No fresh air, for another, and floating above our own filth. You've been becalmed, Sir. Pestilence can result. I think it a good idea to get them off and to have a wee stretch of the legs, as it were. We've been on these ships a long time, and a bit of marching and drill ashore will do no harm"

Lacey nodded in agreement and quickly prepared the reply. A shout to the sentry got the letter on its way.

Eight bells were sounding to mark the end of the forenoon watch, as Lieutenant D'Villiers, somewhat aggrieved and not feeling in the best of fettle himself, despatched himself on his errand around the ship. He had been instructed by Major O'Hare to inform all Officers that a ship was about to leave for Plymouth and this was their chance to get a letter home. His calling on Captain Heaviside resulted in his leaving with a letter to be sent, the good Captain merely needing to seal up the results of his daily communication to his wife. Calling on the cabin of Carr and Drake, however, brought results of a very different kind. From within the room that reeked of a night "born of the bottle", two faces peered at him, both shaded by a blanket. Which was which he could not determine, but the mouth of one opened to enquire the reason for the intrusion.

"There's a boat leaving this afternoon, bound for England. This is a chance to get a letter home. Thought you'd like to know."

There was no reply; the only acknowledgement that he received was the replacing of the blanket over what he thought was their faces. It was he who finished the one sided conversation.

"Well, thanks for your concern! Only following orders. Wish I didn't have to bother." He shut the door.

"Henry, Henry. We've got to do something. If they don't receive a letter along with all the others, what are they going to think?"

The reply was a noise more akin to something from the animal kingdom. On hearing it, Drake sat himself up, swung his legs around, found he was going the wrong way and fell out of bed. From his position on the floor he uncovered Carr's head.

"Come on. If we help each other, we'll get it covered."

He cudgelled his befuddled mind into action, inside his aching head.

"As we live in each other's pockets, they'll expect the content to be much the same. I'll get washed, then you. Oh, from now on, I'm keeping a daily letter on the go. I'd advise you to do the same. I've been lazy. We can blame mal de mer, a bit, but I don't think it'll stretch too far. You think of something, then I will. That'll take up a page or two, then finish with affection and the promise of a better job next time. We've been in action; that sort of thing."

All this reached Carr's ears in various levels of sound quality, for one because Drake was washing his face, then drying it, then pulling his shirt over his head. For two, Carr's head hurt so badly, that there was nothing else that he could think of. He managed to sit up.

"God. If the Navy drink like that, it's a wonder half their ships aren't sunk by collisions or some other nautical mishap, or they all just get lost. Leave that water there, dear fellow, I'm going to stand up and attempt to reach it."

This he did, and he washed himself whilst Drake uncovered the pen, ink and paper. In this way, painfully, slowly, with many pauses whilst they battered their thoughts, and with little editorial deliberation, two letters were fashioned and made the postbag on time. Drake ensured the conveying of the same down into the longboat waiting at the side, and then his attention was drawn to the Tansy. He had heard the expression "water carnival' before, but what he saw, moving with the speed of black treacle over a cold plate, away from the side of the Tansy, best answered to that description. Three large barges, each pulled by four large sweeps, each with two oarsman, was ladelling its way towards the shore, each crowded full with the women, wives, children and the camp followers that they had brought with them. Each barge had at least three musical instruments, each playing a different tune, giving the occupants a magnificent choice as to which to dance to, which they did.

Jigs and reels were being described all up and down the deck, whilst the children and anyone else who could climb, were festooning the rigging of the single mast with as many items of flags and bunting as they could lay their hands on. All aboard were waving to others on the corresponding vessels, waving hats and coloured scarves, shouting to each other, singing to each other. The celebratory affair was added to when the three passed, at a speed that would make the bovine tramp to milking look like a stampede, through the local Spanish fishing fleet. Spanish songs, shouts, and lewd gestures added to the cacophony and the fairground confusion. The families were going ashore.

The significance of the sight was not lost on the likes of Deakin, Halfway and Miles. Nor the Officers such as Drake, Rushby and Carr. If the families were going ashore, then surely they would be also? Drake looked anxiously around and was relieved to see Major O'Hare.

"Excuse me, Sir, but I see that the families are being taken off. Does that apply to us also?"

"Yes, Mr Drake, indeed it does, but only for a few days, whilst the Ipheion is repaired. You may pass the word around, and tell all to make ready, but remember how much you wanted this when you are marching and drilling up and down the open spaces of this place, and finding out just how much a slow sea voyage takes your wind away."

Drake heeded little of the last point of wisdom. He was smiling from ear to ear.

"Yes Sir. I'll pass the word on, Sir."

Their own disembarkment was a far more dignified, orderly and speedy affair. The troops, with their Officers, sat erect on the seats of a flotilla of longboats, looking for all the world like some kind of landing force. The men marched off to the barracks, the Officers to whatever applied; Officers' quarters in the barracks or a billet in the town. All now being veterans of barrack life, all settled in quickly, which freed the late afternoon and early evening for exercises at double time, especially forming square and advancing in column. Very soon Drake came to appreciate O'Hare's final words. What he could easily cope with back in Somerset, now had him gasping for breadth, and he was not alone. That night all settled quickly to a night ashore, to find silence that highlighted almost eerily what they had grown used to, the sounds that accompanied a night on a ship moving at sea.

* * *

The next day was Sunday and its laws and traditions were obeyed. Whilst the men were confined to barracks there was no drill and Officers' privileges allowed a visit to the town, with orders to return in time for evening Church Parade. It was Drake who provided the driving force.

"I think, as we are here, that we take a walk up there."

Both Carr and Rushby looked at Drake in puzzlement, but all was made clear when they saw that he was pointing to the top of The Rock.

"We should get you, Barnaby, you and your sketchbook, up to the top. To make a recording, as it were. Parade back here in five minutes."

The walk to the town was short and the town itself quaint and charming; narrow walls, gleaming white, leaned in upon narrow cobbled streets, shaded and cool, with the inhabitants themselves providing the enhancing colour; bright dresses, scarves, hats and sashes. Finding the way to the top was easy, it was simply a question of taking any road that led uphill and soon they were on the single road to the summit. Several Gibraltarians, mindful of the attractions to visitors of reaching the top, had set up a donkey station where the ascent became steep and their Spanish keepers, on spying the three Officers, began, with gestures and blandishments, to try to steer them to where the animals were tethered.

"Senors! Subirse les burros. Montar a burro a la cima. Trez pesos."

Drake turned to the others, but they continued walking.

"I think he wants us to ride a donkey to the top. Should we, do you think?"

It was Carr who replied.

"I won't hear of it. We're Light Company!"

The climb was indeed steep and the mood became more sombre as the white dust road continued up the hill to a summit that seemed to remain stubbornly the same distance away. However, their mood soon lightened as, from some way off, they spied two red coated Officers, descending the track, each mounted on their own donkey. It was Rushby who stopped, his eyesight being perfect, and exclaimed his conclusion.

"I do believe, yes, yes it is, I'm sure, Lieutenant D'Villiers and Captain Carravoy."

A careful look from their own eyes confirmed the same for Drake and Carr. Without a word all three stopped, the better to study the spectacle. The comedy grew as the distance lessened. D'Villiers was doing his best to maintain a dignified seat in the saddle, but the absence of stirrups was making that impossible. The rapid gait of the donkey was throwing him around at

261

all angles, whilst he tried to control the animal with the reins, this being made more difficult with the donkey being eager to return, it knowing that this direction took it back to food, drink and rest. D'Villiers attempted manipulation of the reins was, in fact, superfluous, the keeper was running alongside holding the bridle of each. D'Villiers was clinging on, with nothing to cling on to.

But the picture created by D'Villiers was one of sedate dignity compared to what was happening to Carravoy. His legs were longer than the donkey was tall, consequently he was required to lift his feet off the ground, making it necessary that his knees stuck either up or out at an absurd angle, depending on which way he felt precarious. He was also holding the reins, but his anxiety over his position made his elbows stick out to improve his balance. Thus looking for the entire world as though his legs and arms were wings and the donkey was about to fly. All three stood regarding the display, but it was Carr, as his character dictated, whose expression and stance most conveyed the feeling of farcical disdain; arms folded, head to one side, slightly smiling. Both Grenadiers pretended not to notice their three watchers, but Carr soon put a stop to that.

"Any thoroughbred in that mount of yours, d'you think, Carravoy? He's managing a most elegant trot! Some dressage, post ride, perhaps?"

Carravoy looked over with eyes that could have melted stone, but made no reply, which was just as well, for they were being bounced around so much that speech was impossible. Only when they had passed did the three allow themselves to laugh out loud, which caused D'Villiers' head to turn, his expression as angry as the thorough shaking passing up through his body to his jaw would allow.

When the comedy show had turned a corner and was out of sight, they continued on to make the summit and all agreed it was worth the climb. The view was absolutely breathtaking on that bright blue day; they could see the far mountains of the Spanish interior and the corresponding peaks of Africa, equally clear across the white flecked Mediterranean. Rushby lost no time in sketching, while Carr and Drake picked out the details. Their three transports were out in the bay, tiny in the anchorage below, idling around their anchors. Their prize now stood alone at the quayside, the Ipheion having been moved to the repair dock and she was now a peculiar sight compared to her seagoing appearance, there was a conspicuous gap where her foremast should have been. Whilst Rushby hurried into his second sketch, with ambitions for a third, Carr and Drake stood above the view, saying little, each with a foot on the stone kerb. The grandeur of what was before them occupying their thoughts, giving birth to a sombre mood. It was some time before either spoke.

"Here's why you joined the Army, Nat. Most live a lifetime back home and never see the likes of this. Memorable don't do it justice."

"I'll not argue, Henry, but unlike them, we go on to who knows what? In two weeks we could be in a battle. There's not many back home that would accept this, knowing what could come just a while later."

"You're right, Nat, but that's our lot and I'll settle for it. I'm not afraid, we punch our weight. No one's going to roll over us."

"Have you any idea where we're going? Now that we're here in Gibraltar?"

"Naples or Egypt would be my choice. Which of the two, it's impossible to say."

Hc turned to Rushby.

"How goes with the sketching, Barnaby? We daren't be late for Church Parade."

"Five more minutes, and I'm done. I say, this really is the most stunning place. Thanks for bringing me up here."

"Bringing you, Barnaby. Nonsense. Sooner or later, you'd have got your own self up here. Your artistic temperament would have driven you on and up, I feel most sure."

The trip back down was a pleasant stroll, although the gradient turned it more into a long stride lope than what could be termed a walk. They were not late for Church Parade, they took their place with time to spare and the service was well conducted by a Naval Chaplain. However, upon returning to the barrack room, they found waiting for them a tall Grenadier, bearing a letter.

"Captain Carravoy said that I was to give you this, Sir."

Carr took the letter, expressed his thanks and returned the salute. Inside he opened and read the letter. He looked at Drake.

"The Grenadiers are challenging us to a cricket match!"

The following day Carr paraded his Light Company early.

"The Grenadiers want to play us at cricket. We must respond. To lose is one thing, to not even manage to enter the field is quite another. Us three Officers will play, naturally, and can I count on you, Ellis and Fearnley?"

His two Sergeants nodded, apprehension growing in their faces and Carr returned to his men.

"That's five. We need eleven. Six more, so any volunteers, any who've played before?"

John Davey's hand went up.

"Where have you played, then, Davey?"

"Only on the Village Green, Sir. Estate against the Village, but I'll give it a go, Sir."

"Good man. Five more needed."

Another hand went up.

"Me too, Sir. Same kind of thing."

"Well done, Parker, that's seven."

He looked along the ranks. There was no more movement. Joe Pike spoke up.

"Beggin' your pardon, Sir, but I'm not sure what this cricket thing is."

"Put simply, Pike, someone throws a ball at you and you hit it away with a bat, enough to give you time to run to another point, called a wicket. You have to do that more times than the opposition. So, that's explained that; consider yourself on the team."

Pike stood nonplussed. Carr made another note, then regarded the ranks some more.

"Right, never mind those of you that think you can hit a ball with a bat. Are there any good throwers and catchers? If you threw a stone, would you hit what you had thrown at?

Two more hands went up.

"Jones and Steel, good, only one more needed. What about you, Miles?"

"Beggin' your pardon, Sir, but this game you describe be well outside of anything I've ever done. There weren't much room for cricket in the stews of Bristol. I'd rather not, Sir."

Another hand went up. John Byford, as near to a Gentleman Ranker as the Company had. A good soldier, but never inclined to draw attention to himself.

"You can include me, Sir. I played at school."

"Right, good. That's the team. It's firing range this morning, then Officer's choice, which is cricket this afternoon and evening."

After the midday meal, the teams assembled on the field beside the Parade Ground. A wicket was chosen and measured, then 22 pairs of army boots walked all over it in an effort to improve the surface, which done, the creases were blancoed on. White range posts were sent out to mark the boundary and the wickets were assembled. Captains Heaviside and Reynolds had been recruited as Umpires and so Carr and Carravoy took themselves in their direction for the toss. Before that ritual it was agreed that leg before wicket would constitute dismissal. Carr lost the toss, Carravoy elected to bat and for the first time ever they shook hands. As Carr placed his field he soon noticed that they had an audience, a large one, navy, army, and civilian.

D'Villiers and a Grenadier Sergeant came to the crease and things began badly for the Lights. Rushby volunteered to open the bowling, along with Jones and, the delivery being regulation underarm, he found any amount of speed or turn very difficult to generate. D'Villiers and his Sergeant monotonously slogged Rushby, in particular, to all parts of the field and soon the Grenadiers were on 42 for no loss. Carr put himself on at the other end with no different outcome. However, things looked up slightly for the Lights when D'Villiers made a slog too far, right down Byford's throat and he was out; caught. Carravoy came in and Carr decided to look for another bowler, but he had no idea who to ask. Instead he called for volunteers and Drake thought that he should offer himself.

Drake managed a quicker ball, but Carravoy and his Sergeant were clearly both adept batsmen and the score ticked on, but Carr's men were getting quicker around the field. With the score on 72, Carravoy called for a chancy run, which proved to be too much the case, and his Sergeant was run out, Drake taking the throw and knocking off the bails. Carr clapped and encouraged his men, but the third wicket proved to be a bloody affair for the Lights, Carravoy being joined by another Sergeant, and they soon passed the 100, then soon to 130. Time to change the bowling again, so Carr threw the ball to Steel.

"See what you can do."

Byford came forward with some advice to Steel.

"Pitch it at his legs, try to tie him up a bit, and get some more fielders on the leg side. He might get a mite frustrated and sky one, or go for chancy runs."

Carr listened and nodded to Steel. The advice had some effect. Carravoy, in particular, being tall, struggled with Steel's faster and more accurate bowling and one crept through to nudge Carravoy's leg stump and dislodge a bail. He was out, but he felt more than satisfied with his innings; a half century, and the Grenadiers on 161 for three. In came a Corporal and the pair kept the score moving. Straight balls, even down the leg side were giving them little problem, runs were added. Time for another change. Carr looked at Byford.

"Anything you can do?"

Byford nodded and took the ball. Holding it in the tips of his fingers he was able to impart some spin. He sent five balls spinning to the off side which cost some runs, but the sixth he kept straight and it met the Corporal's left leg. Had it not, it would have hit the wicket.

"Howzat?"

Heaviside lugubriously lifted a finger. 182 for four. There followed a succession of Grenadier rankers. None could be described as sophisticated batsmen, more agricultural, but each added to the score. Carr rotated Byford, Steel and also Jones, who proved to be fast and accurate, but the score ticked on, reaching 252 for eight. Another change, perhaps?

"Davey. You want to try?"

Davey took the ball, and looked at it. It was very much battered and bruised, a veteran of many games. He paced back to his mark and waited. Reynolds dropped his hand and Davey ran up to deliver the first full toss of the afternoon. The ball took the shoulder of the bat and flew to the astonished Rushby, who grasped it in front of his face, as much for self preservation as to dismiss the batsman. Last man in. Byford came on at the other end and, at the cost of two more runs, bowled the last man. Grenadiers: 254 all out. A formidable total.

Carr hefted his bat, and looked at Drake. No words were necessary. There was a distinct danger of huge embarrassment. They walked out to polite, if not solid, applause and Carr took guard. Carravoy opened the bowling and, whilst he was not difficult to hit, he was consistently on the wicket. Carravoy

clearly knew his cricket and his field placings made runs difficult to come by. Nevertheless, the score was moving as Carr
and Drake hit the ball into the spaces. Things changed when a
very large Grenadier came on at the other end and achieved the
fastest pace on the ball of the day. Drake was clean bowled for
18. Rushby came on, hit a few and then perished, mishitting a
ball that skied off to be caught at deep fine leg. The Lights were
41 for two. Ellis joined Carr at the crease, looking even more
apprehensive than when he first knew he was on the team.
Carr advised him to block a few, get his eye in and then see
what he could manage. What he managed was to get out second ball, leg before wicket.

Fearnley took Ellis' bat as they crossed over and arrived at
the crease. One ball to survive from the giant Grenadier, but
not only did he survive it, for, either by luck or judgement, he
glanced it past his legs for three runs. 44 for three. Carr was on
strike and Carravoy had given the ball to another Grenadier to
bowl, but the smug look that was growing on Carravoy's face
was there for all to see. Carr went to Fearnley.

"We've got to hit some runs, Sergeant. Hit the damn thing.
Do or die!"

Carr returned to his crease and practiced what he preached.
He took a swing at everything and so did Fearnley. Fortune
favoured the brave and the score moved on, despite dropped
catches, near run outs, bails failing to fall and turned down
appeals. 82 for three and Carravoy was becoming irritated. Victory looked certain, but not the desired crushing defeat. However, his spirits revived during the next over. Carr took a mighty
swing and was caught at deep mid wicket. Two balls later
Fearnley was clean bowled. Byford joined Davey at the wicket,
the score on 84 for five.

Byford soon demonstrated himself to be the most cultured
cricketer at the crease so far, for either side. Davey plainly had
a good eye, but it was more strength and timing than technique, but Byford, with great economy, dealt with all that was
dealt to him, defending the dangerous balls, despatching the
bad. Whilst Davey bludgeoned whatever he hit and trusted to
good fortune with what he missed, Byford played into the gaps,
kept the strike and moved the score on. It was a genuine
cricketer's performance. The score moved on, not quickly, but
the scorers were regularly troubled. 156 for five, then Davey's

luck ran out. An attempted haymaker went straight off the edge of the bat for him to be caught at gulley. Parker took his bat as they crossed.

"Just keep it village green, Parker. Nothing else for it.

Parker proved to be just of Davey's ilk, but without his luck, nevertheless he hit a handy 18 before being clean bowled. Jones and Steel proved to be no more than bowlers with a bat in their hand and scored few, but Byford was edging the total upward. To Carravoy's great frustration he was keeping the strike and scoring regularly. Jones stayed with him for a while, before being stumped and Steel lasted a little longer before edging a catch with the last ball of an over. Last man in; Joe Pike. Carr had a quick word before a very uneasy Joe advanced out to face the fray.

"We're 201 for nine, Pike."

Joe looked bemused. His Captain may as well have been speaking Latin.

"I can't see us winning, but we've not been shamed. Just do your best and get what you can."

Pike marched forward, the last batsman of the day, carrying his bat as though it were a musket with bayonet fixed. Carravoy saw little threat but saw enough to put himself back on, also his large, fast, Grenadier. Byford was playing everything, the weak link lay with Pike. The same took guard, but he was told by Heaviside that he was stood square in front of his stumps and must move. It was the good Captain who lined him up with the middle stump in order to receive the next ball. Carravoy bowled. The result was a clean, ferocious crack, heard before the ball sped back between Carravoy and the wicket to speed on for four runs. The next two balls produced much the same result, a four and two, Byford urging Pike on for the second run. The last three balls brought a four, a two, and another four. Pike was driving the ball back up the wicket with perfect timing and precision. Carravoy had been hit for 20 runs. Byford leaned on his bat and grinned. The large Grenadier was back on against him. Byford blocked the first, hit the next for two, then could only manage a single. Pike was back on strike, so Carravoy set his field placings to cover almost all of the "vee" either side of the wicket, to stop any drive, leaving no one behind the batsman. Pike hit the first hard and clean. It penetrated the field but was stopped. Only a single. Byford back on strike, and the last ball of the over brought two. Byford went to Joe, who now had strike.

"Well hit, lad, but he's going to stop you. Anything you hit back at the bowler they'll stop and he'll bowl it straight, wanting you to drive. Try to hit something off to the side where there are few fielders. Don't hold your bat so square, give it a bit of an angle."

Joe Pike thought he understood and took guard. He twisted his bat slightly as Carravoy approached. The ball was not quite straight and the angled bat drove it off through midwicket, off to his left. No fielder there, four runs. The next five balls went off at much the same angle, three to the right, two to the left. 12 runs; 242 for nine. Byford played the next over in his same untroubled fashion, garnering six runs. Joe was back on strike. The whole of the Light Company and the Grenadiers and the families of the same, and most of the crowd, lined the boundary. Carravoy spread his field wider, but still no one behind the batsman save the wicketkeeper. Pike hit the first ball sweetly, but a fielder just past Carravoy half stopped it. Byford shouted, "No". No run, but the next ball was turned into a vicious drive, an unstoppable four through midwicket again. Two to draw, three to win. The next ball, got the two, a clean hit up to the boundary, but a fielder was waiting and they took two runs. Carravoy looked around at everyone looking at him. Another ball like the last would cost them the game, which seemed lost anyway, but there was nothing else for it but to play the game out. He placed the ball at the tips of his fingers and delivered it at Pike with all the spin he could impart. Joe watched the ball onto his bat and followed through, then he heard the shout from behind him. The spin had taken the ball to the edge of his bat, and Joe had played on. A bail was dislodged. It was a draw.

Byford looked at Carravoy and waited. He knew what should happen now, and it did. Carravoy came over and shook his hand.

"Well played."

"And to you, Sir."

He then walked down the pitch to do the same to Pike.

"Well batted, Pike. I though we were going under. You had a very good knock, but bad luck."

"Thank you, Sir."

The Lights came onto the pitch to applaud their opponents as they and the two batsmen trooped off. Carr placed himself in Carravoy's way.

"Good game, Carravoy. One of the best I can remember being in. It seems us Lights have some hidden talent. I had no idea. Well played to you and to your men."

Carravoy managed a half smile. Being that close to defeat did not sit well, but the requirements of the occasion placed stronger demands upon him than his bad feeling; he knew the ettiquette. He offered his hand and Carr took it.

"Yes indeed, Carr. You nearly did for us. Well played also, to you, and to your men.

* * *

The progression of their days in Gibraltar were signalled by the changes that showed on the Ipheion. From only one mast, then came the crane hoy that lowered in the second, then the replacing of the top mast, the spars and the rigging. A restored Ipheion meant that their days in Gibraltar were over, and emotions were mixed. It meant a renewed acquaintance with life on board a cramped transport, but it also meant an end to the most intense three days of training that many had known. A fair proportion of the time had been drill on formations, and the battalion could form square in a time between 30 and 45 seconds, depending on their original formation, but twice that amount of time had been spent on the firing range. For hour after hour they practiced volley by ranks and half company volleys. When they marched away from the range it was as if they were marching through snow, such was the depth of empty cartridges, but Lacey was growing in confidence with his men. His half hunter regularly told him that, when required, all came reloaded to the "make ready" within 20 seconds, and the bullets were kicking up the sand at body height, even at 100 yards range. On the last day, with the last volley, both Lacey and O'Hare looked at each other and agreed wordlessly, needing only a half smile and a nod of the head. Their musketry was up to the mark.

Early the next day saw the families wending their way to the quayside and boarding the same barges that had disembarked them days before, only this time there was no carnival atmosphere as the barges inched their way out to the Tansy. Most

270

sat on the deck or lined the sides, although from somewhere could be heard a cheery fiddle. The barges returned and took the stores along with the wounded from the fight with the Madelline who should recover in time for the forthcoming campaign. The battalion was to parade at 9 o' clock and so prior to that, Carr, Drake and Rushby toured the barracks of their Light Company, checking the equipment on their men, and searching floors and shelves for missed items. The Lights were in good heart from their honourable draw when all expected a thrashing, and Joe had acquired a knickname; "Tailend", although it didn't last long; Joe was easier.

The battalion paraded for the last time on the Marine's Parade Ground, in fours, Grenadiers and Light Company in the lead. With each man carrying full equipment they marched through the town to the quayside, this being at Staveley's request and they soon saw why. He had paraded his Marines and Seamen along the High St and all gave three cheers as Lacey and O'Hare led their men through. Their victory over the Madelline was clearly still prominent in their memory and still worth any celebration. A flotilla of longboats quickly took them out to their transports, but this time there was no favourable offshore wind, the South Westerly that had pushed them in, still prevailed. The three vessels needed to be towed out to gain some sea room and pick up their faithful Ipheion, then they sailed close-hauled SSE to confuse the spyglasses over in Algeciras. Unlike their leaving of England, few lined the stern rail to watch The Rock sink into the mist of the horizon and so when they were clearly alone on a lonely blue sea, they hauled their wind and set a course East. It was the 1st June 1806. Summer was building in the Mediterranean and over the next two weeks all were grateful for the steady South Westerly that blew through the stifling cabins, 'tweendecks, and corridors of their laden carriers.

Dawn of 15th June saw the mountains of Sicily rise from its own heat haze, as had The Rock, and many lined the rail to examine their landfall and speculate if this was their final destination. With the wind still strong and Southerly, Fallway elected to sail along the South coast, which occupied all the next day, but there was no shortage of interest as smokey Etna dominated the far horizon and, for many, the sight of a volcano was as much a subject of fear and superstition as it was of curios-

271

ity. However, whichever emotion the volcano caused, grew, when as the day faded, they finally made their turn North into the Straits of Messina and the mountain provided an eerie red glow on the larboard side as they used their fair wind to push them North. Dawn of the 16th saw the Port of Messina and Fallway's choice proved wise; with the wind still holding, the transports were able to ease right up to the quays and the battalion disembarked. Enquiries of the sailors enabled the identification of the town beyond the quay, but that did nothing to improve their opinion of the confused jumble of cargo, filthy carts of all sizes and decaying fishing tackle that cluttered up practically the whole of the quayside and plainly added to the stink of sewage and rotting garbage that invaded their nostrils as they assembled to disembark.

A mounted aide de camp, a Major, was waiting for them on the quayside with an escort, and so Lacey disembarked first, accompanied by O'Hare and other Staff. The Major approached Lacey as he came down the gangplank.

"Good morning, Sir. I am Major Willoughby. Welcome to Sicily. We saw your approach up the Straits. General Stuart's Headquarters is up in the town, Sir, and I have a guide here," indicating a soldier of the 78th Highlanders in full Regimental dress, "who will take your men to camp. It's through the town and a little further. However, I am instructed to take yourself to the General as soon as possible, Sir."

Lacey turned to O'Hare.

"I must attend the General. Take over and get the men to their camp and settled in. Give priority to unloading food off the Tansy. Requisition a wagon or something, if you have to."

Lacey mounted a spare horse and followed Willoughby up into the town. The ride was short and Stuart's Headquarters soon became apparent, not only from the sentries but also from the bustle of red coated soldiers going in and out. However, Lacey was given priority and ushered straight in to meet the General. He found himself saluting a youngish man of middle stature with thinning blond hair. He looked up from a map of Calabria just across the Straits, as Lacey placed his orders on the desk and introduced himself.

"Lieutenant Colonel William Lacey, Sir. 5th Provisional Regiment."

Stuart spent no time on pleasantries.

"Provisional! Before that, Detachments, I assume. I've already enough green troops as it is. I was told to expect another Battalion, commanded by you, yes, but Detachments! Are you up together, your internal structure, I mean? Are your orders carried out?"

Lacey drew himself up to his full height.

"Sir, I can confidently say that the 5th will carry out any orders that you decide to give us."

"Hmmm. Big words, Lacey. I hope so. Now, I'm invading the mainland on the 30th. Landing here."

He stabbed his finger onto the map, at a point where blue met green.

"As far as I know it's Regnier over there with about 6,000 men. There's another two, at least besieging Gaeta, North of Naples. I've got just over five, so I need you and your men in good order. Don't get too comfortable in your camp tonight. Tomorrow you march to Milazzo, which will be your embarkation port. You'll be staying there until we leave. Get your men there and await orders. Use the time well. One further thing. I'm taking your Lights and Grenadiers away. I'm creating a Light Battalion and a Grenadier Battalion. The Lights will be under Lieutenant Colonel Kempt, the Grenadiers under Brigadier Cole. I trust that both have Officers that know their business. However, you'll still be with your Grenadiers, you and your Line Companies are also under Cole. Now, good day to you!"

Lacey made a salute to the top of Stuart's head and left the room. He obtained directions from a Clerk as to the likely whereabouts of his men, mounted the horse he'd been given and took what he thought was the right road. He was soon re-assured; he could see the end of his column climbing a hill not too far ahead. Once on their camping ground, whilst the men did their best to create a satisfactory camp, Lacey made his Headquarters in a room borrowed in a nearby farm, then he sent out for all Officers, Captains and above. All arrived within five minutes.

"Tonight's camp is temporary. Tomorrow we march for Milazzo, about 20 miles away, a day and a half's march. That's our embarkation port, for we are invading the mainland on the 30th. Today's the 16th. O'Hare, I want you to ride ahead now and find us a campsite with enough room to keep the men busy and up to the mark. I expect to arrive around noon the day after tomorrow. For the rest of you, make no elaborate preparations today. We march at dawn after a night spent sleeping in our greatcoats. One further thing, something that disappoints me, but it's orders."

He turned to Captain Carr.

"Carr, your Lights are being removed from my command to become part of a Light Battalion under Lieutenant Colonel Kempt. Carravoy, same for your Grenadiers, but we will be in the same Brigade, both of us under Brigadier Cole. Both of you, expect to meet your respective Commanders very soon. That's all, Gentlemen. Good afternoon.

Carr left the farmhouse immediately and sought out his Company. They were on the far edge of the camp and already settled in with fires going to brew tea. He called over Drake, Rushby, Ellis, and Fearnley.

"We're crossing The Straits to invade the mainland, on the 30th June. But, and this I don't like, we will be taken away from the 5th to become part of a Light Battalion and in a different Brigade. We won't be under Lacey's command, but we must make the best of it. The good part is that we will be operating as Light Infantry in a Light Infantry Battalion. Tomorrow we all march out of here to Milazzo, our embarkation port, which will take two days. I'd say we've got seven or eight days in camp before we embark and in those days I expect us to train under our new command, and I want all that we've learnt about being Light Infantry honed up to a state of perfection. I won't have us looking incompetent alongside other Light Companies. Clear?"

"Sir."

All spoke in unison. This was a different Carr, it was plainly noticeable, different especially to Drake and Rushby, and they were struck by it. No longer the languid, somnolent Carr. This was Captain Carr, Officer Commanding, giving his orders, clear and decisive. Things were different, as they were different about him. They were now on campaign, sooner or later to face the enemy.

"Good. Now go and tell the men."

The march to Milazzo was hot and testing. Mile after mile of brown dust road, under a hot sun that climbed high in the sky, to beat down almost vertical. However, when a stop came, shade was found under the verdant olive trees that lined the road in an unbroken swathe of deep green, and many clear, if narrow, streams ran off the hills to their left to keep their canteens full. Nevertheless, the heat took its toll. Many veterans soon discarded their shakoes for white kerchiefs that were knotted, bandana fashion around their heads. This was widely copied and soon almost all the battalion showed as a long red column with grey legs, on a brown road, topped by a thick collection of white dots above red jackets. Deakin, as ever, marched with Halfway.

"You ever been this hot? Not me, least not since the West Indies."

"Can't recall. Not even during a fierce mid-summer. This is just about the most damn burnt up place I ever clapped eyes on. If it weren't for these trees here, I'd say they'd had a grass fire through here just yesterday morning."

Deakin grinned at his longstanding companion and uncorked his waterbottle, offering it first to his friend.

"So, we'm over the water, onto the mainland."

Before taking a drink Halfway asked,

"Who told you where we're goin'?"

"Found out from the Lights. They've been told everything."

"Ah, invasion force. I don't like it. They can catch you on the beach, with their guns and then cavalry. A beach is perfect for cavalry. It can be all over in ten minutes. I don't like the sound of it."

"Well, bain't you cheerful this morning."

Gibney was marching off to the side of their column. Deakin turned to him.

"How do you reckon to a sea landin', Sar' Major?"

"It depends. Depends on the state of the sea, what the beach is like, and if tha' escort can get in close enough to cover thee with their guns. Get all three right, and thee's got a good chance. I'd say it's likely we can get all three, with the beaches in these parts and a sea that's not wound up. But, I'll tell thee one thing, I'd rather be goin' ashore off some boat than have to go up into some damn breach, thee knows. Up over some town wall."

"True, Sar' Major. True. You'll get no argument from me."

They did not march into Milazzo, for them it remained in the distance a collection of bright orange roofs with a single church dome, backed by many tall masts. They met Major O'Hare and then, on his direction, marched off the road to a clear, gently sloping hillside and settled to making a good camp, as this was to be their home for some days. The baggage train was close up

275

and soon tents and stores were scattered within their secured area. Lacey again called for his Senior Officers.

"We've got seven, perhaps eight days here. First we spend a day on checking equipment. I want the men to check everything they've got, every stitch and buckle, and we'll inspect again before embarkation. Nothing is to give way once we are over there. I don't want even a single button to come off, much less the sole of a shoe. All, and I mean all, Officers to inspect, don't just leave it to your Sergeants. Then we keep the men busy for as long as we've got. I want them in the best of fettle, able to march and run, keep formation and change formation. Finally, I want each of you to come up with some situation that we may have to face, and a solution. If I agree then we'll practice it. O'Hare, could you stay? The rest of you, dismiss."

They all saluted and left, with the exception of Major O'Hare.

"Stuart suspects our internal cohesion. As we're ex-detachments, it's the right question. What do you think?"

"The men respond to their orders from the drums and bugles well enough. As good as I've seen. What worries me is how soon do we know what's happening, so that we can give the correct order. I would suggest that each Company have a Lieutenant or NCO who is to act as a runner back to us, to carry anything that the Captain thinks we should know. They stay with their Captain at all times. That'll do no harm, perhaps even some good. Cohesion is all about us knowing what's going on, then good orders, quickly obeyed. Also, we've got two good Junior Majors, Simmons and Maltby. They could be encouraged to give an order before getting it confirmed. That's how I see it."

Lacey nodded. He had always regarded O'Hare as a good Officer. Now he was sure of it.

"I agree. Can I leave that with you?"

"Yes Sir. I'll see to it."

Lacey looked at O'Hare.

"Between you and me, Padraigh, I don't like losing our Lights and Grenadiers. I don't know what he has in mind over there, but the Grenadiers are assault troops and the Lights are skirmishers. I can't see where the need will come for a whole battalion of each. On top of that, Stuart's concerned about internal cohesion, but he's setting up two battalions where the Officers, as yet, don't even know each other's names! I don't like it. Keep a special eye on Carr and Carravoy, will you. I want their companies right up to the mark, in all ways. They may be put to the test, and it could be severe."

* * *

The battalion settled to a state as close to domestic bliss as could be contrived in the middle of a Sicilian hillside in late June. The camp followers soon created their family enclaves and the warm weather gave no problems with creating a few of the basic creature comforts. The day of "making and mending", little of the former, much of the latter, passed with little more than some irritation from the old soldiers, Tom Miles in particular, when Ellis came to make a check on progress.

"You think I don't know what happens, when a strap comes off yer pack!"

Ellis tugged it anyway.

Lacey and O'Hare were invited to dinner to meet Brigadier Cole and the other Senior Officers of the Brigade, and, as predicted, orders came for Carr and Carravoy to take their companies to a point different from the rest of the 5th for manoeuvres. Carravoy and D'Villiers found the move most conducive, for Brigadier Cole proved to be a tall aristocratic Officer, eminently the right sort, and the Grenadier Battalion was to be commanded by a Lieutenant Colonel Mallory, who turned out to be a friend of the Carravoy Family. Carr's encounter, on the other hand, proved to be much more of a military examination that any form of social re-acquaintance. The Light Companies were paraded and Kempt walked slowly up the line to inspect. Carr found himself being stared at by eyes that could pierce fog.

"Name?"

"Captain Carr, Sir. 5th Provisionals."

"Some of your men don't have muskets. Something different instead. Explain."

"They are Baker Rifles, Sir. They are accurate up to 200 yards, perhaps more. Our Colonel, Colonel Lacey, bought them for us at his own expense, Sir, with instructions that they be given to our best marksmen. The idea is that we pick off the enemy's Officers and NCO's first, Sir, and early. I have trained my men in just that drill. Sir."

"So you think you can bring down their Officers at long range."

"Yes, Sir. But more than think, I am confident that my men can."

"Let's see."

Kempt ordered a dozen targets to be set up, the time for which gave Carr a chance to talk to Davey.

"That's just under 200 and he's going to be as much worried about the rate of fire as the accuracy. What do you think? Do the bullets need to be wrapped in leather?"

Davey considered.

"No, Sir. We'll wrap the first, but not the rest. Under 200, I don't think it's needed, Sir, and those targets are man sized, they're not bulls eyes. We just have to hit them."

"Right. Pass the word along."

A dozen men were selected, including Davey, and all came to their mark, ready loaded.

Kempt took charge. He had his watch at the ready.

"I want six rounds, at those targets. Make ready. Present. Fire."

All twelve went off with the sharp bark peculiar to the Baker and all targets jerked with the impact. The reloading proceeded smoothly and all completed their six inside two minutes. Sixty-one hits were counted, out of the possible seventy-two. Kempt walked over to Carr.

"Return your men to their ranks."

"Sir."

The Lights and Grenadiers continued to train with their new battalions and, for a succession of days, all companies marched up into the hills and beyond. Each day saw a long sequence of exercises, marching, and musketry, until finally they could march back down to take their rest. All returned to camp soaked in perspiration and all felt the need to get clean, so that at the end of the day, the stream alongside the camp soon took on the appearance of an open air battalion bath house. This drove the women and anyone else in need, further from the camp, up-stream, to obtain clean water. This included, in particular the Mulcahey family, they being high in number and all grown enough to be capable. Mary O'Keefe, Bridie Mulcahey's young-est sister, was often despatched on the trek, high up the hill, with two buckets to fetch the necessary. It was day's end and the evening meal needed preparation, this now being the main meal of the day, for they were on campaign, and Mary was labouring back with a full pail in each hand.

"Can I help you, Miss? I'm just going back down myself, and I can carry those if you wish."

Mary set down the buckets and turned around to see a soldier that she had certainly noticed before, but had never come near. Joe Pike, wearing no tunic, just his shirt, had finished cleaning himself, and was just fitting his haversack around his shoulders as he left the stream in its little valley to come up to the path that ran back down to camp. Mary's green eyes widened to their fullest extent and the sideways tilt of her head matched her coquettish smile, but all this was lost on Joe. He was waiting for an answer. It came.

"Why, yes, kind Sir. I'm sure I'll be fully obliged for your help."

Joe walked forward to the buckets, but Mary did not step back. Joe had to awkwardly reach around her and, as he straightened up, his eyes looked full into hers, and she didn't look away. Confusion flooded his mind. He was looking at her for the first time, and he couldn't look away either, not for a long count to five, at least. She broke the moment.

"The water. They'll be needing it."

"Yes, right. As you say."

Off they went down the hill, part of the procession of cleaned up soldiers. Joe could not bring himself to look at her again, all the way back down, but she, on the other hand, was making a thorough appraisal of him. Tall, well muscled, good looks by any standard and carrying the heavy buckets as though they were empty. He was obviously kind, but equally obviously, painfully ill at ease, spending most of the journey studying the ground.

"My name's Mary. Mary O'Keefe. I'm with Pat Mulcahey's family. He's been made up to a Corporal. Do you know him?"

"Yes, sort of. He's friends with some that I know. My name's Joe. Joe Pike. I'm with the Lights. He must be in another Company. I've not seen him for some while now."

"He's in Number Three. Captain Heaviside."

"Him I do know."

In thus halting fashion the conversation continued until the Mulcahey encampment was reached and Joe set down the buckets. Bridie Mulcahey, Pat and the children were all around the fire. Mary made the introduction.

"This is Joe. Pike. He's helped me with the water."

Pat Mulcahey looked up.

"Joe, yes. The last time I saw you was in a Taunton pub. And some shenanigans."

Joe smiled but said nothing. However, Bridie could see all the signs in her sister's face as she stood regarding Joe, who was looking anywhere but at her. Bridie elbowed Pat in the ribs.

"Now sure, after a kindness such as that shouldn't we be inviting young Joe here to sup with us tonight? Yes, is how I'm thinking"

Pat Mulcahey looked at his wife in confusion. Food was scarce enough without adding guests.

"Yes, that's fine, if he brings over his ration, then sure, he's welcome to eat with us. I'm thinkin' that's the right of it."

His wife elbowed him again.

"Sure, isn't it the old skinflint that y'are. Things aren't that bad that a guest has to bring his own makings over to our fire to get fed."

Joe at last spoke up.

"You're all very kind." At last he managed a glance at Mary. "I'd very much like to eat supper with you, and Mr Mulcahey is right. I will bring my ration and add it to yours. Pleased to. I think that in the Lights we get a bit extra."

Bridie replied, after a black look at her husband, who was still rubbing his ribs.

"Well, that's very kind of you. And you're very welcome. If you fetch it now, I'll add it to our pot."

Joe nodded and managed a smile all round, but was again thrown by the knowing grins he received in return from the Mulcahey children. He beat a hasty retreat back to Miles and Davey, who were both preparing their rations prior to cooking.

"I'm eating with the Mulcahey's this evening. They've invited me over. I need to take over my ration."

Miles looked up frowning.

"And what brought this on?"

"I carried Mary O'Keefe's water buckets back for her."

Davey looked up.

"Oh yes, and what happened from that?"

"She's got green eyes, dark hair, and soft brown skin."

"Green eyes, dark hair, and soft brown skin! Well, that tells us all we need to know. Give him his portion, Tom, he's lost to us."

Joe emptied his haversack of his washing items and held it open for the dried peas and potatoes. He opened his clasp knife and hacked off his portion of the salt pork and returned in thus ungainly posture to the family estate of the Mulcaheys. The ration was handed over and immediately added to the family pots. Joe remained standing, as awkward as a Parson at a pagan wedding, until Mary moved over where she was sitting, although there was already plenty of room, and patted the ground next to her.

"Sit down, Joe."

Joe obeyed and soon became the object of gentle questioning that revealed his story up to his joining the Army. The food came and Joe found it most palatable. Mrs Mulcahey, well experienced with Army rations, had found some herbs to add to the flavour and a little flour gave each a dumpling on top of their portion. With the meal ended, Joe sat with Pat Mulcahey in the midst of the family, Pat contenting himself with his evening smoke, whilst the children chattered around him, and Joe and himself talked farming and carpentry. With the pots washed, Bridie pronounced that more water was needed, which confused Pat who could see that there was still plenty, and Joe and Mary took themselves back up to the stream in the last light of the day, the full orange sun now low on the horizon. After a while both returned, Joe with full buckets, Mary with a chain of small blue flowers circling around her hairline. Joe had remembered how he had made similar for his younger sister. All had then said good night, whilst Mary's waving good-bye had set off giggling amongst the Mulcahey children, a sound soon silenced by Pat himself.

"Hush now, the lot of you, and keep your impish selves under those blankets."

Joe returned to Miles and Davey, thoughts so far away he would have walked past their fire, had Davey not shouted to him.

"He's returned, love's lost dream. And how was the meal at the Mulcahey's."

"It was nice, very tasty, she put something extra in it, herbs I think, and we each had a dumpling."

Tom Miles natural character immediately rose to the surface.

"So you're sayin' it were a lot better than you'd have got back here?"

John Davey sprung to Joe's defence.

"Now, just how much of a surprise is it, that Bridie Mulcahey is a better cook than you?"

Tom Miles gave Davey a sideways scowl but said no more. Joe slumped down and stared at the fire.

"Green eyes, dark hair, and soft brown skin."

Joe Davey looked sideways at him and grinned.

"That's right, lad. Now you'd best turn in. You've another day in the hills tomorrow. Could be our last, I think."

It was. The next day was the 23rd and orders came around that they were to embark at dawn of the 25th, sooner than all thought, so that day was their last day of exercise. Come the evening meal, Joe ate with his two messmates, but, with no surprise to them, the meal finished, he wandered over to the Mulcahey family and soon he and Mary could be seen together talking, sat a little way off from the family. The 24th was final inspection day and all gave their equipment a final check. As the whole battalion sat on the dry grass in the warm sunshine, Mary came over to help Joe make his check. Joe made the introductions and John Davey bid her welcome. Tom Miles said nothing and so Davey did the talking for him.

"This be Tom Miles."

Miles looked up from biting through a button thread.

"He doesn't say much, but generally what he does say is worth listening to, and the rest you takes no notice of. It's not hard to tell the difference."

Miles at last spoke.

"And is it my fault that you've caught me with a mouth full of cotton! I'm pleased to meet you, Mary. We were just making some tea, if you'd like some."

With the last he gave a challenging nod in the direction of John Davey. Mary smiled and Tom returned his best rictus grin. Davey explained.

"Take that as a greeting. The best we've seen for many a long week."

Mary grinned. "I'll make the tea, if you like."

All nodded and Mary began. When all had a mug of the good brew, she took up Joe's tunic and checked the buttons. One did not gain approval and she set about a repair.

The afternoon saw assembly by companies and the two Sergeants of the Light Company made a pre-inspection before the Officers. Ellis thoroughly checked Miles' musket and, although it was perfect right up to the new flint, Ellis gave Miles a black look the equal of the one he was receiving, and the animosity from Miles intensified when Ellis had the audacity to check the cleanliness of the touch hole in the priming pan. For an hour knapsacks and all else were pulled, tugged and tested, musket slings and shoe soles also not being allowed to escape. The Lights all passed inspection.

They were to march down through Milazzo an hour before daybreak on the next day and so that evening was spent with friends and family, and sweethearts, as in the case of Joe and Mary, for they could be seen in their usual place, just off from the Mulcaheys. Just as there had been a parting back in England, this now was the parting for the families that had been allowed to follow their menfolk. The soldier in each of the families Mulcaheys, the Hills and the Nicholls, sat long into the night, holding their wives and looking at their children. Reveille sounded whilst all was still dark, but not in any way chill, and the men filed out from their family areas to form up in their companies. In the poor light of the re-kindled campfires farewells were made, and in just such a yellow glow Joe and Mary stood facing each other holding hands, but saying nothing. When the last call for assembly was given, Mary placed her right hand on Joe's chest.

"Come back safe."

Joe smiled down at her, even through the dark, then he turned and ran to his company. A Corporal showed his displeasure.

"Where've you been, Pike?"

Tom Miles answered.

"Leave him be, Corporal. He had more of a good bye to say than most."

Orders rang out and the battalion marched out onto the dusty road and entered Milazzo.

* * *

283

General Stuart himself was observing the embarkation. He sat his horse, accompanied by his Staff, just off the road where it entered the port. He saw the 5th approaching and studied their passing. Grudgingly, he had to say to himself that he liked what he saw. All in step, each man well turned out and with the bearing of one who is fit and capable. He followed the 5th into the town and approached Colonel Lacey.

"Lacey. It seems your men are up together. First impressions are good, but will they fight as well as they look?"

"I have no reason to think otherwise, Sir."

Stuart nodded.

"I hope your confidence is justified. Now, Willoughby here has your embarkation orders. I'll see you on the other side. Good luck, Lacey."

"Thank you, Sir."

Willoughby handed over the orders and rode off.

The orders showed that they were using their old transports, which were waiting for them at the quayside, amongst many others. The Lights were to be in the Tansy, the Grenadiers in the Llewellyn, the remaining eight companies and their supplies in the Bidewell. The 5th assembled on the quayside. Carr, Drake and Rushby came up to Lacey and O'Hare. Carr spoke.

"Permission to take the Light Company off to our transport, Sir?"

Lacey made no direct reply, neither did O'Hare. Lacey merely offered his hand.

"Good luck, Carr."

"Thank you. Sir."

O'Hare made the same to all three, and perfect salutes were exchanged. Whilst the Lights marched on, Lacey led his men onto the familiar deck and took himself down to the equally familiar cabin, accompanied by Major O'Hare. There he found the Senior Officers of the Brigade assembled and all toasted the success of their forthcoming venture. All settled aboard their ships, but from there nothing happened. An unseasonal Gregale was blowing steady from the North East making any exit of the harbour very difficult. Aboard the Tansy, Kempt used the idle time to consult with his Officers, that being Captains and above. Carr found himself looking at a large, hand-drawn map spread on the cabin table.

"In case you haven't met him, this is Major Greelish, my Senior Major."

The Major stepped forward. His most striking feature was a large blond moustache, then one would note blond hair of the same shade, then the narrow pale blue eyes, but Greelish had the powerful frame of a cavalryman.

'It's a pleasure to meet you, Gentlemen."

He shook hands with those nearest and nodded a greeting to those more distant. Kempt continued.

"This is the Bay of St Euphemia, on the Calabrian coast. We land here, at the Northern end, close to the village that names the bay. The landmark is a squat tower just off the beach. The advance party will be two companies of us Lights, a company of Grenadiers and the whole of the 78th, all under the command of Lieutenant Colonel Oswald. Carr, Moresby, I've volunteered your companies."

Kempt looked steadily at both, enough to gain their clear understanding.

"Once there, intelligence says that Regnier is some way off, but the army will advance from our landing, in column along the beach, our Battalion leading. That will give order of deployment, making the whole army ready for any battle, but minus the 20th. They have been despatched in small ships further down the coast to demonstrate at various points and distract the French. With a good wind Stuart hopes they will rejoin in time to take part in the likely engagement."

Kempt leant further over the map, using it to illustrate his explanation.

"Now, this is our understanding of the ground beyond the bay. As you can see, inland looks like a wide saucer of lowland, perfect to allow us to position ourselves to the South, and then advance inland in formation. Carr, when we march along the beach, I want yours in the lead. When it comes to it, your company will form our right flank, where your Baker rifles may come in useful. That's the best I can say until we know more about the enemy's dispositions. Now, back to your men, and see they're settled in."

All day the ships sat at the quayside and inside the men cooked in the Sicilian heat. The transports were crowded to the maximum with stores and supplies, besides men, some also with horses and artillery. Sat in the enclosed harbour, the opening of ports and hatches did nothing and come the afternoon, men were going down with heatstroke. Stuart gave his orders. Come dawn they would get out to sea, whatever the circumstances. The devilish Gregale still held and so all were towed out, just far enough for sails to be set and the fleet to sail North of North-West, thus gaining enough sea room to tack and sail close hauled on their desired Easterly course. After two slow days, they were joined by a small fleet that had embarked at Faro and, escorted by HMS Apollo, HMS Endymion and the brave Ipheion, they held their course for the Bay of St Euphemia.

Deep in the hull of the Bidewell, Quartermaster Sergeant Pearson had his men preparing for the invasion, numbering each item, whether bundle or barrel, by their order of priority, so that the most important would be landed first. He made good use of Sedgwicke when it came to reading the manifest and establishing identity, then, where possible, the stores were re-arranged, those with priority moved under the hatches. Sedgwicke had established a good working relationship with Pearson and now, with emotions high, he felt able to converse with him on a rough level of parity, himself up to a superior and Pearson down to a subordinate, that being.

"Is this your first campaign, Sergeant? First on a foreign shore, that is?"

"No, Percy, it ain't. I went to Flanders in '94 with the Duke of York. I was a ranker then and part of that bloody mess of Tourcoing. 'Tween you an me I don't relish goin' up against the French again, yet 'ere I be. Still, at least as Quartermaster I got a better chance of keepin' out of it. Then, we got kicked out with our tail between our legs and I expects the same 'ere. The only bright spark be the absence of mud and rain, like there was there."

Sedgwicke said nothing, but reached out a hand to steady himself as the Bidewell took a rare lurch in the gentle sea as the coast of the mainland came steadily closer. On the evening of the 30th in the last light that remained in the Western sky the horizon changed from the level blue of the ocean to the gentle brown and green of the Calabrian Hills. The Endymion had cracked on and made the correct landfall whilst there was still light and, guided by her lights, they joined her. The signal light shone from the Apollo, "Land at first light."

* * *

Captain Roul Linois was enjoying himself. They had descended on the small village at just the right time, their evening meal, and he was helping himself to bread and fowl taken from the table of a terrified Calabrian family, now cowering in the corner of their single room. All around, out of the half dark, came screams, shouts, and shots as his Voltigeurs searched the hovels from top to bottom for food and anything else of any worth. Several villagers lay already dead, their peasant blood staining the hard packed earth of the village centre, and some bleeding out their lives in their own doorways. Between mouthfuls, he yelled orders at his enthusiastic men, giving instructions as to where a special search should be made. Another peasant met his untimely end, blasted out of his own house through the back door by two shots from close range muskets. The light was growing, not from anything celestial, simply from burning houses. This was satisfaction indeed for the past trials of partisan warfare.

His men assembled back in the square, carrying what they had found. It was a good haul, including livestock, but Linois knew that it wasn't all there was. He ordered the family to be brought forth and lined up against the wall. The family consisted of a husband, his wife, two sons and an elder daughter. Linois took a swallow then a swig and looked at the family.

"Tirer la femme et les garcons. Marque la fille"

The wife and sons were summarily shot and the daughter staked out, and spread-eagled on the hard earth, her dress ripped open from hem to bodice. Linois turned to the translator.

"Demande' a lui. Ou' est la nourriture il haez cache?"

The interpreter asked the question and the Father, in a state of shock and hysteria, motioned the interpreter to follow him. Linois motioned to four soldiers to follow. After a few minutes they returned with five sacks of grain. Linois looked at the interpreter.

"C'est tout?"

The interpreter nodded. Linois walked over to the Father, drew his pistol and shot him through the head. He then walked over to the girl, unbuttoning his trousers. Rank had its privileges.

Chapter Nine

Maida

Moving by touch, as much as by sight, the two companies assembled on either side of the main deck of the Tansy. Little could be seen despite the best efforts of two candle lanterns at either end, the most that could be utilised in the face of the order that no lights were to be shown. In the poor light that fell more upon their shoes rather than their faces, the orders were read to both Companies, Carr's words forming a precise echo to those of Captain Moresby.

"Once you are out of the boat, if we are under fire, get up the beach and find some cover. If not under fire, form up in skirmish order."

Over the side there was nothing to see, no colour, neither sea, nor sky, nor any tone even to the ship's side, as both Companies descended ladders and netting into the waiting longboats. A bashful moon, away to their left, low down and but the sickle of a new phase, did nothing to add any light. Dawn was but a suggestion on the Eastern horizon, as they felt their way down, reaching out a tentative foot to engage reassuringly with the gunwale of the mercifully stable boat below. Encumbered by full kit, they sank gratefully onto the benches within each longboat and more than one placed his hand onto the side of the goodship Tansy, as farewell to the sound and safe ship that had brought them there. As each longboat filled with soldiers they pulled off a short way to allow others to take their place and receive their complement and so, for those in the first boats, there came a long wait while the landing battalion assembled to enable them to set out all together. As a file, Miles, Davey, and Joe Pike sat a bench together, with three other Lights filling the bench to their right. Each gripped their empty musket. None were to be loaded as yet, there was to be no risk of an accidental discharge to warn any possible occupying force that they were on their way. As the most experienced soldier there, Tom Miles was the one that Joe Pike sought answers from.

"What's going to happen, Tom? What's it going to be like?"

"Can't tell you too much, boy, this be a first for me, an all. All I can say is, get off the beach, quick, unless you'm ordered otherwise, and get to some cover. Scrub, or dunes or something, then wait and see. "'Tis cavalry that worries me, on an open beach."

John Davey joined in.

"We'll be alright, Joe. We did alright on the Madelline, didn't we? And this is on dry ground!"

A voice joined in from somewhere in the dark.

"Ah, but that was a sea fight, and you don't get too many cavalry in fights at sea."

The light was growing, a horizon could be located, dark below less dark, but a black square block, silhouetted, was clearly discernable in front but just off to the left. The order was passed around, in no more than speaking voice.

"Form line abreast."

The sailor on the tiller gave the command, "Give way all" and the oars creaked as the manoeuvre was completed, then came the final order, "Ahead together" and "Give way all" was heard again. A look either side, even in the growing half light, would have shown a long succession of landing boats as Colonel Oswald's advance battalion pulled for the shore, but few even glanced that way, by far the most were intent on the shoreline before them. The order came to load and all did, albeit awkwardly, whilst sat on the crowded seats. The pitch of the boat became more regular as they met the surf before the beach and then came the crunch of gravel under the hull. Daylight had arrived during their row in. The sailors leapt out either side to steady the craft and all stood up to disembark over the bows, which had driven up, out of the knee deep waves. One of the sailors joked with Miles.

"There you are soldier, you've not even got your feet wet."

"Thanks, mate. If you're ever in The Hatchet, in Bristol, look me up and I'll buy you a drink."

"Who shall I ask for?"

"Duke of Cumberland."

Once out they formed up, in their threes, with Officers and Sergeants in front, all anxious, waiting for orders, staring at the dune grass that marked the end of the beach. Suddenly, from behind them, came the roar of cannon fire and they heard the rush of shot passing above their heads. Both the Apollo and the Endymion were firing at battle speed at targets inland. Oswald came to the centre and waved them all forward. Carr turned and repeated the order.

"In files, move forward."

They advanced into the dune grass and through it, until it thinned, where they saw the object of their supporting cannon fire; enemy infantry. 150 yards ahead was a battalion of what looked like mixed troops, some in sky blue but most in a strange combination of dark green with a wide crimson centre. They were suffering from the accurate Naval gunfire directed from the mastheads, the grape shot ploughing up huge gouts of earth or smashing bodies to pieces from direct hits. The several prone bodies at their feet gave testament to the accuracy of the cannonfire just witnessed. Still no orders, so Carr gave his.

"Rifles to the front. Skirmish order."

John Davey moved ahead of Joe Pike.

"150 yards."

Some adjusted their sights. Davey had already done so.

"Make Ready. Present."

Davey levelled his sights onto an Officer.

"Fire."

The Officer fell. From the way he twisted twice, he was probably hit by two bullets.

"Advance to 100 yards."

They ran forward and both companies either side followed, either from their example or their own order, it was impossible to know. The cannonballs were still singing over their heads, a lot lower than on the beach. At 100 yards Carr resumed the engagement.

"Two ranks."

His men formed up.

"Front rank. Make ready. Present. Fire."

45 muskets crashed out in response to the order, soon followed by the second rank. Drake took over, co-ordinating the fire, whilst Carr looked for Oswald, but couldn't see him. Davey was looking for another enemy Officer to target, found one, but was annoyed when it took two shots to bring him down, whilst Miles and Pike loaded and fired at either side as rapidly was they could. A Major arrived that Carr didn't know.

"Are you Captain Carr?"

"Yes Sir."

"Oswald wants you now. Follow me."

Whilst shouting to Drake to hold there, Carr followed the Major off to the right. After some time he found himself on the edge of the dunes with Colonel Oswald, the new Major and Captain Carravoy. Carr recognised that they were behind Carravoy's Grenadiers, who were all firing furiously. Oswald gave his orders. He had a strong Scottish accent, and needed to shout above the din of the muskets, and the distant roar of the naval bombardment, but here there were no cannonballs rushing overhead.

"Carravoy. I want you to take that farmhouse to our front. Carr, I'm pulling you out of the line. A company of the 78th will relieve you. I want you to support Carravoy on his left by taking the barn and paddock of the same farm. Bring your men back to here when the 78th arrive."

Carr doubled back, only part way with the Major, who soon angled off to the rear. Carr found his company continuing the fight and so far no just one dead, two injured. The 78th arrived, led by the same Major and they formed up behind, so Carr ordered his Company to follow him and they set off at the run, still in two ranks. Three minutes brought them back to Oswald where the Grenadiers had formed four ranks and they immediately began their own advance. Carr ordered skirmish order and in their three's they advanced. When they came under fire they advanced by filing, the first fired, then the second advanced on, then the third, until they reached the fence. The paddocks were lightly held and soon cleared; also the barn, the enemy leaving five dead and wounded as proof of the accuracy of the Lights musketry. Carr ordered them to add what could be moved to the back fence as fortification, then take up firing positions and be ready to receive a counterattack.

Carravoy led his men straight at the farmhouse and was relieved at little opposition, just some ineffectual fire that seemed to come from elsewhere. Two of his Grenadiers stove in the wide frontdoor and they entered to find the family disappearing down into the cellar via a large trapdoor in the floor. He turned to one of his Lieutenants, Josiah Berkeley

"What's hello, in Calabrian?"

"Haven't a clue. Blessed if I know. Bon something."

Carravoy had to satisfy himself with grinning at the anxious face of the farmer as it passed out of sight beneath the floorboards. His men were arriving.

"Get to the back, man the windows and doors. We are required to hold this place."

He took himself upstairs and the first view he had was to the side, seeing Carr's men lining the walls and fences of the paddocks; this he liked. The view from the back window he did not like; something of the order of two Companies, in French blue, were advancing at his building in thick skirmish order, they would get to him first, not to Carr, the farmhouse was plainly their objective. A view from the remaining side he liked even less. There were no British troops there; he was the far right flank. This was his first engagement and the weight of command was suddenly very heavy. What happened with the Madelline didn't seem to count. Should he hold, or retreat? He decided that he had to make some attempt to hold the building, if only to delay the French attack, and then hope. He issued his orders and his men increased in number at the windows and lined the back garden walls. At less than 100 yards he gave the order to fire. A ragged volley came from all around. The French took their casualties, but then came on. Carravoy's men reloaded and kept up the fight, but the French were not stopped, they were creeping forward in threatening numbers. He called for Berkeley.

"Go back around the front to the paddocks and find Carr. Tell him I need support. Tell him three Companies are attacking us. Go now."

Carr was looking to his front. There was nothing, just some fugitives that they had just ejected. The main conflict was off to his left, and then he heard the eruption of musketry from the farm on his right. He could see nothing of their assailants, but plainly there must be some. Berkeley arrived, anxious and breathless.

"Captain Carr. We are under attack. Three Companies. Captain Carravoy asks that you give some support."

"Three Companies? That's nearly half a battalion."

"That's what Captain Carravoy said."

Carr looked over the paddock wall. Still nothing in front, just the odd remaining fugitive. He took his decision.

"Tell Captain Carravoy he can count on my support. Go now."

Berkeley hurried off.

"Drake. Take your section forward then right, around to the back of the farm. Two ranks. Pitch into any French you see. Keep a lookout to your left. If any French appear on your flank, retreat back to here and hold. Understood?"

"Sir."

"Rushby, your section to follow me."

Drake took his men over the walls and off to the right, but they were soon lost to Carr's sight as he led Rushby's section past the front of the farm building. In its shelter he halted his men.

"Two ranks. Reload."

This was quickly done and Carr led them out beyond the building where immediately he saw what he was up against. The French had pushed right up to the farm walls in numbers and were pulling at the gates and fences, but a force nothing like three Companies. Carr led his men further on to form at 50 yards range on the flank of the attacking French and then he heard the controlled volleys coming from the other side. Drake was in action and Carr commenced volley by ranks from his own command. Several blue figures collapsed like rag dolls. An Officer tried to lead an assault towards them, but this died before it began when his chest collapsed with the impact of two musket balls. Opposed from in front and assailed from both sides the French broke and ran. Carr ordered a ceasefire and walked to a garden gate, but to use it he had to pull away a dead Frenchman. He walked up to the back door and knocked politely.

"Anyone home?"

The door was opened by Carravoy, with Berkeley in attendance. Carr spoke first.

"Thought I'd better check and ensure that everything was alright. Using the tradesmen's entrance seemed appropriate."

"Thank you for your trouble, Carr, but in the end there was no need. We were seeing them off comfortably."

"Berkeley here made it sound rather urgent. Three Company strength."

"Well, he's a worrier. Come the end, things were well in hand."

"Yes, I'm sure, but whatever, there's a few less Frenchmen that we all no longer have to concern ourselves with, and that made it worth the trouble. So, if there's nothing further, I'll get back to my own paddock."

He tipped the rim of his shako with the pommel of his sword and left, taking his men with him. Back in position they were all drinking water and sheltering from the now hot sun, when the Major arrived and he looked around and saw the French dead and the wounded prisoners. The Lights had dragged them into the shade and were doing what they could, including sharing water.

"Right, Carr. Job done, I see. Hold here and await further orders. The 78th have pushed into St Euphemia and so we are now consolidating. Most of the army are coming ashore. Well done."

"Thank you, Sir."

The Major then took himself into the farmhouse by the front door and, after passing through, he saw the extensive remains of the fight on the other side when he looked out from a back window.

"Well done, Carravoy. Things plainly got very hot on your side, the fiercest action of the landing. But you held them off, as I can see. With no support?"

"Almost, Sir. The Light Company did appear around the flanks, but we largely did the job ourselves."

"Well done, well done indeed."

"Thank you, Sir, but my Grenadiers are a match for any company of Frenchmen. We didn't have too much trouble changing their minds."

"Well said, Captain. Be assured that your fine performance will be reported to Colonel Oswald."

"We're grateful, Sir."

* * *

Carr and Carravoy held their positions and rested until noon, when orders came to move North to St Euphemia. Correctly forming fours they marched to their new position. InevitablyMiles had something to say.

"Did you see them packs that those Frenchers carry? Made out of finest cowhide I'd say. I've a mind to make sure one comes my way, first chance I get. Their boots look a cut above, too."

Ellis overheard.

"And what happens to your old pack, Miles? Fine you'll look on parade with some brown and white cowhide job on your back. You'll be flogged for wilful loss of the King's property."

"Alright, I know, I know. But if this campaign goes on a long while, these of ours will fall apart. They always do. Come that time, Regulations falls by the wayside and that's when you'll see me wearin' one. Boots an' all."

"Until that happens you keep wearin' the one you got."

All around grinned at the exchange, until they found themselves marching over the ground that they had first fought over and saw a few Calabrian civilians burying bodies, some being the mangled remains of those brought down by the cannon fire. Even the hardest veterans looked away. They passed Engineers digging fortifications above the beach they had landed on hours before and many of these, their labours creating a severe thirst, walked alongside both companies to share a drink from their canteens. Next they passed a curious square tower which they recognised as the square block that they had seen as they came in on their longboats at the dawn of that day. Finally they reached St Euphemia where Colonel Oswald was waiting for them, and he called Carr and Carravoy over to him.

"The landing battalion is now disbanded, therefore your Companies are returned to their original commands. My thanks to you both for what you did over on the right, especially you, Carravoy. My Major tells me you held that farmhouse against a strong French attack. They'd have turned our flank were it not for you, and you held it practically unsupported, something on your flanks, but you in the centre, where it was hot. Your men must be bonny fighters. What's your Regiment, again?"

"5th Provisionals, Sir."

"And your Colonel?"

"Lieutenant Colonel Lacey, Sir."

"Well fine, good, I'll mention you to him when I see him. Now, good day to you both."

Carravoy knew that Carr had heard every word and turned away as soon as he could. Carr could not resist making a comment, even though it was at Carravoy's back.

"Practically unsupported? Something on your flanks? This new hole in my head must still be giving me delusions. I'd better check with my men, find out what really happened."

With that he returned to his Company and they sought out Kempt's Light Battalion. The men made camp and collected their rations, but Carr was livid. Drake and Rushby could see it and busied themselves with their letters and sketching, leaving him silent, simmering within his own dark thoughts.

As their pork and peas bubbled in the pot, Davey, Miles and Pike sat cleaning their firearms and attending to other required maintenance. Their cartridge boxes were half empty but that was corrected with the arrival of Percival Sedgwicke, leading a mule. Davey greeted his old barrack room companion.

"Hello old Parson. Does that mule speak English or have you learnt the local lingo?"

The other two grinned and made their greeting.

"How's things, Parson. Still looking after our rum?"

Sedgwicke was moved by their cheery greeting and laughed with them.

"Yes, yes, of course, but I'm here on a different errand. How many cartridges do you need?"

Each examined their cartridge boxes and made their answer so that Sedgwicke could count them out from the panniers on the mule. All was good humoured, but he still felt awkward in their company. These were hard and capable soldiers, high status, but that was part of the problem; to him their capability in battle elaborated their coarseness and insensitivity and it caused him no small discomfort. With such as these he could never be "at ease". He stood silent and awkward. John Davey detected only his discomfiture, not its cause and, as in the past, he came to his aid.

"Well then Parson, you must be on your way round. We'll be seeing you some more, no doubt?"

"Yes, yes, and good luck to you all."

"And to you, Parson."

Sedgwicke led his mule around the rest of the 5th Light Company and returned it to a stable in the village; he then took himself back to the beach. The waves had risen during the day and the landings were not going well. Stores were coming ashore and men also, but it was all that the sailors could do to prevent the longboats broaching over on the beach and spilling either passengers or cargo into the boiling surf. Sedgwicke knew that he had to return to the Bidewell and he climbed awkwardly aboard an empty longboat, failing to avoid a soaking from a coursing wave that scoured along the longboat's side before crashing onto the hissing shingle. His was the last boat for the day. Evening being near, Stuart halted any more attempts to land. It would be completed the following morning, the 3rd July. Wet, but not cold with the day being so hot he returned to the hold of the Bidewell and sat himself down near Pearson, and began to remove his soaked clothing.

"Hello, Percy. Found a new way to keep cool? How's the landing?"

"I think it's stopped. I saw no other boats passing me as I came back."

"Really? Well then, that's us done for the day. Time to get our rations."

"Seems the landings have gone well. We've pushed the French back and have got ourselves ashore."

"Ah, you mark my words, Percy. Johnny Frog is just letting us gather up on the beach. They'm biding their time, all the better to see us out of here. I've seen it before. They'll take more beatin' than we can put together."

At this moment, General Stuart may have agreed with him, as from the top of the square tower, the Bastione di Malta, looking South East he could see the myriad pinpricks of light from the French campfires on the heights just to the West of the village of Maida, above the River Lamato. The impression given was that his own force was outnumbered. He could only hope that an undisturbed 3rd July would give him time to complete his landing and get all his stores ashore.

On that day, Sedgwicke and Pearson, both good Storesmen, completed their portion of the task by emptying the Bidewell of all that was required to go on shore. It was completed by the end of the morning and the afternoon was spent in a leisurely check of what remained, matching the stores to the manifest. Then the rumour began to circulate around the ship; the French army had been seen. Then came the order; all Storesmen to go ashore and make preparations to follow the army out to meet the French. Full weapons and equipment to be carried.

* * *

Lacey had himself woken early and emerged from his tent to immediately see Major O'Hare.

"Are the men ready? The orders were to be ready to march at dawn."

"Yes Sir, they are. Formed up and ready."

4th July was another slow dawn, but, beyond the camp, Lacey had enough light to see his eight companies formed up and stood easy.

"Have the men been checked? Cartridges, spare flints?"

"The Sergeants and NCO's are doing that now, Sir."

Lacey nodded, reassured. He looked at the breaking dawn.

"Well, Padraigh, a clean sun up. Let's hope we see the sunset, eh?"

"Good luck to us all, Sir."

"Amen to that."

The inevitable Major Willoughby rode up.

"Please to march your men out to their position, Sir. Most are already in place."

"Very well. I'll lead the men there myself."

Lacey walked over to his men, now clear in the growing sunlight. O'Hare preceded him and shouted the first order.

"Parade!"

All came to order arms.

"Three cheers for the Colonel, boys. Let the French hear you!"

The men cheered lustily, some raising their muskets to the brightening sky.

"Huzza! Huzza! Huzza!"

Lacey drew his sword and brought it before his chin to salute his men.

"A bright day to clobber the French, lads. We'll see the right side of them before this day is done, and that's the backside!"

Laughter was interspersed with the shouts of agreement as O'Hare and Lacey marched to the head of the column. O'Hare turned, half right.

"From you, Gibney."

"Parade, by the left. Forward march."

Each left foot rose and hit the sand. The 5th marched on and took their place behind the Grenadier Battalion of Cole's Brigade. The army, now formed up and facing South, marched off and Halfway and Deakin looked around.

"Where are we in all this?"

"We'm in the middle, Toby. Last Brigade in the middle column. Last battalion in the last Brigade. Bringin' up the rear."

He stepped out to the side to obtain a better view.

"There's another Brigade ahead of us, that must be Acland, with his Scots girlies, another out on the sea shore, that must be Oswald, with those funny Swiss buggers. What looks like the Lights is inland on our left, and if I'm not mistaken, that's

Carr, Drake and Rushby, and that mean sod Ellis, leading that column. Our Lights must be the leading Company. Led by that cheery piece of work, Kempt."

"You think there'll be a battle, Ned?"

"I wouldn't bet nothin' against it. We'm for a fight, certain sure."

The march South soon saw the loss of any kind of form that would apply to a parade ground. Miles swore and cursed, joined by those around him as they pulled each other through the swamp and mud where the plain met the dunes. Deakin and Halfway, contending with their own slog through the sand dunes and weighed down by the same full kit, noted that the beach column were staggering around the equal of themselves as their boots sank into the soft, loose shingle of the sea edge. The supply train, following on and containing Sedgwicke and Pearson leading forward a string of mules and donkeys, could choose for themselves and used the high beach, this being marginally easier for both men and animals.

For over an hour they heaved themselves onward, full equipment and packs weighing more and more as the treacherous ground continued and the sun grew higher. At last the order came to halt and rest. The men sank down and reached for water canteens and haversacks containing biscuits. Sergeants made their rounds and many an inexperienced soldier got a musket butt in his back for tipping precious water over his head, rather than drinking it.

Carr, Drake and Rushby were halted just behind Kempt and his Staff. Beyond they could see a river, seemingly wide, and fast flowing over its last yards to the sea. It seemed shallow, not deep.

"What river's that, Nat?" Rushby asked.

"I believe it's called the Lamato. And I'd say that our walk along the beach is done. Inland now to deliver our greetings to Mr Frenchman."

Officers were galloping about on foam-flecked horses and Carr, noticing movement to his left, saw the whole General Staff, with Stuart in the middle, canter up to Colonel Kempt. After a short discussion involving much arm waving, Stuart galloped off to their right, to Colonel Acland and his Staff, at the head of the middle column. Kempt came up to Carr and returned Carr's salute.

"We're marching inland, deployed as a firing line, two ranks. Your Company will take its line from the river there and, you being the right flank, I'm going to support you with two Companies of Corsicans and a Company of Sicilians. I may well send the Corsicans over the river, if required I'll ask you to support them. Until then, deploy your men, and await orders. Good luck, Carr."

Kempt nodded in reply to the salutes from Drake and Rushby and stalked on to issue his orders to the rest of his Captains. All around, in all columns, men were scrambling to their feet, and obeying the orders "Order Arms" then "Shoulder Arms". The last tots of rum were being issued, those still without, eager to receive their ration. Tom Miles, Joe Pike and John Davey were being served by the same Orderly that had received the bitter end of Miles' tongue way back in Taunton Barracks.

"No thumb in this time."

"No Tom, 'tis full measure. Good luck to you and to Joe."

"Thanks, mate. Come the finish, eh?"

"Come the finish, Tom."

Being at the end of Cole's Brigade, the 5th were the last to receive the order to split their column of fours into two ranks to form a long firing line. Similar was happening all over Stuart's command, but eventually all were formed up to the General's satisfaction. The companies of the 5th were spread fully over the Army's deployment, the Light Company on the far right, the eight Line Companies of the 5th and their Grenadiers on the far left under Cole. Stuart took the time to ride over to inspect that side and noted that the 5th was one of the few battalions that came to the "present" arms as he approached. Stuart had the manners to acknowledge the salute by removing his hat and holding it aloft as he rode along the line.

Lacey was with Brigadier Cole and Colonel Mallory of the Grenadiers.

"Lacey, you hold our left flank. The French have some cavalry, but it's hard to tell their strength. Edge over left to the scrub on the slope, and restrict the open ground; gain yourself some protection. Mallory, I'm giving you artillery front right. Cole, you will have Acland to your right, and Oswald in reserve for both you and him. The 20th may return in time or may not. Landing at St Euphemia the likelihood is that they'll arrive to support you. The French are coming off the heights to our right,

300

their forward units probably coming down and fording the Lamato as we speak. I suspect that they will attack in echelon, they won't take the trouble to form a line, so when you hear the game open on our right, that's where we'll make contact first, so make sure that your men are ready. You'll be in action soon after. I'm advancing from the right. When you see Acland move, that's your cue. Good luck to you all, Gentlemen. See you when it's done." He tugged on his right rein and took himself back with his Staff, back along the line, making a show of rising in his stirrups with his hat in the air, acknowledging the cheers of the 5th and the Grenadiers. He felt re-assured. His left was as secure as he could make it. Both the 5th Provisionals and the Grenadiers looked well led and solid.

Ten, then 15 minutes passed, three 4 lb guns arrived, in pieces and carried by mules, but within 5 minutes they were assembled onto their carriages with the gunners stood ready to pull them forward. Then Cole saw the Colours of Acland's 81st and 78th appear out of the ranks and the whole moved forward. Cole gave the order and his own command began their own advance across the hot, dry, plain.

* * *

Across the reach of time, almost all battles have been fought on open ground, creating the moment when, from afar, the enemy appears in view and the armies present themselves to each other. At first there's a suggestion of a different colour where the plain ends at a wood or hill or even the horizon. Then the colour becomes clearer and is part of a definite line and there may be some sparkle from weapons and accoutrements. Then the colour divides to become a uniform with brazen Colours clear above the ranks, then there's movement; feet and arms march and swing, and shakoes or helmets emphasise the movement of heads. It is at this point that the prospect of battle is wholly real, death now stands at all men's shoulders.

So it was for the men of Stuart's army, as their forward march began. From a mile or more, there was a suggestion of blue in the shroud of brown dust that lifted in the heat haze but then all was obscured again as the dust thickened once more. All eyes were on no other thing as the whole British army advanced in line. Carr in the centre of his Company, with Drake

301

and Rushby off to the sides before their own sections. Together they marched onward with swords sloped across their shoulders, their men with shouldered arms. Carr was one of the few to catch the movement to his right. True to his word, Kempt had sent the Corsican Rangers over the river to enter the thickets and woodland. Carr saw them disappear into the trees and undergrowth.

"Captain Carr."

Carr turned, but he knew the voice. It was Kempt.

"Take your men over the river and support the Corsicans. Secure that wood. Your line of advance is the far river bank. Greelish will be on this side, if you need a decision of any kind."

Carr brought his sword up in acknowledgement.

"Drake, Rushby, over the river. As we are, in two ranks."

They waded through the shallow river; it was surprisingly cold, and before the wood they formed up as they had crossed the river, in two lines. The Corsicans could be heard up ahead, shouting and calling from within. As a beginning, Carr didn't like it, but ordered the advance, maintaining a firing line.

The wood was little more than a thicket of drought-stunted trees, hot, but light, with boulders, but little undergrowth. Carr's Company advanced silently on, each man fixed intently on the spaces between the trees ahead. Suddenly came the crash of musketry at a volume that signalled much more than just a skirmish.

Carr halted his men leaving Rushby in command, then motioned to Drake and they both edged forward to investigate. Too soon they saw the Corsicans, already moving back. Beyond them and very close, in the dappled sunlight could be seen green and yellow plumes atop the shakoes of French infantry, in strength, crowding through the spaces between the trees. The Corsicans were using their muskets, but they were already falling back, their retreat would soon become headlong.

Carr motioned Drake to move back to their men.

"Front rank, make ready. Wait for the order men, let the Corsicans through."

They didn't have long to wait before the gaudily dressed Rangers ran back and through their position, some bravely turning to reload and fire, but they were masking the French from Carr's men. From all around they were shouted at to return, shouts reinforced by angry gestures. Soon came the French and most noticed that these were not tall, forbidding grenadiers, but middle in stature and plainly agile, their swift movements emphasised by a swinging green and yellow tassel besides their shakoes.

"Front rank. Present. Fire."

The muskets crashed out and all was white smoke. Carr let the smoke clear as much as he dared, but at the first appearance of the enemy line he ordered again.

"Rear rank. Present. Fire."

Volleys by ranks began, each rank delivered a volley every 20 seconds. The French were not stopped, but they had taken casualties and were not coming on with such leaping confidence. However, they were returning fire and three of Carr's men were down. The Corsicans had reformed into some sort of line behind, but Carr's men were heavily outnumbered and the French were using the cover to creep up to the British Line. The range was down to 30 yards and closing. Despite their controlled volleys, Carr's men would soon be overrun. He made his decision.

"Retreat by files."

Tom Miles shouted at Pike and Davey.

"I'm reloaded. Get gone."

He peered through the smoke and when it thinned he saw enough of a Frenchman to make him a target, the man advancing forward, crouched, with bayonet extended. He took aim and fired. The ball took the Frenchman on his left shoulder, throwing him spinning into the trunk of a tree, a red epaulette flying up in the air. Miles turned and began reloading as he ran, blowing clear the priming pan and biting open a cartridge. However, some yards back he nearly fell over the prone figure of Joe Pike. He pulled him over and saw that he was not hit, just badly stunned, but there was a huge red mark on the side of his forehead. His shako was smashed in. Miles shouted,

"Davey, Joe's down," then he finished his reloading and fixed his bayonet. The French were coming on, there were two, perhaps three, who were almost upon them. Miles took aim. He shot the first, then met the second, sliding the French bayonet over, before kneeing the man in the groin, then smashing the butt of his musket into his temple. The third man was but feet away with a levelled bayonet and Miles was lowering his own bayonet whilst desperately trying to clear his feet and regain his balance, when a Baker rifle went off alongside his shoulder. The man collapsed, a hideous gurgling sound issuing from his throat. Davey appeared alongside and remained en garde with bayonet fixed while Miles dragged Pike to his feet and lifted him over his shoulder, but the French were up too close. Davey swept aside a lunging bayonet and swung his rifle butt into the side of the Frenchman's head, but hope of escape was fading.

"Tom!"

Miles dropped Pike and turned, levelling his own bayonet, then he heard a voice he recognised, reassured by the loud clear order.

"Miles. Get Pike back and clear."

Carr had returned with Ellis and others. Carr shot the nearest Frenchman with his pistol. For the next he deflected his bayonet with his sword, but a glancing blow from the musket butt of another Frenchman lost him his own shako and reopened his Madelline wound. Carr was first to disengage his weapon and smashed his sword pommel into the side of the Frenchman's head, then cut him across the neck with his sword. Somehow the first Frenchman had disappeared, perhaps the work of Ellis who was fighting nearby. It was Ellis himself who shouted,

"Sir, they've got round us."

"Fall back."

All fought their way back in Medieval style, no one had the chance to re-load, neither British nor French, but the crowding French surely were going to take them. Then it was Carr's turn for relief, when came a sturdy English voice.

"At 'em, lads. Huzzah for the 35th!"

Redcoats were swarming around and past him, '35' on their crossbelt badge, with the reformed Corsicans mixed in. Seeing some Corsicans running from the woods and the retreat then confirmed by Major Greelish, Kempt had sent in the next Light Company, that from the 35th, to support. Carr looked up to see the French running back, the fresh British troops meant that they had had enough. It was not long before the redcoats returned leaving the Corsicans to hold their position. Their Captain came over to Carr and extended his hand.

"Smart, 35th. Kempt wants our return, if you can manage it."

304

"Carr, 5th Provisionals. Thanks for your timely arrival. Things were becoming very sticky. But, yes; thanks once again. Who were those French, do you know?"

"They call themselves Voltigeurs. Light troops, just like us, only better dressed."

Carr grinned, then felt the trickle of blood down his face, but Ellis was pulling out a bandage, and Carr quickly bound his own wound. At a rapid walk they returned to the edge of the wood, where Miles was examining Joe Pike.

"How did you manage that, you clumsy bugger. What gave you cause to hit your head with that tree?"

Joe Pike sat up and was grateful for the water that Davey had fetched from the river in his own canteen to bathe the smarting wound.

"Something hit my left foot, and I fell over, into a tree."

Miles looked down and roughly hoisted Joe's left foot, causing him to topple over, spilling the water over him.

"Looks like you'll be wearing Frencher footwear before I do, boy. You'm lucky, the ball just took away the heel of your boot, and your shako took the hit from the tree."

Joe brought his foot up for his own examination and nodded. Just then Ellis re-appeared.

"You lot. Up and over here. Re-form, and quick."

All ran back over the river, Joe hobbling but keeping up. Kempt had brought the Sicilians up into the line alongside the 35th, extending it, and so the 5th Lights had to form up with many of their right-hand files standing in the river. On reforming and seeing the approaching French line, Carr stood with Nat Drake.

"What price lines against columns now, Henry?"

"None at all. This is man for man. Who's best with their muskets. So here we go. Good luck, Nat."

"Good luck, Henry."

They shook hands and parted.

The British had advanced no further and before them were two four pound guns in action against what was now a clear target. The French line was 300 yards away and closing, and the sight was both magnificent and chilling. The whole line was Voltiguers, the yellow and green plumes and tassels clear on their shakoes, also the red epaulettes and the bright white crossbelts. They were coming on with lowered bayonets, steady and relentless, drumbeats pushing them on, with Officers out front waving their swords and encouraging their men. Tom Miles was not impressed, nothing to do with the French, just with where he was.

"Why be I stood yer, up to my ballocks in freezing water, and on top, something is biting my arse?"

The voice that came from behind was that of Ellis.

"You're here because you're ordered, Miles, and what's biting your arse is not any kind of fish, nor nothin', it's my bayonet. So hold your noise and watch your front!"

Carr heard the argument and grinned. Looking ahead he saw that the French were away from the river, and that he should curve his line around which would get most of them out of the water. He gave the order and dressed the line himself.

"There you are, Miles. Perhaps some plunder this time, eh?"

"Could be, Sir. Them Frenchers look well set enough."

The French seemed to be three deep and they were taking punishment from the British artillery, not least from the two guns before the Lights, firing from further up along the riverbank. The British stood with shouldered arms and all watched intently. None could move their gaze to anything else. The two guns before the lights ceased loading round shot and began loading canisters of thin metal sheet.

"What are those they're putting in the guns, Tom?"

"Case shot, boy. Very nasty. They burst open and out comes large balls, bigger than you puts in your musket. That'll do them Frenchers a lot of no good, wait and see."

French cannon balls were passing just over their own heads, doing damage behind the lines perhaps, but not to them. The two guns roared out and, when the smoke had cleared, there were two clear gaps in the French line, but they closed up and came on. It showed the veteran quality of the advancing French.

Capitaine Rouol Linois felt very confident out before his men. This was no different from Marengo, soon the British line would, as had the Austrians, crumble in the face of this inexorable advance by his Voltigeur Brigade. The levelled bayonets, the persistent, determined march forward, would soon have an effect. However, in the next second his confidence took a heavy knock.

Carr, in the front rank, gave the first order.

"Rear rank. Lock on."

Linois saw the space between the British heads fill with more heads and all was steady, as if on parade. He heard a shouted order.

"Make ready."

Again, as if watching a parade, he saw the muskets rise as one to the vertical.

John Davey knew his role. Find an Officer and bring him down. He said to himself,

"There's one, that stiffbacked jaunty bastard. He's for me."

He then waited for the order. The range was down to under 200 yards and the cannon were loading and firing case shot as fast as they could sponge, load, and prime, urged on by their young Artillery Officer. Kempt was stood just out in front of his men, in the centre, stiff as a ramrod, sword resting on his right shoulder, Greelish 20 yards beyond him. Using a space between the cannonade, Kempt turned to encourage those near, at least those that could hear.

"Steady, Light Infantry, wait for the word. Let them come on."

Barely a quarter of his command could hear, but all were indeed, "waiting for the word." Joe Pike and John Davey were in the front rank, with Tom Miles locked on behind. Joe was frightened. His head hurt, and his left leg felt unsteady.

"Tom, Tom. I be scared. How're we goin' to stop them?"

"You looks good enough to me, boy. Just get a bullet into that line, that's where it starts. See, their crossbelt, aim above where it crosses. If we give 'em enough of that, we'll see 'em off. Then we'll get you your new pair of Frencher boots."

Joe grinned and gripped his musket tighter, if that were possible, bringing the warm wood up against his right cheek. The range was 100 yards and below, 90, then 80. It was Carr who called back the artillerymen; Kempt was too far away. Now there was nothing between the Voltiguers and the British Lights. Kempt gave the order and Carr followed.

"Present."

Linois saw every musket come down level as the order moved down the line. He was close enough to see the open muzzles and suddenly his confidence melted. For his first time as an Imperial Officer, he felt seriously afraid, a fear made worse from its sudden arrival. Death or injury could come in a moment.

"Front rank, fire!"

A pause.

"Rear rank, fire!"

Davey's rifle ball hit Rouol Linois just below and to the left of his sternum as he turned to his men. The ball detached his windpipe from his left lung and smashed a vertebrae out of the back of his jacket. His legs collapsed and he began choking on the blood entering his lungs. He was not alone, the impact of the volley was appalling. Lying on his side he could see that all along the French line men were down, dead or injured, screaming, choking or pleading for help. However, there were no gaps. The third line came up to fill the spaces and the line marched on, stepping over their fallen comrades, but almost all their Officers were down. However, like the veterans they were, they broke into a run, eager to close before the next volley.

Carr looked both ways, along his men. All in the front rank were at the "make ready. The range was down to 40 yards.

"Front rank, present. Fire!"

Another explosion of noise and smoke, paper cartridges fluttering down. The front rank lowered their muskets and began to reload. Carr gave a pause.

"Rear rank, present. Fire!"

They fired. He waited another 10 seconds and saw that his front rank had almost all returned to the "make ready" The French could have that, too.

"Front rank, present. Fire!

Again the appalling din, almost as intimidating as the impact of the bullets.

"Fix bayonets."

The smoke cleared and what had been a terrifying and seemingly unstoppable French line minutes ago, was now bloody ruin. Dead, dying and wounded were everywhere slumped on the ground, 20, in some cases 15, yards from the British line. Any who survived were turning to retreat. Carr looked along his line; all bayonets were in place. He took himself out from the line and waved his sword.

"Charge, boys, charge. Huzzah for the 5th! Huzzah for the King!"

His Company sprang forward into a run, bayonets extended. They may not have been the first Company into the charge but if they were, they were soon not alone. Kempt himself was leading from the centre and Carr led his men on. Their backpacks protected the French from his sword, but not so the bayonets of his men. Many thrust powerfully forward to bring down yet more French. The last thing that Rouol Linois saw in this life was his men running back in panic, with the pursuing British with levelled bayonets, then a boot thudded down onto his chest to end his life.

Miles joined in with gusto, John Davey not far behind, whilst Joe Pike could only hobble up in the rear. The whole Light Battalion were pursuing the French like lurchers onto a hare, but Carr thought more of where his men were going, perhaps too far? Would they be cut off? 300 yards on, he shouted to reform. His call was taken up and passed on by all who heard and his men came to order. They gathered and held their ground, and Carr awaited developments. He looked back to his own line, over to the ground where they had come. In the space between he saw Miles, Pike and Davey. Miles was pulling the boots off a dead Frenchman who looked to be about Joe Pike's size. The dead Frenchman looked to be an Officer and Davey was pointing at his rifle and then at the prone body.

* * *

Charles Carravoy could just make out the sound of the Light Battalion beginning the fight over on his right, for the noise was almost drowned by the rhythmic firing of the three guns to his front, but beyond them was the reason why he would soon be involved. Several lines of cavalry were advancing on Acland's Brigade, who had for some time been suffering from the attentions of French artillery; there was a steady stream of men falling out behind their line. Carravoy looked over to see their Colours being returned to the safety of the ranks and the young Highlanders of the 78th Foot and the 81st Lincolns were hurriedly forming square. Would the cavalry come his way? It would seem not, Mallory looked unconcerned. He was right, the cavalry attack was not pressed home in the face of some long range musketry and they turned to gallop off, across his front, back to the French right. What worried Carravoy most was what could now be seen approaching Acland through the dust thrown up by the disappearing cavalry. Across something like a two battalion front, came a line of infantry, the battalion on his side wearing claret, the other a combination of dark green with a broad red section down the centre. Acland's men had quickly reformed as a firing line and he was leading his men forward to meet what Carravoy could see, it seemed to him to be the French centre brigade. At something just over 100 yards, Acland opened fire and the greens and reds turned and ran, they had seen what had happened to the Voltigeurs to their left, but not so those in claret, they marched on resolutely. At a range of over 100 yards little damage had been done. Their uniform looked familiar and Carravoy looked back to Oswald's Brigade. Half of his men wore the exact same uniform. They must be Swiss, then surely allies. Carravoy started shouting, to no one in particular.

"It's a mistake. They're Swiss. Don't fire, don't fire!"

The 78th Highlanders, or at least their Officers, seemed to be in much the same mind, for they, too, ceased firing. The Swiss came on and at 50 yards levelled their muskets and gave the Highlanders a volley. Carravoy kept shouting,

"It's a mistake. Don't fire. It's a mistake."

His anxious shouts were soon ended. Mallory galloped up, in a flaming temper.

"Carravoy! Why is that enemy line not feeling your fire, damn you? Take a turn to your right front and support the 78th. At your best speed if you please!"

"But Sir, aren't they Swiss."

"Swiss or not, they stand with the French. You give them whatever fire you can."

Carravoy gave the order and his Grenadiers wheeled around to face the French Swiss. It was over 100 yards, but he ordered volley fire by ranks and the muskets crashed out. The 78th also arrived at the correct decision and had begun their own volleys, supported on the far side by the 81st. Met by such concentrated fire, some at 50 yards range, the Swiss stopped and courageously held for 10 minutes, but then, alone and unsupported, they fell back. Acland's men marched on.

Far over, on the left of the British line, Cole and Lacey were in anxious conversation. Having angled over to their left, they were close to the scrub-covered hillside, and the whole was filling with Voltigeurs, creeping forward through the cover and beginning an accurate fire on the end of the 5th Provisionals' line, and even more threatening, also moving on and past their front. Should they send one or perhaps two Companies out to clear the Voltiguers? However, French cavalry were also massing in support of these French Lights, the two Companies could be cut off and ridden down and, alongside the cavalry, more French infantry could be seen advancing in line, with individual sharpshooters out in front, already attempting shots at long range. To make matters worse, French artillery could be seen arriving through the murk. Lacey made the suggestion.

"Sir, if I reform two Companies back at a right angle to our line to face the skirmishers that will at least answer their fire, and give us some protection on our flank from the cavalry"

Cole had realised that if the advancing French did close, his Grenadiers on his far right would not be in action; they were too far over.

"Wait, Lacey. I will bring over two Companies of Grenadiers from our right. They can form up to answer those brigands on the hillside. Hold here, I will get them myself."

With that he put spurs to his horse and galloped off, but Lacey didn't like it, coming from far over, how long before the Grenadiers arrived? He called to O'Hare.

"O'Hare. Bring round No 1, the nearest, to answer those French in the scrub on the hillside. When the Grenadiers arrive, they will take their place, so then return No. 1 to their original front."

O'Hare saluted and ran across to give the order, in this case to Captain Reynolds. The Company broke apart but soon reformed as a firing line opposing the Voltigeurs, but the French Brigadier must have seen the threat that they were posing to the British because he had reinforced them. No. 1 was heavily outgunned, even though the range was over 100 yards, however, Reynolds was answering the French with volley by ranks and the French began to fall, but so too were his own men.

Deakin and Halfway, both stood in the middle of No. 3, and facing the oncoming French line, were as worried as Lacey. An eruption of smoke from the French position added to their worries, French artillery had come into action but at least firing round shot not case, nevertheless there came cries and screaming from over on their right. Then a shell fell short in front of them and exploded, setting fire to the tinder dry grass, which quickly spread, adding choking smoke to the dust and heat. Both pulled up their neckerchiefs to cover their mouths and noses and many copied, but the smoke stung their eyes.

"This be turnin' into a bad battle, Jed."

"You'll get no argument from me."

"Who do you think we'll be fightin', Jed, them in front or the cavalry?"

"Them in front, Toby. Those bastards be aimin' to close. We'll be muzzle to muzzle afore long. But what I don't like is them sneakin' along to our left. They'm gettin' behind us. B'ain't good."

Then he turned to see what he first heard. Grenadiers were doubling behind them, their kit clashing together sounding nothing like musical, but it was a sweet enough sound to him for all that. Cole was with them and he saw what Lacey had done in his absence and was both impressed and reassured as Reynold's company quickly dissolved to make way for the Grenadiers and then reform on their original front. One of the Companies he brought over was Carravoy's and his Grenadiers formed on the end of the 5th line, forming a corner with the members of their own battalion. Before riding off Cole gave Carravoy his simple orders.

"You're in command, Captain. Stand with your men and give all the fire you can. Keep Johnny over there!"

Carravoy brought his sword up before his face, which was good because it hid the anxiety that was growing there. He was never more grateful than when he found Major O'Hare standing beside him.

"Hello Captain Carravoy. Welcome back to the Battalion!"

Carravoy made no reply and O'Hare could tell that, despite the reassuring tone he was trying to use, it caused no change in Carravoy. He was almost in a state of shock from all the noise, screams, and rapid changes of ground.

"Right. Off you go, but don't run, it gives a bad impression. Steady your men, then volley by ranks. But you may find yourself having to go to independent fire. Get as many bullets into those gombeens over there as you can. Good luck to you now."

Carravoy took himself off and joined the front rank that was just forming, but already some were falling from enemy fire. He gave the orders and volleys began. The man beside him uttered something between a grunt and a sigh and collapsed on the ground at his feet, choking out blood onto the dry earth. Another fell, three files up, making no sound, just falling in a heap. Carravoy felt his self control going and his voice cracking, but he kept his place, fear of shame and fear of the enemy both vying within him. His one consolation was that his men were loading and firing as though at a practice, standing firm, asking his pardon when they needed him to give them room to reload.

Cole looked over to his left. It was still perilous, all the more so because the Voltigeurs were receiving yet more reinforcements and the French cavalry were massing behind them as if to turn this flank, at present held only by the two deep line of Grenadiers. Also he was being menaced in front by an advancing French Brigade, supported by artillery. He looked for Lacey.

"Lacey. We must extend back further from the Grenadiers opposite the skirmishers and also form them four deep on that side for cavalry. Should I bring over more Grenadiers, or can your men move quickly enough out of the centre?"

"It must be done quickly, Sir, in case the cavalry come soon upon us. My men are nearest. Pull 6, 7, and 8, out of the centre and close up the Grenadiers from the right to fill the gap. That will bring them into the fight that's coming on our front."

"Very good."

He turned to his Aide de Camp, at his side but just behind.

"Madden. You heard that?"

"Yes Sir."

"Get them over, at the double. Then on to the Grenadiers. Tell them to close up at their best speed."

The Aide de Camp galloped off and Lacey followed, only jogging on foot. He didn't like a three Company hole in his front, he wanted to be there himself to see all quickly set to right. Madden had got there first and the three Companies were already turning out of the line. He continued his run, but stopped when his men were passing him on their way to their new position, shouting as much to the men as to their Captains.

"Form fours as you go, men. You're against cavalry."

Lacey's remaining companies were watching the approaching French infantry to their main front, reacting to the sight as they saw fit. As he passed the last Companies, Lacey heard both Officers and Sergeants encouraging their men, but in different ways. Some uttering dire threats.

"If any one of you bastards takes one backward step you'll get my halberd through you, see if you don't."

Elsewhere he heard different forms of encouragement.

"Get off your ten, boys. Just get off your ten. That'll see these Crapauds away, you see if it don't. Ten good shots'll do it."

Lacey reached the beginning of the now huge gap, and didn't like what he saw. The French line was little more that 150 yards distant and the Grenadiers had not moved. The French had to be halted. He saw no choice but to create a long range firefight, it would decide nothing, but it would hold off the immediate danger.

"Prepare for volley fire by ranks."

The word was passed along and Lacey saw his men, the five companies remaining, all come to the "make ready", steady and waiting. The French were now 100 yards away.

"Front rank, present. Fire!"

He let the smoke clear a little.

"Rear rank, present. Fire!"

The Captains took over and the volleys continued. Lacey waited for a gap in the smoke and looked. He saw that the French were halted but were now stood returning fire. He then heard what Deakin had heard earlier, the Grenadiers were closing up behind him. The firefight was set up, albeit at long range. There was nothing for it now but to stand up to it and trust to his men.

Cole was organising the Grenadiers to receive cavalry and was wholly relieved to see that the 5th Provisionals were arriving already in fours. They ran to their places, but instead of receiving the still threatening cavalry, what happened was that the Voltigeurs crept closer and increased their fire, a four deep line being impossible to miss. From the outset, Cole's new line began to take casualties.

On the main front the requirement was now to fire as often as possible and the Captains had ordered independent fire. The smoke and noise from the opposing lines was indescribable, each man could do nothing but follow the orders he gave to himself. D'Villiers was stood in front of his men, stock still. He couldn't move even had he wanted, but his men wanted him back to clear their field of fire. They had called out "Come back, Sir," but he had remained out front, sword sloped back over his right shoulder, so the NCO's moved the men up, causing a curve in No.3 company, but they were now firing either side of him.

His mind was shutting out all the noise and the mayhem; he didn't notice the noise from the bellowing muzzles no more than inches either side of him. In contrast, Heaviside was walking up and down behind the two deep line, giving encouragement in the way that would have worried the men, were it any different, and causing many a wry grin to pass across faces now stained with dust and gunpowder.

"Stand and deal it out to them, men. Thou comest to me with a sword, and with a spear, and with a shield: but I come to thee in the name of the Lord of hosts. First Samuel. 17, verse 45."

The range was down to 75 yards, as the French inched forward. These, too, were veterans of Morengo. It was a pure test of will with each side having two battalions, but the British had one advantage, in a two deep line every man could fire; the French were in three lines, the third line taking no part, only there to fill the gaps from casualties. Both sides were under artillery fire, but the British were firing case shot, the French continued with solid. O'Hare looked along the line of No. 3 Company. This was far from his first battle, but nevertheless emotion rose within him. The 5th Provisionals were holding their line, edging forward, loading and firing like veterans, their musket barrels moving smoothly through the angles required to reload and fire. Halfway and Deakin were close to him in the front rank, with Gibney and Mulcahey locked on behind. Gibney had discarded his halberd and had prised a musket from a deadman's fingers. Each was matching the other load for load, firing at the flashes seen through the smoke before them; four reloads per minute.

The exchange of fire continued, ten minutes and beyond. No. 1 Company had been in action for almost 15. A runner, an NCO in No.1, part of O'Hare's messenger network, came to him and saluted.

"From Captain Reynold's, Sir. Our Company is runnin' low on cartridges. Some of the lads have fired more than 40, Sir. Only close on 10 left. Were takin' the cartridges from the dead and wounded already, Sir."

"Thank you, Corporal. Return. Give Captain Reynolds my compliments and tell him to hold his fire to three per minute. I will see that ammunition arrives soon."

He looked for an Officer, but there was none. He turned to an NCO.

"Corporal."

The NCO turned to face towards him, his face was sweat-stained and filthy with dust, white eyes emphasised in the grime. His left ear was covered by a kerchief, and black grains of gunpowder adhering to parched lips. His "Britannia" shako plate showed that he was "old Norfolk".

"Name, please Corporal?"

"Harris, Sir."

"Take yourself back at the double to our supply train, Harris. I want more cartridges up here in five minutes. Clear?"

"Sir."

Harris ran off.

Sedgwicke and Pearson were both in a state of high agitation, but for different reasons. Sedgwicke could see the lines of wounded being attended by the Surgeon and his Assistants, their screams loud even above the sounds of battle as amputations were carried out with nothing to ease the pain beyond a piece of wood locked into their mouths. Some were obviously beyond help with nothing more to ease their dying than a mouthful of water, others lay waiting their turn with the Surgeon. He wanted to go to them to give them the Peace of the Last Rites, but Pearson forbade it. He was himself in a state of near terror being so close to the fighting which was evidently very fierce, but he was enough of an old soldier to realise that this fire fight had gone on for some time and would soon need more ammunition. He was involved in his own argument with the other Storemen who were saying that they should take the cartridges up anyway. The mules were loaded and ready, but a look forward and to the left showed him the clouds of dust and that meant cavalry, and some hundreds of yards ahead he could see the firefight between the Voltigeurs and the line opposing them. He wanted nothing to do with going further forward, but a runner was coming back. Harris went straight to Pearson.

"Major O'Hare wants the ammunition brought up. Straight away."

Pearson looked at Harris. His appearance alone told of the ferocity of the fight.

"I wants volunteers to take these mules forward."

Harris was incensed and even leveled his musket at Pearson.

316

"Bugger your volunteers. The damn lot of you is needed. "'Tain't just about getting' the new up there, 'tis also about takin' the cartridges along the line, to give to the lads. Now get these mules up there, or I'll put one in you, an' I don't care if I swing for it. The rest of you, load your muskets, they may be needed. We're goin' back up."

Their muskets were already loaded and were swung up onto their shoulders. Sedgwicke seized the bridle of a mule and began to pull it forward, as did others so that the mules moved towards the conflict. All the Storemen were pulling a mule, wherever it was in the train and all were moving bar Pearson. Harris placed the muzzle before his nose.

"You an' all. Sergeant Quartermaster!"

The mules were moving up, but the fight was coming their way. The French Voltigeurs, chosen for their initiative, could see the supplies and these elite soldiers soon worked out why they were needed and where they were going. Bullets began to sing around the group. One hit a mule and the animal bucked and reared throwing its burden around like mere parcels until a Storeman shot the animal and cut its tether. The train moved on, but into greater peril. A Voltigeur Officer, of high courage, was leading six of his men across to intercept the mules. Harris walked forward to meet them. At 40 yards he shot one, but was then shot himself, collapsing over in a heap. The Voltigeurs knew what to do, shoot the muleteers then drive off the mules and so they came on to do just that, but they needed point blank range amidst the milling animals.

The Storemen raised their own muskets and fired. Sedgwicke pulled the trigger, but nothing happened, he hadn't fully cocked the hammer. Two more French were brought down, which left four including the Officer. The Storemen were reloading frantically, when a volley from the right brought down all the remaining French except the Officer. A Lieutenant of the 5th's Grenadiers had noticed where the Voltigeurs were running and had pulled some men out of the line to meet them, but the surviving Officer ran on trying to drive off the mules. The nearest was Sedgwicke's. He swung at Sedgwicke with his sword and he instinctively raised his musket to take the blow, but then the Officer collapsed against him, mouth and eyes wide in shock. He had been shot from behind by the Lieutenant's pistol.

"Well done, men. Now get all this forward. It's urgently needed."

The mules were urged forward again, escorted by the men from the 5th. They noticed Sedgwicke.

"Well done, Parson. There must be rum on they mules, don't 'ee think lads? B'ain't that so, Parson?"

The men all laughed, as did Sedgwicke, then they had reached the firing line, the smoke swirling back into their faces. Pearson was in a complete state of terror, and so the Corporal Storeman; the one "three fingers missing", took over, as the boxes of cartridges on half the mules were broken open.

"Right lads. Get a haversack, two would be better, fill it and then give 'em out. Ten each. Never mind their cartridge boxes, stuff 'em into their pockets. Parson, take these other mules on to the end of the line. Do the same up there. You two go with him."

Sedgwicke and his two companions dragged the reluctant and frightened mules further along the line, stopped and took off the boxes. The mules ran off as soon as they were unburdened, but the cartridges were exposed and Sedgwicke and the two filled their haversacks with the white paper cylinders. Three lightly wounded soldiers came and did the same. All ran off to different parts of the line. Some soldiers came back from the line to claim their own from the open boxes and also take some back for their comrades. Sedgwicke took himself into the bedlam of the firing line and as he came to each soldier he rammed about ten down into his right hand pocket.

He came to one soldier who mumbled his thanks before collapsing against Sedgwicke with blood pouring from what had been his eye socket. But Sedgwicke kept on and then he reached Deakin and Gibney. Deakin noticed him first and held his pocket open for the cartridges.

"Hello, Parson. Look who's here, Pat, Toby, 'tis Parson. Glad to see you, Parson, there b'ain't many Storemen like thee in this firing line that I've seen."

Gibney joined in, whilst priming his musket.

"Percy, my boy. 'Tis pleased we all are t'see thee. Ah'm fine for now, nearly a full box, but get th'sen on down the line, there's lads there as is very short. Good lad, Percy, well done to thee."

In the time it took to say that, he had brought his musket to the "present" and sent another ball into the French line.

Sedgwicke moved on, lifted himself at what they had said to him, "in the midst of mortal peril", their simple words of praise and greeting.

Cole sat his horse and looked, both to his left and to his front. Lacey was close by, but each said nothing. The situation was stable, Cole was holding the flank and his men were putting up a stubborn fight, but they were getting the worst of it. A look along the line showed a redcoated figure prone at the feet of almost all those remaining in the line and the drummers were helping the continuous stream of walking wounded back to the Surgeon. In between his main concerns it struck him that he could have no complaints about the 5th Provisionals; they were standing their ground and making a fight as well as any Line Regiment he had seen or heard of. However, he knew that if the French Commander knew his business, soon he would release his cavalry onto Cole's weakened line, but he had to hold. Defeat here could lose a battle so nearly won.

The minutes wore on. He could see the punishment his men were taking and he had little idea of what was being inflicted on the French, but clearly they held the initiative and they were closing the range, both on his main front and also the Voltigeurs to the side. The psychology of battles told them that they held the upper hand. Suddenly Cole heard two heavy volleys behind and to the left and he looked fearfully over, to be quickly and wholly reassured. Above the smoke he could see two British Standards which he recognized as those of the 20th East Devons, the Union Flag that was the King's Colour and the pale cream yellow of their Regimental Colour. The 20th had forced march up from the beach and were advancing in line along the scrub covered hillside, already pushing the Voltigeurs before them, these being those that remained standing after the first crushing volleys, but now the 20th faced a threat of their own. The French Commander, as a last throw of the dice, at last sent his cavalry forward at their firing line. The full Regiment was riding at the charge and Cole's anxiety returned. He saw the 20th's Colonel address his men but could hear nothing of what he said above the din of his own ongoing firefight. What he did see was the whole Regiment come to the present and await the cavalry onslaught. At 50 yards one volley from each rank brought the French horsemen to a total halt as the front riders were brought down in a heap of men and horses and the mounts of those behind refused to ride on through the struggling shambles. The job was done; the French turned and rode off, the Voltigeurs running beside them.

The 20th marched on, breaking formation as they picked their way through the remains of the French cavalry, then re-forming like veterans beyond. In no time they were level and then beyond the 5th Provisionals, pushing onto the flank of the main French line to their right. Lacey and Cole grinned at each other and shook hands, but O'Hare, from where he was, knew there was still fighting to be done.

"Fix bayonets."

The firing lessened as his men obeyed the new order. He walked out to the centre of his men with his sword unsheathed in his right hand; he swept it back, then swept it forward.

"March on, boys!"

The whole line moved forward, not in a headlong charge but a steady inexorable advance. They could see the French before them begin to retire, not as beaten men, but in an orderly re-treat, still facing the British at first, but then turning to march off. O'Hare took his men onto the French position, then halted. Ammunition was short, as was water, and French cavalry were still around. His advance was the last act of the battle. The French were beaten, everywhere they were in retreat

Deakin found his water canteen, he was the only one that had any left. He drank himself, then passed it to Gibney, who passed it onto Halfway.

"Where's Pat?"

All looked around. Mulcahey was no-where to be seen, cer-tainly not amongst those robbing the French dead, but there were several prone red coated shapes lying within the area they had just advanced across. Deakin looked at Halfway, his face grave.

"Take a look at those back there, will you, Toby?"

Halfway left the line and began his search. The third lifeless figure revealed what he didn't want to see. It was Mulcahey, with the left side of his chest caved in. The French artillery must have changed to case shot to cover the retreat and Mulcahey must have been close on the last casualty that the 5th suffered. Halfway closed the eyes and laid him out, first remov-ing the knapsack into which he put any items from the pockets and his ring. His kerchief was clean, but there was nothing else of any value that could be called personal and was not soaked in blood. He stuck a musket into the ground using the bayonet and placed a shako over the butt, then returned to Deakin and Gibney.

"He's back there, Jed. They got him. Must have been the last shots they fired."

Deakin draped his wrists over the muzzle of his already grounded musket and lowered his head, then raised it to look with hatred at the French, but all that could be seen of them was dust and a few wounded, limping into the distance. Then he turned back to Halfway.

"Did you fix on the body."

"Yes, the one I marked. And I've got his bits and pieces, such as were of any value."

* * *

Cole rode out to just beyond the point of the advance, but could see little more than anyone else. It seemed sensible to hold his position and the men stood for some while, drinking and eating, sharing also what had been found in the French knapsacks. He was relieved to see General Stuart and his Staff approaching at a fast canter. As he approached, Stuart looked at the casualties strewn all over, both British and French.

"Cole, good to see you. I had no idea that things were so tight over here. Well done, my word yes, well done. Evidently with you the French made a real fight of it, unlike elsewhere. Well done again, to you and to your men."

"Thank you, Sir, but if you get the time, please pass that onto Lacey and his battalion. Provisionals, yes, but they conducted themselves as well as we could expect from any Regiment. Better. They stood and fought like hard-biting veterans. They should be told."

"If you think so. Yes, I will. Now, pull back. The French are gone, so we're returning to the beach. To re-supply if nothing else."

Cole saluted and instructed his Staff as Stuart rode off. The line began to retrace their steps, but Halfway and Deakin made a stretcher out of a French greatcoat and two French muskets and carried the body of Patrick Mulcahey back to their lines, but they didn't add his body to the long row already assembled by the Drummers. Again the Battalion was told to hold and rest, and the lugubrious collection of Catalonians came to begin the task of interring the dead but Deakin sequestered two shovels from them and he and Halfway dug a grave themselves. Whilst Halfway and another dug out the last few shovelfuls, Deakin himself went to Sedgwicke.

"There's a job for you, Parson. The bastards got Pat. We've dug a grave and need you to say the words. It's just up here."

Sedgwicke felt the same uneasiness he always felt with such as Deakin, but nodded all the same. His emotions were mixed, he felt pleased that they had called upon him, but also felt sadness himself, remembering the kindness that Mulcahey had shown him all those months ago back in that cold barn. Attended and helped by several others of their Company, Mulcahey was lowered in, his face covered, and Sedgwicke conducted the ceremony. All stood in reverent silence, a silence made more profound after the hellish mayhem that had existed only an hour before. Despite their own wounds and exhaustion, all joined in the familiar prayers and gave Amen. With that the grave was closed.

* * *

Stuart could see Lacey and O'Hare supervising the tending of the wounded, and Stuart, mindful of his promise to Cole, rode over to them. Both came to the attention and saluted.

"Cole tells me of the conduct of your men, Lacey. "Hard biting veterans" was his description and so I offer my thanks. This was clearly the point of decision and I knew little of it."

Lacey made the reply.

"Thank you, Sir, that's very gracious of you."

"No, not at all. You held your ground until supported, and the support didn't come from me. I confess myself as fortunate that it was such as yourself and your men on this side, or things could have turned out very different. Be assured, I will mention you efforts in my dispatch of the battle. I've named it Maida, by the way. St Eupemia sounds too much like some kind of Christian Festival. Right, get your men back to the beach."

He touched his hat and rode off, but Major Willoughby lingered.

"Just thought you'd like to know. Elsewhere, the French gave practically no resistance at all. Over here was indeed the "point of decision" as the General put it. On our right and in the centre the French dissolved entirely, before you they remained intact. As the French collapsed, we on the right and in the centre ended up very disheveled. Had you given way, from here the French could have rolled up our entire line with their cavalry. I'd like to add my own plaudits."

O'Hare shook his hand and added his thanks before Willoughby rode off. Lacey looked at O'Hare.

"Seems we've built a reputation, Padraigh, but at a price. What's the "Butcher's Bill"?

"48 dead and about as many wounded, and half of them will be amputees. That's nearly a Company."

"Yes. I'll stay here and do what I can. You take the men back. Food and drink for them, if you can find it."

The 5th Provisionals formed "fours" and marched back, their column soon parallel to that of the 20th and some water canteens were tossed across, back and forth. It wasn't too long before conversation and comments equally crossed the space, the distance between them making for an easy exchange. The tone was genial, each had just witnessed the deeds of the other, but still with an edge; Regimental rivalry was never far below the surface.

"Who are you?"

"5th Provisionals. Who are you?"

"20th. So you're not a Regiment?"

"No."

"Then you got no nickname. Nor no nuthin'."

"No."

Someone in the 20th, perhaps with a brighter spark between his ears than most looked across and noticed the variety of uniform, the yellow of the Norfolk, the buff of the Somersets, and other various facings from ex-Militia.

"Where'd you get all they different jackets from? Off some army rag and bone merchant?"

No reply. If there was, it was drowned in the laughter coming from the ranks of the 20th.

"That's it then. The Rag and Bone Boys."

At that point their paths parted company, the 20th up to St. Euphemia, the Provisionals and the Grenadiers on down to the beach. There they found themselves picking their way over whole rows of full infantry kit and clothing, including kilts and tam 'o shanters; the 78th had got there first. A look into the sea told the story; the whole of Acland's Brigade were splashing and jumping about in the sea, washing away the sweat and grime of the past morning, and not a few bathing minor wounds in the salty water. O'Hare led his men further along the beach, just as Acland's men were quitting their portion.

"Come on then boys, your turn. Get off your kit and get in the briney."

His men needed no further bidding. The idea of a wash and a splash in the clean ocean after the foulness of the day was too good to waste a second. In under a minute weapons and straps were off and down, boots and clothes soon followed, and the whole battalion was whooping and leaping down the beach to dive and crash into the clean and curling surf off the beach. The Grenadiers soon followed and half a mile of beach became a spectacle of naked soldiery, chasing and cavorting in the regular waves. O'Hare and Lacey looked at each other and within two minutes they, too, were out in the ocean, Lacey demonstrating powerful swimming technique that looked as though he was crawling through the water. However, the relief of the water on the bodies of everyone was more than matched by the relief in their minds, that the battle was done and they had survived, and this gave an edge to the screaming and high frolics that exhibited itself up and down the beach; diving through the waves, splashing each other and chasing each other around with large bundles of wet seaweed. But it was too good to last. A Major, as agitated as his horse, galloped onto the beach and continued, on to the nearest men, still cutting energetic capers in the crowded water.

"Where is your Commanding Officer?"

"Don't know, Sir. Along here somewhere."

"Who is your nearest Officer?"

"Him there, Sir."

They pointed to Captain Reynolds, or his piece of ocean, him imitating an aquatic jack in the box by ducking under the water and then springing up and out as high as he could.

"I say. You. Are you an Officer?"

"Yes Sir. I am."

"Get you men out of the water and formed up. The French have reappeared and are no more than musket shot away. There is absolutely no time to lose, they could catch you here. Form up on the other side of the dunes, immediately."

Reynolds responded in kind.

"Pass the word. Out and formed up. No time to dress. Muskets and cartridge boxes. Move! The French are on us."

Starting with those around Reynolds, the men quit the sea and ran to their clothes and equipment. Those who, out of modesty, tried to pull on drawers and trousers, were quickly persuaded otherwise by being pushed on up the beach. Most managed their boots, but nothing more. In minutes the whole battalion was drawn up, in two's beyond the dunes, looking once again across the Plain of Maida, where, but two hours before, they had fought, what was for them, a most desperate battle. The Major was there before them, rising in his stirrups and shielding his eyes as he peered into the distance at a cloud of dust. The Grenadiers appeared to their left, as naked and dripping as they, save for a cartridge box across still wet chests. Other battalions added to the line to the left and right, but all in some stage towards complete dress. Orders came from the Major.

"Load and make ready."

His order was being obeyed, when Lacey and O'Hare arrived, at least wearing cotton drawers.

"Report, Major."

"There has been a sighting of activity out on the French positions, Sir. General Stuart has ordered that the army be drawn up in readiness."

"The French have returned, you say? The last I saw of them, they were in no state to resume any kind of engagement. Unless, of course, they've received reinforcements."

He turned to his servant, the one time Clerk Sergeant, who, dutiful as ever, had gathered up the Colonel's effects and was standing close, awaiting orders.

"Walker. My Dolland glass."

The spyglass was handed forward and Lacey trained and focused it upon the nearing dust cloud. He studied and refocused for a minute.

"Well, Major. If they're anything, they're cavalry, and for another thing, the French must be desperate for mounts because what they are using have all got horns, and as for troopers, there are none mounted that I can see. If you want my opinion, our bathe has been interrupted because of a herd of buffalo!"

He handed the glass to O'Hare.

"What do you make of it, Major?"

O'Hare allowed himself a long look.

"Certainly some sort of cow, and all milling about in a most unsoldierly fashion. Would you care to look, Major?"

The Major did, but gave no opinion. He closed the glass and handed it to Lacey.

"I'll report to General Stuart."

He mounted his horse, face turning as red as his uniform, and rode off. O'Hare gave the order.

"Back to dress, boys, before the milkmaids show up!"

Gibney looked at Deakin.

"Well, there thee goes, Deakin, and that were about the only medal showing thee and I'll ever be party to!"

Chapter Ten

Of Orders and Volunteers

"Captain Carr!"

Carr knew the voice, but the sounds of many approaching feet, crunching through the beach gravel, told of more. It was Kempt, just returned from his pursuit of the French, accompanied by General Stuart and Majors Greelish and Willoughby. Stuart spoke first.

"Carr. I need to know the status of the French, have they halted or have they continued away, to licks their wounds? If they have halted, then they still present a threat. I have no cavalry, at least not at present; therefore under the command of Major Greelish here, I want you to take your company along the road as far as Catanzarro, 20 miles East of here. You get yourself to Maida, then as far on again. Find out as much as you can, but go no further. Greelish here will be mounted, and two Dragoons from the 20th will be his escort. As soon as you have discovered all you can, he will leave you and return poste haste. Leave immediately."

"Where will we find you, Sir, when we're finished?"

"The army will be marching South, through Monteleone and onto the fortress of Scilla. It's the major road South from here, from the one from here that you are taking East. Returning to here and continuing South will bring you to us.

"Yes Sir. I'll make my preparations immediately."

Carr turned to Major Greelish, who swivelled his moustache down to Carr.

"I will parade my men back here in 30 minutes, Sir, if that's acceptable?"

Greelish returned a curt nod, which Carr took as being the only answer he was going to get. Greelish left to make his own preparations, but Major Willoughby motioned for Carr to stay.

"The General has chosen you because you are the only Lights in anything like good order. Kempt's men are still returning in dribs and drabs after gallivanting after the French as far as Maida and beyond. The General hasn't said so, but he's pleased with the way you handle your men. Get to Catanzarro, take a look, then get back. Find out what you can, but take no chances. Good luck, Carr."

"Thank you, Sir."

Carr saluted and ran off, quickly finding Drake and Rushby.

"Nat, Barnaby. No peace for the wicked; Stuart wants us off on scouting duty. He wants us to find out what the French are up to, are they gone, or are they still around? If the latter, what are they about? Get the men back to the supply wagons and get them full with ammunition, water and food. After our walk to find the French, we then have to catch up with the army, who are moving South from here, so expect a lot of marching."

Drake and Rushby ran off in their turn to find their Sergeants. Many men of the Light Company were stood washing in the Lamato, but soon, all over their position, they could be seen replacing jackets and packs and arranging their straps and crossbelts, making comfortable for the forthcoming march. Miles began to question Sergeant Ellis.

"What be we about, Sergeant? The rest of the army is takin' their ease. How come we'm movin' off so soon?

Ellis' reply was heavy with sarcasm.

"Why, the General has particularly requested that your precise talents, Private Miles, be applied in a special mission against the French. An' if you goes, then we has to an' all. So we all credits you with our selection for this particular piece of work. So get your kit on. We has to form up to get ourselves over to our supply wagons. So move yourself!"

Miles returned a black look and attended to the careful placing of his own equipment, his mood not lightened by Ellis' caustic reply. Soon they were marching back and found the wagons and the Storesmen already waiting with ammunition, water, and biscuit. Each man was also to receive a ration of salt pork and peas, and the three items of food, wrapped in kerchiefs, each added to the bulk and weight of their haversacks. Water was being consumed copiously. It was early afternoon, ferociously hot and eye-searingly bright, with dust everywhere, any movement raising a cloud that hung in the thick air. Deakin and Halfway were also at the wagons filling several canteens and so they joined up with Miles, Pike and Davey to talk in the small time remaining. Their pleasure at seeing each other was genuine. Deakin asked first, gallows humour, asking what each wanted to know.

"Alright lads. No holes, nothin' missin?"

Miles replied, "We're all fine, but Joe here got a whack on the head, but made up for it with a nice pair of Frencher boots. How was it for you?"

Deakin's face fell.

"It were bad, a tough fight. They got Pat. We buried him more or less on our line, far over. He's lying with a lot of our lads; the French paid us out well before deciding to give best. The 20th came up just in time, good lads all, and finally saw the Johnnies away. But, thur 'tis, Pat's gone."

Silence fell between them, each with their thoughts on Pat Mulcahey, but it was broken by Joe Pike. Anxiety lay heavy in his words.

"How will his family know? What's going to happen to them?"

Deakin answered.

"They may find out in a bad way, or the worst way. The bad way is that a muster is sent back, and from that, someone tells 'em. Or it could be the worst way. They don't see Pat comin' off the ship when we finally gets back to 'em."

"What will happen to them?"

"Don't worry about that, lad. We takes care of our own. So, how did it go on your side?"

Miles took a deep breath, but the words died in his throat.

"Light Company. Form up!

Miles changed his comment to a parting reply.

"We'll be seein' you, then, Jed, Toby. We'n sent off on a mission to look for the French. If you finds some bottles of local, hold one for us."

The last each saw of the others was their grinning faces as they parted company and the three Light infantrymen formed up in their ranks and marched back to where Carr and Greelish were waiting. Whilst Drake, Rushby and the Sergeants made their inspections, Carr approached Greelish.

"What are you orders, Sir?"

Greelish looked at him in annoyance and impatience.

"Surely you heard the General, Carr? We are to go through Maida and onto Catanzarro."

"Yes, Sir, but what formation would you like us to advance in? From here forward we can't be certain about what we are going to meet."

Greelish's appearance did not change.

"I leave that to you. Your job is to get me to Catanzarro."

Carr was surprised that this Major, him being no less than their Commanding Officer, would give no opinion on the best formation they should use and so he made the only reply he could.

"Yes Sir. Of course, Sir."

"We have six hours of daylight left. Can your men do 20 miles in that time?"

"Yes Sir, or something very close to it."

Greelish repeated his curt nod and Carr saluted and changed his attention to his Company, already in a column of fours. He turned to Drake.

"As we are, Nat. We're going back across the battlefield. Ellis!"

"Sir."

"Yourself and three men. Out front as a picket, 300 yards. Keep your eyes open. There are still Lights coming back, but there could still be French. Those Voltiguers looked useful and some may still be around."

"Yes Sir."

In the early afternoon of the day of the battle, Carr's Company retraced their steps forward across the unaltered scene of the French defeat. French dead, many with bayonet wounds in their backs, broke up the rhythm of their march. Some French wounded, still suffering from their wounds cried out piteously, but most harrowing of all, was the scurrying off at their approach of Calabrian peasants robbing the dead and abusing the wounded. Clearly intense hatred dwelt within them for their French occupiers and now was a chance for revenge. Cries of pain came from the distance and evidence of their work could be deduced from missing fingers, missing ears, and cut throats. Come dark, this work could begin again in earnest.

Willoughby was correct. Kempt's Light Battalion was returning, pushing French prisoners before them and sweeping up any French wounded who could walk and had taken themselves to the Lamato to try to bathe and tend their wounds. Many of the Lights were plainly the worse for drink, pillaged from somewhere, and their raucous, drunken shouts accompanied the march forward of Carr and his men. Thus, there was more human traffic, in various conditions, coming past them in the opposite direction than they themselves formed on their scouting mission. Greelish led the main column, with his two Dragoons either side, and a servant with a packhorse behind them. Carr placed himself 100 yards in front where he could see his advance picket. From the discarded accoutrements and dead, dying, or wounded Frenchmen, it was plain that they were following an army in flight, more than retreating, being pushed and pursued. Two hours hard marching brought them within sight of Maida. Returning Light Infantry had long ceased and the village seemed quiet. Carr halted the column at an enclosed farm and waved Ellis on to discover what was in the village, but Greelish immediately rode up.

"Why have you called a halt, Carr? We have to get through Maida and beyond."

"Yes, Sir. But the French may have re-occupied it and established a rearguard. I've sent my picket forward to take a look."

"Damn your caution, Carr. If the French are there, we'll all discover it soon enough without hanging around waiting for some of your scoundrels to come back and tell us."

"Yes, Sir. But the village could mask cavalry and at this farm we are safer than being out in the open."

"Carr, your worries would insult an old woman. March on."

The Company left the farm and followed Ellis towards the village. Ellis had spread his men far out to expand the ground they could see, but tension fell from all when he turned and waved them forward. As they approached the village, the lessening distance enabled them all to see red-coated figures moving between the houses and some in blue, plainly prisoners. They marched into the village and Carr was pleased to see a familiar face. Captain Smart had recognised him and was walking his way, bearing a broad grin. They shook hands.

"Carr. Glad to see you came through."

"Smart. You too."

However, before the conversation could develop, Major Greelish rode up. Both came to the attention, Smart recognising his Battalion Major.

"Carr. 15 minute break, no more. Smart. Report."

"Yes Sir. Colonel Kempt told me to hold here until mid morning tomorrow. Following Colonel Kempts orders, the 20th Lights are out in front somewhere; they pushed on South West from here, to a place called Borgia. They are under the command of Major Colbourne of the 20th. They may return through here, they may not, which is why I must hold no longer than ordered."

"What of the French?"

"Can't really tell, Sir. We have seen some dust, but that's all. I have a picket about half a mile forward, but they have sent back no word."

"Where did you see the dust?"

"In the direction of Catanzarro, Sir."

Greelish nodded and dismounted.

"Get me some water, for my mount and myself."

Carr had listened to the conversation then took himself off to his men, who had settled to a break without waiting for orders. Miles, Pike and Davey were filling their canteens from the small trough filled with fresh water from the nearby well, filled by themselves by drawing a bucket. Davey was still filling his canteen, when alongside his shoulder came the head of a horse which buried its muzzle in the cool water, right alongside Davey's almost filled canteen. Davey turned angrily to the rider, this being one of the Dragoons, his face framed in the Westering sun, causing Davey to squint.

"Well that's damn nice to you, mate, to fill my canteen with horse slaver. You had but to wait a small time and I'd have finished. A damn poor move, I call it. Damn poor."

The Dragoon leaned forward over his horse's shoulder. His build was heavy cavalry, big and powerful. Davey noticed a scar, running from the outside corner of his left eye, down to the corner of his mouth.

"I don't give a shit for thee and thy canteen. My horse is thirsty and I b'aint goin' to keep him from what he needs."

Davey met the challenging stare.

"I hope thee and I meets again. I really do."

Miles had heard and seen all and was pulling the now needed fresh water up from the well, whilst Davey emptied his canteen onto the ground.

"And just what did you get up to, this morning, in all the fighting that was happening round and about? You looks too spic and span to have been too much involved. Back at the back, polishin' your brasswork, was you? Safe and sound and out of it? I never did know cavalry that got up close with the enemy still formed up and steady, but you comes up soon enough when the likes of us as broken 'em up. Back in the rear, nice and safe, till the job's nye done!"

The Dragoon's face turned purple with anger. He jerked his horse's head out of the water and in Miles' direction. The next

332

move was to ride Miles down, but Miles, recognising the signs, had whipped his bayonet out of its scabbard and fixed it on the end of his musket with equal speed. This he followed by adopting the 'en garde'. The two remained locked in a ferocious stare, neither making a move, until Lieutenant Drake came running over.

"Miles. What the Hell is going on here?"

Miles came immediately to "order arms".

"Oh, nothin' Sir. I was just demonstrating a point to this here cavalryman, Sir, about how we defends ourselves against horses. Sir."

Drake looked almost as angry as the Dragoon.

"Drill, is it? That's what you say. Now remove your bayonet and get yourself back to the others. We move in five minutes."

Drake watched his order being obeyed, but took full notice of the malevolent look that Miles gave the Dragoon as he turned away toward the rest of his Company. The Dragoon pulled his horse towards the opposite direction, giving Drake as contemptuous a look as he had given Miles, but Drake had concerns of his own. Time was up and the Company needed to be reformed. His orders sounded around the abandoned village, repeated by Ellis and soon they were advancing on, this time with Fearnley and two others out as picket. The way out of Maida to Catanzarro was a good road and quicker progress was made, but Greelish was still left fuming whenever Fearnley called up Carr to decide the way of coping with anything threatening or suspicious. Carr was concerned. They were the most advanced of the British forces and the trail of discarded equipment, although lessened, was still there. They were still following the main French army on its retreat. Greelish's impatience and the way it was communicated to Carr with insults and sarcasm were not lost on the men under Carr's command. Tom Miles soon voiced the conclusions of many others.

"This stiff-backed bugger's goin' to get us killed, caught out in the open by a regiment of Frog cavalry. Any damn child knows that cavalry will be somewer', covering a retreat, an' they'll look on doin' us as sweet revenge for what happened to 'em this mornin'."

Ellis overheard and for once delivered no rebuke. He agreed too strongly.

"We all thinks it, Miles, but you 'as to say it. If we follows orders, Captain Carr's that is, and follows our drill, we'll get out of it. Just keep a watch out to your flank, same as the rest of us."

The first they saw of Catanzarro was smoke on the horizon Then, as they crested the last ridge, it was plain that much of the village was on fire, but from their distance there was no sign of the French and they approached, in close skirmish order to enable them to spread out for infantry or close quickly for cavalry. However, as the details emerged before them, Carr formed an opinion that he shared with Drake.

"Those buildings haven't been on fire for even an hour, they're still burning fiercely. Any longer, they'd be burnt out. Whoever set them alight is not long gone."

They eased their way forward, but pickets out to the flanks signalled no cavalry and so they entered from both the main road and the narrow alleys. However, nothing could prepare them for what they found in those alleyways and inside the houses. The deeds inflicted on the inhabitants by the retreating French were not done to force the disclosure of food, this was pure revenge. There was no living thing remaining in the village. The French had killed every being and every animal remaining and the stench of burning flesh pervaded everywhere. The evidence lay within the houses, doorways, and alleyways. Within minutes of the Light Company entering the village came the sounds of retching or curses and oaths heaped upon the heads of the French and damn them until the next time we meet. Miles looked at Davey, both with ashen faces.

"I never saw the likes of this before, John, not never! Give me another chance to pay these bastards out, just one, that's all I ask. Women, kids, and old 'uns. What harm do they do? None. Killin' the likes of them, done just to make 'em feel better. And they wouldn't waste a cartridge! Oh no. Butts and bayonets was just fine for this Devil's work."

Joe Pike was supporting himself on his musket, his face green from vomiting.

"Why do they do this, Tom? Why, what's the purpose?"

Miles' reply was angry and impatient.

"How do I know, boy? They b'ain't yer to ask. All I knows is, that some armies is worse than others, and this Frencher army must be one of the worst. All I can tell 'ee, is what you can work out for yourself. This is just spite, pure spite, takin' their defeat out on anyone, in this case those as is just easy and to hand and can't fight back.

Greelish and his Dragoons had ridden through the village to a hilltop just beyond and he could be seen studying the darkening horizon. Carr remained in the village centre, with Drake and Rushby. All were looking down at the large number of horseshoe prints, still showing in the dust and the mud besides the well, and fresher compared to the equal number of boot marks. Drake looked up at Carr.

"Cavalry?"

Carr's reply was testy, borne of anger.

"What else? Last out to cover the retreat. Blood's still running in the gutters."

"Do you think it's the whole population?"

"That I doubt. There aren't that many, just those who left their evacuation too late. Either that, or didn't see the need. We have to do something about the dead; we can't leave without doing something. Any suggestions?"

It was Rushby who answered.

"We need houses for our own billet tonight, Sir, but there will still be enough left for us if we fill two or three with all the wood we can find, place the bodies on the wood inside and then set fire to it. I think that's the best we can do."

"I agree, well thought of, Barnaby, but not houses on the French side. I don't want them seeing fresh fires. Can I leave that to you both?"

"Yes Sir," in unison.

Carr walked out to join Greelish, still peering and focusing forward. Carr did not want to interrupt Greelish still trying to carry out his mission, but it was plain to Carr that, with the fading light, he had no hope of carrying it out within this day. He politely cleared his throat. There was no reaction. He had no choice but to stand and wait. Eventually the telescope was lowered.

"Sir. I've set the men to dispose of the bodies. I would suggest that we billet here for the night in the remaining houses, and see what can be seen with daylight."

"Seeing by daylight seems rather an obvious comment to make, Carr! Personally, I'm not spending a night in any of that squalor. I'll pitch camp outside, with my servant and escort. You suit yourself."

Alarm bells rang in Carr's mind.

"Sir, may I request that you make your camp behind the village. The French expect a burning village, what they do not expect is new campfires in addition. That will tell them we are here and bring cavalry down upon us."

Greelish's face lit up, as though possessed of a revelation.

"You know, Carr, I think you may have hit upon an idea. Get a dozen of your men to go off down the hill and forward to our left. Beyond half a mile. I want two dozen campfires lit out there. Then we'll see what the morning brings."

Carr was horrified.

"Sir, with respect, that could bring a regiment of cavalry down on us."

"Not here, Carr, there, out there. And we'll be here, watching what goes on."

"Again, Sir, with respect. Any cavalry that comes this far to reconnoitre and finds a lot of decoy campfires will also come to the village to inspect that. We could be one company against half a regiment."

Carr looked and sounded anxious. A look at the Dragoon escort showed that they agreed with him, but Greelish continued.

"You worry more than a village full of old washerwomen, Carr. We are here to discover a French presence or not. I have given you an order, see that it is carried out."

With that he turned his horse back to the village, leaving Carr red with anger on the hilltop. With one last stamp of the ground, he returned to the village. Soon, Fearnley and eleven men could be seen leaving the village. There was enough daylight left to light their way, but when the campfires could be seen dotted and sparkling a half a mile off, Fearnley and his men returned in the light of the funeral pyres that were still roaring on the site of the three cottages.

Ellis, Miles, Pike, Davey, and many other veteran Light Infantrymen looked in horror at the bright spots of yellow light, such as could be seen for miles. Two more could also be seen, but safely behind the village.

"Who ordered that?"

"'Tweren't Carr. 'Twer' the Major."

"How'd you know?"

"One of they Dragoons told I. The one without the scar. They b'ain't happy neither. Sendin' signals to the French."

"I d'reckon that Major knows as much about Light Infantry work as I d'know about sewing a dress. I don't like it; we'll be lucky to get out of 'ere in one piece."

This from Miles, but it was Ellis who ended the dialogue, and his tone matched the worry of the conversation he had just listened to. His words surprised many, they showed little faith in the Officers who had led them there.

"Get back to your billets and get your food inside you. If your building is on the outside of the village dig a loophole through the wall, we may have to defend this place. Check your kit and flints before you turn in. I wants all of you up and ready way before dawn. My guess is that we'll be fightin' our way out of here or holed up defendin' it. If you're on sentry go, take a mate with you and keep yourself very awake."

They obediently did as ordered. The three found their place on the hard earth floor of their hovel and placed their kettle on the good fire alongside those of three other messes that were sharing with them. The pot was filled with their pork and peas, which was covered in water. This home itself had suffered little from the French depredations and all around on the walls hung the now heart wrenching remnants of family life, that once provided small comforts before the wars of nations descended on their small community. This was not lost within John Davey, he had been raised in just such as this. He saw the bunch of herbs hanging by the fireplace to dry, put there by whom, a Mother, a child, a Grandmother? But whomever, they would not return to benefit from this small domestic comfort. Davey ran his fingers down one stalk to gather a tiny bunch of leaves and said a quick prayer as he threw them into the pot and started stirring.

The three Officers were attending to their own affairs when their food arrived, prepared by their own Servant, who, having placed it on the table, yet still stood anxiously shuffling about.

"Beggin your pardon, Sirs, but what may be happenin' in the mornin'? I needs to make my arrangements, Sirs."

It was Drake who answered. Carr was deep in thought, staring at the fire and fingering his medallion.

"Why, Morrison, we wake up, take breakfast, confirm that the French have gone, then march back to the army."

"Yes, Sir. I hope so, Sir. I do so very much hope so."

The servant left as Carr came to the table and Rushby ladled out the food and the biscuits. When each was settled, Drake looked at Carr.

"You know what may well happen, tomorrow, Henry. What's your plan?"

Carr toyed with his food, and then looked up, turning his face towards both.

"We can't leave until good light, because that's needed for maximum visibility to give Greelish a good look. Then I hope we march off unmolested."

His voice became heavy with sarcasm.

"If the French do come riding out of the dawn, as I strongly suspect they will, Greelish will ride off to convey to General Stuart the stunning and wholly unpredictable news that the French have cavalry patrols behind their retreat. That leaves us on our own. If they arrive at first light, we will have to hold here. We will have to stay here till dark and hope to sneak away, or, the cavalry will get worried that they are being left behind and give up. If the French come later, as we are marching back, Greelish will still ride away. On our way here I made a note of defensive positions between here and Maida. Almost every mile, there was something, a groups of rocks, a paddock, a farm, something. We march to each to minimise the time we are out in the open. What worries me most is that there are too many bits of woodland and also valleys off to the side so that some cavalry could get close, and once they've penned us in, they won't let us out. However, I'm hoping they will decide that they can't stay long or they'll lose touch with their main army. Whichever happens, it isn't much of a plan, but it's the best we've got."

"You expect us to be fighting our way out, Sir?"

"Yes, Barnaby, I do. The odds are not good; when have we ever ignored campfires? Ellis has already told the men to be up before dawn and doubled the sentries and we've gathered barricade material at entry points. As soon as the light is good enough to see far enough, I hope that Major Greelish will order our withdrawal, then we won't need any barricades. Then we hope."

After eating, they saw to their rest and soon two slept whilst the third patrolled the sentries. Dawn came as a sudden clear blue that told of another blistering hot day to come and the light was growing rapidly, quickly pushing out the visible distance. There was no morning mist; all moisture had been burnt off in the heat of the previous days. Carr emerged from their billet to find Drake alone in the main street.

"Morning, Henry. The men are at the defences. Greelish has ridden forward to his hill. He's there now. Ah, biscuits and coffee. Well done, Morrison."

Carr took two biscuits and a mug of coffee and began his walk to Greelish, off in the distance and clear in the full daylight. Carr was able to announce his presence by saying "Good Morning", but Greelish remained up in his stirrups, his telescope pressed against his right eye. Finally, it was closed and Greelish looked down.

"Nothing. I can see nothing, Carr. My little ruse has told us a great deal. Had the French seen the fires, we would be seeing them, riding to investigate. We can ride back and report."

"If I may make a point, Sir. It's plain, Sir, that the infantry have gone, they have abandoned two defencable villages, especially this one. They have been pulled right back to regroup. What we can confidently predict, and should allow for, are the usual cavalry patrols that any prudent General would send out. Cavalry will be in this area, Sir, either near or far."

"Your rank does not allow such high level conclusions, Carr. I am with you to make the judgement on what the French are about. We ride back."

"Yes, Sir. But may I respectfully suggest that you don't part company from us just yet. I doubt the French would ride directly across open country at an enemy camp to their front, as that is. They will use what cover they can to get close to those campfires before being seen. There are valleys and woodland either side, and the French know this country better than we do. They may yet come, but onto our flank, even from ahead, cutting us off, if the country allows."

Greelish's face fell. What Carr had said could not be argued with.

"There may be some merit in what you say. I'll stay with you an hour or so, and then take off. General Stuart needs to know what I know."

"Yes Sir. Of course."

Those mounted trotted back, leaving Carr to walk, but all was ready. Drake had already sent Ellis with three men out on flank picket to their right, and Fearnley the same to their left, and the column was ready to go. Drake ordered the march and they left, leaving Carr alone between the many blackened and collapsed walls, their charred and exposed roof timbers pointing accusing fingers at the clear, benign blue of the arching sky. He didn't fail to notice that his men had placed three crude crosses before the still smoking ruins of the three cottages used to cremate the bodies. A line from Henry V came into his mind, one drummed into him at school. "I was not angry since I came to France until this instant." He nodded in that direction and marched out himself, promising himself some form of revenge, large or small, but wholly personal.

* * *

The clear morning air, cool from the night, was gone, now twisted into unseen columns by a myriad of heat thermals that rose from the baking ground. Even at half a mile, for Carr pursuing them, the loose column on the road merged and danced into red shapes that moved in the heat haze in conjunction with their slow progress along the hard, dry road. At two miles the thick and swirling air turned the column into a red smear from which individual figures could not be discerned, even through a good Harris "three-draw telescope", purchased in London by an Austrian General and taken from him as French booty at Ulm. However, it was clear enough to conclude that British troops were on the road.

* * *

Carr did not first catch up with the column, instead he ran out to Ellis and his three pickets, these on the side of the decoy camp. Ellis had placed himself at the rear.

"Ellis. You and Byford, concentrate on the flanks, but mostly to the rear, you especially back towards the decoy camp, for as long as you can see it. Your front two concentrate on the flanks and to our front. If you see anything you don't like, fire a musket and halt. Pass that on. I want your best watch, mind, your best."

340

"Sir."

Carr loped off to convey similar to Fearnley and his men, then he took himself back to Ellis. His unease showed in everything he did, checking his pistols, adjusting his sabre, but above all, jogging to any vantage point that became available.

Time passed. The Company maintained close order on the road, whilst the pickets, frequently changed, remained out wide, ever watchful, mindful of Carr's explicit order; "Your best watch". Whilst the tension lessened with every step, the impatience within Major Greelish grew. Mounted on a good horse and tied to footbound infantry because of the remaining small possibility of cavalry appearing, which he needed to witness, he fumed at allowing himself to remain beholden to Carr's anxiety of cavalry arriving unseen out of some hidden valley. He told himself that the miles were stretching out between them and the retreating French and they were going in opposite directions. His patience finally snapped and he summoned Lieutenant Drake to the side of his horse, Carr was again out with Ellis.

"Drake. I've decided I know enough, I'm leaving now. Pass that onto...."

A musket went off over on the right and all looked over to see the white smoke still hanging over the solitary figure, the second in the picket line, but Carr was already closing up to him.

"What did you see, Hoskins?"

"Over that ridge, Sir. It looked odd, Sir. It could have been birds flying low, but it was too, well, crowded Sir, sort of. It looked like black things, Sir, small and lots of them, moving just beyond that ridgeline. There were a few bits of sunlight glintin', too, Sir."

"What about horsehair plumes on top of cavalry helmets. Could that have been what you saw?"

"Yes, Sir. I reckon that could explain it as much as anything else."

"And you're certain you saw something?"

"Oh, yes Sir. There was something out there, alright."

"Well done, Hoskins, first class. Now reload and get back to the column."

Carr closed up to each picket and shouted at them to rejoin the column. He began his own run; 300 yards back to the road and the rest of his men. He stopped once and turned, but saw nothing, but the second time he turned, he saw them. Their Commander must have heard the shot and decided that they had been seen. No point in delaying the attack any longer to give the British time to prepare some kind of defence. He had wheeled his troopers left and came on at a fast canter, up over the last ridge that had concealed their attempt to get ahead of the British and, with that, the Commander saw that their charge would cut their quarry off, anyway.

Carr had 200 yards to go, the cavalry had over 600, but on fast horses. Carr would regain his line, but what then, how far to the nearest of his refuge points? He could see that Greelish had taken his own decision and, with his escort, was spurring his mount away along the road, rapidly attaining a gallop, Dragoons and servant behind him, with the bundles on the pack horse bouncing to alarming heights in the rush to be away. As they rode by, Miles left the ranks to get near to the scarred Dragoon as he rode past in pursuit of Greelish.

"All right, mate. Johnny's arrived, so off you go. We'll cover your backside for you!"

Any reply was lost in the dust and the pounding hooves and Miles now had his own orders to attend to. Carr was shouting orders, despite his laboured breathing from his long run.

"Close up. Rallying square. Fix bayonets. Rifles to the front, out here now. On me."

Carr had halted just off the road and he held out his sword to show where he wanted the line. The cavalry were still some way off, but his worst fears were confirmed. It was half a Regiment of cuirassiers, French heavy cavalry, 400 or more. They had body armour and long swords, but worst, heavy horse pistols which, from under 50 yards were as accurate as a musket. As his riflemen formed up on their position, Carr made a quick examination of where they were and the worst of his fears, at least, fell away, their chances were close to good. A dilapidated paddock that he knew was their next safe haven was not too far, but no time to ponder, the growing sound of hooves called his attention away.

"At 200 yards. Get the Officers, or their horses. I don't care, just bring them down."

He looked along his line, just over 30 men, some adjusting their sights, but most stood with their weapon, at the "make ready", bayonet challenging upward. Still time, so he looked for one of his Officers.

"Rushby, keep in close order and get the men behind those walls."

He pointed to the paddock, reassuringly closer to the Company than himself. Rushby saluted and turned, shouting orders. Carr returned to his major concern.

"Present"

The rifles all came level. He gave them time to settle onto their targets.

"Fire."

The rifles exploded as one, and the smoke drifted across their front, but not enough to prevent Carr seeing that almost 20 riders had been downed and all but one of the leading riders. The French now had a barrier of struggling men and horses before them, but not enough to substantially check their charge forward. They avoided their fallen and came on. They had received a check that they didn't expect at that range, but they soon recovered.

"Retire."

All ran to catch up to the small square, each side three deep, that Drake and Rushby had formed and, still holding good order, was running on to what worryingly now appeared to be little more than a series of short walls, with scattered stones in between. The riflemen merged into the outside rank and their run continued. Drake took his own decision. It was over 100 yards range, but his men were loaded and a volley, if delivered quickly, would keep the cuirassiers at a distance, giving more time to reach the paddock. He had seen for himself that they were faced with heavy cavalry and if they were allowed to catch up and simply ride around and use those damn pistols, then there was little hope. A quick volley and then move.

"Halt. Face your front. Second rank. Present. Fire."

Again the explosion of fire and more horses and riders fell.

"Rear rank. Present. Fire."

The same effect, and all turned to the walls that were now quite near. They all tumbled over and through the gaps, but the paddock was no kind of a defensive work, there were as many gate wide holes in the walls as solid stonework, and the whole was too big for the 80 odd men to man sufficiently. However, there were the ruins of a small building in a near corner, probably a feed store, with all walls intact at least to chest height. Drake led the way and all crowded in, but it was too small for them all, and the floor was covered by stones from the collapsed walls with as many fallen stones outside as in. The last men were coming up, including Carr, which added to the crush, but the French were also urging their horses through the gaps. Drake gave his orders.

"My section, back outside, get these stones piled up, make something you can lie behind from this corner to the wall. Lieutenant Rushby, your section man the walls, give us covering fire. Anyone left inside and doing nothing, throw stones out for the wall."

The work began, fear giving strength to those that had the task to throw, lift and pile the awkward stones. There was no hope of building a careful wall, but a long heap grew out from the corner of the hut to join with the main wall. A few brave or foolhardy cavalrymen charged up to the hut, but were brought down by the muskets and rifles of those within, but with their demise came the pistol fire. Some cuirassiers, perhaps those with more battle experience, dismounted their horses and began sending pistol fire at the building, using the paddock walls as cover and, with the number of men they had, it was a heavy weight of fire. The Light Company began to take casualties, very soon there were two dead and three wounded, four of these amongst the work group outside. Carr took command, and gave his orders. The pile of stones was now sufficiently high to provide cover for anyone lying down.

"Stop work and take cover. Reload and wait."

He looked around. The men inside the hut were answering the pistol fire that continued as heavy as ever, continuing to smack and buzz against the stonework, but with all now behind the walls, it was wholly ineffective. The siege that he had foretold was now upon them.

"Cease fire. Rifles only and pick your targets carefully. Conserve ammunition."

What worried Carr now, was the French edging along the outside of the paddock, up to their ruin and making an attack over the wall; they certainly had enough men. The remains of a narrow window, only the lower half, the top half defined by a lopsided dry and rotten frame, looked out over the open ground outside, but that told them little of what was happening immediately under the wall. What to do, make an exit so that they could climb out and fire along the wall, which would expose those venturing outside to pistol fire, or hold what they had? He looked out through the window, gingerly easing his head around the dried out frame. Cuirassiers were riding around the outside, pistols held up to their shoulders, looking for targets. Two pistols balls sang through the opening to smack against the inside wall, but he had seen that the outside level was nearly three feet lower than the inside, making the wall a high enough obstacle to any attack. Carr decided; they would take the risk and hold what they had. He turned to those sheltering along the wall.

"I want firing positions over the top of this wall, one yard apart, one foot down, like a castle. Use the stone to raise this window, the rest add to the inside wall."

The work continued. Firing positions were made and they began a serious defence of their small enclosure. The number of wounded mounted, but none serious, as all were from flying fragments of stone or spent bullets; now it was the French who were suffering. They could make no progress across the paddock and several of those riding around outside were being picked off by the accurate fire from the rifles, but Carr was still worried about French creeping up below the wall of the hut. He drew his pistols, cocked both and looked out through the heightened window. He waited for a gap in the cuirassiers riding around outside, then put out his arm followed by his head to see that there were indeed some cavalrymen crouching down to the right. He fired his pistol at one, then shot back in as a cavalry pistol was fired at him. He took his other pistol, eased it around the window frame and fired it, unaimed and blind, but down at where he thought the troopers were. He looked at the inside wall of his command and saw more with rifles there firing across the paddock than at the outside wall. He tapped five of them on the shoulder.

"You five, fire outside. Make them ride far out. Lieutenant Rushby, send pistol fire around the sides of this window."

He looked for a tall soldier, and found one.

"Saunders. Get yourself hoisted up and look over the wall from time to time. Choose a different place each time, but tell us where the French are."

The soldier reported and, with Drake joining Rushby, both Officers sent pistol fire down and along the outside of the wall. With them firing blind, how effective it was couldn't be seen, but heavy stones heaved over the top of the wall added to the defence of this one point where the French could get close, and the huge Saunders reported no serious gathering of French building an assault.

Miles, Pike and Davey were outside, crouching behind the recently built parapet. They had added to the height and made two firing positions. Davey had his own, whilst Pike and Miles took turns at the other. Davey was concentrating on cuirassiers firing around a gate post, but Pike was at his place, waiting.

"Can you see any, John? They seems a bit more scarce, or are they just keeping their heads down more?"

"Can't tell, Joe. Bullets is still comin' in, so they'm firing from somewhere. So, don't ease off, and don't show too much of yourself."

His rifle went off and a cuirassier disappeared.

"I reckon that did him a bit of no good."

He drank some water and began reloading. Miles had been reloaded for some time and was waiting for Pike to fire, but with no impatience. He knew they were holding their ground, no need for two to fire when there wasn't a target for one.

"I'll tell thee one thing, I reckon these are the cavalry bastards as did for that village. At least from the same Regiment. We're holding them off, and 'tis them as is getting' killed. I'm happy to stay here for a while and see to the likes of a few more. I wish that they would come over that wall, then we'll see who gets paid out."

The wounded were being attended to by Sergeant Fearnley, for both he and Ellis carried a basic medical kit. One of the wounded was serious, shot in the chest, but the other three would be walking wounded, the worst had a ball pass through the outside of his arm. Water and linen was the best he could do, but for now it was sufficient. Sensing movement, he looked around and was shocked to see Lieutenant Rushby with his left hand inside his jacket, up to his right shoulder. He was white with shock and unsteady on his feet.

"Sit down, Sir, and let me take a look."

Fearnley carefully removed Rushby's jacket and immediately saw that there was no exit wound, but that could be both good and bad. The removal of the shirt revealed the wound. It was certainly made by a bullet.

"Where can you feel the hurt, Sir? Has it gone inside, like?" Rushby took a deep breath and swallowed.

"It feels all close to the surface, but it aches through and through."

"All right, Sir. I'm going to have a look. Bite on this."

He placed a short length of wood, already pitted from previous teeth marks, into Rushby's mouth. A bullet or dislodged stone smacked into the wall above them and buzzed elsewhere.

"I need to see if I can feel it, Sir. I'll be as careful as I can."

He probed with the thin knife and Rushby gave a stifled scream and clenched his fists hard. Tears emerged from between his clenched eyelids. Soon Fearnley felt what he hoped he'd find.

"Whatever it is, it's not too far down, Sir. With a bit of pushing aside, I can probably see it, even. We should try to get it out, Sir, if you're willing?"

Rushby nodded and Fearnley smiled back, himself twice the age of the young Ensign.

"That's it, Sir. It won't be too bad. You two," he gestured to two unoccupied soldiers, "take his arms, and hold him steady, push him back against the wall. It's going to hurt and so he's going to move, or try."

With no small skill, using the knife and some basic forceps, Fearnley eased open the wound and peered in. Another soldier mopped the blood. Rushby strained against the hands that held him and screamed again, as much as the wooden gag would let him. Fearnley continued to work and for over an agonizing minute, continued to probe. A sigh and a grin spoke of his success and a bloody object was held up within the forceps.

"It's a ball alright, Sir, but I'd say you was lucky. It's all out of shape. It must have hit the wall somewhere then went on to you. That took the force out of it, and it took nothing of your shirt in with it, Sir. That's good. I'll just clean you up and put a drop of rum in there, like I've been told. I don't understand why, but 'tis what you do, and I do know it'll sting. But I'm afraid it's not over, it'll need stitches."

"That can wait. Rum for now, then see to the others."

Fearnley was not wrong and Rushby winced as the rum was trickled in, but then grinned. He was relieved and held up the cleaned ball in the fingers of his left hand for examination, noticing that it had been flattened over at least half its surface. He took a drink of water from one of the two soldiers and grinned again.

"My thanks to you all, especially to you Sergeant. I know nothing of these things, but I'd say that was a fine piece of work."

Drake came to make his enquiries and Rushby held up the ball.

"Ricochet. I was lucky. How goes it outside?"

"Oh, we're holding them off, and I'd say they're the one's suffering. There's quite a few lying outside, but there's a lot of them still and we're bunged up in here. It's stalemate. But you rest, and don't worry."

At that moment there came three clear notes from a bugle.

"What's that? Theirs or ours?"

Fearnley answered.

"Theirs Sir. That's no bugle call that I've ever heard."

Drake ducked along the wall to reach Carr.

"What's happening Henry? Does that mean anything? Are they reinforced?"

"Can't tell yet. But they're still circling around with their damned pistols and we're still taking fire from the walls outside."

But over the next few minutes the fire slackened and then ceased. Carr peered through one of the crude embrasures. He could see nothing. He called to his men.

"Any of you. Can you still see any of them?"

No reply, so he gingerly raised his head, continuously peering around. Looking over the wall, on the Catanzarro side, he saw that the French were forming up, well out of range, and heaving their wounded onto the several spare horses.

"Rifles up. Maximum range. Keep firing."

Those with rifles re-opened fire on the clear target, but no more French fell. They were, it was now certain, out of range.

"You can stand up, lads, and take a look. We've fought them off."

However, inside himself he knew the main reason. Casualties were one thing, losing touch with the main army was another, but what came next surprised even Carr.

"He's got a bloody nerve!"

A young French Officer, highly idealistic, had ridden slightly in their direction and was holding his sword up in salute to acknowledge their defence, both brave and soldierly. Carr sprang up onto the wall, half withdrew his own sword and then slammed it back into its scabbard. Two or three of his men shouted "Catanzarro" at the top of their lungs to be joined by others, and others vigorously gestured the traditional English "V" sign in the Officer's direction. The main body of cavalry were on their way and the Officer realised that no honourable rejoinder would be replied and so he, also, sheathed his sword and turned his horse away to canter after his command.

"Damn him and every Frog bastard that he rides with."

Rushby had been looking over the wall.

"It may not have been this Regiment, Sir."

"They're from the same damn army, aren't they?"

Carr descended from the wall. He turned to Drake.

"How many dead?"

"Three, Sir."

"Get them buried. And badly wounded, can't walk?"

"Three again, Sir."

"Send out some men. Try to get some loose horses to carry them. Not all will have gone off with the French. We stay here until sunset. I'm not risking them turning around and hoping to catch us out on the open road. Tell the men to rest and eat. We're marching through the night. How's Rushby?"

"A bit shook up, but recovering."

Carr nodded."

"Right. Get things done."

Some men went out and did indeed return with horses, four not three, two with blood on their necks and saddles. Their saddle blankets were a rich dark green, edged with gold, embroidered with a gold "N" and "33'eme C". Carr seized the blanket's corner and raised it up.

"33rd Cuirassiers, eh? That's a number I'll damn well remember."

* * *

General Stuart stood by his horses head, alternately stroking his neck and feeding him apples, specifically carried from England, each being handed to him by a servant as and when required. He was in a most excellent mood, the fact of his victory against the much vaunted French had thoroughly sunk in and, between apples and pats, he regarded his passing army. His Staff, an inevitable accompaniment, sat astride their horses and also watched the men progressing along the pale sand and chalk road that led South to Monteleone, Scilla and Reggio. Stuart could hear from the comments behind him that his Staff shared his own good opinion, that the men looked in good heart, Appearance notwithstanding, they were sunburnt and dusty, and undressed with jackets and shakoes slung over packs, but all had the bearing of men victorious and it showed, they were upright and talkative, sharing banter back and forth between the ranks. He didn't expect marching in step, but they were marching with purpose, at a good pace. Optimism grew further within him that they could soon take the towns between themselves and Scilla and, by taking advantage of low French morale after their unexpected defeat; they could capture the fortress at Scilla and complete the campaign with the capture of all facilities that would enable the French to invade Sicily.

Deakin and Halfway were in their usual place in their marching column, with Gibney, as usual in his place outside the ranks, marching alongside. Their uniforms, once bright red, were now covered with chalk dust, so their appearance now matched the pink of the Swiss. Those of the Swiss, from the same dust, had turned to a subtle shade of grey. Halfway was closest to Gibney.

"How come we'n marching South, Sar' Major, away from them Frogs that we just saw off. Don't we need to go after 'em?"

"Well now, Corporal, bein' as I'm not privileged to that kind of information, there's not too much I can say, but I do know that there's French holed up in towns and villages this way, and, I suppose, they has to be dealt with first. 'Sides, do I take it that thee's itchin' for another fight, seein' as we just 'ad such a bad one, day 'fore yesterday?"

"No, Sar' Major, no lover of battles, me. Just curious. Like most, I likes to have some idea of what's goin' on. 'specially as we'm in the land of the enemy."

Deakin joined in.

"Land of the enemy this may be, but the civilian part of it is much to my liking. They'n more than happy to see us. I've a haversack full of good bread and some kind of pie, and fruit, and a bottle besides. But speakin' of the fruit, what I got off 'em is a bit of a mystery."

He fished one out from the depths of his haversack. It was round, red, and orange, but no kind of orange. It was hard. He turned to the soldier on his left.

"Here, pass that along to Captain Heaviside. I've got plenty. Let him have a look at it. He might know what 'tis."

The fruit was passed along and Heaviside pronounced judgment.

"It's a pomegranate. You eat the seeds, nothing else, they're surrounded by a kind of jelly. Pick them out; you'll find it quite pleasant. "And ye shall eat the fat of the land. Genesis, chapter 45, verse 18."

"Yes, Sir. That's a comfort. Now we know. Pomegranate."

He produced two more.

"Here y'are Toby. One for you and one for Gibney."

The fruit was accepted and disappeared into already weighty haversacks, but their mood was good. The sun was fierce, as always, but a steady sea breeze kept them at least merely warm and blew away inland the dust from the thousands of marching feet. They had passed through no town, nor even a village, but every farm and hamlet they met had greeted them well and supplied them with food, wine, and water. They approached another collection of small houses and the people were at their doors and fences, cheering and waving, with water buckets set on a plank table and a pile of oranges. In front men were falling out to refill canteens and take an orange, as if they didn't already have enough. Halfway made the observation.

"I d'reckon, Jed, that these people is more happy to see us than any Irish we saw, when we was in the 9th. It's like we was Jesus Christ in a redcoat the way they do cheer and shout at our passing. We never saw the likes in Ireland."

"No argument there, Toby. But in Ireland we'm the occupying power. I daresay that if the French were to march in there to kick us out, like we'm kicking the French out of here, then them Irish would cheer them just the same. 'Tis all about whose got their boot on your neck and whose takin' it off."

"You reckon we'm as bad to the Irish, as the French have been to this lot. I'm hearin' wicked tales about what they does to get food out of these people. You can't say we'm as bad as that."

"No, but any injustice is felt, large or small. If you'm put upon, you thanks the one's that takes it away, or you should.

Anyhow, look, it's fallout time. Let's find some shade, get some sleep."

At the tail end of the 5th, Sedgwick was suffering in the heat. A red rash was building around his wrists and neck, where his skin met his cuff and collar. A state of undress was wholly unacceptable to him, that being to remove his jacket and besport himself in his shirtsleeves, but this was his state now, with a damp rag about his neck that did ease the irritation. However, back under the shade of the supply wagon, with the sea breeze supplying air that was bearably warm, he did feel a modicum of greater comfort. But he suffered also inside, spiritually. On dry land he had hoped to be able to often frequent a proper place of worship, but he had visited two and found them wholly distasteful; he'd been greatly affronted by the pomp and the eye-searing colour and opulence, this even in the lowliest, along with the all-pervading stench of incense. Here was Popery writ large, much too large for his Low Church training and persuasion and so each was no place for devotion; instead a pained, but silent rehearsal of a possible argument between himself and the incumbent Priest, were he there and could speak English.

Also a debate had continued intermittently within himself over approaching Captain Heaviside, that obvious and self-ordained Man of God, to investigate the possibility of the two forming a Bible Group or some such Prayer Circle. However, counter to that, it was beginning to set itself within him, that they were both, now, several classes apart. Nevertheless, today saw Sedgwick with spirits higher than usual. On the day of battle, had he not carried out his duty to carry ammunition to the firing line, had he not been under fire himself, and had he not been singled out, by the base and common soldiery, to conduct the service at the burial of one of their number? Today was one of Percival Sedgwicke's better days.

If Percival Sedgwicke's spirits were higher than typical, those of D'Villiers and Carravoy were lower that usual. Each realized that they had almost "funked it", as expressed in their terminology, in the recent conflict. The Grenadier Company had been returned to the 5th Provisionals and, when came a fallout from the march, D'Villiers had taken himself away from the 3rd Company with its lugubrious and pious Captain and sought Carravoy amongst his Grenadiers, but conversation passed between them but little. In his mind, D'Villiers again ran through a conversation with his Sergeant the day after the battle.

"The lads are proud of you, Sir."

He had been shocked.

"How so?"

"Because you stood out front, Sir, daring the French. You set a good example, Sir."

But this brought little comfort. He knew why he had "stood out front"; he had been frozen with fear, which gnawed deeply at his own self-esteem.

Carravoy also had his own devils. He had lied about the extent of Carr's help at the farmhouse, and he had been exposed to Carr over it, he had been sworn at by his Commanding Officer and, finally, he knew the reason why he had remained amongst the Grenadiers, when desperation was irresistible within him. They, but ranking soldiers, had stood firm and calm, needing no example from him, rather the reverse, whilst he was panicked and terrified. Each would have liked to confide in the other, but D'Villiers was much Carravoy's junior, and confessing to fear in that measure would be very much "bad form" and self-demeaning. So each sat, saying little, other than conjecture on the next few days.

O'Hare was passing and saw both, including the black cloud that hung above them.

"How now boys. You two look as though you came for a wedding and found a funeral!"

The two began to get to their feet.

"Ha, no. Don't get up. Don't get up."

He stood and regarded both for a short while, giving them time to look up at him, then back down in embarrassment."

"So, you both came through it? Hale and hearty, nothing left behind, neither blood nor bits?"

Both looked up and nodded.

"And you were damn near terrified from start to finish. Yes?"

Both now did look up, faces showing the shock of hearing the truth from this socially inferior, but deeply experienced Officer.

"Well now, let me tell youse. That's just how it is for everyone, everyone of us, first time. And that was a bad one, make no mistake. No one has the nerves to cope first time, 'specially that one, and stand up to it like it was nothing. So listen. You

353

didn't run. You didn't disgrace yourselves. You just surprised yourselves about how damn scared you were. Well, as I'm now saying to youse both, that's how it works, there's nothing special about the pair of youse. So cheer up and call yourselves veterans."

With that he left. Carravoy said nothing, he had other remaining worries, but D'Villiers managed a cheery "Thank you, Sir", which was when the headache started and he began to shiver.

The orders were passing around to form up, but Toby Halfway was going through the same as D'Villiers was just starting.

"Jed. I don't feel right. Hot and cold and a swaying head. Right now, the shivers. I got an ague of some sort, been comin' on all mornin'. Do you think it's that new fruit, pomme summat?"

Deakin looked at his friend and it stirred bad memories. He had seen this in the West Indies, long ago, but it remained vivid.

"Toby, do your joints hurt and perhaps your eyes, too?"

"That's right, Jed, that's comin' on too."

Deakin grew fearful. Swamp fever; and he remembered the foul, swampy ground they had inhabited before the battle. He unbuckled Halfway's greatcoat from his pack.

"Now just sit back down, Toby, and wrap this round you. Here, Peters, get his kit off him and keep him still and warm until he feels hot. When he feels hot try to keep him cool. I'm going to find Captain Heaviside."

He took himself off and found his Captain just closing his Bible and stowing it in his pack.

"Sir. It's Corporal Halfway, Sir. I'm certain he's got swamp fever, Sir, I saw it when I served in the West Indies and I had it myself."

"You're certain?"

"Not bein' a medical man, not wholly certain, Sir, but he complains of exactly what I know swamp fever is made up of, Sir."

"Where is he now?"

"Still in the shade, Sir, bein' cared for by the lads."

"I will pray for him."

"Yes, Sir. Meanwhile, Sir......."

"Meanwhile, Corporal, you see that he is cared for, and I will inform Colonel Lacey. Dismiss."

Deakin knew that he was now required to come to the attention and he did so, then he saluted, then marched off."

Heaviside was as good as his word and found both Colonel Lacey and Major O'Hare, Lacey just rising from his table to enable his servants to pack it away.

"Sir. I wish to report what I believe to be a case of swamp fever, Sir."

Lacey looked at O'Hare. His expression worried.

"That's six."

Carravoy joined them.

"Sir. Lieutenant D'Villiers, Sir. He isn't feeling at all well."

"Right. Captain Heaviside. I want you to organise wagons for the sick. Empty as many as you need and give the supplies to the men to carry if they cannot be carried in the remaining wagons. Pass the word that the sick are to be taken back to the rear to be carried in them."

Heaviside saluted and went off, leaving the three Officers together. Lacey looked at O'Hare.

"The other enemy, Padraigh, the one that takes no sides."

O'Hare nodded. No reply was needed. Meanwhile, Heaviside was turning the world of Sedgwicke, Pearson and the other storemen upside down.

"I want as many empty wagons as you can put together. Cram the others full with what cannot be carried and send to the Captains of all Companies for men to carry what can be carried. Expect a number of sick men. Get it done at your best speed. Then expect another role for yourselves; that of medical men. We've been hit by swamp fever, so you'll want plenty of drinking water and a strong preparedness to care for them."

He turned to Pearson.

"I'm making you responsible, Sergeant. Very responsible. Clear?"

Pearson nodded and saluted, but Heaviside didn't see. He was turning away, but Sedgwicke saw this as his chance.

"Captain, Sir. I was wondering if I may have a word, Sir. I think you may know that I'm........."

"Storeman! The word crisis is not unknown to you, I feel sure."

"Yes, Sir, I mean no, Sir."

"We are in the middle of one right now. See to your duties."

"Yes, Sir."

Heaviside turned away and almost collided with the Battalion Surgeon, hurrying back in accordance with Lacey's orders.

"Sir, I'm fairly certain it's swamp fever."

"How do you know?"

"One of my men has had it in the past, Sir, and the symptoms match what happened to him."

"Yes, thank you, Captain. That's useful. Knowing that early gives me a chance. I'll do my best."

"Sir."

Heaviside took himself back to his Company, passing a number of evidently ill men being helped back to the waiting wagons. By now Deakin had returned to Halfway, now very hot, with Peters draping a wet rag around his head.

"Now listen, old mate. Captain Heaviside has seen the Colonel and it looks like they'm clearin' wagons. I saw the Surgeon go back, so I d'reckon there's more of you. I saw them fussin' around D'Villiers, perhaps he's got it too. They'll take care of you. Look after yourself and do like they say, so's you gets well."

He turned his head towards the sound of "fall in".

"Right. Let's get you back to the wagons. Peter's give us a hand here."

With Halfway's kit draped around their own necks and shoulders, Halfway was walked and carried back to one of the supply wagons. They came to the first and looked in, to be rebuffed by a harassed storeman.

"Officers only. Try the next one."

They turned to confront Lieutenant D'Villiers, being helped by his servant; clearly unwell, but not as advanced as Halfway. They reached the back of the next wagon, already half full, and helped him up. As Peters laid him out, arranged his kit, and placed his rolled up greatcoat as a pillow, Deakin topped up his canteen, and propped it up by his side. He heard orders being shouted outside; he knew he had to leave. He lifted Halfway's hand and squeezed it; the response was weak, as was the smile from the half-lifted head.

"There's your water, to your left. We'n away now, old son. See you in a while when you'n back on your feet. Do like you'm told now. For now then; so long."

Peters smiled and patted Halfway on the chest. Both climbed down and ran to catch up with the now marching column.

Stuart's army marched on, trailing their sick and wounded with them, until they reached Monteleone, the first garrisoned obstacle on their march to Scilla. It was a dirty white jumble of a variety of buildings, some well founded, some of the poorest. The town filled a dish-shaped valley, with some buildings creeping up onto the higher slopes and a bleak, grey castle that hoisted its higher battlements above the highest buildings, but, these being low and squat, that was no remarkable achievement. Oswald's Brigade, the Swiss and the 58th, were at the heads of the column, but Stuart held them back and rode up to investigate, taking Oswald, Cole, Acland, and Kempt with him. Their attention focused on the castle, still flying the French tricolour, and French infantry were manning barricades across the main road and others on the edge of the town.

Stuart pondered. Was it a demonstration, to see that honour was satisfied, or a serious defence? Time to ask the question.

"Kempt. Is Carr's Light Company back with you yet?"

"No, Sir."

"Right. Oswald. Get your two in column, either side of the road. Cole. I want Lacey's out on the left, pushing around their flank. Then we will see, Gentlemen, just what these French have in mind."

The group split as the riders went back to their various commands. Cole soon reached Lacey and salutes were exchanged. Respect between the two had grown.

"Lacey. Oswald is sending his two forward, in column either side of the road. Yours are to march up and overtake Kempt's Lights and position yourselves to menace their right flank."

"Line or column, Sir?"

"Line, but three deep, I'd say. If you do have to go in, you'll need skirmish order."

The orders were given and soon they were marching up the road, past the Light Battalion that had been called off the road and were resting up on the grass verge, using the shade of some ragged olive trees. The silence did not last long.

"It's the rag and bone boys! Must be some kind of shoddy shop up in that town. Short of a few bits and pieces, are you lads?"

However, many amongst the 5th, now bloodied in battle and knowing it, were not inclined to take such comments without some measure of reply.

"That's alright, boys, you just take your ease. A bit of quality's needed, and so they're moving us up. Don't boil your pork and peas just yet; you can do that after we've got you in. We'll light you a nice warm fire."

The banter continued then faded, as the 5th marched past and moved off to the left of Oswald's two columns, but they had barely extended out before the tricolour came down and the Sicilian Royal Standard was run up. The town had surrendered. Oswald's 58th were ordered straight in and they dismantled the now unmanned barrier from the main road, before advancing on. Lacey spread his companies around the edge of the town, giving each an entrance, be it alleyway or garden and they entered the town, passing between the houses. There was barely a soul to be seen, but cheering could be heard from the direction that they assumed would be the main road. Deakin, Stiles and Gibney were moving on between the houses, bayonets fixed, following Captain Heaviside. Old men and crones stood at their doors to watch their passing, toothless grins and crablike hands reaching out to touch them, declaring a greeting. The suspicious redcoats smiled and nodded in return, whilst still maintaining a careful watch on all windows and corners.

Suddenly, they heard a ferocious commotion from up ahead, many voices, both male and female, loud shouts, and different languages. They had reached a main side road and from around a corner came a large group of men, followed by several women, but the focus of the group was a struggling figure, trying to stay on his feet whilst being dragged, kicked and pushed down towards the centre of the town. He was evidently French and a ranking Officer as shown by his ribbons, medals and epaulettes, but he had taken a fearful beating. His mouth was swollen and one eye was shut. There were bleeding cuts on his face, and he bled also from holes in the knees of his now filthy breeches, evidence that he had been dragged, seemingly over some way. Whilst he was being hauled along, he was all the while threatened with cudgels, staves and menaced by a variety of sharp farm tools. Heaviside turned to his men and gave orders to a large group.

"You men, follow them down. If it looks as though they are going to kill him, put a stop to it. Shoot if you have to. That Frenchman is a prisoner of war."

The group, including Deakin and Stiles, followed the rapidly expanding group into the square. The crowd was so dense that the soldiers could do little to carry out their orders, if needed, which looked likely. The Frenchman was plainly an object of intense hatred, the gathering group spat at him, threw any kind of object at him and several did their best to get close enough to aim a kick. He was dragged to the horse trough and allowed to sit in the water and mud with his back against the rough stonework, but it was plain that he had little time left to live. A man emerged from the crowd and urinated on him to the delight of all watching, whilst behind his tormentor several men were gathering with axes and staves. When the urinator had finished, they walked forward, weapons raised, eager to finish the job. Then a pistol shot rang out and Major Willoughby forced his horse through the crowd, followed by a squad of 58th, with bayonets fixed. Willoughby placed his horse before the Frenchman and the soldiers completed the guard. The Frenchman kneeled in pleading supplication beneath Willoughby's horse, hands clasped together, tears and cries emerging from his damaged eyes and mouth. Other British Officers, mostly Staff, were arriving on the Square. Willoughby called out to them.

"Get the interpreter, let's try to find out what's going on here."

The interpreter was found and came through the crowd. Willoughby leaned forward over his horse's shoulder.

"Ask them what this man has done."

The interpreter did as he was bid and the result was a cacophony of shouts and arm waving from all who could hear, but the most telling gestures were to the graveyard, visible on the slope of the hill, with several, over 20, fresh graves marked by dark brown earth. Others pointed to a gallows, till now unnoticed, and a wall with its plaster shattered at chest height. The interpreter looked up.

"Sir. They say he is, was, the Commandante here, and he has killed many. He killed them to get them to tell where the food was, and..."

The interpreter turned to one townsman, perhaps more imposing than the others, to ask another question. Willoughby identified the word "masse".

"He killed the townspeople here because of the attacks by the masse', their partisans. Now they say that he must die too, Sir."

Willoughby made his reply.

"Tell them this. If this man is to die, it will be after a hearing at least, to find out what he has done, and then with proof."

The interpretation was made and it produced little angry response from the crowd, save more insults and approbation being spat and hurled at the distraught Frenchman. Willoughby looked for a solid building and found one, probably the Town Hall. He turned to a Sergeant in his escort.

"Take this man into that building. See that he is cared for and kept safe."

The Officer was hauled to his feet and escorted away, at last given some protection from the kicks and spittle, but several townspeople were now running to the next occurrence. The surrendered French Garrison, now weaponless and under close escort, were being marched into the Square. Many people, mostly women, ran up close to the ranks of the redcoat escort and peered in and through and soon began pointing. The subjects identified did their best to reduce themselves in stature and hold their heads low, in the faint hope of not being seen, but Willoughby could see what the issue was. Plainly there were more involved than just the Commanding Officer.

"Halt."

The prisoners and escort halted and the townspeople ran up and closed in. Willoughby followed and spoke to another Sergeant.

"The prisoners that these people are pointing at. Get them out."

With many mistakes and terrified protestations, five Frenchmen were hauled out, identified with shouts and gestures for the redcoats to move left or right or beyond, to the correct member of the accused. With no more pointing fingers being thrust into the French ranks, Willoughby considered the task complete. Again to the Sergeant.

"Get those five over to that big building. See that they are kept safe. There's going to be a trial."

The interpreter heard the last sentence and conveyed it to the crowd. Willoughby couldn't be sure of their reaction, to him it sounded somewhere between growling and cheering, but for now the issue was settled. He was grateful when Stuart rode in.

"Sir. There has been some disturbance. We had to prevent the locals from killing six of the French just surrendered. One was the Commanding Officer. They accuse them of murder, Sir. There are fresh graves in the graveyard, and over there," he pointed to the corner of the square, "is a gallows and an execution wall. I think we need to mount some kind of trial, Sir. We will antagonise the locals if we don't hand them back or make some kind of a show. I think it clear, Sir, that some civilians have been killed."

Stuart looked pained.

"I wanted no delay here. The quick capture of this place has given us a time advantage that I don't want wasted on some kind of trial. It's only just gone Noon, time yet for 10 more miles."

Willoughby thought.

"May I suggest, Sir, that some Senior Officers remain here, to conduct a trial, with one battalion, while the rest of the army pushes on to Scilla. What you leave here should be able to march out by morning."

Stuart looked at Willoughby.

"Right. Cole and Kempt will stay. Cole as Senior can be the Chairman. Lacey can make up the third. His battalion stays, and you accompany me. I want the army through here in an hour. Each battalion makes up its water then moves on. No other delay."

"Sir. And the prisoners just surrendered?"

"March them with us. They can embark at Reggio. It won't be long before that will also be ours, I feel sure."

Staff Officers bustled about with orders, and the 5th Provisionals formed up on the square, to be dismissed to find what point of rest they could, and soon be plied with oranges and pomegranates, but an enterprising baker selling soft, flat bread was more welcome. Things improved further when a seller of dried fish also arrived, then someone selling cheese, and the picnic atmosphere grew around the square that hitherto had been the scene of high drama and near murder. The soldiers lounged and watched proceedings, whilst giving scraps to the children. Kempt arrived, with a face like thunder, and all watched as himself, Cole, and their own Colonel entered the Town Hall. The interpreter, with the imposing local, had gone around to gather witnesses and these formed a group outside the build-

361

ing, but they were not noisy, all remained decorously serious and sombre as befits an ongoing trial.

Some soldiers went to the trough for a wash and tried to clean some clothes, with the strong hope that they would dry soon enough on stones that were hot enough to hurt from the fierce, high sun. The witnesses went in and later re-emerged. Several of those that came out waved their arms and shouted to the sky, with pleasure or with curses, but for the soldiers of the 5th, it was impossible to tell. All the while the army marched through, wasting none of the short time they were given to get water, or to buy from the hastily erected stalls.

Deakin, Stiles and Peters, sat on a wall and played with the children, giving of their rations and showing them how the firelock on their muskets worked, making a fascinating spark. Stiles did more looking around than the others. He and Peters were friends of long standing.

"B'ain't no young girls around here."

"What's that to an ugly bugger like you?"

"Well, I'm just sayin'. I suppose they keeps 'em locked up."

"Up in the hills more like, in some cave. Stashed 'em up there as soon as they knew the Frenchers was comin'. Can't say as I blame 'em, if half of this lot is true."

The army finally passed through, and it did not go unnoticed that the wagons for the sick and wounded halted at the Church and the patients were taken in. Deakin went over to ask if he could visit but he was turned away. However, what did come next into the town was a cheering sight. Their Light Company, led by Captain Carr and Lieutenant Drake, at last had caught up, all weary and dusty and grateful for the place of rest. All made straight for the horse trough and soon the village pump was earning its place in the town's list of expenditures. Miles, Pike and Davey came straight over to Deakin and the rest, removed their kit and prepared for a clean up themselves. Deakin was the first to speak.

"How goes it, boys? Not too many a long mile? Did you find the French?"

Miles replied.

"More like the French found us, after our new Officer gave 'em the wink with a whole campful of fires."

"Which Officer."

"Oh, some Major they landed us with. He took off when the French came on. We lost some men and picked up wounded. Lieutenant Rushby for one. Where's Toby?"

"Sick. Swamp fever, and he b'ain't alone. They'm in yon Church. Lieutenant D'Villiers too. Anyhow, here's your bottle. Nothin' like a forced march to work up a thirst and put an edge on your appetite."

Miles forced down the cork and drank, before handing the bottle to Davey, who, with Pike, had collapsed in the shade of the wall. Miles, ever curious, looked around.

"What's happening over there? Some kind of village meeting?"

"No. A trial. Seems the French have been a bit too handy with the rope and their muskets. Them's fresh graves up there."

Miles looked, then turned back.

"Ah, we saw some of that, the worst of that. Place called Catanzarro, an' I never wants to see the like again. Bastard French cavalry, probably the ones we had to fight off. An' this lot have been up to the same game. 'Tis some army we'n fightin'. They thinks no more of killin' a civilian than they does of squashing a bed bug. I've got no time, no time at all."

At that moment the crowd at the Town Hall parted and the noise rose to a crescendo of taunts and abuse as the six were led out, all tethered as prisoners, a halter from the neck of each one, back to the bound wrists of the one behind. The Commandante was last, followed by the three Trial Judges. The six were marched to the corner of the square that contained the execution wall, where they stood in abject misery, some sobbing. They knew what this corner meant. Soldiers of the 5th were much in evidence at the sides, keeping the townspeople away, so it was probably true that the taunts and jeers of the townspeople did not add substantially to their misery, but it added to the glee of the townspeople.

Lacey looked along to Kempt and Cole, all stood on the steps of the Town Hall.

"There should be a Priest, Sir."

Kempt looked black, but acquiesced.

"There's the church, see if he's home. Send the interpreter."

Minutes passed before the interpreter returned.

"He says he won't do it, Sir. They killed of his flock. They are beyond Christ."

Kempt's look turned even blacker.

"What about your Chaplain? Lacey."

"We haven't got one, Sir. We're Provisional."

"Well, what, for the Love of God, can be done?"

"We have a storeman who used to be a Parson, before he was defrocked, then sentenced to time in the army."

"Well, damn well get him, get some of your men for a firing squad, and let's get this business done."

Lacey saluted and walked forward to his nearest Officer and told him to fetch Sedgwicke from the wagons. The Officer did as he was ordered and soon emerged with a dusty and bemused ex-Parson Sedgwicke, not at all looking the part, but he placed himself before Lacey and saluted.

"Sir?"

"Sedgwicke, isn't it?"

"Yes Sir."

"Right. Six French prisoners have been convicted of murder. They have killed some of these townspeople. They are going to be executed. We have no Priest because the local man has refused. I want you to make some kind of a show. Do you have a Bible?"

"Yes Sir."

"Get it. This must be done quickly, for everyone's sake."

"But Sir, they're probably Catholics."

"I don't care if they're Mohammedans. We are a civilised army and we do this properly. If it needs to be in Latin, then that's what I expect. Now get your Bible."

Sedgwicke did an immediate about turn, went off to his wagon and returned, lips still silently mumbling what he thought was the required phrase, finally to come to attention before Lacey,.

"Right. Get yourself to the water pump there and wait."

Lacey walked on to find Heaviside, leaving Sedgwicke trailing in his wake, him bemused and becoming more than horrified with the growing thought of what he was about to be part of.

"Jacob."

Heaviside was taken aback by the use of his Christian name.

"We need a firing squad. Find some good steady men, but they must be volunteers. We can't order a man to kill anyone in cold blood, that's not who we are. It'll be done as three, then three, so ideally we need nine men. Private Sedgwicke will do the absolution. He used to be a Parson; best we can do. Go now, see what can be managed."

Heaviside saluted and took himself first to the men of his own Company, starting with Deakin, Stiles, and Peters. As he approached, the men got to their feet.

"Men. The six French have been found guilty of murdering a number of these people and they are going to be shot immediately. I need volunteers to form the firing party. Can I have some volunteers?"

Deakin and his companions stood uncertain, but Miles had heard all.

"I'll volunteer, Sir, and all you have to do is go to the Light Company. We've just come back from a village where every living thing was shot and butchered; by French cavalry, we think, Sir. Day 'fore yesterday it were, and it's still strong to mind in us all. I'll step up, Sir."

Miles looked at Pike and Davey.

"What about you two?"

Davey spoke first.

"Not me, Tom. I'll not volunteer for cold blooded shooting. Can't bring myself."

Joe Pike looked down, then looked up, at Miles then Heaviside. He nodded his head.

"Yes Sir. You can include me."

Heaviside said nothing, but then did as he was advised. The Light Company was a little way off and he went first to Carr and Drake, leaning against a shady wall, drinking water and eating biscuits.

"Carr. Drake. Pleased to see your safe return."

Through full mouths both gave their thanks as Heaviside continued.

"I'm asking your permission to call for volunteers from amongst your Company. We need a firing party to execute six Frenchmen who have been found guilty of murdering civilians from here. Miles and Pike have volunteered. They mentioned some unsavoury work that you witnessed a day or two back. Do I have your permission?"

Carr gave the reply.

"You have my permission, Captain Heaviside. We saw it too and, were I a ranker, I would volunteer. Ask away, they are over there. And if you want an Officer to conduct the thing, then look no further than me!"

Drake looked disturbed at Carr's blunt eagerness to be involved in what most took to be a very unpleasant task, but he was more surprised at the response when Heaviside went and asked the men. Before he had finished speaking he had 22 men. He selected 16 to add to Miles and Pike and thanked all the men for making his task so easy. Uniquely, he did not finish with a Bible quote. Heaviside returned to Carr and Drake. Before he was close enough to speak, Drake straightened up. His heavy expression and tone made it clear that he wanted no part. He used a good excuse to take himself away.

"I'm going to check on Rushby. They've taken him into that church."

Heaviside came up to Carr.

"Captain Carr. If you would? Private Sedgwicke there, will act as a Priest."

Carr levered himself off the wall and went to his men.

"Volunteers for the firing party, form up, two ranks. Ellis, Fearnley, to me."

The ranks were formed and Miles and Pike took their place within.

"Ellis, Fearnley, take Sedgwicke with you and stand up the first three."

"What about blindfolds, Sir?"

Carr spat back the reply with some force, surprising both Sergeants.

"Take off their jackets and rip them apart. That's how. These don't deserve to die like soldiers!"

Carr turned to the two ranks.

"First nine, follow me. Load when you get there."

Carr heard the sounds that accompanied the selection of the first three, a choke and a wailing cry from one of the prisoners or perhaps two, loud cheers and cries of approval from the crowd. Carr arrived just as the three were positioned and their jackets removed, Ellis and Fearnley ripping out blue cloth as needed. Carr arranged his men and walked along the rank, giving each soldier his target. Meanwhile Sedgwicke passed along to each prisoner, offering his Bible to each face to be kissed before the blindfold came. To each he mumbled what he thought to be the correct Latin.

"Et ego te absolvo a peccatis tuis in nomine Patris, et Filii, et Spiritus Sancti."

Each prisoner crossed himself at the end of the words, awkwardly, with bound hands. The crowd was silent. Sedgwicke took himself off and well to the side. Carr took his cue.

"Make ready. Present."

Joe Pike leveled his musket at the opening of his target's shirt, the centre of a chest now heaving with fear. The memory of Catanzarro came livid into his mind.

"Fire."

The muskets erupted and the smoke and echo swirled around the square. The three had been blasted back against the wall, their blood both splattered and smeared down the plaster as the balls passed through them and their bodies slid down to slump at the base. The crowd remained eerily silent.

"Order arms. Sling arms."

The squad swung their muskets behind them, the slings over their shoulders. Carr checked each prone and bloody figure. All were very dead.

"Get these bodies over to the Church steps, away from this crowd. Sergeants, the next three."

He took himself to the remaining nine of the Light Company and brought them over, again allocating targets as the three condemned arrived, but this time, the three contained the Commandante and the abuse and gestures rose and continued with heavy vehemence. The two soldiers arrived and stood, but the Commandante slumped to his knees and even rolled over. Ellis and Fearnley hauled him up, but he collapsed again. Carr knew his French was poor, but his anger spilled over, sickened at this man who happily butchered others, but didn't have it in him to stand and meet his fate with the same backbone as that of his own soldiers. He strode forward to stand above him.

"Est ce que je dois attacher vous a' une chaise?"

There was no reply, nor change, he remained slumped forward, cheek against the dirt and sand.

"Ellis. Get into this building and get a chair for this bastard. And a rope."

Ellis entered through the door and a minute passed, then two. The abuse of the Commandante continued unabated and increased, if anything, as Ellis appeared with a rickety chair and some rope. The sobs and cries grew louder as the prostrate

Officer was hauled up again and lashed to the chair; throat to the back rail, hands and feet to the legs before and behind. Carr nodded to Sedgwicke, who looked green and pale, and then to Fearnley, who had used the time to prepare more blindfolds.

Sedgwicke repeated his first performance. From the soldiers came the required response, the kiss of the Bible and the genuflection, but from the Commandante came nothing. Sedgwicke again hurried to the side as Fearnley tied the last blindfold.

"Make ready. Present."

He made a pause, which was filled with a last anguished cry from the Commandante.

"Fire."

Again the crash of the muskets echoed around the square and the result was the same on the two standing but with the seated Commandate the chair was blown over backwards and his head hit the wall, breaking his neck. A sound something like a groan came from within his body, to be terminated by a gout of blood that erupted from his mouth and nose.

"Order arms. Sling arms," but the order was lost in the cheering and shouting.

Carr again made a check, then turned to the squad.

"Get these bodies over with the other three."

Carr followed his men as they carried the shattered bodies across to the Church. He peeled away to go to Colonel Lacey.

"Have you any further orders for me, Sir?"

"No Carr. That was satisfactorily carried out. And welcome back. I understand that things got a little rough on your scouting mission for General Stuart."

"Yes, Sir. Rough is an understatement. On another subject, Sir, I don't know if you recall the first conversation we had about what can happen in a rebellion. Well, I take that back, Sir, what I saw was worse, far worse. So, if there's nothing further, Sir."

"No, Carr, nothing, but please ask Captain Heaviside to report to me again."

Carr went straight to Heaviside who immediately came to Lacey.

"I want you to bury those men, Heaviside, but wait until dark, which won't be too long. I want the graves hidden, you do whatever is necessary, you understand? I have too strong a suspicion that these townspeople will dig them back up and do something appalling. Do your best to hide the graves. I think that right."

Heaviside saluted and ordered his men to carry the bodies into a house on the square, where they were wrapped in sheets that were found inside They waited until the dead of night. Scouts were sent out to detect any locals that may be near and the bodies were carried out the back door. An abandoned stable was found and pickets set up to keep anyone away. The rank straw was cleared, then respread, as a ruse. The bodies were interred in a ploughed field behind and the surplus soil scattered. All returned through the deep darkness for a few hours sleep before the march out at dawn. But, come the day, as they took the road South to catch up with the rest of the army all six bodies were hanging from a tree, their clothes filthy from the attempted burial and their faces badly mutilated.

Chapter Eleven

Scilla

Those able to make comparisons would conclude that Scilla was misplaced, a bad throw by one of the higher Greek Gods, who, when engaged upon creating the world, aimed an earthly segment at the coast of Greece, but missed and hit the toe of Italy. In peaceful times Scilla would be regarded as favoured beyond fairness. It had an appearance more classically Aegean, visitors left with memories of the town being bathed always in clear yellow sunlight that reflected continuously from the gentle waves of the surrounding azure sea and holding to a history that some say went back to the Illiad, and even beyond that, to the realms of mythology. If so, then mythology had come again, only this time out of Pandora's box; violence between nations, the protagonists being the new power of Republican France, and the old of Britain and her allies. Fate had decreed that this small jewel of a harbour town was to be a scene of violence and occupation that would stretch out for almost two years.

The arrival of the 5th Provisionals at Scilla found the place swamped in the business of siege, the object being the ancient and much adapted castle perched on a dramatic promontory that projected from the harbour out into the Straits of Messina. The battlements were topped by the tricolour of France, but such was the setting that only the red and white stood out from the background of the clean sky blue that was reflected off the Straits, a view further enhanced by the addition of the Lipari Islands rising just above the far horizon.

Upon enquiry Lacey had been directed to the British camp the other side of the town and this required a march through streets devoid of civilian life. What life there was, being pro-vided solely by lines of British soldiers labouring with heavy materials through the narrow alleyways up to the vantage points that gave purchase to the siege against the castle; heavy timber and two handed baskets full of earth and sand. From the depths of the town the 5th began their climb and, with height, the pan-orama revealed itself, the drama and strength of the castle, derived from both its position and its structure, and the pictur-esque shape of the town, crouched behind its defender, and sending feelers out either side around the sheltered beaches.

The siege had not yet started, there was no noise of gunfire and as they climbed, the men of the 5th turned from time to time to see what their newly gained height had revealed, but all that could be seen of the forthcoming siege was a battery revetment erected behind and above a row of houses, the steep slope allowing a sight of the castle walls, but the earthwork as yet contained no artillery. The other regiments, arriving earlier, had taken the immediate slopes for themselves and so the 5th were forced to climb higher than any other battalion, but, once reached, their view was perfect of the town, the harbour, the beaches, the sparkling sea and the castle. On their chosen ground the 5th settled in. The men had no tents, but in that sunshine, with that view, none felt the need. With the advent of the siege, orders were that the Light and Grenadier battalions were to be reformed and so those two Companies peeled off to where those of the same ilk were camped, but, as chance would have it, they remained near neighbours to their comrades of the 5th.

Tom Miles turned one more time to examine the panoply that stretched out before him as far as his eyes could see as he removed his kit and let it fall onto the warm grass.

"Well, this'll do me. I'm all for a nice restful siege, if it means sittin' 'ere for a week or two. I've done with marchin' about this place, for at least a good while."

As usual, his opinion was voiced loud enough to inform the whole battalion and so it was overheard by another old Norfolk veteran, this being Carr's "tall soldier" Ezekiel Saunders.

"You could be right there, Tom, were it not for one thing. Some of us may well have to go up over one of them walls, and I'd settle for a week's marchin' rather than climb some ladder to say hello to some Frencher hid behind a battlement. 'Tis usually Lights or Grenadiers as gets the job, and that gives me an' you odds even."

Miles moved his gaze to the castle, particularly the walls, but made no reply. However, all was also overheard by their Officers. Carr, Drake, and Rushby stood regarding the view, Drake leaning forward on his sword, mopping his forehead with his soft forage cap, whilst Morrison set up their tent and the other components of an Officer's camp. Carr tried to open the conversation.

"You ever been involved in a siege, Nat?"

"No. Outside my experience."

"Also myself. Something new for us both."

But there was no reply. Carr wanted to talk about the siege they were part of, but Drake had walked off, following Rushby who was looking for the best angle for his sketching and to see if his wound would, indeed, allow some artwork. Since Monteleone a distance had grown between Carr and Drake, and it was Carr that felt the change. He knew it had everything to do with the execution, but with time, the heat of his anger had abated, and now two emotions competed within him. He still hated the French for Catanzarro, but, with time, he now found cause to question within himself his eagerness to volunteer, when the requirement for a King's Officer would be to wait until ordered, then carry it out quietly and with due dignity. To have brashly volunteered, as he had done, created a doubt about himself that gnawed within him.

His attention was distracted by a water wagon labouring up the hill, with a double team of mules. Nothing so unusual, apart from the fact that this time it was escorted by none other than the estimable Sergeant Major Gibney and half a minute's viewing told him why. The men of the 5th, thirsty and filthy, were eager for the water and many were running in its direction. Gibney placed his significant being in front of the spigot.

"Now then, now then. Lets 'ave thee good and orderly. One bucket, each mess, each day. Water has to be hauled all up here and none's to be wasted. One bucket, each mess, each day. Percy; good man. Thee takes the bucket, thee turns ont' tap and thee turns it off. It be thee as does the dolin' out. Understood? Right. Carry on."

Sedgwicke nervously took the first bucket, placed it under the spigot and turned on the tap. The water splashed and splattered and he anxiously debated within himself how much of a margin to leave, if any. He filled to the brim.

"Too much, Percy. Some'll get spilt as 'tis carried on back and that's waste. Two inches down. Carry on."

With Gibney overseeing no one dared argue. It was Sedgwicke who got the black looks when two inches looked like two and a half.

Morrison had made their camp and Carr sat on one of the portable chairs. Despite his mood of self doubt he smiled. Here was a battalion of battle-hardened men, ready to kill if ordered, yet still subject to the tiny human minutiae, innocent in its domesticity, that still applied, even to men ready to stand a firing line and blow others to perdition. He shook his head, hoping to get himself out of this "black dog" depression. He remembered some words of advice, amongst the first he had been given in the 6th Foot, back over what seemed an age; "First, your men". He rose and began a tour of his Company's ground, passing by Drake and Rushby, and suggesting they should do the same.

"See how the men are."

Although a suggestion, they took it as an order.

O'Hare was taking his ease outside the Command Tent, in fine humour, a good cup of tea held in his right hand, his left drumming out the beat to an Irish ditty that was circulating in his head. As with Carr, some minutes before, O'Hare's attention was drawn to the track up to their camp, but this time it was Lacey riding up, allowing his horse to take the hill in its own time. O'Hare knew that Lacey was returning from Headquarters in the town and, as was everyone, he was eager to hear of their immediate future. Lacey arrived and dismounted, handing the reins to a soldier who appeared, as if from nowhere.

"Any news, Sir?"

"Nothing that could be said to apply specifically to us. The castle is well prepared bar one thing. Water. And in this heat that'll give them a serious problem. The locals report that a great deal of time had to be spent clearing out the castle's cistern because it was full of rubble, and they will not have had time to re-fill it. He's got a good garrison, but has to support it through this month, July, one of the hottest. Stuart was right. Getting quickly through Monteleone was a bonus. However, the castle's modern. It was rebuilt back in the eighties after an earthquake shook the whole place apart. Apparently this is a bad part of the world for such. Oh, and one piece of good news, although not unexpected, Reggio fell to us, on the 10th, without a siege! It's got a harbour. We can expect both supplies and reinforcements to come up from there, not over those damn mountains that we've just had to wend our weary way through. So, apart from the French now probably somewhere up in Naples, this is the last French hold in this part of Italy. Once this is captured, the job's done. Home perhaps, who knows?

"Who knows, Sir? But something in my water tells me that there'll be other serious doings that will be occupying us in this here sunny part of the world."

"Well, Padraigh, only time will tell. What I can say is that the bombardment starts tomorrow, albeit by light guns, but 24 pounders are on their way and from that point on, this affair will become serious."

"Yes, Sir. And the assault?"

"Oswald's men probably. They are manning the houses immediately opposite. I'm hoping that Stuart will leave us out. We had a tough battle, I don't need to remind you of that, whilst Oswald's were in reserve, but I expect Stuart to use one of either the Lights or the Grenadiers. That'll be our contribution. But I for one have had a basinful of glory this campaign, I'll be happy to spectate and cheer, when the time comes."

"Amen to that, Sir."

Lacey took his leave, then O'Hare finished both his tea, and his ditty.

* * *

The sun was setting, way off to their left, throwing long shadows on the grass made yellow by the dying light, shadows now so distorted they told nothing of their origins. As politeness required, the three had dined together, but Rushby had taken himself off to the Surgeon to check on his wound, hopefully to confirm what he thought; that it was healing nicely. Fearnley's stitching had been of the highest order. The remaining two sat in silence, which Carr finally broke.

"Let's take a turn around the camp. Check on the men."

They both rose and Drake reached for his soft foraging cap, for some reason now his favoured headgear. Carr waited and remained bareheaded. They walked for some minutes in silence, for them that in itself being almost unique.

"Is there something you want to discuss with me, Nat? Now's your time to speak freely."

"About what, in particular?"

"The choice is yours, but something's been bothering you since Monteleone. The execution, I suspect; could that be what's weighing on your mind?"

"Now you mention it, yes. When I was in the 9th, I saw a few. Looters and deserters, even a rapist. Myself amongst other Officers, and I was not untypical, looked upon the affair with some distaste, possibly the worst detail that one could be given. To avoid it gave a feeling of extreme relief, certainly in my case. I would not have volunteered for such a thing even if my Soul depended upon it; a cold blooded shooting."

Despite the conflicting debate that existed within himself, Carr angered.

"They were damn murdering bastards and I, and eighteen of my men, saw them off to the Hell they deserve. What we see in Catanzarro, and happened in addition in Monteleone, was cold-blooded murder; of innocents! We saw women and children, not shot, but clubbed and bayoneted."

Carr waited for some reply. None came, so he continued.

"What we witnessed in that village was very different from what you describe. Those weren't the occasional deeds that accompany the presence of an army that chance dictates contains the worst men that life can offer, and who anyway, act as individuals for their own personal gain. What happened there was different, it was both organized and condoned. Paying out someone for a defeat. I awarded the retribution to myself. I volunteered, and so did the men, don't forget. They didn't feel the need to indulge in a deep internal debate on the morality of such. They simply saw evil men and blew them to Kingdom Come. I take a measure of comfort from saying that we stood against such bestiality, and, in any case, I saw the thing properly carried out. I heard what the townsfolk wanted to do to them. With us it was at least quick and with due form."

"I can understand where you're coming from, Henry, I saw it in Catanzarro too, but to appear so eager, well, it set you apart."

"Not for the first time that that's applied to me, Nat, not for the first time, but I ask you to remember that this is a real campaign, with all that throws up. For me, this has resurrected what I saw in the Irish Rebellion. This isn't a Shorncliffe Review, this is the real dirty business of fighting a war, with civilians in the middle; and in this case against an enemy that does things in a far different way to what we've been brought up to hold to. To us, our honour and integrity are everything. We are appalled at the idea of living off the land, stealing, and carrying out reprisals. I feel now, that I rose up, struck a blow, as it were. My motives contained no pleasure, I assure you. Eagerness perhaps, yes, but born of the wish to stand up against it, "use might for right" if you prefer.

Carr paused, and sighed, his anger now vented. Once more no reply. He continued more calmly.

"But to volunteer, "conduct unbecoming" and all that. Well, yes, that's a thought that's grown in my mind over the past couple of days, but I make no apologies. I stand by what I did. And, as I say, they weren't murdered; they were cleanly shot, like soldiers. They were lucky to get that."

A new point came to mind.

"You fought the French before, when you were with the 9th. At Castricum. You saw nothing of such things during that?"

"No. It was us doing the retreating."

Drake paused, as the pair walked on. Eventually, after some thought, he came to a conclusion.

"Very well, Henry. I think you wrong, and I stand by that, but you've earned the benefit of the doubt. We've gotten used to you coming at things from a different angle, and the job was cleanly done, I'll grant you. We have your cool head to thank for that."

He paused again.

"Now, the battle and marching done, and in camp, we must write letters. Back to our tent. It's as well that I'm in close attendance, to give you a hand with some choice phrases. When it comes to writing fond letters with appropriate sentiments to such as Jane Perry, it's well understood what a dullard you are."

Carr grinned and placed his hand on Drake's shoulder before they turned back to their tent.

* * *

The camp was woken by gunfire. As all turned out, many stuffing shirts into the tops of breeches as they emerged from tents and blankets, their enquiring looks were extended beyond the positions of their own empty batteries to the white smoke coiling back on the West wind over the battlements of the castle. Two feluccas and two transports were sailing away from the beach on the larboard tack, using the high tide. They must have made the turn late or misjudged the strength of the wind blowing to the castle because they had all slipped to leeward and their mistake had taken them within range of the battery mounted on the seaward side of the castle. They were well within

376

range, as shown by the fall of the ranging shots that were significantly beyond the four vessels. O'Hare was soon joined by Lacey.

"That's going to cost them. Who are they, do you know, Sir?"

"My guess is the 20th going to Reggio. Stuart mentioned something about it the other day. Oh my, pray God, get them through it."

Laccy was aghast as three heavy shots struck home on the hull of the transport nearest to the castle; the ship that also happened to be the largest, therefore the favoured French target. Splinters flew up from her side and the foresail shivered with the passing of a fourth ball. Another missed the stern and skipped across the water leaving a trail of white eruptions across the surface. O'Hare added his own prayer but perhaps more practical.

"Pray God they don't lose a mast, then they will be lost. They'll drift ever closer."

The importance of masts carrying sails was emphasized by all ships spreading more canvas, more than was prudent as they sailed across the strong beam-on wind, and all heeled over until the sea washed through the scuppers of their maindecks, but all gained speed and turned into the wind as close as they dared to narrow the target they made to stern only. The gunners were firing at will, with all the speed they could. Three more hits were scored, but nothing vital such as mast or rudder and all escaped. An Officer stood closeby made a telling observation.

"Someone will face a Court for that. All the quicker if there are casualties."

Many nodded as they stood and observed the final French shots, but all fell short and the guns fell silent. Yet still they watched as the four ships safely made an offing into The Straits sufficient to tack down to Reggio.

"That was close, O'Hare, damn close. I could see the whole damn army making an unprepared assault on that castle to come to the aid of that ship."

"Perhaps, Sir, but I don't see General Stuart taking extra casualties to save the contents of one ship. That's the game we're in, Sir. We all take our chances."

"If you're right, I'm glad it wasn't a decision that I had to make, nor anyone, thank God."

"Amen to that, Sir. And I think some breakfast, after all that excitement."

Whilst breakfast was taken pleasantly in the open air, there was plenty to divert the partaking observers. The French were plainly upset at what had been happening in the town opposite the castle, the result of the work of the files of burdened soldiers that the 5th had seen on their first entry through the abandoned streets. With their lighter guns in the battlements opposite the town, the garrison was making brisk practice on the buildings immediately to their front, for what reason it was impossible to tell from a distance, but bricks and tiles could be seen flying upwards through the smoke.

The following day the noise was doubled because the British were firing back, opposite the same French light batteries. A breastwork had been constructed within musket shot of the castle walls for the army's lighter siege artillery and the smoke informed the observers that it must be two pieces, also that they were heavier than Field Artillery as the battlements before them soon started to show significant damage.

The bombardment continued over the subsequent days and those with an appreciation of sieges and castles lost no opportunity to demonstrate their knowledge. Major Simmonds, the second in the battalion, was one such. Not a bombast by any means, nevertheless he held court to whoever would listen.

"Now, you see, this castle has natural strength, obviously, stuck on a rock, with height in most places. However, being on a rock gives no possibility of building ravellines to protect the walls. They are a sort of triangular block of whatever, built in front of wall, but just a bit lower, which exposes the surface of the ravelline to gunfire from the main wall. It's called a glacis. Without ravellines, the walls are exposed all the way down to our gun fire. Eventually, we'll get a breach, and when it's practical, we'll get the go. At least some of us."

Lacey had ordered his good Dolland glass permanently set up upon two tripods, focused carefully upon the crumbling walls. Most Officers passing by availed themselves of the opportunity to obtain a detailed view of the increasing wreckage of the battlements and the cleft that grew below, like a hit from a giant axe. Through that particular piece of damage, when it became large enough to be deemed "practical", the assault would go.

Most dawdled and dreamed upon the hillside, listening to and watching the gunfire assault, those with a glass having the advantage. Carr was different. He allowed his men two days rest, then had them out and away, over the hills, practicing their drill, advancing up and back against various imaginary foes in a variety of situations. Surprisingly he overheard little grumbling from the men. Boredom had set in and being off and away to sample the generosity of inlying villages had a major appeal. Soon other Companies in the Light Battalion copied their actions when they saw the 5th Lights return in the evening, marching smartly back to camp, all in step and obviously in fine fettle. Both Lacey and O'Hare observed and nodded with satisfaction, remarking the same to each other.

The considerations of the siege lay outside their concerns until one evening, when Carr was ordered to the tent of Kempt, and Carravoy similarly to the tent of Colonel Mallory. Both Colonels conveyed the same orders, Carr listened dispassionately whilst Carravoy listened with growing apprehension that knotted his stomach. Kempt spoke to his Senior Officers as though dispensing retribution for some heinous misdemeanor.

"Both the Light and the Grenadier Battalions will be involved in the assault under the command of Brigadier Oswald, with his 58th in reserve. The Grenadiers will go for the breach, whilst we, the Lights, will attempt to the right, that being the wall above the rock where it can be climbed. Where the wall begins there is a ledge. We can carry our ladders up the rock and then place them for the final climb up the wall using the ledge. Mounting two assaults will split the French forces, and the French, those who will be forced to man the battlements against us, can be enfiladed by long-range musket fire from the upper windows of the houses. If we get in, all well and good, if not, we've provided a diversion. The Grenadiers will have the continued support of the battery. Any questions?"

Carr asked the first question.

"Are the ladders available now, Sir?"

"Yes."

Carr again.

"Where can we practice, Sir?"

Kempt looked at him coldly, but he had anticipated the question.

"Wherever you go, be out of sight. There are some cliffs to the West of here, around the headland. That may serve."

"When can we anticipate the assault, Sir?"

"Today is the 17th. Three 24 pounders are anticipated on the 22nd. They will join the breaching operations on the 23rd. So, three, perhaps, four days after that."

The meeting broke up and Carr returned to his two Lieutenants.

"We're for the ladders, when the time comes. We're to assault the wall to the East of the main breach where there is a ledge part way up the rock. We set up our ladders there and mount an assault. Oswald may intend us to be a diversion or a genuine assault, only time will tell, when we get onto that ledge and see what can be done. Support will come from muskets back in the houses."

Rushby was in a mild state of shock, but Drake spoke up.

"Light duties again! And what if this ledge is not practicable?"

"Then we are a bunch of done birds on a nicely exposed perch."

He paused.

"You're exempted, Rushby."

"But, Sir!"

"No arguments, you're still an invalid. Climbing up rocks and ladders is not for you. I'll lead your Section."

He paused again.

"We get our ladders tomorrow and practice around the headland to the West. We leave whilst it's still dark. I don't want the French to see what we're about. I'm sure they've got spyglasses upon their loftiest towers. Now; tell the men to get some sleep."

The following dawn saw the campground of the 5th Lights again deserted, but that had become common. The mid morning, however, saw Lieutenant Carravoy make a shallow climb to the tent of Major O"Hare.

"Sir. Might I have a word, Sir?"

Throughout the night Carravoy had remembered his words condemning O'Hare, after their examination in The Mess, "Irish lackey" came clear to memory, but now all was different. It seemed from another age in another world; life and attitudes back in barracks had been made irrelevant by his fear and shock of the recent battle and, after, it had been O'Hare that had offered comfort, that drawn from his long experience. He didn't have to but he did because it was needed. Carravoy sought words drawn from that experience just now, but he was to be disappointed.

"There's little I can say to you, Charles, but one thing. "Go on" doesn't sound well from an Officer. It's "Come on".

Carravoy was taken aback, but O'Hare continued.

"You must lead your men. We took the Commission, we wear the uniform. The idea of assaulting a breach puts depths of fear and terror into anyone, but men do it. Men even volunteer, like the "Forlorn Hope", the volunteers to be first into a breach knowing that the enemy will almost certainly have packed explosives under the rubble to blow the first wave to God or Perdition. They still do it. It's little comfort, I know, but some. You have, at least, what most don't. Close artillery support, firing grape at the defenders over your heads, as you climb. That's a real bonus. But above all, lead your men. Your Grenadiers are amongst the best I've seen. They'll get you through it."

Carravoy wandered back, only marginally less despondent and realising now within himself, what else could O'Hare have said? He could only point out the obvious, remind him of his duty and emphasise the small comforts. He returned to his tent and poured himself a stiff brandy and, perhaps surprisingly, his mind lifted somewhat from his fears. The brandy was surprisingly good, taken from a dead French Officer at Maida. He promised himself another, before he went up the ladders, then he looked at his hand. It was still shaking.

Meanwhile, Carr and his men were puzzling their way through the problems of a two-stage assault on a castle wall. Drake made a start.

"We aren't going to get all the men onto that ledge. The rifles should stay back and send fire through the embrasures. Keep the French heads down."

Carr agreed and moved the discussion on.

"If we're to assault the embrasures, we need a continuous stream of men going up, and coming up quickly. That means ladders up to the ledge and then up from the ledge. How many have we got?"

"Six, but we could get eight."

"Right. Get eight. That means four routes up."

"So, that means carrying a ladder up a ladder, to be set on the ledge for the next stage."

"Yes."

"How?"

Ellis and Fearnley had been stood quietly and respectfully by. It was Ellis who spoke.

"Sir. May I suggest hauling them up by ropes, Sir. Four lads go up the first ladder, with ropes down to the second. Then they pull them up, Sir. Four lads should be able to manage the weight, then they holds it steady for the lads followin' to use it and climb on up."

Drake clapped Ellis on the shoulder.

"Splendid, Sergeant. That's just what I was going to say. Do you agree, Sir?"

Carr spoke as Ellis and Fearnley grinned.

"I don't agree that you were going to say it, but I do agree with the idea. We've brought rope, so let's start with the six we've got. First question. Can four men haul up one ladder? Go and get the men organized."

John Davey swung his Baker around his shoulder and held the sling taught.

"Well there you are, boys. I knew that volunteering for this bundook would do me a bit of good. I'm sent to the rear to give you covering fire, leavin' you to the house painting."

Miles looked at him with murder in his eyes, Joe Pike simply with wholesale concern. It was Miles who spoke, with his usual venom.

"Then just you make sure that you raises your sights when it's us goin' through the gap, or embrasure or somethin'. I don't want a ball from your Baker goin' through the back of my skull, nor nothin', that's all."

Davey just grinned insolently and eased his crossbelts.

"I'll be back over here. Ready with a fire goin' for when you're done."

Miles' brow darkened even more, but it was the inevitable Ellis who called them away.

"Miles, Pike. Over 'ere. Pike. You're one of the rope haulers. Miles, you follows the ladder up, then carries on up to the top."

"Oh, now, b'ain't that just fine. Up to shake hands with those friendly Frencher boys, waitin' with a loaded musket, or somesuch."

"Not quite. Before you shakes hands, we'n givin' you a couple of fused charges to lob in first. They'm wrapped round with chain and lit before you goes up. One with a short fuse that you throws first, one with a long, that will have burnt short by the time you comes to throw it."

"How do I carry two, if I'm to climb a ladder at the same time?"

"The short you carry. The long with the lad behind. He'll pass it up."

"Oh my, this be gettin' better 'n' better."

They found a cliff with a suitable ledge half way up and began their practice. Four strong men, such as Pike, could haul up a ladder to their ledge with more than adequate speed and on up went such as Miles to lob one pebble, then a second, further up the cliff. For the next day they took two more ladders with them, and practiced all, frequently exchanging roles. Carr and Drake were pleased and the men themselves took pleasure in slickly applying their newly acquired skill. On the 21st, having taken their meal on the beach to await the dark, they returned to camp. They were intercepted by Kempt.

"What's your verdict, Carr?"

"It can be done, Sir, and I think effectively. I just hope the ladders are long enough and whoever worked it out got their sums right."

Kempt expected a simple "Yes Sir", not the comments nor implied criticism, but he gave Carr the benefit of the doubt. He was the first to train his men and deserved credit for that; nevertheless, stern Commander that he was, his voice had an edge.

"Yes Carr, but we all have to place our trust somewhere, in such affairs as this."

"Yes, Sir."

On the 22nd the three 24 pounder guns arrived. They had been taken from their supporting frigates and were plainly ex-navy, for two reasons, firstly, they were manned by sailors and secondly they were the long naval pattern. They were quickly set up in the battery behind the houses and lost no time in pounding the walls. The long barrels gave extra velocity and accuracy and their power was immediately apparent, the battlements crumbled under the rapid fire of the three guns. The crews manned the guns in relays and continued through the day and on through the night, making good use of clear moonlight and torches lit in the British positions opposite. The morning of the 23rd saw no cessation and the battlements were now a wreck, with the French battery silenced, all guns dismounted. There was now a definite cleft beneath the left hand bastion, which Oswald declared practical.

"Send for Carr. I want to try a small demonstration. I want him marching along the cliff, back to here."

A Staff Officer galloped off and soon found Carr and his men shaving the last seconds off their times with the ladders; others, such as Miles, were practicing with real fuses in real charges. The Officer shouted down.

"General Oswald wants you back in Scilla. March back, carrying your ladders"

"But Sir, it's broad daylight, won't that give the game away?"

"Those are your orders. Immediately, if you please."

"Yes, Sir. Right. Pack up, we're marching back. Carrying the ladders."

They left the beach, gained the cliff top and progressed back, ladders carried in plain sight on their shoulders. They reached the edge of Scilla to be greeted by General Oswald himself. Carr couldn't fail to notice the new damage inflicted on the castle.

"Carr, take your company to the beginning of the beach, that being opposite the breach. The French have no cannon there any longer and you are at very long musket range. Make some kind of a demonstration to show the French what's in store."

"Such as what, Sir? Parade with the scaling ladders, and the like?"

"Yes. That sort of thing. Make a lot of noise. Try to give the appearance that you are looking forward to it."

"Looking forward to it? Yes Sir. How long, Sir?"

"Two minutes should do it."

"Permission to carry on, Sir?"

"Yes. Go to it."

Carr returned to his men, Drake in particular, with Ellis and Fearnley nearby.

"The General wants us to make a show in front of the breach. I'm not utterly certain what he has in mind, I don't think he has, but it must be something about showing the French what's on its way, and there's nothing they can do, and it won't be pleasant. So, we get ourselves opposite the breach, show them the ladders and give them the impression that we can't wait. So, forward, the Light Theatrical Company!"

Ellis took himself in front of his section.

"We are going to the castle to show the French our lovely ladders that we are going to climb to say hello. I want you bastards grinning like madmen, like you can't wait to get up there and deliver them a bit of murder and mayhem."

The Lights took themselves through the streets, still echoing from the sound of the two batteries pounding the walls even more, the acrid smoke from the heavy charges joining the echoes that bounced off the eaves and walls of the buildings. Eventually they emerged from between the last houses and the first shingle of the beach crunched beneath their boots. Ellis and Fearnley took over.

"Line up now, and lay them ladders out front. A bit of cheering won't come amiss an' all. And remember; grinnin' like berserkers."

They lined up and began their performance, cheering, grinning, and pointing to the scaling ladders. Their cheering was lost in the gunfire but it placed the necessary rictus grins upon their faces.

Davey and Miles were sharing the custody of a ladder.

"Tom. You got one of your charges?"

"Yes."

"Well, knock off with the cheering and go out and toss it up a few times, make sure the fuse is showing, smooth it out like, let the Frenchers see that we know what we'm about."

Miles did as he was bid. He drew out the fuse and, as much as his face could show joy, he looked pleased to be a "charger", tossing up the canvas bundle with its protruding fuse, up to be caught, then tossed up again.

The spectacle lasted for its two minutes, when Carr called a halt and they ceased and began to file back. Ellis gave the last instruction.

"The French have their glasses on you, boys. Don't forget to wave goodbye, now."

All waved their farewells and it was Ellis himself who gave a last insolent grin and a wave before disappearing behind a corner. The guns continued.

Come late afternoon, Lacey, eye pressed to his Dolland glass, saw the main gate of the castle open and a group of blue-coated figures emerge under a large white flag. They walked forward across the causeway until they were lost from sight behind the roofs of the houses. Lacey spoke, to nobody in particular.

"Hello. The French have come out to parley. About, four or five, I'd say. Under a flag of truce. Here, take a look Padraigh, although now they're on our territory, as we speak, but they've left the gate open."

O'Hare looked but saw nothing but the gaping and defenceless gate. Nevertheless the pair kept a watch for about 30 minutes using the naked eye, until they saw the white flag and the blue figures re-emerge into the space before the castle. Lacey returned to the spyglass, but only to see the party disappear between the flanking towers of the gatehouse and the heavy gate close. Throughout the night speculation was rife and many arose early to view the castle. At 7.00 am the French tricolour came down to be replaced by a white flag. Cheering erupted all over Scilla and the encampment. Cheering for success but also from a relief that was tangible. None more so than within the chest of Captain Carravoy, he took himself into his tent and did his best to control his breathing. A brandy helped, despite this being before breakfast.

* * *

The whole army was required to parade, by battalions, to accept the French surrender. It was to be conducted with the full honours of war, and the 58th and the Swiss formed a Guard of Honour where the causeway from the castle met the town. The rest of the army was stepped up the hillside, the 5th Provisionals at the top, their Lights and Grenadiers now returned. With the cessation of gunfire, from the most unlikely of places, under houses, out of roofs, and in from the countryside, the civilian population returned. Stuart anticipated the kind of trouble that had arisen at Monteleone and ordered that the civilians be confined to the beach and side streets and not have access to the road out of the town. However, Willoughby made the point that standing them on the beach gave them access to a huge amount of pebble ammunition, so Stuart changed his mind. They would be allowed to stand alongside the road as it emerged from the town, but held well back.

At exactly 11.00 o'clock, the heavy castle gates swung open and the French emerged, preceded by the Commander, closely attended by a Sergeant carrying the tricolour that had been hauled down the day before. Then came the Officers, then the garrison, with sloped arms. The artillerymen simply marched. General Stuart was waiting. Salutes were exchanged and the tricolour handed over. After further salutes, the French column marched on, through the silent streets, and then they emerged from the town, out onto the road that led South West to Reggio. Here the ranks broke up, with each man required to surrender his musket and add it to the growing pile of the same, and each Officer required to surrender his sword to a waiting British Officer, who added it to another growing pile on a table. The clatter of the surrendered arms being added to the heaps reached right up the hillside, for all were watching in silence, including, surprisingly, the closeby native Scillians. The French then re-formed their ranks and stood in silence; they were now prisoners of war. The British now all marched down to the road, battalion by battalion, and marched on. Scilla was finished with, and the French tailed onto the last battalion, followed by the supply train.

The army marched on through the growing heat, and the heightening sun, but all were in high spirits. The route was easier out of Scilla than the tortuous mountain road into it, and besides, all could deduce that they were marching to evacuation, back to Sicily. It was an easy coast road and a day's marching brought them alongside the Straits proper, with a good detailed view of Sicily itself, even Messina, where they would disembark after crossing. High spirits and cheerfulness was the norm, but this did not apply to Corporal Deakin. He missed his friend Halfway. Miles was back with the Lights, as if he was any kind of company anyway, Stiles and Peters had their own friendship and Pat Mulcahey was dead. During a break from the march he approached his Company Commander, Captain Heaviside.

"Sir, beg your pardon Sir, but do you know what is going to happen to the sick and wounded, Sir?"

"What I heard, Corporal, and I've no reason to doubt it, is that they will be brought down from Monteleone to Scilla, and evacuated from there, sparing them the march that we are now making."

"Back to Sicily, Sir?"

"Yes. Where else? Those that survived we will meet up with there. I'm able to tell you, Corporal, that swamp fever took its toll, nearly as many as battle casualties, and so they were given special facilities and cared for according to the needs of their special ailment."

"Yes, Sir. Thank you, Sir. That's a comfort."

Heaviside nodded and resumed his reading, for the 254th time, a number which he would have known had he started a count decades back, of the Gospel according to St Luke. The bugle call came to reform. As they stepped back to the road, Deakin felt able to confide in Gibney.

"The sick and wounded is goin' out from Scilla, Sar' Major. That should include Halfway. The Captain says we should meet up on the other side. Let's hope, eh?"

Gibney had no real friendships amongst the men, just some he spoke to more then others, but he remembered that it was Halfway that he had been locked on behind throughout their desperate firefight at Maida, and they had all drunk from Deakin's canteen at the finish. That counted for something.

"Aye. Let's 'ope. Halfway's a good lad that I wishes well unto. Aye, here's hopin' he'll come through."

The next day saw their arrival at Reggio, a wholly unspectacular place, just a fishing village with grandiose thoughts that it might be a port, on a coast that would have been thoroughly exposed were it not for the close proximity of Sicily, about eight miles across the Straits. As a port it had no natural assets, but an ancient mole jutted out, then curved back, as yet devoid of shipping other than small fishing craft. For the 5th Provisionals, the place reeked as bad as Messina, a memory their sense of smell quickly brought to mind, and all were grateful to march through and out into the fields above and beyond.

The army counted itself as on holiday. Out in the fields and hills their situation was almost the equal to that of Scilla, but without the tension of the ongoing siege. As the men made their billets and the Officers waited for their tents to go up, all was smiles and joviality. They had won and they had survived. It was not long before whistles and flutes could be heard around the camp and all added to the atmosphere of joy layered upon peace. Carr, Drake and Rushby sat on the folding chairs that had been the first items of their camp unpacked, waiting for some tea. Rushby was sketching, the wound in his right shoulder now offering no impairment. All were pleased to see an old friend approaching, Captain Matthew Smart of the 35th. His beaming smile matched that of all three.

"How now, you types? Taking your ease prior to the forthcoming short cruise? Nice spot you've found for yourselves."

Carr turned in his seat.

"Morrison, another cup for Captain Smart."

"Sorry, Sir, we've only three."

"Then he can have mine, but make sure there's enough brewed for four."

He turned to regard Smart.

"So what brings you this way? From the fashionable heights of the 35th to the unsociable depths of the 5th Provisionals?"

"My errand is twofold. Firstly to ensure that you polysorts are not doing anything to disgrace yourselves, but secondly I come with an invitation. Colonel Kempt, or should I say Acting Brigadier Kempt, requests your presence at dinner. This evening. He feels the need to make some gesture of thanks to his Captains for our performance, and, well, it's unfortunately unavoidable, but that does include you. Ex-detachments notwithstanding."

Carr grinned, as did they all, at the dry humour.

"Where?"

"A large pink building in the square. You probably passed it. The residence of the owner of a local fishing fleet. A Signor Trezetto.

"When?"

"Seven-thirty for eight. How's your uniform."

"Feeling sorry for itself, but we'll get it up to the mark, or at least Morrison will."

The tea arrived, at least three cups of it, and all remained chatting amicably about all sorts, from where to find a good London cobbler to the surprisingly low performance of the French over the past campaign. The debate swung around poor leadership, or poor formations, to just plain poor troops. Eventually, Smart took his leave and left the three to their own company. Rushby was busy sketching and so Carr and Drake shared the conversation between themselves. Eventually Drake gave voice to his main worry.

"Major Greelish will be at the dinner tonight. You will watch your "P's and Q's", Henry, won't you. Don't say anything controversial. Just the usual dinner talk, you know the thing. Horses and hunting are usually pretty safe."

Carr made no reply, nor did his face convey any reassurance.

"Seriously, Henry. You've done yourself a lot of good. There's not a Company in the whole damn army that's made a better fist of things than ourselves, and that's down to you. Take what you've gained and hold it. "Puncher Carr's fading into the past. I'm still talking about Greelish. I know he was a clot, but from his point of view he had a job to do and he had his orders, too. I know we lost men, but it was Stuart himself who gave us the infernally chancey job in the first place. We're back with the 5th and Greelish is no longer our battalion Officer. Come tomorrow we need have no more to do with him."

Carr rolled his eyes over to Drake.

"You're right, Nat. As with affairs such as this, you're right, always right. I'll do no muck raking, even if he does, although what he can have to complain about, I can't imagine. Why should Greelish want to say anything derisive when we got him there, and got him back? I agree to all you've said."

"That's sense, Henry. Your record over the past month speaks for you by itself. Let that do the talking and be satisfied."

Carr sprang to his feet, propelling himself out of his chair by the arms so violently that the structure squealed and creaked.

"Yes, yes, Nat. Yes. Absolutely yes. Now, my uniform and shako, and, and, oh my God, my boots. They haven't been cleaned since Gibraltar. Morrison! Get my jacket up to parade ground standard. Throw out my boots and the blacking. To those I will give my own personal attention."

The boots emerged, placed not thrown, with the blacking, rag, and brushes lodged carefully besides the pair. Carr started on one, but Drake began on the other.

* * *

Carr arrived on time, in fact five minutes early. He found the building more easily that he had anticipated. A servant opened the door and Carr immediately removed his shako. It had been the most difficult item to bring up to standard and it showed.

Others had arrived before him and had placed theirs on the hall table. He made room for his at the back and continued through. Kempt was in the small reception room that led to the dining room and, as much as that flinty countenance could show pleasure, it was there up to the maximum as he extended his hand in greeting. Major Greelish stood at his right shoulder.

"Captain Carr! Glad you received the message and equally glad that you could come."

Carr took Kempt's hand, which was returned with a grip of appalling ferocity. Carr was immediately cheered up.

"Good evening, Sir. Yes, Captain Smart came and passed it on. Thank you for inviting me. I've been looking forward to it, it's a pleasure to be here."

Carr realized immediately that the last was an unnecessary flummery, as though it were he that was gracing the occasion, but Kempt showed no reaction; instead he turned to his right.

"You're very welcome, Carr. Truly. Now, you remember Major Greelish?"

Carr's hand came up halfway, but not that of Greelish. He merely nodded.

"Captain Carr."

Carr let his hand drop, but his good mood was not shattered. What rose within him was insolence, not umbrage.

"Good evening, Major. Pleased to see you made it back, Sir. And your message was passed on in good time, I trust? And General Stuart felt well informed?"

Greelish's face reddened, his white moustache standing out in even starker contrast, and his eyes narrowing, but he said nothing whilst furiously working his moustache with his upper lip. Carr remained standing, sporting a pleasant, open grin that, in this context, conveyed considerably less respect than that required; more like an exchange amongst equals. What arose inside him was the thought that the incompetence of this Officer merited no deference from himself, whatsoever.

"Well, Sir. I'll pass on in."

Carr soon found Smart, stood by a table populated by several small glasses of aperitif.

"Matthew, you've found your spot I see. What's this?"

"A local drink. They call it a vermouth. It's very good. Try one. I've had two."

"Two! Now, why am I not surprised?"

Carr took a glass and sampled the clear liquid.

"Mmm. You're right. But one will do for me."

"Well, campaign done and dusted. Back to clean beds, better food and shaving every day."

"I hope you're right, but I think not. The French are less than 100 miles to the North. Beaten but not defeated. I have a strong feeling that they'll be back, at some time as yet undetermined. The question for you and I is, will we still be on this mainland or safely cocking a snook at them from across the water in Sicily?"

Before Smart could reply, an immaculate Orderly came into the room and announced with a ringing cut-glass voice that dinner was served. Carr and Smart entered the dining room and found it to be wholly in the Calabrian style, dark panelling reaching up to a high ceiling that was unpainted, but nevertheless ornate with intricate white plaster. What colour there was in the room was provided by dour portraits, that glowered threateningly through assassin eyes, down onto the newcomers. Complementary dark tapestries and curtains occupied any remaining spaces. However, the candlelight brought up the highlights of a glittering table, silver and crystal, with a silver centrepiece of a fishing vessel complete with crew heaving in a bulging net that seemed in great jeopardy from bursting.

There were no place cards and so Carr and Smart took their places alongside each other half way along the table. Smart was examining the cutlery and Carr was in his usual dinner daydream twirling the stem of a glass in his fingers. The Orderly re-entered the room.

"Gentlemen. Brigadier Kempt."

All stood to pay their respects as their Commander entered, but not alone. As his Senior Major, Greelish attended his Brigadier, walking just behind his left shoulder. Kempt reached his place and took his seat, the signal for all to do the same. The courses arrived, the first two being fish accompanied by a cool white soave. The meat course was lamb, but some indulged in a vigorous discussion by floating the idea that it may be goat kid. Whatever, it was excellent meat accompanied by a light chianti. The excellent food and wine soon added to an atmosphere already merry and convivial from the thought, either at the back or at the front of everyone's mind, that their fighting was done. Kempt, stern Commanding Officer that he may be, proved to be a most agreeable host, amusing and entertaining all with anecdotes from many campaigns that stretched across the world. The spaces were filled with talk of homeward journeys and fair winds and what could be taken back for the family as a gift, momento, or keepsake. There was much information exchanged of feminine items that could be purchased, at very reasonable prices, from the shops and markets close to where they now sat. Carr listened with deep interest, both for himself and to enable him to inform Drake.

Carr was enjoying himself immensely; he was of a lighter spirit. He made no analysis as to why, but deep within himself the gloom of the past year that could well up at any moment, was beginning to thin. Several Officers wanted to take a glass with him, wishing him good luck and better health. It was plain that he dwelt within their high regard, their raised glasses and good wishes showed that he had been well favoured within their now dissolved battalion, and the growing thought added to his new feeling that his fortunes were taking a better turn. There was much hilarity and jesting over the theatrical performance of his men that persuaded the French to surrender, there was even a rumour that Carr had advanced towards the walls of the town and gave a speech, in French, but addressed to his men, to stir up their spirits and ardour ready for the likely assault. Carr spoke up.

"That was no speech, that was a Punch and Judy Show."

Gales of laughter came from all quarters of the table and noisy rapping on the table, with many managing a passable imitation of "that's the way to do it". However, there was one face that did not reflect the bonhomie that circulated around and up the table, that of Major Greelish. Carr did not notice, but Matthew Smart did.

"Our Greelish, there. Seems to be giving you the evil eye. Anything serious between you two?"

Carr didn't look and decided not to care.

"If there is, I'm unaware and I don't see why. We did that bit of scouting for him up to Catanzarro, after we left you in Maida. He did his job and I did mine. Where any ill feeling should arise from, I can't say. Anyway, leave him to stew, in whatever juice he cares to make for himself. It's in the past. Here, have some more of this pudding. It's made from fruit and egg white, and sugar! It's delicious."

With that he spooned an extra helping into Smart's bowl. Cheese and fruit finished the meal and, after the Loyal Toast, Kempt produced some port to go with the local nuts that now stood within arm's reach of all there gathered. Greelish had said little throughout the meal and his temper had bridled at the attention that Carr was receiving. It had not gone unnoticed with Greelish that many regarded Carr as a "quality cut above" and this rankled, his own opinion of Carr was anything but. With the arrival of the port, talk could turn to "shop" and several Officers along the table were asking Kempt for his opinion on the future of Light Infantry within the British Army. His reply was frank and honest.

"I'd say this campaign has proved little, in a major way, that is. Our impact upon the battle was no more than that of good steady infantry, which applied everywhere in our army, as much as I'm aware. There wasn't much, as I saw it, of our being called upon to act any differently from most other battalions."

He paused and looked down the table.

"Except for Carr down there. Your Company had to carry out what could be described as Light Infantry tasks. Do you feel you advanced the Light Infantry cause, at all?"

Carr took a swallow of chianti. He had drunk no port. He remembered Gibraltar.

"Well, Sir. There were two extra things that my Company was called upon to do, that could be described as particular to Light Infantry. One was to hold that wood, but we didn't. We got kicked out and needed Captain Smart here, with his 35th, to help us out. The other was after the battle, scouting forward after the French. That we did, and we got back. But I will say that the trouble that we found ourselves in, we got out of, because of our Light Infantry training. We carried out our drill and that saw us through."

He took another drink. All were listening and some feeling was building up within Carr.

"Whether our Light Infantry example will spread further through the British Army, I can't tell. But there's one thing I'll take issue with you over, Sir, if I may, in saying that the performance of our battalion was no more than that of any good steady infantry. We smashed those Voltigeurs in one minute with no more than two volleys and a bayonet charge. Not many battalions could have done that. So, perhaps we advanced the Light Infantry cause that way."

Cheers and pounding of the table. One Captain, tipsier that the others rose to his feet and proposed a toast.

"Gentlemen. We've had no toasts yet. I propose one; to Kempt's Lights and the memory of Maida."

All repeated the toast, which gave rise to yet more cheers and pounding. As the noise faded away, Greelish leaned forward, his expression serious, even indulgent.

"So then, Captain Carr. If there is such a thing as a Light Infantry cause, if it is to be advanced, then we need success at Light Infantry work. In your opinion, what matters? What brings success?"

The serious tone and question had silenced the table, but Carr's reply was instant.

"Speed. Do the right thing, do it well, but above all, whatever you do, do it quickly. The French understand the role of their Voltigeurs perfectly. 'Rapid and intimidating' are their watchwords and they are conquering Europe with it. Except," and he raised his glass and grinned, "this part of Calabria."

More pounding and cheering, and those that weren't pounding raised their glass in response. Greelish waited for the noise to subside. His chance had arrived.

"Now, I've served alongside Captain Carr, and if he is to be emulated, then there is one trait that is of some concern. I have noticed that he lives in terror of cavalry. Does that apply to all Light Infantry, or just yourself? A permanent worry, ever uppermost in your thoughts. Yes, Captain, would you not agree?"

Kempt, not inexperienced with atmospheres at dinner parties, instantly sensed the change, as did most there. The word "terror" had been used. He didn't like it and it was inappropriate. He decided that the evening was best ended there and then, but he had no loyalty to Greelish. He spoke before Carr could reply, speaking as Kempt, the Brigadier, not Kempt, the genial host.

"And I say that any Infantry Officer, Infantry mark you, who is way out unsupported in advance of his army, and if he is not worried about cavalry, then, well, he is a damn fool!"

Many around the table grinned and nodded, glad for their host's intervention. Greelish reddened, but said no more. Kempt continued.

"Gentlemen. I consider it time that we returned to our Regiments. Tomorrow our transports arrive, and we embark. I wish to thank you on two counts, firstly for your attendance this evening, which has added to a most convivial occasion, and secondly for all of you carrying out your duties so well over the past few weeks. I wish you well for the future, and for your future careers.'

Thanks and similar good wishes were passed back down the table and all rose and left. Smart, understanding both the delicacy and the potential of the situation, ushered Carr up and out, through the reception room, still with some unclaimed aperitifs, to the table with their shakoes. They were amongst the first to reach it, and each claimed their headgear and set a course for the door. Outside, both shook hands.

"Good luck, Smart. To you and the 35th."

"You too, Carr. If you ever wish to transfer into us, you can count on a good word from me."

Carr grinned.

"Yes, perhaps. One is ever unaware of what our Lords and Masters have in mind for us, especially in a battalion of detachments. But, whatever, I wish you good fortune."

Each turned and parted. Smart disappeared around a corner as Carr placed his shako on his head. It reached over his eyes, it was the wrong one. Too big. He re-entered the door and went quickly to the table to select his own, where he found himself shoulder to shoulder with Major Greelish, who viewed him with a look of both dislike and disapproval.

"Sir. It seems I've walked off with the wrong shako. I took this one. It's much too big. I do hope that it isn't yours? Sir?"

Greelish took the shako and quickly gave judgement.

"No, Carr. It isn't."

"Well. I'll just put it back then, and take my own."

Carr reached to the back and correctly found his own battered affair.

"Good night then, Sir. It has been a pleasant evening."

There was no reply. If there was a stony look in his direction, he didn't see it. He was off out the door, grinning from ear to ear.

* * *

The following day proved Kempt's inside information to be correct. Transports began to arrive at the ancient mole, both sides, inside and out, and the army began to embark, battalion by battalion, with all their attendant paraphernalia following the men into the ships for the short journey to Messina. The ships were sailing in relays, there were not enough for the whole army but the whole operation was helped by a stiff South Westerly that gave a helpful beam wind for both journeys, laden out, empty for the return. The 5th Provisionals were to be the last and, as they shuffled down the hillside, the last in the queue, they were allowed to take their ease and watch developments. The sight of the whole army gradually distilling itself towards the small harbour carried it's own message that they would be on that ground for the hours of daylight, at least.

Deakin, Davey, Pike, Miles, Stiles and Peters sat in their usual argumentative group. Ezekiel Saunders seemed to have also attached himself to their company. No one seemed to mind.

"Zeke, how come you b'ain't a Grenadier?"

"Too intelligent!"

All laughed, save one. Their attention was on Joe Pike, displaying a wholly morose figure sat on the ground, head down, musket leant back over his right shoulder. Miles could not resist the need to comment.

"What be you so down in the dumps for? B'ain't we goin' back over to Sicily there? That, at least, be a better camp than what we've got to put up with 'ere. More water for a start."

Pike made no reply, but Deakin spoke up.

"Leave him be. Whatever 'tis, it's his dumps and he wants to be in 'em. Can't see as it's doin' you no harm."

"Well, seems to me we got cause to be cheerful. Not sat there like a Vicar on a Sunday with no one come to Church. What ails thee, boy?"

Joe looked up. He did look miserable.

"We're going back over and I've got nothing to take back for my Mary. I saw lots of good things on sale in the market place, but I've no money to buy anything."

Peters guffawed,

"You b'ain't alone in that Joe. Ain't none of us got no coin, and we all knows that pay don't come regular on campaign in the British Army."

Unusually for him, Miles spoke in a more sympathetic tone.

"What did you see there, then? Was there anything special, like?"

"Well, there was the usual, I suppose, bracelets and scarves; stuff like that. I just don't like taking back nothing, that's all."

His words hit home with them all. They all well understood affection for kith and kin and all knew that Joe was hurting. It was Miles who took charge.

"Right, Joe. We'll go and see Mr Carr and see if he'll let us off for an hour. He's got a sweetheart, in fact they both have, him and Drake, so I'm hopin' that our askin' won't fall on deaf ears. We'll get somethin' for your Mary. You can pay me back come payday."

Deakin looked up.

"And how do you expect to pay?'

"There's other things that acts as coin besides round bits of shiny metal with some bugger's kisser stuck on it. I think I might have just such."

"What?"

"Never you mind."

"Well, if you do have the wherewithal, bring back a nice feminine piece for me. I'll pay you back soon as."

"What do you want a girly present for?"

"Never you mind."

Miles and Pike left their knapsacks and muskets on the ground in the charge of their messmates and took themselves over to where their three Officers were standing, idling and chatting whilst watching other battalions file past. Miles spoke up, addressing all three.

"Sirs. Beggin' your pardon, Sirs, but me and Pike was hopin' to nip over to the market place and make a couple of purchases, Sirs. With your permission, Sirs. It'll take about an hour."

Drake and Rushby made no response, it was Carr's decision.

"Where are your knapsacks and muskets?"

"Our messmates is takin' care of them, Sir. They won't go astray."

"And the nature of your errand is what?"

"Joe Pike here, Sir. He has a sweetheart that he's goin' back to, and he don't have nothin' to take her back. And Corporal Deakin wants somethin' similar, Sir, but he won't explain why."

Carr grinned.

"Well, Miles. I do recall making you a promise about plunder."

"Yes Sir, that's right, Sir. When we was up against the Madelline. Sir."

Carr turned to Drake.

"Well, Lieutenant? They're both in your Section. Any objection?"

"No, Sir. None. But no more than an hour, Miles. Clear?"

Miles and Pike hurried between the nearest two buildings and the shops and market immediately came into view.

"But Tom, what've you got to pay with? We've not been paid, none of us."

"You remember that Frencher that John said he brought down? Well, you got his boots, but I got his buttons and buckle. And I d'reckon that they'm silver."

He reached down into his right hand jacket pocket and his hand emerged with two bright buttons.

"A couple of these should do it. But what Jed's got in mind, I can't imagine. Anyway, what do you think? A couple of headscarves?"

Joe brightened up considerably, his even white teeth showing clear in his tanned face.

"Sounds just fine, Tom."

They did a circuit of the town square and fingered the wares on several stalls, to be accosted by each stallowner, who wanted to show them everything that he had displayed. Eventually they settled on one particular stall with bright cotton headscarves, all of a fine weave, and a selection of jewelry. Joe selected two scarves and Miles threw a button onto the table. The stall keeper picked it up and examined it carefully. Then he drew a knife and applied it to the button hole emerging from the back. The soft metal marked easily. However, he shook his head. Miles responded by adding the second button, but then added a brooch and a set of earings to the two scarves. Again the stallholder shook his head. Miles, unsurprisingly, immediately took umbrage.

"Listen, you chisellin' Eyetalian skinflint. We've just kicked the damn Frogs out for you. If 'twern't for us, you wouldn't 'ave no market! No bloody town, even!"

Of course, the stallholder understood not one word, but the tone was unmistakable. Miles took both buttons off the table, pocketed both, and made to walk off which produced a torrent of Italian from the stallholder accompanied by furious and animated beckoning with his hands to return to the stall. He took the large brooch off the pile and replaced it with a small one. Joe spoke up.

"That brooch is none too impressive, Tom. It's not much bigger than a button."

Miles responded by withdrawing the buckle from his pocket and simply holding it up, at the same time maintaining an enquiring look on his face. The stallkeeper removed the small broach and replaced it with the large. Miles shook his head. The stallholder looked pained, then, the expression on his face told that he had had an idea. He went off sideways to the next stall, spoke to that stallowner and threw two coins on the table. He then returned with a large sausage and larger piece of cheese. These were added to the bargain. Miles looked carefully at the new additions. Both looked wholesome. He paused a second then threw the buckle onto the table. The stallholder grabbed it and held it shining up to the sun. Meanwhile, Pike quickly stuffed the scarves and jewelry into his haversack and Miles did the same with the food.

"Get gone, boy. Quick."

They both hurried away, dodging through the crowd, but they did not get far enough before they heard the same stallholder bellowing at the top of his voice, a word that sounded like "Arrafony".

"Tom, what's up? What's wrong with him."

"Well boy, perhaps I weren't wholly truthful about that buckle. The buttons is silver, true enough, but I got my worries that that buckle may just be plain pewter. We'd best hunt on away now."

Rapid walking brought them back to their camp. There had been few developments, certainly none that applied to the 5th. Their messmates were on the same patch of ground. On the way back, Joe had chosen one of the scarves, plus the earings, leaving the second scarf, the brooch and the two items of food. Miles laid all four out before Jed Deakin.

"Which do 'ee want?"

Deakin examined all four.

"What do I want with a piece of cheese? Nor a sausage?"

"I don't bloody know! Thee'ce b'ain't told me nothin' about what thee wants anythin' for. Make your choice an' we'll settle on a price for payday."

400

Deakin took both the scarf and the brooch.

"Three and six."

"Done. See you next payday."

The sausage and cheese were then divided around the group and, with fresh army biscuits they made fine fare for them all. However, Deakin insisted on a portion for Toby Halfway. All looked at him, posing the silent question.

"And if he's no more, then we'll pass it onto Paddy's family."

Nods of agreement circulated the group.

* * *

The day was dying and the 5th Provisionals had at last reached the quayside. Three large transports could be seen just offshore, hove to in the rose-tinted light that still shone clear from the Westering sun. They were waiting for three more of their build to clear the mole and set sail before they could re-set their canvas and edge in to embark their own final contingent. Colonel Lacey, with Majors O'Hare and Simmonds, paraded from one end of the battalion column to the other, ostensibly checking that all was well and properly stored, but in reality that excuse had long been exhausted, now it was just for something to do and to pass time chatting to their Officers. The dice, penny whistles and flutes had long been put away, and so now all just leaned and lounged on whatever wall they found themselves alongside. The Light Company, being last, were still in the town, confined to the sights in the main street, whist the Grenadiers, the first, were up onto the mole and had the view across The Straits, with the first lights winking in Messina, as the parting sun lengthened and deepened the shadows. Etna fumed and brooded away to the South West, sending a plume of smoke in their direction that dispersed on the good Southwesterly, but nevertheless leaving a smudge on the roseate sky.

O'Hare found time to idle in the company of Carravoy, who stood eating pomegranate seeds, teased out for him by his servant and arranged for him in a china bowl. Carravoy had returned to his old confident self and there was a hint of regret within him that he had exposed so much of himself to this Irish Officer. O'Hare was his usual cheerful self and remarked on the fine view and the red glow from Etna, but, receiving only monosyllabic answers, he moved on. He himself concluded that Captain Lord Carravoy was back to normal. He passed Captain Heaviside, inevitably reading his Bible, therefore beyond idle conversation. Once more, amongst several occasions on that day, he reached the supply wagons but this time saw Sedgwicke and Sergeant Pearson. He recognized Sedgwicke from the "figgy duff" incident and was pleased to return their salute and stop.

"Sedgwicke, isn't it, and Sergeant Pearson."

"Yes Sir", in unison.

"I've not had the chance, not many idle moments have there been, but well done to you both for bringing up the ammunition during the battle just gone. Well done, well done to you both."

"Thank you, Sir," also in unison. O'Hare moved away.

Sedgwicke looked at Pearson. They had little in common, but they had learnt to work together and that, at least, had built a form of relationship, but it was Sedgwicke who was possessed of enough intelligence to think of something to say that could start any kind of conversation.

"Well, now we depart, Sergeant. One good thing, a great deal of stores have now been used up. Less work for us, I think."

Pearson didn't turn his head. He continued to gaze back over the low hills behind the town, now empty.

"They'll find something for us, don't you worry. And them Frenchers b'ain't gone. This is just first off, there's more to come, you mark my words."

Sedgwicke held his peace and turned away. He saw no need for misery with embarkation now so near, away from danger and back to comfort.

O'Hare passed on, but the supply wagons were the end of the column, so he turned back to retrace his steps. In a short while he saw the three transports that were holding them up ease away from the quayside, their timbers now almost pink in the growing sunset. He passed each Company again.

"Not long now, boys, and you're off terra firma, at least for a short while, then a bit of a rest, perhaps a bit of sport, or entertainment who knows?"

Nods and smiles came in return. Lacey was respected, but O'Hare was genuinely popular, the Officer who had stood with them throughout the battle and then led them forward at its close. From practice made perfect throughout the day the last three transports were warped in and the men filed aboard, maintaining single file as they entered the companionways that led to the lower decks where they would spend the short journey, following the lanterns down and through. Having found their place all sat, lounged, or slept despite the sounds of the sailors winching their supply wagons onto the waiting decks. Soon the deck beneath them took on life as they swung away seaward and the ship heeled to the quartering wind and lifted and dipped in the gentle swell. Some had the pleasure of the open deck, but this gave little to see. The night had won and the coast of Sicily was now but a dark shadow, with only the cluster of lights that marked Messina to show that there was, indeed, human life in front of their bows, either side of the lifting bowsprit that defined their direction. Messina was reached in the early hours of the morning and huge fire beacons burning within the harbour gave safe passage up to the quayside. In the dark, no buildings could be seen as familiar, but what was familiar was the reek, from both the quayside and the black water trapped beneath them. It seemed that what had greeted them weeks before was still rotting and had been joined by a ton or so of additional noisome substances.

Orders came to file off the ship and march straight up and out to the fields beyond, there to parade for a roll call and there spend the rest of the night. Each man, burdened with his kit, filed down the gangplank and followed the man in front off the quay and into the main street. Shapes that looked vaguely human lay bundled in the corners and spaces between the many crates and barrels as they proceeded up the gentle slope. The light of burning torches lit their way, but these were few and far between and mostly they could do little more than follow the man in front. Deakin, Stiles and Peters, members of Number Three Company were in the upper half of the narrow column. They entered the light of a burning torch where Deakin saw what he had been dreading. The Mulcahey family must have been waiting all day and now into the night and they now stood anxiously examining each face as it passed, Bridie with the four children, and Mary O'Keefe, Bridie's sister. They saw him and ran forward.

"Jed, Jed. Where's Pat? Is he behind you? Is he all right?"

Deakin couldn't speak, he couldn't find the words, but his silence told everything. Even in the poor light he could see Bridie's face change and the grief do its work.

"He's dead, Bridie, he went in the battle. I'm so sorry. We all are. We didn't know he was gone. It must have been quick, that's the best I can say."

Bridie had collapsed against him and the children were leaning against her, crying with their own anxiety at their Mother's distress. Deakin placed his arms around her and gave what comfort he could. Mary came and laid a hand on his upper arm.

"Jed, what of Joe? Is he all right?"

"He's fine, Mary, just fine. He'll be up shortly; he's back there, with the Lights. You won't have long to wait."

Mary ran down to the next burning torch and stood anxiously, hands holding the grey pinafore up to her chin. Captain Heaviside came up alongside the last of his Company and immediately saw that one of his men had fallen out.

"Corporal. What's this, what's going on?"

Deakin released himself from the sorrowing figure of Bridie and stood to attention.

"Beggin' your pardon, Sir, but this is the family of Corporal Mulcahey. I've just told them, Sir, about Pat, Corporal Mulcahey that is. Permission to fall out, Sir?"

"Granted, but I expect you there at Roll Call."

Deakin placed his hands on Bridie's shoulders. Her forehead fell against his chest, her sobs somehow made more heartrending by the half-light.

"Come on now, Bridie. There's no gain in standing here. Best to follow on up to the camp and get these children settled."

Bridie stood upright and Deakin picked up the two smallest and started up the dark road, to follow the continuous double file of troops. It wasn't long before they were caught up by the Light Company, with Mary alongside Joe, hugging his arm as though the safety of, not just herself, but the entire world depended on it. The others were closeby. Deakin spoke, naming no names, but it was clear who he was talking to.

"You lot. Take up one of these children, they'n fully worn down. We has to get them up to camp."

Each child was taken into the arms of a marching soldier and Deakin returned to Bridie. His hand gently pushing her shoulder moved her on whilst at the same time delivering comfort, albeit in small and inadequate measure.

"Now don't you worry none, Bridie. You'll be looked after and taken care of, you and the children. The lads'll make sure of that, for Pat's sake, as much as for yourself and the children. He was a good man and a fine comrade to us all. He took not one backward step in that battle but stood there with us, shoulder to shoulder. We've got his things somewhere, what we took out of his pack."

Then Deakin remembered who had removed the personal items from Mulcahey's pack, it was Toby Halfway, and where was he? He said no more but walked on beside Bridie, with each child now asleep in the swaying arms of Davey, Saunders, Miles, and Joe Pike, the mighty Saunders carrying the heaviest. They reached the field where they had first settled on their first arrival in Sicily, back in June and formed up by Companies to allow the Roll Call in the growing dawn, and in the light of a lantern held by their servant, each Captain called the Roll. The spaces of silence created by no answer were filled by the distant keening of those whose loved ones should have answered but were now left behind, buried in a grave soon to be ignored by a peasant farmer desperate for the precious space to grow his lifegiving crops.

* * *

The next day, after a short sleep, the battalion awoke and set about their new peace time duties, mostly cleaning and mending until new kit could be issued. Deakin and his comrades made a billet close to the Mulcahey family, as much to see that they received some rations, as to provide comfort in their time of mourning. Whilst checking a boot Deakin looked up and noticed Lieutenant D'Villiers crossing the camp in the direction of the Grenadier Company, hoping to find Captain Lord Carravoy. Deakin pulled on the boot and hurried across to intercept and place himself before the Officer; Deakin standing rigidly to attention.

"Beggin' your pardon, Sir, but can you help me over what happened to Corporal Tobias Halfway, Sir? He had the swamp fever, Sir, and I was under the impression that you had it, also, Sir. I was hopin' that you could give me some information, Sir, as to his whereabouts."

D'Villiers felt himself to be wholly affronted by the sudden appearance of this Corporal, barring his way to where he wanted to go and his face showed it.

"How the Devil should I know, Corporal? We weren't treated in the same room! The one thing that I do know is that some died, surprise, surprise; and were buried. Some in the ground and some dropped over the side of the boat that brought us back, I think they call that burial at sea."

Deakin silently took a deep breath.

"Yes, Sir. But perhaps you can direct me to the Infirmary where you stayed, Sir?"

D'Villiers looked at him, trying to think of a reason why he could also condemn that request as being unreasonable. He couldn't, which didn't improve his temper.

"Back in the town. A large building...",

then he thought, to work it out.

"...off to the right as you go back in."

"Thank you, Sir. I'm very much obliged for your help, Sir."

Deakin peeled off an immaculate salute, which was not returned, so he held it until D'Villiers was thoroughly past and Deakin could see nothing of his face. Proprieties observed, Deakin took himself immediately to the tent of Captain Heaviside, where he found the good Captain, not reading his Bible, but poring over his muster rolls. Heaviside looked up as Deakin opened the tent flap and did his best to simulate a polite knock, this being on the tent pole.

"Excuse me, Sir. Beggin' your pardon, Sir, but I was hopin' to get down to the town, Sir. The reason bein', Sir, to find out about Corporal Halfway. He's one of yours, Sir."

"I am very well aware of who my Corporals are, Corporal. Deakin, isn't it?"

"Yes, Sir. Deakin."

"You haven't received my orders, given to Corporals and Sergeants?"

"No Sir. I may have been elsewhere. Sir."

"Hmmm. Yes, but go tomorrow. Right now I want you here, checking on the men. As of now, we are stood down, but that can change. You check the kit and musket of each man to find out what needs replacing, or even re-issuing, so that their pay can be docked. Go tomorrow, and make sure that I find out about Halfway. If he's dead, as seems likely, I'll need another Corporal."

Deakin made no reply, but simply saluted and left. His immediate return was to the Mulcahey family. Bridie was wearing a black armband, but was busy about the family area, making a stew for the forthcoming dinner.

"Bridie. Are you still getting rations for the family?"

She ceased her stirring within the blackened pot and looked up. The pot contained Deakin's ration, handed over earlier.

"Yes, Jed. No change so far."

"Right. That may continue, it may not. It may not when the muster is brought up to date. Depends on the Purser and the Colonel. I'm hopin' that Lacey, seemin' a decent man, will see that you'm still supported. Any change, you'll let me know."

She smiled, which he returned. Her greatest dread was being abandoned with no way of returning home, but she felt more at ease and re-assured. Jed Deakin could mount a watch over her and her children as well as anyone she knew.

For the rest of the day, Deakin followed the orders given and checked each man's kit and musket. Few were missing anything, and all that was missing was minor. Any major item lost or destroyed had been quickly replaced by taking one from the dead. His major task was to record what had been fairly worn out, mostly boots, breeches and hose. Pay had arrived, the first since leaving England, and many were totting up their meager coins, rueing lost items and cursing their stoppages for food and clothing. Deakin spent the evening with the Mulcaheys, talking to the children and seeing them wrapped up against the chill of the night. With the children asleep he sat beside Bridie. She looked at him and smiled, then turned her face to study the fire. Jed was a family friend of long standing, she saw nothing unusual in the time he was spending with them, acting as the good friend he had always shown himself to be, and properly filling the space left by the death of her husband and his friend. She was grateful.

However, he had made up his mind and drew from his pocket the scarf and brooch, but the pocket furthest from Bridie. Now was as good a time as any.

"Bridie, I've got no family, never have had. I couldn't even tell thee if my Mother nor Father was alive. So, now you've got no man, I was thinkin' that perhaps, if you'm willin', you might see fit to take me on, like. You know how I do feel for you, and for your children, too. I don't know if religion could cause a problem, but if you sees it as fittin', then I was hopin' we could hook up together.

He paused to gauge her reaction.

"How does that sit with you?"

Bridie looked at him and smiled, at the same time doing her best to repair her hair, a stray piece had come out from her headband. She had no doubt regarding the quality of Jedediah Deakin. She paused a slight while and regarded the fire.

"Alright, Jed. I'm willing. We'll take each other on. But we don't sleep under the same blanket for a month or so. I don't think that would be fitting. It's too soon, if you follow my understanding."

"I do, Bridie, and I'm in agreement. Yes, that's fully right. Pat was a good messmate, so due respect is right.

He brought the scarf and brooch up from his left and passed them across to Bridie.

"I brought you back these, 'cos that's what Pat would've done."

She took them and held them in her hands, studying one, then the other, letting the scarf fall from her upraised hand, to regard it in the light of the fire.

"They're lovely, Jed. Both."

She smiled and leant over and kissed him. Deakin spoke further.

"To be held in Pat's memory, I should say. Perhaps your eldest, Jenny, could have the brooch. I don't know. Your choice.

He paused. They sat in the light of the fire, each regarding the other and both smiling.

"So. That's all right, then. I'll tell the Captain, and he'll pass it onto the Colonel. That'll keep you on the muster, and the children. You'm my common law wife, until we decides to make a change, or not, that is."

She spoke softly, still holding the gifts. Her late husband's memory re-kindled. A tear appeared to roll down her cheek, sparkling in the reflected light of the fire.

"Right, Jed. That's a comfort."

He took her hand and squeezed it.

"We'll be fine. Right. I'm for turnin' in. Tomorrow I go to see what happened to Halfway, and I'd best go early.

Early next day saw Deakin leaving the camp. Rising early was part of his nature and with the first crack of dawn, he was awake and donning his uniform. He wasn't challenged at the camp entrance and he knew that his errand should be short. The road back to Messina was not long but winding and skirted by olive trees that would block his view, however, soon he was looking at the outskirts of Messina and then looking over to the right to see if a large house or some such was obvious, but it wasn't. Cursing D'Villiers for a damn numbskull, he continued on, hoping to meet an Officer or NCO or anyone. A red-coated figure emerged some way off from a track that joined the main road. He felt disappointment, the outline told him that this was just a soldier, unlikely to know; he could see the cross belts, the rolled blanket behind his head, the erect musket and the figure showed no arms because his thumbs were tucked into his webbing and musket sling. They drew closer and the face grew familiar, but more thin and haggard than he remembered, he didn't look in the best of health, but a few more yards made him certain.

"I reckoned I'd be needed to guide you back to camp. You couldn't find your arse if they fixed a candle on it. And you've gotten thin!"

The two did no more than slap each other on the arm and grin.

"Come on. I've got something saved for you. I know how partial you are to a bit of cheese, and there's some sausage, too. And by the way, I've taken on Pat's family. There's a chance that me and Bridie will get spliced, so you'm the uncle now, you'll have to be their uncle Toby."

The two quickly fell into step, side by side.

* * *

Obediah Hill stood before the ancient olive tree at the entrance to their camp. A tree taller than most of its genus, the venerable olive provider had a conveniently long trunk on which notices could be fixed and he was regarding one, evidently the latest; for it had suffered no wind damage, as yet. His mouth worked with his thoughts, such that the movement extended back to his extensive sideburns that covered half his face forward from his ears. The notice was brief and to the point.

409

Challenge for a Prizefight
A match made for 25th August

Purse of 30 Guineas
Winner takes all

To fight Nat Pearce of the 20th Light Dragoons
Champion of the 3rd Brigade, Light Cavalry.

Colonel Reede-Smythe
20th Light Dragoons.

Hill removed the notice and walked with it through the camp to where he knew the Light Company was bivouaced. He looked around but almost immediately saw the person he was looking for and walked forward.

"Davey. Be this of any interest to you?"

John Davey took the notice from the outstretched hand, a hand much misshapen from the working of a flintlock. Davey took his time to read it.

"What about Saunders? He's big enough."

"True, but he's no pugilist. Ain't never been in any ring, and if this Dragoon be some kind of champion, he'll know what he's about."

Silence fell, as Davey again read the words, but it was Hill who broke it.

"30 guineas, John. You could buy a small holding for that, or some kind of cottage. I'll not push you; I'll wager this Dragoon's no dunce in the ring, but I thought you'd like to be made knowing, at least."

Davey's face became deeply serious, almost depressed.

"Yes, Corporal, I'm obliged. Thank you. I'll give it some consideration."

"Right you are, Davey, but just one thought. This Dragoon's been on a ship, and then been riding his horse for nearly a month. His wind won't be too sound, whilst you, you've been marchin' and jumpin' about to the tune that Carr blows for you. That'll be one thing in your favour. Small, but it's there."

Davey nodded and they parted company, with Davey still holding the paper. He went and sat with Miles and Pike, and Mary who was still clinging to Pike's arm as though she hadn't let go since they were re-united by torchlight. The scarf was tied about her neck and frequently checked upon. Miles noticed the paper.

"What's that you got there?"

Davey handed it over and Miles read it slowly. His reaction came immediately after he had read it.

"What's it to you? You ever done any prizefighting?"

Davey nodded.

"Fairgrounds and such."

Miles again regarded the notice.

"30 guineas is a tidy sum. Very tidy." Miles paused. "What do you think?"

It was Davey's turn to pause.

"I suppose I've got to give it a go."

"There's no "got to", John. Prizefighting can really do you up, even kill you."

"I know, but like you say, 30 guineas is a tidy sum.

He looked again at the notice, then looked up.

"I'll give it a go."

Miles paused and looked at Davey, but saw nothing that spoke of any eagerness, but, nevertheless, what he had said; he had said.

"Then we've got to take up the challenge quick, 'fore someone else does. And we've got to get you trained up. 25th August is just over three weeks from now."

Miles turned and looked inquisitively at Joe Pike.

"Joe. Me and thee will go and see Cap'n Carr and get us three released from all his practicing and drill. John here has to be brought up to fightin' condition, not just for the honour of the Light Company, but also for the honour of the 5th Provisionals. That's what we'll say. Mary, can you drag up an old sheet from somewhere? He needs rags to bind his hands. There's an Infirmary just down the road, perhaps they've got one that's no good no more."

He stood up and rubbed his hands at the prospect, grinning malevolently.

"Right."

Davey looked up at him, grinning himself.

"It seems that you'm takin' charge. How much do you know about it?"

"Some. My Father was a prizefighter. I got some memories."

"Begat by a prizefighter! Now that explains a lot."

Miles returned an evil look, as he, Pike and Mary walked off on their errands.

The two soldiers found their three Officers, sat, as usual, together in conversation. Miles spoke first.

"Excuse me, Sirs, but I don't know if you're aware, but there's notices been put up concernin' a prizefight, Sirs."

Carr answered.

"Yes, we've seen them."

"Well, John Davey was thinkin' of takin' up the challenge, Sir, and if you sees fit, Sir, then he'll go on ahead."

"It's his decision, Miles. If he wants to fight, he needs no consent from me."

"Ah, well now, Sir, beggin' your pardon, but that's not quite how it is. You see, a prizefight is a hard business, and he'll need to be trained up, brought up to condition, like. So, the permission we needs from you, is to be excused drill and such, to get him good and ready, Sir."

"We, Miles? How so, we?"

"Well, Sir. He'll need trainers to hone him up, and we were thinkin' that that would be me and Pike, here, Sir. You see, Sir, I knows a bit about the prizefightin' game and what I know would bring him up to, well, a higher standard, Sir. Then, less likely to disgrace the Regiment, Sir."

"We aren't a Regiment, Miles, but I take your point."

Carr turned to Drake and Rushby, who had been listening intently.

"What do you two think?"

There was no answer, but first Drake nodded, then also Rushby, who finally spoke.

"We train them for battle, Sir, I think Davey should be allowed to train for this, and with his trainers. Besides, over the past weeks, they've never let us down. It's arguable that they deserve this indulgence."

Carr turned back to Miles and Pike.

"Very good. Permission granted. But how can you be sure that Colonel Reede-Smythe will choose you for the match?"

"Ah, yes Sir. Now, that's the next thing, Sir. I was hopin' that you could square things with the Colonel, Sir, ours, that is, and then you take Davey to this, I mean, Colonel Reede-Smythe and tell him that we take him up. And the sooner the better, really, Sir."

Carr nodded and gave an understanding smile.

"Right, Miles. I'll go and see Colonel Lacey. Bring Davey back down to here in 15 minutes.

Not half an hour later, Carr, Davey and Miles exited the camp and turned inland, which soon took them to the ground occupied by the 20th Light Dragoons. They had progressed almost in silence, nothing passed between them that could be described as social exchange, other than Davey answering two questions for Carr: "Can you put up at least a reasonable performance against this man? Are you sure that you want to go through with it?"

The presence of Carr got them straight past the camp guard and on to the quarters of Colonel Reede-Smythe, this being a large farmhouse; no lowly nor common tent for him. Carr beckoned to an Orderly and dismissed him to announce their presence to the Colonel and convey the reason why they had come. Carr turned to Miles and Davey.

"You'd both best wait. I'll see him first and see what he has to say. Then it's up to him if you come in or not."

They were taken upstairs and Carr was shown into what looked like a back bedroom, with no bed, but a large, rough-cut dressing table, resting on the crude oak floorboards. Bright sunlight shone in through the small window, showing motes of dust floating on the air currents that circulated the room to reach a portly, bucolic middle-aged man, with ruddy cheeks, white whiskers and thinning white hair, but his cold blue eyes stared out from above his full cheeks with what could only be described as greedy malice. He was sat behind a small table, the only other piece of furniture in the room, and his countenance did not, overall, display any kind of greeting. He didn't bother to get up, and his tone was challenging from the start, which could come from the reason for their visit, or the plain attitude of superiority that cavalry always felt towards infantry.

"So, Carr, is it? And you have a man to make a match with mine?"

"Yes, Sir?"

"Where is he?"

"Just outside, Sir."

"Jenkins!"

The Orderly entered.

"Fetch Pearce."

The Colonel's face split into a shark-like grin as he brought the tips of his fingers together with his elbows on the table.

"Any good, is he, your man? Bring him in."

Carr returned to the door.

"Davey."

Davey entered and came to the attention. Reede-Smythe spoke as though Davey wasn't there. They could have been discussing a horse in the stable below.

"He'll need to be bigger than that, Carr! We're almost looking at a mismatch."

"Well, Sir. If you've had other offers..."

"No, Carr. In truth, none. My man has a bit of a reputation, you see."

They stood in silence whilst Reede-Smythe sat equally silent, still maintaining his smirk and posture.

Waiting outside the door, Miles heard footsteps on the stairs and a large figure emerged from the gloom of the stairwell. Miles was the first to recognition.

"Hello, mate. Did you get back well and sound? Not too hard a ride back was it? No Frogs to cause you worry? Well, that's no mind, 'cos they didn't get past us."

He was looking at the scarred Dragoon from the well at Maida. The Dragoon immediately recognized Miles.

"Be it you I'm fightin'?"

"Oh no. He's in there. You'd best knock."

Pearce took the advice, and heard the "enter". It wasn't long before he recognised Davey whilst he came to attention and the remembered dislike narrowed his eyebrows. He was almost a foot taller than Davey, and broader, with huge hands at the ends of almost simian arms.

"This is my man. Corporal of Horse Nathaniel Pearce."

Carr said nothing, not being sure if he was supposed to say anything. Eventually he concluded that he should respond.

"Yes, Sir. So; as you choose, Sir. Is the match on?"

"If you choose it, Carr! Your man is giving about two stone, I'd say. What does he say? He's the one in the ring."

Carr looked at Davey, who nodded stiffly, still remaining at attention. It was Reede-Smythe who reacted by springing up out of his chair, more rapidly than his bulk seemed to make possible.

"Right, Carr. Last points. Under Jack Broughton Rules, and with mufflers. Yes? We can't have two soldiers going hors de combat because of smashed hands. You agree?"

"Regarding Jack Broughton Rules, Sir, I am wholly unaware."

"Then ask your man."

Carr looked at Davey, who nodded again.

"We agree, Sir, but we have no mufflers. If you have a spare pair, we'd be grateful."

"We have. I'll get them sent over. Until the due date, then; at five o' clock. Unless you care to start the betting. Shall we say five guineas?"

"At what odds?"

"Four to one on your man."

"Make it three!"

* * *

The next day saw the three, Miles, Pike and Davey running up to the woods behind their camp, but Davey had a log across his shoulders. Once in the woods Miles wound an old tent around a tree and Davey, with his hands bound with strips of sheet began pounding the tent for all he was worth. Then Miles had him 'bunny hopping" around a series of obstacles, then throwing the log to Miles and then to Pike then back to Miles. A break came for midday meal, which saw them back in the trees shadow boxing. More pounding of the tent and "bunny hopping" saw out the day. This proved typical, the content for each day, but what was often added in was Ezekiel Saunders holding up a haversack full of cloth for Davey to hit, at his head height, then down to body height. The next week saw another addition. Late afternoons, after their training, ten men from the Light Company came into the woods with them, each with a canvas bag full of small stones, that each had been asked to prepare. From a variety of angles these were thrown at Davey's head and body and he was expected to block or avoid them as they came in quick succession. Miles final trick was to have Davey chase a chicken around a pen, trying to catch her. The final day before the fight arrived, and training finished with light shadow boxing, then with Saunders and his haversack, then finally with the bags of stones.

That evening found them all at their camp fire, the meal finished, with Mary O'Keefe repairing the stitching on the mufflers, that had proven to be old and much worn. Miles, as usual was holding forth.

"Now remember, John. Broughton rules allows for holds. Keep movin' and dodge away. Make him chase you and get him tired. Make him miss too. If you can get some hits into his body as you go, all the better. Dodgin' and movin' is your best chance. He's a big bugger, but no cavalryman was ever any good on his feet. Sway and move. He'll tire."

All this being illustrated by very enthusiastic swaying and moving from his own body.

"Yes, Tom. You've told me all this before."

Joe Pike took the chance to examine what he didn't understand.

"This Colonel's putting up 30 guineas, that goes to the winner. Yes?"

Miles nodded.

"So how does he make any money? He's giving it to the winner."

Miles leaned forward, forearm draped over his knee as though indulgently addressing a rather ignorant child.

"He puts up the money to cause the fight. To make it happen, like. Then, bein' as he fancies his man as a winner, he gets the same sum back, and more, from the bettin'. If his man wins, that is. Understood?"

Joe Pike nodded, the motion of which disturbed Mary, mending done, she having reclaimed his left arm.

"Right, sleep. Big day tomorrow. The fight's in the afternoon, after trainin', but there's no substitute for sleep before midnight. One hour before's worth two after, my Father used to say."

"Yes, Tom. You'm the trainer."

The next day dawned, and the clear sky told of a hot one. Miles immediately required Davey to drink plenty of water.

"You can't drink during the fight, but with fightin' in this heat you'll sweat plenty." They ate their food and spent the day back in the woods flexing and shadow boxing. Pike, Miles, and the whole Mulcahey family did their best with the stone bags. Mid afternoon saw them leave the camp and walk to a field that was two over from theirs, dedicated as neutral ground, but some men of the 20th had been busy, erecting a ring with ropes and painting a square yard in the centre. The ring looked to be about seven yards square, erected in a natural amphitheatre, a dip with a slope going up and away on three sides. Miles took a look and returned.

"I'd like that ring bigger, but it's about right. This Reede-Smythe's missed a chance to take space off you. We'll settle for that."

They took themselves off to the shade of some trees and watched the shadows move around as the sun swung across to its final horizon. Davey continued to sip water. After a while, Miles bandaged his hands. Spectators began to arrive, in 10's, 20's then 100's. The word had circulated around and all had seen the notices. A crowd was building. Miles looked around and over.

"'Tis a fair crowd that's buildin' here, John. If 'tis a good fight, they'll pass the hat round to be split between the two. That can raise a tidy sum, a pound or two, sometimes more."

"Shouldn't we be goin' down, and take our corner?"

"Not yet, John. No point in waitin' in the sun. Bide 'ere until the opposition arrives."

With that there came an outburst of cheering, markedly from those in cavalry uniform. Pearce had arrived and was making his way to the ring, accompanied by his Seconds. Reede-Smythe led the way, still bearing his shark-like grin. They reached the ring and chose a corner.

"Come on then, John, time we joined the party."

They left the shade of the trees and walked down the slope to the ring. The cheering at his appearance grew louder, his support coming from those with a uniform that included a red jacket. This was plainly a contest that was more than a simple fight between two men, this was cavalry against infantry.

It was Joe Pike who was carrying the bucket of water and Miles bid him stay outside the ring when himself and Davey entered. They went immediately to the whitewash square in the centre and waited. Pearce and his Second came forward to stand the line opposite. Miles took the initiative.

"Jack Broughton Rules, yes?"

The second nodded, but Pearce had fixed upon John Davey with a look of pure hatred. Davey replied with a happy grin.

"I told you I hoped we'd meet again."

Miles looked at Davey quizzically, then continued.

"We has to choose Umpires. Do you have one?"

The Second replied.

"Yes, our Colonel."

"Right."

Miles looked around and saw Major O'Hare. He went over to him.

"Sir, will you act as Umpire?"

O'Hare raised his shako.

"Yes, I certainly will, and I'm sure that Major Willoughby there will act as third, if you have no objection, Colonel?"

Both Major and Colonel raised their hats and nodded. Miles returned to Davey and motioned him back to his corner and began to put on the mufflers. Davey began deep breathing. They waited a good five minutes, as convention required, to allow all bets to be placed, which was furious and fully occupied the time of waiting.

Carr, Drake, and Rushby were stood somewhat back from the ring, but still with a good view. Carr turned to Drake.

"Jack Broughton Rules. What do you know?"

"Ah, now I've been making enquiries. The fight goes on until one man cannot stand and defend himself at his line on that square, there. Any man can go down on one knee for 30 seconds if he cannot continue, but after that he must get back to "toe the line". If a man goes down, or is knocked down, he cannot be hit, but he has 30 seconds to return to the fray. By toeing his line. A Second can help him to get there, that's why he stays in the ring, but after that, it's up to the fighter."

"So it can go on and on?"

"Yes, that's right, on and on, until one of them cannot put up any kind of fight, any more, which is shown by not returning to their line on the square."

The gloves were on and Miles accompanied Davey to his side of the square. Pearce and his Second did the same, each Second with their hand on their fighter's shoulder. Davey raised his guard, whilst Pearce raised both his fists cocked for punching. Both Seconds removed their hands and the fight began. Davey took a pace back whilst Pearce sprang forward and swung aimed punches at Davey's head, but Davey swung his body left but dodged right, leaving Pearce sawing at thin air. Davey sent a clean left into his right ribs, a left hook to his jaw, then jumped away. The clean piece of boxing brought a roar of approval from the redcoats in the crowd, but Pearce was after him. He wasn't slow despite his size. For some minutes, this formed the fight. Davey moving and dodging, never keeping his head still, moving around the ring. Pearce was throwing heavy punches from all angles and Davey was doing his best to dodge, or block, or ride the punch if he had to. Davey threw some blows of his own, but it was plain that it was Pearce who was running the fight, taking it to Davey, who was using all his skill to avoid the continual stream of heavy blows aimed at him.

The fight began to settle and the ferocity of Pearce's attacks lessened but not significantly. If Pearce had planned to pound Davey out of the fight within a few minutes, it hadn't worked. Davey still circled and weaved around the ring, making Pearce chase and throw punches when he felt in range, but many were missing. Pearce attempted to grapple and make a throw, but Davey dodged away and cuffed the side of Pearce's head for his trouble. The crowd had grown almost silent. This was an exceptional fight, one that Gentry would pay pounds to see, the boxer against the brawler, but Pearce had settled to a steady level of aggression. The punches still came thick and fast, unscientific, but still they came. Pearce, the experienced champion, was getting both the range and the measure of Davey and punches began to land more frequently. Pearce managed to sieze Davey across the waist and threw him into a corner, then began a flurry of punches with all the strength and energy he had. Davey swung and twisted and tried to cover up, but the rain of punches was unavoidable. Davey dropped to one knee, but Pearce still took the chance to land a blow on the top of his head. The timekeeper shouted the seconds as Miles came forward with a wet cloth to wipe his face.

"That's right, John. Take your chance if he locks you up. But look, that last took some out of him. He's breathing hard. Do as you've done, and hit his body when you can."

Davey rose up and immediately placed his foot on the line. If Pearce is feeling it, why give him the rest? Pearce bored in, hoping to finish it, but his eagerness made him clumsy. Dodging the 'haymaking' punches Davey crashed two hard punches, right then left, into Pearce's ribs and sent a precise right into the side of Pierce's head. Pearce staggered and his chest heaved for breath. Davey sent another left into his side, but Pearce seized him and bore down upon him, making Davey take his weight. Davey wrestled his way out and stepped away, but not so far as to let Pearce stop and rest. Davey remained within range, continuing to feint and move, looking for an opening whilst tempting Pearce to continue to swing and miss.

More minutes passed as the fight continued, Pearce continuing to hunt, Davey continuing to dodge, weave, and run, making Pearce lumber after him. Pearce attempted his wrestling move again, and it worked, locking Davey into a corner and pummelling him with heavy blows. Davey dropped again, but this time he protected the top of his head from the blow that came. Miles attended him, carrying a wet cloth and dry rag.

"Right, John. How're you feelin'?"

Davey grinned.

"Well, I've sure felt better and been in better places, but I'll say not too bad."

Miles ignored the joke and continued wiping Davey's face with the wet then the dry.

"It's workin' John. He's wearin' out, not carryin' his gloves so high. We've got to drop 'em further. Start hittin' his arms and body too, when you can. But make his damn arms ache."

Davey went to the line, but Pearce wasn't there. He was taking a rest against the ropes listening to the seconds. 28, 29, then he was there and the bout continued. Davey was encouraged. He didn't know what he himself looked like, but Pearce certainly looked none too fresh. Davey began to work, boxing closer and taking risks, but throwing more punches that almost all connected. Pearce was a boxer who relied on his size and strength, ready to take blows if that placed him in range to deliver his own huge punches. Avoiding a punch was not in his technique and Davey's punches steadily attacked Pearce's arms, shoulders, and midriff. Now the crowd noise grew, this was genuinely a contest of science against strength, with both boxers now trading blow for blow. Davey was taking punches, but they now lacked power and were swinging and clumsy, easier to block and ride, whilst releasing shots of his own. Davey landed a two handed attack into Pearce's ribs, but took a heavy blow to the side of his head. Davey dropped again. It had hurt and he would take the time, but also to assess Pearce. Although on one knee, Davey looked carefully at him. He felt tired himself, he didn't have much more, but Pearce, back in his corner leaning on the ropes, looked exhausted. Miles came again with the wet cloth. He looked worried, but it was Davey who spoke.

"Now or never, Tom. This is it, win or lose."

Davey came to the line first, straightened up and motioned Pearce to his place. The insolent challenge was clear. "Get to your line and let's get this settled." Pearce pushed himself off the ropes and came to his line. Davey immediately feinted with his left then crashed in an overarm right that broke Pearce's nose. Pearce bellowed with rage and the toe to toe exchange began. Davey was relying on his movement and defence to avoid and block the punches from Pearce that were becoming fewer and easier to predict. Davey put everything he had into an attack to Pearce's body, then switched to his head. Three heavy blows battered Pearce's head from side to side. He swayed and tilted forward. Davey stepped aside and Pearce sagged to his knees. The count began as Davey went to Miles to have his face wiped. Miles was like a child at Christmas.

"You've gott'n, John, You've gott'n. One more like that and he's gone."

Davey could hear the yelling of the crowd, he could make out very few words, but he could hear Reede-Smythe screaming for Pearce to get up. Pearce was still on his knees over the square, but his Second was manfully attempting to get him to his feet. Eventually, Pearce pushed himself off the flattened earth as the count reached the middle twenties. His Second led him to his mark and propped him up, as Davey came to his mark. The instant the Second let go of Pearce, Davey stepped forward and slightly to his right and crashed a vicious left hook into the point of Pearce's jaw. He collapsed like a puppet whose strings had been severed. The count began and Davey waited. Pearce's head moved slightly but that was all; his length was fully measured across the ruptured grass of the ring. 28, 29, 30. Davey raised his arms in triumph, Miles ran forward shouting something, but it was lost in the din of cheering.

* * *

Dusk was changing the light as Davey, with Miles, Pike and Mary in attendance, washed himself in a large tub of clean water. Everything ached, but he had enough in him to return thanks to all those who came to shout their congratulations. His prize money rested in its leather bag on the trestle besides the tub. It wasn't long before Obediah Hill came along, carrying another, which he dropped onto the table besides the original.

"Ten pounds, 16 shillings, and eight pence. Your share of the hat going round. All the lads threw in. That was some fight, Davey, many said they hadn't never seen the like. Mr Carr put in £5, saying somethin' about sharin' his winnings. So, what happens now, to the money, I mean?"

Davey tried to reply, still out of breath.

"I sends it to my Molly, she's with my Mother. I've got a letter, it was waitin' here when we came back. Our local Vicar wrote it. She reached my Mother's, the child too."

Hill looked anxious.

"Are you going to send it all.?"

"Yes. This makes it up to 40 guineas."

"John. Forgive me saying this. But it that wise? You wants to send 40 guineas to Molly Dixon! And you reckon she'll be back there, with the money to greet you when we reaches home? I'm sorry John, but that's the question."

Davey bridled at the words, not severely, but he didn't like what was being implied.

"Yes, I do reckon she'll be there. That's what it's all about. With that money, I can make a good home for her, Tilly and me. I trust her."

"Your decision, John, I meant no offence, I just think it needed sayin', is all. If you'm fully sure, this is my advice. You could, through the Purser, send it back with a letter of credit, that only you can cash when you gets home, if you produce a receipt, signed here by the Colonel. That'll keep it safe from any twisted courier and safe for only you."

"What if I'm killed. She won't be able to get the money as my wife because we aren't church married. If I'm killed, then she can still get the money if she gets that letter of credit signed by the Colonel. That will allow the bearer to draw on the battalion's account. She can find him when the battalion returns. That's what I want, and that's what we'll do."

Hill could see that Davey was unmoveable.

"I hope you're right John, and, well, good luck to you all the same."

The next day saw Davey enter the Purser's tent, down through a corridor of cheering wellwishers. He handed over the prize money and obtained a receipt and a Letter of Credit. This he took to the Colonel's tent and waited an hour for Lacey to see him. Lacey studied both.

"Where do these go?"

"The receipt I keep, Sir. The Letter of Credit I'm sendin' to my wife, Sir. You may find yourself signin' it again to release the money, Sir, when we gets back home."

Lacey nodded, drew the pen from the inkwell and added his signature to both.

"There you are, Davey. A good performance yesterday. Well done."

"Thank you, Sir,"

Davey took one pace back, saluted and left.

Lacey returned to his correspondence. One letter demanded his attention before that of all others. It was in a heavy paper cover, sealed with the stamp of their new Commander, General Henry Fox. He opened it and read to halfway down, when he allowed all the breath to leave his body. The orders read;

"...to prepare three companies from your command for embarkation to the fortress of Scilla, there to form the garrison. Command will be a Major and a Second, chosen by yourself."

Lacey threw the letter across to O'Hare, who was taking his ease at the tent entrance. After O'Hare had read the letter, Lacey posed the big question.

"Who do I send?"

"It has to be our best, Sir. The Grenadiers, The Lights, and Number Three.

"Will you take command?"

"Yes."

"I'll give you George Simmonds as Second. He knows all about castles and sieges and such. You can have Gibney too. Oh, and some storemen. Sedgwicke seems fairly competent. And Pearson, too, as the Senior."

Chapter Twelve

An Active Garrison

The collection of soldiers emerging from the castlegate, were plainly in holiday mood. Those beyond earshot, needed only to observe the antics and horseplay, whilst those within hearing, would draw their own conclusions from the shouts and hoots of laughter. Evidently, some of the garrison were off to their favoured "sbara" in the town, off duty and out for enjoyment. They progressed ingloriously along the causeway, close to the many fishing craft drawn up on the beach to their left, the proud crafts' painted eyes mystically glaring forward from their bows, their stare made more intense by the contrast between the fierce black and white of the eye and the bright reds, blues, and greens of the rest of the hull. The local fishermen gave the capering soldiers less than a glance, as they worked or lounged, mending nets or discussing tomorrows fishing ground after this day's fishing in The Straits. The day had been good, proven by the baskets of fish being carried up to the town along both sides of the causeway, for fish were also coming onto the causeway from the other side, landed from the boats that called the alternative beach their home.

Another group of soldiers followed, through the same gates that had not been shut for a year, a fact made plain by the build up of pebbles and shingle against their lower sections, which would need some serious shovelling should the time come again when they needed closing against the arrival of another determined foe. This group was less raucous and had an observer been told that these were family men, they would not have been surprised. Steady and sober, they turned right at the end of the causeway to take the streets that led through the town up to the family encampment. A close observer would have noticed full haversacks on many, enough rations for a family. This had given the men cause for cheer equal to that of the preceding group, although it gave rise to nothing as demonstrative as those previous. A supply ship had just arrived, her bowsprit emerging from behind the seaward castle wall, barely moving to the onset of the regular, harmless waves.

The workday done, soon the town square would fill with its civilian inhabitants, themselves come to spend the back end of the day relaxing, taking a drink of wine outside the sbarra, talking to friends and watching what came. There was nothing special about the day, but some of the garrison of soldiery, containing many who looked to the town for entertainment to break the drudgery of duty and drill in an ancient stone castle, usually livened up most evenings. Usually there was music and dancing of the traditional kind, and many of the soldiers had learned the steps and moves over the past months, their red jackets adding both contrast and colour to the dancing lines of men, women, boys and girls. As the family men passed on up through the town it was clear that this evening would be no different, the drums, fifes, whistles and fiddles were all gathering, and it was common, and this evening was no exception, to see redcoat musicians amongst the accompaniment.

Deakin, Halfway and Davey were amongst the second group, certainly counting themselves as "family men", and with them Joe Pike, who considered himself as thoroughly "attached". Tom Miles was with neither. He was on sentry on the seaward battlements, displaying an aggrieved scowl to match that of the lowering battlements that he was guarding. The four "providers" passed the last of the town and took the well defined path up to the family tents, just out of the town and up the slope. The criss-cross of deep and well worn tracks evidenced the length of their stay over the past many months, as did the many additions to the tents; stone walls, pig pens, chicken runs and kitchen gardens, even a cow. Nor did any family members now sit on the ground, rough and robust furniture now civilised the entrance to all the family tents, and even most of those tents that were inhabited solely by male soldiery. Bridie Deakin, as she now called herself, greeted her men and then her main man with a kiss. She cooked for them all, and all took their ease on the stools and benches, handing across the rations just landed, salt pork, fresh biscuit and flour, dried peas and beans, and even potatoes. The supply ship had been very welcome. All sat in the late afternoon sunshine, enjoying the cool breeze. It was August, 1807.

However, the ship had not proved to be so welcome to the Commanding Officer, Major Padraigh O'Hare. She had brought despatches from another new Army Commander, General

Sherbrooke, with disturbing news, such that O'Hare had called his Second and his three Captains to his quarters for a conference. They were in the highest room in the castle, light and airey, with the sound of the lapping waves joining the bright sunlight that entered the open window. O'Hare wasted no time on pleasantries; Major Simmonds and Captains Carr, Carravoy and Heaviside listened intently.

"The French have re-invaded. They have taken several towns, including Catanzarro, and the Calabrian insurrection after our victory at Maida is now largely suppressed. If they are determined to clear us out also, well, the Neopolitan Army and the Masse' will hold them up, but eventually they will reach here. There may be two strands to their assault. There is a rumour that they will start with Reggio. That makes sense, a quick gain to deprive us of a port, and gain one themselves, rather than belabour their way down to here, fighting across the hills, to slowly close on us. I'm saying when they come, not if, and they'll take Reggio; I can't bring myself to trust any Neopolitan Army to resist a long siege down there."

Simmonds spoke up.

"They held out at Gaeta, that fortress North of Naples."

"Only with our best support. General Sherbrooke says nothing about making such an effort with them, nor us, for that matter. His silence speaks volumes. Without orders we can only assume that we do the best we can, and then withdraw. Gaeta notwithstanding, the Neapolitan Army has done nothing since of much military note. We have to assume that the French will push them aside and then they will reach here, and then we will be under siege. What's your assessment? You first, George."

Major George Simmonds, the siege and fortification specialist, placed the fingers of both hands to cover his mouth. He took a breath, removed his fingers and spoke.

"Well, we've rebuilt the damage that we inflicted, and it's better than before, in my opinion. What gives me greatest comfort is the stairway we've cut in the rock down to the beach facing The Strait. We can both receive supplies, reinforcements and evacuate out of the enemy's direct field of fire. However, what we did, so can they. A battery of 24 pounders will eventually reduce the defences of this place to make it untenable, then it's our decision; how much of a fight do we want to put up? For how long?"

426

O'Hare turned to Carravoy.

"Charles?"

"I think that Major Simmonds is most accurate in his assessment, Sir. I've nothing to add apart from to emphasise the question that when defeat is inevitable, the weighty decision is; how long do we attempt to hold out?"

"Henry?"

"I say we make them pay; for every foot of rampart. We put up a fight and show them that we don't give in when a bunch of ladders are thrown down before us. It's about creating respect, Sir, and making them worried, afraid, for the next time they're faced with a red coat."

"I don't follow you."

"Well, Sir, they came at us at Maida as though we were nothing. To advance without even firing a volley, as though the mere sight of their bayonets would make us turn and run, shows me that they hold us in contempt. I say that we hold this place to the absolute last point of expediency, to show them that when they see redcoats it means that what comes next will be hard and costly. Wherever and whenever, we show them just how good we are. This is just a small incident at the start a long war, Sir."

O'Hare looked down and smiled slightly at this firebrand speech. Carravoy looked astonished, shocked at so outward a show of feeling. Heaviside's face showed no change, neither did that of Major Simmonds. O'Hare continued.

"As you say, possibly, but is this place tenable? Can we make a stand here, with a chance of evacuation, having dealt the French a bloody nose? I say yes. Any disagreement?"

All four shook their heads, but Carr with enthusiasm, Carravoy resignedly, face down. O'Hare did not fail to notice.

"Right. I will now reply to General Sherbrooke informing him that we are prepared to withstand a siege, we'll put up a fight, to quote Captain Carr, but I'll also point out that left to our own devices evacuation is inevitable. However, we are prepared to stay here and do as much damage to the French as we can. Any comments?"

Carr spoke.

"No Sir. None from me."

The other three allowed silence to convey their acquiescence.

"Right. From now on we are preparing for a siege. Major Simmonds, what's to be done?"

"First is to prepare sandbags. We cannot have enough. Firstly, to pile behind the battlements to give them weight when the shot begins to strike. That'll also stop chunks of stone flying back into the castle. Any left over, go to the gate, for when the time comes that we are thoroughly locked in. Next, is the obvious, to check our stores and weapons and set up secondary magazines closer to the battlements where we will be returning fire. If I had my way, we'd demolish the houses opposite to give us a bigger field of fire, but my guess is that that would not be very politic. Relations with the locals at present are good."

"The first two, yes. The last, no, as you yourself have deduced. These people will be in for enough misery as it is, without us blowing up their homes. To still keep the Masse' on our side, and local support, is worth more than a few feet added to any glacis. So, we start with shoring up the battlements, any bastion first, or both together?"

The question was directed at Simmonds.

"Both together, left and right. The French will start by attacking both.

Through the rest of August and through September the daily activity was to be the winching of bags and sacks, full of sand, up to the embrasures atop the two bastions. As the stack of sandbags grew higher, so did the tension, for the work on the battlements sent an obvious message to both townsfolk and garrison. It was reinforced by both fact and rumour that came over the mountains of French preparations to the North and their being seen in closer and closer locations. September turning into October saw the Masse' in almost continuous conflict, skirmishing with the French as they probed into the hills, and the Masse' themselves trying to impede the French by blocking passes and tearing down bridges and revetments. A telegraph semaphore erected on the seaward side of the castle gave O'Hare daily communication with General Serbrooke, but the news coming into the Castle showed the inexorable French build up of men and material to begin the siege. October saw the first storm in The Strait, closing communication, and this forced O'Hare's decision. He issued an Order of the Day. It read simply: "10th October. All dependants and relations of the British

428

Garrison are to prepare for evacuation, weather permitting, on the 13th October. Signed Major P. O'Hare. Officer Commanding.

Gloom spread through the camp, and not a little through the town, relationships had spread beyond British soldier exclusively with British female, but stoicism was the only possible response and tents were struck, livestock sold and half grown vegetables pulled up prematurely and examined for any worth. On the morning of the 13th, soldiers and their families, all burdened, progressed into the town and onto the beaches. One large transport awaited their arrival, 5 minutes' sailing away, lifting and leaning on the choppy sea, mercifully the good side of "rough", in no way stormy, but nevertheless, not calm. With the state of the sea, the local fishermen had volunteered their craft to take the women and children off the beach and out to the waiting transport. All were grateful, their local skills and knowledge would make everything safer and speedier.

The soldiers and their families waited and parted when their turn came, affection and sadness obvious amongst all, but shown at different levels of intensity. Jed and Bridie Deakin, held hands for a second or two, kissed and smiled gently whilst their comrades lifted in the children, lifted high to prevent their getting wet, then Bridie herself climbed the short ladder. However, Joe Pike and Mary OKeefe clung together until the very last second, she crying and him doing his best to re-assure.

"I came back last time, didn't I?"

Eventually, the last act was the last boat slanting under shortened sail out to the transport. All soldiers involved were allowed to the uppermost battlement and watched as the transport turned into the wind and set only cautious sail to take them back across The Straits. White handkerchiefs waved from the decks for almost an hour, until a bank of rain tracked in from the South West and hid all but the white sails, turning them to a ghostly grey. Jed Deakin looked at Joe Pike as they pulled themselves away from the battlements.

"Well, that's it for family life, at least for a while. Back to messmate livin' and cookin'. And sleepin'." He placed his hand on Joe's shoulder and eased him away.

* * *

French cannonfire, both grape and solid, was stripping the roof off the hovel that served as a shepherd's hut on the Aquile Ridge, the last high ground to the East, that topped the hills leading down to Scilla. Slate and timber were falling down upon the defending soldiers, whilst the thick walls were proving more durable to the light mountain guns, but plaster and mortar falling off their insides told their own story that these also would not last long. The hut was the centre point of a defensive line of hedges, embankments and stonewalls that through November and December had held the French away from a sight of Scilla, but now they were mounting a serious assault, evidently soon to be successful. The hut was drawing fire, and its continued occupation would only mean death or injury for any defenders. Carr shouted orders to the few occupants remaining as another solid shot sailed through the roof and out the other side.

"Get out and take cover. Wherever you can, keep firing, but await orders. Saunders, Pike, stay by me."

He climbed some stairs to a half loft containing a high window that looked out over the French positions. Through his Dolland glass, what he saw, he didn't like. The French were climbing the ridge in full column, two companies wide, and at least as deep, more than one battalion, with cavalry on the flanks. Another shot smashing into the walls drew the comment that confirmed his inevitable decision.

"A full Boney assault! So that's that."

He shouted down to his two messengers.

"Pike, you go to Lieutenant Drake, Saunders you to Lieutenant Rushby. At 100 yards, two ranks, ten rounds rapid, then retreat in files. Warn them of cavalry. I'll try to organise the Masse'. Go."

Pike and Saunders shot out the back door as a cascade of plaster and brick dust showered Carr descending the stairs. His two messengers had turned right, but he turned left. The hut was the join with the Masse' irregulars and he ran behind their position, their firing places matching that of his own men, walls and earth embankments topped with hedges. He found the Masse' Commander, Michael Sciarpa, looking intently through the trees at developments with the French. There was nothing of the brigand about him, in fact he was a lean, smallish man, dressed in a long black coat, who had more of the look of a schoolmaster, than someone who had been fighting the

French as an irregular for almost two years. Perhaps he had been a schoolteacher, for he had an understanding of basic English. Because of the continuous roar of musketry, Carr had to tap him on the shoulder. Sciarpa turned round and laughed to see Carr. He started a greeting, but Carr cut him short.

"The French are making a big attack, with cavalry, cavalleria. Tell your men, fire ten, rapido, then retreat, ritirata, quickly, veloce."

Sciarpa nodded, then slapped Carr on his upper arm, as though it were Carr that needed reassuring. Then he ran along his line.

"Dieci colpi, i compagni. Rapido, poi ritirata"

Carr ran to his men, first Drake, then Rushby. Both sections were ready, behind a chest high wall, muskets held at the make ready. He reached Rushby just as he gave the order to fire, immediately matched by Drake. 40 muskets roared out and the firing by ranks began. Carr looked over the wall to see the result, but had to wait for a gap in the smoke as it blew back. The column was taking punishment, from both sides, the Masse' also were making their presence felt, but the progress of the dense column was inexorable. It would have taken the firepower of a whole battalion to stop it and all that Carr had was his Company and twice again of the Masse'. The equivalent of three companies were punishing the column, the rifles felling the Officers, but the drums in the centre were driving the men on. Despite the front rank being continuously stripped away, the ranks behind stepped over the dead and marched on. However, what pleased Carr was the fact that the punishment being given to the column was holding back the cavalry.

The ten rounds were finished and the order was being given that rifles were to load and hold fire. Drake and Rushby gave the order to fall back and soon it was just Carr stood at the wall. The column was maintaining its pace, but the cavalry was coming around its flanks. Time to go; and Carr ran after his men, passing through the riflemen holding their first position 100 yards back in the first cover, a thin line of trees. Carr held there with them, waiting. Seconds passed, then a minute, but no cavalry. Shots were still sounding over to the right where the Masse' were, mixed with some screams. It seemed to Carr that the Cavalry had thought better of the wall and had turned left to the bank where the Masse' were. Could he support them? He thought not. He motioned his men to fall back and felt reassured when the firing died away. The Masse' must have escaped, melting back into the trees, rocks, and scrub.

With his men still spread out in skirmish order, Carr led his command down the hill to the town. They had just lost the last ridge before the town itself and now the French would be taking their first view of Scilla itself, albeit way beyond cannon shot. He was pleased to see the Masse', still in numbers, moving down behind him from far over on his left, over to the South. They would maintain a picket line, the French would not have a free march down to Scilla. As there was no pursuit from the French, Carr called in his men and sent them to their billets and tents, some on further into the castle, where also went Drake, Rushby and himself. Carr immediately reported to O'Hare.

"The French are within sight of us, Sir, they've got the Aquile Ridge which makes them about two miles away. They attacked in way beyond battalion strength, supported by cavalry. Ourselves and the Masse' held them up and took a toll of them, Sir, but there were too many."

O'Hare nodded.

"What're your casualties?"

"Two dead and four wounded, Sir."

"Seriously?"

"Two, Sir."

"Arrange for their evacuation. There's a transport in the morning. Now, get fed and get some sleep. Well done."

Food and rest were also uppermost in the minds of Carr's men. Miles, Pike and Davey filed in through the door of one of the abandoned houses that were growing in number throughout the town. Some of the Masse' had followed them into the town and the word was spreading that the French had reached the last ridge and were now watching Scilla, causing even more families to abandon their dwellings and make for the hills. There would be no drinking, nor dancing, nor music in the town square this night.

Pike hung up his pack and musket and took himself off to the Castle to collect their rations, leaving Miles and Davey to occupy themselves, which meant giving priority to cleaning firearms, then checking the rest of their equipment. Each had little to say; it had been a long day, climbing the ridge, making a fighting retreat against heavy odds, then making their way back down, but Davey felt the need to ask something of his more experienced messmate.

"What're our chances, Tom? This is lookin' none too good."

Miles was in no good mood. A dislodged stone from the wall had hit his upper arm and it was becoming numb and stiff.

"It don't take too much figuring, does it? Sooner or later we'll be holed up in that castle, with the Frenchers where we are now. Then 'tis all about if the Navy can get us off, wind and tide permittin'. But I'll tell thee one thing, John, they'll not take I, I b'ain't spendin' years in some French prison, I'll jump and take my chances with the sea. If I get ashore, I'll join the Masse'. The French b'ain't collarin' me."

Davey made no reply, he busied himself with cleaning his Baker rifle. Both were content with the silence, and both looked forward to Joe Pike returning with the days rations.

A similar gloom had settled over the evening Officer's conference in O'Hare's quarters; himself, with Major Simmonds and his three Captains sat around the perimeter of a small table that held a map spread out on its surface. The progress of the French was clear, the pencil marks on the map, with the date of their addition, told their own story. The latest was the rectangle drawn on the Aquile Ridge and the date, 1st January 1808.

"A happy New Year, Gentlemen."

"And to you, Sir."

All smiled at the irony.

"Not too much happiness, it would seem, except, of course, amongst the French. Perhaps they are doing the occasion justice. No matter, to work. We are making them pay for their gains, but they are closing us in. However, be not downhearted; remember our objective, to vigorously resist as long as it remains prudent. So, I'm looking for our next chance to give them a bloody nose."

He leaned over the map.

"I'm told, via the telegraph, that the French are moving battalions down to Favazzina and Calabra, both on the coast to our North East. "

He pointed to each in turn, on the map.

"Intelligence also says that they are moving up to Porticello, on the opposite coast, to our South West, between here and Reggio. From what I'm told, it looks like one battalion.

His finger followed the coastline and passed over Scilla, to reach Porticello, midway to Reggio.

"I propose an attack on both Calabra and Porticello, not Favazinna. At Calabra the French will feel themselves protected by Favazzina, and at Porticello they have seen that all our operations against them so far have been on the opposite side of Scilla. A night attack on both will hit the French and delay their operations. My only concern is our access to Calabra, with the French forward at Favazinna and now up on the Aquile Ridge. Captain Carr."

"Sir."

"Get in touch with Sciarpa. Ask him to scout the gap between Favazinna and the French positions on that ridge. Could a column get through and get back? Also ask him to scout the road to Porticello. Can we use the high road, or are there French, so that we should use a side track?"

"Yes Sir. And so's you know, Sir, we've found some boxes of French Navy grenades down in what was their armoury. They could prove useful."

O'Hare nodded indulgently.

"Yes Carr. It'll give them a headache at least."

Carravoy now asked the question that he anxiously wanted an answer to.

"Which companies, Sir?"

"Captain Carr's Lights attack Calabra, your Grenadiers go for Porticello. You can count on Masse' support sufficient to double your numbers, or at least close. Number Three will hold the castle."

"When, Sir."

"When we hear back from the Masse'."

* * *

Carr, Drake and Sciarpa lay at the top of a steep hill overlooking Calabra. Whilst the rest of his command slept, for they had used the night to get there unseen, he studied the objective, making notes and drawing a map. Whilst drawing he passed his Dolland Glass to his companions to enable them to make their own study and perhaps make their own suggestions. One good thing he had noticed; the main road both exited and entered the town almost at the beach, furthest from them, whilst the houses, being nearest to them, rose up the slope in a semi circle. Any French on guard and awake would be at the road, so the attack should go in between the houses where any French occupants would be asleep. He crawled to Sciarpa.

"Any French sentries, sentinelles, you can take care of, yes?"

Carr drew his hand across his throat in the obvious gesture. Sciarpa grinned.

"Yes, Capitano Carr, we can take care. No problem."

Sciarpa grinned again. The more Carr saw of him and his men, the more he liked. Friendships had grown between the men, also. They were tough and skilful, their knowledge of irregular warfare honed over the years of fighting the French occupation. Carr had sent half the Masse' up into the hills, to hold their flank against the French up on the Ridge, the remainder would join in the attack. Carr looked again through his glass and found what he wanted. A large building in the middle of the town, which was the object of much French attention, with supply carts arriving and leaving. Carr turned again to Sciarpa.

"Do any of your men know Calabra?"

"Si, Capitano. Many lived here before French arrivare."

"Can they guide us to that big building in the middle, nel centro?"

Sciarpa looked through the Dolland, took it from his eye and nodded, repeating his reassuring gesture of slapping Carr on the upper arm. Carr laughed, then turned to his Lieutenants.

"Right, Firstly, we go in as three columns, down the centre three streets. Nat you on the left, Barnaby you on the right. Fan off and do as much damage as you can. I'm taking the Masse' in through the centre to fire that big building, so give me two minutes to get there before you open the Ball, but I want two files, six men, from each of your sections. A five minute action, no more. When you hear the bugle sound recall, you get back and regroup on your entry points as a two deep firing line. Clear? Secondly, each man to have one of those French grenades we found, and I want three haversacks of cartridges for my column. If we're going to burn that building, that's what we use. Now, get some sleep."

Simultaneous to this moment, Captain Lord Charles Carravoy was attempting a similar reconnaissance but without anything like the success. If anything, they were lower than the town, for they had needed to quit the highway some way off to avoid French eyes and take to a track that petered out into a field of reeds. These provided good cover for his sleeping men, but the edge of the reedbed was a ditch, then it rose to the road. Carravoy and his two Grenadier Lieutenants were lying sprawled at the road edge, legs down into the ditch, with Carrvoy warming the eyepiece of his spyglass against his eyebrow, it growing hot from agitation. His two Lieutenants, Ameshurst and Berkeley, were down the bank from him, heads besides their removed shakoes, the frontplate of which showed them to be "ex Holyboys, old Ninth".

"I can't see a damned thing, and somehow we're to make a successful attack, somehow, with no idea of the geography of this place."

Berkeley spoke up.

"Can I make a suggestion, Sir?"

He didn't wait for an answer but carried on.

"If you discard your red jacket, Sir, and put on a coat and hat borrowed from the Masse', then you could walk on a mite further, Sir, looking like some kind of farmer. Perhaps go into one of the fields to get a better viewpoint."

Carravoy looked at him, but it was Ameshurst who built upon the idea.

"Yes, Sir, even better, Sir, perhaps one of the Masse' knows this place and can draw a map, then you'll have a better idea of what you're looking at, Sir.

"I have no paper. Either of you?"

Ameshurst answered.

"Yes Sir. Here's some, and a pencil."

All three withdrew and found their interpreter who quizzed their leader, Nicolo Di Ui, Sciarpa's Second in Command. An ex inhabitant came forward and a crude map was drawn. There was nothing special about the town, a main road, a church beside the square, some houses. Carravoy debated within himself the need to get closer and the need for the disguise. In the silence Berkeley spoke up.

"Looking at this map, Sir, it seems our points of entry are here, and here, Sir, assuming we don't go straight up the main road."

Ameshurst continued.

"No indeed. For our first attack, bad idea, but we need to see what's there, Sir. There could be fences and pig pens. Geese! They make a hell of a row. I'll go if you prefer, Sir."

Carravoy looked at them both, from one to the other.

"No. I wish to see for myself."

He turned to the interpreter.

"Can you get me some clothing? A coat and a hat?"

A hat and coat came forward and Carravoy looked at both with utter distaste. The hatband inside was a greasy circle and the coat was torn and filthy, worse inside than out. Nevertheless, Carravoy took off the jacket, put it on and then the hat. He was about to depart, when Ameshurst stopped him.

"Sir, those breeches, Sir. They are, well, rather white and clean; they stand out in huge contrast to the rest of you, Sir. Any Officer putting a spyglass on you would immediately smell a rat, Sir. A bit of dust rubbed on, Sir. To take the edge off, as it were."

Carravoy did the dusting himself, then took himself onto the road and forward, carrying a pole found nearby. The two points of entry matched the map and were easily identified, one, over the far side of the main road in line with the church tower, the other on their side by a large birch tree. Both were clear exits to the fields in which he stood. French uniforms grew in evidence and so he poked around with the pole and decided that enough was enough. He itched all over and his head was sweaty. He shouldered the pole and returned, but he had enough sense to go way past the waiting men before he turned into the reeds and walked back up to them, having already discarded the hat and coat.

"Right. Seems simple. The entrance beyond the road is distinguished by the church tower, that's yours, Berkeley. On this side, the other entrance is shown by a big tree, with trailing branches, that's yours, Ameshurst. I'll be with the Masse'. When I hear you engaged, I'll go in down the main road. We attack when it's dark, but whilst there is still enough light to see our navigation points."

Berkeley looked at Ameshurst.

"What do we do when we get in there, Sir."

"Shoot as many as you can, what else? Do you have any grenades?"

"Some, Sir, but not many."

Carravoy made no reply. He knew that he had made no requisition.

"Well, use what you have. So, into the reeds and wait."

This proved to be unpleasant; mosquitoes and crawling insects created much discomfort which intensified with the dying of the light, but eventually the tree and the tower were just discernible on the grey horizon. Dimly lit windows beckoned along the edge of the town, but gave little light outside. Carravoy went up onto the road, followed by Berkeley and Ameshurst and their men. Berkeley and his section crossed the road and entered the fields, Ameshurst took his along the verge between the road surface and the reeds. Carravoy waited five minutes, then led the Masse' along the road, with Di Ui just behind him. Shouts and musket reports soon came to him from either side, followed by explosions. Grenades were being used. The Masse' filed past him and split into two lines as they progressed on close to the walls on either side, jogging into the town, muskets at the ready, moving faster than Carravoy felt prudent. French uniforms emerged from the houses closeby to be clubbed, knifed and bayoneted by the eager Masse'. The sounds of fighting were ahead on both sides, both his sections were penetrating deep into the town.

Eventually Carravoy and the Masse' entered the square. There were no French apart from a few fugitives running across to the far side, two were dropped by a volley of shots from the Masse'. Shouting in French grew in volume. Carravoy peered forward into the pitch dark, but his ears told him more than his eyes. Many running boots were coming up the road that entered the square on the far side, and it seemed that they would soon reach where they were. Uniformed shapes moved through the poor light from the windows of the houses they passed on the road they were plainly using.

"En avant, mes enfants."

Dim shapes ran off to both sides, many men, as was told by the heavy sound of military boots on cobblestones. Carravoy halted and the Masse' began to retire, backwards, their faces to the threat. He soon joined them.

"Prêt vos mousquets. Tire'"

A volley erupted from the far side of the square. The muzzle flash threw a brief silhouette of Carravoy and his men onto the walls of their side of the square. Several Masse' grunted and fell, two were picked up by their comrades and both were dragged and carried away. Carravoy felt a blow on the outside of his right thigh, but he kept on running, shouting "Retreat." He and his Masse' ran on up the road and sunk gratefully into the reeds. Shouts and shots came from both sides, Berkcley and Ameshurst were still in action, but the sound was coming closer and then muzzle flashes told Carravoy that they also were now in retreat. Minutes passed and Grenadiers began to reach them, breathing heavily from their fast run back. Carravoy was about to question them, when cannon roared out from the main entrance to the town; more than one, and grapeshot whistled down the main road, at chest height. Rather than risk troops in a night action with the Masse', the French were traversing the area with cannonfire, barrels at zero elevation.

Carravoy waited and waited and more of his Grenadiers returned in one's and two's. Eventually Lieutenant Ameshurst came in, bringing in about a dozen of his men. Carravoy seized his arm.

"What happened?"

"On our side, Sir, we got in and did some damage, knocked a few over certainly, but I can only say that the French reacted with astonishing rapidity, Sir. Within minutes we were facing whole companies of them. We had no choice but to fight our way out. Has Berkeley returned, Sir?"

"No."

Ameshurst raised his voice, above the cannonfire.

"Any here from Two Section?"

An answer came from the dark.

"Yes, Sir. Miller here, Sir."

"What of Lieutenant Berkeley?"

"Can't say, Sir. The last I saw of him he was organising a rearguard. He sent us back, Sir. That's all I know."

* * *

As Carravoy was re-gathering his men, Carr was leading his forward. Close to the town they came up to a Masse', kneeling on the prone shape of a French sentry, blood from the sentry's gaping throat soaking the collar of his uniform and glinting in the weak light from the town. Carr took his centre column straight in, the two borrowed files of Lights leading the way on either side, filing quickly on from position to position, the remaining two files and a menacing group of Masse' just behind. Many of the Masse' irregulars began to copy the simple tactics of Carr's men as they advanced rapidly forward. A group of French soldiers emerged from a house to be quickly pounced on and silently dispatched. Carr shouted to his first two files.

"First two files. Hold here. Cover us when we come back."

Carr and the Masse' ran on and he soon saw their target building just as the sounds of Drake and Rushby's attacks came to him. The building was easily identified, it had the highest windows, all showing dim candlelight. Carr, with his six remaining men and the Masse' ran on and reached the door, finding it fully open, both door wings, and populated by a group of astonished French soldiers, unloading a wagon. Carr didn't break stride but ran straight in, leaving the doomed French Storemen to be dispatched by the Masse' irregulars. Inside were more French who were quickly shot or pounced upon by the eager and vengeful Masse; Carr himself felled an open mouthed French Officer, amazed to see red uniforms bursting into his warehouse at gone midnight. Carr looked for the best place to begin his fire. Barrels could be seen in the torchlight and some were smashed in to reveal brandy and some kind of oil. The contents were thrown together over some sacks that seemed to contain clothing, and Carr placed his sack of cartridges on top as did his two fellow incendiaries with theirs. The three of them broke open several cartridges, then one of the soldiers sparked two cartridges in the pan of his musket and tipped the fizzing powder onto the highly combustible pile. The result was an instant and violent conflagration that spread quickly across the warehouse, feeding on the contents of other smashed-in barrels.

"Time to go."

Carr both pushed and motioned his men out and back around the building, ignoring the cries of wounded Frenchman left at the doorway, with the contents now well alight, blazing inside with flames now issuing through the lower building windows. Carr, his Lights and the Masse' sprinted back the way they had come.

Miles, Davey and Pike held their position at the corner where Carr had placed them. Three more redcoats of the other file showed dimly across the street at the far corner. The garrison was coming to life, light showed in all windows around, and voices shouting in French were increasingly being heard. A light came on in the window behind Joe Pike, but Tom Miles had been giving the doors and windows of their closest buildings his full attention. He fired his grenade, waited for the short fuse to burn to the casing, then hurled the black sphere through the window. The loud explosion was followed by screams and then the door opened. Miles shot the first Frenchman to emerge, then smashed forward with the butt of his musket. Joe Pike fired through the door as Miles fixed his bayonet, but no more came forth. Miles shouted across the road.

"You lot. Get your grenades in through those windows. Anyone in there, get 'em dead!"

The three did as they were bid and the three explosions went off in quick succession, starting a fire. Davey looked on into the town, in the direction where Captain Carr and his men had disappeared. The rapidly spreading fire in the target building began to illuminate the streets around them and several figures could be seen. The three opposite were firing up the street to their right, but there was nothing off to Miles' left. From somewhere a bugle sounded recall. Davey spoke urgently.

"Tom, looks like they're comin' back. Get loaded, and you Joe. We could be needed."

The six of them spread across the road as Carr came up with his six and the Masse'.

"My six, form up."

Soon there were twelve across the road, and the Masse', seeing what was happening, stopped and filled the gaps and a solid line soon formed. The French had quickly recovered, good Officers gathering men to mount a counterattack, and one group, at the charge and many in number, came directly after Carr. They were silhouetted perfectly by the burning building.

"Present. Fire!"

More than five dozen muskets were emptied at the pursuing group, causing many to stagger and tumble as they ran into the heavy volley. The French stopped. What else was down that dark street? Carr motioned all back to their first point of entry. Once out, on either side he saw Drake and Rushby's sections forming their own firing line. The Masse' were joining on where they could, thoroughly enjoying themselves; they knew how to fight, these Inglesi! Carr waited. An explosion erupted from somewhere in the town. Rushby's section fired a volley. Carr counted the seconds of one minute. No more French appeared.

"Job done, boys. Time for the off!"

* * *

The atmosphere at the Officer's conference was as cold as the January wind sighing around the battlememts outside their high room. Carravoy sat head down, hands gripping the table edge, head lifting in ill temper, whilst Carr, untypically, sat erect and alert. Simmonds and Heaviside remained upright and stone faced. All knew of the loss of the Grenadiers and the loss of an experienced Officer, but their commiserations on his return had done little to raise the spirits of Carravoy. Frankly, he found them patronising, especially those from Carr.

"Don't let it get you down, Charles. It sounds as though you hit a whole battalion of those damned Voltigeurs. That's why we wish each other luck. We have to resign ourselves to this from time to time, or give up the game."

"You attend to your affairs, Carr, and I'll attend mine."

The frostiness still pervaded, but O'Hare was moving on.

"What is your assessment of the Masse' for holding a pre-pared position? You first, Carr."

"I have every confidence, Sir. They understand the principles of a firing line well enough and can load as fast as a trained soldier. If we integrate them within our companies, Sir, that is, they fight as small groups alongside our men, then I see no problem, Sir."

"Carravoy?"

"Mine behaved as a disorganised rabble that ran at the first threat. However, I'll admit they are keen to fight, and, as Carr suggests, in small groups alongside our men, there are grounds for confidence."

"Any other comments?"

Carr spoke again.

"They are excellent nightfighters, Sir. They would control the area between our lines and those of the French, giving us warning of any night attack, and the Masse' themselves are very adept at night raids. That'll keep the French on edge, and awake!"

At last some humour. Heaviside and Simmonds each managed a half smile.

"Good, because I am withdrawing to the town. Our perimeter will be in three sectors; Carr facing Favazinna and the Aquile Ridge, Heaviside in the centre, Carravoy facing the Reggio road. We'll use the Masse in both the ways you describe, Carr. Talk to Sciarpa, will you? You two seem to have "hit it off" well enough."

Carravoy became even more sour. Barely audible, he mumbled.

"One damn brigand with another."

Carr heard, but let it go. O'Hare was closing the meeting.

"Get off now, the three of youse Captains. Tour the town and decide on your sections. Heaviside, yours is the largest , Carravoy, yours to be the smallest."

It was the only reference that O'Hare made to Carravoy's defeat, but it rankled with Carravoy the most.

Carr took himself directly to the house where Sciarpa had his headquarters. The Masse' Commander, and others, greeted him with loud shouts and waving arms.

"Saluti, Capitano Carr, Saluti."

He then pressed a glass of fierce spirit onto Carr. He had one of his own, so Carr had no choice but to down the appalling liquid in unison. This time there was an interpreter and Carr had no trouble explaining to Sciarpa what O'Hare wanted the Masse' to do. Sciarpa grinned contentedly and nodded vigorously. With all in place, Carr left to go, but Sciarpa stood up and held his sleeve.

"Il mio buono compagno, comrade, Di Ui, dice, he say, altro Ufficiale, other Officer, he is fool, buffoon."

Carr bridled to the criticism of a fellow British Officer, however, resigned to his mission, he nodded slightly, but made no reply, and left.

* * *

Deakin and Halfway were leading a squad of men up the slope from the town, none carried any packs or haversacks, just "weapons and water", but many carried axes and billhooks.

"How far back did Heaviside say we had to take down these trees from the houses, Jed?"

"Hush! I'm countin'"

Deakin had reached 200, that being long exaggerated paces, each of which to him meant a yard.

"Right, we'll start with this one. Any up to here is cut down. Captain Heaviside wants a 200 yard field of fire, that's to here. A time to break down, and a time to build up. Ecclesiasticus, 3, 3, is what he said."

He placed his hand on the trunk of a mature olive tree and looked up through the bare branches at an iron grey sky, such as to subdue and chill even the lightest spirit amongst them but all were heavy that day. He took off his coat and hefted his axe. Halfway was nearby.

"It do seem too much of a sin to cut down trees as prime as these. What if we was to cut down fruit trees as good as these, back home?"

Deakin made no reply, but swung his axe to make the first connection with the hard wood. Soon it was felled, and Deakin straightened up to ease his back, then to see Sergeant Major Gibney marching up."

"Right, thee's started."

"Yes, Sar' Major."

"Well, see that what thee's felled, gets burnt. A felled tree's better cover than one in place and growin'. But take what thee' can for firewood."

"Yes, Sar' Major."

Davey, Pike, and Miles were engaged on a similar task of destruction. Their's was the noisiest; smashing out window frames, ripping up floorboards and nailing layers of them across the window opening, but leaving a narrow horizontal gap for a musket. Upstairs, in the few periods of quiet, could be heard other Lights picking loopholes in the walls.

Miles turned to Davey, who was holding a floorboard in place for Miles to nail up.

"Be that thee? Whimperin'?"

"What have I got to whimper about, besides havin' to spent too much time in the company of the likes of you!"

"Well I can hear whimperin' and I hears more and more of it, the more of these boards we rips up."

Davey looked down through the spaces between the joists. It wasn't bare earth, it was ceiling laths with plaster pushed up between.

"There's a cellar down there."

Miles met his gaze.

"Might have a few bottles, but how d'you get in? There's no door outside. Try the scullery."

They took themselves to the furthest back room with its tubs and sink and searched for a trapdoor. They could see nothing obvious in the room, but they opened a cupboard and its floor was a trapdoor. Miles pulled at the ring handle and the door came up. Davey found what they next wanted.

"Here. Here's a candle."

This was ignited from Mile's tinder box, and the yellow light of the candle showed narrow stairs down. Davey ventured down with Miles in close attendance, the candle held forward and down. The whimpering turned to crying. Reaching the bottom of the stairs showed the source. A collection of women and children were cowering in the corner; what they took to be the Mother, a Grandmother, and four of their children including two girls in their late teens. Even in the far gloom they could see that they were all filthy and unkempt, the remains of food scattered around and half empty sacks of supplies close by. Miles reacted first.

"For Christ's sake Mother, what the Hell are you playin' at? You should be long gone, up into the hills. When the Frenchers find you, well, I've seen what they do. Don't stay here, for the love of the Livin' God."

All was, of course, wholly unintelligible to the cowering and terrified women and children. Miles turned to Davey, whose face showed deep concern even in the poor light of the candle.

"What's to be done?"

Davey's reply was immediate.

"They can't stay here. When it starts, this place could be burnt down. If they do stay and the French find 'em, well, we've seen it."

He paused and thought.

"They can't go now to the hills. The French have closed in."

He thought again.

"Is there a fishing boat still on the beach?"

It was Miles' time to think.

"I recall seein' a couple, still fishin' and sellin' to us."

"Right, let's get them to the beach."

He raised his voice to a shout.

"Joe, get down here. The door's in the scullery. Bring some lads with you. "

A muffled reply filtered down, but soon the thumping of heavy boots told that Joe and others were on their way. Davey motioned the group of civilians to come forward. They had calmed down, clearly the soldiers meant them no harm, they were redcoats and had they meant any harm, it would have been done by now, but none moved. The Mother pointed to the Grandmother and advancing the candle showed that she couldn't stand, she was crippled, hence their hiding, not fleeing. Joe appeared down the stairs. Miles turned away from regarding the family.

"Joe, get a chair down here. We've got to get the old dear out. She can't walk."

Joe called back up the stairs and a small chair was passed down. The frail old woman was lifted onto it and carried to the stairs, then passed up, almost horizontal. Davey posed the question.

"How'd they get her down here in the first place?"

"What's that bloody matter? Down's easier than up. A boat off the beach is what matters now, and quicker the better."

All processed down to the beach, carrying the old woman at shoulder height as though she were some kind of religious relic. They came onto the shingle and were relieved to see a boat still there, stern swinging with the waves, half in and half out of the churning water. The crew were there unloading fish, hard at work. The soldiers carried the woman down to the boat.

"How do we make these understand?"

"Well, Tom, you're good at sign language. Start signin'!"

The fishermen looked up at their approach and stopped work. Miles went up to the first. He pointed vigorously to the civilians, then to the shingle, then made an expansive gesture out over the waves. The fisherman looked at Miles as if he was a lunatic, then one of the girls came forward, laughing, stood besides Miles, and began to speak. It was a short conversation, soon concluded and happily. Miles looked at her with bad temper. The fisherman motioned the party to the boat and all the family were helped aboard, many hands, both fisher and soldier lifting up the Grandmother, still in her chair. Miles, Davey, Pike and the others turned to go when the old woman began to talk furiously, at the same time pointing at Miles and motioning him back to the boat.

"What's she want?"

"Well, go back down there and find out."

Miles went forward, reached the boat and looked up at the wizened, but now kindly face. She began genuflecting down at him whilst reciting weighty Catholic prayers. Miles indulgently remained looking up until a shower of water came down over him, thrown from a tiny glass bottle, and the names Frances of Paola and Saint Gaetano were loudly intoned. Tom Miles, temper rekindled, raised his hand to his forehead. All the soldiers were laughing loudly, which didn't improve his mood, but John Davey knew the significance.

"Leave it Tom, don't wipe it off. She's just blessed you. I think she just made you her Godson!"

The gales of laughter redoubled all round. Miles looked up, the water still dribbling down his face and he drew upon the few words of Italian he knew.

"Grazi, Mother, Grazi. Arrivederci."

The woman and children waved as the boat was launched and the soldiers waved back, but the gesture was unaccompanied by any cheerfullness, rather accompanied wholly by sorrow; more sad civilians uprooted by war.

On the new steps at the rear of the castle, Storeman Sedgwicke looked down upon the strange events with curiousity, but he reached no conclusion regarding what it was about. He quickly turned away to give his attention to the last few barrels and sacks; his head ached, as did his body, and he was mortally tired. Storeships had been arriving, which had determined the hours of his working, not by the hours of day or night, but by the tide and the vagaries of the wind. Thus working through the night and by lamplight, had been common. Not only did he have to carry the supplies into the main store, but also some up the stone steps to the secondary magazines level with the high battlements. He had been working all the previous night, and his brain could not be cudgelled into further analysis of what he saw below on the beach. Some lightly wounded men, those with at least halfway sound arms and legs were providing aid to both himself and Pearson, but Pearson had not half the capability of any of them. The last stores were brought in, then came the decision on which would go further up. Boxes of small mortar shells, the heaviest, were the most obvious, so himself and two soldiers took two boxes between the three of them,

Sedgwicke in the rear. The twisting stairway was carefully negotiated and then they were out in the blast of the wind that existed at that height. Still keeping single file the boxes were lugged into the store behind the battlement, the walkway being now very constricted by the sandbags, then they emerged back once more to repeat their journey. One of the soldiers looked over the battlements to the hills beyond.

"Here comes our company, Parson. Johnny Frog in all his glory."

Sedgwicke followed his gaze, but that did not take in all that there was to see. He had to shift his view from side to side, for all around the circumference of the semi-circle of his view could be seen blue columns emerging from the trees and woods that covered the high ridges. Also, equally dense columns emerged from the grey mist that blurred the horizon to the South-West.

* * *

The Lights were on dawn "stand-to" in their houses, peering through the slowly lightening gloom towards where an attack may materialise, if at all. Several loaded muskets were ready to hand, propped against the wall. No-one spoke, all were concentrating on the small patch of ground revealed by their loop-hole or window slit. Footsteps sounded behind them, but no-one turned to the sound, so intent were they on what lay beyond the fortified wall of their house, but they did turn at the sound of Captain Carr's voice.

"Miles. Pike."

Both lowered their muskets and turned. Captain Carr was carrying two Baker Rifles.

"From now on, I want you using these, they're both from casualties. They're too useful to be left idle. If you've any problems, ask Davey."

Both took the rifles and Pike examined his carefully, but Miles had a question.

"Beg pardon, Sir, but we've heard that the French have taken Reggio. Any truth in that, Sir?'

"Yes, I'm afraid there is. They took it on the 2nd; too damn easily from what I hear."

"It's February now, is it Sir?"

"Yes Miles, Spring's on its way, but I think that the only heat we're going to get in here, will be coming to us from 200 yards out there!"

"Yes, Sir, but we'll hold 'em off, Sir."

Carr smiled and nodded, then left. Miles returned to his window slit.

"Reggio. Pity. I sort of liked that place."

"Ah, right. That's where you crooked that stallholder!"

Shapes appeared in the half dark, but they soon removed their fingers from within their trigger guards. Masse' were coming in whilst the half dawn still hid them from the French. This had been their routine for more than a week. Each day they heard the sound of skirmishing up in the woods, as the Masse' bickered with the most advanced French. Each night also was punctuated by shots, but now the British recognised these as French muskets, the Charleville had a lighter bark than theirs, being smaller bore and longer. In the dark the Masse' did their work with long, sharp knives.

The morning wore on, from breakfast to midday meal, then Pike, at the window turned to his resting companions.

"There's something going on."

Davey, prone on the floor, spoke from under the bandana covering his eyes.

"How'd you know?"

"There's a lot more firing. Has been for some minutes. And look, all the Masse' are coming back, some are wounded."

All in the room that were either lying on the floor or sat against the wall, bounded up to their positions. Ellis came through the door and shouted.

"Stand to."

He left immediately to go elsewhere, almost embarrassed by the needless order. All around the perimeter the Masse' were retiring in, none walking, all running, which told all that this was serious. Cannonfire sounded, but it came to them as echoes, its origins and targets impossible to judge, but what mattered to the soldiers at their loopholes and firing posts was that nothing was hitting them.

O'Hare and Simmonds up on the highest point of the battlements, looking for developments, both using spyglasses, O'Hare to the hills, Simmonds to the plains further around to the right. Both saw lines of blue coated infantry, but only O'Hare saw field artillery that was accompanying the attack on Carr's ridge front, but none elsewhere, and he took note of the size of the guns. The French field artillery was of a heavier calibre that the British, eight pounds rather than six, and the French had advanced them as far as they dared in front of their infantry. From there they were employed for counter battery fire against the castle, rather than the houses and barricades that were the objectives of their infantry.

"George, what do you judge to be the distance of those pieces before Carr's sector?'

"Two hundred and fifty, give or take."

"I agree. I want our batteries up here to concentrate on the infantry. Get a message to Carr to get his rifles up to his upper windows and do what he can against their gunners. You'd agree?"

"I would and consider it done."

O'Hare screwed his face as he raised his glass to his eye once again.

"You know, I'm of a mind to say that this fellow doesn't know what he's about."

Simmonds didn't enquire who O'Hare was referring to, but dashed off a note which was handed to a runner who sped down the steps with equal haste. Soon Ellis was re-appearing in the downstairs room of Miles, Pike, and Davey."

"You three, and anyone else with a Baker. Get upstairs. Captain's orders."

The three identified, plus another, ran up to the bedrooms that faced out to the oncoming French. Ellis was with them and he indicated the loopholes.

"Look out through these. You can make out their cannon. Pick off the gunners. Never mind the infantry, get the Frogs that man those guns."

Miles was not convinced.

"But those cannon aren't aimin' at us, it's the infantry that's comin' for us. Who takes care of them?"

"You obey orders, Miles, or I'll see you swing. The infantry'll be taken care of."

Miles lifted the unfamiliar Baker through the nearest loophole. Davey had adjusted his sight for him.

"Swing, will I? I don't know how he can tell unless he looks along the gunbarrel same time as I!"

It was Davey who replied.

"Just get those gunners, Tom. They'm the danger, either now or later."

Davey pulled the trigger and brought his rifle in to begin a rapid reload. Miles looked along the sights and lined the foresight with the backsight and a French gunner about to use a ramrod. He pulled the trigger. Through the thinning smoke Miles saw the gunner cling to the muzzle of his gun, without the ramrod, and slump to the ground to lie prone beneath the barrel. He raised his eyebrows in delighted surprise and began his own reload.

All around the perimeter the firing lines waited, soldiers and Masse', two deep or three, many with spare loaded muskets. Heaviside stood at a barricade, D'Villiers at his side, the former quoting from the Bible, the latter barely able to speak.

"Is not the Lord gone out before thee? Judges, Chapter Four, verse fourteen."

"Y'yes Sir. But, will our men stand, Sir? There seem to be thousands of French."

"He will not fail thee, neither forsake thee: fear not, neither be dismayed. Deuteronomy, Chapter 31, verse 8.

He turned to look fully upon D'Villiers.

"And neither will our men, Lieutenant, properly led."

He climbed up besides those men and judged the distance to the advancing French. Then he shouted to all, near and far.

"Right, men, we'll give them 50 more yards then give them some more of what they got at Maida. Aim low men, better to blow off a toe than nothing at all!"

His men grinned and chuckled at the grim, but familiar humour, then they heard what they had expected in the first place.

"Let no man's heart fail because of him; thy servant will go and fight with this Philistine. First Samuel, Chapter 17, verse 32."

Heads shook in amused disbelief, mouths that were set in a grim line managed a smile, and fingers flexed around the stocks of their muskets and many checked again the priming in the pan. Heaviside stepped down and returned to D'Villiers. When close to him, he leaned forward and whispered.

"Draw your sword, Lieutenant, and stand up alongside your men. Let them see that you are there. At fifty yards open fire, you give the order."

D'Villiers drew his ornate and expensive sword and did as required. Meanwhile, his friend, Lord Charles Carravoy was awash with a mixture of emotions; fear again, but also some determination; this time they suffer. Carravoy looked at Ameshurst, stood with his men, all at the make ready, and then at Gibney stood where Berkeley should have been. The sight of the absence of Berkeley and presence of Gibney gave a final push to Carravoy's competing emotions. Gibney was closest, and carrying his musket he sidled over to Carravoy.

"Beggin you pardon, Sir. But when do you want us to open fire, Sir? At what range? And will you give the order, Sir?"

Carravoy's reply was to ignore Gibney and shout, at the top of his lungs.

"At under 100 yards we will open fire. Take your orders from me."

From somewhere came a shout.

"We'll give 'em some back for Porticello, Sir."

Carravoy ignored it. He was intent upon the approaching French. He was both impressed and intimidated by their perfect alignment, their regular step to the beat of their drums. In addition, their fine uniform and the bravery of their Officers, advancing out in front, sword moving as they marched, but fear arrived within him again as the sound of their massed drums grew louder. Suddenly, from behind him he heard the roar of their own artillery from the castle and the unmistakable whine of grape whistling overhead to fling men backward to the earth as though they were discarded dolls. Carr and Heaviside, observing similar before their own positions, shared the same thought, as though linked by telepathy.

"They can have some more of that, before we open fire."

O'Hare looked at all before and told himself, "So far, so good."

He was indeed content. The French artillery fire against the castle was wholly ineffective, firstly because the battlements were new and reinforced, secondly because so few cannon could maintain a high rate of fire, such was the toll exacted amongst the gunners from the accurate fire from Carr's riflemen. He continued to watch, then smoke billowed from Carravoy's position, then the sound of the volley came to him. Seconds later came the same from Heaviside and Carr. Ranks of Frenchmen were swept down as if by a giant hand and the punishment continued as the volleys by ranks crashed out. The French stood it for

a minute, their Officers urging them on, some with their shakoes on the ends of their swords as they danced before their
battered ranks. But to no avail, first the centre fell back, then
those before Carr and Carravoy. The British muskets ceased,
then his heart missed a beat. The Masse' leapt over the barriers
to pour forward after the fleeing French, there were some
redcoats amongst them, but mercifully few. He turned to his
bugler.

"Sound recall, loud as you can."

The notes rang out and the redcoats stopped, but not the
Masse', barely a few stopped on seeing the redcoats halt at the
sound of the recall. He put his glass to his eye and swept across
the landscape, then he saw what he dreaded, French cavalry
trotting forward in perfect formation, mercifully not a massed
Brigade, but enough to do severe damage. He could only hope
that the recall would save some. The Masse' were now split in
two waves. Some, blood up, were pursuing the French killing
as many as they could reach, others, perhaps with less revenge
in their hearts but certainly more prudence, had pursued as
far as they felt the risk allowed. These had stopped and were
making their way back, but for those far out, there was now
little hope. In two squadrons, fanning out on either side, the
French charged, not a headlong gallop, more a cold blooded
canter. The slower speed would still catch the Masse', and give
more time for a precise and fatal blow. These had now realized
their danger and were running back, dropping their weapons to
aid their flight, but now many were being ridden down, the
French Dragoons choosing their blow carefully, either a chop
down onto the back of the neck or to just overtake and send a
backhand swing back into the face.

O'Hare saw a Masse' Commander, Di Ui, he thought, rallying those closest to the British into some kind of firing line. He
succeeded in establishing some kind of order, but his failure to
achieve a perfect line was of more benefit, what he achieved
was a solid block of men that could at least make their way
back to the barricades. The Dragoons saw this obvious target
and charged for it. The result was casualties on both sides,
Masse' killed with swords, and Dragoons by musket fire, and
bodies in Dragoon blue and colourful Masse' civilian marked
the surviving Masse's passage back to the British lines. The
French had inflicted severe casualties on the Masse', and lost

453

men themselves doing it, these to be added to those lost in their main attack. O'Hare resignedly called the day a draw, but allowed in favour of the British.

* * *

Lieutenant Barnaby Rushby closed his greatcoat collar against the rain that was an infrequent event for this part of Calabria, but it was falling and it was wet. It was coming through a hole in the roof that hadn't been there when he first came on duty, but the roof didn't have his attention. He was looking for but hoping not to see the dreaded black dot. He had been told that if you could see it rise a little at the top of its trajectory, then you had half a second to get out of the way, because a cannonball was coming straight at you. He could be seen peering anxiously through the narrow firing slit of a top window of the house his section occupied. He waited for gaps in the smoke that shrouded the French gunline, through which to see the feverish activity exhibited by the French artillerymen, who were creating "black dots" for the opposing British as fast as they could.

If O'Hare's conclusion that the French Commander did not know what he was about was correct, in the days that followed he showed that he had learned his lesson. His field artillery had been pulled back out of musket range and ordered to concentrate on the houses and barricades from which the British and the Masse' had taken such a heavy toll of the attack the previous day. The heavy, Naval thunder of newly arrived siege guns added to the weight of shot now sent against the flimsy houses and temporary barricades. The British and Masse', holding their positions, had no choice but to sit and take it or withdraw. The guns in the castle could not reach their French counterparts to give either aid or succour. The worst of the punishment came on the Light Infantry sector, where the French had placed their siege guns, up the slope to give greater range.

Carr and Drake were in discussion of their plight in the upstairs room next to Rushby's, when a shot came in through the outside wall at such velocity that it went out the back, having punched a neat hole in both walls. Both looked at each other, final realisation now shared between them.

"Get your men out and behind the baricades. They are more able to resist shot. All of them, and maintain a watch from there. Rushby's to hold the next row of houses. I'm off to see the Major."

Carr found O'Hare and Simmonds observing all from their usual high vantage point intent on the action before them. Carr coughed politely. O'Hare turned and beckoned him forward.

"I know what you are going to tell me, Captain, that we can no longer hold the outer perimeter of houses. It just causes us casualties with no gain. Moving on from there, I'm of the growing opinion that the whole town itself is untenable. If we withdraw from the outer houses, do we move back into them when the French attack again? I think not; that may well involve us in costly street fighting. I believe it is time to withdraw to the castle. Your opinion?"

"Total agreement, Sir. It's why I came."

Carr thought his reply, especially the last addition, sounded a trifle insolent. He added another "Sir".

O'Hare said nothing, so Carr continued.

"I've pulled half my company back to the second line of houses, Sir, the rest are maintaining a watch from the barricades."

"Very prudent, Captain. I've just issued an order exactly to that effect. You and it must have crossed over, but I'm glad you're here, as my unofficial liaison Officer. I will withdraw at night, but the castle won't hold us all, us and the Masse', who are still almost twice our number. Resisting a siege is a job for soldiers and artillerymen, not irregulars. They will add little to the defence, but add to the evacuation when it comes and add to the food and water we need brought to us. Also, if the castle does fall quickly, the Masse' will be captured and we all now know what the French do to civilians who take up arms against them. They have to be taken off, so I'm sending a semaphore for transports to cross over tomorrow. Please convey this to Mr Sciarpa and ask him to be ready."

Carr saluted and left. He re-entered the town, still echoing to the sound of heavy shot demolishing roofs and walls, and hurried to Sciarpa's headquarters. The greeting was the same, also the fierce libation, but Carr soon got them down to business and the interpreter passed on O'Hare's orders. Sciarpa sat back, then sat up, then narrowed his dark brown eyes, his expression showing an affront to both his honour and dignity. He began a rapid dialogue with the interpreter, who nodded rapidly. Sciarpa finished by pointing at Carr.

"Cio gli dire."

The interpreter began.

"Signore Sciarpa says that the Masse' have taken too many backward steps and they do not quit their sacred soil to leave the French to, how you say? Burn and pillage. The Masse' will attack them once more. We that break through will continue the fight in the hills. We will not go. This night we attack."

Carr was astonished, almost horrified. He began a reply, speaking urgently.

"If we take you off in ships, we can land you anywhere, all of you, to continue the fight behind the French lines. Translate."

The interpreter did so and Sciarpa's face changed from outrage to interest. Carr continued.

"You will have all your men, and the more men the more damage you will do. The fight will go on."

Carr motioned in the direction of Sciarpa for the translation and the interpreter obliged, but this time Sciarpa replied, at length, with much pounding of the table. The interpreter turned to Carr.

"Signore Sciarpa says that he likes what you say, but they must make one more attack. They will not walk quietly away, like cur, dog, how you say, with tail between legs? We now make plan, and the plan is to be done, or the Masse' will attack to break out. The honour of the men of Calabria says it must be so."

At the finish Sciarpa nodded vigorously. Carr looked at him and could do no more than offer his hand across the table. Sciarpa took it, then they started talking.

* * *

It was a half hour before dawn and three British Officers stood on the high bastion that overlooked the town. It was still dark, but a keen February wind came out of the full blackness that closed in on all sides. O'Hare, Simmonds, and Carr had instinctively huddled together for warmth.

"I hope this plan works, that you've cooked up; Captain."

"So do I, Sir, but they were adamant, I'm afraid, Sir. A matter of honour. One more attack, if not on our terms, then on theirs. I don't think we had much choice, Sir, and I think we'll do the French some damage, if we get the timing right."

Major O'Hare replied, scepticism seeping through his Irish brogue.

"Ah, yes, you're right there, Captain Carr. As in so many things, timing is everything."

Carr looked at his watch, then to the East. A clear streak showed just above the horizon, his watch showed 15 minutes before the due hour of dawn. He fired his pistol and the instant reply was a cannon report and the reply to that, although not so immediate, was an outburst of firing, explosions, and shouts at the French lines opposite Carr's Light Company. The Masse' had sprung forward, out of the dark, one massed attack at one point, launched just yards before the French lines from positions they had silently taken up an hour before dawn. The sounds of the conflict grew fierce, but nothing could yet be seen apart from the flashes and explosions that seemed to be progressing up the slope. Were they pushing further? Carr looked again to the East and saw that what had been just a streak was now a whole section of illuminated sky. The ground of the attack was in the shade of the hills behind, but soon that same light would reach the slope that was taking the force of the Masse onslaught. He looked again and anxiously watched, his pulse rate as high as though he were up there, immersed in the fight with them. Minutes passed as the light grew. Fires were burning and frantic shapes could be seen manically entering and leaving those areas of dancing light. O'Hare raised his own glass, the rapidly breaking dawn had given him the amount of light he needed.

"They're in, Carr, no doubt about that. They're capering about on his gun line."

He raised his glass a little.

"And they're up to and firing the French camp. I do believe many French are running back beyond that. Pray God, many don't follow them."

He closed his glass.

"Enough, Carr, sound your guns."

Carr again fired his pistol and the signal guns began, at fifteen second intervals. Carr lay down his pistol and took up his own glass and focused it.

"I do believe they're obeying, Sir. I see them coming back. Now, the part with the most concern. It's full light and they're out in the open, but, if it works!"

He moved his glass up slightly.

"Well, this is it, it's started."

Carr, as had O'Hare, had seen the inevitable cavalry coming down the slope to counter-attack. The Masse' were now highly vulnerable, a disorganised crowd, streaming back in retreat, with several hundred yards to cross before reaching safety. Carr saw his own command advance out a short distance in files of three to give some covering fire, but the distance was yet great. The cavalry were at full gallop, eating the ground between them and their intended victims. However, few French troopers noticed some white posts in the ground beside them as they rode past, so intent were they on the hated Masse'. At that point every cannon in the castle that could bear opened fire and maintained a barrage as fast as the gunners could load. The smoke hid much, but through the gaps they could see that the cavalry charge was now a forlorn hope. The British gunners had used the range posts perfectly and the grapeshot had hit the French horsemen at just below maximum range, turning men and their mounts into bloody rags. The first lines had almost all fallen, hindering the passage of the remainder, whilst the incessant grape shot continued to take its toll. Many of the Masse' had stopped their running to turn and observe, then striking contemptuous gestures at the suffering French, but soon all had run between the covering files of the Light Company. The few cavalry that survived were either brought down by the riflemen or scared off by the formed up company. Carr turned to Major O'Hare, but he couldn't hide his pleasure.

"Well, I think that worked, Sir. At least after a fashion. I better go down and see Sciarpa. I expect he's quite pleased with himself."

O'Hare nodded his assent and Carr descended through the castle. The Masse' were all back in the streets, forming a very lively jumble of elated men, all shouting and congratulating themselves, pummelling each other's backs and shoulders, whilst waving both weapons and trophies in the air. Carr was at a loss to decide where Sciarpa was, but his headquarters seemed as good a place as any, and indeed that's where Carr found him, not inside but out, sharing the triumph with his men. As soon as Sciarpa saw Carr he ran to him and dragged him over to wall, mounted it himself, then hauled Carr up beside him. He took a pistol and fired it. It did little to quell the noise, but all at least turned around, then Sciarpa started shouting, whilst gesturing towards Carr. The speech lasted for little more than a minute, but during the pauses, Sciarpa pointed at Carr and the crowd responded "Urra". Carr knew when the speech had finished because Sciarpa seized him, kissed his cheek, just one; standing on a wall made kissing the other very perilous, then Sciarpa undid his own red bandana that was the Masse' badge and tied it around Carr's neck. Carr stood upon his wall, wholly nonplussed, but he regained enough presence of mind to shake Sciarpa's hand and shout.

"You're all brave men."

Sciarpa, showing a better command of English than hitherto, translated.

"Il Capitano dice che siamo degli uomini coraggiosi."

He beat his own chest.

"Courage, si?"

The result was an outburst of more "urras", and they both descended from the wall. Carr felt in danger from all the backslapping, some from hands still containing weapons, but the interpreter had arrived. Carr took shelter behind him.

"Tell Signore Sciarpa that the transports are waiting. Please lead his men to the beach and to the boats. The British are now giving up the town."

Sciarpa listened to the Italian, then came and stood before Carr and seized his upper arms and shook Carr once.

"La buona fortuna, Carr di Capitano. You are molto uomo. Much man."

Sciarpa walked away without looking back and that was the last Carr saw of him.

Chapter Thirteen

Full Siege

Storesman Percival Sedgwicke sat hunched in terror at his small table, trying to maintain accurate records of stores booked in and issued. His superior, Storesman Sergeant Pearson lay on his bed, hands forming a "dead Bishop", his eyes staring at the ceiling. Sedgwicke did his best to concentrate, but his attention was drawn every half minute, or less, to small flakes of masonry falling down the wall at his side, in addition the accompanying dust was clogging his pen. Inside their store, beneath the level of the battlements, they had heard the beginning of the bombardment as loud thumps against the outside wall, but now, with the damage having penetrated deeper, the sounds of impact were louder and the signs of it more potent. Sedgwicke winced visibly as more thumps came in quick succession and the whole of the inner surface of a stone came away, to leave a neat indent half way up their stores wall. The debris falling onto a barrel added to the effect.

"Now what did I tell 'ee, Percy? These Frogs be something special, you think you've knocked 'em back, but they just springs back at you. We'll be lucky to get out of here in one piece, you mark my words."

He looked up to discover what Sedgwicke was up to.

"Why in the Lord's Name are you doing all that bookin' in and out for? No one's going to check, nor nothin'. You're wasting your time."

Sedgwicke made no reply, he simply cleaned his clogged pen once more. The truth was that the familiarity of his routine was a huge comfort. He was more afraid now than at any time since setting foot on Calabria and he sought solace in the commonplace.

What Sedgwicke could hear, O'Hare could also feel, through his feet. On the highest battlement he could see the smooth operation of the French batteries and feel the impact of the shot through the ancient stone, but neither of these had his attention at that moment. He was not depressed, far from it, his men had, so far, given a very good account of themselves, but what he saw through his telescope told him that the "day of prudence" was now not so far into the future. From the direction of the South West, teams of bullocks were drawing heavy artillery along the coast road. What the French had captured at Reggio they had now brought up to use against Scilla. He estimated that these additional heavy siege pieces would be in action some time tomorrow; he had pondered the battery positions built in a prime position but held empty and now he knew their purpose. He turned to a Sergeant held in the role of aide de camp.

"Officers meeting in my quarters. 15 minutes."

At the due time all entered close upon each other and took their seats. Their mood matched O'Hare's, serious and somber but businesslike and confident, their performance so far against the French spoke for itself. O'Hare began.

"You may have noticed, as I just have myself, our opponents arriving with additional siege guns, undoubtedly to be slotted into the empty battery opposite. From then it will only be a matter of a short time before we must leave. Major Simmonds, your thoughts, please."

"Well, Major. We have kept the French to a slow rate of fire. At first our riflemen made good sport amongst their gunners, and our batteries being on a higher level than theirs, took a heavy toll also. However, our batteries are now slowly being destroyed. The sandbag reinforcements delayed this significantly and we've got some guns back into action, but our fire is slackening, whilst theirs is increasing. At first we forced them to build facines to protect their embrasures, which slowed them up having to roll them back and forth each time, but they have now perfected their technique and are firing at maximum. These additional guns will undoubtedly put all ours out of action within a day or so. Then we will be left only with the rifles as any method by which we can do them any damage."

"What then?"

"With counter-battery fire no longer of any concern to them, they will concentrate on breaching, and with the number of guns that they will have this will take two forms. Firstly to create a breach and secondly to completely destroy the parapet above it, giving any defenders no more than an exposed platform to stand on, exposed to grapeshot from their guns as their assaulting parties scale the ladders."

"How long?"

"We're down to the last few days."

"So, gentlemen, are we at the end of "prudent resistance", do we evacuate now, or hold on a while longer?"

There was a moments silence, but during it, Carr leaned forward, looked at the others and saw that no-one else was going to start, so he did.

"We still have opportunities to do them damage, Sir. I've looked at the cliff and the castle wall they've got to scale to get up, and it's a horror. We could at least drop our mortar shells onto their heads as they mill about down below, and also this castle's concentric, I believe that's the term," he looked at Simmonds, who nodded, "so we give them the outside wall then carry on the fight from the inner."

O'Hare grinned.

"Anyone else?"

Simmonds began again.

"We will not stop them getting in, when they come. They have the guns, they have the manpower. The issue is do we stay and fight the siege some more, then fight a rearguard, with the French at our heels and all the risk that entails, or evacuate now before they assault?

O'Hare looked from Simmonds to Carr.

"I hear you, Captain Carr, but my priority now is to get all the garrison away. I don't see how we're going to do them any more significant damage other than when we fight our way out, that means waiting for them to attack and then mounting a perilous rearguard action, which could jeopardise our chances of complete evacuation. However, the final decision isn't mine. I will telegraph General Sherbrooke and inform him of developments and my forecast for the next few days. Meanwhile, do we ask our artillerymen to maintain the unequal contest? They've taken significant casualties. Major Simmonds?"

"For counter battery fire, no! That will only cost lives and delay the French very little from the inevitable. We can pull some light guns in off the parapet and hold them back, ready to redeploy to cover the causeway, if, or more like when, the French attack. If we wish to at least mount some show of resistance I would suggest Captain Carr's riflemen on the topmost embrasures. These are untouched and too high to make any difference if they were destroyed. Our cannon are gone, so it makes more sense for the French to concentrate on breaching. Johnny's target is the assault walls. So, accurate rifle fire from above will keep them nervous, if nothing else."

O'Hare turned to Carr.

"Captain Carr, can that be so?"

"Yes Sir. But, with respect, Sir, I do think that we can fight off one attack, at least, we've ...."

He was interrupted by O'Hare.

"Yes, Captain, I've heard you. You may yet get your wish, but from this moment, I am planning to avoid it. You have your orders. The matter's closed. Good luck, gentlemen, dismiss."

* * *

Joe Pike pressed the hard walnut against his cheek, closed his left eye, let the muzzle drop down, then squinted along the barrel. He waited for the two fascines to open and when they did he followed the edge of the left one across with his foresight, hoping to see a blue uniform, but none showed. The heavy cannon fired and all was enveloped in white smoke. When it cleared, the fascines had been rolled back. Another heavy ball had added to the almost total dismemberment of the parapet down on the left hand bastion below him. Pike shifted his aim to the window of a house behind and his perfect eyesight detected the suggestion of a pale face. He fired and withdrew from the embrasure, his place taken by another rifleman, ready and loaded. Joe Pike joined Sergeant Ellis and John Davey who were both cleaning their rifles after a long morning plus much of the afternoon at the battlements. Sedgwicke was close by, practically on his knees, giving out cartridges, and water. On the castle roof it was warm, despite the early month, and all were thirsty from the long session of firing. Davey gave him a cheery smile.

"Hello, old Parson. Delivering the necessary? It's all right, you don't need to crawl, the Johnnies can't see you up here."

Suddenly, the soldier who had replaced Pike jerked back with much of his head missing, dust and stonework flew up and back. Ellis gave him but a glance.

"That's grapeshot."

Davey's face showed his surprise, besides his concern.

"Forget what I said, Parson, you may have the right of it."

Sedgwicke was alternating between shades of white and green, overlaid by a look of utter horror. He took himself to the seaward battlement and was violently sick.

Ellis had reached the same embrasure, but peered carefully around the stonework. He saw the telltale cannon smoke swinging away from the upper windows of a house, one row back and higher than the main French battery. Their position was confirmed by significant holes in the wall beneath the windows.

"Those bastards have got some light guns up into those houses behind. Any of you scored a hit in the main batteries yet?

There was no reply, other than the shaking of heads.

"Right. When you see a muzzle poke out of those holes, send your shots through the hole and the window above. Concentrate on them; there's more purpose."

They answered the light cannon until the light failed with the growing dusk, then they were told to stand down and return to their quarters back in the castle. Whilst filing down the stairs they were passed by the Grenadiers going the other way, up to man the battlements, both as sentries and to be there to make the first resistance to any attack, now regarded as imminent. In their quarters, the Lights found Sedgwicke again, now recovered, and this time with the barrels of salt pork and sacks of dried peas. This time Tom Miles showed his appreciation, his words dispelling the impression created by his hellish appearance after hours on the firing line.

"Well done, Parson. You're a good comrade, it's the truth and that's your due. Full ready with what's needed. We're grateful."

Many echoed Miles' words, and Sedgwicke's grin split his face as he doled out the rations, giving more than measure. There was plenty still in stores and none would be taken back. Around their cooking pots, all heating upon the large fire, there was little conversation, one stirred the broth whilst the others saw to their equipment. Just the simple exchange of glances, nods, and smiles that conveyed amongst them the shared acknowledgement of another day survived.

Captain Carravoy and his Grenadiers had reached the walkway above the main beach that looked out onto The Straits, the walkway led seaward back to the newly cut steps. The change in the weather added to his black mood. With him was Lieutenant D'Villiers, off duty, but seeking conversation. Lieutenant Ameshurst and Sergeant Major Gibney walked together along the battlement, checking the sentries, whilst the remainder of the company took shelter from the fine rain in whichever holes and corners offered themselves. Carravoy and D'Villiers leaned over a crenellation that was sheltered by the looming battlement above and watched the tide go out. Small waves rose from the calm sea to flop exhausted on the hard shingle, creating white surf that the ebbing tide slowly pulled back towards the foot of the steps that led down to the beach at the rear of the castle. They said little; in their own way, each had learned to cope with the constant danger, but the high anxiety from being always under the French assault was a permanent drain on both their nerves and their temper. Eventually D'Villiers spoke the question that had been growing within him since their own guns had no longer been able to reply their own defiance.

"Which do you think, evacuated, prisoner, or dead?"

Carravoy shrugged.

"Your guess is as good as mine. We have O'Hare in charge here, with Sherbrooke pulling the strings over there, and Simmonds chipping in, as and when. O'Hare wants us out and I agree, but Sherbrooke has to decide. Carr doesn't, damn fool that he is; he wants us to stay and carry on this hopeless charade. I swear he'd send the lot of us down the river if it meant the killing of one more Frenchman. The man's a lunatic, a dangerous lunatic, but he's been overruled, by O'Hare, thank Heaven. So now, it's all about Sherbrooke saying yes, the boats coming over, and us getting out before our French friends get in. Personally, I have little trust in any of them."

At that moment Gibney approached out of the dark, came to the attention and saluted.

"Beg pardon, Sir."

Carravoy turned to face him.

"Yes, what is it?"

"One of t'sentries, Sir, the one closest to the French. He's worried, Sir, thinks he's seen something, something white, Sir, and heard equipment janglin' too. Sir."

"Which one?"

"Henshaw, Sir. He's old Norfolk, Sir, and seen a bit."

"He's probably got the jitters about a night assault, like we all have."

"Like we all have, Sir. Yes Sir."

Carravoy detected the condescending tone, but Gibney continued.

"But 'tis an extra low tide tonight, Sir. Chance perhaps for the French to get around the side of us, see what can be done. Shall I take some men down t'steps, Sir? Take a look, like, just in case?"

Carravoy's annoyance was hid by the darkness but the concern of a veteran Sergeant Major couldn't be ignored.

"Very well. Take ten men. And tell Lieutenant Ameshurt I've asked him to take charge. He at least has a level head."

"Shouldn't we warn Major Simmonds, Sir?"

"No, let's see what we have. Almost certainly it's a false alarm."

Gibney roused up the nearest ten men and told them to check their priming and fix bayonets. He took up his own musket and did the same. Ameshurst eased his sword in its scabbard and checked the priming pan of his own pistol, but he did not replace it into his waistband but let the weight of it carry his arm down to his side. Ameshurst left the battlement and went to the walkway that led to the steps.

"Sergeant, form on me. All of you, at the "make ready". Right, come on."

He led forward through the almost complete darkness to where the walkway joined the steps.

"Henshaw says he saw white, you say?"

"That's right Sir. White."

"Hmmm, could be crossbelts."

He turned to his men, speaking just above a whisper.

"If the Sergeant and myself fire, you fire in pairs, then drop to your knees to be clear for the next behind. Then it's bayonets. Am I understood?"

Several "Yes Sirs" came from the dark and Ameshurst began his descent. Gibney's bayonet led the way, the barrel against Ameshurst's right arm. To Ameshurst's left was the open drop to the beach. The steps were wet from the rain and water trickled down the rock to their right and the sound of the waves grew with each step descended, but they were now out beyond the narrow band of surf. One of his men hissed in an audible whisper.

"Sir, I'm sure I heard something, Sir. Like someone swearin'."

Ameshurst stopped.

"No lower. Hold here, I'm not losing any more height. I go on alone."

Ameshurt fully cocked his pistol, but Gibney, even though it was a hanging offence, grabbed his arm.

"Sir, if thee goes down there and if there is a gang of Johnnies, that's a death sentence, Sir. They'll have you against this rock like a rat on a wall."

Gibney saw Ameshurst's teeth grin white in the gloom.

"Yes, Sergeant, thank you for your concern. But we must check, right to the bottom. If they are there, we must hit them early, the sooner we can hit them before they ascend too far, the better"

"Then I'm comin' with thee, Sir."

"No you're not. Stay here and command the men. Now; I'm going, we've wasted time."

Ameshurst drew his sword, transferred his pistol to his left hand and continued down. Gibney watched his back disappear into the gloom and the fine rain. Ameshurst slowly descended, one step at a time, to listen and peer forward. A sound came up, was it the scrape of a musket butt on the stone? He crouched down and waited, counting the seconds. If he reached thirty, he'd go on. He didn't get to five. A figure with a sword and large epaulettes grew out of the dark and rain below him. Ameshurst raised his pistol and fired. The figure jerked back amongst the white crossbelts behind, and Ameshurst looked over down to the sea. The water was full of wading men, all with muskets held high, and he knew at that moment that his muzzle flash had been his death sentence.

Gibney heard the massive volley that was loosed at Lieutenant Ameshurst and gave his own orders.

"Fire by ranks, aim down t'steps."

He fired his own musket then knelt to reload as the soldiers behind obeyed Ameshurst's last orders, the muzzles of the first two muskets erupting above his head, but Gibney realised that these muzzle flashes were showing their own position. He waited for all to fire.

"Up ten steps. Do it again."

Thus the small squad began a fighting rearguard back up the way they had come. No French came up to them, but bullets were slamming into the rock above the steps as the French fired at where their muzzle flashes showed them to be, or had been.

The sound of Ameshurst's pistol jerked Carravoy out of the mood of angry depression that he had sunk further into. Realisation came quick, clear, and disconcerting, that his men had been right and he had been wrong.

"Sergeants! Get the men up and along the walkway. The French are attacking this side. Sentries, with me."

Carravoy, with his sentries, ready and loaded, ran along the walkway. D'Villiers was caught up in the rush and joined in, not sure what to do, he had no weapon. Carravoy soon saw the muzzle flashes of the French; he emptied his own pistol then ran on to meet Gibney's squad making their retreat.

"Form here. Rapid fire."

Up on the highest battlement, surrounded by his Number Three Company, Captain Heaviside had been composing his next prayer for the safety of his family when he heard the sounds of the ferocious action beginning below.

"Alert! Alert"! Man the right battlements. Pick your targets. Rapid fire."

His men ran to obey, but Heaviside was thinking elsewhere. He grabbed the first NCO he saw.

"Deakin. Get ten men to the front battlement. Light the torches and throw them over, far out, the causeway especially. This may just be a diversion for the main attack. If you see anything coming, send a runner to the Major and a runner to me. Clear?"

"Yes Sir."

Deakin already had Halfway at his side and the two of them each stopped five more. They ran to the front battlement, fired twelve of the torches kept there and flung them far out off the battlements. The burning brands each arced down towards both the beach and the causeway and they hit the stones with a burst of sparks.

"You lot. Get to an embrasure and keep your eyes very open. If you sees anything, shout, at once!"

Unsurprisingly, Deakin and Halfway were at neighbouring embrasures.

"You think this is the main attack, Jed?"

"Don't know. Time will tell. But one thing I do know is that this is the end of the cannonin'. From now on they'm comin' at us."

At the steps, the weight of fire hitting the French was now appalling, as from both above and from the side the Grenadiers and Heaviside's men kept up an incessant fire, firing in relays from the embrasures and walkway. The French were trapped, stood waist deep in the cold waters, and burning torches had lodged on the steps to give enough light for the British above. Soon any French left alive were making their escape, wading painfully slowly out of the light, giving no return of fire to betray their position. Soon there was no-one left for the British to fire at; the surface of the sea close to the castle rock was covered in dead bodies, half floating, their lifeless limbs moving in slow motion with the waves of the incoming tide that would return them to the beach from which they had come.

Carravoy seized Gibney's arm to turn him around. Gibney obeyed the tug on his sleeve and saluted.

"What're our casualties, Sergeant?"

"Three wounded, two dead. Sir."

"Lieutenant Ameshurst?"

"Missing, Sir, but I think he must be dead, Sir. He went down alone, Sir, to take a look. He fired his pistol, then a whole volley was fired at him. I don't see how he could have survived, Sir."

Carravoy's spirits sank further. His final Lieutenant dead, acting bravely, as had Berkeley. However, at that moment there came a great commotion amongst his men on the walkway, mostly shouting "Glad to see you, Sir." From amongst them came a dripping Ameshurst, boots squelching as he walked. Gibney couldn't stop himself from clapping his huge hand on the Lieutenant's shoulder, another hanging offence.

"Thee's got out, Sir. What did th'do?"

"Well, I remembered your wise words, Sergeant Major, about rats on a wall, and as soon as I fired, I jumped into the sea. There were French all around, but to them I was just another face on the water, looking dead. My main worry was being shot by you people, but you're all such rotten marksmen, I survived. When the French had all gone, I got back onto the steps, and climbed back up. Here I am."

Laughter and congratulations came from everywhere; Ameshurst was well liked, and Gibney took off his own jacket and put it around Ameshurst's shoulders. Carravoy's emotions oscillated between relief at Ameshurst's survival but also jeal-

469

ousy. Ameshurst had properly handled both himself and his men, on top was his own personal bravery. The result was a return to Carravoy's irritable depression.

* * *

The following morning O'Hare ordered that a white flag be hung above the main gate. A resplendent and immaculate French Staff Officer came onto the causeway and saluted. Each side understood, this was a truce to allow the collection of the dead. The foreshore close to the castle rocks and many yards beyond it were thick with the casualties of the abortive night attack. Throughout the morning not a shot was fired, nor was there any sound as parties of French soldiers gathered up and carried away their casualties. When all had been taken away, the same French Officer came forward and gave the same salute. The truce was ended and the French guns fired anew.

However, military activity, of sorts, had not ceased altogether. O'Hare stood at the side of his signalman as he called out the letters for his co-signaller to write down. The first sentence was already complete and it was the one that O'Hare wanted.

"Evacuation 17th. Transports ready."

He waited for the completion of the final sentence.

"Heliades and Ipheion escorts. Captain Baines in command."

O'Hare turned to his Sergeant Aide de Camp.

"All Officers, all! In my quarters. 15 minutes."

Carr, Drake, Rushby, Carravoy and D'Villiers climbed the stairs together, but not a word was exchanged. Heaviside, Ameshurst and Simmonds, were already present. There were not enough chairs and so the latecomers stood. O'Hare himself stood to speak.

"Gentlemen, we evacuate day after tomorrow. You take only what you can carry on your back, you will convey the same orders to the men."

Carravoy took a step forward and raised his hand.

"What about what our servants can carry, Sir?"

"They have their own possessions and I would regard it as extremely churlish were any Officer here to require a servant to discard any of their own possessions to make room for those of their Officer! I hope I have made that clear. But, to the real business. The French will see our transports and will probably attack, no matter their state of readiness. They will want to pay us back, we've caused them a butcher's bill far higher than they feel merits the bargain."

He let that sink in, then continued."

"Major Simmonds and Captain Heaviside, I want an evacuation plan by the end of today. You will assume a coincidental assault. Dismiss."

All left, with different thoughts in their heads. Carravoy and D'Villiers; which luxuries to sacrifice, Simmonds and Heaviside mulling over the kernel of a plan, the others speculating on their possible role in that very plan. They returned to their Companies, informed their men, then left it to their Sergeants. Miles was the first to make a comment.

"Well, that's bloody easy. Every damn thing I own goes into my two sacks, I've bugger all else that could be left behind."

The orders reached the storesmen to send all food that was left up to the men, but not the surplus rum. One rum ration for the following day, the rest to be tipped away. Sedgwicke and Pearson rolled the spare barrel out of the store and Pearson stopped at a convenient drain, but Sedgwicke stopped him from removing the bung.

"No, we must tip this at the back, at the sea. A lot of rum washing ashore will tell all to the French, I fear."

Pearson nodded assent.

"A blessing to have an educated man!"

For the rest of the day, with the bombardment as background, all within the castle busied themselves with their affairs. Drake was scribbling a note.

"What's the French for "occupants"?"

Carr replied without looking up.

"Blessed if I know. Some kind of habitue' would be my guess."

Rushby spoke up.

"It's the same. Their occupants is the same as ours."

"Right. Job done."

This time Carr did look up.

"What's that?"

"A note to the new French tenants."

"And it says?"

"Les nouveaux occupants plairont-ils la feuille la maison comme ils le trouvent ?"

"And in English?"

"Will the new occupants of this house please leave the place as they find it?"

"Oh very droll. That'll raise a few French smiles, gallic grins, no doubt."

He stood up and walked to his equipment.

"Right, I'm done. Ten minutes we're on duty. Top battlement till dawn."

It proved to be a long quiet night, the only noteworthy event being the arrival of Captain Baines in the small hours, guided in from his ship, the Heliades, by a single lantern. From that moment, their Naval guest, O'Hare and his two planners were locked in conference. Dawn came, Spring clear with a good light, and with that the bombardment resumed, concentrating on the already ruined left bastion, but enlarging the breach. Carr and Drake had stood themselves down, it was but minutes to their relief, when Rushby came up.

"Sir. The French; they're coming out and carrying ladders."

Carr and Drake catapulted themselves upright and ran to an embrasure. The French were on the same spot as they themselves were, over a year ago, carrying ladders as they had done, but these waving them up and down. Carr was immediately incensed, very angry.

"Damn cheeky bastards. Do they think we fell out of the same chamber pot as them? Where's Davey? Get him here."

Davey reported and saluted.

"The French are trying the same theatre as we. Remember?"

"Sir."

"We shouldn't shoot them, by all the rules they are giving us a chance to surrender, but you see that Officer, the one with the sword, grinning?"

"Yes Sir."

"Take off his hat, he's being bloody rude, but don't hurt him, at least not too much."

Davey grinned and began a careful loading of his rifle, including the piece of thin leather around the ball. He settled himself at the embrasure, took aim, took a breath that he held, then fired. The ball wrecked the hat, lifting the crown up and over as a ragged blue disc, but the strap held and Officer's head was jerked back. He began shouting at his men and all ran back through the gaps in the houses, the Officer now wholly comical with his dismembered hat hanging down behind his head. He scuttled off behind his men, this all much to the amusement of the British on the battlements, them making sure that their laughter and catcalling was loud enough to reach across the space to the French. At that moment Carravoy and his Grenadiers arrived; they had heard the shot.

"What's going on, Captain Carr? Why the shooting?"

"Oh nothing, Captain. Nothing of any concern. Just putting the enemy in his place, is all."

Carravoy peered through an embrasure. There was nothing to be seen and Carr and his Officers returned to their quarters where there was a feast of food, perhaps not in quality, certainly in quantity, but also there were their written orders for the evacuation. Carr broke the seal and read. He finished his mouthful and spoke.

"We're the rearguard. I want every sand bag, grenade, mortar shell and spare musket you can lay your hands on."

* * *

The day of the evacuation broke as Spring clear as the previous, but the scene at sea beyond the castle was very different. All not on duty or not held in wait, watched proceedings. The frigate Heliades and their beloved Ipheion were off the castle with two heavy transports in between, but the wind was not helpful; from the East and slightly offshore. Both warships were manoeuvering to bring their guns to cover the beaches. The handy Ipheion had got in place to cover the harbour, and she was now losing all sail, save the bow stay sails that would hold her in, but the heavy Heliades was held up by the wind, too far out and at a bad angle. She could not bring her guns to bear on the vital bay that contained the steps down from the castle; the route of the evacuation. O'Hare and Baines stood at the battlements as the sailors on Baines' own ship struggled to find the correct set of the sails. Both showed anxious faces; the plan was awry from the start, so both agonized over their next, crucial decision, to start without gun cover, or wait. The boats for the evacuation sat obediently alongside the transports, waiting the signal to move forward. For these small craft, the beam wind blowing along the coast was perfect for a rapid to and fro.

Lieutenant Rushby came breathless out of the stairwell and ran to Baines and O'Hare. He faced O'Hare and saluted.

"Sir. Captain Carr sends his compliments, Sir, but I am to tell you that the French are massing before him. Probably for an attack, Sir. He thinks that they have worked out what we are doing."

O'Hare did not fail to smile, despite the anxious drama all around him.

"That's most astute of Captain Carr, Lieutenant, and I am grateful. Now return to your post."

Baines dropped his telescope.

"I heard. We've got to start. We've no choice."

"Agreed. As you choose, Captain."

Baines looked at O'Hare. Both deadly serious, each knowing that disaster was more likely than possible. Baines nodded to the Midshipman at the next embrasure, ready with a lighted match and he applied it to the tail of a signal rocket. All watched the fuse burn up, and then followed the blue arc of smoke up into the sky to be terminated with a green explosion. Each lowered and moved his gaze to the ships boats as they rowed for position, set their sails and began their short journey.

Meanwhile in their respective bastions Captains Carr and Carravoy were experiencing similar emotions, but for different reasons. Carravoy, at an embrasure, could hear everything but see nothing of what was causing the sounds of a serious conflict beginning, beneath him there was no activity; whilst Carr, also, could only hear. The French guns were still pummelling the bastion he was to defend and he and his men were sheltering back in a dark passageway, to advance any further into the murderous barrage meant certain injury and probable death. He turned to Drake and Rushby.

"We're damn all use here, until the bombardment stops. Nat, hold your section here, but I want your riflemen. Barnaby, you and your section with me up to the roof, top battlements. Nat, when the French are on the ladders, I'll come back. This will need careful timing."

Baines and O'Hare had taken themselves to the rear of the castle, into the main, seaward battery where they could oversee the movement of the evacuation boats. Six boats were closing with the platform that terminated the steps down from the walkway; six was more than enough for one company. Suddenly the water erupted around the leading boat. Her bows shattered, her speed drove her under the water, her crew clinging to the wreckage. O'Hare looked back to the beach and had enough angle to see a whole French field gun battery on the beach, well within range of the platform. Their over eager Officer had fired too soon, a minute later would have wrecked more boats, but luckily for the British, excitement got the better of him. Baines began shouting through a speaking trumpet for the boats to steer for the shelter of the cliff at the back, where they would be out of French sight. The evacuation had halted almost before it had begun.

Major Simmonds, having stationed himself on the roof, the topmost battlements, had seen the field guns arrive and knew immediately their threat, confirmed with their first volley. He looked over to the platform at the base of the steps. No boats and he knew why, but what to do? The castle guns were all out of action and the Heliades was practically stern on. He turned to see Carr and his Light Company emerge from the stairwell and file over to the left to take position above their bastion.

"Captain Carr!"

"Sir."

"Can your riflemen do anything about those field guns?"

Simmonds pointed out and down through an embrasure that overlooked the beach. Carr ran over and peered through the same.

"Why, yes Sir. Well within range."

"Then get them over here and commence firing."

Simmonds watched Carr run the short distance to his men.

"Change of plan, lads, rifles only, over here."

Carr returned with about 25 of his Command. Each file of three quickly found an embrasure and began rapid fire, talking turns. To see the effect, Simmonds peered through the embrasure used by Pike, Davey and Miles, but it was Miles who found the need to make a comment.

"Don't worry, Sir. Like shooting fish in a barrel."

Simmonds looked again, and saw, and grinned. The artillerymen were taking casualties already. He turned to his NCO runner.

"Get a message to Major O'Hare. French artillery under effective fire from rifles. Suggest evacuation recommence. Now run!"

The breathless Corporal reached Major O'Hare and delivered his message. O'Hare was unsure, and Baines shared his apprehension They would not know how much the French fire had been reduced until their boats presented a target, but Baines nodded and raised his speaking trumpet to the boats waiting below.

"Round to the steps. Begin evacuation."

Their sails were set for the perfect wind and were soon out from behind the cliff. Nothing came for several agonising minutes, then one shot, then another, both missing. The boats reached the platform and Number Three Company began their embarkation, with Captain Heaviside, standing stock still at the side, overseeing the calm transfer and quoting continuously from the Bible. D'Villiers fidgeted nervously at his side.

"Deliver me not over unto the will of mine enemies: for false witnesses are risen up against me. Psalms 27, verse 12.

"I am with thee, and no man shall set on thee to hurt thee. Acts Chapter 18, verse 10. Moresby, blast you, your musket does not go into the water!"

The boats queued and filled, sporadic roundshot came, but missed, poorly aimed by gunners reluctant to show themselves to carefully lay a gun. Number Three was embarked and away. Deakin and Halfway, now afloat, looked back. A shot hit the water yards away, but what held their attention was the noise and the smoke surrounding the castle. The Ipheion was serving her guns at battle speed, at a target unseen. Flashes and explosions everywhere. It looked like the Devil's Citadel.

"How many more lads is comin' out of there, Jed."

"Any more'n us, will be lucky."

Captain Carravoy strode impatiently up and down his battlement, smacking one gloved fist into the palm of the other. He had set a few men to fire at the field artillery, they were beyond effective musket range, but at least they were in some way active. Gibney patrolled the men, checking all was "full right", and Ameshurst stood calmly at the bastion entrance. Suddenly shouts came from the Grenadiers to the left. Carravoy ran to the last embrasure and saw the main French attack cross the causeway, the bombardment still thundering above their heads, a whole battalion strong, followed by another.

"Over here, all of you. Make that column feel your fire. Independent, rapid fire!"

Within a minute, Carravoy's bastion was wreathed in musket smoke, but not enough, thankfully, to spoil their aim, the

East wind blew the smoke clear, giving them a clear view of the attacking column. Carr, from high above, had seen the blue and white legions between the houses and knew there were but minutes before the main attack was launched. He saw the masses lurch forward and shouted, loud, for both left and right to hear.

"Grenades, to hand and ready!"

He knew their six inch fuse would burn for 20 seconds.

"Light."

He counted 10 seconds.

"Throw and commence."

The grenades went over and more followed, then fused mortar shells. At that moment grapeshot hit their embrasures, but too far to their right. Ellis reacted.

"Keep out of the embrasures, lads, just lob 'em out and over, but do give 'em some air."

Rushby looked at Ellis

"What's cricket got to do with it, Sergeant?"

"Yes Sir. Gibraltar's a long time past."

Carr, meanwhile, was descending to the passageway that led to the threatened bastion. He went immediately to Drake, waiting in the passageway with his section.

"When their cannons stop, Nat, then we go."

He looked behind.

"Ready lads! I don't know who invited these Crapauds up to our fine abode, but I believe that we show them what happens to people we don't welcome!"

The cannonade stopped.

"Follow me!"

The bastion was now but a platform of wrecked guns, broken stones and shattered sandbags, but Carr's men crossed the space just as the ladders were appearing. Grenades and shells continued to descend from above, their continuous explosions mingled with the screams of those they killed and wounded. Carr's men ran to the edge and began to fire down, then, with no time to reload they used their butts and bayonets. It lasted but a minute. Drake had been detailed to watch and soon it was obvious that more French were climbing the many scaling ladders than less than half a company could resist. It was retreat back or die there.

"Back, lads, fall back.

477

Carr heard and shouted to withdraw. Fearnley dragged back a wounded man, and the giant Saunders carried another. They all sprinted to the end of the passage and scrambled over the high sandbag barrier waiting there.

"Reload. Grenades, make ready."

Seconds passed, then a minute. Loud and urgent French echoed off the dark stones of the narrow passage. Two French grenades came bouncing down the flagstones to explode with a mighty report inside the passage, but they did no harm, the fragments hit the sandbags.

"Send two back. No fuse."

Two were lit and the rope fuse was allowed to burn almost to the casing when they were thrown, to bounce down the passageway. The noise was the same, but at the French end, then silence.

"En avant, mes enfants! Vive la France!"

White crossbelts, angry faces and high shakoes filled the passageway.

"Fire."

This was not for the muskets, but for a light cannon, one of two, held ready and loaded. The noise was deafening and the smoke dense, but it's grapeshot charge couldn't miss. The second was fired. Then four muskets sent their bullets at the French to join the grenades going over, all then being a hell of noise, smoke and screams. In relays of four, using ready loaded muskets stacked against the wall, Carr's men sent death and injury amongst the French. Both cannon fired again. It terminated the short fight and no more French came forward. The East wind cleared the passage of smoke. It was a charnel house of dead and dying, two, three deep, white crossbelts now red with blood.

"Reload, boys, and hold. Lieutenant Drake, you have command. I'm going to the Major.

Carr ran back along the passage and emerged onto an open courtyard that narrowed up to the main bastion. As he ran he heard a huge explosion, then another.

"Oh Sweet Jesus! Mortars. The whoresons are using mortars."

He reached the main bastion and went immediately to Major O'Hare. He didn't forget to salute.

"Sir. The French have the left hand bastion, Sir, but we are holding them out there. They can't get through the passage, Sir."

O'Hare looked at Carr, then at Baines, then back to Carr.

"Thank you Captain. We've been short of good news, and that's welcome. I'm evacuating the Grenadiers, then your Lights. Return to your command."

Carr did not return to the passageway, instead he went up to the roof, where all was silent. He went anxiously over to his riflemen.

"Why aren't you firing?"

It was Ellis who answered.

"No point now, Sir. See for yourself."

Carr looked over and, indeed, saw for himself. The French had fired two houses in the town and the smoke, carried on the wind, was shrouding their cannon. The increased cannonade from their direction told that the guns were again fully manned. Carr looked for Major Simmonds and saw him at the rear, at the battlements that overlooked the sea, but Simmonds saw Carr and ran up to join him as a mortar bomb exploded immediately beneath their battlements. Carr waited neither for Simmonds nor for orders, but called to his men, all now idle, all grenades gone.

"All of you. Into the stairwell. We're not long for here."

His men immediately abandoned their positions and disappeared down the stairwell, Simmonds with them. A second mortar bomb exploded on the roof, at the embrasures on the right where the rifles had been. More grapeshot hit the front embrasures. Lieutenant Rushby staggered and fell.

* * *

Captain Carravoy did not feel well. His leg hurt badly, but that was nothing compared to the pain that was splitting his head. The order to withdraw his Grenadiers had come and his men had filed quickly off the bastion. He was the last and just into the passageway when the mortar hit, squarely onto what had been their position moments before. A second earlier and Carravoy would have been blown to pieces, but in the passageway he was hit in the leg by a piece of shell and the blast had blown him off his feet, sending him into the passage wall, render-

479

ing him practically senseless. He staggered to the junction with the main passageway and collapsed.

Above him on the roof, Carr, Ellis and Davey were bending over Rushby, the long rent in the back of his tunic all too obviously showing where the fragment had hit.

"Get him off the roof, before the next arrives."

Each taking an arm, Carr and Ellis dragged the prone figure down into the stairwell. Carr turned Rushby over, but his body was seemed lifeless and his face drained of colour. Carr feared the worst, but he determined not leave him there.

"Ellis. Take charge. Get the men down to the walkway. Hold there."

Then to Davey.

"With me, let's get him down."

Rushby was again hoisted up and carried down the stairs, his lifeless feet bumping over each step. Davey spoke what they both thought.

"I think he's gone, Sir."

"Keep going."

They continued down through the castle, all passages now echoing with the intensifying conflict.

Drake, still at the sandbag barrier and still holding the passage to the bastion, heard running feet behind him. It was O'Hare's runner.

"Sir. Your orders are to pull back, Sir. To the walkway."

"Thank you. Inform Major O'Hare that we are on our way."

The NCO saluted and disappeared into the gloom and smoke.

"Right. We're going back. Drag these guns along, or the French will use them on us."

The recoil ropes were quickly released and his men took up the drag ropes and the guns were hauled back, along the passages to the walkway. They halted at the end of a long passageway and trained the guns back down it. Drake looked back down through the gloom, expecting to see the French, then he turned to the sounds of running behind them and saw Ellis and the other Lights out on the walkway and passing the entrance to their passageway, all heading on for the steps.

"Ellis! Where's Captain Carr?"

"I think he's still on the roof, Sir."

At that moment the French from their bastion came to the end of the passage, having followed Drake's exact route, the only route possible. The first of Drake's guns roared out.

Deep concern had come again to O'Hare and Baines. The evacuation boats were returning for the second time, but they were coming under fire again from the French field guns on the beach. Baines immediately used the loud hailer to order a halt, the sheets were cast loose and the sails fell slack, then the boats coasted forward and stopped, just out of the French guns effective range. Baines ran to the end of the battery wall, cursing the wind and his own crew at the same time, but before he reached the last embrasure a cannonade roared out that could only be naval. He reached the embrasure and peered through. His crew had launched a boat and towed their ship's head around, and, at extreme angle back to the stern, the whole broadside of 24 pound guns had been loosed at the French artillery on the beach. The result was plain, despite the smoke. But one gun remained in place, the rest had been blasted back up the beach, by, he surmised, the use of chain shot or bar shot. The single remaining gun had been abandoned. He ran back to overlook the evacuation boats, but they had seen for themselves the demise of their tormentors, and were already moving forward. Soon they were at the landing stage and the Grenadiers were jumping aboard.

The same runner as before again reached Drake, holding back the encroaching French.

"Sir. You are to fall back, Sir."

"Agreed. Tell the Major you've told me."

The runner disappeared, then Drake turned to his Sergeant, Ben Fearnley.

"Hold here, Sergeant. You hold here. Behind you is the only escape for Captain Carr. I'm going to get him."

Drake tapped two men and they ran out onto the walkway, but they turned left to get to the roof passageway. Still running they reached the bottom of the stairs, and were hugely relieved to see Carr and Davey, coming down and carrying Rushby.

"How bad is he?"

"Can't tell, but it seems pretty bad."

The two soldiers took over the burden of Rushby and with Drake anxiously examining Rushby, they started for the walkway, Carr was the last and he turned to make a final check, looking back along the passageway. His last glance saw the prone figure of Carravoy dragging himself forward on his elbows. Carr's companions had gone, so there was no point in shouting and the sounds of battle came from every direction. He ran back to Carravoy, saw immediately a wound in the back of his head and the blood on his leg. He turned him over. Carravoy looked pale and faraway. Just then a mortar shell came bounding down the stairs from the roof, the fuse spluttering and malignant. Carr ran back drew out a handkerchief, stuffed it into the fizzing fusehole and pressed down upon it with all his weight. The seconds were agonizing and the two looked at each other, each expression clear that this could be their last moments on Earth. More seconds passed. Nothing. Carr ran back to the prone Carravoy.

"Come on, Charles, or we'll miss the boat."

He wrapped Carravoy's left arm around his shoulders and hoisted him up. Becoming upright, Carravoy seemed to find some use in his unwounded leg, even to regain the power of speech.

"Thank you, Carr. I seem to be not quite feeling my usual self."

"We'll count that as a blessing! You've got a hole in your head. You are catching me up, but I've got two and yours is at the back. And that was a fine linen kerchief. I expect a replacement."

They emerged out onto the walkway, and turned the corner when the mortar went off with a huge roar and the explosion came out of the tunnel as though it were from the mouth of a cannon. Each looked at the other but said nothing, then both limped and stumbled to the passageway entrance where Drake and some Lights were still holding back the French. As Carr and Carravoy passed they turned and all fell back to where Miles, Pike and Davey were forming a rearguard at the walkway gate-arch, halfway along. Rushby remained a lifeless figure at their feet and Carr examined him again, but felt more certain than before. He could feel no pulse. Miles spoke.

"We're pretty sure he's gone, Sir. Best you go on, now, Sir. We'll hold them off from here, then file back."

Carr gave no argument. Miles was right, best to let this file of three do their work together as the last rearguard. He turned and followed the Lights helping Carravoy to the top of the steps. All descended down.

Back at the gate, Miles fired, then Pike. The French had emerged out onto the walkway and in force. Davey shouted to his companions.

"I'm loaded. You two, get gone."

Joe Pike shouted a protest.

"Get gone. I'll jump into the sea if I have to. Get gone."

Davey sighted along his rifle, and both Miles and Pike knew argument was useless. They ran for the top of the steps and there they stopped and waited, taking position and waiting for Davey to file back. Davey was just sighting on the leading Officer when the whole of the walkway, now crowded with French, dissolved into blood, dust, stones, spinning weapons and shakoes. The Heliades had trained her guns on the walkway and fired grapeshot as soon as the French emerged. Davey lowered his weapon and turned to leave. At that moment Rushby groaned. Davey looked down at him.

"My Lord, Sir, you do choose your moments."

At the bottom of the steps, on the platform, the last were climbing into the last boat, this being the longboat rowed over from the Heliades to join the evacuation. Carravoy was carefully helped in and Carr looked up to see Miles and Pike holding their positions at the top of the steps, waiting for Davey. Grenades were arriving on the platform from the French arriving on the battlements above, but they were quickly kicked into the water, however some were bouncing off the steps above. Carr's mind was settled when two, then another, then another, exploded on the walkway above, sending dust and smoke out over the cliff.

"Miles, Pike. Retire, that's an order."

Miles and Pike heard and looked at each other, then at the smoke that filled the walkway. The arch had disappeared behind the smoke. Miles counted, three, then four seconds, then he looked at Pike, and inclined his head back. Pike knew the gesture and followed him down the steps, their careful pacing of each step soon turning into a run. The boat was pulling away and they had to jump. Miles gained his feet in the boat and took one last look back to the top of the steps, then gripped the man in front, who happened to be Captain Carr.

"Jesus!"

Davey was at the top of the steps with Rushby thrown over his shoulder. He re-adjusted his burden, then began down. Shouts of encouragement came from the boat, intensifying from relief and extra hope as more grapeshot smashed into the walkway behind him and some also into the embrasures immediately above. Davey had reached the bottom, but the gap was now too far to jump, certainly too far to throw Rushby.

"Throw me a line."

A light rope snaked over and Davey spent agonizing seconds lashing it around and under Rushby's armpits, but this done he lowered him into the water. The line went immediately taught as Rushby was hauled out to the boat. More grenades hit the platform, one into the boat but it was quickly thrown overboard. Davey threw off his tunic, kicked off his boots and dived in. He emerged at the surface halfway to the boat and a powerful breaststroke took him to the side in time to push Rushby up as others pulled from above. Davey was then roughly hauled up himself to land in the bottom of the boat. He opened his eyes, looked up and found himself looking up at Miles.

"Now wer' did you learn to swim?"

"There's more than one way to get clear of the Squire's men!"

Miles pulled out his bandana and wiped his messmate's face.

"Thievin' poacher! You nearly had me worried, there. At least for a while!"

Chapter Fourteen

A Righteous Outcome

The long column of soldiery drew little more than a glance. Countless such parades had passed to and fro from London and Chatham, marching, and counter-marching, up and along the Old Kent Road, to embark, or disembark, as required. All this had now become very familiar over the years since war became formal and active between Britain and France. This latest addition in the long sequence, as it dropped down into Deptford off the wide expanse of Blackheath, was merely the latest; a long column in ranks of four made up of tanned, hard-eyed men, three mounted Officers leading but most Officers marching on foot before their Companies. NCO's in step, but detached alongside. The good people of Deptford were undiverted, being well used to this to-ing and fro-ing that reminded them that they were still at war, so the only stir amongst the population came via the inevitable small boys that attached themselves to the sides of the column, to be sworn at and shooed off by the stone-faced Sergeants and Corporals.

Some, who afforded them more than a glance, saw enough to give rise to more than simple curiosity, and their examination then became more prolonged. Their jackets were not red, more like pink, and several bore items of uniform that were holed and patched, dirty, even bloody. Several boots were almost falling apart, held by twine that itself was wearing out and made a fringe beside the departing sole from the upper. Some knapsacks were two-tone cowhide. There was little about the sight to afford it the description of "stirring and military", but it did not require an old soldier to discern that these were, perhaps not parade ground, but certainly hardened soldiers. Such as they were becoming more common throughout the British Army, there was nothing ponderous about their gait, nor anything slouched about their demeanour. These were plainly veterans, making a hard march. The 5th Provisionals had returned home, although London was counted as home for barely a small proportion. Orders were to march to Camberwell, remain there the night, then march on to Horse Guards for an 11.00 o'clock parade. The three mounted Officers at their head,

485

said little to each other. It would have been difficult anyway, each was riding in echelon, behind and to the side of the other, but Lieutenant Colonel Lacey occasionally allowed himself a look back to examine his command, and each time his sense of satisfaction grew; his 600 odd men were marching perfectly in step, muskets on the right shoulder, arms swinging in perfect unison. However, from time to time he extracted a letter from his inside pocket that caused him more than mere satisfaction, it caused an open grin. He read it again, whilst allowing his horse to find its own direction, then turned to look at his second in command, Major O'Hare. At the same time he held the letter out and back, in offer.

"Would you like another read, O'Hare?"

"I think I would, Sir."

He urged his horse forward the extra three yards and took the letter, then reined his horse back. The words brought the same expression to his face as they had to his Colonel.

Lieutenant Colonel William Lacey – Officer Commanding: 5th Provisionals.

Sir,

Upon disembarkation, you are to proceed with your men to Camberwell Green, there to receive new uniforms and equipment as required. You are then to march to Horse Guards Parade, for 11am 19th May 1808, where your Battalion will be formally conferred as the 105th Foot. The Prince of Wales Wessex Regiment.

His Royal Highness, The Prince of Wales, has instructed the Commander in Chief, to award the 5th Provisionals a Number and Colours such as will designate your Command as a Regiment of the Line. This award has been bestowed in recognition of your service during the recent conflict in Southern Italy, as described in the Campaign Reports of General Sir John Stuart and Major General Sir John Coape Sherbrooke.

God Save the King

Secretary to the Commander in Chief, General Sir Henry Livermore.
11th May 1808

Having read the letter once, then once again, Major O'Hare urged his horse up alongside his Commanding Officer and returned it. Each shared a smug look as the letter was returned to the inside of Lacey's jacket.

* * *

Camberwell Green was reached in the mid afternoon and found to be a prim and proper village green surrounded by neat houses, with cared for doors and windows that soon flew open with the arrival of the hundreds strong body of soldiery. Before too long the word went around and a variety of stalls and barrows arrived around the edge to display their wares and produce, but already waiting along one side was a long array of low carts each loaded with a particular item of uniform. All was to be changed, except weapons, these were to be cleaned and made fit for parade. By single companies they paraded past the carts to be laden with the new item; jackets, haversacks, knapsacks, boots, canteens, greatcoats, stocks, scabbards, cartridge boxes, blankets and breeches. At this last cart they found Sergeant Major Gibney, regularly intoning a solemn command.

"Tha' breeches is not to be changed until parade int' mornin'. This is to stop thee causing disturbance to t'local ladies around these parts, and second, so that they is new and clean for parade tomorrow. Don't sleep in 'em!"

Old Norfolks ruefully surrendered their "Holy Boys" shako and looked askance at the common GR in the centre of the replacement, with flags either side, a crown above and a lion below. 105 was shown on their canteen and a simple 105 on their crossbelt badge, but their jacket facings were the subject of much comment as they returned to their messes, none more so than from Tom Miles.

"What kind of bloody facings is this, bright green? We'll stand out like a bunch of May Queens. We've gone from "Rag and Bone" to "Paddy's Own". 'Tweren't no soldier as thought this up?"

It was his nemesis, Sergeant Ellis, who spoke up and answered amidst the laughs and guffaws that met Miles' comment.

"You wear it, Miles, and like it. And, on top, that's got to go."
"What?"

He pointed to Miles' back.

"That Frencher knapsack you bin totin' since Maida. The brown and white cowhide job you looted. You can store it, or sell it, but it's regulation issue from now on."

"So I gets another flimsy affair, courtesy of His Majesty, that'll fall apart after the first soakin'. This've lasted I a year nor more. I'm for keepin' on'n."

"Your choice, but you parades with regulation. Now get your new brass work polished up. I'll be lookin' 'specially at yours come mornin'. There's a cart there with brickdust and blanco. You're back in England now, so parade includes stocks and hair queues."

"England you say? Now there's a fact that's so far escaped my attention!"

Miles took himself over to the said cart, passing two of his Officers, each discussing their own concerns. Of the two, Captain Henry Carr and Lieutenant Nathaniel Drake, the latter appeared the most anxious.

"Do you think they'll be there?"

His Captain, Henry Carr, displayed a nonchalant air, hands clasped behind his back. He inclined himself in Drake's direction.

"Can't say, not with anything like certainty. As soon as we landed we sent off word, post haste to Taunton. That was six days ago. If everything has functioned as it should, then they'll be there, but ......?"

He looked at Drake and raised his eyebrows as if to say, "It's in the lap of the Gods".

"Now, we must attend to our uniforms. Morrison is doing his best, but I feel we should lend a hand. Important day tomorrow."

Both walked off to busy themselves with the affairs of the forthcoming parade, but two Officers remained standing almost in the centre of the green, deep in conversation, and their talk was none too cheerful as could be seen from the morose look on their faces. Captain Carravoy and Lieutenant D'Villiers were each discussing their futures.

"Well, Royston. We're back in the capital. What is your mind regarding a transfer?"

D'Villiers face screwed up in thought, betraying the lack of a clear decision.

"Probably, yes. One hundred and five is hardly high ranking, is it? Which is the point, there's no status whatsoever. I mean, what's to be gained by saying, I'm in the Hundred and Fifth? And I've had enough of Heaviside; he issues and enforces his military edicts with the same fervour as those of his religion. He thinks me incompetent. I've had enough, so I've written to my people to take it up again. What about you?"

"Not sure. Remaining with the one oh five, the "Heroes of Maida" may not be so bad, but it's likely that I'll attempt to purchase a Majority somewhere. Perhaps even an exchange. That's something you could consider. This battalion now has a reputation as one that fights, and for some, that makes it worth exchanging into. Casualties means dead men's shoes to fill. Whatever, go or stay, I'm not too concerned either way, there's merit in both."

Both nodded in mutual agreement, then, hearing horses, they both came to attention to salute their Senior Officers who were riding off The Green to the main road.

Storesman Sedgwicke also came to the salute with their passing. He also was engaged in a philosophical ponder, but less on his future. He thought of his family, in particular his sister, who had kept him supplied with adequate funds. He had written, but would she reply, would she journey to the capital for this rare opportunity to see him? His thoughts then turned to the Church that faced out onto The Green. A Cleric of some sort was polishing the brass handle, oblivious to the bustling activity displaying itself behind him. "There but for fortune" entered his head several times, but he busied himself with the new uniforms, and held to the hope that he could gain some time to enter and pray in an English Church, perhaps that one, for the first time for over two years.

* * *

General Perry was in a state of high agitation, sat in the Outer Office, this being the office of the Under Secretary to the Secretary of the Commander in Chief. He occupied, fortunately without his knowledge, the very same chair as used by Captain Carr back in October 1805. Everything about his uniform, and person, that could be examined, pulled at, and adjusted had suffered exactly that fate, and several times over. Nothing in

489

the office had changed over the intervening years, all remained as it had over the decades before that. As ever, the notes from the striking clock marked the hours and the most rapidly moving object in the room was the feather of the Under Secretary's quill, the only motivator for the motes of dust that hung in the few shafts of sunlight. Discounting Perry's agitation, the quill was all that moved, besides the hands of the clock, which stood lugubrious as any Undertaker.

Perry looked upon the black-coated and black-featured Secretary with a look as black as the subject of his gaze, but the Secretary, with studied calm and careful concern, slowly went about the methodical tasks as required by the Under Secretary to the Secretary of the Commander in Chief. He completed each task, slowly and carefully, as though any approach less ponderous would place the fate of the whole British Army in deep jeopardy. Perry had arrived without an appointment, feeling certain that his rank, the equal to that of General Livermore, would gain him rapid access. That had proven to be an illusion, and the tall sentinel of a clock had now rung for two quarter hours, the deep chimes beating more and more upon General Perry's patience. Just at the point where he was about to give vent to his deep frustration, the door to Livermore's Office opened and the subject of his occupation emerged, but this did nothing to quell Perry's temper. He who came out was nothing more than a Major aide de camp, and this inferior had been given priority over him for the past half hour. The Under Secretary raised his head at a speed that told it was too heavy for the shrivelled neck muscles, and at the top of the rise he spoke, the thin lips extending into a rictus grin, but his eyes held the chill of a Gorgon.

"General Livermore will see you now, Sir. He knows you're here."

Was that last a cutting remark to emphasise Perry's secondary priority? Livermore knew of his presence, but still kept him waiting? General Perry's conclusion did nothing to improve his mood and he rose and hurtled through the open door. General Livermore was standing in respectful greeting, hand extended towards a fellow General Officer. When Perry ignored it, Livermore changed the gesture to one that merely indicated a seat, which Perry had already taken. When both were seated, each stared at the other, expecting the initiative to come from the opposite side of the desk, but Livermore began, having taken full notice of Perry's liverish complexion.

"General Perry. How do you do? What is your concern?"

"My concern, Sir, is that one of my battalions, namely the 5th Detachments, now Provisionals, have returned from attachment abroad. As I see it they are still under my command. There has never been any official communiqué informing me otherwise. This being the case I wish them returned. I intend to split them over my four Militia Battalions and thus bring those up to strength. I expect to take the order back with me."

Livermore listened whilst adopting his common pose. Sat back, elbows sat securely in the cup-size recesses of the chair arms, created by countless adoptions of such pose, his fingers erect and opposed. He had become curious.

"Please inform me, General, I beg, why would you wish to break them up? They have been serving together for over two years. With some distinction, as I am able to detail for you, should you so wish."

"Distinction be damned! Abroad or not! They're a disorganised rabble, I both saw it and saw the result. Poorly commanded, poorly officered, and poorly trained. Too many criminals and rejects; and on top, Lacey made poor appointments. Officer corps all wrong. Their remaining as a discrete battalion makes no sense; indefensible; illogical."

Livermore made no immediate reply to the tirade. He merely found the hole in his left ear with his left hand, then raised his eyebrows, whilst allowing an inscrutable smile to form on his lips. Eventually he spoke.

"I'm afraid that you must take the absence of a letter removing them from your command as an oversight, General. Back in October of that year, things were a little, er, fraught; and such things result during such times. That will be rapidly corrected. Regarding their forthcoming status, well I'm afraid that is now out of your hands. The Prince of Wales himself has requested that the "heroes of Maida" be made a Regiment bearing a title that includes the words, 'Prince of Wales Own'. "His Own", if you appreciate those words. The victory of Maida caused more than a little stir, you see, certainly up here in the capital; down there in Taunton, perhaps not. We are now faced with a Royal Command, no less."

He paused, both to give room for an indulgent smile and to allow the fact to sink in.

"Maida had them dancing in the streets, General. It was the theme of Society Balls, if you understand, to dress with a Calabrian flavour. When Stuart came home, he was hailed as the 'Hero of Maida', and made a Knight of the Bath, and then, unsurprisingly, people began to read accounts of the battle, including his Princely Highness."

Frustration and increased anger began to rise in Perry such that he gripped the arms of his chair enough to turn his knuckles white. This was going wrong. What he had taken to be a foregone conclusion was slipping; probably had, slipped away. The Prince was involved, Perry's cherished ambition was vanishing, like ice in a kettle. Livermore opened a file, extracted some papers and continued.

"Regarding 'disorganised rabble', well, for a start, I read in Lacey's first report that they sent you a French tricolour, captured by them off a privateer that tried to capture them. Any truth? Did that not give you pause?"

Perry wasn't sure whether to nod his head or shake it. Livermore waited for some verbal addition, but none came, other than the intensification of Perry's mouth and eyebrows knitting further together. Livermore continued.

"Also by way of contradiction, in his report General Stuart describes their holding of his left flank as, and I quote, 'a most gallant and well-conducted defence of their part of the line. At one point the battle could have turned on the outcome, for they were assailed on two fronts, yet they bravely stood their ground, finally advancing forward to confirm their victory."

Livermore set down the paper and raised his eyes to study General Perry.

"Gallant and well-conducted. Bravely, General, it says. All this is unknown to you?"

Perry shook his head, his face now showing clenched jaw and deeper colour. He said nothing.

"You do get newspapers down there? Don't you General?"

Perry nodded, suddenly feeling exposed.

"And you knew nothing of the stand of the 5th? As just described?"

No reply.

"Then I will continue. People such as myself read these reports, and credit has been apportioned; in my view justly."

He sought a further paper.

"General Sherbrooke adds more, this being in his report on the defence of Scilla by three of their companies. He says, using much the same words, 'a gallant and well-conducted defence of the castle, against great odds, causing the enemy heavy casualties that made their eventual gaining of the castle a costly bargain'. End of quote. They may have left you as a disorganised rabble, you must look to yourself as to the reason for that, but on active service they have behaved as well as any Regiment we have. Better. You may not agree, but the Prince of Wales would."

He resumed his fingertip pose; to allow both the rebuttal and barb of the last two sentences sink in. Perry's face continued to register deep anger and resentment, then confusion was added. It was Livermore who continued further.

"As for who's command they are now under, that also has been settled."

He found yet another piece of paper.

"They are now under the command of Brigadier Sir Henry Fane, whose Brigade is now numbered as the Sixth, amongst an army about to embark for Portugal under the command of General Sir Arthur Wellesley. Those two gentlemen, it would appear, are perfectly content to acknowledge them as a "Regiment of the Line."

Silence fell, filled only with the gentle ticking of Livermore's mantle clock, but he had had enough. He emerged from between the two deep wings of his chair.

"Well, General Perry. If you have no further business, then I bid you good day."

Perry's ire and frustration remained unabated. Up until now he had always gained his own way, his rank procured it, but here it was, writ large; he was unable to act upon a most cherished prejudice. In fact his justification, were he to continue to voice it, would now be condemned as absurd. He rose from his chair and took himself out of Livermore's presence and into the outer office, stepping around the mighty bastion of the Secretary's desk to set a course through the red mist for the door. Movement to the right caught his attention, this being Lacey and O'Hare rising to attention. Perry ignored both, he reached the door and seized the handle, wrenching open the door to make an explosive exit, so fast his coat tails rose in the slipstream. Slowly, the door swung back of its own accord.

His disappearance was observed by General Livermore himself, who had emerged from his Office, knowing who waited outside.

"Lacey! Amazed to see you're still vertical, and in one piece, and with all functioning."

He advanced towards his old friend, hand extended before him, to take that of Lacey with a grip from which O'Hare swore he could hear cracking bones.

"General. May I introduce my Second? Major Padraigh O'Hare."

"You may, you may."

O'Hare's hand received the same treatment. Then Livermore turned to his Secretary, who, within the presence of his Senior showed more animation than he had shown all day.

"Wilson. No more appointments today. I'll be at my Club with these two Gentlemen. We have much to talk about, both past and present."

He took the arm of both and propelled them to the door, which he himself opened, and then on past the "present arms" salutes of both Coldstreamer sentries.

* * *

It was the first hour of a morning in the best of an English May. Bright clear sun had climbed over the roofs surrounding The Green, and shone bright upon the preparations for a military parade, a parade made more sparkling by the pristine newness of all uniforms there displayed. Officer's faces shone to match the sun and there was no significant gloom either amongst the men, despite the preparations of hair queues and the return of the hated stocks. The veterans amongst the ranks had spread the word that a Royal Parade always resulted in a double rum ration. That was the subject of conversation as each attended to some other's hair queue, or laced up a stock, particularly Privates Peters and Stiles of Number Three Company.

"That's a point. We 'aven't tasted rum since the double we got at Scilla."

"Ah, and not just rum. I've heard that today could be a pay day, an' all."

"Which is another point. Awarding colours and such from some Royal often results in some bit extra from the very Royal coffers."

"That is something I'll believe upon seeing."

Jed Deakin had been listening without identifying. The two were like twins, same size and same voice. He was busy giving a final shine to his musket brass, when he looked up and saw the Colonel walking purposefully in his particular direction, carrying what looked like a scarf and some badges.

"You two! Attention."

Both sprang up to join Deakin, but Lacey soon stood them easy.

"Deakin."

"Sir."

"You're a Colour Sergeant. Get these sewn on before we march off. This sash goes with it. Do you know the drill?"

"Yes Sir. Seen it many times, but a Colour Sergeant should have a sponson, Sir."

"We'll have to dispense with that. You have your musket. You'll march in the Colour Party. After me on the way to, out in front after it's done. Clear?"

"Yes Sir."

Deakin saluted, which Lacey returned, then strode off. Captain Heaviside had been both watching and observing.

"He shall reward every man according to his works. Matthew, 16, Verse 27."

Deakin stood shocked.

"Yes Sir. I'm sure that would explain it, Sir."

"I'm sure it would, Colour Sergeant Deakin, but I do feel that your magnificent Badges of Office should be sewn on, as Colonel Lacey said, to fully confirm and display your new standing in the eyes of us all. 'Every tree is known by his own fruit. Luke, Six, Verse 44.' Best see to it."

"Yes Sir."

He took himself off to Bridie and the family, wearing the sash, but examining the new emblems. Four badges, two being the stripes, two being crossed flags. He was showing the badges to Bridie long before he reached her, and she seized his arm in delight, and then kissed him. Mary O'Keefe ran up and did the same.

"Oh, Uncle Jed. That's grand."

495

"Yes, only we've but an hour to get them sewn on."

Bridie took charge.

"Don't you worry one little bit, Jed. Me and Mary will take an arm each. It'll be done in no time. Take off your jacket and put it over your shoulders. Just stand still, it'll be easier if it's still on you."

Deakin did their bidding then both took hold of an empty arm and immediately began cutting away the recently re-sewn, but old, and very faded, Corporal's stripes. Meanwhile, Colonel Lacey was off on another errand, seeking another. He found him in the Light Company.

"Davey."

John Davey rose to attention without needing to look; he had recognised his Colonel's voice.

"Sir."

"Davey. I'm struggling to put this in a way that can be called diplomatic, so I'll just say it straight out. You're a convicted felon, Davey, sentenced to time in the army. Were you anything other, in recognition for your actions back in Scilla, I could recommend you for a Commission, such as is awarded for singular acts of bravery. You know what that means, it would make you an Officer."

"Yes Sir. I understand."

"My hands are tied, that is beyond my gift, but what I can do is make you a Chosen Man. That's one beneath Corporal and on a par with Lance Corporal. I hope you will accept."

"Accept Sir? Yes Sir. Thank you very much, Sir."

"Right. Well, here's your stripe. It goes on your right arm, just above your elbow"

He handed over the broad white band. Lacey genuinely felt this to be a paltry recognition of so high an act of bravery, he felt that more should be said, but this time on a personal level.

"I understand you have a...er...wife back here in England?"

"Yes Sir. My Molly. She'll be wholly pleased. Sir."

"And you hope to meet her, here, in the capital?"

"Yes Sir. I've sent word, Sir. Parson, I mean Private Sedgwicke, wrote the letter. I'm lookin' forward to it, Sir, and to see little Tilly."

"Right. Well. Good luck to you Davey, I'll leave you to get that sewn on in time for the parade."

"Yes Sir."

Davey came to the salute, which was immaculately returned by his Colonel.

* * *

The parade had been stood still for almost an hour, studying the brickwork of the Horse Guards, and being partially entertained by a preening Staff Officer, going about his showy business across the washed and polished flagstones that fronted this most important of military buildings. Mercifully they were stood at ease, the ranks with grounded arms, the Officers with swords point down, both hands folded over the pommel. There was little noise, merely the distant sound of polite conversation that had slowly reduced in volume as each topic was exhausted and others proved difficult to find. The crowd had swollen at first, then drifted away with the absence of the most important of presences. Now, but only the very interested remained, these being family that the hastily written and posted letters had summoned from many and varied parts. The Noon Gun sounded from The Tower, its echo rolling through the streets and across the river and parks to inform the good citizens of the capital that half the day was done. Silence returned, but not for long. Suddenly the band struck up and, over an hour late, an escort of Lifeguards trotted onto the square, helmets, swords and breastplates all painfully reflecting the midday sun. Behind came two huge open landaus, the first, it would seem, full of feathers, the second noticeable for two rigid poles, with the length that was erect in the air thickened by a long leather case for half its length. Both were in the charge of four, what seemed to be, tailor's mannequins, as rigid as the poles in their charge. After them, yet more burnished Lifeguards.

The whole cavalcade swung around to face the direction from which it had come. From the first landau came the sound of much laughter and giggling, whilst the door of the second swung open from the inside and down stepped two General Officers, one being Livermore, followed by two Majors, these carrying the encased colours. All four fell in on each side of the door of the first landau, the two Generals on one side, the Majors on the other. A foursome Honour Guard.

Two footmen then leaped from the back and one ran to unfold the gleaming black foot rest and the other to open the door, to then stand rigidly with the handle in his custody, partly for fear that it would, by some phenomenon, swing back, but mostly to convey to his Princely Highness, that he was, indeed, holding open the door for his High Prince. This act revealed a collection of glasses and bottles on the floor of the landau. A figure within the coach stood up, or rather a collection of feathers around the arc of a huge bicorne hat elevated itself, then an ample white waist-coated stomach presented itself at the opening, then two pudgy hands came forward onto the rails beside the doorway. Finally a mirror-bright black dancing shoe placed itself on the first step, followed by another that crunched the pale yellow gravel. At that moment Colonel Lacey, standing before his men, roared out a command with all the volume he could muster.

"Parade. Atten shun."

At all sections of the assembled ranks, movement came as arms arrived to the "Order".

"Parade. Present arms."

Even more lifting and whirling of polished steel and brass, as the parade, in perfect unison, presented their weapons to His Royal Highness, The Prince of Wales. However, this, His Highness, appeared wholly oblivious to what was going on. He was sharing a joke with a female companion, but some words did drift over, which seemed to include, "hush, present, flag, serious." At last His Highness turned to the parade and all could at last make out a face, albeit at the rear of a mighty collection of sashes, decorations, epaulettes, tassels, feathers, and fringes. He was a tallish man, but overindulgence came plainly to mind, both of his frame and of his person. His four escorts sprang to attention plus salute and allowed the decorated figure to pass, before falling in behind as the Prince advanced forward, him knowing enough so that he made straight for the nearest soldier, assuming him to be the Commanding Officer. In this he was correct; Colonel Lacey stood waiting. At five yards distance The Prince came to a halt and turned to the General Officers.

"And who have we here, Livermore?"

"Colonel Lacey, Your Highness. Commanding Officer of the 5th Provisionals."

The Prince walked up to Lacey, still stood at the "Present Arms", the lower blade of his sword pressed against his nose.

"Put away your sword, Colonel, you're making my Lifeguards nervous."

He grinned widely, and the formality began to fall away, as Lacey sheathed his sword.

"We heard all about your exploits, Colonel. Well done, well done indeed."

"Thank you, your Highness."

"You have to call me, Sir. I'm in military uniform, that of some high rank or other. I'm not sure which."

He turned back to Livermore.

"What am I Livermore? In the Army, that is?"

"You are a Colonel in Chief, Sir. Of a number of Regiments."

The Prince returned his attention to Lacey.

"There you are, Lacey. A Colonel in Chief, no less."

He paused and resumed his tipsy grin.

"Yes. As I say. Very well done indeed. Maida gave me an excuse to celebrate for at least two weeks."

He leaned back and raised his voice.

"We gave 'em one Hell of towelling. That's what I say."

"Yes Sir."

"And Scilla. The defence of Scilla. They got more than they bargained for there, too. Am I right."

"Yes Sir, absolutely right, but that defence was conducted by my Second, Major O'Hare, just behind me here."

The Prince's face fell a little at being ever so slightly contradicted, but he nevertheless peered around Lacey and said "Well done Major". O'Hare, already at stiff attention, could do no more than mumble, "Thank you, Sir" past his erect sword.

"Now then, Lacey. We are calling you the 105th The Prince of Wales Wessex Regiment. Does that suit?"

He left no room for an answer.

"We would have called you some kind of Somerset, but it seems that Somerset is rather full. How many, Livermore?"

"Two, Your Highness. The 13th and the 40th. Not to mention the Yeomanry."

"There you are Lacey. Full. So, you are to be the 105th Regiment. The Prince of Wales Wessex Regiment. Now, when this is done, I want to meet all your Officers and get all the details of what we did. Maida and Scilla. All the details, mind. In that tent over there."

He pointed to an open-fronted tent off to the side.

"I've provided some refreshments. When you march off, you'll stop on The Mall, I've made arrangements for your men, but I want you to bring your Officers back."

"Yes Sir. Thank you, Sir. They'll be greatly honoured."

"Right. Let's get these Colours handed over, then get on with the interesting stuff. Is all ready on your side?"

"Yes Sir. The Colour Party is formed behind me."

"Good. I think we have the right ones. Emerald green, yes. Chosen by my wife, so I regard myself as blameless. Now, if you'll stand aside, we'll get this done."

Lacey saluted then marched off to stand beside O'Hare and draw his sword. He nodded to Gibney.

"Colour Party. Atten shun!"

No movement, they already were.

"Colour Party. By the left. Forward march."

He allowed them to take five paces.

"Colour Party. Halt."

Meanwhile, the two Majors had uncased the Colours. One was a huge Union Flag with a laurel circle in the centre that contained the Roman Numerals CV. The other also held a Union Flag, but only as a minor part, confined to the top corner next to the flagstaff. Its colour was bright green, and in the centre was a circle of myrtle leaves, a shrub common in Calabria, and in its centre, also the numerals CV. The Prince took this first, the Regimental Colour, from the nearest Major and carried it, needing two hands, to the nearest Ensign. The Ensign dropped to one knee to minimise the lift that the Prince would need to give to the standard in order to drop it into the cup of the plain leather holder. On one knee he proffered the cup with his left hand and, with his right, guided the base of the shaft into the cup. The Prince, well experienced, then held the shaft steady whilst the Ensign took the shaft just below the cloth with his right hand and rose to his feet and came to the attention.

The Prince then turned and obtained the King's Colour, the Union Flag and took it to the second Ensign. He also had dropped to one knee and was holding the cup forward. The process was repeated, but the Ensign had difficulty in standing and simultaneously retaining hold of the Colour. His right side was weak and he grimaced in pain and the standard lurched from the vertical. The Prince raised his own hands, but Jed Deakin, Colour Sergeant beside the Ensign, seized the shaft with his left hand and returned it upright. The Prince was shocked and the Ensign speechless with embarrassment and the pain besides, but Deakin spoke up.

"Humble apologies, Your Highness, but our Ensign hasn't quite recovered from his wound, yet, Sir."

The Prince looked at the Ensign, now thoroughly red, compared to the bright pink that he was just seconds ago. The Prince's face showed no little sympathy.

"What is your name, Ensign?"

"Rushby. Sir."

"And where did you get your wound?"

"Escaping from Scilla. Sir."

"Were you the last one out?"

"So I'm told, Sir. But I was unconscious at the time, Sir, slung over the shoulder of one of our men. It was he that got me out. Sir."

"Was that your only wound?"

"No Sir. That was my second. I was wounded just after Maida, Sir."

"Well, I can think of no-one more fitting to carry the King's Colour. Have you a secure hold now?"

"Yes Sir. Thank you, Sir."

The Prince of Wales turned to Colonel Lacey.

"All done, Colonel. You're a Line Regiment now. March your men away."

The last syllable was long drawn out and almost covered Lacey's reply, who then turned once more to Gibney, and nodded.

"Colour Party, left wheel."

The four, with their Colours, swung through 90 degrees.

"Colour Party. By the left. March."

The Colour Party began their journey to the end of the column that had remained patiently at attention in four ranks. Lacey, O'Hare and Simmonds followed and seamlessly picked up the step. More orders rang out and the whole parade changed face and stood ready to march away. The Colour Party and the Senior Officers came to a halt at the end facing The Mall. The final order rested with Colonel O'Hare.

"105th Regiment. By the left, quick march."

The band struck up a marching tune, "Ye Sons of Albion" and, with Colours released and flying, the 105th Foot marched away and onto The Mall. Good chance would have it that this was the side where the spectators and families had been allowed to gather and the music from the band had competition

501

from their cheers and shouts, all being accompanied by the waving of hats and handkerchiefs.

* * *

They didn't go far. The marching off was merely for ceremonial purposes and the men, at least, had spotted a trestle table with kegs of rum, and further on, that which was most wished for, pay desks with their own Regimental Purser or his Clerks ensconced thereto. The parade halted and broke up, the men falling out into St James Park. Gibney was left in charge with the other NCO's, as the Officers returned the way they had come, and the Colours were furled and left with the Colour Sergeants. This was the men's chance for celebration and their families and well-wishers soon came the short distance down The Mall to join them. Families long parted were reunited amidst scenes of deepest joy and emotion. Many a son and daughter now measured their height against that of their Father and all were now some way further up to his shoulder, in some cases past, but more poignantly, hands were held and faces gazed into.

John Davey was sat on a fence rail with Miles, Peters, Stiles, Pike and Mary, all being entertained by Deakin holding out the King's Colour. The Regimental Colour was equally on display closeby and all took no small pride to see the word "Maida", in a scroll to the right of the centre design. Tom Miles alone felt the need for a sour word.

"One battlehonour. Don't measure up at all to the list of the old Ninth."

However, he was quickly told to "shut his gob", mostly by the women, and if he wanted to spread some misery, then he had better "bugger off somewhere else", but the rum cheered them all and also they sat contentedly waiting their turn at the Pay Table. Percy Sedgwicke was seen by Jed Deakin walking through the assembly, looking for someone perhaps, but certainly looking forlorn.

"Parson! Come and sit with us. Have you got your rum? Be 'ee lookin' for someone?"

"Yes to the first, was and found to the second."

"Well, come and sit with us for a while. Somehow we've got extra."

Deakin tipped a tot extra into Sedgwicke's cup, causing his spirits to rise, but he couldn't dismiss the image of his sister, just departed, who had given him money, but who could barely bring herself to look at him, he in his common soldier's uniform. Deakin broke in upon his depressed thoughts.

"This'll cheer you up, Parson. Now we'n a Regiment, we'll get a Chaplin. He'll be lookin' for assistants, I shouldn't wonder.

Deakin was right. Better cheer did arrive in the complex world of Sedgwicke. He looked cheerfully at Deakin, drank more rum, and also felt it.

John Davey was taking the time to examine the look of his Chosen Man stripe when he heard a voice that caught his breath.

"Hello, John. It's me."

Davey turned and there was Molly and Tilly, and a baby cradled at Molly's hip. She was wearing a plain dress, well made and of good cloth, her lovely hair shiny and well kempt. The doxy was gone. She looked a well-set wife and mother. Davey allowed his rifle to fall in the direction of Joe Pike, but it was Mary who caught it just in time. Davey himself was up and embracing Molly with his left arm, having lifted up Tilly to cradle her in the crook of the other, but mostly he was looking at the baby held up to him by Molly.

"This is John. I named him after you, 'cos you weren't around to say. He were born Christmas 'fore last. That makes him 15 month old. He looks like you, 'specially so according to your Mother."

Davey was lost for words, and for some time, but Molly said no more, and Tilly clung to his neck. Eventually he found some words to say.

"Did you get my letters. Parson wrote them. Did you get my pay? And did you get the note, you know, the note signed by Colonel Lacey?"

"Yes we did, and it's all safe, and the bank advanced money on the strength of it, but nothin's been done with it yet. You'll have to decide. Your Mother's thinkin' of a smallholding, that'll grow food and make some money. She says you can always build a shelter or house on your own land. That'll come of its own time. But it's up to you. You won it. I hope it weren't too hard!"

"Ah, no Molly. He fell over at the first punch!"

"I don't bet. I'll get the story from someone else."

But she said no more, Davey had taken them all in his arms.

* * *

The fare provided in the tent was sumptuous; all the delicacies of English cuisine, plus a few French, and certainly French wine, shipped through Portugal. The crowd was a mixture; immediate friends and family of the Officers, few of these being of any high social standing, but also many were there by being of self-described high society, the latter particularly wishing to rub shoulders with the principal socialite in all the land. They, and they were many, had drifted back with the Prince's arrival. Himself was in his element, a full glass of chilled Chablis, a piece of quail pie, and victorious soldiers able to give him the full details of what had been done, how, and by whom. What's more, details described by soldiers highly mindful of his personage, and who, therefore, would hold back no answer to his searching questions. He had interrogated both Lacey and O'Hare regarding the tactics and dispositions, and now he was looking for details. His eyes fell on the wounded Ensign, stood with two other Officers, and concluded that a wounded man must have been in the thick of it and so over he went.

Carr, Drake, and Rushby immediately noticed the imposing and colourful figure that was heading in their direction and so their own conversation ceased immediately and all came to the attention.

"Gentlemen, gentlemen, forgive my intrusion but you must allow me to ask regarding what we did in the Maida campaign. You were at both the battle and the siege, I take it?"

Drake, being more at home in titled company, was the first to recover and fashion an answer.

"Yes Sir. We are all Light Company, and so we were at both.

"Light Company, you say? So, let me see if memory serves, you were under Kempt?"

"Yes Sir. That's correct."

"And you saw them off with two volleys?"

"Well, Sir. Two would have done it, but we got off three."

"Three! Ha. Well, stap me and sink me! But did you blast 'em? Send 'em tumbling back?"

"Why, yes Sir. I'd say that was about the best description of what actually happened as any I've heard, Sir."

"It is? You really don't say? My, but didn't we do well. And what of Scilla?"

"Captain Carr here, Sir. He's our Commanding Officer. He knows more of the details, Sir. He commanded the rearguard out of the castle and personally rescued one of our Officers who was wounded."

Carr cleared his throat and took a gulp of wine.

"Well Sir, we fought them all the way as they closed in, from the mountains down to the last boat. But we made them pay, Sir. For every yard. I can safely tell you that."

The Prince changed the subject.

"Your Colonel tells me that some of your Company were armed with rifles, Baker or some such."

"Yes Sir. About 36 had Bakers, bought by our own Colonel, Sir. They proved invaluable, more than once we gave the French a nasty surprise. Twice, for instance, we forced them to abandon their guns with accurate rifle fire. It was a major factor, as you can imagine. And French grenades were highly useful, too, in our hands, when they were scaling the walls."

"Bakers" you say. That we must remember and make enquiries. Would you recommend them for Light Infantry?"

"Oh, yes Sir. Beyond question. They give you a very valuable advantage, Sir, in the skirmishing prior to the main line versus line engagement, and even during that. You can open fire before they do."

"Bakers. Right. Got that Thresher?"

He turned around to half face a stone-faced Major, stood behind the Prince to hold his glass or furnish him with more quail pie.

"Now, back to Maida, what of the other flank, the left, where things got a mite anxious?"

Drake answered again.

"I'm afraid we can provide no detail, Sir. We remained on the right. But..."

He looked around.

"That tall Officer there, Sir."

He pointed to Carravoy stood just outside the tent in the close company of D'Villiers and both their families.

505

"He is Captain of our Grenadiers, Sir. He was on that side and it was his men that formed the new front when the Voltiguers threatened to get around our flank, Sir. He was shoulder to shoulder with the men, Sir. Part of the whole thing."

Something in the Prince's mind now told him that there was a better place to be. He took a mouthful of his pie, grinned with bulging cheeks, raised his glass to them all, sipped from it, then left, making a bee-line for Carravoy and his ensemble. Rushby visibly relaxed.

"God, I thought he was going to mention the flag. I've never felt so mortifyingly shown up. Toppling the standard."

It was Carr who spoke.

"Well, you can put that thought right out of your head. I've heard of able-bodied Ensigns who let the damn thing tumble onto the King's head. The King! You have a honourable wound and what flag falling there was I didn't notice. I thought it was all part of the business of handing over. So dwell on it no more. That's an order. You're a hero of Maida and the siege of Scilla, wounded twice. Go and find some girls to boast about it to. That's another order. I don't doubt that if you walk outside this tent, then they'll find you! Go."

Rushby went, face alight, in much better humour, and the two remaining looked at each other, but it was Carr who spoke again, predicating his words with a long sigh.

"Are your people, here?"

"No. Too far, too little notice, but they may get in this evening. Rushby's are though. Yours?"

"No. As you say, too far."

He took a deep breath.

"Suddenly it's damn stuffy in here. Let's get outside and pray that his Royal Highness doesn't delay us here too long. There can't be much more that anyone can tell him about our brush with Johnny. Pray he departs soon."

It was Drake who replied.

"Food first!"

"Oh, yes. Food."

They both filled their plates and took them to eat in the open air. The space they found for themselves was close to where the Prince of Wales was grilling Carravoy and D'Villiers before the enthralled and deeply honoured audience of their immediate families. Drake finished first and returned for more. In his absence Carr's attention came suddenly to an approaching female figure that he instantly recognised as Cecily Fynings. She was alone. He gave his plate to a passing servant and came to the attention, but she broke that by holding out her hands, which he took without thinking, but the absence of Jane Perry disabled his thoughts. He stood silent, but she soon compensated.

"Henry. It's lovely to see you, but you've got thinner, and brown, and you've another wound. It's plain you've not been taking care of yourself."

Carr had recovered.

"Hello Cecily, it's wonderful to see you. Are you looking for Nat? He's gone for food. He should return in the time it takes for him to pile his plate high for a second time, so I'm afraid he should be quite a while."

She laughed and looked at him, but he refrained from the question he longed to ask. Then she answered what was unspoken.

"Jane couldn't come. Her Father forbade her. Your Regiment, and you in particular, I'm told, are high on his list of persona non grata. She was forced to remain in Taunton. But, be assured Henry, she dearly wanted to come."

Her hand went into her purse. It emerged with a folded letter, pure cream, high quality paper, held closed by a neat red seal.

"She gave me this to give to you. It was done in secret, apart from me. She told me that you are to go somewhere that is absolutely quiet to read it."

Carr took the letter and ran his fingers over the smooth side that bore no seal. Then he slid it inside his jacket, just before the arrival of Drake, he carrying a plate from which much was in jeopardy of falling off. Drake had not seen Cecily through the crowd but his face showed both joy and surprise as he saw at close range his dearest Cecily. The plate would have fallen had Carr not had the presence of mind to anticipate the danger and he perceptively took it from Carr just before both Drake's hands came forward to grasp those of his beloved. Once again it was Cecily who compensated for a soldier's loss of words.

"Nat, what is that uniform? That dire green! Who concocted that?"

Drake adopted a tone of mock indignation.

"Now then, dearest. Regimental honour is at stake. This is the uniform of the 105th Foot. The Prince of Wales Wessex Regiment. Who dreamed up the colour scheme, I've no idea, but it is to be neither mocked nor denigrated."

She laughed.

"Right, in that case it is to be lauded and applauded, but, if we ever walk out together then you must give me warning that you are going to wear it. It will inform my own colour scheme in a very major way."

Now they all laughed and Drake returned his attention to his plate, at the same time feeding Cecily the choicest pieces. Carr began to feel out of place and intrusive, when he felt something hit his shoulder. It was more than a mere tap for attention, more like a blow. He turned and found himself facing Lord Frederick Templemere, his cane raised and he being accompanied in echelon and either side by Lord Charles Hopgood and Lord Anthony Mahon. All three were dressed in the height of fashion, from the finest cloth; mock military uniforms, with wide striped collars, these now being "a la mode" this season. Carr was taken aback and in his moment of surprise Templemere spoke first.

"Ah, it is you Carr. Found you at last. Now, I'll think you'll agree that you and I have some unfinished business."

Carr stood, still in shock, but he noticed the scarring on Templemere's right cheek. It idly crossed his mind that the surgery to reconstruct the shattered bone must have been agony. With that thought he recovered.

"Unfinished business, Templemere? Not as I recall. Our business came to a conclusion in that water meadow. Was there something else?"

Both Drake and Cecily had noticed the new arrivals and detected the hostile tone. Drake let his plate fall to the grass and advanced to stand beside Carr. His drew on his aristocratic breeding to lend him the required authority.

"Captain Carr. Could you introduce me to these gentlemen?"

"Yes. Lieutenant The Honourable Nathaniel Drake, this is Lord Frederick Templemere. I'm afraid the names of the other two gentlemen have eluded my memory."

Both gave their names.

"Your servant, Sirs. Now, is there an issue here?"

Templemere replied.

"None that concerns you, Captain Drake. My quarrel lies with Captain Carr here."

He shifted his gaze to look disdainfully at Carr. He pulled off one of his white kid gloves.

"Carr. You prevented me from continuing our meeting by striking a foul blow. Our affairs are unresolved. I challenge you to continue the duel and to meet me to try for a fair conclusion."

With that he struck Carr across the face with the glove and threw it at his feet.

Carr made no move, but quietly replied.

"I resigned once from the army to meet you, Templemere, I'll not do it again. You ended up unconscious at my feet. I could have killed you but I let you live. The affair's done."

Templemere replied in a voice dripping with contempt.

"Then I call you a coward. Here and now, before these witnesses, here assembled."

Drake took a step forward. His voice grew louder.

"The Hell with you, Templemere. You know full well that any Officer who fights in a duel will end up Court Martialled and cashiered. An Officer must refuse, he has no choice."

Templemere remained studying Carr.

"Your affairs are your own, Carr. I take it that you refuse to meet me, so again I call you a coward. I strip you of your honour."

It was Drake who replied.

"Your own honour is sullied, Templemere, to call out a man whom you know is forbidden to take you up. Captain Carr here has met you once. You may have disliked the outcome, but that's your affair. You called him out and he met you. It's done. You should leave."

"I'll not. I'll not until I hear Captain Carr say that he refuses to meet me. Then once more I can call him a coward. Then I will leave."

The raised voices and the sudden movement had silenced the crowd for some yards around them. The circle included Carravoy. He had heard and, seeing Templemere there, easily deduced the issue. He walked over and stood beside Carr.

"Lord Fred. It is good to see you again, but I would wish for better circumstances. Lieutenant Drake there is perfectly correct. Captain Carr is forbidden, by Military Orders, from meeting you in a duel. However, on top of that, his personal courage and bravery are beyond question. I myself have both witnessed and benefited from his conduct under fire. In the face of the enemy. I, too, think you should drop the matter and go."

"I'll not. Not until I hear Carr say what I require him to say."

"How now, Templemere. Still causing bother, are we?"

Templemere's face froze. He had recognised the voice, even though it was laced with deep sarcasm, and in turning he recognised the unmistakeable figure. The Prince of Wales, having moved on to interrogate Captain Heaviside about the defence of Maida town, had heard the commotion and took it upon himself to get involved. Templemere bowed, very low.

"Your Highness."

"Yes, yes, Templemere, quite so, but these Officers, in fact my Officers, are quite right. A Commissioned Officer is forbidden to duel, and that's the fact of it. You sully yourself by pushing this further. All I can say, is, that if you count yourself as a weapons man, then you should join the army, there's plenty of fighting coming up, I can tell you, enough for even you. But; as long as you choose to stay out of it, I fail to see how you can call anyone a coward, especially someone with a record of actually standing up against the Johnnies. Up close, as it were, toe to toe. So, if you don't want to do that, but still want to go around getting involved in duels, well, then again, all I can say is, that that does make you a bit of an insect, you know, bit of an arse, as it were. Were I you, I would take myself off, back to my sheep or whatever. More immediately, and to the point, uninvited, you're ruining my party. And stood on my Parade Ground."

He paused.

"I'm surprised you're still here!"

Templemere visibly reeled at the deep derision, delivered with perfect cadence, the Prince's voice rising and falling to produce just the required level of sarcasm, but Templemere's face showed intently all the shock of such a tirade coming from the mouth of the Prince of Wales himself. He knew, that from that moment, he was finished in society. Hopgood and Mahon did too and sidled off, leaving Templemere alone. He could do nothing but bow, words wouldn't come. He picked up his own glove from besides his feet and hurried away, through and out of the condemning crowd, spurred on his way by looks of either hatred or those that displayed delight at his very public and thorough discomfiture.

Drake, Carr, and Carravoy came to attention before their Colonel in Chief, but he had lost all formality and spoke conversationally.

"Yes, gentlemen, at ease, but I'm taking my leave. Done enough, and learned enough, certainly for one day. Thresher!"

He turned to the ever present attending Major.

"Go before and organise the carriage. I believe the ladies are already within."

He turned back to the three. Each was astonished as he shook their hands."

"Remember, this is for Old England. Old England."

With that he nodded, then turned away as each saluted his back and Thresher escorted him through the crowd and away. Carr now turned to Carravoy.

"I have to thank you for that, Charles, for your support I mean."

Carravoy's face remained stern as he looked at Carr. A silence grew before he replied.

"I don't like you Carr. I think you are wholly the wrong kind to be an Officer, a bad influence and a bad example. However, I'll not stand idle whilst you are called a coward. I know, that to you, such a word does not apply."

The abrupt end gave warning of the abrupt taking of his leave. Carravoy turned and was soon lost in the crowd.

* * *

They were paraded in Winchester High Street, drawn up, sixteen ranks deep, in front of the Town Hall. The June heat was making itself felt, but what was far more irksome was the seemingly interminable speech being made to them by the Lord Mayor, delivered through one of the windows of the dour, solid, granite building that served as the centre of administration for this worthy city. "No way of avoiding it," had been Lacey's first words upon receiving the letter inviting them to parade in the High Street, it being delivered by hand, to their camp on the previous day. The Regimental Standards, uncased for such an occasion, stirred fitfully in the occasional breeze, but what pride there was dwelt more within those attached to the Regiment who watched, among these being Bridie Deakin and Molly Davey, now friends by their common circumstances, but their relationship was warm enough. Mutual support permanently made up their Orders of the Day and so their friendship had grown. Bridie took care of baby John whilst Molly pointed out all the sights to Tilly.

At last the final words echoed back from the bright and colourful shops and houses behind them, that made such a contrast to the dour Town Hall before, and the Mayor called for three cheers for The King. Lacey turned to Gibney, who took over.

"Parade. Remove shakoes."

"Three cheers for The King."

The huzzas rang out mechanically around the confined space.

"Replace shakoes."

The Colours were furled and cased and the parade marched off, but few failed to notice the carts up a side road that would follow them out into the city fields. The Mayor had laid on, at Council expense, a good supply of beef, bread, and beer. Once beyond the houses the column halted and the lines dissolved to reform again at the supply carts and for the men to draw their share. The sunny, lush, and airy fields provided a welcome contrast to the scene of the Mayor's speech; the open spaces with many varieties; emerging blossom in the many orchards, and the bright green of new growth in the intervening cornfields. Lacey joined O'Hare and Simmonds under a convenient tree and sat himself in one of the collapsible chairs. Each already knew their orders. Lacey was clearing up the details.

"Padraigh. Have you sent word to Taunton? They can expect us on Thursday?"

"Yes, Sir. I sent a rider yesterday, immediately after Church Parade."

He paused. A ball of rags had come tumbling between them, a misthrow from one of the children attached to the Deakin, Davey, Hill family ensemble, who were enjoying their picnic some yards away. It was Tilly who came to fetch and it was O'Hare that rolled it back to her. All three Officers allowed themselves to smile and grin.

"A month isn't long, Sir, before we re-embark."

"No, but it may be a mite longer. We'll be brought up to strength, we'll drill ourselves senseless, then march off. Weymouth again, I would assume."

"Do you know anything about Arthur Wellesley, Sir.?"

"Not a lot. He made his name in India, nicknamed the "Sepoy General", and he achieved a couple of stunning victories, but against the natives. There was a siege, too, so I've heard. He was in that North German mess around the Elbe in the year five, since then he's been dabbling in politics. Now he's got the Portugal Expedition, and that includes us."

Simmonds spoke next. He sounded anxious and concerned; Wellesley would be a new Commander.

"How do you think it will go, Sir?"

"Impossible to tell. I know that the French have wiped the floor with both the Spanish and the Portuguese armies, but their people are putting up a fight, just like the Masse'. All I can say, is that we met their best at Maida. And on equal terms, line against line. And they were veterans whilst we weren't. What they will put against us down in the Peninsula, won't be any better."

He sat forward and slapped his hands on his knees.

"Now, I think I'll take a walk amongst the men. Give them an hour, Padraigh, then re-form."

With that he rose and marched off, hands clasped behind his back, heading straight for the gambolling children. O'Hare did not follow his progress, for his attention was immediately taken by Captain Carr who had suddenly emerged from the throng and approached with an air that demanded attention. He addressed himself to Major O'Hare.

"Excuse me, Sir, but I was wondering if I might borrow a horse. There is an acquaintance of mine who lives quite near, and I would very much like to visit."

O'Hare went into thought, but it was Simmonds who answered.

"I've a spare. Tell my groom you can have Jerome. He's good for a long journey."

O'Hare now spoke.

"Be mindful, Captain, that we need you in barracks come Thursday."

"Yes Sir. Be assured, I'll be there."

The horse was identified, saddled and bridled and, after packing a few items for himself, Carr led it back to where his company was enjoying the Mayor's generosity. He spoke to Drake and Rushby, both sat entertaining Cecily.

513

"I'm taking my leave for a couple of days. I'll see you Thursday, back in Taunton."

With that he mounted the horse, but Drake couldn't fail to notice that Carr was wearing his sword and there was a Curaissier pistol in the saddle holster.

"Henry, what are you about? What are your plans?"

Carr pulled the horse's head away.

"See you Thursday."

* * *

The estate was close and Carr arrived in the late afternoon. It was immediately apparent that it was extensive and fashioned from great wealth. He spent some time in a convenient copse crowning a conveniently overlooking hill. From here, through his Dolland, he examined the buildings and watched the comings and goings of the staff and servants and it was not long before he had a fairly certain idea of the purpose of each of the buildings around the estate. There was little happening apart from the common day to day. There were no visitors and no one left. The afternoon wore on and Carr sustained himself on bread, cheese, apples and water. A road skirted the sidewall of the gardens that decorated the rear of the main house and, as the day turned to evening, Carr walked his horse along it. Jerome gave him enough height to see what he wanted over the neat brickwork, then he let himself into the first field he came to, hobbled Jerome, and left him to contentedly graze. Carr then walked back to a side gate of the garden, which he found unlocked. He entered and walked to the centre of the immaculate lawn that lay just below a plain terrace that came out from a series of glazed doors. He stood on the lawn and waited, which gave Carr ample time to examine his surroundings. The whole was bathed in the clear yellow light of an immaculate 1st June evening. The lawn was pristine, bordered by scarlet flowering shrubs and the manicured grass swept up to halt cleanly at the quarrystone pavings of the terrace, themselves terminating at the tall, authoritative, glazed doors. Above all rose the red brick and tall chimneys of an early Georgian stately home, secure in its status and grandeur.

In almost no time a servant crossed the terrace and immediately noticed the tall Officer, statuesque upon the lawn. Thor-

514

oughly disconcerted and confused he hurried through one of the glazed doors. Soon a figure appeared behind the glass and the door opened to reveal Lord Frederick Templemere. The look of hatred masked any degree of surprise. He rapidly walked off the terrace and came up to Carr to stop within feet of him.

"Carr, damn you. Leave; before I set the dogs on you."

Carr ignored the instruction.

"My Lord Fred. I trust my timing is up to the mark. You've not yet had your dinner? Nothing intoxicating imbibed? Fresh as a daisy?"

Templemere said nothing, content with his look of loathing, but his confusion grew.

"My Lord, I note that somewhere over yonder, I think there," Carr waved his hand to a large building behind and to the right, "you have a somewhat well appointed indoor ride. You were correct, back there on Horse Guards; now you've chosen to make it so, we do have unfinished business. I suggest that we go in there, and conclude the matter."

Templemere's mouth stretched into a smile that did nothing to dilute his look of vehement dislike.

"You mean, Carr, that you and I go in there and fight a duel?"

"Almost correct, my Lord, I mean that you and I go in there and have a fight. Omit the duel. No rules, no Seconds, simply you and I and two swords. We go in there and we fight it out. In the way that soldiers such as myself have to fight it out, against an enemy. That is, fighting to stay alive. That's my offer. If you have the stomach for such, I'll wait here and allow you to prepare yourself. If you decline, I'll leave the way I came, but if that, then on your honour, our matter now counts as settled."

Templemere's expression changed to indecision. What had immediately come to mind was a formal duel, but Carr was offering something from a battlefield. He studied Carr further but discerned nothing. Carr stood relaxed and expressionless, awaiting an answer. Templemere felt doubt rising within him, a combat outside the rules of duelling, but his hatred of Carr rose to supremacy. Then something flickered in Templemere's eyes.

"Very well, Carr, as you suggest. Alone and man to man. You'll wait whilst I prepare myself?"

Carr nodded.

515

"I'll take myself into The Ride, if that's acceptable?

He spoke the words to Templemere's back. There was no reply, so he began to make his own arrangements, but he merely needed to remove his jacket and shako, which he transferred to his left arm. With Templemere out of sight through the windows, Carr walked off the lawn in the direction of The Ride, but, when out of sight in some bushes, he doubled over to the right, through the bushes to stand on the path of his entrance but well hidden. Minutes later, Templemere burst out of the doors, a pistol in each hand, accompanied by three retainers each with their own pistol. Carr could clearly hear the shouted instructions.

"There's a damn trespasser in The Ride. Probably a thief. I want him shot, d'ye hear? Shot. You two go that way. You, with me."

All four disappeared from the lawn in their chosen directions. Carr left by the side gate he entered by. He found Jerome and rode him, the long way around, to his crowsnest copse. He unsaddled him, hobbled him again and sat to observe. Lord Templemere and more retainers could be seen out beyond the outmost buildings, gazing further to the far hedges and trees, but then returning. The long June evening saw no more activity. Carr walked Jerome to a stream to drink, then returned to his lookout. He ate and drank the last of his supplies, then settled for the night.

He was awoken by the growing sunlight. It would be a stifling day. The estate was still and silent, the first movement being maids and cooks beginning their dreary dawn duties. Carr settled to wait further, gambling on the time honoured habits of the aristocracy. It came, but not in the form he expected, but better than he expected. The double doors of the stable block came open and out came, not a horse, but a phaeton, a light carriage, fast and dangerous. Second to a thoroughbred horse, it was the preferred mode of transport of all society rakes and dandies. The horses arrived shortly after and were harnessed to its shafts. Lord Fred was indulging in his pre-breakfast exercise, a fast carriage ride around his estates. Carr shifted the focus of his Dolland glass and identified The Ride, a dark orange track that snaked around the extensive Templemere domain. He followed its course until it disappeared into some woodland, the furthest point from the house. A half mile further on, it re-emerged. Carr saddled Jerome and set off on a wide curve, to get to the wood and wait.

He entered the wood and rode across through the short bushes and thin, light starved grass until he cut the ride. It was well built and maintained, perfect for a fast ride in a phaeton. He saw no need to hide, once in the wood the carriage would be confined to the track by the close trees. With Carr on the track, Templemere would be forced to stop. The wood was dense, pierced only by the track which now, with the risen sun, was improved by dappled sunlight playing innocently on its surface. Rooks cawed eerily above him, a breeze disturbing their treetops; something moved off in the undergrowth. Carr blindfolded Jerome to keep him settled, and soothing words calmed him further. Carr chose the exit to a blind bend and, thus, he first heard, rather than saw, Templemere's approach. He reached for his pistol from the saddleholster behind, checked the priming, then cocked it. The instant he saw the horses, Carr rose in the stirrups and took careful aim.

Templemeres face registered shock and terror; Carr's cold, deadpan face above the stark, black, gaping muzzle of the pistol, and behind, his blank right eye sighted down the barrel. Templemere dropped the reins and leapt from the carriage, rolling over and over from the momentum until he could gain his feet and take off through the trees. Carr whipped off Jerome's blindfold and started after him. It took no more than a minute. Templemere was no kind of a runner and Jerome felt no hindrance from undergrowth that slowed the fleeing Lord. Carr came up beside him, took his right foot from his stirrup and crashed his heel into Templemere's back, between the shoulder blades. Templemere fell headlong to the turf, to roll over beside Jerome's hooves, then he looked up further to find himself once more the subject of the staring muzzle of Carr's dragoon pistol. Templemere's eyes widened further, then came confusion as Carr spoke.

"My Lord. I note that your buggy contained your sword. Some morning exercise, I presume. Would you care to go and fetch it?"

Templemere could not take his eyes from the pistol and failed to move. Carr bent his arm and pointed the barrel skyward. He then sat the horse with his left forearm folded on the pommel.

"Your sword. Lord Fred!"

Carr waved the pistol in the direction of the phaeton and the removal of the pistol levelled at him released Templemere's legs from the lock that fright had placed upon them. His face grew more composed, which grew as the seconds passed. He wasn't going to be shot and in a swordfight he had a very good chance. Without a word he gained his feet, brushed himself off and turned towards the phaeton which had stopped but a little way off, the horses attending to their grazing. Carr pointed the pistol at Templemere's back, expecting something similar, perhaps, to the previous evening, but when Templemere's sword came out from the scabbard with a theatrical hiss, Carr holstered the pistol, dismounted and tied Jerome to a nearby bush.

Templemere was swishing and bending his sword as Carr drew his. Templemere, now with a sword in his hand, had much recovered.

"Now then, Carr, I hope you've been practicing."

"Shut up, Templemere, you're in a fight."

With that Carr advanced upon him. Templemere adopted the 'en garde', out of habit, but Carr engaged his blade and forced it over. Templemere tried to disengage but Carr bore straight in, and fast, keeping their sword hilts locked together. He then head butted Templemere hard above his left eye. Templemere reeled back, and Carr took a step forward to follow him and send a left hook hard to his head, connecting with the scarred right cheekbone. Next he hooked his left leg around Templemere's right and barged him over. Templemere lay sprawled, stunned and in shock, both blows were spreading acute pain, across his face and into his head. Carr placed a boot on Templemere's sword, then stood over him, his sword at Templemere's throat. Templemere's face registered pure dread, his eyes bulged and his mouth quivered. Carr took a moment to examine what he saw. His mouth twisted with contempt.

"Once again, Lord Fred, I have the choice to kill you or let you live. I'm going to let you live, but remember; this is what I do, this what I can do, wherever, and at anytime I choose. If you confront me again, ever, with your damn challenges and insults about cowardice, then next time I will most certainly damn well kill you!"

He leaned forward and seized Templemere's shirt front, pulled him up and then slammed him back into the turf. Templemere's head met the soil with a thump. Carr gave him one last withering look then returned to Jerome. He mounted and, paying Templemere no more attention, rode off to take Jerome the short way out of the woods, but the long way around the estate. He reached the turnpike and set Jerome to an easy trot. He allowed himself a smile that grew wider as he reached or Jane's letter inside his coat, still unread, seal as yet unbroken. Tomorrow was Wednesday and in the evening was choir rehearsal. If he rode all day and through the night he should st make it.